SAUDI

She reached out in bewilderment for her husband. But already Rashid and Ibrahim had disappeared into one tent, and the flaps were being lowered. She was alone among these strangers swaddled like herself from head to toe in dire black. Like it or not, she was borne along toward another tent by these figures screeching torrents of words she could not understand. It was like a nightmare to be in the resolute grip of these faceless strangers. It was so hot and she was so dizzy and disoriented she almost forgot that the women under these shrouds were her new family.

She was inside the shade of a tent, the flaps were lowered, she was drawn forward, fingers plucked off her cloak and veil; through the eye slits of her mask she saw bright lantern lights and many moving shapes coming closer, throwing off their own cloaks and masks and surrounding her, untying and peeling off her mask, laughing and gaping at her. Sunny stared from one face to another, wondering who all these women could be. She smiled uncertainly as the laughing, joking, chattering horde closed in on her.

Also in Arrow by Laurie Devine

NILE

SAUDI

Laurie Devine

ARROW BOOKS

Arrow Books Limited
62-65 Chandos Place, London WC2N 4NW

An imprint of Century Hutchinson Ltd

London Melbourne Sydney Auckland
Johannesburg and agencies throughout
the world

First published in Great Britain by André Deutsch 1985
Arrow edition 1986

Set in Lectura by Photobooks (Bristol) Ltd

Printed and bound in Great Britain
by Cox and Wyman Limited, Reading

ISBN 0 09 940950 X

For Roberta B. Cohen

Far are the shades of Arabia,
Where the Princes ride at noon
'mid the verduous vales and thickets,
Under the ghost of the moon. . . .
They haunt me—her lutes and her forests;
No beauty on earth I see
But shadowed with that dream recalls
Her loveliness to me:
Still eyes look coldly upon me,
Cold voices whisper and say—
'He is crazed with the spell of far Arabia,
They have stolen his wits away.'

WALTER DE LA MARE

PROLOGUE

Sunny Shannon sat on the hilltop and tried to decide whether to take him back again, whether to forgive and forget, whether she should or would dare trust that man - and herself - again. He had been her husband. He was the father of her children. She had never loved, and never hated, anyone as much as she had loved and hated him. After all the guilts and wonders and shameful secrets of the twenty-six years of their loving, was it possible to begin anew together? Was their love rare enough for the miracle of resurrection? Today, after weeks of doubts and hesitation, Sunny was determined to finally decide whether she would marry her husband again.

Sunny sighed. This was not a simple matter of romance and passion and kisses in the moonlight; not even a question of whether she loved him or whether he loved her, or even whether they were compatible or complemented each other in some necessary way. This decision - like, it seemed, every decision now that Sunny was older and wiser or at least no longer young - was far more complicated than that. Whether she chose to marry him again or leave him again, she would lose something important.

Sunny smiled and remembered that old cliché about two people looking at a glass and one seeing it as half full and one as half empty. She hadn't used to be so pessimistic. She used to be the golden girl, the true believer in anything and everything. She wondered what had happened to all that true belief.

She decided it was better to think of her decision in another way. Surely, whether she chose to marry him again or leave him again, she would gain something important?

Or would she?

It was possible to win at life, wasn't it?

Sunny brushed her long graying blond bangs away from her large tired blue eyes, but still she couldn't see her way toward answers. Once, when she was much younger, she had believed it was not only possible, but her right, to win at life. She had wanted it all, and she had believed it would be possible for her to have it all. But Sunny had not felt invincible for a very long time.

From her hill she looked out over the sweeping vistas of the prettiest little town in New England. Still River was a tiny fertile village tucked into the larger rockier town of Harvard, an hour's drive northwest of Boston. The Still River she had known as a child had been small and tight and insular and perfect in its way. Tight-fisted old Yankees and struggling Irish and German immigrants used to make their yeoman livings off Still River's rolling farms and orchards. But now this village, and many others like it, had been turned into a tiny Boston bedroom suburb, a subdivided temporary resting place for overpaid computer engineers and corporate executives and others who had a yen to live like the gentry. They built split-level architectural dreams and hired gardeners to see to the landscape. They bought outlandishly expensive Jeeps and ordered their backwoods clothing from L. L. Bean. Still River was no longer the simple country village Sunny had once called home.

Yet from where she sat on what had been her favourite childhood lookout atop the highest hill in the nest of meadows and orchards and farmland that was Still River, calm beauty still reigned. The winding sparkle of the Nashua River lay before her like yarn carelessly unwound from a skein. Over the town's grassy knoll of a Common, the white steeples of the Protestant churches reached out to the heavenly blue sky. Still River was idyllic and peaceful and pastoral. Sunny took a deep breath of the clear fresh bracing air and felt that she was home. But she had been born far away from here in that other wildly exotic world she also called home. Yet it had been a joy to grow up in this placid New England town. Today, after she finally made her decision, would she say goodbye to Still River or settle in here for life?

Sunny lay back on the blanket she had stretched out on the dewy grass under an apple tree. Already this morning someone was mowing a meadow, and she could smell grass and hay and even a touch of mint. She could hear birds twittering in the woods, and when she shut her eyes the birdsongs seemed to grow louder. She looked up at the fluffy clouds which arranged themselves in shapes and forms that reminded her of dunes in the desert. She had loved those dunes that were white and red and golden, dunes that were high and drifting and fantastic, dunes that were an infinity of shifting desert sand. Sunny stared at the white clouds drifting high over Still River. She had seen clouds like this from the other side, flying high above the earth on her way halfway around the globe to live in another world with her husband. Could she, would she, do that again?

If she remarried her husband, she would have to return to Saudi Arabia and live with him in his country. Could she, would she, do that again?

Sunny remembered, as if it were yesterday, when she had first gone to Saudi as a bride. She had been so young, so innocent, so bedazzled by bright and shining illusions. Sometimes Sunny could hardly remember how it had felt to be that young and credulous. She had been the world's greatest champion of romance. She had fervently believed every fairy tale she had ever heard about Princes Charming and white horses and Arabian nights and living happily ever after. In her own life she had staked everything on living out her own real-life fairy tale just like the ones she had made her grandmother read her over and over when she was a little girl. Only later, after her fall from grace and giddy believing ecstasy, had she learned that romance, like all the other quicksilver thrills in life, was not always what it appeared to be.

Ahead, a translucent morning mist made the White Mountains of New Hampshire and the Green Mountains of Vermont seem a shimmering mirage. Sunny wondered in her heart of hearts if she had ever cast away her belief in fairy tales. Wasn't it true that she didn't regret her dreams, only that her dreams had not come true? Sunny's emotions shamed her in a way. She was an independent woman. She had a fine education and an absorbing career, and she was a good mother. But maybe, she thought, all I ever wanted, maybe all I still want, is to live happily ever after with my one true love. Here, now, today, I can decide to go off with him again, and maybe this time it will be different from the way it was before. Maybe this time we *will* live happily ever after.

Sunny laughed and wondered what Dr. Rosen would think of such reactionary yearnings. Wise and wonderful Dr. Rebecca Rosen, her psychologist, had been worth every penny of the thousands of dollars she had paid for those three sessions each week for seven grueling years. If she rang up Dr. Rosen, would she tell her what to do? But Sunny's therapy, like so much else that she had loved in her life, like so many people whom she had loved in her life, had terminated. Besides, one of the whole tiresome points of therapy and adult living was to know yourself well enough to make your own decisions and then muster the maturity to be able to live with them. Mostly Sunny could do that now. Yet, a little, she missed her old wild willful rebel self. Once she would not have lain here like this agonizing over whether to love her husband. Once she would have just plunged in.

Once, in fact, she had done just that.

And once she had suffered the consequences.

Sunny remembered how she had fallen so absolutely in love that nothing on earth or in heaven - nothing! - could ever have kept her from being with him. In her saner, older, more cynical moments now, she wondered if she had really loved him so desperately or if she had just once read, and believed, too many bad novels about endless loves. Sunny stared at the clouds. She had loved her husband desperately, all right. She could never forget or belittle the joy and the fierceness and the heat of loving him. That was real. That was true. And so, against all sane and cautious advice, she had married him and gone off with him to his magical medieval kingdom between the seas.

Saudi. If she remarried her husband, she would be remarrying Saudi as well. They were one and the same, indivisible.

Saudi: how she loved and hated it. To her, Saudi was all black and white, a hot place on eternal emotional fire. Gentle and brutal, pure and corrupted, gorgeous and squalid. . . . No one here in America understood a single thing she ever said about the white light and the dark shadows that were Saudi. Either people here thought Saudi was one big playground for superrich playboy princes or they thought it was all dunes and derricks and wild-eyed religious fanatics. The Saudi she knew was so much more complex - so much better and yet so much worse - than the myths and the lies that shrouded it.

Saudi was the country everyone loved to hate. The West hated Saudi for quadrupling the price of oil and triggering the panic of the energy crisis and fueling an international financial recession. Even other Arabs were jealous of Saudi for its money, despised Saudi for its arrogance, and ridiculed Saudi for its ignorance. What we should do with those filthy Saudis, Americans sometimes told Sunny after they had a few drinks, is either bomb the place off the map or land the Marines and take back 'our' oil fields.

Just as soon as Americans finished recommending we 'nuke the Gulf,' they invariably wanted to know how it had felt to wear the veil. And then there would be prurient questions just under the surface about what sex was like there, was it better or was it worse, with the men so much the masters and the women the slaves? Men here and in Europe acted as if Saudi Arabia were some sadomasochistic dream come true. Although Sunny nursed her own female grudges against Saudi, she could not tolerate the smug and superior way the West carped on about the sorry plight of Arab women. No one listened when she tried to explain that the personal freedom of Arab men too was severely curbed in such a rigid traditional culture. And when she went a step further and spoke with longing of the joys and serenities and emotional warmth of living in the heart of a loving Arab family, Americans rolled their eyes and changed the subject.

Sunny heard a whinny, and she looked up at the faithful old chestnut mare who was her life's companion. She scrambled to her feet and threw her arms around Princess Camey's neck and buried her head in the Arabian's thick mane. She picked thick bunches of fragrant sweet grass and fed her mare by hand.

And then, after looking around to make sure no one had come upon her and was watching, Sunny followed her impulse: she searched in the grass until she found a cluster of daisies. One by one, she pulled the petals off a flower: he loves me, loves me not, loves me, loves me not . . . loves me not. In irritation she threw away the ill-omened daisy. It wasn't until the fourth flower that the petals said he loved her. Sunny threw away the other daisies. She would quit while she was ahead.

She considered that perhaps she *should* quit while she was ahead and send her husband back to Saudi alone. Certainly that would be her most prudent choice. But Sunny wasn't sure it would be right. She clung stubbornly to her belief that there were right and wrong in the world and in her life. She knew that many people thought it childish to believe in absolute right and wrong. But if that made her childish, then she would choose forever to be a child.

Would it be right to marry him again? After all the tangled web of rights and wrongs in his life and in hers, after all her father had done to and for him and his, after all the guilts and shames and secrets passed on even to the third generation, how could she possibly unravel what was right and what was wrong?

Sunny sat up straight and tall. She squared her shoulders, and she felt a thrill of pride and strength surge through her. It was her life, and she would live it as she wished. She had that right, and she would take that responsibility.

Her exhilaration faded. She had again decided only to decide. Back to square one.

She would begin again by defining the question. Wasn't she trying to decide whether to risk her own hard-won independence on something as dangerous and unpredictable as loving an imperfect man?

Sunny felt like kicking herself. She wasn't a female saint dealing with a male sinner. She too had made a lifetime of mistakes - with her parents, her husband, his brother, her children. She was at least as imperfect as her husband.

The proper question was whether she, an imperfect woman, could let herself trust an imperfect man. She must decide if she dared to risk the interdependencies of sexual love.

Sunny reached thirstily into her backpack. She had set out bright and early this morning without even a cup of tea, but her indomitable grandmother had insisted she take along a thermos. Sunny was forty-two, yet sometimes she felt past her prime, second best to her spry old grandmother. She wondered whether that was because she was truly getting old or because, for a very long while, both by choice and by chance, she had been living a life without love. Until the two of them had come together again, she had felt that all her old juices had just dried up. It hadn't been much comfort, Sunny thought, that many of her women friends were just as lonely. It wasn't enough to blame such emotional deprivation on the historical accident of living in loveless times.

When Sunny came across two apples as she rooted for the thermos, she bit into one and absently fed the other to her horse. Finally she unscrewed the lid and poured lukewarm tea into a plastic cup, and then she reached down in the backpack to see what else was there. She caught her breath when she lifted out the familiar folds of the coarse, heavy black fabric of her *abba*, the cloak she had worn in Saudi over all her other clothes. Sunny could have sworn she had taken this monstrosity to the town dump years ago. But as she shook out the folds of the *abba*, two more foul black things and a lovely cedar box inlaid with an intricate arabesque of mother-of-pearl fell onto the blanket. Gran had packed not only food and drink to sustain her but her old cloak, mask, veil and photographs to help her decide.

Sunny stared at the *hegab*, the mask, and remembered her shock the first time she had seen one. At first she had refused to wear it. But in the end, of course, she had bowed to the inevitable. Why, she wondered, did everyone rant on so about veils when it was the masks women wore along the Gulf that were really the atrocity? This particular mask was a face-size slab of dense fabric, of sewn-together layers of opaque, cheap rayon and taffeta and polyester, with two slits only as wide as button-holes for the eyes, a slight fullness to make room for the bridge of the nose, and three ties at the back to hold it in place.

Sunny took a last thoughtful sip of tea and decided to put on the damnable mask. Romance might be fantasy, but this was reality. If she decided to marry him again, she would have to wear it whenever she went out in public in Saudi. And so she would make this mask too part of her decision. As she tied it on tight, she fought down a moment of claustrophobic panic. Then she remembered how she had to breathe with the mask on, in quick, nearly breathless shallow pants through flared nostrils and parted lips. But Sunny was not about to stop with the mask. She shook out the seven thicknesses of the gauzy gossamer black veil and threw it over her head. Now she could hardly even see the sun. She drew the cloak around her shoulders, then pulled it up in place on the crown of her head so that its enveloping folds were like blinders.

Now she was in utter darkness. Was this what she wanted? The darkness of blind love?

In a sudden rage Sunny tore off cloak and veil and mask. How could she even consider going back to Saudi and putting on the blinders again? When she put on this cloak and veil and mask, she felt and looked like an animal. Like an animal.

Sunny waited until her anger was under control before she finally opened the beautiful antique box sent her from a Middle Eastern bazaar nearly forty years ago. Inside the fragrant box were photographs redolent with cedar and musk and unsolved mysteries.

Her mother as a pretty baby, a lovely girl, a beautiful bride. Gran and Gramps with her father, a little boy in short pants. Her father in his high school football uniform, in his Stanford graduation gown, in Arab robes and head scarf. Her father posed beside a familiar Arab. Sunny turned over that photograph. '*Abdullah and Tom, 1936.*' Yes, both brothers looked like him. Sunny turned the photograph over again and looked more closely at the faces of her grinning father and that scowling Arab. All that had happened, in a way, was because of these two men. Of the one's bravery and the other's secret guilt. In a way, Sunny thought, not only I but my child had to pay for what happened that terrible day between these two men. In a way, the brothers had paid a high price too. Was that debt - now, finally - paid in full? Or did she - and he - and their last remaining child still have more to pay? Surely, by now, enough blood had been spilled? Sunny sighed. She would have to go back to where it had all begun, in Saudi, when she was just an infant.

Sunny sifted through the photographs until she found first the original black-and-white snapshot and then the copy she had had made years later in a shop on Mt. Auburn Street in Cambridge. She had loved this photograph so much that she had had it enlarged and painted in romantic old-fashioned sepia tones. Her mother, her beautiful mother, was holding her snug against the swell of her breasts. Her father had his arm around her mother, and he was gazing adoringly, as he did in all these photographs, into the eyes of his Sally. A little apart from the Shannon family grouping stood that same dusky Arab in tribal robes and head scarf. They were all standing together beside the pier and the boat that was about to cast off and take them out into the Gulf. Sunny stared at the treacherous sapphire water beyond her parents and the Arab and the boat. She supposed it didn't matter why they had left her behind on the Saudi mainland while they sailed off to the nearby island of Bahrain. But what was important, what was so very important, was what had happened to her parents, and this somber dusky Arab in his dusty tribal robes, that day in the Gulf.

Sunny turned over the sepia-toned photograph and read the date and the inscription in Gran's spidery handwriting: '*Sally, Tom, and the baby. And the Arab. July 5, 1938. Their last picture together.*'

1

Sally Shannon danced with her baby on the hot bright sand. As she danced in her white dress in the white heat, she waved a lacy white parasol over their heads. Framed in the dusty sepia monotones of Saudi's gold air, gold sky, gold sand, she spun around and around on the beach with the baby held tightly in her arms. As she turned, the sultry Persian Gulf wind made the long white sail-like fullness of her skirt billow out so that Sally fancied she and Sunny could magically ride the crest of the waves all the way home to America without even needing a boat. 'Escape!' she whispered conspiratorially to the baby. 'We're getting away!' Sally laughed a rich happy laugh, and she pirouetted again until the baby too let out a gurgle of pure joy.

'Away!' In her exhilaration Sally held the baby up in the air as though, she thought, Sunny were some ancient pagan sacrifice she was about to make to the implacable gods of the sun or the sea or the sand. But at that ominous thought, Sally was suddenly dizzy with foreboding. Last night she had dreamed that she, Tom, Sunny, everyone she loved were all gathered together at the Ritz in Boston, fronting on the cool swan lake and the bright blooming gardens, when suddenly there was a rumble and a rolling, walls and ceilings were crashing in on her and them, and after a while Sally was standing in the rubble and she was alone and she didn't know whether everyone she loved was dead or if she herself was the one who had died. After the nightmare Sally had wished for a sound commonsense reason to postpone their weekend holiday away from Saudi. She was embarrassed to admit to her husband that since she had come to Saudi she had found herself more and more often bereft of sound commonsense reasons for everything and anything. Most of the time she blamed her odd new moods, her lurid new nightmares, her disquieting new tendencies toward superstition on nothing more significant than the awful, damp, disabling heat. None of them were at their best in this heat. It was the maddening heat that had made her do as their Arab houseboy suggested. Just last week she had put a bluestone charm in Sunny's crib to ward off the Evil Eye.

Sally could feel an itchy prickly-heat rash budding on her chest and at the back of her neck and where her thighs rubbed together when she walked. She could feel sweat beading her forehead, in her armpits, under her breasts. As she lifted her arm to blot the perspiration off her forehead with the sleeve of her dress, she got a whiff of herself. When she worked up a sweat out in the sand patch she called a garden, the wet smell of work was sweet and decayed. When she made love with Tom on their gummy cotton sheets, the hot smell of sex was yeasty. When she sat too long waiting in the sun, the steamy smell of impatience was thick and stagnant. But the strongest, gamiest smell of all, the smell that would not be masked by cornstarch or deodorant or cheap jasmine cologne, was the rank animal smell of her own fear. Sally wiped off her face and rubbed in the sweat under her arms and breasts, yet still she could smell her own fear. She sighed. Only a moment ago she had been laughing and dancing on the sand. She tried, always, to laugh off her misgivings. The worse she felt, always, the more she laughed. She had been acting positively giddy ever since she had come to Saudi.

She clutched the baby close to her as the fears took over again. Anxiously she looked from the glassy sapphire sea before her to the relentless orange sun above to the gritty white sand beneath her. Dangers and menace were everywhere. There were snakes and scorpions in the desert and sharks and eels in the sea. There was early death from oasis fever and cholera and malaria and a host of other sicknesses that never struck back home in New England. There were the daily torments of the heat and the humidity and the swarms of big black flies and the packs of big brown rats. And always, there were the filth and the backwardness and the suspicion of hostile Arabs who wanted the infidel Americans to stop looking for oil and go away and leave them to their medieval squalor.

After being worn down by two years in Saudi, after barely surviving a difficult pregnancy and an even more difficult delivery, Sally could recite a litany of fervent curses upon this cursed land. Yet it had not always been so. When Sally had been fresh to Saudi, she had written rapturous letters home about its virgin beauty. Once, this exotic landscape had seemed to her paradisiacal. Once, the Arabs had seemed to her wise and serene and larger than life.

But Sally had exhausted all her romantic delusions about Saudi. Now she only wanted out. She thought she was pregnant again. Sunny was only four months old, and Sally thought she was pregnant again. She could not endure another pregnancy here. She was ashamed she did not have the stamina to stick it out in Saudi. She would have liked to be an altogether heroic pioneer woman who thrived on hardship. But she was only Sarah Maguire Shannon, a sheltered, fragile, and very homesick twenty-three-year-old American girl. This weekend, when she and Tom were away for a breather on the nearby island of Bahrain, she would tell her husband she was going home. He could break his contract with the oil company and come home with her, or he could serve out his remaining eighteen months here alone. If he insisted on staying, she would wait for him back on his parents' farm in Massachusetts. She would hate to be separated from him, for she loved Tom almost more than she loved her own life. But she had to think about the baby in her arms and the other one still in her womb.

Always Sally worried that Sunny was in mortal danger here. She wondered if she should take her with them to Bahrain as they had planned or leave her here in Saudi with the neighbors who had already offered to baby-sit.

Sunny was on formula. She might be better off in a crib in the compound. But while they were away Sunny could catch a sudden fever or there could be a freak accident or she could be bitten by a scorpion. Everywhere along the desolate backwaters of the Persian Gulf, man was always at risk. For her baby, for herself, for her Tom, there was no security here. All of them, all the time, were in mortal danger.

Sally shifted Sunny into the crook of her left arm; she threw her parasol down on the sand; and with more superstition than piety in her heart, Sally made the Sign of the Cross. 'In the name of the Father, and the Son, and the Holy Ghost,' she murmured. As the sun beat down, Sally prayed ardently to exorcise her fear. But she was still afraid when, after a long while, Sunny let out an insistent wail.

Sally shooed away the flies that had settled on the baby's face and picked up the delicate white parasol Tom had bought her the last time they were in Bahrain. Sally loved the incongruity of this pretty confection from another world trimmed with lace and ruffles and ribbons teased into bows. She perched the parasol on her shoulder and began the long trudge with the baby back down the beach toward the dock. She breathed not only more easily in the shade but more happily at the thought of how she must look now with this absurd parasol. Especially in the summers, marooned here in these brutal endless Saudi summers, there was only so much reality any of them could stand in the flyblown oily stench of the camp, the desert, the wells. In contrast to the harsh definitions of bleached-out sky and desert, Sally's silky blond hair, her delicate white dress, her lacy white parasol conjured up another, more softly ambiguous world.

She fluttered her eyelashes at the intensity of the blinding spotlight that was the sun; she patted the baby; she tried not to let her eyes settle into a wrinkly squint. It was noon, and already the light, the heat, the heavy damp air were too much. There was nothing at all moving in the air except too many waves of heat: heat so overheavy it seemed to transform stationary objects - a tent, a palm tree, a broken-down truck - into wavering shimmerings of mirage. Sally was stifling in the high-necked, long-sleeved, floor-length white cotton dress styled like a Victorian nightgown. But it could have been worse, Sally consoled herself. The American wives had to cover up their necks and arms and legs so as not to offend Saudi's puritanical Muslims. But at least the American wives were barefaced, not masked like those pitiful Arab women.

She staggered at last around a bend and could see the four tatty date palm fishermen's shacks, the single dusty street, the cluster of dusty warehouses, the rickety pier, the rusty boat, the huddle of gesticulating men. They had planned to avoid the heat by casting off very early this morning, but the engine had refused to catch. The boat's captain had assured them he would have it repaired in no time flat, but so far they had been waiting for three hours. She had passed the time combing for shells along the beach, playing with the baby in a nearby cove, and taking yet another roll of photographs of them all lined up on the pier. But now Sally was impatient either to cast off for Bahrain or to cancel the whole trip. Again she considered sending the baby back to the compound. It was terribly hot now, perhaps too hot for the baby to be out with them in the open boat. The American mechanic who had been called out to repair the engine was just about to climb back into his truck, and she could send the baby back with him. She stood irresolute in the baking sun.

'Sally!' Tom shouted to her from the launch. 'The motor's working! We're ready to cast off.'

Sally wavered for an instant more, then called out to the mechanic. When he pulled up near her, she explained she wanted him to drop Sunny off at a neighbor's. 'Two days, baby. Mummy will be back in two days.' She kissed a light butterfly kiss of goodbye on the baby's moist velvety cheek.

'Sally! Let's go!'

She kissed the baby again on her tiny rosebud lips, then tried to run out to Tom on the pier. But as the heat slammed against her, spots as alive as electricity danced before her eyes, and she reeled and almost fell. Yet despite the heat, the sweat, the smell, the leaden weight of her own legs, Sally managed a radiant smile as she walked the length of the pier. She waved to the captain, to the crew, and to Abdullah, her husband's guide, who was along today to buy supplies for Tom's next expedition into the desert. She could not stop herself from blowing Tom a kiss, even though he had told her once, twice, a trillion times that she shouldn't be affectionate with him in front of the Arabs. Sally felt a thrill of sexual desire course through her as Tom stood intently watching her. She could never get enough of him. Here in the Saudi heat their physical passion had swelled and throbbed and all but obliterated her. She liked it best when he took her in the sweatiest hours of the hottest afternoons, rutting together naked and twisting on the foam iron bed. This man with his jealous possessiveness, his unpredictable depressions, his single-minded intensity focused ardently on her was in her blood. She tried to read his sunburnt face, but his beard, his sunglasses, and his Arab head scarf hid him from her. Impulsively she threw him another reckless kiss, and the lightness of her laughter hung in the heavy air. She was very pleased with herself as she proceeded toward the fifty-foot, motor-driven *Calabria* which would carry them the twelve miles from the pioneer American oil fields on the coast of Saudi Arabia to the more established and better-provisioned British-run oil concession on Bahrain.

'Dammit, Sally. Don't do that in front of *them*!' Tom gestured toward the Arab sailors who were gawking at his wife and muttering excitedly about her in their guttural tongue. 'And why did you send the baby back? You said you wouldn't go without her.'

She could see he was annoyed with her, with the Arab crew, with the morning's frustrating delay. As she twirled her parasol, she gave her husband her steamiest, most seductive smile. 'I wanted to be alone with you.' She took his hand, and as he swung her on board their bodies touched for an instant. Again the wanting of him raced through her. 'Alone, Tom.' Their eyes locked.

'Later,' he muttered hoarsely. He kept his hand on her waist long enough to feel her damp pliant flesh under the thin cotton, but as he steered her toward the far side of the deck he saw Abdullah narrow his eyes. At once Tom took his hands off his wife. An Arab never touched his woman in public, and a part of Tom yearned to be an Arab. Especially Tom wanted Abdullah's acceptance and respect. In the four long, arduous years Tom had been in Saudi, Abdullah had been his guide and his companion but not quite his friend. They had trekked together, hunted together, thirsted together, run the gamut of all possible human privations together. Yet always Abdullah had kept his emotional distance. The Arab men were, in a way, as veiled as their women. Abdullah was as elusive as shade in the desert.

Sally felt Tom pull away from her, and when she saw Abdullah scowling she felt like spitting in his face. 'It's rude to stare. Don't you know, Abdullah, that it's rude to stare?' Boldly she stared back at him. She knew he didn't like her. She was certain he thought she was as wanton as a whore. It used to infuriate her that these Arab men were as they were, that they treated their own women worse than their camels, that they looked her over as if she were meat hanging from a hook in the souk. Now she was past caring about anything, pro or con, about the Arabs, except that she resented the way Tom imagined that the Arabs were Indians and he was a cowboy and Saudi was Hollywood. Despite all evidence to the contrary, Tom persisted in believing the Arabs to be noble savages. Sally swept haughtily past the sullen ignoble savage she detested.

Abdullah leaned his sinewy mahogany-colored body against the boiler-room wall. He straightened his long white nightshirt-cut robe that was called a *thobe* and his flowing red checkered head scarf that was called a *ghutra*. Thoughtfully he watched the retreating backs of the perplexing foreign man and the crazy foreign woman. He had not understood the English words that witch had hurled at him, but he had heard her contempt. How, Abdullah wondered, could Tom allow his pale woman to act so shamelessly? She even kissed him and rubbed her body against him in public. Abdullah brooded yet again over why Allah had seen fit to make him a guide for the *Nazrani*, these Christian followers of Jesus of Nazareth who had invaded and degraded his world. True, Tom had a good enough heart. Time and time again, in the desert, the man had shown fierce manly courage, generosity, and patient endurance. In time, with just a little more comradely knowledge of the desert and the Arabic language, Abdullah might even be willing to accept Tom as a brother. Yet when this man was around his woman, he paraded his emotions far more childishly than Abdullah's two young sons would ever dare to do. Abdullah shrugged. Who was he, after all, to try to comprehend the mysteries of why the infidels were as they were? He turned away from the Americans and feasted his eyes on the sandy flatlands and hills stretching to the horizon. He wished once again, very sharply, that it had been his fate to pass all his days in the wild, simple infinities of his desert. All of his Al-Murrah tribe had always done so. To be as they had been, always, forever, had been all he wished for in his life. Abdullah sighed a resigned little sigh. It must have been written in the great book of life that his destiny was different from his ancestors'. Five years ago the Saudi king, Abdul Aziz, had signed a pact to allow the infidels to search the desert for oil. The king had asked the elders of Abdullah's tribe to assign one of their own as *rafiq* protector for the Americans. The best of the Al-Murrahs had all drawn lots, and Abdullah had been one of the losers. It had become his fate to shadow the geologist Tom Shannon.

Abdullah allowed himself a final glance of longing at the shore. It was midsummer, and the black tents of the Al-Murrahs would be pitched at the tribal wells to the south on the fringes of the deep red dunes of the Empty Quarter. His wife, his sons, his father were many days away, even by the fastest racing camel. Abdullah squared his shoulders and made himself stop dreaming and padded over on his bare feet to do his duty. Tom Shannon and his woman were formally under his *dakhala* protection. It was a matter of Abdullah's personal honor and the collective honor of the Al-Murrah that he safeguard these Americans against all dangers, even at the price of his own life. Impassively Abdullah stood a little apart from the Shannons at the far edge of the deck.

Sally glared at Abdullah. 'Is he going to hang around us all weekend?' She shuddered. 'He gives me the creeps. He's always sneaking around, listening, giving me dirty looks.'

'C'mon Sally.' Tom looked around to make sure the Arab sailors couldn't see them. Abdullah he would trust with his life, his wife, all the treasures of the earth. But those leering sailors were strangers. It was very bad form to let one of the wives make a spectacle of herself in front of the natives. The sailors were on the other side of the deck, and so Tom put his arm around her shoulders. 'Don't be like this, honey. He's only doing his job.'

'Is it his job to spy on us? Tell him to go away, Tom. Your Arabic's good enough for that. Get rid of him. Please?'

'I can't insult him like that.' Tom decided not to risk an argument by delivering another lecture about Arab manners and mores. He had not been off alone with Sally since the birth of the baby four months ago, and he intended to make the most of this occasion. He pulled her closer to him and let his fingers play on her shoulder. 'Forget Abdullah. We're as good as alone. You know he doesn't understand English.'

'But I hate him watching us.' She took his hand. 'I

wanted to talk to you. Really talk, about something important.' The engine caught and drowned out what else she had been about to say.

Their launch cut loose of the pier, away from the muddy waves slapping the weedy beach, out beyond the breakwater into the azure sea that, on this July morning, was as steaming as hot soup. Flocks of black, big-beaked birds rose squealing from the sandbar that guarded the mouth of the port which had been newly dredged by the Americans. On shore the terrain was gravelly bluffs, scrubby vegetation, salt flats, and mountains of sand and rock way off in the distance under a hovering haze.

Sally watched the dunes and the dusty palm groves and the limestone, oil-rich hills and mesas of the shoreline recede into what camp cynics said was always the greatest beauty in Saudi: the loveliness of leaving it behind. She wondered, as she always did when she looked at how small the human settlements were against the vastness of the desert, at the fragility of man's hold on life here. From the shade of her parasol she stared at the oil-company camp with so much naked hatred that if there were any righteousness in the world, it would have exploded into a ball of fire, and she and Tom could go home where they belonged. In Massachusetts now it would be summer, a lush green sweet summer, not desolate and burnt like the summers here. At home the tomatoes would be ripening on the vine, the fireflies would be winking like neon at night, the air would be heavy with the smell of roses and honeysuckle and freshly mown grass. Sally raised her arm and waved goodbye to the land as if its oil derricks and pipes and tanker trucks were not forlorn and detested but instead home sweet home. For one rapt instant she half-believed and altogether hoped that the oil encampment had suddenly been whisked seven thousand miles back to New England, where poets call landscapes of mountains and green pastures and bubbling streams God's country. But even the heat shimmers couldn't disguise this black oily blot on that sea of endless sand. Sally put her weary head on her husband's broad shoulder. This was Saudi, not home. This wasn't God's country. This dead, acrid, sulfurous land was of hell and the devil and damnation.

She would tell him now, before she lost her nerve. 'I want to go home, Tom.'

'We'll be home soon enough. We'll only be away two nights in Bahrain.' He smiled down into her blue eyes. 'You're worried about leaving Sunny behind, aren't you?'

He had misunderstood. 'I'm worried about all of us.' She would be blunt. 'I want to leave Saudi. I have to leave Saudi. I hate it here. Let's go home, Tom.'

His arm grew slack around her shoulders and he was silent as he watched the receding shoreline. He wasn't surprised she wanted out. Sally was as fragile as a fern, and a fern could not for long survive this withering life in the desert. Mostly he regretted bringing her here, even though she had hounded him to let her come, even though he doubted he could have lasted this long here without her. They had been in love, it sometimes seemed, for all their lives. They had started as childhood sweethearts back in Still River, and later, when he was away at college in California, she had written him at least a letter a day. They had married just after his graduation, and then they had been separated for two excruciating years while he looked for oil in the Arabian desert.

Just as soon as the oil company had allowed the wives to come, Sally had rushed to his side. In those first steamy months here, she had been brave and intoxicated with the sheer adventure of life in this fantastic other world of masked women and black tents and lumbering camels. They had camped in the desert, shopped in the souks, sailed on the Gulf, and most of all they had been overcome by the sensual heat of this place. But then she had become pregnant, and she was sick all the time, and frightened, and as fretful as a baby. Now, mostly, he felt guilty for inflicting Saudi upon her. What made it worse was that she knew he loved it here and that he had never been happier than when he was searching these pale bleak Arab deserts for oil. Yet he knew she couldn't stand much more of Saudi Arabia. Not long ago, in their bungalow, he had found her poring over an album of dried flowers she had picked one summer day in Massachusetts. She had looked so wistful as she had lifted a tiny sweetheart rose to her lips and then so despairing when her touch had turned the brittle gold petals to a powder all too much like sand. His heart had ached as he had watched her weep over that rose dust. Too, he felt her sometimes sobbing in dry heaves in the heat of the nights, and when he would hold her closer to comfort her, she would cry out for him to tell her how it could be that it was so arid and brown and parched here – 'So dead,' she'd always say; 'it's so dead. . . .'

Now as she looked up at him, two tears as clear as Persian Gulf pearls coursed down her cheeks. 'I'm going, Tom. I'm taking the baby and I'm going home. With you or without you, I'm going home.' She hesitated, then went on. 'I'll wait for you back home if you stay on here for the rest of your contract. But please, Tom, come home with me. Please!'

But Tom's gaze was drawn as if to a magnet away from his wife and back to the Saudi shore where he believed the biggest jackpot on earth was hidden. The rich oil fields of America were shallow puddles compared with the deep black viscous seas of oil that lay under the Middle East. Shortly after the turn of the century the British and then the Russians and finally the French had begun to drill the petroleum fields of Iran and Iraq and the Persian Gulf. The Europeans had persuaded backward and impoverished kings and shahs and *shaykhs* to sign 'concession' agreements for paltry sums in exchange for monopoly mineral rights over entire blocs of countries. Even though the Americans had come late to the Middle East oil bonanza, they had been blessed with a fantastic stroke of buccaneer luck. Five years ago, in 1933, a consortium of American oil companies had paid the king of Saudi Arabia a down payment of only thirty thousand British pounds in gold for granting them a sixty-year monopoly concession over the eastern half of his country.

And now Tom wanted the satisfaction of finding the best fields himself and seeing those wonderfully stinking black geysers spurt into the sky. He thought of the Number Seven as his own. He had decided where to drill, and then he had insisted they go deeper and deeper, long after others had wanted to give up. He would never forget the day that well came in, for Sunny had been born just hours after commercial quantities of oil first gushed up from it. Lucky Seven; lucky Sunny, born the very day an explosion of liquid black gold promised that Saudi was sitting on buried treasure. March 4, 1938 - his, and Saudi's, lucky day. And now, just when everything was about to burst wide open here, Sally wanted him to give it all up and return home and live a boring, predictable life in Massachusetts?

Tom let his arm drop away from his wife's shoulders. He resented her ultimatum. She had known about his work when she married him. Any other young wife would thank God her husband managed to keep a steady and high-paying job like this even in the depth of the Depression. He had first signed on for this hardship post because he earned three thousand dollars a year more here than he would have in the Texas or California or Oklahoma oil fields. He had needed the extra money so he and Sally could get married, so they could save up to buy their own home, so he could help his parents pay the mortgage and keep their farm in Massachusetts.

As Tom heard Abdullah restlessly pacing the deck on his panther feet, he wished he could go on the prowl with his Arab. Sometimes Tom simply wished Sally *would* go away. Being with the Arabs took him back to his childhood, when the boys all banded together, when they scorned the prissiness of girls, when they whooped and hollered with an excess of young innocence. The hardships of life in Saudi were difficult enough to endure without a wife who refused to make an effort to understand these people Tom believed were romantic and wild and free and more moral than any white men he had ever met.

At first his infatuation with the Arabs had been a matter of smells and sounds and sensations, the aroma of cardamom-scented coffee freshly roasted at dawn, the lonesome tinkle of faraway camel bells in the dead of night, the thrill of cool wet water on hot cracked skin. As time had passed, he had become more and more drawn to the primitive tribal life of the nomadic Arab 'Bedouin.' He had begun to press for assignments that would take him farther out into the desert. He had taken to sleeping in a black goat-hair tent. He had ridden the high dunes by camel. He had hunted gazelles with a falcon on his wrist. He had sat silent and motionless in his dusty robes for hours beside flickering campfires. He had begun to experience a wild fierce leaping joy as he flirted with Arab life here in the vast scorching solitude of this endless desert.

The boat's engine coughed and died. Black smoke rose in a cloud from the engine room. The American captain screamed at the Arab sailors, the crew ran frantically about, the smoke died down, and the boat sat still in the quiet sea while the men worked to repair the engine again. In the hot, humid climate of the Gulf, mechanical breakdowns were daily occurrences. It took a stable of maintenance engineers to keep the trucks, boats, and airplanes running.

Tom reached into his shirt pocket and pulled out a cigarette. He lit it slowly and took a deep reflective drag. Moodily he stared at the coastline. Always, when he thought about Saudi and oil and the Arabs and himself, he ended up with a mass of contradictions. He loved the oil business, and he loved the primitive life of the Bedouin, but common sense told him the two were probably mutually exclusive. Saudis were not just any Arabs, any Muslims; they were Wahhabi Muslims, members of a strict and puritanical sect who were as different from the masses of freewheeling Muslims as fundamentalist Southern Baptists were from Roman Catholics. Saudi's Muslims did not drink alcohol, smoke cigarettes, dance, sing, go to the movies, or otherwise engage in any fun-loving deviltry. The Wahhabi strain of Islam was the state religion in Saudi. Religious police flogged men who refused to join the five-times-daily prayers in the mosques. Criminals were punished according to the harsh medieval code recommended thirteen centuries ago in the Koran. Murderers were beheaded, the hands or feet of thieves were severed, adulterous women were stoned to death. In the towns women covered their faces when they ventured from their walled houses, for they lived by a strict code of seclusion.

Saudi Arabia was one of the most remote and isolated backwaters of the world. But Tom had drawn up the geologic maps and run tests on the oil from the Number Seven well. Saudi Arabia had so much oil that someday it would surely be one of the richest states on earth. Yet Tom worried that a sudden influx of great wealth might destroy this brave, simple, ancient way of life. When he camped with the Arabs, Tom often felt he was witnessing the end of a world. Still, he tried not to get carried away with misplaced romanticism. Health care, education, new and plentiful water resources, electricity, roads, trucks, telephones, and indoor plumbing would make the lives of these Arabs less difficult. Still he feared they might lose what was the best in them, the inner harmony and integrity of their desert hearts and souls. Sometimes Tom thought that all he and the other Americans were bringing to Saudi was muck and stench and ambiguity and trouble. Always, when he tried to come to rational conclusions about Saudi's future, he ended up feeling uneasy, ambivalent. But still Tom hated to expel himself from this arid Eden. Before this culture vanished forever, he wanted to understand and experience all Saudi had to offer.

Tom threw his cigarette in an arc out into the Gulf. He could understand why Sally did not share his enthusiasms. The Arabia he loved, the Arabia of camels and campfires and camaraderie, was a masculine world that would forever exclude her. Of course she hated it here. She had all the hardships but none of the joys. He loved her, and he wanted her to be happy. Maybe she *should* wait for him back in Massachusetts.

As the engine roared again and the boat lurched along the channel toward Bahrain, Tom reminded himself that whatever ultimately happened to Saudi, what mattered was his wife and daughter. Maybe he should go home with them to New England.

Sally had been watching the play of emotions on his face, and now she sensed it was time for her trump card. 'I'm pregnant, Tom. I'm going to have another baby. That's why I have to go home.'

'Pregnant! Sally! Honey! You're sure?' When she nodded, he threw his arms around her and hugged her tight.

'A son,' she murmured. 'I'll give you a son.'

He had to protect her, coddle her, adore her. A son! He would do whatever she wanted. 'Okay. You win. We go home.'

'Really, Tom? Truly? You'll go home with me?'

'I'll give my notice when we get back from Bahrain. They know all the trouble you had having Sunny. They won't like me leaving, but what the hell. I'll have you home before the first frost.'

'Frost! Imagine, Tom, cold nights and frost and ice and snow. Knee socks. Earmuffs. Mittens!' Sally laughed her tinkly silvery laugh. She was suddenly so full of high spirits that she furled her parasol and sat down at the edge of the deck, peeled off her sandals and let her legs dangle almost but not quite into the deep clear water. She made a face and pointed to an undulating nest of sea cobras listlessly tangled on the sea floor. She flinched away from a school of jellyfish, for even one brush of those pretty pink tentacles could make her lie in sleepless pain for weeks. She shaded her eyes with her hand and scanned the shimmering surface of the sea for any sign of sharks.

As he sat down beside her, he was relieved he had finally surrendered in this, the last battle of their war over Saudi. Tonight, in their hotel room in Bahrain, he would make slow tender love to the cradle of her body. But now he was content to sun himself beside his pregnant wife. He looked out to sea. 'There! Over there, Sally!' Tom pointed to flashes of silver fins skimming the waves.

Uncertainly Sally shaded her eyes. 'Sharks?' She was thankful that in her two years in Saudi she had not yet spotted a shark. Yet always she had known those killers lurked just under the surface of this sea. When she got back home, she would swim only in highly chlorinated swimming pools. Back in Still River, she would court no more dangers. Already she had endured a lifetime of dangers in Saudi.

'No,' Tom finally said. 'Looks to me like the "great" barracuda. It's funny ones that size would be swimming in a school. Usually they're loners. Must be mating. Or spawning time. They're the deadliest fish in the sea. Worse than sharks. A helluva lot of swimmers who have been reported killed by sharks were really done in by barracuda.' Tom shook his head. 'Barracuda have razor teeth, and they'll go after anything that moves. They've been known to rip a man to pieces, even this close to shore.'

'Ripped to pieces?' Sally shivered in the heat and edged closer to her husband. Unhappily she followed the progress of the barracuda fins, only one more menace in this world that teemed with deadly danger. Even though he had told her they were going home and she had nothing more to fear, she burst into tears. 'Tom,' she sobbed, 'I'm afraid here. So afraid.'

Just as he was patting her shoulder and telling her she had nothing to fear, there was a menacing rumble from the engine room.

In the next dreadful moments, Sally clutched Tom's arm as the boat's vibrations increased. She clawed at Tom as the deck pitched violently back and forth. She tried to climb into his lap as the boat heaved in the water. She was in a panic as she remembered the portent of her nightmare, the rumbling and rolling just like this, then walls and ceilings crashing in, the smell of death all around her. She had thought the nightmare was a premonition of danger for her baby; she had left Sunny back in Saudi to save her child; but now, as Sally clung to Tom, she saw the truth. *She* was the one who was in danger; it had always been she who was in mortal danger here, she who never should have come, she who was about to die. Her fingernails were sharp and pointed, and she ripped Tom's flesh as she raked him in her terror. She screamed as a sudden blue flash from the engine room was brighter, for an instant, than the sun. She shuddered when a louder clap like thunder echoed over the water.

He held her close to him as if nearness gave him some power to save her. She was crushed against him, screaming, when the explosion rent the air. Smoke belched over the deck, and there was a whoosh of hot air. The two of them were thrown off their feet, still in each other's arms, their eyes wide and staring. In an instant they were sprawled back in a tangled heap on the deck. There were more agonized screams from the far side of the deck, frenzied shrieks in Arabic and in English. Sally panted in Tom's arms. Her body trembled against him.

A deafening boom sounded, white light crackled, the stern blew apart. Tom and Sally were pressed tightly together; she clung desperately to him as the deck collapsed under their feet. She fell on him, they fell together, they and what was left of the wooden deck slid into the hot water of the Gulf. Tom concentrated on only one thing: hold on to her, hold on to Sally, save her. He had to get his Sally away from this boat before there were more explosions, before there was gasoline in the water, before the water was on fire with burning oil. He tried to swim with her in his arms, but she fought him. She flailed at him, she screamed and she hit at him, she went under, he grabbed for her, finally he brought her up coughing.

'Oil!' he screamed. 'Swim! Fire! Sally!' Again she tried to hit him. As she screamed she took in another mouthful of seawater; she was choking as he treaded water and held her up by her long yellow hair. 'Sally! Sally!'

A final series of explosions drowned out his cries. Hot oily air whirled in currents above the water. The last struts which had been holding together what was left of the launch finally gave out. Flaming planks crashed near them in the water. Steel drums bounced on the waves. Smoking bits of wreckage sailed through the air, splashed, sank. Faint human cries drifted on the wind. The surface of the water was slick with black oil, and some of it began to burn. Around them the water hissed with fire. The flames raced closer.

Sally suddenly grew very still in her husband's arms as she watched the approach of the fire. All her life she had been afraid. But now, at its end, at last she found calmness and courage. She knew she would die soon. She looked into her husband's eyes. So much to say. Forgiveness. She had to tell him that she forgave him for doing this to her, for bringing her to this place of death, to die by fire in this water. 'Forgive,' she murmured. 'I forgive.' She had so much more to say to this man. Always she had loved Tom; in life, in death, she wanted to be with him. Always with him, never alone. She clung to him. She would die alone, even if she was in his arms. 'Don't leave me,' she begged him. 'Don't leave me here, Tom, alone. Promise! Promise!' Her eyes pleaded. 'The baby. Sunny. Home. Back home. The baby . . . ' Her eyes, now, were glassy as she watched the fire leap higher and felt it singe the hair on her head. 'Oh, my God,' she prayed out loud. 'Oh, my God, I am heartily sorry for having offended Thee. . . . '

But even if she had given up, even if Sally was saying her farewells to him and making a good Act of Contrition, Tom was still frantically trying to save the two of them. He swam away, he thought, from the worst of the fire, toward a floating oil drum. He wrapped Sally's limp arms around the drum, he told her to hang on, he promised her he would be back as soon as he found something more buoyant that they could use as a lifeboat.

'Tom! No! Don't leave me alone!'

He ignored her plea and struck off alone. He was concentrating on swimming in hard clean strokes, on looking for a bit of wreckage that could serve as a raft. He was some distance away from Sally when the oil drum she was clinging to caught fire.

Sally was very quiet. She did not scream; she moved her lips in prayer as she fried in the hot oil on the crest of the water. She burned like a torch for a long moment, but then strong arms gripped her, pulled her from the flames, drew her away from the burning oil. Bravely Abdullah cut through the simmering purple water with the white woman in his brown arms. His honor and his tribe's honor and his race's honor required that he save this woman and this man who were under his protection, even if he had to forfeit his own life. When he felt her body go slack, he told himself she had only fainted. He surged through the water to where he saw Tom clinging to a floating hatch cover. Abdullah tugged at Tom's arm and shouted something in his ear in Arabic. Tom stared at Abdullah in bewilderment, and when he saw Sally in the Arab's arms he clutched at his wife. He kissed her, he stroked her hair, he did not seem to notice that her body was stiff and burnt and dead. Again the Arab screamed at him and gestured at the top of the hatch cover. In Tom's panic, he forgot what little Arabic he knew. He shook his head at Abdullah. He kissed Sally's closed eyelids. Without Tom's help, then, Abdullah pushed and lifted and dragged Sally out of the water and atop the hatch cover. He had to struggle even harder to get Tom up beside her.

Abdullah clung to the listing side of the makeshift raft. He paddled with his free hand now left, now right, now swerving sharply until they were mostly away from the burning oil. He looked anxiously out at the sea. He had seen that school of barracuda not far from the boat just before the explosion. By now the great savage fish would be coming closer. By now they would have felt movement and tasted blood. Abdullah looked at the small refuge he had secured for the Americans atop the hatch cover. Tom and his dead woman not only took up all the room, they also were all the weight it could bear without sinking. Abdullah had thought there would be room up there for all three of them. He had not realized the woman was dead until her body was out of the water. He had to make Tom let go of the woman and get up there in her place. If Tom wouldn't let her body sink into the sea, if he himself didn't get out of the water, if the barracuda were as close as he feared they were - even submerged in the water, Abdullah broke into a sweat. He wished that either he spoke English or the American spoke Arabic. His life depended on making Tom understand what had to be done. Abdullah plucked at Tom's arm, he pointed at the woman, he gestured with his free hand that Tom had to let the woman go so he could take her place.

But the American brushed him off like a fly. Tom shut his eyes and held Sally close to him in his arms. He was in shock. He still had not understood that his wife was dead.

Abdullah clawed at the foreigner. '*Min fadlak*, please! *Nejdah*, help me! *Min fadlak!*'

'Sally!' The American crooned that single word under his breath. 'Sally.'

'*Nejdah!*' Abdullah thought he could see sinister silver shadows on the crest of the waves. Allah, not so soon! Allah, not now! 'Allah!'

The scream seemed to bring the American almost to his senses. He stared at the Arab as if he were trying to recall who, exactly, he was. 'Abdullah!' It began to dawn on Tom that this Arab wanted him to let Sally slide down into the water. But Tom held Sally in a tighter grip. Give his wife's place to this Arab? Tom turned away from Abdullah's pleading eyes.

The Arab made a desperate calculation: the speed at which the barracuda were coming at him, the amount of time it would take for him to scramble onto the hatch cover and push off the body of the foreign woman. . . . There wasn't time. His time was too near, now, for any evasions. *Maktub*, it is written. . . . It must have been written - Abdullah looked up at the sky - that his own time was now. But his sons - his wife and his two sons - who would care for them? Desperately Abdullah screamed at the American. '*Awladi!*'

Reluctantly Tom tore his eyes off Sally. Dully he was beginning to realize she wasn't breathing. His head swiveled back to Abdullah, and he seemed, finally, to be trying to understand. 'Sons? You're trying to tell me something about your sons?'

'*Waladaine*.' If he spoke as if to a three-year-old, the American might understand. 'Two boys. *Enta sadet awladi!*'

'My two boys? You . . . help . . . my sons?'

It seemed to Abdullah that the American was understanding at least the gist of his last desperate request.

And then it seemed suddenly that Tom understood even more than that. He looked down at the Arab in the water, over at the slashes of barracuda fins coming toward them, and then at the space his - dead! - Sally was taking up on top of the hatch cover. To save Abdullah, he would have to let Sally's body slip into the sea. The barracuda would get either Sally or Abdullah. Tom told himself he had to let go of Sally, yet he could not bear to do it. The last fatal precious seconds when there was still a slight chance of saving Abdullah slipped away as Tom held Sally's body tightly to him.

'Allah!' In the water Abdullah screamed to God for help. 'Allah! Allah! Allah!'

Finally, as Tom watched the glide of the barracuda coming closer, reality hit him. Sally was dead, but Abdullah was alive. He could do no more to help his wife, but he *could* save his friend. He shifted the weight of his wife's body in his arms and braced himself to do what common decency and humanity required. It would nearly kill him, but he would let her go. He would let her go. Just as soon as he was sure he could rescue Abdullah, he would let her slide into the water. He stretched out his hand to Abdullah. He reached out, he caught the Arab's hand in his, he tried to pull him to safety.

But his generosity had come too late.

'Allah!' The Arab screamed in agony as the barracuda were upon him. 'Allah. . . . '

Tom Shannon shut his guilty eyes so he would not have to see the bloody thrashing in the water. He kept his eyes shut for a very long time so he would not have to see once more that the wife he still held so tightly in his arms was dead. When, finally, he opened his eyes, there were neither pools of blood nor pools of oil atop the sapphire blue coldness of the Persian Gulf. But drifting near him among bits and pieces of wreckage from the boat was that absurd white lacy parasol of Sally's.

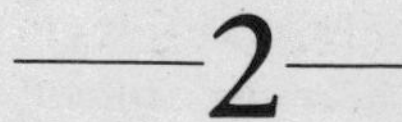

2

Tom Shannon feared God enough to touch the graven image on the burning-hot religious medal of Saint Jude, the patron saint of lost causes. Sally had given him the medal, which he wore on a chain around his neck. 'Sally,' he said aloud, as if invoking her name were a prayer. He gunned the engine and crossed himself as he stared down the mightiest slipface of the steepest dune of the Dahana. Even Saint Jude, he thought, would have to abandon him today. In the three weeks since that doomed boat had exploded in the Gulf, he had longed for deliverance. Yet now, when it counted, he shrank from the brink. His sweaty trembling hands slipped off the steering wheel.

Tom knew he was altogether lost in every way that mattered, even though he knew he was in the Dahana high-dune country, in the withered heart of the Saudi desert, exactly forty-two miles north and eighteen miles west of the American camp at Dhahran. In the more innocent happier days of only a few months ago, Tom had been the first to map the geologic makeup of these golden apricot dunes that divided the coastal Gulf lowlands from the high gravel plains of central Arabia. He and Sally had thrilled to the beauty of these Dahana dunes. They had camped not far from here, they had sunk up to their knees in these soft sands, they had made love at high noon in the hot shadows of one of these gorgeous supple drifting mountains.

He told himself he must not think of that now. Especially he must not think of kissing, touching, loving her. He must think only of doing what had to be done. Of doing what he had decided to do. Of committing his final mortal sin. Of killing the killer.

He had killed Sally and he had killed Abdullah.

He had killed Sally just by allowing her to come to this godforsaken country. He should have known Saudi was no place for a woman. He should have taken the money he had saved in his first years on this cursedly overpaid job and run all the way back home to her in New England with it. He shouldn't have been so greedy for more money that he put his wife in jeopardy. Greed, he remembered, was one of the seven deadly sins. Deadly greed.

He had killed Abdullah even more surely than he had killed Sally. Even when Tom squeezed his own eyes tight shut, he could not escape the memory of those fiercely pleading dark eyes. Abdullah, who had saved Tom's life so many times in the desert, had deserved better. A dog deserved a better death than Abdullah's. He had let that poor man die that dreadful death because he had valued the corpse of his wife more. Tom stared at the Saudi sand mountains and wondered again if he would have made the same choice if it had been not Abdullah but an American in the water. Tom wanted to believe it had been only his own fatal misunderstanding of Arabic that had caused Abdullah's death. Yet on that high noon in the Gulf Tom had had a very long and absolutely damning instant of hesitation after he understood both the words of the Arab and the menace of the barracuda. He was as guilty as if he had sunk a dagger into the Arab's heart. Into his friend's heart.

It was time, Tom told himself with finality, to begin paying for his sins. He was bitterly ashamed, he was heartily sorry and now he must offer his penance. Here in the supple, shifting sands of the Dahana, it was time for him to die.

Nervously Tom licked his lips, and his tongue came away with a flaking layer of dead skin. When the blinding searchlights and the frantic rescue party had found him drifting in the Gulf the night after the explosion, he had been tantalizingly close to death. He had been suffering from shock and exposure, and his body had been covered by patches of first-degree burns from the tropical sun. He had begged the doctor in Dhahran to let him die just as Sally, Abdullah, the American captain, and one of the Arab deckhands had died. But the doctor had treated him and congratulated him for being blessed and surviving the accident with nothing broken. Tom had despaired that he was cursed. From now on, in his life, everything was broken.

Tom looked down the four-hundred-foot drop-off of the dune. He reached for the hand brake. Surely he would die if he forced the truck down here; then he would be as damned as he should be. Suicide was a mortal sin.

But then he flinched as if the hot metal of the brake had scorched his fingers. Long ago, when Tom was an altar boy, back at St. Theresa's, Father Healy had refused to bury suicides in consecrated ground. He had branded suicide the one unforgivable mortal sin. Fleetingly Tom wondered if he could set the truck rolling to perdition down the slope and then, at the last instant, make a good Act of Contrition and therefore get the grand slam: death and paradise with Sally. Tom supposed God wasn't amenable to such childish bargains or such sly moral trickery. If he was going to do it, it would have to be with the full knowledge of his own imminent damnation.

Again Tom brooded on the ends of Sally and Abdullah, and again the despair settled over him. His mother had once told him he was 'black Irish,' one of those brooding sensitive Celtic souls given to self-laceration and gloom.

Grimly, before he could change his mind, Tom snapped loose the hand brake. He heard the motor whinny like a wild mustang, and, as he tried not to brace himself for the impact that had to come, he felt the truck buck under him in the loose sand at the crest of the dune. He took a last very deep breath, he hit the gas and eased the clutch, and he let his grip on the truck and life itself begin a sickening, deep, satisfying slide down, all the way down, to hell. Illogically, he waited one second, two seconds, a dizzy half-minute, for the truck to burrow deep into the sand, at least six feet down like Sally's grave. But he was trying to defy the laws of physics. The inflated balloon tires were custom-made to ride the crust of the desert sands. As the truck proudly skimmed the down-crest, Tom jammed his foot harder against the accelerator. The truck jerked ahead faster, and Tom's chest slammed into the steering wheel. Skid, he urged the truck. Roll, burn, be done with it. He tried to dive-bomb it to earth like a plane. He screamed as the truck careened down the slope, 'Sally!'

He was prepared to die when the truck hit what he thought would be the tightly packed wall of sand in the valley between the two deep dunes. He wanted nothing more at that moment than the end of his guilty life. He floored the gas pedal and waited for the end.

Instead, the truck began losing speed two-thirds of the way down the dune where the angle of the slope slackened. Frantically Tom hit the accelerator, he spun the wheel, he pounded his fists on the steering wheel. But the truck rolled gently into the valley, then shuddered in a rain of sand and stopped. The engine coughed but did not die. The tires began hissing escaped air as they sank deep into the soft sand.

Tom lay against the steering wheel and spent a lingering

instant wondering if this was death. The engine coughed again, and when it finally quit and left him in that terrible empty silence of the desert, Tom sighed.

Shakily he righted himself. He should have known his truck could take that dune, that it was better at keeping its balance than he was. And surely, too, he should have remembered that the sand at the feet of the Dahana dunes was as soft and as drifting as newly fallen snow.

He climbed out and stood awhile looking up. From the bowels of the dunes, even the grainy yellow sun looked as if it could have been made of sand. He took a deep breath and felt particles of sand in his lungs. He wiped the perspiration off his forehead with the back of his hand, and he looked at the sand that stuck to the sweaty hairs. He listened very hard to see if he could hear the sound of the sand moving on the ground, in the air, all around him.

He had failed in his first try, but there was no reason why he had to fail again. He had tried to go with a bit of dash, with the throttle wide open. But death would maybe come with more certainty, and certainly with more suffering, if he simply set off by himself in a long deadly one-way walk through the dunes. Maybe the others would find the abandoned truck in a week or so, but probably they would never find his own remains. Tom shuddered. It would take either a greater courage or a greater despair than his to court a death like that.

He was suddenly so parched he reached inside the truck and, instead of water, by mistake pulled out his canteen of whiskey. He unscrewed the cap, smelled the liquor, and considered that there were easier ways out. Tom held the canteen above his head and poured the liquid fire down his throat until he choked. The second chug of the whiskey hardly burned at all.

It was then, as he was beginning to see the blurry sodden shape to the unwanted years ahead, that he remembered Sunny, the one he could hardly believe he had forgotten. He loved that little girl who was all he had left of Sally. Yet with Sally gone, it hurt too much to hold their baby in his arms. Tom fortified himself with another drink. If he had buried himself in the dunes today, Sunny would have been an orphan. Maybe, Tom thought, I'm not much of a man, and probably I wouldn't be much of a father. But surely I'd be better than nothing for that baby.

He looked wistfully out toward the beckoning wilderness beyond the Dahana dunes. Without Sally he did not want to live.

But Tom screwed the cap back on the canteen and threw the whiskey inside the truck. He would have to get to work digging the wheels out. If he was going to live for the innocent victim of that Gulf tragedy, he would have to extricate himself from these infernal dunes.

He stood transfixed. Sunny was not the only child victimized by the accident. Just before Abdullah died, he had pleaded with him to help his sons. Possibly he could redeem himself by living for all three of those children instead of dying for Sally and Abdullah.

Tom squinted speculatively at the sky and guessed he had four hours before sunset. In the back of the truck were boards he could use as levers to pry the tires out of the sand. He was still weak from the shock and the burns and the exposure. But if he kept his wits about him and didn't waste any effort, he could have the truck moving in an hour and a half. Tom squared his shoulders and began to work up a sweat so he could get back to the American compound to take up his new lease on life.

Inside the dark shadows of the black tent spread like a bat's wings deep in the desert, Tom brightened as he heard brass pestle hit brass mortar to announce the coming of the coffee. He had been in Saudi long enough to know that negotiations would not even begin to begin in earnest until he and Abdullah's male kinsmen and the interpreter had drunk their tiny ritual cups of fruity Arab coffee and then their large ritual glasses of sweet Arab tea. Tom's knees ached and his buttocks were numb as he politely sat with his heels tucked under him on the itchy camel-hair blanket. He was no stranger to the sluggish rhythm of Bedouin life. He had squandered many an hour haggling in dirty tents with dusky tribesmen. Yet tonight he was here to pay his debt to Abdullah and society and himself, and he was impatient to get on with it. He was willing to pay for Abdullah's sons to attend the mission school on Bahrain, and he had brought the minister himself to convince the Arabs the boys would profit from a Western education. Tom studied the faces of the somber Al-Murrah tribesmen who were Abdullah's extended family. Already Pastor Guttman had whispered they must be careful tonight. The family thought Tom was acting as if he owed them something, and so they had concluded Tom must be responsible for Abdullah's death.

Even when the missionary reminded him that the ancient 'eye for an eye, life for a life' desert code still was the law, Tom had shrugged off Pastor Guttman's warnings. Abdullah's father would make tonight's final decisions, and Tom instinctively trusted the fairness of Ibrahim. The gray-bearded and weathered old man looked like a patriarch not only of the Al-Murrah tribe but also of the Bible, Elijah about to ascend into heaven in a tornado of fire. Tom's mind wandered back to New England, where his mother used to mark her devotions in her missal with garishly colored prayer cards depicting all the suffering saints. Tom and his friends used to trade the grimmest and gaudiest back and forth the same way the Protestant boys traded baseball cards. Ibrahim looked just like Saint Sebastian about to be martyred in a rain of arrows.

Tom rocked on his haunches to try to shake some circulation back into his legs. Slyly he angled his wrist so he could see the face of his watch. Ibrahim and Pastor Guttman had been at it for more than an hour, and still Abdullah's father had not given the slightest hint he knew more was at stake than reassurances about the health and comfort of everyone squatting in this hot hairy tent.

Tom stifled a yawn. With the air of a shopper about to

part with his money, he speculated whether the two boys performing the coffee- and tea-making rituals were Abdullah's sons. Vainly he studied the two pairs of deep brown doe eyes for a reflection of his friend. Big-eyed, scrawny, grubby Arab urchins all looked alike to him. These boys were dark like all the Al-Murrah, not Negroid of feature but with tawny bronze skin. Some of their tousled black curls were carelessly tied back in frayed braids, and the rest framed their long thin hook-nosed Semitic faces in greasy tangles. These boys looked too malnourished and neglected to be Abdullah's sons. Tom looked guiltily away from the ragged boys. Surely their lives had been better and happier when their father was alive.

One lad had stoked wood on the fire, and the other expertly, and with great ceremony, poured a mix of waters from three different jugs, representing three different desert wells, into a tarnished brass beaker. Before putting the water on to boil, the bigger of the boys paused and looked over at Tom. When he saw the American dividing his attention between the two of them, swiftly he sent the other lad away to gather more wood for the fire. Finally, as he looked up at Tom from under the long eyelashes that fringed his lustrous eyes, the boy reached into a sack and took a handful of pea-green coffee pods and began grilling them in a skillet. When the beans had sizzled to an aromatic beige, the boy scooped them into the brass mortar and pounded them until the camp rang with a sound like Sunday church bells.

Next the boy called out something to someone out of eyesight and padded over to where a hanging blanket partitioned off the women's living quarters. The pair of small brown bare feet Tom glimpsed under the blanket might, he decided, belong to Abdullah's widow. He watched a slim brown hand reach out with a handful of tiny gray seeds. The boy returned to the fire and pounded these seeds until the cardamom and the coffee were a uniform gray dust. He added the spiced coffee to the boiling water and carefully set the beaker on and took it off the fire until the contents had boiled three times. Then he strained what remained with a length of date palm, tasted a few drops himself, and nodded in satisfaction as he picked up a stack of thimble-size cups in his other hand. The boy smiled at Tom as he artfully offered him the first and most honored cup of the viscous orangish swirling liquid dynamite.

'*Zain*, Muhammad,' said Ibrahim, nodding with benign approval.

Tom rewarded courteous little Muhammad with a gracious guest-to-host smile and took an exquisitely small swallow of the tiny cup of bitter brew. In his years of making desert camp with Abdullah, he had learned not only how much of this peppery, clovelike coffee he should drink to be polite but also how much he could drink without coming down with diarrhea. Fewer than three cups wasn't very polite, but more than four wasn't healthy. Tom took the two more sips necessary to finish that cup, then held it out again. He watched another smile light up Muhammad's face and was sure, then, that this one was Abdullah's son. Tom smiled back. Under the grime and the grease was a little boy with anxious, needy eyes. Again Tom felt that stab of guilt. Was this one Abdullah's favorite?

Tom watched Muhammad smile at him too eagerly as he poured the obligatory second cupful. Again Tom savored it slowly, as if it were fine cognac, and again he watched Muhammad smile in an exaggeration of delight as he poured him another. This time either the coffee or the need of the fatherless boy was too bitter for Tom's taste. When he held out the empty cup again, he jiggled it to signify he had had enough.

As Muhammad moved on, first serving coffee to the missionary, then to Ibrahim, finally to the tribesmen, Tom turned his attention to the smaller boy still at work brewing the sweet black Bedouin tea over the open fire. He was a younger version of Muhammad, with the same slight build and a matching mop of black hair. Yet when the boy suddenly looked over at him, Tom caught his breath. This one had extraordinary wild-animal eyes. He had never seen eyes like that on a child. Tom was relieved when the boy stopped staring at him with those accusing eyes. Except for their size and their eyes, these two boys were as nearly alike as twins. Surely they must be the brothers he had come for.

In the four weeks that had passed since he had decided against death in the Dahana dunes, Tom had plotted how best to discharge his responsibilities to the sons of Abdullah.

At first he had thought he might raise them as his own sons, send them to the new oil-company school in Dhahran, let them live with him and Sunny in their American bungalow. But Tom's supervisor had taken him aside in his air-conditioned office, poured him an icy beer, and told him that was impossible. Tactfully he had explained that the monopoly oil rights in this country were worth billions, and so the Americans working here must never in any way overtly offend the touchy Saudis. These particular Muslims regarded much of Western civilization as immoral and decadent, possibly contagious in its sin, and so the Saudi king had insisted the infidel oil workers live apart in a quarantined foreign compound. The American oil company had decided to humor all the royal whims. So long as the flow of oil was not in jeopardy, the company was determined never to interfere in Saudi domestic affairs. Unless and until the natives asked for schools, hospitals, electricity, roads, other such amenities of modern civilization, the oil company was not about to provide them. Tom's boss could not bend the rules and let him raise two Arabs as his own. Those boys could neither live within the American compound nor attend the American school.

Tom had hunted all over eastern Saudi Arabia then for a school for Abdullah's sons. But all he found was mosques in a few of the larger towns where old blind men would squat every morning trying to teach boys to recite the Koran. Tom was intent on more than that. They must learn to read and write and count not only in Arabic but in English. They would have to study history and science and mathematics. If and when Saudi ever stumbled into the twentieth century, he wanted these brothers to be ready to assume a glorious role in it. But the only Gulf establishments where all that might be possible were Christian missions in Bahrain and Kuwait. If Tom could secure Ibrahim's permission tonight, he would use some of Sally's insurance money to send the boys to the Dutch Reformed Church mission school on Bahrain. Tom liked to think that twelve-mile journey offshore would be only the first step. If they were as bright as he hoped, maybe someday he would send them to Beirut or Cairo for a secondary or even a university education. He could do no less for the sons of Abdullah.

The smaller boy was using a dirty rag to wipe off even dirtier glasses before he set them down in a circle on a misshapen tin tray and poured in the thick syrupy tea. But instead of following his brother's example and serving the foreigners first, he took the tea to Ibrahim. The old man scowled at this violation of the rules of hospitality and pointed to the guests. But the boy defiantly remained kneeling on the worn faded Persian rug in front of his grandfather. Ibrahim raised his hand as if about to strike him, but instead he leaned over and wiped tears from the boy's eyes. 'Rashid, *ya* Rashid,' he whispered. Ibrahim's expression, as he stroked the boy's matted curls, was very tender.

Tom stared in fascination at Rashid. Clearly this spirited one with the burning brown eyes was the favorite. And a boy like this one had probably been Abdullah's favorite as well. Tom bit his lip so he would not further offend this boy by smiling. For the first time it occurred to him that he might enjoy lavishing time and attention on Abdullah's sons. He would have his work cut out for him with this stubborn one who so evidently scorned to serve the infidels. Tom was just remembering that in Arabic *Rashid* meant 'the upright' when Muhammad snatched the limelight and the tray. He swatted Rashid on the back and served the tea and more anxious smiles to Tom and the minister.

Tom could contain himself no longer. He leaned over and asked Pastor Guttman if these were Abdullah's sons.

'*Nam.*' Ibrahim nodded his head. '*Abnaa* Abdullah.'

Tom looked at Ibrahim with growing respect. This old one was smart enough to deduce what had been asked in an alien language. Tom recalled what he knew about Abdullah's father. Ibrahim, like all the Arabs, was younger than he looked, perhaps in his late forties. Before the turn of the century, when Ibrahim was no older than Muhammad and Rashid, he had learned the ways of the Bedouin with another boy who was to grow up to be the king of Arabia, for the tribe of Al-Saud had sent their Abdul Aziz to learn desert craft from the noble tribe of Al-Murrah. Later Ibrahim had fought under the standard of his boyhood friend when Abdul Aziz had ridden to victory over most of the Arabian peninsula. When after twenty-four years of warfare Abdul Aziz had united virtually all the tribes to form 'Saudi' Arabia, Ibrahim could boast that he was the friend of a king. Legend had it that Ibrahim and King Abdul Aziz were still allies and comrades. They were two of a kind: proud patriarchs, fierce fighters, shrewd bargainers. Even so, Tom wondered if a man like this could be a visionary. Ibrahim, like many of the Arabs, suffered from the effects of degenerative eye disease. His left eye was entirely blinded, and he could see but dimly out of the other. Tom had a moment's doubt whether a mostly blind Saudi nomad could possibly have the foresight to let the sons of his son learn strange and threatening infidel ways.

Ibrahim proceeded with the formal introductions. 'Muhammad *ibn* Abdullah *ibn* Ibrahim *ibn* Khalid Al-Murrah.' Muhammad stepped forward and smiled at Tom.

Gamely Pastor Guttman tried to recover lost ground.

'Muhammad, the son of Abdullah, the son of Ibrahim, the son of Khalid, of the People of Murrah.'

Ibrahim pointed to the younger one. 'Rashid *ibn* Abdullah *ibn* Ibrahim *ibn* Khalid Al-Murrah.' Rashid hung his head.

'That one's Rashid,' the minister said.

'So,' Tom said. He took a tentative sip of the sweet black tea and examined more carefully the boys he hoped would soon be his charges. Muhammad was sly and ingratiating but so obviously insecure that Tom wanted to reassure him with a bear hug. Haughty Rashid was even more intriguing, although Tom suspected that underneath all that bravado he was just as frightened as his big brother. Suddenly he wished he could simply hold out his arms to them. He wanted them to crawl up on his lap, hug him, trust him. He shouldn't be planning to bargain for them as if they were a pair of racing camels. Tom took a deep breath and remembered not only who he was but who the Arabs were. There were rituals and courtesies which must be honored. But although his desire to cuddle the boys passed for the moment, a tenderness for them remained. Whatever he had to promise this wily old Arab, he would take on responsibility for them. He caught the eye of the missionary and nodded just once.

Ibrahim, who had been watching Tom intently, sat back on his haunches and smiled broadly.

The minister shook his head in exasperation. The Reverend Hans Guttman was a tall, spare, prematurely gray-haired man who had come to the island of Bahrain more than a decade ago to perform God's work among the heathen. But he had more success redeeming minds and bodies than converting souls. He rarely was able to convert even one zealous Muslim to his faith, but he did teach the sons of the merchant class how to read and write. At night, too, by the light of a kerosene lantern, Pastor Guttman did some writing of his own, for his life's work was a study of Arabian folkways, fauna, and flora. Seldom did the insular Saudis let a Christian minister travel out to the tribes in the desert, and so Pastor Guttman had been delighted to accept Tom Shannon's offer to be his interpreter tonight. He was eager to take these Al-Murrah back to Bahrain, but he had expected an intricate and satisfying haggle over terms with Ibrahim. Tom's artless giving away of the game had ruined tonight's sport.

Tom thought of his misadventures shopping in the souks. The Arabs always seemed to know not only the maximum amount in his heart that he was willing to spend but also the exact amount he happened to be carrying in his pockets. Sally had always said he was the world's worst bargainer. Sally . . .

Tom could not bear sitting in this hot, dusty tent with his cramped legs curled painfully under him for one minute longer. He had killed Sally and he had killed Abdullah, and so now he must begin to pay his penance. 'Say whatever you have to say,' he told Pastor Guttman. 'Give him whatever you have to give. But I want those boys.'

The missionary sighed. 'It may mean blood money,' he warned.

Tom shrugged. 'So be it.'

Ibrahim nodded, sure he would be able to get whatever he wanted tonight. He didn't have to be told why his son's American friend had come here tonight with the *Nazrani* preacher. Every Bedouin in eastern Arabia knew Tom Shannon had been asking too many questions about Arab schools, and Ibrahim had understood why when he saw the American openly appraising Muhammad and Rashid. For the past hour Ibrahim had been pondering whether the American's offer would be a blessing or a threat. For long centuries Arabia had been sealed off from the rest of the world. All foreign influences had been regarded as infidel and suspect, and so little had changed in Arabia since at least the days of the Prophet Muhammad in the seventh century.

Ibrahim looked into the flickering campfire and remembered the portents of his dreams. Even before the Americans had come to drill for black gold, he had dreamed that men with red faces would come to unleash a heavy stinking black mist. At first he had thought this mist must be evil, but then in another dream he had known it was good, that it would make his dry barren Saudi an Eden again. He had remembered his dream when the king had asked his tribe to provide a guide for the Americans. After his only son, Abdullah, had drawn that fateful lot, Ibrahim had begun to believe his family was destined to play a role in the great flowering of Arabia. Even Abdullah's brave death had not shaken Ibrahim's faith. Allah, he reasoned, must have had some great mysterious design when he cut down Abdullah in his prime. And surely Allah would not have sent Tom here if He did not want the boys to go to school in Bahrain. With a stony face Ibrahim prepared to bargain the best possible terms for his grandsons' future. When he had heard the preacher out, he would stipulate that they must come home to the black tents six months out of every year. Further, he would forbid that they be taught Christian heresies or ever touch alcohol or tobacco or pork. He would also demand blood money for the death of his son. Pastor Guttman wearily sighed again while a new gleam of satisfaction lighted the eyes of the Arab as the two settled into their negotiation.

Tom looked back at Abdullah's sons sitting cross-legged and silent, and he wondered about their ultimate destiny. So far only one workable well had come in, but already back in San Francisco plans had been drafted to make the Saudi east coast one giant oil field capable of someday fueling all the West. Tom had seen blueprints for a port, a refinery, pipelines, pumping stations, supply centers, and cities and towns large enough to shelter thousands. The vast change and the vast wealth that would come with the oil could be a mixed blessing not only for Saudi but for these two young sons of Abdullah. With character, discrimination, and intelligence a man or a country could make the most of great wealth. But the weak and the venal could just as easily be ruined by too much too soon. Already these boys differed in their responses to him and all he appeared to represent. Muhammad was eager to fawn on him, but Rashid all but spat in his eye. Tom mused whether this younger Saudi generation would embrace or reject the West.

Tom must have dozed off while Ibrahim and Pastor Guttman hammered out their terms, because he was groggy and heavy-lidded and still half in a dream world where Sally was a little girl in an oil-stained First Communion dress when he became aware that the bargaining was over and the tent was crowded with even more tribesmen. He nudged the minister and was told he had to pay Ibrahim three hundred and seventy-five dollars in blood money before Abdullah's sons could study half of every year at the mission school in Bahrain. He nudged the pastor again and was told to be quiet, that a desert storyteller had wandered into the camp, that the performance was about to begin, that the two of them were staying overnight here in the tent of Ibrahim.

Tom rubbed his eyes and stared doubtfully at the wizened old storyteller. He was very, very old and very, very dirty. His robe was tattered, his head scarf was askew, his eyes were diseased and filmy and bloodshot. Yet he had a compelling otherworldly aura. Tom had heard of these wild poets of the desert who wandered the wastelands much as troubadours had circuited the courts of medieval Europe singing their songs and reciting their stories. Pastor Guttman promised to translate the gist of the Arab's story for Tom.

Finally it grew so quiet they all could hear the giggles of the women gathered just on the other side of the hanging blanket. Ibrahim made a loud hissing sound, and even the feminine laughter died away. The wind howled outside in the desert, and the circle of Arabs drew closer together. After long moments of perfect silence the storyteller began a quavering monologue that at first made the hackles on Tom's neck rise. He was alarmed at the eerie, groaning sound of the Arabic, but he was reassured when the minister leaned over and told him they were about to hear the most beloved love story ever told in the black tents - a sad story, a beautiful story, the story of love won and love lost, of love dead and love resurrected, the story of Layla and Majnun.

Tom leaned his back against a camel saddle and listened. At first this didn't sound to Tom like a love story. All the grating sounds of Arabic seemed to him to ring with war and violence and retribution. Yet as Tom truly listened for the first time in his life to Arabic as it is spoken among the Arabs, he finally began to appreciate its gentle rhythms and beauties. The voice rose, fell, grew faint, died, grew stronger, filled the tent with a roaring and shouting and a triumph. In fascination Tom listened. He could understand only a word here and there, but somehow, as though he had suddenly been given the gift of tongues, he comprehended the heart of the age-old story.

A young man and a young woman fall in love. They sigh, they look, they long for each other. Darkness falls, they are apart, still they love. They are together briefly, hotly, and then there is disaster. One of them - He? She? Tom could not tell - dies, and the other mourns and grieves and wants to die with the wanting for the return of the other. Always, forever, he, she, mourns that eternal loss. Their love is perfect, devout, everlasting. . . .

For hours the storyteller wove his spell. For hours the Arabs listened and murmured their affirmations - 'Truly!' they cried out. 'Yes!' '*Akmal*, "continue"!' 'It is thus!' - every time the storyteller paused to catch his breath.

Finally, when he sighed his last sigh and spoke his last word, Pastor Guttman leaned over and whispered a very loose translation in Tom's ear. The Arabian maiden Layla loved a young Arab prince, and he loved her, but destiny did not allow them to marry. The young man became so maddened with love that he went out to the desert and lived like a hermit, forever forsaking society, living only to write beautiful poems in honor of his love. Everyone in Arabia thought the young man was mad and so everyone began to call him *Majnun*, which means in Arabic 'the crazy one.' When Layla died young of a broken heart, Majnun found the grave where she was buried and lay on the hot sand and languished there until he too died and was buried next to her. United in death, Majnun and Layla finally could lie together side by side.

Tom listened and nodded and had tears in his eyes. In a way, he decided, this story was his own. He too had loved truly. He too had buried his young love in the desert. He too was maybe even a little crazy with the losing of his love. He liked that poetic image of the grieving man throwing himself on the hot sand of his lady's grave. Losing all for a grand love - his Celtic soul could understand that, admire that, maybe emulate that. 'What were those names again?' he asked the minister.

'Layla. The girl's name was Layla.'

'And the man?'

'Majnun. They called him *Majnun*, "the crazy one."'

'Majnun.' Tom repeated the word. He liked the sound of it. 'Majnun.'

Tom let out a sigh of relief as he drove through the front gate of the American compound and headed out for the open desert. He was grateful to Pastor Guttman for translating last night in Ibrahim's tent; he was glad the clergyman was going to take on Muhammad and Rashid; but the longing was in Tom to be off by himself in the desert.

The terrain grew wilder and more desolate as he drove aimlessly toward the interior. He wished he could have reached the Dahana dunes before nightfall. In a way Tom loved even the monotonous stretches of the monochromatic desert, but most of all he loved the Dahana dunes. Abdullah had been leading the way the first time he and

Sally caught sight of them, and Tom still remembered his feeling that he might too easily lose himself in the towering womanly undulations of the dunes.

Tom consulted his compass, he looked up at how far the sun was from the horizon, and he calculated that he should stop soon if he wanted to be able to give the sunset his undivided attention. Yet he drove a while longer just to put as much distance as possible between himself and the compound. Dhahran and all it represented depressed him more and more. He remembered reading about the early Christian monks in Egypt who had turned their backs on the civilization of Alexandria and gone out to the desert to be holy hermits. Looking out at the Saudi desert, Tom could understand that impulse. Something about the vastness of the desert and the smallness of man made God as inescapable as grains of sand here. No wonder the Middle Eastern deserts had spawned so many religions. Mystics and prophets and saints had repeatedly heard the terrible and wonderful insistent thundering voice of God in these deserts. As Tom parked the truck and spread his blanket and bedroll in the sand, he felt a sudden wisp of an impulse to be like those ancient hermits who had left home to find God in the desert.

Tom swigged whiskey from his canteen and savored the burn of the liquor on his empty stomach. The bleakness of the desert mirrored the bleakness in his own soul. He threw the liquor out of easy reach and made himself eat a tin of corned beef. He had not come out here to drink too much whiskey and feel sorry for himself. He had the rest of his life to drink and mourn. Tonight he had an important decision to make.

He was satisfied he was doing all he could for the sons of Abdullah. He would pay their tuition and living expenses at Pastor Guttman's school, and he would continue financing their education just as long as they kept on learning. Someday, when they were grown up, he would do his best to get them jobs here in the oil industry.

But now he had to make a more torturous decision. He

had postponed deciding about his daughter for too long. One of the American wives in Dhahran had been temporarily taking care of Sunny. But the oil company didn't allow a man to keep a child out here unless he had a wife. He would either have to go back to America with Sunny or send her home alone.

Tom sighed. In the chaos of those last flaming moments before Sally died, she had said something about Sunny and America. Tom supposed she must have been trying to tell him to send the baby back home to safety. Again he sighed. Sally's mother had died years ago, and Sally's father had remarried and moved to Maine and started another family. But Tom's parents had already offered to make a home for the baby on the farm. His parents would love her and raise her to be a fine young woman.

Tom resisted his thirst for more whiskey. He would not get drunk and evade this decision. He could hardly bear to think of Sunny. She was his little girl, and he wanted to take care of her forever. Yet every time he picked the infant up, he remembered Sally dead in those same arms.

Tom gave up and crawled over on the blanket to reach the whiskey canteen. He tormented himself with the same old regrets. He should never have let Sally come out here. Like a Victrola needle stuck in a groove, Tom repeated his refrain: this was no place for a woman, no place for a woman, no place for a woman . . .

He wiped the tears off his cheeks and looked out at the horizon where the sun was setting in a fireworks of purple and indigo and mauve and blood red. Always he was soothed by the tints of each day's end reflected down on the spreading sea of land. Since Sally had died he had felt closest to her spirit when he kept his vigil watching the Saudi sunsets she had loved. If there was anything left of Sally in this world or the next, she was hovering near him now. For a moment Tom could almost feel Sally's soft skin next to his. But when he reached out as if to touch her, his hand came back with a fistful of colorless sandy dust.

Yet Tom believed that perhaps Sally had been here after

all, to grace him with a comforting thought. It was wrong to remember their years together here as one long ordeal. In the beginning she had loved the primal romance of the desert, its silent infinities, the way the light caught the sand and bathed it in glowing hues at sunrise and sunset. He had not lured Sally to certain death here. She had chosen not only to come to Saudi but to stay.

Tom shivered. Sally would be in Saudi now forever. Desperately he clung to the absolution of Sally's last words. Before she died, she had whispered that she forgave him.

The desert chill was already upon him even as he watched the last flickers of purple light flame at the horizon. He supposed he should go home to Still River with the baby. Surely, even if he couldn't get another job that paid as well as this one, he could find some sort of work. It was almost September. The leaves would be streaking yellow and orange and red and brown. The apples would be hanging heavy on the trees. His mother's hands would be raw from canning. Tom yearned with every particle of his being to go home.

Suddenly the blue-black darkness of the Saudi night had fallen like a veil. Tom leaned back on the blanket, took another gulp of whiskey, and looked up at the sky. On how many nights just like this one had he and Sally lain like this? The stars and the moon were always so bright they would stretch their hands up to the sky and pretend the heavens were within their grasp. Tom mourned a moment for the innocence of those nights with Sally. It might be worth staying in Saudi just to be able to feel sometimes still near to his love.

He knew he had only been teasing himself with thoughts of going home. He could never leave Sally in this place where she had been so afraid. In the water just before she died, she had begged him not to leave her here all alone. If he were to go back to New England with the baby, he would have to leave Sally's body, Sally's soul, Sally's all here, alone. But he could not be untrue to her. He would be like that man in the Arabian story. He would be *Majnun*, 'the crazy one,' living in the shadows of a lost love in the desert.

He would send Sunny home without him. With the kind of money he made here, he would be able to buy her a horse, clothes, anything her heart desired. He could treat her like a princess. He could love her even from halfway around the world. Tom swallowed hard. He had always been clumsy with the baby. He had always felt shy and insecure holding that fragile infant. Yet he would miss clasping that little live bit of Sally in his arms. He wiped his eyes and told himself it was best to send Sunny as far away as possible, from him and from this hell.

This hell of Saudi. . . . Yes, he decided, that was it. Saudi was his own private hell.

Tom let out a deep sigh and stretched out, hoping sleep might come now that he had made his decision. Since Sally's death he had not been able to get a good night's sleep unless he camped out alone like this. Soon, Tom warned himself, his fellow Americans would begin calling him a hermit. *Majnun*, he muttered to himself; I'll tell them just to call me 'Majnun.'

As he tried to fit the contours of his body into the sand, he wished he could take comfort in finally providing for all three of those needy children. But still he lay awake, haunted by what had happened to his wife and his friend. He despaired of ever being able to atone for his moral failure on that fateful day. 'Oh, my God, I am heartily sorry,' Tom began to pray out loud. Abruptly Tom broke off his Act of Contrition. He did not need a priest to tell him what penance was required. He would stay here all his days. His penance would be to live out his damned life in the desert. But no matter how he atoned, no matter how many years he lasted, there would never be absolution for what had happened that bitter afternoon in the Gulf.

Tom stared at the bright stars and wept until the sun rose.

3

'Sunny! Sunny!'

The eight-year-old girl looked dreamily up from her book and frowned. Gran was looking for her again. Gran probably wanted her to help fix supper or clean up her room or something horrible like that. Maybe, if she was lucky, Gran would give up and go back to the farmhouse. Sunny cocked her head and tried to figure out where Gran was calling her from.

From far enough away, Sunny decided. She smiled and went back to one of her very favorite passages in what she was absolutely convinced was the best book ever written. Dashing Colonel Lawrence was just about to lead the cavalry charge of the wild Bedouin warriors astride their purebred Arabian horses and racing camels. Sunny turned the page and stared raptly at a full-color illustration of those great-chested, princely horses. She took riding lessons every Saturday morning at Miss Jennings's academy and so she liked to think she knew gorgeous horseflesh when she saw it. Someday, Sunny promised herself again, I'll have a copper-colored mare of my own. She heaved a sigh of great longing for the horse of her dreams. But then she got caught up in Colonel Lawrence's escapades again. The Camel Corps was swooping in to destroy the Hejaz Railway operated by the evil Turks. She gazed at another illustration, of camels in full battle array, and she reconsidered. Would she rather own a camel or a horse? What she really wanted, she greedily decided, was all of it: a camel and a horse and a tent and robes and headdresses and veils. Sunny hugged the book closer to her. She could almost feel the strong desert wind streaming her pigtails out behind her. She could almost feel the hot coarse sand scorching the soles of her feet. She could almost hear the wild deadly cries of soldiers closing in for the kill. Here in lush, wet Still River, she could almost believe herself to be in hot, dry Arabia.

'Sun-nee!'

Guiltily Sunny looked up from her dog-eared copy of the juvenile version of *Lawrence of Arabia*. Was it wise to ignore Gran like this? Was it chivalrous? Would Colonel Lawrence hide from his own grandmother? From where she sat atop her favorite hill way out in the orchards, Sunny loked out over acres of white blossoms that hung as thick on the apple trees as icing on one of Gran's delicious devil's-food cakes. She couldn't see her grandmother anywhere.

'Sun-nee!'

Gran must have gone off looking in the wrong direction. Still, Sunny thought, it wouldn't be long before she wised up and headed for the apple orchards. Gran was very wise. Sunny supposed she had, at most, another half-hour. Sunny looked wistfully down at her two favorite books. She wouldn't be able to complete this campaign with Colonel Lawrence or dip once again into *Tales from the Arabian Nights*.

If she hurried, however, she would have just enough time to pore over her Mother Box. Sunny reached into the waterproof canvas bag she had lugged out with her. Carefully she unwrapped the beautiful wooden box her father had once sent her. As she opened it and inhaled the scent of cedar, she remembered what Gran had read aloud to her on the enclosed card from her father: 'A beautiful box for my beautiful princess.' Lovingly Sunny ran the tips of her fingers over the intricate pearl design. Gran said the box had been made in Beirut from Lebanese cedarwood. In Damascus, Syrian craftsmen had inlaid this Lebanese cedarwood with mother-of-pearl. Her father had bought this perfect present for her in the bazaars of Bahrain. Beirut! Damascus! Bahrain! Sunny assured herself again that she was the luckiest girl in Massachusetts. No one else she knew had ever been given such an exotic gift from such an exotic father. All the other fathers she knew were farmers who lived right here in Still River. Those other fathers considered a trip to Boston as close to foreign travel as they ever wanted to come. Sunny stared at the fragrant, lovely box. She was very loyal to her father, even though she did not remember ever seeing him, except in treasured photographs. She would not admit even to herself that she would have given anything and everything - even her Mother Box - if she only could have a homebody father like all the other girls.

Sunny lifted a handful of her mother's letters up to her nose and wondered if her mother had smelled like cedar too.

Thoughtfully, then, she traced the ink-smeared addresses on the envelopes. So many letters. Her mother had once written very many more letters in those two years she had spent in Saudi than her father had written in all the years that were to follow. Why, Sunny wondered again, didn't Father write her more often? He sent her countless presents, but he wrote her only once a year, at Christmas. He didn't even send a letter with her birthday presents every March. Even though she wrote to him every month now, even though she tried to make him her confidant by telling him of all her heart's desires - like how much she wanted an Arabian horse and how much even more she wanted to be with him - Father still would not break his silence with her except at Christmas. And then, when he did, his brief letters were so dry and full of facts: how Saudi oil production had fallen nearly to zero during the World War, where in the desert they were exploring for new fields, how they were gearing up now the war was finally over. Often he included oil production figures, but only occasionally - exactly three times in the past seven years - had he slipped and called her 'my princess.' Did Father love her at all? Gran insisted he did; but although Gran never lied, Sunny did not quite believe her grandmother. If Father really loved her, surely he would have made some effort to see her. He had never once come home to visit her in Massachusetts.

Sunny wished she had brought her bankbook with her, so that she could look at the growing balance. For the past two years she had been saving up most of the birthday and Christmas money her father sent. Ever since Gran had first read out loud to her about Colonel Lawrence and Sindbad and Aladdin, she had been certain it was her destiny to be with her father not here in drab New England but in fabulous Saudi Arabia. In school, even though some of the other kids laughed at her for it, she had begun to tell everyone that she was not American but Arabian. She wondered if her three hundred dollars was enough to buy an air ticket and surprise her father out there. She felt terribly sorry he was all alone. Didn't Father know that he - and she - would feel so very much better if they, and maybe Gran and Gramps, could all be together? Sometimes at night, when Gran was knitting and Gramps was smoking his pipe and listening to Jack Benny and Fred Allen and Fibber McGee and Molly on the radio, Sunny liked to climb up on Gramps's lap and shut her eyes and pretend that she was sitting on her own dear father's lap. If she ever got to know her father, she wondered, would she learn to call him 'Dad' or 'Daddy'? If she ever did get to know him, she supposed, to call him 'Father' would seem too formal and stiff.

'Sun-nee!'

Gran. Sunny regretted she would not have enough time for her usual ritual of slowly sifting through her mother's letters, touching each one in turn, wishing all the time either that Mother had printed her letters home or that her teachers would hurry up and show her how to read flowing script like this. Yet Gran had once read her mother's letters out loud. Sunny could pick out a familiar word here and there, and so she went straight to the letter she loved most. She opened it carefully so she wouldn't rip the delicate airmail envelope. With a stubby finger she traced the lines. Mother was describing her birth and how

Mother had felt when she first saw her face and how Mother had tingled when she had tugged at Mother's breast and how Mother had laughed when she had accidentally wet on Father's best suit. Sunny squinted, then, at the wonderful passage of the letter where Mother described how they had come to name her. She knew this family legend so well it didn't matter that she could not quite make out the actual words. Father wanted to name her 'Elizabeth,' after Gran, and Mother wanted to name her 'Mildred,' after her own mother. It wasn't until Mother was well enough to walk outdoors that they had come to a compromise. Mother had pointed down to the ground and then up to the sky.

'Choose, Tom,' she said. 'She's the first American born in Saudi. What else can we call her but "Sandy" or "Sunny"?' Father had laughed, but it had turned out Mother wasn't joking. She had looked down again at the baby laughing in her arms. 'Such a sunny baby,' Mother had said. And then Mother had looked up at the sky again, 'There's only one sun and only one Sunny.' And that had been that. Sunny sighed. Yes, her mother had loved her. Her mother had loved her so, so much . . . Sunny touched her lips to the proof of that letter.

'Sun-neeeee!'

By the timbre of that voice, Sunny could tell that Gran was starting to get mad. She knew she should stash her mother's letters back in the inlaid box and beat Gran back to the farmhouse. Instead Sunny lingered over the photographs. Here they were at their wedding at St. Theresa's, her mother the world's most beautiful bride, her father the handsomest bridegroom. Here they were camping in Saudi, dressed in Arab costumes. Here they were, her mother holding her, safe and secure, in a bundle of blankets in her arms.

'Sunny?'

Sunny couldn't bear to put her mother's letters and photographs away without revisiting, at least for a moment, the Saudi her mother had so evidently loved so much. What would it be today? Her mother's version of how the desert looked at sunset? The dune mountains? The sapphire sea? No, the sky. She would let herself read, again, printed in tiny letters on the back of one of her mother's photographs, about how the crescent moon had looked, lighting up the purple sky one midnight. Reverently Sunny looked at the blackness of the underexposed photograph and tried to imagine instead the beautiful Saudi night. 'Camping one night,' Sunny read out loud in a thrilled whisper, 'at the edge of the Abqaiq sands. The violet sky brilliant with a million -'

'Sunny! So there you are!'

An irate Bess Shannon stood, hands on her wide hips, peering up at Sunny from the foot of the hill. She was a formidable, rawboned country woman with a shaggy white head, gentle poet's eyes, and water-melon breasts that were just now heaving as she tried to catch her breath. 'All the way up there!' The old woman climbed laboriously up the hill. 'Didn't you hear . . .' She caught sight of the books and the cedar box and the letters and the photographs in Sunny's lap. 'What's that? Sally's stuff?' Bess's voice was kind but gruff, like Bess herself. 'What are you doing with Sally's stuff out here?'

'I just wanted to look at them.' Sunny wished with all her heart that she had been more cautious and put her mother's mementos away when she had the chance. It wasn't that she thought Gran would disapprove of her reading the letters or confiscate the photographs. She just didn't want Gran or anyone to know how much they meant to her. She didn't want to share what little she had left of her mother with anyone. Not even with Gran, whom she loved more than anything - except Gramps, of course, and the thought of her mother and the idea of her father and perhaps the fantasy of Saudi. 'I read the letters sometimes.'

Bess reached down and fingered the worn envelopes. 'I'd say you read them more than sometimes.'

'Every day.' Sunny gnawed her lip. 'I look at her

pictures and I try to read her words, and then I try to figure out what she was like.'

'Come here, child.' Bess plopped down on the grass and pulled Sunny into her wide comforting lap. 'Now suppose you ask me whatever it is you want to know about your mother.'

Shyly Sunny pulled out one of the photographs of her mother. 'She was very beautiful, wasn't she?'

'Pretty as a picture.'

'I guess I don't look anything like her.'

Bess gravely studied her granddaughter, as though she did not already know that Sunny was a cherub of a child with rosy apple cheeks, alabaster skin, clear trusting blue eyes, and thick bouncing yellow pigtails. 'Honey,' she said, 'you're the spitting image of her!' Bess squeezed her tight for emphasis. 'Why, I remember little Sarah Maguire - I always called her by her proper name, Sarah; never did like those silly nicknames like Sally - why, I remember pretty little Sarah when she was even younger than you are now.' Bess had loved little Sally Maguire, and she mourned her still. It had been an evil day, Bess thought, when pretty little Sally followed Tom out to Saudi to die. Sternly she steered her thoughts away from such murky channels. 'You're going to grow up to look just like your mother.'

'Yes?' Sunny's believing blue eyes danced. 'Really?'

'I wouldn't lie to you, honey. You're going to grow up to be just as pretty as your mother.'

Sunny took a deep breath and, on impulse, told Gran her great secret. 'I'm going to *be* just like her, too. I'm going to live in Saudi Arabia!'

'Are you now?' As far back as she could remember, Bess had listened to Sunny prattling on about that country of bleakness and misery and death, but she had never realized the child was deluded enough to want to go there. Bess herself had no use for Arabia. She had gone to the library to read up on Saudi when her son had first gone out there, and she had been very quickly repelled by almost everything about it. To her mind, Arabs were filthy dirty, they tended to religious mania, and - most unforgivable of all to her mind - they treated their women worse than she would treat even any of the farm animals. Bess debated whether it was more important to discourage Sunny's Arabian fancies or to encourage the girl to have an imagination and a will of her own. With some reluctance, Bess decided that for the sake of Sunny's character, she would have to risk cultivating even this most ridiculous of whims. So this year Sunny wanted to be a Saudi nomad? Next year she would probably want to be a cowgirl or a nurse or a teacher. She would grow up all too soon and surrender her dreams and settle for being a wife and mother. It wouldn't hurt to humor her now. There was no harm in dreaming great dreams, just in trying to live them. She smiled indulgently at her granddaughter. 'So why do you want to go to Saudi?'

'Because it's wonderful there.' Sunny pointed to her books on Lawrence and the *Arabian Nights* and to the box of her mother's letters. 'Everyone says it's wonderful there. Colonel Lawrence, my mother, everybody!'

'I see.' Bess pursed her lips. She knew very well from Tom's guilt-stricken communications that in the end Sally had detested Saudi Arabia. She must have sent those highly colored letters home just to keep everyone from worrying. Bess was uncertain how much, if any, of this she should tell Sunny. She did not want to glorify one single facet of Sally's life in Saudi. God knew, she thought, this family had suffered enough already - Sally dead, Tom as good as dead, Sunny all but orphaned - and all because of that cursed country. But Bess thought there could be no real harm in Sunny's keeping her fondest fantasy alive. After all, she was only eight. She didn't have to face the dark side of life just yet. She stroked back a loose tendril of Sunny's golden hair. 'Yes, honey, your mother and everybody writes wonderful things about Saudi Arabia.'

'I'll write you wonderful letters just like my mother, Gran. You'll see. I'll go to Saudi just like her, and I'll love it there, just like her. And I'll finally get to be with my father!'

Gran swept the little girl into her arms. 'My poor baby,' she crooned. 'My poor little lonely baby. It's not right, Tom, not right, no matter what you say in your letters. . . .' The old woman became aware of the drawn face of the little girl looking too attentively up at her. Bess bit off what she was just about to say, that her son should get out of Saudi Arabia and come home and take care of the daughter who needed him. She looked deeply into Sunny's eyes, sighed, and shook her head. 'Enough, child. Let's go home. Supper's ready.'

'Next!' The airline ticket clerk frowned when it seemed that no one had stepped forward.

Even when Sunny stood on tiptoe, she was not tall enough to see over the top of the counter at the Boston airport. But resolutely she spoke up to where the clerk must be. 'I want to buy a one-way ticket to Saudi Arabia.'

But the clerk hadn't heard her. 'Can I help you, sir?' He motioned for the graying businessman who was next in line to step up to the desk.

But the man, who had little girls of his own, smiled and took Sunny by the waist and lifted her up to the platform where suitcases were routinely weighed. 'This little lady's ahead of me. Seems she wants to go to Arabia.'

The clerk looked blankly down at the small blond girl with the pigtails and the determined look on her face. 'You want to go where?'

'Arabia. I want to go to Saudi Arabia.' Sunny opened her purse and handed her savings-account bankbook to the ticket clerk. 'I have money. I can pay. I have enough to pay whatever it costs. At least, I think I do. I have four hundred and twenty-five dollars.'

'In your savings account?' The clerk tried to hide a smile, and then he looked at the balance and whistled. 'Where'd a little girl like you get all this money?'

'From my father. He's in Arabia. He's the one I'm going there to see.' Spunkily she lied a small lie. 'He's expecting me.'

'What's your name, little girl? And your phone number?'

She smiled as she recited her name and number. But then the clerk called his supervisor and whispered what sounded to Sunny like her secrets, and finally he tried to make her get out of line and wait behind the counter until someone arrived to take care of her. Stubbornly Sunny stood her ground. 'I want my ticket. I can pay, and I want it. I'm going there today.'

'Let me see your passport.' The clerk held out his hand.

'My what?'

'A document that proves you're an American citizen.' The clerk looked grave. 'If you don't have a passport, I'm afraid you can't leave the country. That's the law, miss.'

'You're making that up.' Sunny had managed to get this far without a passport. She had played hooky and walked all the way to Ayer station, and taken the B&M train to Boston, and then a bus out to the airport. She was not about to be turned back now for a make-believe reason.

But just then a tall slim woman in a tailored uniform like a flag came rushing up. 'You must be Sunny? The little girl who wants to go to Arabia?'

'That's me!' Sunny smiled at the pretty woman in the patriotic suit. 'Are you going to sell me my ticket now? I want to get there today, and I guess it's a very long trip.'

'A very long trip indeed. I'm Miss Palmer, Sunny, and I'd like you to come with me.'

'Are you the stewardess? Are you going to be on the flight to Arabia too?'

'Let's talk about that over an ice cream sundae.'

Sunny wavered, but then she gave pretty Miss Palmer her hand as they walked through the terminal toward the snack bar. She had finished her sundae and had just begun to tell Miss Palmer all about Colonel Lawrence's daring campaign against the Turks when her grandparents swept in.

'Sunny!' Bess picked her up and hugged her. 'God, girl, what are you doing here?'

'We were worried sick, Sunny, when the airlines people called us up and told us you were all the way down here by yourself, telling some damn-fool story about Saudi.' John used his handkerchief to mop the perspiration off his face. 'I just about scared your grandmother out of her wits, speeding all the way in here.'

Sunny hung her head. She hadn't meant to frighten her grandparents. She had meant only to join her father. She had planned to write them wonderful loving letters from Saudi. 'I'm sorry. Really, I am.' Tears ran down her cheeks. 'But I told you I was going to Arabia. Don't you remember, Gran, that day out in the orchards? Weren't you listening?'

Bess rocked her in her arms as if she were an infant. 'Hush, now, honey, that's enough for today.'

'I want to thank you, miss, for being so nice to our little girl.' Sunny's grandfather reached for his wallet. 'I think I owe you something for the ice cream and whatever else you gave our Sunny.'

'It was our pleasure.' Miss Palmer smiled at Sunny. 'I'm just sorry we couldn't get you where you wanted to go.' She laughed. 'Next time you remember to get a passport, young lady. In a few years, when you're all grown up, you come back to us, and we'll be happy to fly you wherever you want, even to your Saudi Arabia.'

'I'll remember. And I'll be back.' Sunny smiled through her tears. 'I'll get to Saudi, and that's a promise.'

On a Saturday morning early the next spring Sunny slid out of the front seat of the pickup and was puzzled when, instead of leaving her off in the driveway, Gramps parked, and then he took her by one hand and Gran held her other one and they all made for the barn. Usually

Sunny walked the three miles to Miss Jennings's 'riding academy' by herself. But for some mysterious reason, today, on the morning of her ninth birthday, both grandparents had insisted on coming with her. And for some equally unfathomable reason, Gran and Gramps were flushed with excitement.

Miss Jennings waved to them from astride her horse in the ring, where she was gamely trying to show one of the clumsy Wilson girls how to make her nag canter. 'Now?' Miss Jennings called out to them.

'Right now,' John answered.

To Sunny's surprise, Miss Jennings curtly dismissed the Wilson girl, dismounted, and disappeared into the barn. Gran and Gramps were grinning and beaming at Sunny as expectantly as if this were Christmas morning and she were about to catch her first glimpse of the decorated tree in the parlor.

When Miss Jennings reappeared a few minutes later, she was not alone. Prancing behind the riding instructor was the most gloriously beautiful chestnut horse Sunny had ever seen - a large, high-spirited, copper-colored horse with a luxuriant black mane of hair and huge tender eyes and a swishing black tail. Sunny stared in rapt astonishment at the dream come true: an Arabian horse just like those in the picture books.

'So what do you think of her?' Bess asked.

'She's a beauty, don't you think?' John asked.

Sunny continued to stare with saucer eyes at the magnificent horse. She opened her mouth to ask if this gorgeous creature was really an Arabian, but her voice came out as a wordless squeak.

Her grandfather seemed to read her mind. 'She's a purebred Arabian.'

'Take a closer look,' Bess urged her.

With reverent hesitation Sunny approached the horse, which was hands higher than any she had ever ridden. The mare had a thicker neck, a broader rib cage, more muscular quarters. And, Sunny reflected, remembering what she had read once about this breed, Arabians had larger hearts than any other horses in the world. Shyly Sunny smiled up at the horse. Books had prepared her for the size and stature of an Arabian, but not for how very pretty its face could be. This mare had long pointy ears, a dainty muzzle, flaring nostrils, and eyes that were too intelligent and humane to belong to a mere animal. This mare was the horse Sunny had always dreamed her father would someday give her as a token of his love.

At that thought, Sunny's mouth dropped open and she looked back at her grandparents. 'Is it for me? Is it mine? Is *she* mine?'

'Happy birthday, honey.' Bess hugged her, and then it was John's turn. 'Your father bought her for you,' he said.

'From Saudi? He sent her all the way from Arabia?'

'Not quite. But he did send us a big check and very specific instructions.' John still had his arm around Sunny, and as they walked closer to the horse, he pointed. 'So many hands high; the neck and rib cage just so; a bay mare; only the best bloodlines.'

'I picked this one out in Virginia,' Miss Jennings explained. 'Believe me, Sunny, this mare is the best there is.'

'Oh,' Sunny said. She edged reverently closer to the most beautiful horse who had the best bloodlines in the world. When, finally, Sunny stood just in front of the horse, the mare inclined her head and seemed to be studying the girl. Then the horse shook her proud head and whinnied.

'She *likes* me!' Sunny reached up on her tiptoes, and when the mare dropped her head, the girl threw her arms around her neck. The horse nuzzled her.

'You like her?' John asked.

'Like her? Of course she likes her!' But Bess's misty eyes, as she took her husband's hand in hers, belied the gruffness of her words.

'I'll have to register the mare,' Miss Jennings said, 'so you'll have to tell me, and as soon as possible, what you're going to call her.'

'*My* horse,' Sunny said happily as she rubbed the mare's muzzle. 'You mean, what am I going to call *my* horse?'

'That's what she asked you,' Bess said.

'You'll laugh.' Shyly Sunny looked back at her grandmother.

'Only if you say something funny.'

Sunny took a deep breath. 'Princess Camey.'

'Princess what?'

'Camey,' Sunny explained patiently. 'Short for "Camel."'

'You can't call a horse a camel,' John said reasonably.

'It's her horse,' Bess said. 'She can call it Gramps if she wants.' She beamed at Sunny. Always she encouraged the girl to do as she pleased.

Sunny looked gratefully back at the radiant faces of her grandparents. She didn't want to tell either of them where the inspiration had come for the first word of the mare's name. She would call the horse what her father called *her*. Every time she said the horse's name out loud, she would remember how her father sometimes called her his own princess.

'Princess Camey,' Miss Jennings repeated. 'Not a bad name, really.'

Sunny patted the horse's neck. 'Good girl.' Sunny laughed in delight when the mare began licking her face. 'Princess Camey!' She and her horse would ride together over the hills and valleys of Still River, through the Enchanted Meadow, around Hell Pond, maybe all the way over to the Old Mill. They would imagine that grassy hills were sand dunes, that Bare Hill Pond was the Persian Gulf, that apple orchards were palm groves, that dirt was sand. Sunny threw her arms around the mare's neck again. She and Princess Camey. Always they would be together. Never would she be lonely again. Always she would treasure her horse, her friend: the proof, finally, that her father loved her.

4

'Boomtown,' Tom Shannon grumbled to the two attentive Arab youths as he waved his hand in an arc that took in all the shadowy piles of sand and bulldozers and half-finished construction littering the oil-company compound at Dhahran. 'Wouldn't be surprised to turn around someday and see the "Hard Luck Saloon" there on King's Road, and dance-hall girls, and Wyatt Earp.' Tom shook his head, and he was so busy being disgusted he did not consider that if there were a 'Hard Luck Saloon,' he would doubtless be bellied up to its bar. He pursed his lips in sober disapproval as he watched two drunken construction workers stagger home in the dawn light toward their bunkhouses in that part of the compound known as Whiskey Gulch. 'Sodom,' he muttered under his breath with the thirsty righteousness of the drinking man who knows his own demons. 'Gomorrah.'

'Sir?' Muhammad hid a yawn but nonetheless managed to speak in his most cultivated British accent. 'Beg your pardon, sir.' It was not so very early in the morning that Muhammad would let a chance go by to demonstrate that the seven years he and Rashid had spent on British-run Bahrain had not been wasted - at least, not on him. The brothers had also spent two years taking college-preparatory courses in Beirut, but it was still the British he had loved to shadow and imitate on Bahrain who had made the most impact on Muhammad. 'I daresay you sound as if you don't like it here, sir.'

'Damned right I don't like it,' Tom snapped. Three frustrating days cooped up in Dhahran with the demanding company executives flown over from the States had made him edgier than usual. 'And I've told you before to drop that phony accent. You're not Brits. You're Arabs. Got that?'

'Mr. Tom,' Rashid replied gravely, 'I never forget that.'

'Not you, Rashid.' Always the solemn, watchful dignity of the younger of the brothers made Tom feel apologetic. He was sorry he was in such a bad mood that he had picked on Muhammad. Most of all, at the root of it all, he was sorry he had let Abdullah die that day long ago in the Gulf. Often this summer as the Al-Murrah brothers spent their holidays working by his side in the oil fields, Tom had felt like unburdening himself of his guilt to Rashid. But in the end he had kept his silence. He had not been to confession in more than ten years, and he did not mean to do it now to a Muslim boy. 'I meant that for your brother.'

'Sure.' Agreeable Muhammad took the rebuke with good grace. He had been quick-witted enough to deduce, long ago, that foreigners - Americans or British or French, it made no difference - liked their Arabs to be smiling, good-humored, and very, very grateful. And while it was true that Mr. Tom in many ways was an exception to all the rest of the infidels, the American had his own predictable pattern of abuse. He would yell at him now, then try to make it up to him later by giving him money or excusing him from work or granting him some other suitable bribe. Muhammad just now was more interested in perfecting his American slang than he was in Tom's moodiness. 'Okay, boss.'

'And don't call me "boss."' Tom glared at Muhammad. At times like this, when Tom was sick to death of Dhahran and impatient to be back in the desert where a man could breathe, he couldn't stomach Muhammad's obsequiousness. 'Stop the fawning, now, will you please?'

Muhammad rolled his eyes so comically that almost anyone would have laughed - anyone but Rashid, who seldom found his brother amusing, and Tom, who wasn't watching.

But as he tramped ahead of the boys, he regretted

lashing out at Muhammad, who was, after all, good-hearted and always joking. He should be giving him the fatherly direction Abdullah would have wanted. Tom reproached himself for being a failure as a substitute father, and then he kicked a large gray rock up in the air as he thought of Sunny, and that he was a failure as a real father as well.

It seemed to Tom that he always ended up creating a furor when he came back to Dhahran. This trip he had raised holy hell with the company team from San Francisco about America's support of the newly born state of Israel. Saudi Arabia had sent a token force of Bedouin to fight as soon as the Zionist state was proclaimed last May. And after the United States rushed to recognize and support Israel, some Arabs had vowed revenge by disrupting America's oil supplies. Yesterday Tom had pounded on his supervisor's desk and asked why the oil companies weren't lobbying in Washington for a saner American foreign policy. He knew the Arabs, he said. He camped with them, talked with them, understood them. Palestine to the Arabs was a gut emotional issue, and someday they would make America pay dearly for coming down on the side of the Jews. But the men from San Francisco had taken Tom aside and whispered soothing secrets in his ear. The oil industry would continue to do all it could to hold the line against American support of Israel. But in the meantime, the United States ambassador in Jeddah had been assured by the royal family that whatever happened in Palestine would not affect the American oil concession. Moreover, Saudi Arabia had sabotaged an Arab League effort to shut down American oil production. Saudi Arabia would never turn against America. Tom's boss had patted the back pocket of his trousers. Saudi Arabia, he said, was right here.

Tom kept grumbling his favorite complaints under his breath as he and the Arab boys walked to the motor pool from his friend's house at the far end of Dhahran. To

Tom's way of thinking, every change that had come here since Sally died a decade ago was for the worse. And almost everything had changed - even the official name of the American combine that ran Dhahran. Toward the end of the war Standard Oil of California, the largest stock owner in the original Saudi oil concession, needed capital to gear up for a massive postwar boom. High-level corporate American wheeling and dealing resulted in Texaco, Jersey Standard, and Mobil's becoming partners in the oil-concession cartel that was renamed the Arabian-American Oil Company, or Aramco. And that was only the beginning. During the wartime oil-production cutbacks, American wives, children, and all unessential personnel had been sent home, so that there had been fewer than two thousand Americans left in Dhahran. But now, in this summer of 1948, there were at least eight thousand in residence. Besides the oilmen, hundreds of construction workers had been imported to build everything from bunkhouses, schools, and a hospital to roads and even swimming pools. Tom thought most of the new people flocking to Saudi were fortune-hunters. As he remembered it, he and the other pioneers had come here not only for the high pay but for a love of adventure and the thrill of surviving life on the edge.

But since those good old days, Saudi had lost much of its mystery. Now American newcomers came fully briefed on the brutal climate and the isolation and monotony of living a restricted life inside a sequestered compound. To recruit and hold its staff, Aramco paid them at least twenty percent more than Texas companies. It was said that if Americans could 'stick it out' in Saudi for twenty years, they could retire to Florida as millionaires. To sweeten the pot, Aramco offered not only high salaries and lavish vacations but a life-style that did its best to replicate a quiet suburb in Southern California.

But as the gap in living standards between Americans and Arabs had widened in Saudi, there was even less mixing between the two nationalities than in the pioneer times of fifteen years earlier. American oilmen and their wives dressed up in their summer whites and dined and danced by the country-clubby pool at The Patio. Steaks and eggs and every other Western taste delight were shipped in from Australia and sold in the company commissary. Bevies of single American women worked as secretaries and lived on shady streets known as Petticoat Lane and Virgin Circle. But part of the price for Aramco's trying to create a Little America here in the Saudi desert was that life in Dhahran was artificial and hollow and rife with contradictions.

'Can you believe it?' Tom groused. 'Look at this place! Sprinklers on the goddamn lawns! Sprinklers! In the desert!'

Tom looked up to the peak of Jebel Dhahran, where, in the uncertain dawn light, the gas-flare burn-offs smoked up the pure desert air. He sniffed the wind like an Arab's sleek saluki dog and nearly gagged as he took in a noseful of the rotten-egg smell wafting over from the nearby oil-stabilizing plant.

'This place stinks,' Tom said with finality.

He didn't expect the boys, or anyone else, to respond to his carping. Even here in Dhahran among his own people, Tom was odd man out. The Americans thought him most eccentric because he preferred to camp alone in the desert or off with the Arabs rather than live in the air-conditioned bungalow to which he was entitled. He was tolerated only for his knack for finding oil. But Tom knew that behind his back his countrymen called him by one of the few Arabic words they knew: *Majnun* - 'the crazy one.' He supposed someday he should tell them to call him Majnun to his face, as the Arabs did. To anyone who knew the old love story, the name suggested honor and constancy and high romance.

Perversely, just to increase his own misery, Tom sniffed in the fetid air again. Arabs said the sulfur stench was sweet compared with the other corruptions the oil industry had brought to a Saudi that had been altogether innocent not so very long ago. The Saudis looked the other way and tolerated Americans' drinking liquor within the boundaries of the Eastern Province, and alcoholism had become epidemic among the bored, homesick expatriates. Roughnecks held nightly gambling sessions in the bunk-houses. A certain type of fugitive man who was running away from a nagging wife or a ruined life had begun to turn up in Saudi, so that Dhahran was becoming the American oilman's French Foreign Legion. Tom's Arab friends were worried their country was being corrupted from within by the presence of all these exceptions to their rules. Sometimes when Tom looked at eighteen-year-old Muhammad and seventeen-year-old Rashid, he wondered how long they would be able to maintain the values that had been the pride and joy of men like their father. Muhammad had already begun to turn his back on his own people. Was it inevitable Rashid would go that same sad route?

Tom looked out beyond the high steel fence toward the desert. He didn't know much about the sociological stresses and strains of rapid change. But he was a geologist, and he knew about oil. In the report he had presented yesterday, he had estimated that more than half the world's oil reserves lay under this bleakly beautiful Middle Eastern terrain.

Tom scanned the flat horizon to the east, toward the nearby Gulf coast, where thousands were working overtime to shuttle oil from the bottomless wells of Saudi to the insatiable factories of the West. Postwar rebuilding and retrenching and expansion had created an unquenchable thirst for oil. Even the United States, which until now had always exported its own excess oil, had had to begin to import it this year. High-quality crude was far cheaper to extract here than anywhere else in the world. A barrel of oil that cost sixteen cents to produce in Saudi cost one dollar and seventy-three cents to produce in Texas. Moreover, the long-term oil-concession agreements signed by the Saudi king nearly twenty years ago meant that

Americans had an uncontested monopoly to find and develop and market these oceans of cheap and choice oil.

Petroleum profits were higher and risks lower in the Mideast than anywhere else in the world, and a massive Saudi oil rush was the result. During the Second World War, when it hadn't been possible to ship much oil over treacherous seas, production had been, at most, fifteen thousand barrels a day. But by the end of next year it was expected to be a staggering half-million barrels a day. That boom would not have been possible without an extraordinary expansion of pumping, pipeline, and treating facilities. Even before the war had ended, a pipeline had been laid under the sea to Bahrain and a huge oil refinery had been built along the Saudi coast. Ras Tanura had been transformed into a deepwater tanker port through the construction of a seven-mile causeway and trestle fingering out into the Gulf. Aramco had begun building a massive 'Tapline' pipeline across a thousand miles of scorching desert from the Persian Gulf of Saudi to the Mediterranean coast of Lebanon. Along the way, too, three entirely new towns had been built as well as an international airport, two hundred miles of road, and a railroad linking Dhahran to the Saudi capital city of Riyadh. Tom knew Aramco was planning to double its production in five years, and he wouldn't be surprised if it increased tenfold before it was all over. 'Come on, boys.' Tom resisted his impulse to put his arms protectively around Muhammad and Rashid. 'To the desert!'

Tom felt better after he wrapped a white cotton *ghutra* head scarf around his head and held it in place with a black *igal* cord exactly like those worn by Muhammad and Rashid. He and the other pioneer American oilmen had begun wearing Arab headgear years ago because of the fierceness of the desert sun. Now, long after most of the Americans had begun wearing imported hats, Tom still wore his *ghutra* with pride. He caught a glimpse of his head scarf, grizzled beard, and leathery tanned skin in the rearview mirror. But then the smile died on his lips as he remembered being mistaken for an Arab and overhearing an American call him a 'sand nigger.'

Tom ground the gears of the Kenworth truck painted, like all the hundreds of Aramco vehicles, a vivid and perhaps lifesaving red which an airplane could spot in even the most remote stretches. He passed through the gate and struck out on the new Aramco desert road. Every five weeks he had to come in from his wildcat oil-exploration camp to file progress reports. And by the time he finally finished his paperwork and his meetings and left the alleged refinements of Dhahran behind him, he breathed a sigh of relief. He felt suffocated inside those temperature-controlled shacks they shipped in from America. 'Thank God that's over,' Tom said more to himself than to the two boys beside him.

'*El-hamdulillah*,' Rashid echoed in Arabic. He too was glad to be returning to the desert he loved.

Neither of them paid any attention to Muhammad's soft sigh of regret at leaving Dhahran behind.

Muhammad dozed off, Rashid kept his thoughts to himself, and Tom concentrated on making good time on the smooth asphalt that stretched forty barren miles southwest to the high dunes of Abqaiq. It was mid-morning and time for a break when they arrived at the frontier town. But Tom, who had no more use for Abqaiq than he did for Dhahran, drove out a few miles into the open desert before he pulled over. Remembering his unkind words to Muhammad back in Dhahran, Tom asked Rashid to make their coffee. He watched the younger boy grill the beans and boil the water while the older one languidly yawned and stretched and rubbed his eyes. Tom thought back to their meeting in Ibrahim's tent, and he smiled as if at a very private joke when Rashid poured him the first coffee.

As Tom rolled the potent liquid on his tongue, he looked out proudly to where he had brought in the first whopper Abqaiq well eight years ago. He had been the first to suspect that a rich dome of oil lay under the desert not only here but farther southwest where he had just recently spudded in those new Ain Dar wells. He had a hunch the oil nearly one hundred and sixty miles southwest at Haradh was part of the same geological structure that lay under Ain Dar. Back in Dhahran he had just made his case to sink a necklace of new wells between Ain Dar and Haradh, but the cost-conscious Aramco executives had at least for now vetoed his ambitious scheme. Yet Tom thought the largest accumulation of oil ever found anywhere in the world might lie under the desert forty miles from here. Hastily Tom downed two more small cups of coffee. Their destination lay at the end of an uncertain desert track slicked down and blackened only by a coating of oil, and they would have to cross this in the killing heat of the day.

Again they swung out into the desert, but this time Tom was in a ripping good mood. He loved the challenge of this tough, dangerous black ribbon through the gray wilderness. He came close to contentment only when he was pitting himself against fate in the arid desert. Tom's spirits were pitched even higher a few hours later, after the boys repeatedly had to dig the truck out of the soft deep sand. He would miss Muhammad and Rashid when they left Saudi to resume their college-preparation course – this time at Aramco's expense at the American University of Beirut. In the past few years, as oil production had increased, Aramco had learned to jump every time a Saudi prince snapped his fingers. The oil company had branched out into social and economic development, sending Saudis abroad to schools, building roads, and setting up clinics. Tom was relieved he no longer would have to shoulder all the financial burdens for the two boys. But he had grown fond of silly, maddening Muhammad as much as intense, intimidating Rashid. Now that he was about to lose them, he wished he had made more of an effort to be closer to them both. Maybe it wasn't too late to try. 'So you'll be leaving soon for Beirut.'

'*Inshallah*,' Rashid said as he gloomily stared out of the window at the desert he had never wanted to leave.

'Exactly three weeks from today,' Muhammad said.

Tom tried to imagine how hard it must be for these boys to reconcile the worlds in which they had to live. He knew they both had once had trouble shuttling back and forth between the mission school on Bahrain and their family's tent in the desert. Making the transition from Arabic to English had been easy compared with knowing and doing what was expected of them in two separate lives. Muhammad, with his quicksilver tongue and his love of ease and pleasure, had taken easily to the foreign ways. But Rashid for a long while had been no more able to twist his tongue around English than he had been able to swallow living among the Christian infidels. Rashid had moped during the winters in Bahrain, and Muhammad had sulked during the summers in the desert. But the brothers had always been jealous rivals in both worlds. Tom had once asked Ibrahim how and when this bitterness between them had begun, and the old man had shrugged and said that as with Cain and Abel, maybe their feud was written in the stars. As boys, when they had run fierce footraces and nearly killed their camels vying to be first across the dunes, Rashid had gloried in surpassing his older brother. But then in the foreign schools of Bahrain and Beirut, Muhammad had lorded it over Rashid. Tom wondered if it would still be brother against brother when the boys were men. 'I suppose you're excited about going back to Beirut.'

'You bet!' Muhammad aimed him his most dazzling smile. 'Beirut is simply smashing.'

'What's it like?'

'Glorious.' Muhammad frowned at the barren desert. 'The American University of Beirut is very beautiful. Gardens. Many trees. From campus we can look out over the Med.' Suddenly Muhammad looked uncertain. He tried so hard, always, to say and do the exactly right thing, but it was confusing with all these differences between even the British and the Americans. 'You Americans call it that? "The Med"?'

'We say "Mediterranean."' Tom too looked off into the distance, as if he could see beyond the horizon to another green and peaceful campus. He had missed Sally so at Stanford. He supposed the loneliness of that first separation had contributed to his wretched decision, years later, to let her join him. With an effort Tom turned his mind away from Sally. He would think of her later, tonight, when he lay on the hard ground, unable to sleep. 'What do you think you'll study in college?'

'Engineering,' Rashid said. 'And economics.'

'That's smart.' Tom smiled. This one had always been smart. 'Best background you can have for the oil business. That is, for a desk job in the oil business. That's what you want – a desk job?'

'Maybe.' Rashid smiled one of his rare smiles. 'Or maybe I will be a very big boss.'

Tom nodded an acknowledgment of Rashid's ambition. 'What about you, Muhammad?'

'Who knows?' Muhammad laughed. 'Maybe I will study only the tennis and the girls!'

'Tennis?' Tom was incredulous at the thought of a Saudi tribesman playing mixed doubles on a Beirut tennis court. 'You?'

'Why not? Why not tennis?'

Rashid told him why not. 'A stupid game for stupid people.' Rashid glared at his brother. 'Already, many times, I have told you. We are not in Beirut to play games.'

Muhammad shrugged, but his teeth were bared as he hissed sibilant Arabic words at his self-righteous brother.

Tom ignored the ugly exchange. 'And your friends? What kind of friends do you have?'

'Other Saudis. Boys from the Gulf.' Rashid waved his hand vaguely in the air as if to draw a map of the Muslim Arab world. 'Syrians. A few Lebanese.'

'Not too many British,' Muhammad said with regret.

'More French, of course. And Americans. I am making many, many friends with the American boys.'

'What about your free time? What do you boys do besides play tennis?'

'I never play tennis,' Rashid said.

Tom wished Rashid would loosen up a bit. It wasn't natural for an adolescent - even for a very religious and traditional adolescent Saudi - to be so serious and self-contained. 'But you must do something for fun.'

'My brother prays at every opportunity possible.' Muhammad grinned. He enjoyed teasing his brother. He wished Rashid would tease him back. Life did not have to be as grim as Rashid made it out to be. Muhammad was always vaguely vowing to stop fighting so much with his only brother. They were loyal to each other in their way, but they could not seem to stop slipping into these spats.

'I like to walk outside the city,' Rashid said. 'Sometimes ride horses. It is very green there. But the rain!' Even the thought of Beirut's weather made Rashid shiver in the Saudi heat. 'And it is so cold in the winter. Always I miss the desert -'

'The cinema!' Muhammad's dark eyes danced. He was so excited at remembering the movies he couldn't stop himself from breaking into his brother's boring reverie. 'I forgot to tell you the best thing about Beirut! How I love the cinema!'

'Tennis, cinema, dancing, nightclubs, wine, girls, gambling!' Rashid spat out the angry words. It enraged him that his brother had the potential to be so good and yet chose instead to be so bad. 'Tell Mr. Tom about how you have wasted his money in Beirut! You are a disgrace. You bring shame on yourself, on me, on Grandfather, on all good Muslims!'

'Maybe three times each week I go to the cinema.' Muhammad played deaf to his brother's taunts.

Tom hardly listened to them squabble. Ever since he had thought of Sally and Stanford, he had been resisting his desire for a drink. But finally he gave up and reached under the seat for the whiskey canteen he wasn't supposed to take out of the legal confines of Dhahran. He allowed himself one quick nip.

'I like, especially, your American cinema of the cowboys and the Indians,' Muhammad said. He yawned. Suddenly the desert heat and this not very amusing conversation was putting him to sleep.

'Did I ever show you my wife's picture?' Without waiting for their answer, Tom rooted in his wallet for a dark, smudged snapshot of a squinting, fair-haired woman.

In the glare of the sun, the brothers blinked at the familiar photograph of Sally Shannon. In almost every encounter they had with Tom, there was one especially embarrassing moment when the American stopped drinking long enough to produce this ancient picture.

'Very nice,' Rashid said as if he were looking at it for the first time. He watched Tom take another suck of the whiskey and began to calculate when he should insist on taking over the wheel.

'A beauty,' Muhammad gushed. 'What a beautiful woman!'

Tom grinned happily at Muhammad and forgave him, here and now and possibly forever, for all his many shortcomings. Muhammad might be one of the world's greatest opportunists, and he might not even have much character. But the lad most certainly was charming, and he most assuredly knew a pretty woman when he saw one. Tom took another drink. He felt so expansive and so fond of Muhammad that he reached back into his pocket and pulled out another picture. 'Would you like to see a princess?' he asked shyly as he passed them the color portrait.

Muhammad stared eagerly at the first photograph he had ever seen of Tom's mysterious daughter. The pretty, sweet-faced, yellow-haired girl had cheeks as rosy as Lebanese apples and eyes of sapphire like the Gulf. He whistled as he had heard American boys whistle when they saw glamour girls. 'Who is she? A movie star?'

Tom took another gulp of whiskey and began to get maudlin as he looked down over Muhammad's shoulder. 'That's my little girl! My princess!' Tom took another deep drink from the canteen.

Rashid took the photograph. '*This* is your daughter? But she is really very beautiful. She looks like an angel!'

Tom and Muhammad were both startled at this unusual burst of enthusiasm from Rashid. Muhammad tried to snatch back the photograph, and, when Rashid wouldn't give it to him, the boys broke out into a guttural, growling argument in Arabic.

Watching them, Tom was glad his little princess was far beyond the reach of boys like this. Yet Tom absently wondered what an American girl like Sunny might make of them. Muhammad was a bit too sleekly handsome, a touch too sure of himself, a tad too fluid with his bilingual flattery. And Rashid was too intense and ascetic-looking for conventional good looks. Yet Tom remembered how fascinated he had been the first time he saw Rashid's wild-animal eyes. He still had those mesmerizing fiery eyes. If an artist had to pick only one to paint, Rashid would surely be the chosen. His face was one any artist - or any woman - would remember. Tom tired of his effort to decide what Sunny might think of Rashid and Muhammad. He hadn't seen his daughter since she was six months old. The only clues he had about her were a shoebox of letters in a childish scrawl and a handful of fuzzy photographs. Tom took another long drink.

Muhammad had finally succeeded in getting the picture back and was appraising Sunny as seriously as if he were a marriage broker. Mentally he compared her with other Americans at Dhahran and then with the French girls of Beirut. Tom's daughter was really, he decided, quite special. 'This "princess." She is how old?'

'Ten or eleven, I think.'

'Almost old enough for marriage,' Muhammad pursed his lips. 'You should have many offers. Many very good offers.'

'Tell me, please,' Rashid begged as he took the photograph back from his brother, 'more about your beautiful daughter.'

'Her name's Sunny.'

'But that is too perfect! *Shamsa!* She is like the sun.' Rashid held the photograph away from him as if he were dancing with the girl in it. 'You must miss her so much. Why does she not come here to visit you? She cannot be happy, alone there in America, without you.'

Tom's face fell. He hated it when the girl sent him those pleas that he let her come here. Saudi had been deadly to the mother, and he could not risk it for the daughter as well. Tom tipped the canteen to his mouth.

Rashid sighed under his breath as he handed Sunny's picture back to the American. 'Almost at Ain Dar,' Rashid said after a while. 'I can maybe drive, now?'

Tom let the boy take his place behind the wheel, and they drove in silence until Tom threw the empty canteen down on the seat. He picked up the photograph of Sunny again. 'She is pretty, isn't she?'

'Sure,' Muhammad said.

Tom stared at the photograph and tried to see his daughter as a young man might. Then he sighed and, as he very carefully tucked the picture back in his wallet, asked, 'You fellows have girlfriends?'

'Ha!' Muhammad laughed without humor. 'You joke with us? You know how it is here with men and women.'

Tom did know about masks and veils and seclusion. Yet he supposed there still had to be romances of a sort. 'Boys your age, I bet you have brides all picked out.'

Muhammad comically held his nose and crossed his eyes as if to suggest he was far superior to smelly girls who lived in hairy tents.

Rashid, however, was sighing with regret. 'Grandfather has chosen cousins for us, but we must wait many years. Until we are, maybe, as old as you, Mr. Tom. First we must finish school. And then we must work for many years until we have saved enough for a tent and household goods and gifts for the bride.'

Tom nodded and passed his hand in front of his eyes as though that would clear his head of the alcohol blur. 'How much would it cost?'

'Two or three thousand riyals for one of our cousins,' Rashid said. 'More for a special girl from a good family, or a healthy and very beautiful one, like your daughter.'

Tom calculated that that was at least five to seven hundred dollars - a small fortune for boys like Muhammad and Rashid. If they were lucky, after their schooling, Aramco would give them third-rate clerks' jobs. Yet he could give these boys a thousand dollars apiece and never even miss the money. But Tom thought his largesse had to stop somewhere. He had owed these boys for their father's death, but he didn't want to get them women or set them up in business or buy them houses and cars. Tom shrank away from cementing any deeper ties with these boys, or anyone. Since Sally's death, he had done his best to avoid all human entanglements, especially with emotionally demanding Arabs.

Tom knew Arabs were a decent people, an honorable people, and yet he kept his distance from them because he had discovered that they were above all a gregarious people. If he allowed himself to become even one degree closer to Abdullah's family, there would be constant visits, endless chatter, and he would end up sacrificing his solitude. A man dedicated to a life of despair could not allow himself hope and love and laughter. Yet still Tom considered that no matter what he did, he might always owe these boys. Tom gnawed his lower lip until they could see the derrick for Ain Dar's Number Four, and the moment for generosity had passed.

The truck rolled into the squat cluster of portable buildings, and Tom waved to the men clustered around the well. 'Christ Almighty,' he muttered. 'Looks like they're all set to perforate for another flow test. Let me out here, Rashid.'

'But Mr. Tom,' Rashid begged, 'maybe we all rest now? We drove for many hours. You have had much to drink in the heat of the day. You are very tired, I think.'

'Are you saying I'm drunk, boy?' Tom leaped defiantly out of the cab and glowered up at Rashid. 'That's *my* well. *Mine*. And I'll make sure that whatever has to be done on it gets done right. You two go rest if you're too tired to work.' Tom already was conferring with the other Americans. While Rashid and Muhammad argued about whether to join him, Tom climbed up onto the stabbing board twenty feet above the open well. There were two slams of the truck door. Muhammad flounced toward the showers, and Rashid climbed up the ladder of laced steel to where Tom was shouting out orders to the rest of the crew on the ground.

'I will help,' Rashid said as he anxiously scanned Tom's flushed face. He knew the American had finished an entire canteen of whiskey. But aside from his high color and a slight tremble to his hands, there were no signs of intoxication. Rashid relaxed a little. 'What do we do now?'

'They tell me the drilling's progressed through the first two strata. So I think all we have to do to bring the well in is perforate the casing with this gun I'm about to lower into the hole. We got back just in time for the good stuff.' Tom smiled down at the wellhead. 'I love it when one of my wells spuds in.'

Rashid made another try at talking the American out of it. 'You're tired, Mr. Tom. Let one of the other men do it.'

'Don't be a pest, Rashid.' But as Tom swayed and almost lost his balance, he hit the firing pin of the perforating gun, and the delicate mechanism inside the lubricator jarred, and suddenly there was a hiss so sharp and deadly it seemed there was a nest of vipers with them atop the drilling platform.

'Mr. Tom!' Rashid screamed a warning and tried to clutch at the American. But Tom's reflexes, even in his drunken haze, were fast and true. In the instant just before the mighty explosion began to heave at them in waves from the depths of the earth, Tom shoved Rashid off the drilling platform and away, free and clear, from the well which he sensed was about to erupt into an inferno. Then Tom himself dived off just before the drilling platform shuddered and was lifted high in the air by the first shock waves of the explosion.

There was a roar so powerful it shut off all other sights and sounds and memory for a terrible instant of utter time-stopping deafness. Rashid lay unmoving, but then he coughed, his eyes burned, he raised his dazed head and looked around him. Deadly black brimstone smoke puffed out from the wellhead. Sudden fireworks of red and yellow flames exploded before his eyes, and Rashid held up his arms to shield his face. A column of fire and smoke funneled up into the air. The fire consumed the towering derrick, the fire shot higher into the air, the fire seemed about to immolate every cloud in the sky. Thick and highly toxic black smoke curled everywhere.

Rashid skinned the flesh off his knees and elbows as he scuttled backward, in a panic, away from the conflagration. Finally, he managed to lift himself into a crouch and was about to run as fast and as far away as possible.

But then Rashid made the mistake of casting one final look back. Midway between him and the worst of the fire, Rashid spotted a bundle of blackened cloth and flesh that was moving. Rashid rubbed his eyes. It must be the smoke playing tricks. First he had thought it was Tom twitching on the ground, and it had seemed that body was inching not away from the fire but toward it. Just to prove himself wrong, he called out, 'Mr. Tom?' When that crawling thing turned and looked back in his direction, Rashid screamed louder. 'Here! I'm back here!' He had to let Tom know he was crawling in the wrong direction. 'No, Mr. Tom!' Rashid watched in horror as the American who had been his benefactor for so many years wriggled toward the certain death of the holocaust at the mouth of the well.

Rashid looked around for someone to help, but it seemed there were only Tom and himself in this world of fire and smoke. Rashid hesitated for another long instant, then plunged into the fire storm. He staggered ahead and then he heard warning shrieks behind him. He heard, he thought, someone - His brother? Was that Muhammad? - calling out his name. But then, as the black smoke and the ferocious waves of heat began to beat against him, Rashid could hear nothing but a sort of inner sigh that came from the heart of the fire. Blindly Rashid rushed ahead. He coughed; he faltered; he remembered, somewhere deep in the recesses of his terrified mind, that it wasn't only the flames here that could kill him. Perhaps even more deadly were the poisonous gas fumes. He had to move faster than the smoke and the fire. 'Mr. Tom!' Rashid cried out as he glimpsed something moving slightly, steadily, ahead of him on the ground. He lunged for Tom and came away instead with a handful of charred cloth.

'Go away!' Tom shrieked. 'Let me be! It's time!' Tom tried to resume his slow, agonizing crawl. Hell, now, for him, was finally just twenty feet away. In three minutes, five minutes, eight minutes at most, he would be there.

Rashid ignored his cries and grabbed Tom at the armpits and began dragging him back from the fire.

'No!' Vainly Tom struggled against the greater strength of the boy. 'Let me die!'

But inch by inch, step by step, Rashid pulled the American closer and closer to safety. Just when it seemed they would make it, just when the black smoke had lightened to ash gray, the metal derrick began to lean and totter. As Rashid looked back toward the well, the steel girders at the base of the structure melted like a gutted candle. The white-hot metal screamed shrilly like a woman as the derrick collapsed in a heap. The fire, fueled by an ocean of underground oil that rushed out of the well in a tremendous whoosh of pressure, burned even higher. Rashid coughed and choked and felt flames singe his feet, his ankles, his knees, and suddenly his legs gave out. He stumbled and fell and lay, unmoving, across the now unconscious body of Tom Shannon.

By now, every man in the wildcat camp was standing in a ragged line just a little away from the fire. Already one of them had raised Abqaiq and Dhahran on the shortwave. In a few minutes Aramco's elaborate fire-fighting apparatus would be on alert. A fire over a massive oil field out in the remote desert could spread and burn so fiercely it might take two or three weeks to put it out entirely. The call was already being sounded all around the world that expert fire fighters were needed to put the lid on a spectacular fire at the Number Four at Ain Dar. Even now, airplanes had taken off from Dhahran carrying men and the beginnings of the supplies that would be needed in the next days or weeks to bring it under control. New water wells would have to be sunk at once to provide the millions of gallons of necessary water. A boom would have to be lowered so the wellhead could be capped. Finally, thousands of gallons of mud would be forced down the well to smother the fire.

But in these next moments, while the gas at the wellhead was burning off in a burst of fumes and flames, all the onlookers could do was keep watch and wait. The oil crew stood at the brink of the fire scanning the blackened ground for signs of human life. At least three men still were missing, and one body had already been recovered. The Americans shook their heads and anxiously watched the progress of the fire. The Number Four was miles from the other wells in this field, and so they thanked God there wouldn't be any secondary explosions.

But the terrified foreman knew more than his wildcat crew. 'Get back!' If the fire destroyed the Number Four's master valve and main casing, everything within miles would be sprayed by burning oil. 'Into the trucks! All of you! There's nothing you can do here now! Get out while you can!'

The line of crewmen wavered. A few jumped into the

trucks. More stood rooted by the fire zone, staring as if hypnotized by the flames.

'But my brother is in there!' Frantically Muhammad begged from one end of the crowd to the other. 'I saw him go back in there. I saw him! Help him! Help my brother!'

'There's nobody in there that's alive now, sonny.' The foreman tried to get the hysterical youth into a truck, but Muhammad broke away and headed for the sheet of flames.

'Get back here! Are you nuts?'

'Boy!'

'Come back!'

Muhammad disappeared in the smoke. 'Here!' Within seconds he had stumbled over the bodies of his brother and Tom lying only a few yards inside the pall of smoke. 'Help! Over here!' He screamed and waved to the drillers on the sidelines. One came running and helped drag Rashid to safety, while three of the others carried Tom from the fire zone.

The wildcatters carefully set Tom and Rashid down on the bed of a truck, which immediately roared off until they were out of any possible danger. One of the Americans rooted through a first-aid kit, and another cut off the charred remains of clothing. Tom's legs were terribly burned. Rashid's burns were ugly but superficial.

'Okay?' Muhammad was very near tears. 'They will be okay?'

No one answered. One man applied compresses and unguents to the burns. Another gave the softly moaning Tom morphine for the pain. They tried to ward off shock by covering them both with blankets. Finally, then, there was nothing else to do but watch the fire burn and scan the sky for the first sight of the plane that would take the injured back to the Aramco hospital in Dhahran.

On the short flight back, Muhammad held his brother's hand and tenderly smoothed Rashid's smoky hair back from his temples. When it had counted, he had been there for his brother. But had he been there in time? Muhammad moved his lips in silent prayer beside the brother who had always been more rival than friend. But then Rashid looked up and smiled at him and began to pray out loud. As below them in the desert the intense flaming torch of the oil-field fire lit up the black Saudi night, the brothers in unison whispered prayers for mercy and compassion and an end to this suffering.

5

In the flickering light of the desert campfire it seemed that savage ghosts of the fabled tribal past, the spirits of the Islamic warriors who had once swept out from Arabia to secure much of the world for Allah, were alive and unappeased and dancing. It seemed that the decadent ghosts of the opulent future, the oily spirits unleashed by the subterranean steel drills, were on their feet and rehearsing complicated new steps and dancing. It seemed that the ambivalent ghosts of the uncertain present, the ambiguous spirits of a world neither here nor there, were dazed and unsure and dancing. The long, silent, wraithlike line of white-robed, white-scarfed, brown-skinned men, linked at the shoulders with arms intertwined, wavered, then seemed to sigh and sway one step closer to the black goat-hair tents. For this dance there was no music of flutes, horns, lutes: only the primitive percussion of a donkey-skin drum that pounded slowly, steadily, tiredly, like the heartbeat of an old man. To that somber beat the long line of Al-Murrah tribesmen shuffled their bare feet in the sand, back and forth, left to right, in a monotonous lead-footed dance.

At the end of the line, suddenly, there was a clatter of steel and a flash of light as a man brandished a sword at the crescent moon. Heads turned, teeth flashed, shoulders straightened, until the sword was once again sheathed and the brotherly line was once again unbroken. From time to time, then, at irregular intervals, the hops and shuffles and swordplay of the men were punctuated by eerie, high-pitched, and tongue-warbling screeches of unseen women, the wives and daughters and sisters and nieces and cousins who were assembled in the cloistered privacy of a big black tent. When the women were quiet, the wind, howling in from the bleak wastes of the open desert, filled the void. Then a camel would groan, a child would cry out, a man would wave a carbine, then shoot it at the sky. The drum would beat on as the men continued their ghostly shuffle.

In the dark shadows just beyond the arc of firelight sat one man who was not of the tribe or spirit of the dancing ghosts. Silent and unmoving he sat through this night, as he had the night before. To most outsiders the sights and sounds of this mournful midnight desert dance would seem the mythic essence of grief and dread. But the American with the ruined legs knew better. Tom Shannon knew that the Al-Murrah were not grieving but celebrating.

Tom searched the shadowy faces for Rashid and Muhammad, dancing at their own weddings. That tall dark panther of a youth who set the pace for the others was surely Rashid. But Muhammad was not by his brother's side. Only once, six years ago, when brotherhood had been a matter of life and death the night Ain Dar blew, had these two warring sons of Abdullah stood together. Muhammad was at the far end of the line, dancing a little disdainfully to a graceful inner melody only he could hear. Muhammad, who could fox-trot and tango and samba, was no longer content to mime the shambling tribal hop of his ancestors. Tom's heart ached as he watched Muhammad deliberately dip and sway and prance apart from the others. Again he wondered if it had been kindness or curse to send Muhammad to university in England, where the boy seemed to have majored in confusion. In transit, too, he had lost most of his verve and much of his humor, and in their place was a brittle new awareness of the limitations of his own race and class. Tom sighed under his breath. School in England had been the boy's heart's desire, and so, after Muhammad's heroism at Ain Dar, Tom had given what it was in his power to buy with dollars. Yet he regretted that he had unwittingly helped lead this malleable young man to such a crisis of identity. Tom looked at his brother, who had never been the victim of such ambivalence. Rashid would never want to forget and never would forget that he was a Muslim and a Saudi and an Arab.

In the firelight Tom's eyes were wet as he watched his boys dance. He loved his two young Arabs. He would do almost anything for these boys who had saved his life. Muhammad's years at the University of Manchester and Rashid's at the American University in Cairo were only the beginning of what Tom had determined for them. He had gone on to set up a water-well-drilling business here in Saudi in their names. He had helped Ibrahim get financing for the machinery, he had set up the office, and most important of all, he had shown him where to find water where water had never before been found in the desert. Then he had helped Ibrahim secure an Aramco loan to expand into the lucrative trucking business, and three times a week a fleet of Al-Murrah diesels bisected the Arabian Peninsula from the Persian Gulf to the Red Sea.

Tom's next plan was to get the family dabbling in real estate and imports. Already this entire branch of the Al-Murrah owned a surplus of radios, guns, cars, and trucks, and Tom hoped and prayed he would live to see the day when they might become one of the richest merchant families in eastern Arabia. For Tom's acrid years in Saudi had in a way ended with the oil-field fire. He had resisted Aramco's campaign to pension him off and send him home, for Saudi had begun to mean not only death but life to him. Abdullah's family had become his. He had broken down and confessed to Ibrahim the real story of how Abdullah had died, and the old man's generosity had awed him. Ibrahim had simply sighed and accepted what had happened as God's will. And then Ibrahim had studied Tom silently for a long moment with his dim eyes and said he would have to insist on the letter of the old desert code, a son for a son. Tom would be his son. Tom must replace Abdullah. The American had wept as the Arab had held him in his forgiving arms.

Ibrahim and Tom had grown as close as father and son, and together they had plotted a future for Muhammad and Rashid. The boys were being sent to America on graduate-level scholarships offered by the Saudi government. Muhammad would study civil engineering at Northeastern in Boston, and Rashid would study petroleum engineering in Texas. But Ibrahim had insisted that first his grandsons must strengthen their family ties by taking their cousins as wives. Long ago, even while Abdullah had still been alive, it had been decided that Muhammad should marry his cousin Aisha, who was the daughter of Abdullah's dead older brother, and that Rashid should marry Nura, the daughter of Abdullah's younger sister. Tom's thoughts trailed a world away, back to New England, where courtships were a matter of love and passion instead of family arrangements. Soon Sunny would be going out on dates, and before he knew it, she would be writing him about boys and then babies instead of that Arabian horse he had bought for her. Tom savored the thought of the new treasures he had bought for Sunny one gilded drunken afternoon in the souks of Bahrain. When Muhammad and Rashid went to America, he would have them hand-deliver the gold and the pearls he had bought for Sunny's sixteenth birthday.

Tom yawned and wished they would get on with it. Even after all these years, he was impatient at the roundabout slowness of every facet of Arab life. Yesterday he had accompanied Ibrahim, Muhammad, Rashid, and a pack of other male relatives into Hofuf to get the imam's religious seal on the marriage contracts. Muhammad had pledged to protect and support Aisha, and Rashid had made the same promise for Nura. Neither girl had witnessed the men making their vows, but all the kinsmen had watched the brothers each pay three thousand riyals - about seven hundred dollars - to set up a proper household for their brides. Ibrahim had firmly refused Tom's offer to pay the bride-prices, but he had graciously allowed him to give this wedding feast. Since the Al-Murrah were strict Wahhabi fundamentalists, there could be no liquor, music, tobacco, or any dancing except for that ceremonial sword dance of the men. Nor could there be any barefaced contact between Al-Murrah men and women. While the men celebrated here, the women held their own party inside a nearby tent. The high point of this marriage so far had come when the two hundred guests feasted on twenty-five roasted sheep. Tom would have liked to throw a Western-style wedding that all the tribes would have talked about for generations. But he reminded himself that his own yearning for a tiered wedding cake and champagne and rice thrown into the air was of another world.

Suddenly, as the drumbeat stopped and Ibrahim stepped forward from the line of dancing men, Tom snapped to attention. After two days of ritualized anticipation, the marriages were about to be consummated. Muhammad and Rashid would deflower their brides behind the closed flaps of their separate wedding tents while every man, woman, and child of this branch of the Al-Murrah sat listening for any sounds of fighting or laughing or gasping in surprise or pleasure. The young men could take ten minutes or ten hours, but eventually bloodstained bits of cloth would have to wave outside the tents as proof of the virtue of the brides. As Tom tried to catch the eyes of his boys, he thanked God he hadn't had to do it to Sally the first time with his mother in a ringside seat listening to the sounds of their loving.

He watched Muhammad trading boastful jests with his cousins as he swaggered toward his wife's tent. He watched Rashid throw back his shoulders and hold up his head and tread softly to the black tent where his bride waited. How strange, Tom thought, that in a country as puritanical as Saudi a couple's first sexual encounter was so public. And how odd that a husband's first introduction to his wife was the ultimate in intimacy. Yet Tom supposed that what was about to happen behind the closed tent flaps was only an old and universal story. Like every other human being in the history of the world, Rashid and Muhammad would just have to do their best, with as great grace as they could muster, as they blundered through their sexual initiations. Tom's lips turned up in a smile as he remembered another boy and girl on another night, skin against skin, under white sheets and a calico quilt. He wished some of the magic he had made long ago in a hotel on Cape Cod with Sally would rub off tonight on his boys.

Muhammad blinked in the sudden dimness. Before him stood a bundle of black cloth that seemed like every other shapeless sack that was a Saudi woman. Wearily Muhammad reminded himself that he had to have sexual relations with whatever sort of coarse creature was hidden under these homespun folds. His grandfather, his mother, his aunts, his cousins, and Tom Shannon were sitting outside this tent waiting to hear him take this woman. His virility was at stake. If he took her very fast, maybe they would even make a legend in the tribe about how manly he was. He beckoned imperiously to her. 'Aisha!'

From under the black mask and cloak and veil there was a muffled noise that did not sound like assent.

'Aisha!' His curiosity quickened. It would be easier to do what he had to do if she had a pretty face or a curvaceous body. 'Wife, show me your face!' But Aisha backed away from him - he supposed, in terror. Wistfully Muhammad remembered the women he had lusted after in England, where girls didn't hide their charms. But it occurred to him that English girls might *have* more charms to display. His glimpses of the bare faces of Al-Murrah girls herding the sheep or milking the camels had not left him panting for more. Muhammad took a resolute step closer to his wife. With everyone outside waiting and listening, this was no time for niceties like beauty and passion and desire.

But again she fled from him. She ran from one end of the tent to the other, like a bird beating its wings against the bars of a cage.

Watching the frenzy of her flight, Muhammad finally remembered the custom. Any Saudi bride with an ounce of virtue - and Saudi women measured their virtue not by the ounce but by the pound - was supposed to engage in hand-to-hand combat before she would even show him her face. Muhammad leaned against a tent pole and yawned at the prospect of wrestling mask and veil off his cousin. Yet Ibrahim wouldn't let him go to America unless he did the deed with Aisha. A quick little tussle on a hairy camel-skin blanket, and he could escape from this sordid tent to the far more amusing diversions of Boston.

Muhammad begrudged every second he had to spend in this desert camp. He was accustomed now to the superior refinements of a far more discriminating life. In England he had learned to say 'Chin-chin' and 'Happy days' just before he drank gin and sipped sherry. He had learned to dress in subdued tweeds and well-pressed flannels, and he had even taught himself the linguistic tricks of small talk and sarcasm and witty ironical asides. But there had been a price for this worldliness. Along the way, with all the other subtleties of Western life and Western thought, Muhammad had learned to be ashamed he was an Arab. He was ashamed to be in this Arab tent with this Arab woman. Yet he edged closer to Aisha, seized the dangling edge of her black cloak, and whisked it off her.

'*La!*' Again Aisha lunged away from him.

Muhammad stared at his bride's dumpling figure encased in a tight ruffled orange taffeta robe. Some of her oily black hair hung free now, but her face was still shrouded by her veil and mask. Yet when he caught a glimpse of her terrified eyes, he felt sorry for this twenty-nine-year-old virgin. While he had been off in school in Lebanon and England, she had probably never ceased worrying that he, chosen long ago by Ibrahim to be her husband, would never stay home long enough to marry her. Yet still he resented having to marry this leftover old spinster. He crooked his finger. 'Here, Aisha.'

When she ran from him again, he pursued her. Finally he tackled her and straddled her and tore off her veil and mask. Aisha had sallow skin, a large hook nose, and lips nearly as full as a black slave's. Her deep-set dark eyes, prematurely ringed with bluish circles, stared out at him with dread and yet a sort of breathless expectation.

But he was heedless of her feelings. He couldn't help uttering curses in English, for she was even uglier than he had feared. The rumors that Rashid's bride was the beautiful one had probably been true. All the old slights, the festering resentments burned once again in Muhammad. *Of course* Ibrahim would give Rashid the pretty one. Always his grandfather and his mother and the aunts and the cousins doted on Rashid. When Abdullah was alive, Rashid had been even his father's favorite.

Muhammad glowered down at the bride fate and his grandfather had given him. He reached out and ran his hands over her soft, flabby breasts and waist and hips and thighs. He would have been willing to pay far more than the bride-price to avoid doing what he had to do now. Muhammad climbed off Aisha, and his disgust deepened as some of the sloppy stitches in her homemade robe came undone as he lifted the hem. His homely wife couldn't even sew. She probably couldn't cook, either. At this moment Muhammad despised Saudi food, Saudi clothes, Saudi ways, and especially, Saudi women. Finally he stripped down her white pantaloons. Even as she lay flat on her back, the doughy flesh of her belly quivered. Muhammad stared in surprise at the hairless cleft between her legs. The prostitutes in England had sprouted bushy pubic hair. He touched Aisha's smooth shaved mound, and obediently she parted her legs and began to pant as her aunts had said she should.

Muhammad wanted to run away, but instead he swiftly removed his shorts, lifted his robe and braced himself to do his duty. Something was terribly wrong. Muhammad panicked as he looked down at his flaccid penis. Her fault, he told himself. No man would want to have sexual relations with this beast of a woman. Even when he rubbed himself, he still stayed soft. Fear of the awful shame that would be entirely his if he couldn't enter her made him rub harder and go even softer.

Aisha's sad eyes, as she blinked up at him, brimmed with a mixture of emotions. Muhammad saw hurt and pain, and injured pride, and something else. Could that be sly satisfaction in his wife's eyes? Had this woman shrewdly measured him and found him wanting? Had this illiterate peasant woman the temerity to think she had the worst of this marriage bargain? Instead of looking ashamed that she hadn't pleased him, Aisha was smirking at his limp penis.

Muhammad recoiled from this unnatural woman. Inside him he could feel the budding of a great and bitter anger. This ugly woman, this fat woman, this *old* woman dared to let him see that she was glad he had not been man enough to enter her. Muhammad began to breathe heavily. He would show her, and when he was through with her, she would know never to mock him again. In a fury he threw the hem of Aisha's robe over her face so she would no longer be able to ridicule him with her eyes. In a hot fury he dredged up the sexiest memory of his life. Once he had paid two English whores with blond hair and light eyes to go with him to a cheap hotel room. He hadn't needed any coaxing to be hard enough to push up inside first one and then the other. It had taken two of those wild pink-skinned women to satisfy him. Exultantly, he felt himself harden as he thought of the moist, smooth, white-hot feel of those whores, and before he could go soft again, he forced himself down on his cousin. He pushed inside her with such force that Aisha's membrane broke and she cried out in pain. He pumped hard and fast, and it was all over in seconds.

But as he lay unmoving on the fatness of his wife - the deed done, the custom satisfied - a terrible sadness stole over Muhammad. He stifled a sob, and he lay immobilized by the familiar ache of his own betrayal of the best in himself. Mostly he could shrug off his impulses to be as his father and his grandfather had once taught him to be. Mostly he convinced himself that he had rooted out all vestiges of the Arab in himself. Yet here and now he was ashamed of his callous cruelty. He was supposed to protect this pitiful woman under him. He should have been generous enough to be gentle with her, but instead he had just used this good Muslim woman like an English whore. Without even knowing he was being tested, he had just failed at one of the great tests of manhood. He lay atop his bride and as his penis went soft again, he knew he had been diminished.

Muhammad was grateful his wife couldn't see the tears that fell from his eyes. They lay silently together until Muhammad was absolutely dry of eye and spirit, and then Aisha contemptuously nudged him until he rolled off her. She looked down in gladness at the small pinkish bloodstain on her white pantaloons. Proudly she padded to the entrance of the tent to wave the proof of her virtue for all to see. But as she turned back then to face Muhammad, as she readied the basin of water so that they could purify themselves of the sexual act, between them there was still the utterly uneasy silence of those who have nothing whatsoever to say to each other. And in that bleak silence, they heard, carrying over to them from that other bridal tent, the high clear silvery music of girlish laughter.

Muhammad clenched his hands into angry fists as he heard what he jealously had somehow known he would hear: the sound of an answering deep-pitched masculine laugh as his brother enjoyed his Arab wife in his Arab tent.

Muhammad gritted his teeth. Rashid had won once again.

Rashid and Nura sat laughing as they knelt a bit apart from each other on a Persian rug.

But they had not started their night of carnal knowledge with laughter. Their first moments had been taken up, at Rashid's suggestion, by pious prayers toward Mecca. Never having even been alone with a sexually available woman, Rashid had been stalling for time and praying for courage. Only after he had beseeched Allah's blessings had Rashid proceeded with what he had decided days ago should be the next step in the courtship of his bride.

He had sat cross-legged at some distance from Nura as he plied her with a series of small presents that were not required of him in the marriage contract. First two tinkling silver ankle bracelets he had bought for her in Khan el-Khalili in Cairo, and it had been her delighted laugh at being given these trinkets that Muhammad had overheard. Rashid, then, had said her laugh tinkled like silver. Now, when he gave her the *melabas* candy he had bought for her in Hofuf, he laughed again and called her *y'assal*, a woman as sweet as honey. He gave her a fistful of ribbons that he said were green like sweet grass and blue like the sea and yellow like the sun. He gave her a bolt of red cloth - red, he said, like a woman's lips - so that she could make herself a new dress. He offered her, finally, a bowlful of yoghurt thinned by camel's milk and sweetened with ground dates. He told her he had prepared it for her with his own hands.

Nura laughed again and thanked him gravely for all those thoughtful presents. But when he took a drink from the bowl of yoghurt and asked her to do the same, Nura blushed with dismay. She could not drink without removing her heavy black cloak and veil and mask. Yet the demands of courtesy and hospitality required that she drink.

Gallantly Rashid offered to turn his back while she drank what he had prepared for her.

'*La!*' Oh, no. She would not be tricked into unveiling herself without a fight.

Rashid laughed at the failure of his ploy, and then he made another proposition. He was willing, he said, to respect the honey of his wife's virtue. He would shut his eyes, and after she removed her veil and mask, *he* would put them on while she drank the yoghurt.

She laughed again at the incongruity of a man's wearing a woman's mask. For a moment, she forgot her fear of him and what they were supposed to do together in his tent. It was not long ago, after all, that she and Rashid had been children together, playing around the campfires and swimming together in the deep lakelike desert wells. Everyone said Rashid was a good man, a generous man, a brave man, a true son of the Al-Murrah. She was flattered to be her cousin's wife. She knew, however, that she was supposed to make him chase her around the tent and that by now she should be crying out and moaning and protesting loudly enough to wake the spirits of the dead. Instead she longed to cover Rashid's handsome face with kisses.

Rashid brought her indecision to an end by leaning over and very gently tugging at her cloak and veil. Nura held her breath as her cocoon slipped down around her shoulders and she felt his fingers touch her hair.

'Soft as the Dahana sands,' Rashid whispered.

She sighed and did not back away when his fingers fumbled at the ties to her mask. He played with the ties for a long while, and then seemed to give up. As his fingers stroked the hair at her temples, he whispered to her that she would have to help him remove that mask.

Should she be coy or bold? The tips of his fingers trailed from her hair to her shoulders. The touch of his skin on hers thrilled her. For long tantalizing years she had yearned for the magic hour when this man would finally touch her. In the hot languor of desert afternoons, lying in the heat of the shade, she had imagined his hands in her hair and on her breasts and between her legs. She had waited in an agony of sexual lassitude for Rashid to make her his. And so it was too hard to debate any longer whether to untie her mask. It was possible now only to let herself feel the touch of his fingers.

She sat trembling like a gazelle scenting on the wind the dangerous excitement of a predator. His fingers strayed from her shoulders to where the mounds of her breasts should be. Swiftly he drew the black cloak off her shoulders and Nura sighed. As he eagerly touched his fingertips to her breasts, to her waist, back to her breasts again, Nura could feel her blood begin to pound.

Just as Rashid was wondering how he would ever undo her skin-tight purple robe, to his astonishment this girl who would not even show him her face rose majestically to her feet and threw off her robe. He gasped and his penis went hard as he gazed at her curves and swells and softness. 'Beautiful.' He stumbled to his feet and placed his sweaty hands on her cool, full, high breasts. As he touched them, the tips hardened as if by magic. 'So beautiful!' Nura arched her back so that her breasts pointed even higher. Tenderly, tentatively, he reached out his hands and cupped her breasts. This time his touch made her shudder. Quickly she bent over and slipped off her pantaloons. Carefully she spread them on the blanket and lowered herself so that the white cotton was under her thighs. When she was flat on her back, she giggled, spread her legs, and waited.

Rashid took a deep breath. She was the most luscious and hot and willing woman in the world, and she was his. Rashid stepped out of his shorts and knelt beside her and resisted his eager impulse to plunge right inside her. This Nura with the smooth skin and ripe body was his cousin, the daughter of his favorite aunt, who had been the sister of his father. If he acted like an animal instead of a man, if he pushed himself into this girl laid so invitingly before him, he might frighten or hurt her. Yet he was perplexed.

If he wasn't going to enter her just yet, what else could he do? He had expected it would be more complicated and that it would take far longer to get to where they were now. He supposed they should be talking more. Surely there were words that should be said? But what words? And who should say them?

Nura lay panting. Nura evidently did not share his desire to talk. Rashid was afraid she might laugh if he suggested they pray again. Instead he simply looked at the wonder of her lying open to him. When she panted like this, loudly, so that she would most assuredly be overheard outside, her breasts heaved. He reached out his hand and stroked the satin skin of her breasts which would someday nurse their children.

Nura waited with bated breath as he stroked her slowly, from her breasts to her belly, and then she sighed when finally he buried his hesitant fingers in the dampness between her legs. She was panting in earnest now, as he touched her for long minutes, but then she was impatient for the ultimate. She peered at Rashid from behind her mask. 'I have done something wrong?' Her husky voice was so soft he could hardly hear her. 'I do not please you?'

Rashid blushed and shook his head and wished he dared to kiss every curve of her silky body. He could feel himself getting harder. He was embarrassed enough to try to hide his erection from her; but this young cousin of his, a girl so modest she still wouldn't take off her mask, reached for his penis. He squirmed away from her. He had thought it just another idle tribal boast that Al-Murrah women were hot-blooded. When she laughed at his modesty, Rashid grew even more confused. Did she think they were two camels or two sheep about to mate in a pasture?

But then Nura laughed more gently. 'Husband, they are listening outside. I think it is time, husband, to give them something to listen to!'

Rashid nervously wet his lips. 'You are ready? Now you are ready?' She nodded her head so definitely her dangling earrings made music. Again he stalled for time. 'You are certain?' She spread her legs even wider.

Rashid leaned over his bride even more shyly than before. Gently he fingered her so soft breasts, and he let his hands trail down to her rounded belly. As he wandered inevitably lower, she shuddered. Tensely he stared at the mysterious hairless cleft between her legs. When he was a boy, he had once spread a female sheep's hind legs to study the difference between male and female. He conquered his impulse to bend over Nura as he had bent over that sheep, examining her fascinating differences. He concentrated instead on the possibility of a great shame. He did not know where exactly he should put himself, how to do it and not hurt her. He had been too proud to ask any of the other men. When he had overheard Muhammad bragging that he had done all this before, he had almost broken down and asked his brother for instructions. But at the last minute, Rashid had been too ashamed of his innocence to ask Muhammad's help. 'Allah!' Rashid couldn't help praying, out loud, for God's blessed guidance. He would be everlastingly ashamed if he did all this wrong.

'I am waiting!' Nura laughed up at him. 'I will be an old woman before you take me, husband!'

He could not postpone it any longer. Even as he knelt between her legs and very slowly lowered himself almost on top of her, Rashid continued to fret whether he was doing it right. When the tip of him touched the skin of her thigh, he cried out, for he had swelled so much he feared he would explode out of his own skin. Blindly he thrust it toward her. 'Here?' Anxiously he pushed against her skin. 'Do I put it here?'

'Husband!' In between theatrical pants, she called out his name so that everyone outside could hear. 'Husband!'

He was encouraged enough to grope around until he found a kind of indentation in her. He broke out into a sweat. Please, Allah, he prayed to himself, guide me, so I don't put it in the wrong place, so I don't hurt my little cousin. Very slowly, very lightly, he pushed himself in just a fraction.

'Allah strengthen thee!' Nura managed to gasp in encouragement. 'Allah!'

In triumph then, he let himself go and pushed harder and deeper. But he could go in only so far. He felt her give a little under him. He pressed still harder, still deeper, and then finally he broke through, he was altogether in. And then, just when he thought the ordeal was over, he felt Nura moving under him, together with him; he felt her arms close around him. He gasped out loud. This was wonderful, wonderful. . . . 'Allah!' He called out his pleasure for God to witness. He had never felt this good in all his life. He pushed in harder, deeper, faster. 'Nura! My Nura!' They shook together in delight on the blanket in the sand.

From outside the tent then, after the two of them were finally quiet, they could hear the women's *zaghareit* joy-cries. The women had been listening to the progressive sounds of their intimacies so closely they even knew precisely when to cheer.

Rashid lifted his head from Nura's breast and looked in astonishment at his bride. He had been so obsessed with her body that he had forgotten her face. After what they had just shared, how could it be that she was still wearing her mask? Masterfully he seized the bottom of her mask and ripped it off. For the first time he beheld the laughing brown face of his beautiful Nura. Her eyes were black and laughing. Her mouth was red and laughing. Shyly she giggled up at him. She was more embarrassed that he was seeing her face than she had been to let him take her body.

Timidly, then, she pointed from the gifts of his ankle bracelets to the candy to the bowl of yoghurt and then to the bloodstains on her pantaloons. 'My gift to you,' she said in a very small voice.

He hugged her, then kissed her on her red full lips. Their arms were around each other as they drank from the bowl of yoghurt he had prepared with his own hands.

*

The stars were fading pale. The predawn sky was silver. The desert was as quiet as a dream.

Rashid shifted the gears of the pickup truck, and Muhammad yawned in the seat next to him as the Al-Murrah fleet fanned out over the open desert. Neither brother had looked forward to rising in the middle of the night for this hunt. But Grandfather had arranged it specially for them, and so they had to ride and track and shoot. It would be, in a way, their farewell to the tribe and the desert and Saudi. The day after tomorrow they would fly the first leg of their long journey from Dhahran to America.

As Rashid drove absently in the general direction of the Dahana dunes, he was thinking not of this morning's hunt but of last night's sport. Nura was such a riddle of contradictions. He knew, and loved, every crevice and mound and smoothness of her eager nubile body. But when he tried to talk to her, all she would do was giggle and try to hide her face. How could Nura be so bold in sex and so shy in friendship? It was a lonely ecstasy to lie in that woman's arms.

Yesterday's brief freak thundershower had raised a live green fuzz of grass and fragrant wisps of tiny red, violet, and white wildflowers on the desert sand. What was good pasture for grazing wildlife should be good hunting for the Arabs. Not so long ago, a morning like this would have been a wild joy to Rashid. As a small boy, living here always, and then later when he came home for holidays and summer vacations, they all used to hunt on camelback with the hooded falcons. Rashid would track the game so relentlessly that the tribesmen said he would someday be as famous a tracker as his father and the father of his father and the father of the father of his father. Rashid had loved spying out the first traces of the tracks, following them even over hard flint and then glimpsing the fleeing oryx or ostrich or gazelle. The Arabs would let loose their hawks and hounds. The tribesmen would wave their carbines and prepare to close in for the kill. Always, however, Rashid had loved the game of tracking far more than the gory kill. Muhammad had always been the better marksman. Muhammad had always thrilled to the blood sport of a hunt.

A shadow fell across the sand, and Rashid looked up at the sky. Already a waiting vulture careened overhead. Even the vultures seemed to know that there would surely be slaughter this morning. Rashid hated hunting from a truck. He missed the good old days. There was no sport in running down helpless animals in a pickup. Even the fleet gazelles couldn't outrun a truck. It disturbed him, too, that this morning they would be killing animals that didn't need to be killed. There were still sheep left to be slaughtered from the herd Mr. Tom had bought for the wedding feast. Hunting for amusement for the bored was different from hunting for meat for the hungry. Every year there was less and less wild game in the desert. Equipped with repeater rifles and shotguns, cars and trucks, the Arabs were decimating herds that had always been scant but that now might soon be extinct.

Rashid stuck his head out of the window to squint at the faint trail of very fresh gazelle tracks he was halfheartedly following in the sand.

He gasped and pointed at a herd of four gazelles silhouetted at the crest of one of the first of the Dahana dunes. A bull, two cows, and a calf had been drinking from a small rain pool that sparkled as if it were jewels. But even as Rashid sighted them, the gazelles froze in place, alert to the approach of the alien truck. He cut the engine and stared in the uncertain dimness of the predawn light. It was rare, these days, to see a family of the small deerlike gray animals all together. For a moment he wondered if they were a dream. In Arabian poetry, as on the tongues of Arabian lovers, the highest praise for a woman who pleases is to tell her that she is as shy and trembling and graceful as a gazelle. Nura was like a gazelle. Half-asleep this morning, thinking more of his wife than of this hunt, Rashid was willing to believe the gazelles ahead were a mirage.

'Four gazelles!' Muhammad broke the spell. 'Smashing!' Muhammad was already rooting on the floor of the truck through his arsenal of guns. He picked up a pistol and a big gun that Rashid had never seen before. Muhammad quickly opened the door and braced himself on the running board. '*Yalla!* Let's go! Hit the horn! The others will want in on this.'

Rashid hesitated, then shrugged off his scruples. He supposed he was too sentimental. Those were real gazelles on the rise ahead, and gazelles did make tender meat. He blew the horn as a signal for the others to join them. He aimed the pickup in the general direction of the herd. The animals quivered a long second, then bounded away very fast, toward the north and the dunes that might hide them.

'*Yalla!*' As Muhammad urged Rashid on, he tried to wave his gun in the air. But it was, strangely, too heavy. '*Yalla!*'

The pickup raced up the gentle slope of the dune, then down the other side. The truck chased the gazelles up and down three more dunes. They were gaining on them, but they were still not within firing distance. 'Faster!' Muhammad urged. 'Straight ahead! *Yalla!*'

The gazelles, Rashid thought, were so beautiful and so graceful as they ran for their lives. The gazelles were so wild and so free, the gazelles were so frantic and had so little of a sporting chance against the pickup, that Rashid very surreptitiously began to ease his foot on the brake. If he went just a little slower, if the gazelles went just a little faster, they might reach the safety of the high-dune country just in time.

But Rashid reckoned without Muhammad. 'Right! Swerve right!' Automatically Rashid obeyed. He heard, then, the deadly clicks of metal and looked up just as Muhammad took aim with a fat gray gun he held not high at his shoulder but low at his waist. Rashid stared in utter shock. Surely Muhammad wasn't about to gun down a herd of gazelles with a machine gun? 'No!' Rashid slammed on the brake to try to ruin his brother's shot.

Muhammad pulled the firing pin. *Ratatatatat! Rat-tat-tat! Rat-atatat-atatat!*

The bullets raked the flesh of the fleeing animals.

Ratatatatat! Rat-tat-tat! Ratatatatatat!

First one cow fell, then the bull, finally the other cow. The young calf had been running just far enough behind to miss the line of fire. But now the young animal caught up. It stood piteously bleating and nuzzling its dead parents.

Muhammad took aim again with his machine gun. But this time Rashid was too quick for him. He lunged so hard against the truck door that it flew open and ruined Muhammad's aim. *Ratatatatat!* The gunfire harmlessly ripped a metal path in the sand. 'Enough!' Rashid roared at his brother. 'Let the calf live! We have enough meat! Enough killing, in the name of Allah!'

Sullenly Muhammad glared at his brother. He watched, undecided, as Rashid began to walk toward the grieving calf. But then Muhammad leaned over and retrieved the heavy blunt-nosed Mauser he had dropped in the sand. Just as Rashid was calling out to the calf not to be afraid, just as his brother was almost close enough to lay a reassuring hand on the trembling animal, Muhammad raised his pistol and fired one unerring shot between the eyes of the gazelle.

Rashid stopped dead in his tracks. He watched the calf buck just once, moan, then sink to the sand already wet with the blood of its dead family. The eyes of the calf fluttered shut as Rashid ran the remaining steps. He knelt beside the gazelle, he stroked it; frantically he wanted to make the beautiful young wild thing live. In the last breaths of this young gazelle, Rashid could see the death throes of his own tribal past. He laid his ear against the breast of the animal and tried to hear the beat of its heart. But there was nothing to hear. He saw a dark shadow circling overhead and looked up at the waiting vulture. Rashid pulled his hunting knife from its sheath and held it to the throat of the gazelle. '*Bismallah al-rahman al-rahim*,' he whispered: 'in the name of God the Merciful, the Compassionate.' Swiftly he slit the throat of the consecrated gazelle, as the Koran says an animal must be sacrificed for Allah. As he wiped the blade dry on the sand, the lashes of Rashid's eyes were wet with tears.

Back on the running board of the pickup, Muhammad raised his machine gun toward the sky, in triumph, just as the dreamlike softness of the dawn was breaking. Sharp and ugly staccato bursts of fire rent the air as Muhammad fired his farewell to Arabia.

6

All day long, first on the six-hour train ride from New York to Boston, and now during the hour-and-a-half commuter train ride from Boston to Ayer, the brothers had been sniping at each other. They had argued over who would sit next to the window, whether the window would be opened or shut, whether it was polite to smoke cigarettes, whether it was moral to smoke cigarettes, whether it was polite to fall asleep in their seats, whether Muhammad snored, whether either or neither or both of them were dressed right or wrong for their imminent meeting with Mr. Tom's family.

In two white-tissue-wrapped and gold-ribbon-tied packages, one held stiffly and securely in Rashid's lap, the other carelessly lying on the floor by Muhammad's feet atop a *Life* magazine, were a treasury of Tom Shannon's belated golden gifts for Sunny's sixteenth birthday. Two thick gold bangle bracelets, a thin hammered gold one, another gold bracelet embossed with the Saudi crossed-sword-and-palm-tree coat of arms, and two gold bracelets engraved with Sunny's name in English and Arabic. Two long fat gold necklaces and two short fat gold necklaces strung with charms of a heart, a cross, a horsehead, and a Persian peacock. Three gold rings, one with a ruby set in the coil of a serpent, one with a chunk of Red Sea coral, and one with jade set in an intricate gold filigree that had been worked in India. Three pairs of earrings, one chunky, one dainty, another dangling. As the *pièce de résistance*, Tom had paid a jeweler to string the priceless strand of lustrous pink-sheened Persian Gulf pearls he had been collecting for Sunny for more than a decade. He had joked with Rashid and Muhammad that even though they would be giving Sunny far more than a bride-price, they could look but not touch her. He had laughed as he warned them his Sunny was not for sale.

Muhammad blew smoke rings as he stared out at the New England landscape. It was early September, and already the leaves were beginning to change color. Snug farmhouses were tucked beside thick woods. Red and yellow tractors moved along patchwork fields. From an overcast sky came a fine drizzle of rain. It wasn't England, but it was close. Muhammad crossed his legs as he had seen elegant English gentlemen do and smoothed out nonexistent wrinkles in his tweed and flannels. He didn't need a mirror for assurance that he looked just right. When he met the Shannons, he wanted to appear to be debonair and suave. Finally, here in America, he might be able to play his English act before an applauding audience. He had taken a degree in engineering at Manchester, but what he had really been studying was how to pass someday for an English gentleman. Muhammad's face clouded for an instant as he remembered social slights he had endured in England, despite his best efforts not to give away the fact that he was an Arab. Muhammad had high hopes it would be different here in America.

He and Rashid had spent only an hour in Boston changing trains, but already Muhammad had decided he liked this city which was supposed to be Continental and cultured and mad for all things English. If that advance word was true, Muhammad hoped that maybe the American girls in Boston would be mad for him as well. Despite the pornographic lies he had told the men and boys back in Saudi, Muhammad had been forced to pay for any sex he had had in England. Sometimes, it was true, he had taken English girls to the cinema or out for a meal, but seldom had he managed to coax more than a kiss from any of them. It was Muhammad's great expectation that he would be able to take far greater liberties with American girls. Especially he hoped for endless good times with American blondes. He had heard Arabs talk with enthusiasm about the American blondes who could be found in great wild herds in California. He hadn't heard a word about Boston girls. Muhammad shot a worried look at the other passengers in this Boston & Maine railway car. Mostly on this weekday afternoon they were farmers in dungarees, businessmen in dark suits, and students in open-necked shirts. A few frumpy women sat stolidly beside subdued children. There were no beautiful blondes, but there were a few buxom brunettes and one faded blonde who would do in a pinch. Muhammad took another satisfied drag on his cigarette. He thanked God this wasn't Saudi, where ugly fat women like his wife, Aisha, went around covered head to toe in black.

'Muhammad?' Rashid squirmed on the adjoining seat. 'We go much longer?' When Muhammad did not choose to answer him, Rashid's face creased with worry. 'You make mistake? This wrong train?' Rashid groped for English words. Since leaving Saudi he seemed to have lost his careful fluency. 'Or last stop was right one maybe? We should be here on this train? Still?'

'No mistake,' Muhammad replied.

'But we are on train too long. You make mistake.'

'Only in agreeing to come here with a baby like you.'

'Baby!' Rashid's voice rose in a torrent of indignant Arabic, but he stopped when Muhammad pinched him hard on his leg.

'English!' Muhammad hissed. 'I told you, here we speak only English!'

Rashid sighed unhappily but was too tired and hungry and bewildered to challenge his haughty brother again. Rashid had not had a sound night's sleep since he had left his wife's tent. Last night in that noisy Times Square hotel, he had tossed and turned on a bed that was too soft. He had been too nervous to sleep on their one-night stopover in Rome. He had not even been able to nap while they were in the air for that frightening, bumpy, thirty-hour plane ride on Aramco's 'Flying Camel' DC-6 from Dhahran to Rome to New York. Rashid shivered in his seat on the commuter train. America was even colder and damper than Beirut, and this was only September. He praised Allah he would not be going to graduate school here in Boston like Muhammad. After they delivered these presents to Mr. Tom's daughter, he would go on to Texas, which Mr. Tom had guaranteed was almost as hot and dry as Saudi. But meanwhile Rashid had insulated himself from the cold by wearing nearly all the clothes he owned. He had on a shirt, two sweaters, his new black suit, and a raincoat, yet still he was cold. He looked longingly over at a newspaper left behind on a nearby seat. He wanted to fold it up and tuck it inside his sweater, as he had seen poor Egyptians keep themselves warm when winter winds swept in from the desert. He wished he could wrap a length of cloth around his head, but Muhammad had threatened to stalk away and leave him stranded if he dared put on a head scarf. Muhammad wouldn't even let him pray in public. Already, in the few days he had been away from Saudi, Rashid had missed more of the required daily prayers than in all the years of his life.

Muhammad had been a bully ever since they took their seats on the Aramco plane, for after his years in England, Muhammad claimed to know all there was to know about life in the West. Rashid was discovering, to his dismay, just how different life *was* here from the way it was in the Middle East. Everyone walked so fast, talked so fast, even ate so fast. All the meals he and Muhammad had shared so far in restaurants here had been quick and unsatisfying. Everything tasted strange and heavy and wrong. The coffee was too dark and bitter, and the tea was as weak as water. He worried that some or all of those mysterious hunks of meat he kept getting might be some sort of forbidden pork, and he wondered why the ferocious women who worked in restaurants insisted on giving him food so hot it burned his tongue.

'Littleton!' The words crackled over the heavy static from the speaker placed at the front of the car. 'Littleton!'

Rashid plucked in desperation at his brother's sleeve. At Dhahran the Americans had taken pains to speak far more slowly. Rashid despaired that if he couldn't even understand a message shouted over a loudspeaker in a train, he would never be able to keep up with graduate-school lectures delivered entirely in English.

Muhammad was also beginning to worry. He too had been unable to understand the garbled announcements. Muhammad was less sure of himself here in America than he was pretending to be. For him too, New York had been too fast, too loud, too grating on the nerves. He looked around in vain for a conductor, and he scanned the preoccupied faces of the passengers lining up in the aisle. Muhammad had survived his first confusing days in America by following Mr. Tom's instructions to the letter. After their arrival and one night's rest in New York, they had taken the train to Boston, then telephoned the Shannons at their farm. Mr. Tom's father had told them to take a taxi to North Station and then this 'B&M' train. They were supposed to stay on to Ayer, where the Shannons would pick them up. According to Muhammad's watch, they had another quarter-hour to go.

'Littleton!' The static crackled on the loudspeaker again.

Muhammad looked out the window at the sign over the station. He couldn't quite read all of its faded characters, but he could tell it had too many letters to spell 'Ayer.' He shook his head at Rashid. 'Not yet. But soon.' He smiled patronizingly at his brother as he remembered how panicked he himself had felt during his first months in England. 'Don't worry. We're almost there. And it's going to be smashing, Rashid. Simply smashing.'

Uncertainly Rashid smiled back. Maybe Muhammad was right. Maybe America was going to be all that he had been told it was.

The brothers sank back on the cushions. Very soon they would be inside their first American home and maybe making their first American friends. Nervously Muhammad lit another cigarette. Rashid smoothed out the ribbons on Sunny's present. Muhammad picked up the other package Mr. Tom had sent for his daughter. Carefully he blew off the cigarette ash he had dropped on the tissue paper.

'Ayer! Next stop, Ayer station!'

'That's it!' Muhammad stubbed out his cigarette.

Rashid jumped to his feet and pressed his nose to the window so he could see whether Mr. Tom's daughter was waiting. 'There! That must be her!'

The eyes of both brothers sparkled with excitement as they looked at blond Sunny Shannon, who was even prettier than her pictures.

'Look! Gran! Over there! That must be them!' Sunny pointed past the farmers and families milling around the platforms. Two darkly handsome young men were swinging eagerly down the steps of the train and looking their way.

'That can't be them.' Bess shook her head. 'Those two are colored people. We're looking for Tom's A-rabs.'

But headstrong Sunny was already running toward the two strangers. She was breathless when she stood in front of them. 'Are you the Arabs? I mean, are you my father's friends? From Saudi?' Her ponytail bobbed as she looked from one swarthy, dark-eyed face to the other. Although she was disappointed they weren't wearing robes and head scarves, she thought they were even more dashing than the pictures she had seen of Arabs in books at the library. She hoped these two gorgeous boys were her father's Arabs. 'I'm Sunny.' She was flustered and so she laughed. 'Sunny Shannon?'

Muhammad and Rashid stood transfixed before this vision of a young, blushing, blue-eyed, American blonde.

'Really, Sunny, I've told you never to talk to strangers.' Bess ignored the colored boys and waved to her husband, who was over by the other track talking to a farmer from Acton. 'John! Those A-rabs must have missed the train.' She bustled off, sure that Sunny would follow.

But Sunny was still smiling up at Muhammad and Rashid. 'You're Arabs? The ones we came to meet? You are, aren't you?'

Both of them nodded, unable just now to speak to this erotic vision. Muhammad covertly studied the voluptuous swell of her breasts under her clinging blue orlon sweater. Rashid frankly stared at her curves and what he could see of the bare pink skin of her long legs. He had not expected Mr. Tom's daughter to be like this. So ripe, like this.

Twenty feet away, Bess stopped and turned. 'Sunny!' As the truth dawned on her, she corralled her husband and together they rushed back to Sunny and the boys. 'You're Tom's A-rabs?'

Muhammad and Rashid tore their eyes off Sunny and gaped at the forceful old woman and the meek elderly man.

'We're the Shannons. I'm Missus. This is Mister. And this is Miss. Which of you boys is which?'

Muhammad found his dignity and his tongue. 'I am Muhammad Al-Murrah. This is my younger brother, Rashid. I am delighted to make the acquaintance of the father of Mr. Tom Shannon. And you, madame, his mother.' Muhammad bowed slightly to the elder Shannons, then turned to Sunny. 'And most of all, I daresay, of you, Miss Shannon.' He groped for Sunny's hand and then, standing right there on the worn wide floorboards of homely Ayer station, he bent over Sunny's hand and lightly grazed the tips of her fingers with his lips. Muhammad looked soulfully up at Sunny's pale foreign eyes. 'Mr. Tom's fair princess!'

Before even quick-acting Bess had time to put an end to all such nonsense, the second Arab stepped forward, firmly seized Sunny's hand, and hungrily tasted it with his lips. 'I am Rashid.' Awkwardly he thrust a gift-wrapped package into her hands. 'For you. From your father.'

Muhammad pushed his brother aside. 'And this as well.' He presented her with another package. 'Your father wishes you a very happy birthday, Miss Shannon.' Muhammad smiled at Sunny. 'And just as you say in your fairy stories, I hope you will live happily ever after.'

'Yes, happy,' Rashid echoed.

Sunny laughed as she looked from one dark handsome brother to the other. As she had lain awake in bed last night, sleepless with excitement, she had prayed that one of them would be a dreamboat who would sweep her off her feet and all the way back to where her father awaited her in Saudi. She hadn't bargained for *two* dreamboats. With their black curly hair, their sultry complexions, their lustrous mustaches, and especially with their huge flashing brown eyes, these brothers looked alike enough to be twins. And she could tell they both liked her. She could hardly wait to tell the girls at school that both these boys had really liked her. She would have to remember every detail - what he said, what I said, what the other one said - for when school started again next week. Finally she was going to have a genuine boyfriend. *Boyfriends!*

Gaily Sunny laughed again, and impulsively she ripped the ribbons and tissue paper off her presents. 'Ah!' She held up a fistful of gold bracelets. 'Gran! Look at this!' She rooted in one of the packages and came up with another palmful of gold earrings and rings. 'And this! Holy smokes!' She held up the necklaces so that they gleamed in the sunlight, and then she found the pearls. 'Gramps! Pearls! I think, real pearls!' She slipped on bracelets and rings. She fastened the gold necklaces and the pearls at her throat. She pirouetted round and round on the train platform, as aglow with her father's gifts of gold and pearls as she was with the admiration of these two exotic boys. And then, before Bess could stop her, she linked her arms in the Arabs' and nearly swept the boys off their feet as she dragged them and their suitcases toward the parking lot.

By the time Bess and John had caught up with the young people, Sunny was just about to crawl into the narrow intimacy of the back seat between the brothers. Firmly the old woman wedged Sunny securely in front between herself and her husband and banished the Arabs and their suitcases to the back seat. She saw to it that Sunny didn't make any more of a fool of herself in the car, either. All the way to Still River, on the half-hour drive through winding woods and past placid villages, Bess delivered a monologue. This town founded in sixteen-something, that one twenty years later. A hatchet stuck in a front door over there during the Indian wars. The history of the local apple orchards, who owned how many acres here, and who had cheated which brothers and sisters so they could inherit how much over there. Which house they were passing had genuine pegboard floors, and which had mediocre modern copies. The English and Latin names of bushes and shrubs and flowers. Every word spoken as Bess craned her neck so that she could shrewdly study the two young Arabs in the back seat. They were much cleaner than she had thought they would be, and excessively polite as they answered her questions about her son. But she could hardly understand a thing the younger one said. And the other one with that phony English accent, did he think she was born yesterday?

By the time they pulled into the long driveway that led to the modest gray clapboard Shannon farmhouse, Bess had decided to be at least a little motherly to these two foreigners who had once saved Tom's life. They looked as if they needed a good filling supper and a nice soft bed. If it weren't for Sunny's being so boy-crazy these days, she might even ask them to stay on for a week or so and help John harvest the apples. But it seemed Sunny was going to be a handful around these two, and so first thing in the morning she would have John put them on the train back to Boston. Then she would take pen in hand and give that son of hers a piece of her mind. Did he think Sunny would wear all that gaudy jewelry shopping at the Star Market or ice-skating at Bare Hill Pond? He should have been sensible and sent a check to buy more savings bonds. Sometimes Bess wondered if her son had been out in the sun too long. Bad enough he had squandered thousands of dollars on jewelry Sunny would hardly ever wear. But how could he set these two Arabs on his impressionable daughter, and why hadn't he warned her they were colored? She didn't care what color Arabs were. But because she had assumed they would be white, she had blurted out something back there at Ayer station that might have sounded prejudiced if anyone had overheard her. Devil take that son of hers! 'Sunny,' she said before the ignition was even turned off, 'you take off all that jewelry and come help me with supper. John will show the boys to their room, and then they can take a little rest.'

'But Gran! I wanted to show them Princess Camey.' Sunny smiled rapturously at the boys. 'My horse. My father sent her. She's purebred Arabian.' She laughed. 'Just like you!'

'I'm afraid there'll be no time for that. Supper's at five-thirty sharp.' Bess all but dragged Sunny into the kitchen, where she did not intend to mince words with her irrepressible granddaughter.

'A real New England dinner,' Bess told the Arabs later, after her husband said grace and she set the steaming dishes on the table. 'Chicken fricassee and mashed potatoes and our own homegrown tomatoes and green beans and my best pickles. Don't be shy. Dig in, boys.'

Muhammad and Rashid looked anxiously at the serving bowl in which indeterminate objects floated alongside smaller and equally doubtful orange and green and white things. Another immense dish held a mound of lumpy white stuff. There were also bowls of less ambiguous boiled and raw vegetables. They wondered if the soupy concoction should go on their plates or in the little bowls. And should they eat it with a spoon or a fork? They were relieved to see Mr. Tom's father put a layer of the lumpy white stuff on his plate, then ladle on liquid from the other dish. Gravely they filled their plates just as he had.

Sunny could not wait any longer for answers to the questions she had been saving up for years. 'Saudi! I can't *believe* you're really from Saudi! What's it *like*?' She did not pause long enough for an answer. 'I bet it's beautiful! Everyone writes how beautiful it is. Lawrence! He's my hero.' Her face became reverential. 'Him and my father, I mean. My *two* heroes.' She smiled again. 'I've read Philby too, sort of - some of him, anyway. And Doughty! He was wonderful! He looks just like God in his pictures. And I like Bertram Thomas, too! Did you meet him? Did you meet any of them? I bet you did. I bet you know them all! Freya Stark! I can't believe I almost forgot her! Miss Stark is one of my favorite writers in all the world. I mean, she's a woman, and she saw *everything* there, everything! If she did it, then I can too someday. What do you think of her, Muhammad?'

'Pardon?' Muhammad tried to regather his very scattered wits. He did not have the slightest idea what this lovely demented girl was going on about. He pushed the chicken around his plate with his fork. 'Who?'

'Freya Stark. The writer. The one who wrote all those books about Arabia.'

'Oh, yes, her; smashing writer indeed.' Muhammad was not about to admit to this beauty that he had never heard of that Stork character, or most of those others. He was glad the folds of the tablecloth covered his erection. The obvious availability of this eager nubile blonde was driving him crazy. He winked at Sunny as he picked at his vegetables. 'Simply smashing.'

Brazenly she winked back. Already she was beginning to like Muhammad best. He was smoother and livelier and laughed more than the other one. Even though Rashid was definitely cuter, Sunny thought he was too much of a brooder, like maybe a dark-haired Jimmy Dean. Muhammad was more like a swarthy Cary Grant. He even had an accent like Cary Grant's. When Muhammad left tomorrow, Sunny hoped he would ask her for her picture. Should she inscribe it 'To my Muhammad'? No, Sunny had heard boys did not like girls who were too possessive. 'Love and kisses from your Sunny'? No, that would be too much. Just 'XXX's and 'OOO's? Yes. And if Muhammad didn't know what that meant, she'd just have to give him a big hug and kiss to show him. Sunny giggled, but then she started to worry that the Arabs would think she was just a silly little girl. She turned to Rashid. 'And then there's my other favorite. *Arabian Nights*! I love them too. All of them. All thousand and one!' She forgot she wanted these boys to think she was sophisticated and worldly, and again she laughed gaily. 'So tell me, what do you think of them?'

Rashid had hardly understood any of her breathless words. 'I am so sorry, Miss Sunny, but can you talk more slow?'

'Of course.' She was contrite. 'Here I am, chattering away, and you haven't understood a word.' She still was speaking in rapid-fire English, but she obligingly began to shout every syllable. '*Arabian Nights*! You like them?'

'Nights, days, love all.' Eagerly Rashid nodded. He had never dared to hope that the people of America would love Saudi as much as he did. 'My country very wonderful.'

'Yes, yes, I believe you, but what about *Tales from the Thousand and One Arabian Nights*? You know, Sindbad and Aladdin and all the genies?' When it seemed neither Rashid nor Muhammad understood her, she bounded up from the dinner table and disappeared into the living room to return in triumph to put a thick red linen book down on the table between the two Arabs.

'Ah, yes,' Muhammad said politely, 'I have heard of this book.'

'Also me.' Rashid was enthralled by this merry girl who was even more enchanting than Nura. He looked guiltily away from the glorious Sunny, ashamed of his thoughtless disloyalty not only to his wife but to his benefactor. Even though Muhammad said American girls would be as willing as prostitutes, he must show his respect for Mr. Tom by ignoring his ravishing daughter. But when Rashid could not stop himself from looking up at her, he saw Sunny laughing and trading come-hither looks not with him but with Muhammad. Rashid's exhilaration at being near this girl who was as luscious as a *houri* of paradise faded. Back home in Saudi, Muhammad would never have dared to shame the daughter of an honorable man like this. Muhammad was insulting Sunny and dishonoring Mr. Tom. Rashid glowered across the table at his brother.

Sunny's grandparents were even unhappier at what was happening at their own table. John had watched Sunny flirt shamelessly with these two randy boys. Bess had seen Muhammad looking at her granddaughter as if Sunny were a stripper, and she caught the other one stealing glances at her from under lowered lashes. John seemed to read his wife's thoughts, for he muttered an aside to her that this reminded him of being in France at the end of World War One and eating dinner with some of the natives who didn't speak English very well, and they all just smiled a lot and talked with their hands and laughed because that was the only way they could surely communicate their goodwill. But even so, when he finished his second helping of chicken and mashed potatoes, he firmly took control of the conversation. 'So what do you boys do back in Saudi?'

'Many things.' Muhammad smiled vacantly at Mr. Tom's father as he edged his entire body a little closer to the table. If he managed to slide down a little, his feet might just reach Sunny's. He had once heard an American refer to sex as 'playing footsie.' He would try it with this incredibly bold girl. 'Grandfather's in trucking and water wells and real estate.'

'And we herd camels,' Rashid added.

'Camels!' Sunny was far more rapturous about camels than about real estate.

'I'm a farmer, myself. Forty-eight acres of the juiciest apples in all the world.' John began to describe in great detail the differences in the size and color and usage of McIntosh and Delicious and Cortlands, how each of his orchards was pruned and fertilized and sprayed, how they were picked and stored and canned and trucked, how much he made per bushel.

Rashid could not follow the complicated words this man was saying about fruit, but he did understand that Mr. Tom's father was quite properly outraged by Muhammad's leering at Sunny.

Muhammad, however, did not seem to be taking the elderly man's hint. His face was bland and his toes were rubbing Sunny's heels as he appeared to hang on every word the farmer said about his apples.

Bess stretched her long legs under the table between Muhammad and Sunny. She was not surprised when she caught them intertwined, and she nodded in satisfaction when she felt Muhammad's feet retreat. She smiled for the first time during dinner.

But Sunny was looking in sudden consternation at the untouched food on the plates of the Arabs. 'Maybe they don't like the chicken, Gran.'

Bess frowned. 'But everyone loves my chicken fricassee.' She had cooked this dinner specially for the foreigners. Tom had warned her in his last letter that Muslims didn't eat pork. It occurred to her that maybe they didn't eat chicken either. 'Is it against your religion to eat my chicken fricassee?'

'Oh, no,' the boys chorused. Dutifully they loaded their forks with chicken, and slowly they put them in their mouths and chewed and swallowed.

'Do you eat chicken like this back in Saudi?' Sunny asked.

'In Saudi we eat meat boiled. And rice. And milk and dates.' Rashid smiled politely. 'Maybe I will learn to like your food more, tomorrow or after tomorrow.'

'Gran! They're just not used to our cooking, that's all. We've got to give them something else to eat.' Sunny jumped up and ran into the kitchen. She was worried that if she didn't act fast, the Arabs would leave before Muhammad even kissed her. Sunny had already decided to sit on the glider out on the front porch after supper. As soon as it got dark, there on the glider, she intended that Muhammad kiss her. Five minutes later Sunny paraded back to the dining room with plates of eggs and toast and sliced cheese and fruit. 'Eat,' she urged the Arabs. 'I ask you, please, to eat with me.'

Bess's heart felt like a rock in her chest as she watched Sunny and the Arabs breaking bread and smiling and laughing all together. She felt an edge of fear as she listened to Sunny and the Arabs laughing happily together. She felt very old and tired as she watched Sunny's blond head between those two dark ones as the Arabs signed her autograph book. She felt helpless as the boys showed Sunny how to write her name in Arabic script. She assured herself that a little adolescent flirtation was harmless. These Arabs were here today but would be gone tomorrow. Bess was far more worried about Sunny. She had warned Sunny before supper that she must not throw herself at these impressionable young men, and yet the girl had defied her. Bess wondered if Sunny would have been better off if she had raised her to be less willful and independent.

When Bess caught her husband's eye, he covered her hand with his. Yet she decided it wouldn't hurt to say a novena to Our Lady of Perpetual Help, asking that Sunny never see these two predatory Arabs again. She would begin her novena tonight.

7

Early on a springtime Saturday evening two years later, Sunny was hurrying to a Cambridge coffeehouse in her best beatnik black. She was wearing her clinging turtle-neck sweater, her tight straight skirt, her sexy fishnet tights, her flat ballerina shoes. As she headed down Brattle Street into Harvard Square, she hoped passersby would take her for a Radcliffe intellectual instead of a freshman psych major at Boston University. But then she found herself squinting through her black-lensed sun-glasses at a familiar-looking young man with a bouquet of flowers. She was halfway down the block before it hit her that it was the man of her dreams, here, in the flesh.

'Muhammad?' Sunny turned and called to him as if she were out in the open fields of Still River and not on the urban campus of Harvard. When the boy kept going, Sunny ran after him. For two and a half years she had harbored a crush on this princely young man. He had eluded her once, when she was only a girl, too young to get what she wanted. But Sunny was determined she would not miss this second, even more golden opportunity. 'Muhammad?' When she came abreast of him, she laid a hand firmly on his shoulder. 'Muhammad!'

The young man paused and frowned at the blonde who had accosted him. These American girls, he thought, had no shame, God bless them. The little he could see of her face, behind those weird sunglasses and that long straight loose fall of silky yellow hair, was fresh and very pretty. But Muhammad was already late for a heavy date with a coed from Simmons. Tonight would climax three weeks of diligent pursuit, for finally the girl had signed out for an overnight from her dormitory. If he didn't get to their rendezvous very soon, she would doubtless bolt back inside her heavily guarded dorm. Muhammad tried to sidle past the blonde and proceed on his way.

Sunny died twenty or thirty deaths because he didn't recognize her. She started to back away from this haughty young man in the well-cut suit as she considered the embarrassing possibility that he might not be Muhammad after all. But then she spoke up boldly as her grandmother had taught her. 'Sunny? Sunny Shannon?' It occurred to her that her sunglasses were hiding her face, so she tore them off and smiled expectantly at him. 'Don't you remember? Out in Still River? You and Rashid?' When still he did not seem to be able to place her, a little of her radiance faded. Yet stubbornly she persisted. 'Even if you don't remember me, you *must* remember my father. Tom Shannon. In Saudi. My father is Tom Shannon. Mr. Tom, you and your brother both call him. I'm his daughter. Sunny. Remember me?'

'But of course!' Muhammad let out a wry little chuckle. '*La petite Shannon!* How nice, how very very nice, Sunny, to see you again.'

Sunny waited expectantly for him to kiss her hand. Instead Muhammad transferred the small bouquet of red roses to his left hand and then shook Sunny's hand limply, as the Arabs do.

'So.' Sunny ignored both the roses and Muhammad's reserve. 'So you're still at Northeastern?'

'Alas, yes. The perennial student, don't you know?'

'I'm at BU? Boston University? A psych major? Psychology? I just started this year. I live on campus, but I spend most of my time over here, in "the Square."' Resolutely she pressed on. 'I like the coffeehouses. Folk music? Beatniks?' She ignored the hint when Muhammad consulted his watch. 'How's your brother?'

'Still in Texas.' He shook his head, as if Texas were a terminal disease. 'He hates it there. He's talking about saying *adios* and coming up here to MIT.'

He smiled at her with his lips, but his eyes darted past her toward the kiosk at Harvard Square. Miserably she admitted he seemed in a terrible rush to give those flowers to someone else. She let her growing desperation show. 'I tried to call you. As soon as I got to BU last fall, I called Northeastern, and they told me you didn't live on campus. I got your number from Information. But maybe you didn't get my message?'

Muhammad shrugged as if he were helpless. 'Messages! You know how it is. *Gott in Himmel*, how they get lost! Especially when there are so many.'

This was not going at all as Sunny had hoped. Over the many months since the momentous night when she had met Muhammad, she had fantasized that encounter into a love born at first sight. Yet for a long while she had been puzzled that he had not pursued her. The boys back home in Still River and even down here in Boston were always telling her how pretty she was. She had finally decided Muhammad must be trying to save her the grief of a forbidden love. A man of the world must know that her parochial grandparents would no more want him for a son-in-law than Juliet's family had welcomed Romeo. But here and now on Brattle Street, Muhammad wasn't playing the part of her own personal Romeo. 'I remembered you. I didn't forget you.' Accusation was creeping into her voice. 'Not that night. Not since then, either.'

'But how very flattering!' As Muhammad smiled most sincerely, he wondered what this young daughter of Mr. Tom could want from him. Muhammad consulted his watch again.

This time Sunny did take the hint. 'You're late?'

'Regrettably.'

'Do you have a date?' Sunny looked wistfully at Muhammad, who had grown even handsomer since their first meeting. His shoulders were broader, his tan was lighter, his confidence was greater. He was so very cosmopolitan, so masterful. He had lost some of his English accent, but in its place he had substituted adorable smatterings of French and German. Or had some of those delicious asides of his been in Arabic? She could not stop herself from drawing a little closer to him on the side-walk.

Muhammad nodded, sure now what this girl wanted. But seducing Mr. Tom's daughter could endanger his own future. Muhammad's interest in Sunny perversely began to quicken. He had always been contemptuous of Mr. Tom's drinking. He didn't like having to feel grateful to such a wreck of a man. Muhammad looked Sunny over. She had a mane of pale gold hair. She had such a lovely, innocent face. She had big breasts and long slim thighs and a palpitating animal energy. Maybe, after all, he would give Mr. Tom's daughter the thrill she so evidently desired.

'Roses.' He was taking red roses to his girlfriend. 'Are they for the woman you love?'

He had an impulse to give Sunny the flowers and sweep her off to the nearest hotel, but instead he coyly shrugged his shoulders. He would let this Sunny simmer awhile. When she was altogether heated up, then he would take her. 'You know.'

Sunny didn't know, but she was determined to find out. 'Maybe we can get together another time.' She pulled out a scrap of paper and wrote down her telephone number. 'Call me anytime. Anytime you want, Muhammad.'

He bestowed his slowest, sexiest smile upon her, but then he remembered the sure thing waiting for him by the kiosk. '*Ciao, bella*,' Muhammad called back to her as he dashed away.

'And so,' Muhammad said to Sunny as they sat pressed close together like lovers, on the same side of the darkest corner booth at the Wursthaus in Harvard Square, 'there we were swaying upon the camels at the crest of a Dahana dune. It was hot.' Muhammad caressed Sunny's left hand in both of his and looked soulfully into her blue eyes. 'Hot, *Liebchen*, hot. How can I ever make a girl like you from a place like Still River ever understand heat that burns like that?'

Sunny drew in her breath sharply and sidled just a quarter-inch closer to Muhammad. Her thigh was squeezed against his, and her lips were parted in excitement. It seemed to her it was getting hot even in this air-conditioned Cambridge restaurant. 'So then what happened?'

'We were running low on water. We were far from the nearest well. We were out of food. If our hunt was not successful, I was afraid my own mother would die right there, in the heat and thirst and hunger and loneliness of the desert. We were desperate, Sunny. Can you possibly understand what it is to be desperate?'

'Oh yes!' Sunny assured him. So involved was she with his Saudi story that was even better than Colonel Lawrence's campaigns that she hardly noticed when Muhammad's left hand fell into her lap as if by accident.

'It was then that I saw the gazelles.' Like all gifted liars, Muhammad always sprinkled as much truth as possible into his flights of fancy. He would authenticate his seductive tale by describing how that herd of gazelles had looked the morning he mowed them down with a machine gun. 'Sunny! They were so lovely. So pure, so beautiful, so altogether - how would you say it? - so innocent? Yes!' Muhammad nodded at Sunny. 'Like you, *chérie*! Like you!' When he saw that she had flushed with pleasure at the compliment, he allowed his left hand to creep just a few exquisite inches from her lap to the top of her thigh. He would give her time to get used to his hand on her thigh before he intensified his campaign. This was his third date with Mr. Tom's daughter, and he had not even tried to kiss her yet. But even though it seemed he was going slow with this girl, in fact he intended to take a few shortcuts. Soon, very soon, he would have her naked in bed. Muhammad's voice took on a ring of excitement. 'The hawk was on my wrist. The salukis were at the feet of the camels. I pointed at the gazelles. I dropped my hand. And we were off!' Muhammad's fingers began to explore the taut flesh of Sunny's thigh. A girdle. American girls were such a contradiction. They were horrified at the idea of veiled Saudi women, but they themselves wore these torturous girdles. Somehow he would have to persuade Sunny to stop wearing this armor before the night he took her to bed. Resolutely Muhammad tore his thoughts away from the problem of girdles. 'The hawk flew through the cloudless sky, the hounds coursed through the soft sand, my camel -'

But Sunny was frowning as she interrupted him just before the climax. 'Those gazelles,' she said. 'What did they look like?'

Instantly Muhammad withdrew his hand from her thigh. He knew what was coming. He had used his gazelle-hunting story before on American girls. Some of them got wonderfully excited at the thought of the ultimate bloodletting. Others sympathized with the gazelles. Muhammad had thought Sunny, who went on at such endless length about her precious Arabian horse, would fall in the former group. But even though he saw he had miscalculated, he assured himself there was no harm done. He would merely alter his story just a tad. 'Gazelles, Sunny, are glorious little animals. They're small and gray and deerlike and gentle. Some of us even keep them as pets. Some of them are so tame they eat right from our hands.' To illustrate his point, he took her hands in his, bent over them, and kissed her palms tenderly. He looked up at her from under his lowered lashes. 'An animal like that, as lovely as a gazelle - I ask you, Sunny, how could I kill a gazelle?'

Sunny sighed into Muhammad's eyes. A lover, not a hunter, that was for certain. She was glad he hadn't killed the gazelles. He would have frightened her more than a little if he had. She wouldn't like to think that the man of her dreams, her husband-to-be, was a heartless killer who butchered innocent gazelles. Sunny was so caught up in

Muhammad's story she failed to notice that he had dropped both his English accent and his adorable Continental asides. 'So then what happened?'

'I was giving chase, I was out in front of the others, I could so easily have bagged those gazelles, but instead I let them go. When they disappeared down the far side of a big dune, I called back the hounds and the hawk and led the entire hunting party off in another direction.' Muhammad smiled sweetly at Sunny. 'And then, just when the gazelles were far enough away to be safe, I turned around in my saddle, and I looked back, and there they all were, silhouetted at the top of another dune, standing motionless there, looking right at me. Do you know, Sunny? I think those gazelles were thanking me for giving them their lives!'

Sunny all but clapped her hands at the happy ending. Then, however, her face clouded. 'But what about your mother?'

He looked at her blankly. 'Mother?'

'Did she die? You said she was lying near death, that she would have died if you hadn't brought her back something from the hunt.'

Muhammad thought for a moment. Obviously he would have to save Mother by bringing home freshly killed meat. Sunny would probably not like the idea of killing an oryx, a fox, a hyena, or a wolf. Rabbits - that might do it. Surely this sheltered American girl wouldn't be overly sympathetic about them? 'We got some hares.'

'Hares?' Sunny looked disappointed. There were rabbits even in Still River. She liked to hear about hunting more exotic animals in Saudi.

Rapidly Muhammad disposed of the hunt. 'A brace of hares. Just enough for Mother's dinner. I gave the meat to the women and children. I myself ate only dates and camel milk.' Again Muhammad took her two hands in his. 'It had to be enough.' Enough, too, he thought, of fictions from the desert. On with his own hunt in the here and now. Two more encounters, Muhammad calculated, and she would be ready. She would be eager and trembling by a week from Saturday.

As the waitress brought their hamburgers and Cokes, Muhammad gazed sidelong at Sunny and smiled seductively. A Wellesley girl had once told him he looked like a French film star when he struck this attitude. He ignored the food and lit a cigarette. He had been dying for a cigarette for the past ten minutes, but he hadn't been able to spare the necessary hand. He wished he had dared to order a beer. They had good dark German beer here in the Wursthaus, but he didn't want to disabuse Sunny of her illusions about his being a good Muslim who didn't drink. He sipped his Coke and contemplated the other surprises he had planned for this gullible, dreamy, sheltered little girl a week from Saturday.

They strolled along the bank of the Charles in the growing intimacy of their fifth date. It was dusk, and in the soft waning light they stopped here to look at their reflections in the glassy mirror of the river, there to admire the ivy-covered red brick buildings of Harvard, here again to listen to dance music drifting over the water from a party in the boathouse on the far bank.

Sunny fluttered anxiously by Muhammad's side. Tonight she had left her beatnik uniform in her closet and dressed the way she thought Muhammad wanted her to, in a pretty blue-flowered shirtwaist and no girdle. She didn't feel altogether *dressed* without her girdle, but last week Muhammad had stopped in front of the window of a lingerie shop and scornfully told her a Saudi woman would *never* wear anything so unnatural as a girdle.

She walked as near as she dared beside him. Although they did not touch, her entire body inclined toward his. She wished he would put his arm around her and finally kiss her slowly and tenderly and magically as she had been reading it was done all her life in books and seeing it was done all her life in movies. She had been kissed before, but never by anyone like Muhammad. Up to now she had been glad he treated her with such courtly respect. His intentions could only be honorable. She was certain he loved her. She wondered if he would ask her to marry him here and now or if, like a gentleman of the old school, he would write to her father in Saudi first for permission. She hoped he would ask her here and now. It took an eternity for a letter to go from here to Saudi and back. Cautiously she edged a little closer to her Muhammad. When he did not move away, she timidly took his hand.

But he disengaged himself. 'Not here.' Muhammad frowned at her. 'It is not decent to touch so in public.'

'But you held my hand in the restaurant.'

'It was dark there. No one could see.' Muhammad looked around them at the other couples lying in the reedy grass fringing the river. 'Look at them. No pride. No decency.' He was not altogether acting. Muhammad was still truly appalled at the way Americans touched each other in public. The girls were as bad as the boys. At home in Saudi a man wouldn't even hold his wife's hand in public, but here girls expected him to put his arm around them and even kiss them on the street. Happily, however, Muhammad had learned to turn even his Arab sexual modesty to orgasmic profit. He had discovered that by looking but not touching, by pointing out the passionate couples on the grass but keeping his own hands off, it was possible to raise his date's temperature. 'Would you like us to be like them, Sunny? Would you want what we have to be so . . . like the animals?'

Sunny looked wistfully at the girls, near blissful surrender in the boys' arms. She wouldn't object to Muhammad's at least kissing her once. She wanted to lie beside Muhammad in that high soft grass along the river-bank.

But Muhammad was still stalking at a distance. 'I do not understand how these young people can act like this. Look at them! How they sweat, with their bodies pressed so together! How they moan, with their lips as one! Here, right before our eyes, they are all but . . . forgive me, my darling. I should not even be talking so in front of you. But it is such an outrage that I forget myself!'

With him pointing out and dwelling upon what was going on all around them, Sunny could not but wonder how it must feel. She wished Muhammad wouldn't walk so fast. If they were walking more in step, then maybe he would hold her hand or put his arm around her and then kiss her. She yearned so to be kissed. Why wouldn't he kiss her?

In a way, he gave her an answer. 'You see, my sweet, I am a very private person.' He turned around and gave her his sexy smile. He knew by now that Mr. Tom's daughter was addicted to any and all mentions of Saudi and noble savage romance, and so he had his best shots primed for firing. 'Come closer, my pet. You are so far away from me that I can scarcely see your pretty face.' He waited for Sunny to catch up with him. 'I suppose the reason that I am such a private person is . . .' He paused dramatically. 'Can you imagine, for a moment, what it is to grow up with the infinities of the desert in your soul?'

Sunny looked at him wide-eyed. 'I try,' she said truthfully. 'All my life I've wished I were there, with my father. I'll love Saudi, Muhammad. I'm sure I will. You'll see!'

He was taken aback by her intensity. This sweet Sunny was different from those other spoiled American girls. Even though he cautioned himself that no one could ever hurt him again as long as he always remained emotionally detached, this one moved him. How lonely she was! It was too bad she had grown up without a mother and a father and brothers and sisters, with no one except those two old ones. Muhammad liked Sunny so much that for a moment he actually considered sending her back alone, safe and intact, to her dormitory.

'How wonderful it must have been,' Sunny sighed, 'growing up with the infinities of the desert in your soul.'

He remembered who he was and who she was. He was

an Arab; she was an American. Doubtless, he decided, deep inside she thought she was better than he.

Muhammad looked off into space, as if caught in a reverie of his youth in the desert solitude. In fact he was thinking about sand bugs and water that tasted of camel urine and never having altogether enough to eat. Rage that he had grown up in such privation while this girl had enjoyed such plenty coursed through him. He felt like lashing out at this privileged daughter of Mr. Tom. He had been a fool to nurse protective thoughts about her. Soon enough he would take his revenge - his ounce of flesh - from her. His roommate had a girl in their apartment for the weekend, and so already Muhammad had rented the hotel room for exactly one hour, beginning at nine o'clock tonight. It was now twenty after eight. They would walk awhile longer, and then they would jump into a cab and he would whisk Mr. Tom's daughter to the sure climax of their relationship in a properly seedy hotel in Scollay Square.

Sunny tugged at his arm. 'You were going to tell me about the black tents in the desert?'

His anger faded. He could not stop himself from regretting that it had to be like this. She was so very obviously infatuated. He just as obviously wanted her. Why, then, would this night inevitably have to end in ugliness? He had been through all this many times before. He knew that the sex would be quick and hot, that the girl would cry when it was over, that he would have to take care never to see her again. Sometimes it didn't seem worth the effort.

He walked a few more paces. What the two of them were about tonight, he told himself firmly, was the eternal game between man and woman. There was no place there for honesty and mutuality and emotion. He pitied Sunny, as he pitied all women. But he must never let himself forget that women were different, that they were lesser, damaged in most fundamental ways. This Sunny could no more help being the way she was than a horse could help the way it was. A man might have a special fondness for his favorite mount, but still what he did with that horse was ride it. Sunny wanted to play a bold game, and so he would oblige her.

He stopped, turned, looked out at the river. 'Peaceful, isn't it?' As if she were taking cues from a prompter Muhammad had hired just offstage, Sunny stood close to him, looked into his eyes, and waited. He sighed and outwaited her. Finally she shut her eyes and aimed her lips towards his.

'Sunny! Please!' Delicately he extricated himself from her embrace. He pointed at the nearby couples on the grass. 'We can be seen.'

'I don't care!' Again she put her arms around his neck. 'Kiss me!'

He held her at arm's length. 'No, Sunny.' For a very long and almost sincere moment, he stood looking into her eyes. 'No.'

'Yes!' She struggled to break his grip and be close to him and kiss him.

'You're sure?' His voice was grave. 'You're sure, Sunny?' She was trembling in his arms as he slowly, inch by tantalizing inch, pulled her toward him. When she could feel his breath on her face, he began to murmur her name. 'Sunny, Sunny, Sunny.' She looked adoringly into his limpid brown eyes, and then, just before his lips touched hers, she shut her own eyes and let herself sigh into their very first kiss. His lips gently touched hers, and then he drew them away and brought them back after an exquisite pause, this time more firmly, more insistently, so that he forced her own pliant lips open. He snaked his tongue inside. Wetly, hotly, thoroughly, his tongue explored her mouth until she would have drawn away gasping. But by now he had both his hands in her hair and was pulling her closer to him.

When finally they broke apart, he kissed her at her temples, on her eyes, at her neck, and then put his arm masterfully around her shoulders and half-dragged her toward Mass. Avenue. 'I must be alone with you, my Sunny.'

She was so dazed by the heat of his kiss that even if she were capable of thought, it would not have been to question where they were going or why. It was enough to hold on for dear life to this man who had just made her feel better than she had ever felt in her entire life.

He all but raced her toward the taxi stand in Harvard Square. He tore open the back door of the first cab in the line, deposited her on the seat, and whispered a few words to the driver before he slid in beside her. They were off with a jerk and a squeal of tires, and Muhammad was holding her close and kissing her hands and giving her his slowest and sexiest French-film-star smile.

She looked into his eyes, his beautiful eyes, and wanted him to kiss her again. In a great number of movies she had seen, men kissed women in the back seat of taxis. She pressed herself even closer to him. 'Kiss me,' she whispered.

He held her closer. 'Here? You want me to kiss you here? In this public car?' Dumbly she nodded. She wanted him to kiss her everywhere and anywhere, just so long as it was now.

He made a swift calculation. Was it better for him to kiss her again and thus keep her in a hot creamy blur until he had her just about in bed, or should he play it cooler?

'Kiss me! Oh, Muhammad, kiss me!'

This one was hotter than he had imagined. He would try something different with this one. He would make this one beg. 'I don't know, Sunny. Are you sure?'

'Kiss me!'

'Say "please."'

The pupils of her eyes expanded, and she sighed a little closer to him, reaching out for him, blindly, gropingly.

He caught her wrists before she could touch him, and he jerked her hands back behind her waist and held her pinioned. 'I said to say "please." If you want me to kiss you again, woman, you'll have to beg for it. You want it, don't you? You want me to kiss you, don't you, woman? Woman!'

Weakly, as if she were someone else and not herself, she opened her lips and managed one yearning word of surrender. 'Please. . . .'

Her only reward was that slow, sexy, triumphant smile of his. He neither kissed her nor released her hands from where he held them behind her back.

She stared into his eyes as if hypnotized. Her legs, her arms, her breasts - especially her breasts - felt swollen and heavy. She could not have moved away from him even if she had wanted to. As she waited in a passive swoon for him to tell her what to do, for the cab to stop, for whatever was going to happen to happen, she felt the tension build all through her body. Even in the novels she had read, the movies she had seen, never had there ever been any intimation that love was like this. Love was supposed to be sweet and tender and gentle and full of sighs.

He twisted her hands a little behind her back, and her arms began to hurt. She luxuriated in that pain. She loved that pain. She wanted that pain. She longed for it and for him.

When the taxi stopped, Muhammad threw the cabby five dollars from Mr. Tom's monthly allowance and slid her out with him to the sidewalk. On this street there were flashing neon and women in doorways and packs of men in sailor uniforms.

She blinked, looked around her, and almost came out of the ether. 'Where are we?'

Muhammad had his arm altogether around her and was rushing her along toward a doorway. 'At the gateway to paradise.' He laughed a low throaty laugh and they were inside. It was dark and dingy, and Muhammad was impatiently ringing a push bell atop a cluttered counter. He waited only a few seconds, then reached over the counter to a nest of mailboxes and came away with a key. He had his arm around her as he pulled her up a creaking staircase. Just when Sunny was beginning to balk, just when she was about to dig into the step she was standing on and not move until he told her where he thought he was taking her, Muhammad turned and looked down at her and pushed her against the wall of the stairwell and kissed her hotly until she felt she was nothing inside but liquid.

Sunny was so dizzy she reeled and would have fallen if he had not steadied her. She did not say a word as he led her up three more flights, down a narrow dirty hallway, and into a room with an iron bedstead, a card table, and a naked light bulb dangling from a socket in the ceiling.

She stood very still and watched him as he peeled off his coat, his tie, his shoes, his socks, his shirt, his undershirt. Soberly she watched him carefully fold his clothes and stack them on the card table. He was wearing only his gray-striped undershorts. He had only a little hair on his chest and legs. His skin was a glowing gold.

She was frightened enough, at last, to try for the safety of the door and the corridor and the street and home, behind a double-locked door in Still River or at least the dorm.

'Sunny,' he crooned. 'Come here, Sunny.'

Even though she was scared half to death, she heard the throb in his voice and she could not stop herself from turning her head to look at him even as she continued to try to creep to the door before he could get to her and touch her and stop her. Her hand was on the doorknob; she had just enough time to register the fact that it was locked when he had her in his arms. He was kissing her on the lips again with his tongue as he had kissed her on the riverbank and again on the staircase, but this time his hands were moving over her back and her buttocks, and he was moaning. Panicked, she tried to tear herself away. If only she could get out the door, she would be safe. If only she could somehow get out of this tangle she had suddenly found herself in, she would never, she vowed, ever do anything as bad as this again in her life.

'Sunny. My Sunny.' His hands were insistent. His naked flesh was smooth and rich and everywhere around her, such burning, golden flesh. She tried to twist away from him, but his hands were at the back of her head and he was looking deep into her eyes. She shut her eyes so that he could not again hypnotize her.

'You deceived me, Sunny.'

She heard a catch in his voice, and almost against her will, she opened her eyes. Yes, he was crying. Muhammad's eyes were full of tears; they were coursing down his cheeks.

'You deceived me!' Muhammad wept. 'Lying American woman! You lied to me! You made a fool of me! You acted as if you loved me, you led me to *believe* you loved me, but you don't care!'

Sunny stared in utter shock at this weeping half-naked man.

Muhammad released her and began to pace back and forth. 'Tell me, Sunny. It's because I'm an Arab, isn't it? Because you're an American and I'm an Arab. You don't want to love an Arab, do you? Is it that you think you are better than me? Is there some shame to loving an Arab? Tell me, Sunny, tell me! It's because I'm an Arab, isn't it? Isn't it!' Muhammad sank down on the bed, hid his face in his hands, and sobbed. He was so sure of her reactions he did not even peek out at her from behind his hands.

She hesitated only a moment, then took a few steps away from the door and stood looking down at him. Muhammad seemed so entirely miserable, sobbing here on this comfortless iron cot in this sleazy hotel room. She felt safer now. Maybe she had been wrong to jump to such damning conclusions about his motives. This was the man she loved. At the very least she should try to reassure him. 'Muhammad?' From the safe haven of a few feet, she would try to comfort him.

But he did not seem to hear her. His sobs grew louder. She spoke his name again, and when he still did not respond, she laid a tentative hand on the soft black curls at the crown of his head. She saw him shudder. He began to murmur in Arabic. She listened for a few moments; then she sank down on the bed beside him. 'Muhammad?'

This time he raised his head and looked sadly at her. She had always thought his eyes were very beautiful, but now it seemed to her that suffering had made them more beautiful still. She stared in fascination at his beautiful eyes.

'You don't know what it's like for me here,' he said so quietly she had to lean a little closer to him so she could hear. 'I am so lonely . . . so far from home, with no one here who cares about me . . . who understands me. Everyone here is so cold.' He seemed to shiver. 'I am so very alone here, Sunny.' His eyes seemed to well with unspoken pain. 'I had thought, when we met, that maybe I would never be alone again. I had even thought . . .' He left that thought unfinished. 'But I shouldn't be bothering you with my problems. You don't care for me. No one cares.'

Sunny tried to reassure him. It had seemed, for a second, that Muhammad was on the verge of proposing marriage. She allowed herself to feel sympathy for this man who most probably would soon be her husband. Besides, she thought she knew at least a little about what he was talking about. She had never lived in a foreign country, but she had most certainly felt all alone and abandoned. 'I care, Muhammad. Honestly I do. More than you know.'

He shook his head. 'You don't show me you care.'

She smiled tenderly at him. Such a little boy lost. She put her arm gently around his shoulders. 'Don't cry, Muhammad. . . .'

Just like a little boy he crept closer to her, and then he put his hand on her breast and sighed. They sat like that, unmoving, for a few very long moments.

It seemed after a while to Sunny that his body was heating up in her arms. The very temperature in the room seemed to be rising. She looked over at the window. It was open. She could see the cheap chintz curtain flutter in the sea breeze. The curtains were a print of garish orange cabbage roses writhing on a Kelly green trellis. She memorized the shape of those cabbage roses so precisely she could have drawn them freehand on a sketch pad.

Sunny was beginning to perspire in the heat of this small hot room. She looked down at Muhammad in her arms, with his face against her breasts. He did not seem such a little boy now. She was very conscious that she was holding a full-grown man, a full-grown nearly naked man, in her arms, next to her breasts. She should not be doing this, she thought.

She had just resolved to extricate herself from this compromising situation when Muhammad sighed. 'Sunny, my beautiful Sunny. My own Sunny.' His nearly naked body moved closer against hers and he began kissing her breasts.

'Muhammad?' She tried to laugh. 'I thought we understood each other. I thought you weren't going to do that anymore. Muhammad?'

He was kissing her throat now, he was sucking the skin at the side of her neck, and Sunny did not know what to say or do as his hands caressed the tips of her breasts through the thin cotton dress. Between kisses he was murmuring her name, he was pressing down upon her, he was looking down into her eyes as his lips found hers. His tongue was in her mouth, his body was all over hers, she felt herself sinking, giving. He continued to kiss her urgently until finally, tentatively, she licked the tip of his tongue with hers. She was just getting used to the fierce hot thrill of her tongue in his mouth when dimly she became aware that he was fumbling with the buttons of her dress. She would have used her hands to stop him if it weren't for the fact that her hands were reaching out to try to pull him back against her.

She wasn't as hot, suddenly, with her dress off. It felt good when her slip was off, too, and her bra, and his golden skin was next to her pale skin, all the way down to their waists. She felt his hands on her legs, at her waist; she was being raised, masterfully, wonderfully, for just a second off the cot; and then they were naked, altogether naked, with no clothing between them anywhere. His body was burning next to hers, he was all the time kissing her lips, she was clinging to him, and moaning, and kissing him back.

Just as he was about to arch his buttocks and plunge all the way deep inside her, he heard her call out his name. Some of his own fever broke, and he opened his eyes and watched her trembling in his arms. A thrill of power surged through him. She was utterly at his mercy now. Yet still he did not take her. He wished he didn't like her quite so much. He wished he didn't think she was different and better and finer than all the others he had seduced and abandoned. But he could not bear to ruin this one. Back in Saudi, a girl's virginity was all she was worth. He would let Mr. Tom's daughter off easy. He would have his satisfaction, and yet he would leave her intact. Muhammad glowed at his own noble act of unselfish generosity, and then he began kissing her again, and fondling her breasts, and deliberately and slowly and inevitably turning her over.

He was kissing not her lips but the base of the back of her neck, and she missed his lips on hers. 'Muhammad?' She called out for him. She wanted him to kiss her on the lips again; she wanted to feel his bare skin against the bare skin of her breasts.

For a moment he wasn't touching her at all, and then he was touching her but in an odd place. She flinched away from him. 'Muhammad!' She struggled away from it or maybe him. 'Muhammad!'

'Hold still, now. It will go easier for you if you hold still. And relax! It won't hurt if you relax.'

But she was frightened now, and she tried to scramble away from him, off the bed, out of the room, away. . . . What was Muhammad doing to her? 'Muhammad! Stop! Stop it!' There was a painful pressure between her buttocks, it hurt, how it hurt, something hard and hot was pushing into her. She had never felt anything like this before. He was splitting her apart, and she screamed. She screamed and she screamed and she screamed. He took himself out of her, but then forced in again, harder, faster; that thing didn't hurt so much now as he pressed it further in her, but she couldn't help crying for the sheer shock of it. It seemed he was pumping in her in time with the rise and fall of her sobs. . . .

She did not move when she felt him pull out of her. She heard naked feet padding on the floor. She heard a few muffled sounds; she heard shod feet stepping on the floor; finally she collected herself enough to raise her shamed face from where she had been pressing it into the bedspread.

Fully dressed, Muhammad was looking down at her. 'What are you waiting for, baby?' He consulted his watch. 'Come on. It's nearly ten o'clock. Time's almost up.'

She could not look him in the eye. 'What?'

'Get dressed.' His voice was detached, cold, commanding.

She did not understand any of this, but she did know that she wanted to have all her clothes on now and forever, for the rest of her life. Never again did she want to be naked. Silently she dressed. She buttoned all her buttons.

'Good show.' Muhammad seemed in a terrific hurry to get her out the door.

Now that she was dressed, Sunny felt less vulnerable. What had started off not very long ago as their first kiss on the riverbank had turned into – what? She wondered if this was how it was supposed to be between a girl and boy in love. She sat back on the bed. She wasn't going anywhere until she had some answers.

He waited for her inevitable tears. Always, at this point, the girls cried.

Instead Sunny accused him. 'You hurt me. Why did you hurt me, Muhammad?'

He shrugged. 'You're okay. I didn't hurt you much.' She hung her head in embarrassment. But he continued justifying himself. 'You're still a virgin. Nothing's damaged. Someday you'll thank me for this. Your husband will never know.'

Slowly she raised her head. 'My husband? But *you're* going to be my husband!' When he did not answer her, she repeated herself, only this time with less certainty. 'You're going to be my husband?'

He gave her a few more seconds to let the truth sink in; but when she continued looking so utterly stricken, he began to feel guilty. 'Look, Sunny. I never made you any promises. You came up here with me of your own free will. I could have done more than this with you. I could have done anything . . .' But she had her head in her hands and seemed no longer to be listening.

He felt sorry not only for her but for himself. He hated these unhappy endings to these evenings. He was sure that after he got rid of her back at her dorm, he would have to drink a lot of beer before he could fall asleep. He was impatient, now, to be done with this girl who was making him feel guilt. 'Come on, now, Sunny. Come *on*!' He pulled her to her feet.

'What's the big rush?'

He was unlocking the door and pushing her out into the shabby darkness of the hallway. 'It's ten o'clock. I only rented the room for an hour. You don't want me to have to pay for an extra hour, do you?'

Finally her eyes filled with tears. As she cried with her eyes wide open, she followed him down the bleak stairway.

8

Rashid was so parched he was dizzy as he put one foot unsteadily in front of the other. Slowly he walked down the hot, dusty, sleepy main street of the Texas college town. At times like this, when his physical strength was at a low ebb, he could almost shut his eyes and believe himself to be not here in this alien country but home. This damp, humid heat was like Saudi. This heavy, grainy dust hanging almost visible in the air was like Saudi. This sapping, draining tiredness he felt all through his limbs was like Saudi. He looked up at the yellow sky, where dust clouds all but hid the spreading reddish bruise of the setting sun. At least another half-hour before the sun disappeared without a trace on the far side of the horizon and he could break his fast.

Rashid kept plodding down the hilly street which very definitely was not in Saudi. If he were walking down the main street of a Saudi oasis right now, he most assuredly would be the only man in sight. It was Ramadan - the Islamic month of fasting - and from dawn to dusk during this holy month, life even in the bustling towns of Arabia came close to a standstill. Every Ramadan afternoon a peculiar almost breathless silence would fall during the final minutes before it was permissible to break the fast. No veiled women would be seen carrying buckets to the wells, no robed and scarved men would be seen lounging outside their houses, no camels or donkeys or trucks or cars would be moving down the shadowless streets. Everyone would be inside preparing, with many thanks to God, to break the fast with prayer, water, and food. Rashid missed the camaraderie of shared Ramadan sacrifice. When everyone within sight and sound was languishing through the rigors of the fast, it was not so difficult to abstain from all food and drink during the daylight hours. It was unthinkable, in Saudi, during the light of a Ramadan day, for anyone to eat or drink in public. In Saudi, during Ramadan, not even an American Christian dared to smoke a cigarette as he walked down a street.

But here and now in this hot, dusty, sleepy Texas street, two small children sat on a stoop drinking icy bottles of Dr Pepper, a housewife licked a strawberry ice cream cone as she walked toward him, and a pack of rowdy-looking cowboys drank beer outside a bar at the far end of the street.

Rashid smiled down at the little boy and girl noisily draining their soda bottles. They were so similarly pale-skinned and red-haired and freckled they had to be brother and sister. He longed to lean over and scoop these pretty children up in his arms and laugh and play with them. He missed being able to play with children. At home there were always laughing herds of children everywhere, but here Rashid's narrow world was confined to students his own age.

As he smiled shyly down at the little girl, Rashid thought of the photographs of his own young daughter he always carried in his wallet. Nura had given birth during his first spring in Texas, and Rashid wished he were home so he could play with little Wahda. It would be another year before he finished his studies and could finally go home, but once he was back within the borders of Saudi, Rashid intended never to leave it again. Wahda would be three years old before she even met her own father. Rashid doubted his education could ever be worth the emotional price he was paying for it.

The little girl smiled, and the boy offered him a drink of his Dr Pepper. Rashid gravely refused, but he could not resist affectionately ruffling the boy's limp red hair. If only, he thought, his other encounters with Americans were as sweet. Americans still bewildered him. Rashid trusted his intuition about people, and all his instincts told him that Americans - even Texans - at heart were as naturally generous and warmhearted and friendly as these two. Back in Saudi, Mr. Tom had been like a father to him. Rashid could hardly remember a time when he hadn't loved Mr. Tom. The proudest moment in his life had been when he pulled him back from the certain death of that oil-field fire. Rashid had assumed he would be surrounded by a nation of Mr. Toms in America. But that expectation, at least here in graduate school in Texas, had not been fulfilled.

Rashid was light-headed with thirst and hunger and fatigue as he staggered down the street toward the colored people's chili parlor. Just as soon as the sun dipped beyond the horizon, he could break his fast. Rashid loved chili. He was less ambivalent about chili than about anything else he had encountered in his nearly three years in America.

He wiped the sweat off his wet forehead. It had sometimes seemed to him that he had squandered more than a lifetime here in this dusty college town deep in the heart of Texas. How he hated that song. The rednecks would clap and stamp their feet to punctuate that chorus, 'Deep in the heart of Texas!' From what Rashid could deduce, Texans took pride in being a breed apart. Perhaps it was a good thing he had so little daily contact with real Texans. He prayed to God five times a day that life here in America would improve when he went north to Boston next month. He would know then if it was only the color of his skin that had kept him from making American friends.

Here in Texas in this segregated summer of 1956, dark skin was still anathema. There were signs, however, that perhaps the day was dawning when all this would change. The U.S. Supreme Court had ruled two years ago that the segregation of American schools must end, and even though last winter an ugly mob at the University of Alabama had all but stoned a young Negro girl, still that formerly all-white campus had begun to desegregate. And after an old black seamstress was arrested last winter for refusing to move to the back of a Montgomery bus, a coalition of Negro ministers led by the Reverend Martin Luther King, Jr., had begun a successful boycott of that city's buses. Yet still the Ku Klux Klan burned crosses across the South, and white-citizens' councils ruled below the Mason-Dixon line, and everyone 'colored' had to use separate restaurants and public toilets and drinking fountains.

Ever since his arrival in America, Rashid had been puzzling over this incomprehensible obsession with race.

At home in Saudi skin varied from white to black, just as it did here in Texas, and for the same reason. Black-skinned and brown-skinned Africans had been imported to Saudi and to Texas as slaves. In Saudi, light-skinned slave owners had intermarried with their darker-skinned slaves, just as white and black intermingled in America, although usually not within the bonds of matrimony. But in Saudi, even though slavery still existed, there had never been the American South's revulsion to dark skin. Islam was color-blind. Saudi was not segregated by skin color.

As Rashid had repeatedly failed in his efforts to understand this Southern preoccupation with race, he had searched his memory for similar racial shadings in Saudi. *Allah yebaiyth wajhak* - 'God whiten up your face' - was what one Saudi said as a blessing to another. Back in Arabia lighter skin usually meant higher social status and was considered more cosmetically attractive. A father would probably not want to marry his beige-skinned daughter to a black-skinned man. And if a photographer expected to be paid for taking a flattering portrait of a tribesman, he was well advised to expose the negative in such a way that the man's skin looked several shades paler. But compared with Texas, skin color in Saudi was only a superficial consideration. Far more important was a man's status within his tribe, his wealth in camels or land, and - most important of all - his piety, generosity, and courage. In Saudi there was none of the South's ugly racial hatred. Rashid and the other Arabs enrolled here at the university were very careful not to provoke racial incidents. The Arabs kept to themselves; they shared off-campus apartments together, they cooked their own kebab and rice, and they tried not to use the segregated public transportation or rest rooms.

When Rashid had first arrived in Texas, an Iraqi who had already spent four isolated years here working on his doctorate had tersely told him it was an insult when a Texan called you 'nigger' or 'wetback.' Texans despised 'colored' skin on Negroes, Mexicans, or even Arabs.

Rashid, then, had gone into the bathroom and taken a long, speculative and merciless look in the mirror. His skin definitely was not white, or pink or beige or gray. Or red, like that of the sunburnt Americans who worked in Saudi. But neither was it black or dark brown. As far as he could judge, the color of his skin was a dark gold. His skin was neither darker nor lighter than that of the other members of the Al-Murrah, an ancient noble *sharif* tribe of brave proud warriors. But as Rashid looked in the mirror, he had come to the reluctant and startling and insulting conclusion that even though he and his family were first among equals in Saudi, here in Texas he would be considered inferior, contemptible, and 'colored.'

He supposed he might have made friends among Negro or Mexican students, but there were none in his classes. It was rumored the oil companies had made special arrangements with the college so that the Arabs could enroll. The Arabs debated among themselves whether it was a blessing or a curse that they had been allowed to study here. Some transferred to colleges in California or the North as quickly as they could.

Rashid had resisted the impulse to transfer. This program in petroleum engineering was one of the best in the world. It was important to the welfare of his people that he understand everything about the ocean of oil under his country: where to find it, how to get it out of the ground, how to refine and transport it, and how to make the most money from it. Rashid could almost see a divine purpose to his studying of the oil. On the western coast of Arabia, where the Prophet Muhammad had lived and preached and died, lay Mecca and Medina, the two holiest shrines in Islam. On the eastern coast of Arabia, where Aramco had dug in, lay what might be the richest oil reserves in the world. There could be a holy connection between Saudi as the font of Islam and Saudi as the well of oil. If he continued to study hard, if he learned all the Americans could teach him, if he made himself even smarter and tougher and more imaginative than the

Americans, perhaps someday he might be able to help the brotherhood of Muslims make the most of that God-given oil.

Rashid had nothing against Aramco and Americans like Mr. Tom. He had not begrudged repaying the Americans for discovering and developing the oil. But in the Middle East bonanza years since 1948, the Western oil companies had made nearly ten billion dollars in pure profits. Surely the Arab debt to the West was more than paid in full. Rashid agreed with his fellow students from Iraq that the oil companies must be nationalized. He considered himself a man more of religion than of politics, yet he too, along with the other educated elite of his generation, had been swept along by the currents of Arab nationalism. He was at the university in Cairo in 1952 when Gamal Abdul Nasser deposed the Egyptian king who was even more corrupt and extravagant than the Saudi royal family. Over the next few years Rashid had often listened to Nasser speak of Arab pride and Arab nationalism and Arab socialism. And just this summer, when Nasser had nationalized the Suez Canal, Rashid had cut out a photograph of his hero from a magazine and taped it to the wall above his desk.

Sometimes he thought that what his own country needed was a hero like Nasser. Rashid was beginning to resent the nepotism and greed of the House of Saud. Only fifty years ago, the Al-Saud had been only one of the many warring tribes of Arabia. When Grandfather Ibrahim was a boy, the Saudis had been run off their ancient tribal lands and forced to live in impoverished exile in Kuwait. But since then the star of the House of Saud had risen perhaps too high. The princes spent lavishly in the capitals of Europe while at home destitute tribesmen all but starved to death in the desert. Rashid did not forget that the oil that had made true kings of the House of Saud came from the ancient territory of the Al-Murrah.

He had admired old King Abdul Aziz. But the desert lion who had renamed all Arabia for his tribe had died three years ago, and his son Saud was the worst of his cubs. Saud was weak, corrupt and degenerate, and too fond of his women and his wine. He could also abuse his people. When workers in the Saudi oil fields had gone on strike for higher wages and better working conditions, King Saud had crushed them by calling out troops and imposing martial law. Then, just this past June, a visit by King Saud to Dhahran had triggered a spontaneous walkout by Aramco's Arab workers. But the king had refused to meet with the strikers and instead had ordered a total ban on all union and political activity.

Rashid knew what was behind the crackdown. The king, and the Americans of Aramco, were terrified that what had happened in Iran over the past few years could happen in Saudi. When Muhammad Mossadegh, a popular firebrand, had been swept to power in Iran in 1951, his first public act had been to nationalize the British-run oil industry. But the British had withdrawn their crews from the oil fields, and production had come to a standstill because there were no skilled native crews. Then the British embargoed Iranian oil so successfully that Mossadegh couldn't even sell his crude for one-tenth its former value. Anti-British riots broke out all over Iran, the Shah fled the country, and eventually the American Central Intelligence Agency stepped in to bring back the Shah and give a new consortium of Western powers control over Iranian oil.

Rashid thought the Saudi government had chosen to learn the wrong lessons from Iran. Instead of banning all domestic political activity, the Saudi government should be concentrating on how best to take control of its own natural resources. It was madness to nationalize an industry unless there were skilled native workers to replace the foreigners, and it was foolhardy to expect that one lone oil-producing country could dictate new terms to the powerful Western oil-consuming nations. The radical government of Iran had been bankrupted and brought to its knees because the West had stuck together. Instead of suffering from a shortage of oil, the West had simply bought more oil from Saudi Arabia and Kuwait and Iraq. Rashid thought the lessons of all this were obvious. The Islamic nations would never have a chance to get the better of the West unless the Islamic nations acted in concert.

Yet Rashid was troubled. He had no personal ax to grind against the West. He was grateful to Mr. Tom's country for the opportunities it had given him. And yet sometimes Rashid was ambivalent about even these opportunities. Life had had more certainties for his grandfather's, and even his father's, generation. He worried that his own grandsons might reproach him for not reasserting the old values while there was still time, for it could be that a man lost more than he gained by turning his back so resolutely on the past. He wished it were possible to pick and choose only what one wanted of 'progress' and thus avert what he sometimes saw as the decay and decadence of the West. Often Rashid had longed for the purity and the peace and the simplicity of life in the desert as his grandfather had lived it. His father had been one of the first Arabs to work and to die for the American oilmen. Rashid wondered if the good times had ended or only begun in the lifetime of Ibrahim.

Rashid felt a great protective tenderness toward the unborn generations of all Arabs and all Muslims. He feared sometimes that the allure of the libertine values of the West would triumph over the arduous religious and tribal disciplines of Islam. When he himself had tried to strike a balance between the two worlds, he had discovered the discomfort of belonging to neither. He found himself yearning to end his ambiguity and commit himself, heart and soul, to be either totally Western or totally Eastern. Perhaps it didn't matter which side he chose, so long as he could become a true believer. He wished ardently that he could spare future generations the confusion of trying to reconcile East and West. He supposed one answer would be to wed the religious values of Islam to the scientific technologies of the West. But wishing the best of both worlds for his sons and the sons of his sons would not guarantee it for them.

Rashid's dream was to use the money from the oil to make his people as strong and as free and as moral as the Prophet Muhammad had wanted them to be.

He was aware of the arrogance and the awesome ambition in his great dream, and so he did not confide it even to his Muslim roommates. He had long ago trained himself to keep silent about his innermost thoughts. When he returned home to Saudi, he would have to worry about the long arm of the secret police. If he wanted to rise in the Saudi oil industry, he would have to keep his ideas about oil and money and Islamic power and the corruptions of the House of Saud to himself.

But in this lonely, drowsy, sultry Texas summer, there was no one to share either his dreams or his fears. Until June he had been living in an apartment with a Kuwaiti, two Iraquis, and another Aramco scholarship student from Saudi. But two of them had graduated, and the others had gone home for the summer. Rashid was sticking it out here alone so he could get his degree at the end of the summer, then enroll this fall in a management program at the Massachusetts Institute of Technology. The more Rashid studied oil, the more convinced he became that what mattered was not the physical extraction of the oil from the ground but the engineering of the prices and the power of the industry itself. In Texas he was learning the nuts and bolts of producing petroleum. But in Massachusetts he would begin to study the economic potential of that oil for his country.

Rashid had faltered in his resolution, however, as he sweated through the arid loneliness of this hot Texas summer. He yearned so to be home in Saudi with his daughter and his wife, maybe making a son with Nura, inside their black tent pitched under purple desert skies. He received three or four letters a year from Nura, written in the hand of the local *shaykh*. Always when he read those stiff and formal letters, he remembered that even on their wedding night there had been a gulf between them. Rashid worried that he was growing even further apart from his wife, for there was great peril in leaving home for so long. He did not want ever to belong in this sickly-pale white Texas world. But he supposed living here must be changing him in ways great and small. When he returned home, what if he did not fit in there either?

Rashid tried not to stare at the skinny white woman who was coming toward him on the narrow sidewalk. He knew by now that it was dangerous to stare at the white women of Texas, even when they wore provocative clothing, even when they looked at him in a very seductive way. This particular woman was wearing a low-cut white blouse, a wide red belt that accentuated her meager breasts, a full red skirt that billowed over slender flashing bare legs. Rashid thought her tongue flicked obscenely as she savored every sensual lick of her strawberry ice cream cone. He had not had a woman for three years, since he had lain with Nura under their black goat-hair tent. Here and now, in the abstinence of the daylight Ramadan fast, he felt desire for a woman's soft forbidden flesh.

Reluctantly he tore his eyes away. Besides, he did not want this woman who was as bony as a starving camel at the end of a caravan's forced march across the desert. Rashid had been surprised that so many American women were so scrawny. America was such a rich country, and there seemed such an overabundance of food here. He couldn't understand why so many of the women looked half-starved. He doubted they were all suffering from some dreadful wasting sickness, so he concluded that perhaps these Americans were poorer than they pretended. It was possible they couldn't afford to feed their women.

Rashid's Arab friends talked incessantly, obsessively, longingly about American women. They criticized their skinny bodies, they praised their straight light hair, and most of all they unceasingly speculated about their apparent sexual availability. What man with any juice in him could avoid thinking constantly about sex here? Women paraded around half-naked, billboards displayed ripe white flesh, sex was everywhere here, everywhere. Yet in Texas it would have been very dangerous if the dark-skinned Arabs had dared to touch the white men's women. They tried instead to be content simply to ogle all that fabulous bare flesh. But then Ahmed, one of the Arabs from Baghdad, who had porcelain-white skin, had dated a coed from the Midwest. A very disappointed Ahmed had reported back that even though this girl dressed like a prostitute, she wouldn't let him do much more than kiss her on the lips. After a few frustrating dates, Ahmed was glad to return to his favorite whore at the Mexican brothel on the outskirts of town. Rashid and the others tried, and failed, to fit Ahmed's experience into some elaborate theory about sexual mores here in America. It couldn't be true that American girls were a tease. Rashid's brother, Muhammad, dropped torrid hints in his infrequent letters about wild and willing American girls. From the sound of it, Muhammad Al-Murrah had made Boston his personal harem.

Rashid turned and looked back toward the stoop where the children sat drinking Dr Pepper. The boy reminded him of Muhammad, for in a way his brother was still a lost little boy. When Rashid worried about future generations of Arabs being corrupted by the West, he was really grieving over what had already happened to his older brother. Rashid's great dream of oil and power and Islam would perhaps not recover his own brother's lost soul, but maybe, he thought, it would keep other brothers from losing theirs.

Often Rashid thought Muhammad would have been better off if his feet had never trod on anything but sand. Even as a child in the mission school in Bahrain, Muhammad had been overeager to barter all that he was – his family, his tribe, his religion, the traditions of the desert – for the gaudy trinkets of the West. From the sound of Muhammad's letters, he was leading an utterly compromising life in Boston. Rashid doubted if his brother bothered to pray anymore. He didn't think Muhammad kept the Ramadan fast. He knew he drank alcohol and smoked cigarettes. Muhammad had, most certainly, been overindulging in American girls. Back home in Saudi, if Muhammad had dared to violate a woman, her avenging father or brother would surely have slit his throat as well as the wayward girl's. For the thousandth time, Rashid wondered how it could be possible that American brothers and fathers did not do more to protect the innocence of their young women. Didn't they care? Didn't they love their daughters and sisters? Didn't they want to make certain they were not hurt by predatory men? Didn't they have any conception of family honor?

Rashid did not like to believe Americans were as godless and immoral as they appeared to be. Even those who called themselves Christian and who went to their churches every Sunday still did not appear to make their religion a way of life. He did not envy these Americans. Life, for them, must have no certainties. Life for them must be empty and flat and joyless and terrifying.

Rashid looked back in disapproval at the retreating figure of the woman. He watched her wiggle her behind as shamelessly as a prostitute. Why did American women act like whores? He shook his head, then looked ahead of him on the street where the pack of obviously drunken cowboys were making fools of themselves.

Rashid looked up at the sky again. The yellow was fading to gray now. Surely, in ten minutes or so, even the most devout of Muslims would agree that the sun was down and it was time to break the fast. It was not supposed to be easy to keep this strict fast of Ramadan, commemorating the sacred month when Allah revealed the Holy Koran to the Prophet Muhammad in the desert. But the lunar month of Ramadan was the hardest of all to observe when it fell during the long hot days of August.

The first rays of sunrise had crept over the humpy Texas hills at three o'clock this morning. It was now nearly seven-thirty. For the past sixteen and a half hours, Rashid had not so much as swallowed his own spit. Ten more minutes, and then he could finally break his fast.

Rashid walked a little more purposefully toward the colored people's restaurant. As soon as the sun went down, he would go in and order immediately, eat quickly, and leave promptly. Once, when he had made the mistake of lingering too long in this neighborhood, he thought he had overheard some cowboys making fun of him.

Rashid tried, always, to avoid provocative situations. He had been told by the other Arab students when he first arrived that almost any encounter with these Texans could become provocative. The Arabs especially steered clear of cowboys. Rashid had gone to the movies here in Texas. He knew about cowboys and six-guns and shoot-outs. He knew these cowboys could instantly, unpredictably turn into violent killers.

Later, when Rashid reconstructed what happened next, he would wonder if his own absentmindedness - or was it arrogance? - had contributed to the debacle.

He would decide later that he should have been more cautious, that he should not have walked down that street as if he were the only living man in the world. Most of all he would reproach himself for not paying more attention to those drunken cowboys. All his life he would regret that he had not been able to exert a great effort of will and pull himself out of his Ramadan-induced stupor, so that he could have protected himself while he still had the opportunity.

Yet, in a way, when he looked back upon this day, Rashid could be sorry for none of it. For how, after all, could he regret Allah's will?

But then Rashid could never stop himself from wondering *why*. Had Allah wanted what was to happen to happen for a very particular reason? How strange it was that what turned out to be such a major matter could begin in such a minor way, over a bottle of warm Texas beer.

Rashid sauntered unsuspectingly down the heat-hazed Texas street. As he walked he daydreamed about being home. If he were home waiting out the last excruciating moments of the fast, there would be a hustle and a bustle from the women's side of the tents. Young women would be looking inside the skin that hung on a tripod to see if the yoghurt was almost ready. Girls would be squatting by the open fires preparing the coffee and the tea. An old woman might be overseeing the turning of a freshly butchered lamb on a spit, and her grown daughter might be adding spices to the rice. Rashid leaned against a telephone pole and shut his eyes. Almost he could smell the roasting lamb. He was so homesick for Saudi and all things familiar and certain. He longed for his wife, for his grandfather, for the father he had lost nearly twenty years ago, for the daughter he had never seen. He grieved for a moment, with his eyes tight shut, for all the losses of life.

There were tears in his eyes when he opened them. Rashid wiped them away and looked again at the hills on the western horizon. Today the sunset was a dramatic lingering spectacle of purples and reds and oranges. Unhappily Rashid stared at the lush lurid colors. It was forbidden to so much as lick away his tears with his tongue until the last ray of sunlight was gone from the sky. Rashid settled back against the telephone pole and willed back his reverie of Ramadan at home. While the women were laying out the food for the formal breaking of the fast, the men would be standing watch as he was now, looking anxiously at the sky. Just as soon as the eldest, most respected of the men was satisfied the sun had set, he would cry out a heartfelt '*Allahu akbar*, God is great!' Before the men lined up in the sand to perform the lengthy Ramadan prayers, they would retreat to the coolness of a tent to drink yoghurt and eat dates. Floating on top of the yoghurt would be pieces of freshly churned sweet sheep's butter, and as it slid creamily down the men's throats some of them would mutter '*Allahu akbar*' again, and mean it a thousand times over.

Rashid heard a voice saying something in English that did not sound like praise to God. His eyes flew open, and he saw a ring of big, beefy, hostile red-faced cowboys circled around him. Rashid shut his eyes. In the Saudi desert sometimes, when the light struck a certain way, when a man's longing went a certain way, mirages would spring up from thin air. Rashid hoped for a scientific miracle. Maybe this time the theory of mirages would work the other way and these cowboys would disappear. He heard boots shuffling in the dust. He sensed the cowboys closing in on him. Their bullying voices seemed louder.

'Looksta me like a niggah.'

'Naw,' another was answering. 'Wetback for sure.'

'Niggah!'

'Wetback!'

Against his will, Rashid opened his eyes. The cowboys were so close he could have embraced them if he stretched out his arms. He looked slowly from one flushed, drunken face to the next. He would not be able to fight off these eight big men. He studied their faces to judge just how great a threat they were to him. At first Rashid was reassured, for they did not look like evil men. But then it occurred to him that the devilish face of evil maybe didn't look sinister and cunning but only brutish and stupid, like these cowboys. Rashid backed as far away as he could, until his spine was pressed against the pole. Splinters pressed into his hair as he ground his skull against the telephone pole.

'Niggah or wetback?'

The question was asked almost kindly. Rashid's fear receded a little. The cowboys seemed more curious than threatening. They were gathered around him like small boys trying to decide if what was crawling on the ground was a beetle or a cockroach. But Rashid remembered that even sweet-tempered little boys stomped on bugs. The sweat ran like sap from his armpits. He hoped they could not smell his fear. He would be lost if he let them know he was afraid. But when Rashid remained silent, another of the cowboys took over the interrogation.

'Speak up, boy! You a niggah or a wetback?'

Rashid shook his head. He wished he did not have to dignify them with an answer. But it seemed he had no choice. 'I am an Arab.'

'A what?' Eight puzzled cowboys looked down at Rashid.

'An Arab.' Rashid elaborated when it appeared they did not understand him. 'From Saudi Arabia.'

'I think he means an A-rab,' one of the cowboys said. 'That what ya mean, boy? An A-rab?'

When Rashid did not answer, another of the cowboys stepped in. 'A-rab? What the hell's that? And what's it got to do with this? All I want to know is if this colored boy's a nigger or a wetback. You a nigger or a wetback, boy?'

Reason and instinct told Rashid to play along. He should be humoring them, trying to make them laugh, doing everything he could to defuse this potentially dangerous situation. But instead he found himself staring, as if mesmerized, up at the biggest of the cowboys standing flush in front of him guzzling a beer. The cowboy missed his mouth and slopped some of the beer on his chin. Rashid watched the foamy yellow liquid dribble down and soak inside the cowboy's shirt. Rashid stared at the black, beer-soaked hairs on the cowboy's chest. He was so thirsty he could not tear his eyes off that forbidden liquid.

'Somethin' *wrong*, boy?' The cowboy had misinterpreted Rashid's stare.

Rashid shook his head and tried to smile. But still he stared at the beer on the cowboy's chin and neck and chest. He was so thirsty his mouth could not water.

'Seems to me this fancy-pants niggah here don't like the way you drink your beer!' There was laughter from all the cowboys except the one with beer slopped on his chest.

The cowboy took another swig, and again he missed his mouth. His friends laughed harder. Rashid stared from the drops of liquid on the cowboy's face, chin, and chest to the brown-glassed bottle he held in his meaty hand.

'Looksta me like the niggah wants some beer.'

Rashid tried to swallow and clear his throat, but he was too dry. He opened his mouth to tell them again, more decisively this time, that he was an Arab, an Arab from the Al-Murrah tribe in Saudi Arabia studying petroleum engineering here at the university. But all he could manage was a hacking little sound that wasn't a word in any language.

'Cat got the niggah's tongue.'

'Wetback's tongue! You mean the wetback's tongue!'

While the cowboys continued to argue about his racial origin, Rashid could not stop staring at the bottle that was being held almost level with his eyes. He had never tasted beer. Rashid, like all good Muslims, had never tasted alcohol. He stared in unwilling, thirsty fascination at the drunken cowboys and the beer.

'I think the A-rab wants a beer.

'No!' Rashid found his voice. 'No! No beer!'

The cowboys laughed in delight. Finally, it seemed, just when they were growing bored with this 'nigger or wetback' game, they had found a new diversion. The cowboy in front of Rashid held out the brown-glassed bottle. When Rashid shrank from it in horror, the cowboys guffawed.

'Niggah don't want your beer.'

The cowboys stepped closer. To Rashid they seemed to increase in size and menace. Rashid made a desperate lunge to break out of their circle, but too many arms held him firmly against the telephone pole.

'Can lead a horse to water, but can't make him drink!'

'But this here ain't no horse. This here's a niggah.'

'Wetback!'

'And *I* say that nigger or wetback, this one's going to drink. Hold him, fellas.'

As the cowboys finally closed in on Rashid, he fought them with all his strength. Before they pinned back his arms, he flailed at their faces. Before they pinned down his legs, he kicked at their groins. Still, as they held him pinioned as if he were a woman they were about to rape, he struggled and bucked and spat at them. But the harder he fought, the more the laughing cowboys seemed determined to make him drink. While one seized his hair and yanked back his head, another began to pour beer on his closed lips. A cowboy wrenched open Rashid's jaw, and the beer found its way down the well of his mouth.

Rashid gagged and tried without success to shut his lips and shake off the cowboys. Just like a drowning man fighting off a wave of saltwater, Rashid spat out some of the beer but swallowed more of it. In his mouth was a warm yellow sourness, almost like the evil taste of camel urine from a polluted well. His gorge rose as he realized the enormity of what was happening. Not only was he swallowing forbidden alcohol, he was swallowing forbidden alcohol during the Ramadan fast. But worse even than violating the religious laws, these men were violating his manhood. They were tormenting him as if he were an animal. They were shaming him before not only God but man.

Rashid continued to struggle as they poured the first, the second, the third bottle of beer down his throat. They almost drowned him in a sea of their vile warm beer. He fought so hard that finally the cowboys tired of their game. When they ran out of beer, they stepped away from him and walked, still laughing uproariously, back inside the bar to buy themselves some more cold beer.

Rashid lay where they had left him, crumpled in the dust. He lay paralyzed with shame, wishing his enemies had killed him instead of humiliating him like this. How could they have done this to him? At home in Saudi, no one would do this even to his most dearly sworn enemy. Rashid wanted to die for the shame of it. He crawled up onto all fours, leaned over, and vomited up the foul yellow liquid that had been forced down his throat.

He retched again, and again, until he had the dry heaves. Still he tried to force the poisons from his empty stomach. When no more would come, when he still, nonetheless, felt the poison churning inside, he swallowed hard. Maybe, he decided, he would never be able to rid himself of what had just happened. But maybe it was a good and not a bad thing that he carry this inside him. Maybe he should remember it, ponder it, learn from it, and finally, someday, exact a vengeance for it. In the desert, when an evil was committed against a man, there was always a price that had to be paid in blood or in coins. Sometimes this price was not paid at once. Sometimes a blood feud went on for generations.

Rashid sank back on his heels and looked around him at the dusty little Texas town. He stared at the bar, the chili parlor, the shops where shoes, hardware, groceries, farm implements were sold. Always, all his life long, he knew his cheeks would burn with shame when he remembered the humiliation that had been his here today.

He looked, finally, up at the sky. The last rays of the sunlight had, it appeared, been long ago extinguished from the sky. Today's Ramadan fast was over. It was permitted, now, for him to eat and drink. But now, as Rashid knelt in the dust of this Texas street, the only hunger and thirst he felt was for vengeance. Someday, in some way, he vowed, if God willed it, he would, in time, take his full measure of vengeance.

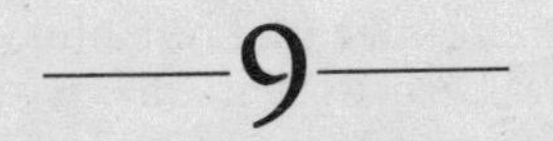

9

Sunny sat listlessly fiddling with the pack of cigarettes at her favorite table in the stone-walled cellar coffeehouse in Harvard Square. She had decided to start smoking last week when she broke off with the latest in her string of tall blond boring boyfriends. Maybe if she learned how to smoke and look sultry, she might attract someone with a little more fire. Ever since that sordid interlude with Muhammad last spring in Scollay Square, Sunny had been playing it safe with boys. She had dated a sophomore engineer from Holy Cross, a junior studying history at Boston College, even a fellow psychology major from Boston University. Each of them had been a waste of time.

Sunny leaned back in her rickety wooden chair. She crossed her long lithe legs and tossed her long thick hair and pretended she was Lauren Bacall as she tapped a Winston out of her pack. She and her roommate had taken turns practicing this sexy series of gestures - legs, hair, hands - in front of the mirror back at the dorm, but Sunny felt foolish actually doing it by herself in this crowded Cambridge coffeehouse. She had the feeling someone was watching her, and she hoped it was her one true love who had finally spotted her across this crowded room. She was nineteen years old, and surely she should have met her one true love by now.

She tapped the cigarette on the tabletop, she sighed a soft, troubled little sigh, she wondered if she should spend less time worrying about men and more time studying. She liked making the Dean's List, and she especially liked her psychology courses. But girls who had started with her in college last year were already dropping out to get married. Everyone told her that if she didn't take her nose out of her psych texts and her favorite old Arabia books and those romantic novels she devoured, she might well end up an old maid.

It was a rainy autumn Sunday afternoon, and *everyone* was here drinking coffee and eating cakes and arguing and smoking. Sunny saw graduate students who were perpetually demonstrating about banning the bomb, bushy-haired poets who made obscenities the stuff of their free verse, even a bewhiskered old man who told one and all that he had once hit the road with Jack Kerouac. Sunny loved being part of the intellectual fringe. She liked it when some of these older, wiser ones let her sit at their tables and listen to them talk about Jim Crow in the South and Bertrand Russell in England and liberating socialism and repressive fascism all over the world. She felt she was a kindred soul to these rebellious beatniks who rejected the boring certainties of middle-class life.

Sunny longed to take risks, do deeds, live her life to the hilt. Ever since she could remember, she had nursed dreams of a life of extraordinary adventure. She thought that if she had been born a boy, she might have become a soldier of fortune or an explorer or a spy. When she had read T. E. Lawrence and Jack London and Robert Louis Stevenson, she had longed to roam the wide world and maybe never come back to a small town as narrow and conventional as Still River. But she was only a girl, so she had contented herself with dreams of high romance and vicarious thrills like sitting in proximity to the bohemians of Cambridge. She didn't like to go out on dates with the beatniks, though. Mostly they were too old for her, bearded and scruffy and not handsome, and all they wanted to do was trick her into trying out free love. In their way, they were as tiresome as fraternity boys.

She had recrossed her legs and rearranged her hair and was about to pout her lips just so for another smoke when out of the corner of her eye she thought she saw someone she knew threading his way through the thick of the tables toward her. She shuddered slightly, assuring herself she must be mistaken. She struck her match, she inhaled, she was doubled over in a coughing fit when the slim dark Arab came up to her table. As she fought for air, her immediate impulse was to throw the muddy dregs of her Turkish coffee in his face. She remembered, then, exactly what he had done to her in Scollay Square, and her mortification overwhelmed her anger. It took all her considerable nerve to raise her head and look the young man she assumed was Muhammad in the eye.

'The daughter of Mr. Tom!' Dark eyes not nearly so cynical as Muhammad's flashed eagerly, happily, even desperately at her. 'Sunny!'

She caught her breath and stared at his sensual, ascetic face. He was so like, yet so unlike, his brother. He had the same shading of skin, the same strong beak nose and lustrous wavy black hair. But where Muhammad had been suave and glamorous, Rashid looked brooding and vulnerable and torturously, intensely romantic. Her imagination ran riot. It was so easy to imagine this one in an Arab robe and head scarf, riding his camel over the sand as he hunted gazelles. She was so intrigued she almost forgot her sordid hour with his brother, who had only played at being an Arab. Rashid, she sensed, was finally the real thing.

She wished she could speak Arabic so she could stun this young man with her linguistic brilliance. She wanted to ask him a million questions about her own father, about Saudi, about everything - as if she knew for a certainty that he had all the answers. The corners of her mouth turned up in a welcoming smile, and she couldn't stop staring at his extraordinary eyes. He looked like some sort of sexually magnetic saint, maybe painted long ago by El Greco. Was El Greco, she wondered dizzily, an Arab or a Greek? Perhaps a Moor? She tried to picture Rashid as Othello. She couldn't help laughing out loud at such a giddy chain of thoughts.

Encouraged, Rashid let out such a quick and hopeful rush of words that he forgot to be careful about his confusing English tenses. 'I see you come through the door. I think, what, her - here? Alone? Yes!' When Rashid laughed, some of the shadows left his face. 'I watch you. I at first am not certain - is it possible, truly, this is the daughter of Mr. Tom? - but then I come closer and I know. You, yes, it is you! You!'

The smile died on her lips, and she was tongue-tied and shy. She reminded herself how his brother had abused her, and she was more than shy, she was afraid. She did not dare ask him to sit down.

He stood there watching her stop smiling, waiting in vain for her to be hospitable. He had been so delighted to meet - by God's wonderful will - the beautiful daughter of the only American he loved, but now he wished he had stayed at his lonely table on the far side of the coffeehouse. Rashid had always been proud and quick-tempered, but after his degradation six weeks ago on that Texas street, his olive skin was translucently thin. He was not going to force himself on *any* American - not he, not now, not ever. Once, it was true, when he had first arrived in this country, Mr. Tom's daughter had been kind. Once, when she had prepared special food for him and Muhammad at her grandparents' house, he had been impressed with her sweetness and sensitivity. He supposed, since he was so lonely and suspicious of Americans even here in Boston, he might have exaggerated the significance of that single act of kindness. Rashid looked longingly at this pretty young American girl, as fair as Nura was dark. Would he have come racing over like this if Sunny were not the sort of girl he had been dreaming of for the past three years? Rashid wished he had been content to watch her from afar. He wished he had allowed himself to keep one last American illusion intact.

In a way he supposed he had been eager to worship this girl.

But he told himself he should never have assumed, just because she was Mr. Tom's daughter, that she was any different from the rest. She didn't like Arabs. She was prejudiced against dark skin. She was racist and imperialist and every other evil that Rashid was beginning to believe Americans were born to be. Rashid could almost taste the sourness of that warm beer in his mouth. He was furious at himself for courting another American rebuff, and he vowed never to repeat this mistake. He would bury himself in his books, he would talk to no one, he would hold his breath until next summer when he could finally go home to his beloved Saudi. 'So sorry to intrude.' His face was a mask of grim dignity. 'So sorry, miss.' He turned to finish making his escape.

It would have stopped there, before it even began, if it

hadn't been for Sunny's great belief in the rightness of her instincts. Without stopping to consider what she was doing, she reached out a hand and bravely touched his arm. 'Wait.'

As he turned and looked warily at her, she wondered at her impulse to reach out to him. Nervously she assured herself he didn't seem at all like his brother. Solemnly she searched Rashid's face. His was not, she thought, a happy face. As she remembered it, he hadn't looked especially happy when she had first met him out in Still River, but now she thought she could read fresh traces of hurt or disillusion in his wounded eyes. Sunny felt a wave of tenderness for this young man wash over her. Perhaps more purely and more simply than she ever was to feel anything again in her life, she wanted happiness and good fortune and no tragedies ever to befall him. She wished it were possible that she herself could bestow all that good fortune on Rashid. All her instincts told her that here before her stood a good man. She was certain, suddenly, as if she had been gifted with second sight, that if she wanted it - if she dared to want it - this good and decent man could play a major role in her life. Tentatively she smiled at him.

'As you like.' He had not forgotten she belonged to a family he must respect. He would stand here and exchange cold politeness with her for as long as she liked.

'Have you heard from my father lately?'

'He seldom writes. I received maybe three letters a year from Mr. Tom.'

'Three a year!' Sunny's lower lip trembled. 'He only writes me *once* a year, at Christmas.'

'Mr. Tom is a very busy man.'

'I suppose.'

His anger evaporated as he watched her fight off tears. She was beautiful and, he supposed, she was rich. She was American, and so she had been born to a lifetime of understood superiorities. Yet he pitied her when she spoke of the disappointment of her father. He wondered why she was here in this coffeehouse by herself. He knew she had no real family except for those aging grandparents. Surely she couldn't be as lonely as she seemed? She seemed as lonely as he was. Her eyes were as guileless as a child's – lovely pale light foreign eyes. Such gentle, trusting, believing, innocent eyes. How could Mr. Tom and his parents let a vulnerable young girl like this go off alone in a big city like Boston? A dishonorable man could come along and take advantage of the innocence of this lovely girl. Again Rashid was reassured that the Saudi way with women was better than the American way. This daughter of Mr. Tom's should be protected, cared for, cherished. . . . 'He always calls you his princess, you know.'

'He does?'

When her blue eyes were ashine like this, Rashid thought, they were very, very beautiful. 'The first time he ever showed Muhammad and me your picture, he asked us if I wanted to see a real princess.'

'Muhammad.' Sunny blushed as she repeated her tormentor's name.

Rashid assumed the flush of red on her white skin was because he had unwittingly reminded her of her father's neglect. He decided to continue with the less loaded topic of his brother. 'Muhammad does not write to you from London? But I thought you were friends. That he watched over you here. No? So maybe you do not know that he works in a bank. He likes it. Always Muhammad likes England more. English girls, too.' Rashid smiled, but she did not smile back.

As Sunny twisted the golden Saudi rings on her fingers, she considered telling Rashid exactly what she thought of his brother. It would be satisfying just this once to speak her mind about the degrading way that devil had abused her. But Sunny looked into Rashid's wild-animal eyes and decided the less said of Muhammad the better. She had not even told her best girlfriend about what had happened to her. Yet what else could she talk about with Muhammad's brother? All her life, she thought wryly, she had yearned for her own princely Saudi *shaykh*, and now that she had one's undivided attention she couldn't even make small talk. It occurred to her finally that he was still standing, and so she moved her used coffee cup and asked him to sit down. 'Coffee?' She smiled. 'They have Turkish coffee here. I always have it.'

A slow smile spread from his eyes to his lips. 'Turkish coffee?' He snapped his fingers. 'You mean *Arab* coffee?' He laughed. 'I get us some, yes?' He was still laughing as he leaped up from their table. He looked so different when he laughed. She wished she could say or do something here, now, forever, to keep this young man happy and laughing.

Her wish came true. Rashid was still laughing as he came back with two tiny cups of 'Arab' coffee, two glasses of water, and two dainty French pastries all expertly balanced on a tray. 'I have very sweet teeth, so these cakes. That's what you say, "sweet teeth"?'

She laughed at his endearingly mistaken English. 'You mean, you have a sweet tooth?'

'Sweet tooth, yes. I have a sweet tooth.' There was a giddiness to their laughter this time.

'Sweet teeth!' Again she laughed, but she shook her head at the pastry. 'No fattening cake for me.'

'Eat! No worry! A girl like you - so beautiful! - you should eat, enjoy.' He handed her a fork. 'For me you must eat.'

Instead she pulled a cigarette from her pack. She leaned back, she crossed her legs, she tossed her hair. She put the cigarette between her lips and waited for him to light it the way men did in the movies. Instead he frowned, reached over, and plucked the cigarette from between her lips and snapped it in two. 'No cigarettes. Not for *you*.'

'No?' If at this moment this fabulous man had swept her into his arms, she thought she might be his forever. He took her breath away.

'No. Smoking very bad, especially for women. You must never smoke.' He picked up a fork and handed it to her.

'You must eat. For the sweet tooth, yes?' He beamed at her.

Meekly she ate every bite of the pastry. When she had finished, she sighed. 'That was good.' She sipped the Arab coffee. 'Tell me, Rashid, do they have coffee like this in Saudi?'

'Pardon?'

'At home. In Saudi? Do they have coffee there?'

'Do we have coffee? Arabs *invent* coffee! In Yemen in Arabia, was the first coffee. Of course we have coffee! In desert every day, every afternoon, every night, coffee, always coffee. First sound every morning - ping! - boy grinds coffee beans. First smell every morning - ah! - the coffee. And what coffee! Best coffee in all the world. Not like this coffee here, old, stale, flat. Coffee in Arabia is much more wonderful, you understand, yes?'

'Oh yes!' Radiantly she smiled. Finally, at long last, she was truly hearing about the land of her dreams. This boy, this wonderful handsome masterful boy, knew everything there was to know about Arabia. She would ask him to tell her all about it. 'The desert! You do love the desert, don't you, Rashid? Is it really wonderful in the desert?'

'Ah!' His face was aglow. 'Yes, Sunny. The desert, my desert, is very wonderful.'

'You'll tell me about Saudi, Rashid? You'll tell me all about it?'

'You want to know about my country?'

'Oh, yes!'

He rose with decision. 'So first I will get you another sweet cake. And then I will come back and tell you all about my country?'

'And coffee. Don't forget the Arab coffee.'

He turned back to her. 'I will forget nothing, Sunny. Always, for you, wonderful woman Sunny, I will remember everything.'

More than two months later, on New Year's Day, Rashid tucked her arm in his. As they crossed Commonwealth

Avenue, he looked anxiously to the right and the left, as if it were only the menace of heavy traffic that made him link arms with her. Yet on this holiday afternoon, the streets were nearly deserted. He continued to hold on to her even when they walked down the center of the mall, although the morning's light snowfall had not made the sidewalks slippery. He reveled in the sensation of hovering over this lovely American girl. He still deluded himself that he escorted her around Boston much as he would have protectively shepherded a sister or an aunt or a daughter back in Saudi. Even though Rashid's loving feelings were neither those of a brother nor those of a father, it still gave him great and gallant pleasure to know that he was watching over Mr. Tom's vulnerable daughter with all the vigilance women deserved from the men who loved them.

Sunny took her hand from inside the fur muff Gran had given her for Christmas and gave his hand a squeeze as she smiled happily up at him. When his liquid brown eyes flashed at her like this, she could read in them the assurance that he surely loved her. Yet still he had not told her so, still he had not asked her to marry him, still he had not even kissed her. Lord, she thought, these Arabs are slow. She brushed away the fleeting memory of that other Arab who had been anything but slow. She hardly remembered Muhammad anymore; but when she did it was always with a shiver of sexual shame. She was glad now that she had never blurted out the truth about herself and Muhammad. She did not want to risk making Rashid angry, or widen the rift between the brothers, or cause any problems in the Arab family she already thought of as her own. Sunny assumed they would marry when Rashid finished at MIT in the spring. Already she had begun secretly shopping for her trousseau, using her father's generous monthly checks to buy pretty floor-length cotton dresses, glamorous filmy nightgowns, and delicate embroidered lingerie. She had even consulted an atlas to begin planning their honeymoon across what she considered the romantic capitals of Europe. She drew a red line from Paris to Vienna to Florence, and then circled Saudi Arabia in a giant red heart.

Sunny sighed as she smiled sweetly up at Rashid. Yet there was calculation in her eyes and her smile and the way she clung to him with her breast snuggled against his arm. She was determined Rashid was finally going to kiss her today.

Even though they saw each other nearly every day, he hardly ever touched her. She ached sometimes with the suspense of the waiting. When they walked as close together as they were now, she could hardly keep from throwing herself into his arms. She wondered why his not touching her excited her more than if he had groped her with the roving insistent hands of every American boy she had ever dated. She quivered sometimes with the wanting of him and his not quite touching her.

The first time she had felt the heat of his nearness had been by accident on the subway. The crowded Green Line car was making a sharp turn near the Boylston station when it jerked almost off the tracks. She lost her balance and was thrown against him, he caught her so she would not fall, and for one moment only she was pressed full-length against him. As he held her, they stared longingly into each other's eyes, and for one heady instant he pulled her even closer. But when the subway car came out of the turn, they had broken apart and looked everywhere but at each other until they were all the way past Kenmore station.

They had touched again, briefly, at a football game on Halloween weekend. When Boston University scored a winning touchdown, she threw her arms rapturously around him, jumped up and down, and hugged him and danced in place and screamed with delight where they stood, bundled up against the cold, in the stadium.

He had finally reached out and deliberately touched her on a cold November evening when they were cutting through the Public Gardens on their way to the library in Copley Square. She had forgotten her mittens and she said her hands were cold as they stood by the frozen pond where the swan boats ply summer tourists, and he took her cold red hands in his warm gloved ones and rubbed her fingers and smiled down at her until she wasn't cold anymore.

They were even more tender with each other just before Thanksgiving when she rooted in her purse and then pulled out the snapshot she wanted him to see. He looked at the familiar face of Mr. Tom, at the American woman who looked so like Sunny, at the dimly remembered and much-loved image of his own dead father. He had never before seen a photograph of his father. He was so startled to see it now, with his father dead twenty years, that he dropped the photograph as though it burned him. Sunny took his hand in hers and stroked it. He shied away from her too, as though singed again. They both looked down again at the last photograph taken of her mother and his father before the tragedy in the Gulf that had, in a way, knitted their lives together. There was an inevitability to his reaching over and covering her hand with his, as though he wanted to transcend memory, as if an effort of his will could rewrite the past from remembered tragedy into a sort of predestined solace.

And now Rashid kept her hand tucked inside his arm as they strolled toward the Christmas display at the far end of the Common. He thought that in her new scarlet wool coat and white fur hat and muff she looked as if she had stepped out of one of those cards Christians sent each other in the winter. As they strolled past the tall ornate splendor of the elegant mansions lining Commonwealth Avenue, Rashid could hear the ice cracking in the trees and feel the snow crunching under his leather boots. A freezing wind howling in from the nearby Atlantic stung the bare skin of his face. All of this was utterly alien to a young Al-Murrah tribesman born to track and hunt in the burning deserts of Arabia's Empty Quarter. This girl, this street, this snow were all of a lovely dream. But when Rashid felt her squeeze his hand again, the sensation of living a dream left him. Sunny was disturbingly real. He had missed her more than he had thought he could miss her, or anyone, for the fortnight she had spent in Still River - so much that he had neglected his studies. Now he pulled her closer to him and wished that the impossible love he felt for this American girl were, instead, a possible love.

But then the nagging litany of sensible reasons why he couldn't have Sunny assailed him again. He already had not only a wife but a child. He had repeatedly resolved to tell Sunny about Nura, but always he changed his mind and decided it was pointless to hurt her. Even if there were no Nura, he and Sunny would still be doomed by too many differences in outlook and culture. Sunny was good-hearted and he loved her, but she was a romantic girl who had dreamed too many dreams of Saudi. He greatly doubted that this sheltered, privileged Christian girl could come camp with him forevermore in the desert, or find a place for herself among the women of his tribe, or ever accept the mask and veil and seclusion. Even with the best of intentions, even with the most endless and adaptable of loves, the two of them would have to endure too many heartbreaks. It was madness to love her. Yet reciting his reservations did not alter the fact that he adored this impetuous, vibrant, voluptuous young American woman. Rashid sighed. He wished he could marry her and raise a family with her and walk beside her like this for all his days.

She interpreted his sigh as a declaration of love. As she matched her strides to his, she reveled in being in step with him, of swinging the weight of her body exactly in synchronization with his. They had just been reunited after the eternity of their two-week separation. She had been out of breath from running up the street from the subway when she flung open the door of his favorite sandwich shop in Central Square. She had come back to him three days early, and she had been so afraid she wouldn't be able to find him - that he wouldn't be having lunch in this particular restaurant, that she would have to flit from library to library searching fruitlessly for him. But then she had seen the crown of his thick mop of black hair in a booth at the back of the room, and she hadn't even waited to catch her breath before calling out his name and running to him. She had loved that sensation of running to him. She would have been happy to make that one simple act the point of her life, running to Rashid.

The snow-covered mall was as silent and pristine as an arctic wilderness. The cold flickering Boston sunlight sparkled on the branches. Sunny was so happy she hummed a few bars of 'Winter Wonderland' as they walked along in their own private land of winter wonders.

'You sing. Never before have I heard you sing. You are so happy, Sunny, that you sing?'

She tried to dazzle him with two of the Arabic words he had taught her. '*Wallah*,' she said, 'you make me so *masrourah* that I want to sing.' Rashid had gravely told her that *Allah* was of course the Arabic for 'the God,' and after he informed her that *Wallah* meant 'by God,' Sunny had begun, with gusto, to sprinkle that oath throughout her conversations. She had, as well, learned a host of other Godly exhortations. *Allah karim*, which meant 'God is generous,' and *bismallah*, 'in the name of Allah,' could be dropped unerringly into almost any sentence. *Inshallah*, 'if God wills it,' was a phrase Sunny had learned to dread. If she asked what time he'd meet her tomorrow, a vague *inshallah* was the answer - as it was, in fact, his response to all her anxious queries about the future. *El-hamdulillah*, 'thank God,' was almost as universal an answer to questions and situations. Did she feel good, bad, hungry, sad, happy? *El-hamdulillah!* She liked the way her tongue flapped on the roof of her mouth on all those l's when she said this incantation fast as the Arabs did. Rashid seemed especially pleased when she told him she had taken a shine to thanking God in Arabic. He taught her, then, that *shams* meant 'sun,' so 'Sunny' was *Shamsa*. She liked the sound of that, too, and beamed when he called her by what she considered his pet name for her. She had also made him teach her the word for 'happy,' and she always grinned when she said she was *masrourah* with him.

'Yes?' He laughed at her adorable pidgin Arabic. 'Then, *wallah*, you must sing for me. You must sing for me a song.'

'Everyone says I have a terrible voice.' Sunny was suddenly self-conscious. 'Besides, I thought music was *haram* - "forbidden." I thought good Saudi Muslims weren't allowed to listen to music.'

He shrugged, sick for once about what good Saudi Muslims were and were not allowed to do. He did not feel like explaining to her the significant differences between one man or one woman's singing a song and Elvis Presley gyrating his pelvis on a stage. He did not even care to educate her about ancient Arab songs that were musical poems of love. He merely wanted the simple pleasure of this woman, whom he was increasingly beginning to regard as 'his' woman, singing him a song. 'Sing, Sunny.' It was not a request but a command. 'Sing to me.'

Sometimes in the past two weeks, lying in her girl's bed in her childhood room in the Still River farmhouse, she had entertained herself with wild fantasies of Rashid in the role of the Saudi *shaykh* and herself the willing, white-skinned, conquered infidel slave girl. Sometimes she was an odalisque lolling on silky divans in the harem. Sometimes she was the booty in a desert raid by savage rival tribes. Never was she anything as humdrum as Sunny Shannon, sophomore psychology major at Boston University, who kept company with Rashid Al-Murrah, a Saudi graduate student studying petroleum management at MIT. Lying on her virginal bed in Still River, she had thrilled to her fantasies of masterful man commanding submissive woman. Yet now, when Rashid had finally given her an order, even though it was a command as innocent as singing a song, Sunny balked. Who was *he* to tell her to sing? To tell her to do anything? She assured herself she would do as *she* pleased, not as *he* ordered. She most certainly would not sing.

But when he asked her again, this time it was not so much command as plea. 'You will not sing for me?' He sensed that he probably should not say what he was about to say, and that he would be leading her on if he said it. But Rashid took a deep breath and plunged ahead. 'At home, in the desert, a woman who feels a certain way for a man will sing for him.'

Immediately her interest soared. If this was in fact a mating rite leading inevitably to their marriage, she would most certainly raise her off-key voice in song. She would tap-dance from Mass. Avenue to Park Street, singing operatic arias, if that meant she would thereby more quickly become Mrs. Al-Murrah. Sunny laughed out loud at the picture that conjured up. Then she wet her lips. 'A song? What kind of song?'

'Any song. Any song you want to sing to me, Sunny.'

She looked into his eyes, and although she racked her brain for the most romantic song ever sung, all she could think of was what seemed to her a childish song. 'You are my sunshine,' she sang, so low he had to bend his head closer to her. 'My only sunshine.'

'I do not hear you,' he said. 'I do not understand.'

She raised her voice and pointed toward the faint yellowish winter sun. 'You are my sunshine,' she sang, 'my only sunshine.' She smiled and whispered an explanation to him. 'You are like the sun to me, Rashid.'

'Ah! The sun! *Shamsa!*' He repeated, in Arabic, her name and the sun's name, which were the same. His voice was husky. 'My Sunny! *Shamsa!* Mine!'

'You make me happy when skies are gray!' She had stopped walking and had turned to face him. 'Happy, Rashid; you make me happy.'

'*Masrourah*,' he whispered – 'happy.'

'You'll never know, dear, how much I love you.' Her arms were on his shoulders, her face close to his. 'Please don't take . . . my sunshine . . . away. . . .'

'Shamsa. . . .'

It was only an instant later that their lips touched, and they kissed under the arching frosted silvery trees of the Commonwealth Avenue Mall. They kissed for a long time, until they were shivering not from the cold but with delight.

10

Sunny snatched the telephone off the cradle at its first ring. 'Rashid? Finally! Be right down!' She sped from the telephone booth in the hallway of her dormitory back into her room to collect her purse and raincoat. Then she paused to look herself over one more time in the full-length mirror beside her desk.

She had decided to make tonight the night.

Anxiously she checked to see if she had lipstick smudged on her teeth, if her hair rippled just so on her shoulders, if her white slip was hanging below her red dress. Rashid liked her in bright reds, oranges, purples - every color Gran had always told her was worn only by tarty girls. Sunny frowned at the apparently wasted vulgar red of her dress. Despite her new wardrobe of hot primary colors, Rashid still kept his hands mostly off her. In the four months since their first kiss on New Year's Day, he had kissed her exactly five more times, and that was counting three pecks on the cheek. He would have to start moving fast if he intended to marry her, and Sunny had begun to despair that Rashid had neither the inclination nor the ability to move that fast. And so she had decided to pop the question herself tonight.

Sunny frowned at herself in the mirror. She had never imagined that her one true love would be the coy one. Every time she and Rashid were beginning to draw closer, he retreated. Yet Sunny never allowed herself to doubt for long that he loved her and wanted to take her back to Saudi as his wife. When she asked him to marry her, his answer would be to sweep her into his arms and kiss her on the lips, on her eyes, at her temples. Then they would go off to celebrate their engagement, and it would all be perfect. He hadn't asked her to marry him because he was shy, or uncertain of how to proceed here in this alien American culture, or as slow-moving about courtship as he was about everything else. She would love him forever, but sometimes he was so slow she felt like jabbing his backside with one of Gran's oversized hatpins. Tonight, for instance, he had been supposed to pick her up at eight but hadn't arrived until ten to nine.

Sunny stared doubtfully at herself in the mirror. Should she ask him to marry her? Was it now or never? It was the last week in April. Rashid would be here for only another month. Banns would have to be cried in church for three - or was it four? - weeks. She would have to break the news gently to her grandparents, who had no inkling of what was afoot and who would probably not be overjoyed. She would have to buy her wedding gown, arrange at least a small reception in Still River, and get her Saudi Arabian visa. She had obtained her first passport, bought presents for Rashid's family, and assembled a carton of her favorite Arab books for immediate shipping to Saudi. She had even engaged a private tutor to teach her Arabic, although she had given up in dismay after a few bewildering weeks trying to grunt and groan just right from the back of her throat. All he had to do was say the word, and off they'd go.

Sunny smiled tremulously at herself in the mirror, and then she crossed her fingers and went to meet her destiny.

'Sunny!' He took both her hands, looked into her eyes, and started to ask her something.

'In here, Rashid.' Brusquely she led him off to a parlor to forestall the elaborate series of ritual questions he always asked about her and her family's health and safety. Sunny knew by now that this was how polite Arabs greeted one another. Usually she was charmed by this, as by all other Arab customs, but tonight she was too impatient to endure the necessary repetitions of 'thank Gods' and 'God willings.'

'Very nice room.' Rashid ignored Sunny's patting the cushion next to her and instead sat at the far end of the couch. He looked around at the cozy overstuffed sofas and the outsized club chairs. 'Why have we not come here before? I think maybe it is more quiet here than in the library. We must study here together, yes?'

'Some other time, Rashid. But not now. Now I want to have a serious talk with you.'

He nodded, then sighed. He had noticed at once that she was not her ebullient self. He set about placating her. 'I know. I was late. I am sorry. I was in the Square and I ran into some students. Lebanese. They invited me to have coffee, and I could not insult them. I –'

'That's not it. So you were late.' Sunny shrugged her shoulders in an admirably executed imitation of an Arab. 'So you are always late. But that's not –'

'You are sick!' He jumped to his feet as though about to sprint off in search of a doctor. 'I knew it! Too thin! Sick! But I will take care of you, my Sunny. I will feed you honey, much meat, rice! Pastries of the French!'

She could not help laughing. 'No, no. I'm not sick. I'm fine.'

'*El-hamdulillah!*' He sat back down. 'But you look not happy.' He took her hand. 'You must tell me what is wrong.'

She steeled herself. She wished she could just blurt it out and be done with it, and that he would immediately say yes, and she could try to forget that she had been the one who had done the asking. She searched his face for signs he loved her. His face was earnest and concerned, but was it loving? She wished she had not initiated this talk.

'You must tell me what is the problem, Sunny. First you tell me, then together we make it fly away.'

She seized that perfect opening. 'That's it. Us.'

He was puzzled but patient. 'I am sorry. Sometimes, even now, my English . . . "Us"?'

'You and me. Us. That's the problem. Where we're going together.'

'I thought tonight to have dinner. One of your American steaks. And tonight you will have a baked potato! I insist!'

She shook her head. 'Not about where we're going tonight. Where we're *going*. Period. How I feel about you. How you feel about me. The point of it all.'

'Ah!' He sighed under his breath and looked away. He had been dreading a conversation like this ever since he had first kissed her. He had hoped they would be able to part next month with these words left unspoken. He loved Sunny now, and he suspected that in a way he would always love the memory of Sunny and what might have been with her. Their love would be as pure and hopeless as those mythic passions of Arabic poetry and song.

'I love you, Rashid.'

Reluctantly he looked back into her eyes. She was such a beautiful young girl, inside and out. He loved her innocence, her trusting nature, most of all her unblemished, strong, spirited, altogether moral character. She was in every way a good woman. To him she was *Shamsa*, as radiant and life-giving as the sun at midday. But he had decided months ago that his love for her would remain undeclared. He had a wife. He could not marry Sunny. He had tried neither to lead her on nor to tantalize himself with possibilities that could never be. Many times he had considered the prudence of ending even their friendship. But he had temporized and rationalized and kept on seeing her. He had convinced himself that if he was very controlled, they could be together as they had been these last months. He had risked the small exquisite dangers of a stolen kiss or two or three, occasional electric touchings of the hand or thigh, whispered confidences in the faint northern moonlight of a Boston winter. But he had been determined to go no further. He had reassured himself he would never do anything to cause this vibrant young girl pain or disillusion. He had intended to love her from a safe distance, sitting like this, a cushion away on a couch. For him, this loving had been fantastical and unreal. He had always known that when he finished at MIT he would leave her forever to take up the threads of his real life in another world. He had tried to convince himself that Sunny surely must understand and accept the limits of how it had to be with them.

But now he looked into her clear trusting eyes and saw that he had been deceiving not only himself but her. He saw, now, what he had refused to see all along. She was not meek but strong, she was not a child but a woman. She loved him, and she meant to have him. And so, in a little while here, now, he would have to tell her why they could not marry. He sighed very softly and shook his head.

'Rashid!' Sunny refused to be daunted by the strange way he was acting. But in her heart she must have understood at least a little of what was to come, for her questions, when they finally came, were phrased in the negative. 'Don't you love me? Don't you *want* to marry me?'

He decided it would only make things worse if he told her how much he did love her. He would say what he had to say and, *inshallah*, then they would part. 'I cannot marry you, Sunny. It is not possible.' He faltered and bit his lip and hoped he would not have to say more.

But she was leaning over closer to him, her face white against her scarlet dress, her blue eyes appealing. 'Impossible! What do you mean, impossible? Don't you love me? I was sure -'

'It's not that.' He wanted to take her in his arms and hold her and comfort her, and himself, but instead he kept his distance, took a deep breath and said what had to be said. 'I have already a wife.' He waited, but there was no reaction at all on her face, except in her eyes - her eyes changed, they dimmed, the sparkle died, the flash was gone. 'At home. In Saudi. My cousin. Nura. We have a daughter. Wahda.' Wretchedly he continued. 'Grandfather said we must marry before we came to America. Muhammad and I both married cousins. His wife is Aisha, the daughter of our father's brother. Nura is the daughter of my father's . . . Sunny?'

She had risen like a sleepwalker and was walking slowly away from him, toward the door.

'Sunny!' Now that it seemed that he had lost her, he wanted her back. He forgot all his resolutions about keeping his feelings to himself, about bowing to God's will, about surrendering without a fight. He ran after her. 'Sunny! But I do love you! Sunny! I love you!'

She kept on going, as though she had not heard him although he was shouting not in Arabic but in English.

Sunny urged Princess Camey on faster, faster, until they were like a wind racing through the orchards of Still River. She dug her heels into the flanks of the horse and wished the Arabian could pick up so much speed that the two of them would glide up into the air like that wonderful wooden horse from the *Arabian Nights* who took the prince and the princess from one magical land to another. Sunny wanted escape to another land, another world, another life, and as quickly as possible. She was sick to death of being all alone in this particular life.

Last night as soon as she had fled to her dormitory room, she had telephoned her grandparents and said she had to come home. She had felt so hurt and broken she could think only of going home. She had packed her suitcase and Gramps had come and taken her back to Still River. She had been glad to be safe and secure, alone in her narrow girl's bed. She had sobbed brokenhearted until she finally fell asleep.

But this morning she had awakened outraged that all the time Rashid had been courting her, he had a wife in Saudi. She had stalked out to the barn and crooned to her faithful old friend that animals were far more dependable and worthy of her own passion and loyalty than lying, deceiving, miserable men. Rashid was even worse than his brother, who had only abased her body. Rashid had abused her heart and her soul.

She had intended only to exercise the mare in the near pastures, then groom her. But once astride Princess Camey, Sunny had not been able to resist trying to outride her demons. She pressed the horse to gallop harder, faster, farther, until finally, at the crest of the hill that had been her favorite childhood lookout, she slid off and absently fed the mare a carrot she had stuffed into her pocket.

Saudi. . . . She had thought Rashid was her ticket not only to eternal love but to Saudi and her long-lost father. Rashid had been more than a man. He had been the fulfillment of all her dreams.

Sunny felt like weeping for the loss of her dearest dreams. She supposed she had been mad to try to make those childhood dreams come true. Yet for her, they could still weave a magic spell. Standing high on this New England hill, she decided to allow herself one final trip back to her childhood fantasy world before banishing all such dreams forever. She was a grown woman, just turned twenty, and her heart had been truly broken. Maybe if she started acting like a mature woman, it would never be broken again. Just one last dream of Saudi, she promised herself; then I'll put all this behind me and I'll be like everyone else. I'll settle for a conventional man and a conventional life and I will dream no more dangerous dreams.

She smiled faintly and cocked her head as though she heard the tinkle of camel bells carried on the wind. . . .

Always, in this Saudi daydream, it was just after sunrise, long before the heat of the day turned the desert into a burning hell. Always she was riding through the silent yawning desert, sometimes astride her camel, sometimes in the saddle of a chestnut Arabian horse who was the twin to Princess Camey. A hot wind streamed her long golden hair out behind her. At first she was alone in the desert, just as she had been alone for too many years in her real life in Still River. But in this daydream she was not lonely. Alone in the desert she felt the joy of solitude rather than the pain of loneliness. She savored the triumph of that difference. Riding hard and fast, she luxuriated in the pleasure of her solitude. Then, in her fantasy, she glimpsed, ahead on a rise of undulating dunes, her tribe's encampment of black Bedouin tents. Waiting in those tents were her father, her lover, her children, maybe even her dead mother who wasn't dead after all but who had been living all these years secretly among the desert nomads. She heard the sonorous prayer calls echo from the cluster of tents. She saw the men in their white robes line up out on the sand to pray to Allah. She glimpsed veiled women scurrying inside the flap of a tent that was their harem. The four wives of the *shaykh* were modestly running for cover at the approach of her and Princess Camey. . . .

A click of a thought - an inspiration! - brought her out of her dream.

She scrutinized that one telling detail from her old familiar fantasy. Wives in the tents! Harems of veiled wives. Plural wives. Four wives per Arab. Muslims couldn't eat pork, they had to pray five times each day, they were supposed to make a pilgrimage to Mecca at least once in a lifetime. And each man could have four wives at once.

He *could* marry her. She could be his second wife.

Sunny nuzzled Princess Camey's neck and considered.

Rashid did love her. She had heard him call that out to her with desperation in his voice as she had walked away from him. She had kept going so that she wouldn't lose total control and scratch his lying eyes out right there in her dormitory parlor. But she had not only heard him. She had believed him. He *did* love her.

She was certain, too, about the polygamy of Muslims. *Everyone* knew about Muslims being allowed multiple wives. So it was possible for him to marry her even though he already had one wife.

Not that she liked the idea of sharing him with another woman. She didn't even like it when she and Rashid were out together and he turned his head to watch an especially pretty girl sashay down the sidewalk. So how could she endure being constantly jealous of another wife? She supposed it was possible that even if he technically had two wives, he could still exclusively love only her. He had probably married his cousin just to honor a family obligation. Sunny decided this woman she was already beginning to think of not as Rashid's 'wife' but as his 'first wife' couldn't be a serious rival. She herself would always be his *Shamsa*, his one true love. Once they were married, he would never touch that other, Arab girl again.

Now that she had decided to set jealousy aside, Sunny even began to warm to the exoticism of being a second wife. Most certainly no one in Still River or even Boston was a second wife. People would be utterly shocked if she told them what she proposed to do. Her grandparents would have a conniption. Sunny decided it might be best to keep this one particularly unconventional detail from them. She tried to imagine what her girlfriends would say if she confided she was about to marry an Arab and go off to join his harem as the second of his wives. In a moment of clarity Sunny realized that even the most daring of her friends might try to talk her out of it or even tell her grandmother. She would keep this one little polygamous fact a secret from all of them.

Sunny laughed and threw her arms around Princess Camey's neck. It would be fantastic to sweep off to Saudi on the arm of the man of her dreams. Their love must have been written long ago in the stars that shone diamond bright over Arabia. Her life was going to be a great epic romance. She would dedicate her life to their eternal love, she would be exalted and transformed by their passion, she would immolate herself upon the altar of their love. All for love, yes, all!

She loved him, and she was going to have him.

Intoxicated by her novel plan to snatch wondrous victory from the jaws of horrid defeat, Sunny swung back into Princess Camey's saddle. Still laughing, Sunny galloped hard and fast until her long hair streamed out behind her in the wind, just as it always did in her Saudi dreams. She felt so young and wild and free and invincible that it never occurred to her that what she might be riding toward, pell-mell, was not her destiny but a fall.

Sunny faltered, she had second thoughts, and she almost called it all off when the squinty old man who was reading the marriage service asked if anyone knew why these two should not be joined together.

As the Vermont justice of the peace paused, Sunny reconsidered.

She had talked him into marrying her.

When she had burst upon him studying in the library, his face had lit up, he had embraced her, he had kept exclaiming her name until the librarian suggested they leave. It was only when they were outside and she told him she meant to be his second wife that the trouble had begun. He had vowed, as soberly as if he were swearing to a legal contract, that he loved her. He had said he would have liked nothing more than to marry her and share his life with her. But then he had made her cry when he said that even with the best of intentions he doubted she would be able to accept the inevitabilities awaiting her in Saudi. Her tears had shaken him. She had been delighted to discover he was so tender-hearted that he had been willing to say or do almost anything to stop her weeping.

So Sunny simply cried and carried on like the wronged heroine in a melodrama, until two weeks later she had worn him down into considering their marriage a possibility. Somberly he sketched the boundaries that would be their married life. They would not be living in a tent out in the desert but inside the Aramco compound. She would not get to see much of her father, who was almost always off in oil-exploration camps in remote parts of the desert. Rashid himself would be putting in long hours not only at Aramco but with his relatives and tribe. His family might never accept her because she was a Christian and a foreigner. She would have to cover her face when she went out in public. She would have to master Arabic. Saudi's enervating climate was all scorching heat and damp humidity. There were snakes and scorpions and even occasional plagues of locusts. Most Aramco wives, even though they lived an American life with their American husbands in the Dhahran compound, found existence there monotonous and difficult and lived only for their frequent vacations.

But all Rashid's arguments had fallen on deaf ears. She would listen awhile, then throw herself into his arms and passionately kiss him until he stopped trying to reason with her.

Only once did he confide to her one reservation that frightened her.

He wished she weren't American.

He said it one night so seriously and thoughtfully she knew he wasn't joking. If she had been any nationality *but* American, he said, if she had been French or German or even British, he would not still be hesitating. It was then that he told her about his humiliation in Texas last Ramadan. He told her, finally, that the more he studied the oil industry the more he believed that the Americans had exploited his country. For the first but not the last time she heard him say that America must be shown it could not continue to cheat and win forever. He confided his great dream of someday using the wealth of the oil fields to right the wrong balances in the world. Someday, Rashid said, there will be a showdown between my country and yours. Someday, Rashid predicted, my country will make your country pay a terrible price. On that day of mortal judgment, Rashid said, how can I help lead the fight or even speak my piece if I have an American in my bed?

Sunny had shivered as she listened to him. His eyes had gone suddenly too bright, as if he were gripped by a fever. She had put a sweater around her shoulders, and for the first time it had seemed to her that this man of her dreams was more stranger than lover. But then the moment of doubt had passed, and she had swept her own fears aside with more kisses, more sighs, more wanting. She convinced herself she had been silly to take fright at his gloom and doom about oil and the future. She was relieved when, after he told her about those cowboys' making him swallow that beer, he had drawn closer to her. Only a day or two later he had finally given in and said that he too wanted marriage.

Sunny's girlfriends had helped her make the wedding arrangements. They suggested she elope to Vermont and be married by a justice of the peace. One recommended a romantic country inn for the wedding night, and another persuaded her brother to lend his car. The plan was to get married, spend a night together, then register the marriage at the Saudi Arabian consulate in New York. Only when they were signed and sealed by American and Saudi law were they going to present Sunny's grandparents with a consummated fact. The week after, *inshallah*, they would be in Europe for their honeymoon. By the middle of June they would be in Saudi.

Sunny stood beside Rashid as the justice of the peace cleared his throat and asked again if anyone knew of any reason why these two should not be married.

The old man had recited this brief service here in this rural hamlet not far from the Massachusetts border for nigh on to thirty-seven years. He was accustomed to young couples who wanted desperately to share a bed as man and wife. The justice of the peace, however, had eyes and ears. He had noticed that Rashid was not white and that he talked funny and that Sunny was more nervous than most brides. But they had their marriage license.

They were here of their own free will. The girl looked to be eighteen or more. They had that lovers' glow that his wife and his sister-in-law, pressed into their usual duty as witnesses, always found so romantic. This was a quickie wedding like maybe a thousand others he had performed, and so he stifled a yawn and continued on with the service.

Yet Sunny almost stopped the proceedings to blurt out that Rashid already had a wife. If he married her here and now, he would be a bigamist, and in America bigamy was a crime. But Rashid's eyes were so warm and glad and loving, and Rashid's hands, holding hers, were so warm and strong that she waited in silence, forever holding her peace.

They recited their vows, and the justice of the peace pronounced them man and wife.

If they hadn't been able to prove that they were married, Sunny was certain the suspicious man behind the solid oak desk of this quaint and venerable inn would never have rented them a room. He had asked Rashid what kind of a 'furriner' he was, and he hadn't been impressed with Rashid's answer. But the Yankee innkeeper had studied the seal on the Vermont marriage certificate issued at Bellows Falls, he had considered the fact that he had too many empty rooms that night, and reluctantly, after making Rashid pay in advance, he had booked them.

While Rashid went back to the front desk to see about some supper, Sunny remained in their room. She looked out the wide windows at blooming flower beds and rolling pastures and forested mountains, and she wished they were spending their wedding night in a black goat-hair tent at the top of a dune in the burning desert. Then she sank down on the deep softness of the massive double bed covered by a handmade patchwork quilt. She could not resist bouncing once or twice, as a child will just for joy. She considered peeling off her clothes and greeting him stark naked upon his return. She was eager for her first real experience of sex. She had by now almost forgotten the disagreeable shame, but not some of the more agreeable sensations, of that abortive hour with Muhammad in Scollay Square. She wanted to be so uninhibited and passionate that Rashid would never *dream* of touching his other wife again.

To prepare for tonight, she had read some purple passages from D. H. Lawrence's *Lady Chatterley's Lover*, although she had been shocked more by the coarse language than by what the gamekeeper did to the lady after he threw her repeatedly to the floor or the ground. Sunny smoothed down the quilt on her marriage bed. She knew what to expect. The earth would move. It would be like crescendos of symphonic music washing over her, like waves beating on the shore, like trumpets sounding and bells ringing and all the dreams she had ever dreamt all instantaneously coming true. The ecstasy of it would make her swoon into unconsciousness.

She could hardly wait!

She knew she was just going to love sex!

Yet when Rashid strode into their room without knocking, she was still demurely sitting on the edge of the bed, her knees pressed tightly together, wearing all her clothes. She waited expectantly for him to tear those clothes off her. But when he merely told her they would have to go down to the dining room to eat, she put on her jacket and followed him demurely out the door. First they would eat; then they would come together in that nice big bed. He praised the heartiness of her appetite at dinner.

At last they were back in the room together. She took a quick shower, she put on her frilly white nearly transparent negligee, she struck a pose framed in the window with moonlight washing over her so he would be tantalized by the outline of her body. He pulled back the sheets of the bed and slowly discarded all of his clothes as she stood breathlessly watching him. Then he beckoned to her, and she ran to him and felt his naked skin through the thin nightgown. He kissed her on the lips until she was dizzy; then he kissed her throat until she was faint. He kissed her shoulders and pulled her negligee down and kissed her breasts. Slowly he slid the nightgown to her waist and then her hips, and when he finally let it fall to the floor, he held her to him and kissed her, and the erotic thrill of flesh against flesh coursed through them. They sank down on the bed, and he kissed her and held her and told her again and again that he loved her.

As his hands and then his mouth found her breasts, she flushed as she remembered this sensation from that other seductive hour when Muhammad had caressed her on that other hotel bed. Rashid sensed a hesitation in her and, remembering another wedding night with another wife, he tried to be more tender. His lips on her breasts were as gentle as though she were not a woman but a delicate tropic flower that would wilt from rough handling. Passion, he thought, as he adored her with his tongue, could come later, on the eternity of nights and afternoons and mornings of their loving.

For an exquisitely long time he stroked her from her breasts over her soft rounded belly to her knees; then he parted her legs and touched her until she moaned. Finally he whispered endearments to her in Arabic as he slowly lowered himself on her and pushed through her membrane and was finally home inside her. Over and over he murmured her name, he continued to kiss her, he was slow and easy and caressive all the way inside her. He drew out his loving long enough for her to recover from the initial shock and slight pain of his entry, and she could begin to think that he felt good, altogether filling her up. If the earth did not exactly move for Sunny, if symphonies did not quite sound, if the slightest little quiver of orgasm never quite shook her, still this first time with Rashid was warm and sweet and loving. 'My milk!' he whispered urgently to her. When he began to shake with his own climax, she did not understand what was happening. 'Now I give you my milk!' he cried out. Instinctively she wrapped her legs around his buttocks and folded her arms and the essence of herself even closer around him. When his shuddering stopped, she crooned to him. She stroked his hair and felt utterly at peace and at one with all the forces of light in the world.

She wanted only to lie naked in his arms and drift blissfully off to sleep. But Rashid disentangled himself from her arms as he told her that all good Muslims knew it wasn't healthy or decent to fall asleep with all those sexual juices still flowing unwashed between them. Rashid bounded out of bed and into the bathroom to take a brisk shower.

Lying alone on the crumpled sheets, Sunny was a little ashamed that she had liked being bathed in sweat, smelling a yeasty sort of sex smell, with Rashid's milky semen trickling out of her vagina onto her thigh. But as far as she knew, everybody except Lady Chatterley and that gamekeeper took hygienic showers and baths right after sex. Gamely she dragged herself out of bed and stood watching him in fascination under the warm stream of water in the shower. She gazed at his long thick penis and the two round sacs that hung below. She wanted to reach out and touch him there. She wanted to know if he always felt as smooth and fierce and wondrous as when he had been inside her, but she didn't quite dare to touch him yet. Rashid was soaping and rinsing himself as thoroughly as a doctor scrubbing up for surgery. 'Must wash,' Rashid urged her as he finally stepped out with his wet golden skin glistening.

As she stood under the water obediently soaping and rinsing with the fervor Rashid had just shown her she must have, she was embarrassed to sense his eyes assessing her naked body. She darted a glance at him from under her lowered lashes, but she was mortified when she saw him frowning. 'Must shave,' he said as he pointed at her pubic hair. 'All Saudi women shave. Or use cream. Tomorrow I will shave you.' She blushed and hid her offending hair with her hands and wondered why the girls in the dorm hadn't told her she should shave before she got married.

Rashid was sound asleep, snugly encased neck to ankle in a white cotton Saudi robe, by the time she came back to bed. He looked so handsome, so virile and yet so childlike as he slept. He was her husband, her lover, *hers* forevermore. She was so excited by the immensity of that thought that she could not settle down and go to sleep. She would have liked to sleep naked next to him, their hot flesh pressed together all night long. He was wearing a robe, however, and so she followed his example and slipped on her nightgown. But just before she crawled into bed, she saw a spot of red on the sheets. She stared at this bloodstain which had been her hymen, and she sighed. Thank God she had saved herself for Rashid; in a way, too, thanks to Muhammad for leaving her virginity intact. She had a sudden, sentimental inspiration. In the morning she would take a pair of scissors and snip out that pinkish-red blotch from the sheets. She would save her virginity all her life. She would maybe even mount it in a scrapbook. Again she sighed.

As she lay sleepless beside her husband in the deepening night, she allowed herself to compare her two sexual experiences with the Saudi brothers. She had been waiting for Rashid to turn her over and hurt her as Muhammad had. She had been willing to endure even that pain to please her Rashid. But instead of hurting her, Rashid had been infinitely tender. She had liked him touching her everywhere. She had especially liked how earthy and sated and giving it had made her feel when he was inside her. And strong. She had never felt stronger or more powerful than when he had come inside her. There had been such a supreme triumph in having him so close, in finally being not empty but full. She savored the remembrance of that feeling of power and satiety, of hunger and want finally appeased. No wonder people whispered so about sex. No wonder they longed for it, chased it, sometimes turned their lives upside down to get it.

'Rashid!' It was the middle of the night, but she shook him until she roused him. 'Just think, Rashid. We can do this every night for the rest of our lives! Every night! Isn't that wonderful!' Rashid's only answer had been to turn groggily away and to pull the covers over his head and go back to sleep.

Sunny had been hoping that after she woke him he would make love to her again. She had imagined he would let go inside her just as the sun came up, so that they would begin the first dawn of their marriage soldered together. Instead she had to be content to lie beside him reveling in her heady dreams. Rashid was wonderful. He was a wonderful man, a wonderful lover, wonderful in every way. And he was a Saudi. He was taking her back there with him where they would live out the great adventure of their lives together. She hugged herself tightly. She was the luckiest woman on earth. Only twenty years old and already she was well on her way to living happily ever after.

—11—

She had the window seat, and she was sitting with her nose very nearly pressed to the double-layered glass as she looked down from the sky at the desert below. She pointed at the barren landscape. 'We must be over it now, don't you think? That has to be Saudi.' She laughed and corrected herself. 'I mean, "the kingdom." That has to be the kingdom, doesn't it, Rashid?' The closer they had come to Saudi, the more often she had heard it referred to in feudal terms. She liked this new name for Saudi. Kingdoms, she thought, were truly the stuff of fairy tales.

Rashid shot a quick, cautious glance around the cabin to see if any of the Arabs sitting nearby were watching them; then he reached over and took her hand in his. He loved her most for her eagerness, her innocence, her vitality, her lust for whatever came next in the bedroom, on the streets, in this airplane. Possessively he fingered her wedding ring. He could still hardly believe this vibrant American girl was his bride. Tenderly he stroked her hand. He wished there was some way he could insulate her from the inevitable shocks of the next hours and days and weeks. He remembered his own first anxious months in America, and he was certain it would be even harder for her to adjust to life in Saudi. In America he had had to adapt to sudden and overwhelming personal freedom. Here she would have to adjust to a sudden and overwhelming denial of that freedom. As a woman married to a Saudi man, she would have to conform to strict codes. He had told her many times what to expect, but often he had wondered if she had really listened. He sighed. They were man and wife, and so it was too late now to change his mind. He held her hand more tightly and was reassured when she turned and smiled at him.

'Look out there, Rashid! That's Saudi now, isn't it?'

He squinted in the glare. Below them was a desolate wilderness of sand, gravel, and gullies. He looked from the dreary humps of bare brown hills to the drearier stretches of lifeless black lava-land. He consulted his watch and yawned. They were nearly three hours behind schedule. They had left Vienna for Paris on an early-morning flight. Then there had been stops and delays in Rome and Athens and a two-hour refueling stopover in Beirut. They had been back in the air for a little over an hour. Dhahran was still four hours away, on the far side of this vast desert, to the east along the Gulf that used to be called Persian and now had chauvinistically been renamed 'Arabian' by the Saudis. He shook his head. 'Below us I think it is still Jordan. But patience, Sunny. Soon enough we will be in the kingdom.'

Rashid was leaning so tantalizingly close to her that Sunny could not resist throwing her arms around him and kissing him on the lips.

He recoiled and shook her off and looked around to see if anyone had seen her kissing him. Sunny was the only woman on the plane and one of only a few Americans and Europeans. Some of the Arabs wearing long white Saudi robes and head scarves were staring disapprovingly at them. 'We can be seen,' Rashid warned her.

She stared at her husband. She had heard that line before from his brother, when Muhammad refused to hold her hand along the banks of the Charles because they 'could be seen' by couples necking nearby. She was suddenly afraid as she tried to read Rashid's closed, forbidding face. Now that she thought about it, Rashid had seldom even held her hand in public in Boston. She was reassured, however, as she remembered that he had been less inhibited during their honeymoon in Europe. He had put his arm around her as they had strolled through the dark romantic streets of Florence. He had kissed her under lampposts in Paris. And in their favorite place of all, in gloriously schmaltzy Vienna, he had scarcely been able to keep his hands off her. But even before their plane crossed the border into Saudi, Rashid had become more conscious of these Arab strangers than of his own wife.

She settled back in her seat and shut her eyes for a moment as if she were tired. She told herself she had to be wrong about Rashid's withdrawing. Surely he would not fail her just when she was about to need him the most. When they landed today in Dhahran, she would not only be seeing Saudi for the first time but probably also meeting her father. They had wired him their flight number along with the news of their wedding. Rashid had cautioned her that it was possible her father was working so far out in the desert the cable had not yet reached him. But Sunny had convinced Rashid, and herself, that he would be there to welcome her with open arms.

Yet as she sat strapped in her seat beside her silent husband, Sunny's stomach began to churn. What if her father *still* didn't want her, even though she had finally flown to him from a world away? Or what if he were as outraged as her grandparents had been at her marrying an Arab? Gramps had shouted that she needed her head examined. But Sunny had felt worse when Gran broke down and cried. She had never before seen her grandmother cry.

Sunny glanced at Rashid, who was sitting stiffly beside her, staring straight ahead, lost in deep thought about his God only knew what. She tried to wish away her growing dread. Already she knew that Rashid loved her best when she made an extra effort to bubble and enthuse and very nearly fizz with good cheer. But now she felt tired, deflated. She wondered whether it was really getting hot in this cabin or whether she was just imagining the heat because they were flying over the desert. She drowsed off into a fretful sleep.

After a while she heard shuffling noises next to her and her eyelids fluttered open. She saw Rashid standing in the aisle. He was taking his carry-on bag down from the overhead rack and snapping open the lock. Her curiosity was aroused. She rubbed her eyes and watched him lift something black from the small suitcase.

'I thought I would get these ready.' He sat back down. 'I bought them in Paris, on a street where Arabs live.' His voice was unnaturally, nervously high-pitched. 'Maybe you should try them on first before we land? Get used to them? You are the only woman on this airplane. It is necessary maybe to wear them even before we land.'

'Of course.' She was as willing as he was to forget their small misunderstanding. She yawned lazily. 'Wear what?'

He shook out a large square of black fabric. 'The veil.'

She blinked, still groggy from her nap, and willed herself alert. She stared at what he said was the veil. All the books went on so about veiled Arab women. But she must have read them carelessly, for she had never imagined that a real veil would be yards of thick blanketlike material. She picked it up gingerly. It weighed heavy in her hand. She examined it curiously. It was fashioned from a number of thin layers of black filmy fabric sewn together at the hems. She rubbed the veil between her index finger and thumb to see if she could count how many layers were in it. But it had been so tightly packed in Rashid's suitcase that the layers wouldn't separate. She held it up before her and could see no light through it. The veil was not transparent but opaque. She frowned. It occurred to her that it must be terribly hot in Saudi. Black absorbed the heat. A woman would swelter under this. It was absurd, she thought, to swaddle women in hot, heavy blackness. She looked doubtfully at the thick, ugly black veil. Vaguely she had assumed veils would be decorative. She had imagined them as spangly and glamorous and entirely seductive. In the movies veils were alluring scraps of thin netting held over the pouting lips and flared nostrils of gorgeous harem girls. In the movies the girls' come-hither cat eyes were always casting yearning looks above the veil. 'What am I supposed to do with *this*?'

'It is easy. Very easy. Just throw it over your head.' He gave her an encouraging smile. 'Later my mother will teach you to pin it fancy. But now you will try it?'

Sunny liked to think she was willing to try anything. She rolled her eyes and shrugged gamely. 'Here goes!' She braced herself for her first heady whiff of life in the fabulous East. She threw the veil over her head and stifled a cry. The veil was thick and black and heavy she couldn't see through it! 'Rashid!' She experienced a second of utter panic as she groped for him. She was blind under this terrible thing. She could hardly breathe. She felt trapped, smothered, buried alive. When she threw off the veil, she was breathing shakily. The hand that held her veil was trembling.

But Rashid was less intent on his wife than on what he knew had to come next. He nervously offered her a shinier, thicker, sinister black square with dangling ties attached. 'Now the mask.'

'What?' She was still shaken by that hideous veil. She

was still concentrating on catching her breath. 'What did you say?'

'Your mask. To wear under your veil. Or usually just to wear by itself, without the veil, with your *abba* cloak pulled around your head.' When he finally risked a glance at her face, he saw she was taking this every bit as badly as he had feared. He had dreaded the moment when she would have to begin wearing the mask. He, like most Arabs, hated shrill confrontations, especially with women, and so he had postponed this one as long as he could. He had gone one step further and avoided even talking about the painful specifics of masks and veils. But now the moment of veiled truth was upon them. She had to cover her face when they landed in Dhahran. He wished this did not have to be. He was not happy about masquerading his American wife as a tribal woman from the desert. He still believed that the strict Islamic moral codes of Saudi Arabia were the righteous path to Allah, but his years in America had left him ambivalent about some of the consequences of Saudi ways with women. He loved his wild, passionate, free, unpredictable Sunny just as she was. He gloried in being able to talk with her about anything and everything. He didn't want to try to transform her into a caricature of an Arab woman. In time, he hoped, it might not be necessary for Sunny to conform to all the old rules.

But the chaotic airport in Dhahran was a circus, and he did not want Sunny to be one of the sideshows. She must cover her face for her own good. Rashid supposed at least a few of the men of his family would be assembled with Mr. Tom to welcome them. It would create a terrible scandal if he debarked from this giant silver plane with a yellow-haired, barefaced, shameless infidel white woman in tow. The Al-Murrah men would assume Sunny was no better than a prostitute. After an introduction like that, the men of the tribe would never respect her and the women would ostracize her. It was imperative she cover her face before they landed.

Rashid cleared his throat and wished, vainly, that he could explain all this to Sunny in a torrent of persuasive Arabic or even that she understood enough of his country and its customs so that no explanations would be required. He prayed to Allah for the eloquence of sweet words, but instead he was so nervous he had to grope even for words that were hectoring and pompous. 'I told you, Sunny, many times, that you would have to cover your face in my country. In the west of Saudi, in Jeddah and the Hejaz, the veil is enough. But it is different in Eastern Province, where we live, and all along Gulf. Others - men, strangers - could see your face under the veil. That would be very bad. So you wear this.' He held the mask up in his hands. 'We call it *hegab*. See, here are slits for the eyes. And it is more full over the nose to breathe. Very modern design! So! It ties here, and here, in the back.' He tried to hand her the mask. 'You try it now.'

For a long moment she neither spoke nor moved. She was so horrified that at first she could not even think of words that meant 'no.' She shook her head and refused even to touch the mask. 'Oh, no,' she finally said. 'Not me.' But then she smiled. 'I understand. This is a joke.' She laughed weakly. 'Some joke!' She turned away and looked out the window. When she finally turned back to face him, there were tears in her eyes. 'How could you even make a joke about something like this?'

He gnawed on his lip. 'No joke.'

'What do you mean, "no joke"?' Her voice was rising. 'You're crazy if you think I'm wearing that!' The two Arabs sitting in the seats ahead turned around to see what was wrong.

'Sunny, please!' He held his finger to his lips to shush her. He could not have his wife acting like this in public. He would have to bring her under control, and quickly. He took her hands and held them not gently but so tightly his fingers dug into her flesh. His whisper was a hiss. 'I *told* you about this before we were married. I told you in Saudi you would have to cover your face.'

'You never said anything about a mask, Rashid! A goddamn mask!' She didn't care who heard her. She wanted them all to hear her. 'I can't believe it, Rashid! I just can't believe it! You actually expect me to wear a goddamn mask!'

He withdrew his hands from hers. 'Do not speak to me like that,' he said coldly. 'Do not use that language to me. Not ever again.'

'I'll use whatever the hell language I want to use!' Childishly Sunny wished she could swear the worst of all possible curses not only in English but in Arabic. She wanted to scream them out loud so that every goddamn Arab on this plane would hear her. They all probably made their wives wear masks too. Defiantly she raised her voice even louder. She screamed to the heavens. 'Goddamn Arabs!'

For a moment she thought he was going to hit her. He raised his hand, she braced herself, but then he stopped and turned slowly away. He shrank as far as he could from her in his seat, the essence of him left her, and the armrest between them became a high wall. In an instant it seemed to her that the man she loved and married had disappeared. In her husband's place was a sullen, detestable stranger.

Rashid covered his face with his hands and tried to master his emotions. He had never been angry at Sunny before, and although it was mortifying to have his woman act so in front of these other men, he didn't want to be angry at her now. In a few hours they would descend from the airplane together as man and wife. Their marriage would stand or fall on the resolution of fights like the one just begun. The mask and the veil were only the beginning. He reminded himself that he loved this temperamental woman. He tried to be more logical and reasonable than she was apparently capable of being at this moment. He reconstructed exactly what had led to her outburst. She hadn't begun to act hysterical until he had shown her the mask. Did she think this was easy for him? Didn't she know, or care, that his whole family would give him a very hard time about bringing home an infidel wife? He had been away from home for nearly four long years of change and challenge. Did she ever stop to think that *he* was nervous about returning? He had not thought she could be so selfish.

Miserably Rashid held his head in his hands. No use striking out at Sunny. She couldn't help acting like the modern American woman she was. He supposed he would have to accept some of the responsibility for this fight. He had been honest with her about many things about his country, but he had glossed over some pertinent details about the segregation of the sexes. In America he had learned to be a little embarrassed, perhaps even a shade apologetic, about the status of Saudi women. Because Sunny had shown so little curiosity, he had convinced himself she wouldn't mind masks and veils and seclusion.

Rashid lifted his face from his hands, sank down farther in his seat, and turned his back to Sunny. He sighed. It could be that he would have to spend the rest of his married life with this woman trying to control his emotions and rationalize their differences. But still they would remain. It would not be easy for him to forgive or forget her public outburst in front of these men. He experienced another onslaught of doubts about their marriage. Gloomily he wondered if they would be divorced before the year was out. Rashid allowed himself a heartfelt sigh. Eventually, if she expected to spend time off the Aramco reservation and among the Saudi Arabs, she would have to give in about the mask. But today he would be the most reasonable of men. If she was still upset when they landed, he would allow her to wear only the veil and her cloak pulled around her face at the airport.

'I'd just like to know one thing.' Sunny had lowered her voice, but she was still spoiling for a fight. 'Just what the hell do you think this is? Just tell me that!'

He never answered her. He sat silent and still, as if he were asleep. But he was not asleep. He sat brooding next to his unreasonable wife.

Sunny too was still fuming as she looked out the window at the barren desert. 'I'd just like to know what the hell you think this is,' she muttered again, mostly to herself.

In a way, it was the air hostess who gave her the answer. There was a crackle of static over the loudspeaker and finally an announcement in Arabic, in German, in French, and finally in English.

'Welcome to the Kingdom of Saudi Arabia.'

Tom Shannon limped in the hot Saudi sun as he waited for Sunny's plane. He hobbled from the arrival gate outside the Customs Hall out to the spot overlooking the tarmac where he had decided he would have the best view of Sunny debarking. He flopped down into the folding chair he had brought with him and peered up into the cloudless cobalt sky through his black-lensed sunglasses. No sign of it yet. Her flight was predictably late. It would have been wiser to wait back in air-conditioned comfort in an Aramco office and send an Arab over here to keep watch. The boy could have kept pestering the airline for the arrival time and telephoned Tom just before it landed. Tom would have had plenty of time to drive over and be waiting when Sunny emerged from Customs. But Tom had not been able to bear to wait wisely in his office. He had not even been able to stop himself from the madness of arriving two hours before the plane was even scheduled to land. He had sent her away, long ago, for her own good. He had always wanted her near him. He was proving that today by keeping this anxious airport vigil. Anyone, he thought, could look at him and see what a caring father he was. Anyone could see that he loved his daughter. Sentimental tears welled up in Tom's eyes. Finally he would see his princess.

Tom began to make his slow, unsteady progress on his ruined legs back toward Customs. When he had arrived here this afternoon, only the shoeshine man had been waiting by this gate. But now a sweaty, yeasty mass of Saudi men in wrinkled white robes and dusty head scarves stood tightly pressed together against the chain-link fence. Tom nodded to some Arabs he knew by sight if not by name, and then he joined a throng of Al-Murrahs. He exchanged ritualistic greetings with them in his heavily accented Arabic. Neither Tom nor the Arabs mentioned Sunny. In his more than two decades in this country, Tom had learned that women were unmentionable in public. But he wondered if these tribesmen knew his daughter had married their kinsman. He and the Arabs consulted their watches, sighed, shrugged. The Arabs praised God and used their head scarves to mop the perspiration off their faces. Almost six, and still no plane.

Tom decided to try the airline counter again. He massaged his aching legs and finally made it inside the terminal. He tried to be civil as he repeated the question he had been asking this insolent clerk all afternoon. When was Flight Eighteen due in?

The Arab shrugged, murmured '*inshallah*,' yawned, did not even bother to look up from his newspaper. Only when Tom threw down some riyal notes did the clerk grudgingly pass on the latest word, mostly in English. 'Maybe forty minutes. *Inshallah*, maybe more.'

Tom almost shuddered. If a Saudi said something could happen in 'maybe more' than forty minutes, in Western time that could mean two or three hours. Tom had promised himself he would not have a drop to drink before he met her. He had wanted to be cold sober, with no telltale smell of liquor on his breath, when he greeted his princess. He hadn't wanted her to know right off that her old man was not only a cripple but a drunk. But Tom had been waiting here in the hot sun for a very long time; in a way, for twenty years. He could not sweat out these final 'maybe more than' forty anxious minutes without fortifying himself with a drink.

He crept out to the parking lot and climbed into the air-conditioned Chrysler he had borrowed for today only from one of the big shots. He reached into the glove compartment, pulled out the thermos, and looked around to make sure no one was watching. Liquor was illegal in the kingdom these days. Liquor had always been forbidden for good Saudi Muslims, but it had been illegal for the past several years even for ex-patriate Americans. Nothing alcoholic could be legally imported here, sold here, drunk here. As a result, Aramco's employees had learned how to build bathroom and kitchen stills so they could make their own *sadiki* - which meant, most appropriately, 'my friend' in Arabic. Tom could see no one looking his way, so he raised the thermos to his lips and took a long, thirsty pull. This particular batch of homemade gin was more potent than usual, and it burned all the way from his throat to his stomach. Still, it made him feel better. He took another drink, then a third. He looked at his watch again. Time was finally passing more quickly. When he guzzled from the thermos again, some of the gin spilled on his shirt. He wiped his wet lips with his hand, then took another bottle from the glove compartment and gargled with mouthwash. It was time, he decided, to take up his station by the tarmac.

But outside, when the heat hit him, he regretted those drinks in that air-conditioned car. He knew it was deadly to drink that much gin, then go out into the sun. He staggered in the choking heat. He was sweating, his face red, puffing from the exertion of walking in this heat.

At the gate outside the Customs Hall Tom signaled to the shoeshine man. He had paid this man to shine his shoes four times already this afternoon, but again there was a fresh layer of sand encrusted on top of the thickly polished shine. As Tom stood motionless while the man buffed his shoes, he tried to see himself as his Sunny soon would see him. He wished he could believe not only that he had done his best for her today but that she would be proud of him. But Tom was drunk, not blind. He could see that this crumpled beige suit he had bought in Khobar for this occasion was too big in the shoulders and too tight over the hips. He had second thoughts about his efforts to make himself a new man for Sunny today. New clothes couldn't help legs permanently damaged fifteen years ago in that oil-field fire. He felt hot and naked and alien without his usual white *ghutra* head scarf. He had cut himself when he shaved off his bush of a beard this morning, and already the sunburn on his cheeks and chin was smarting. He reeked of the medicinal smell of homemade liquor and mouthwash. One look at him, one whiff of him, and Sunny would know he was a wreck of a man. As he limped back to his vantage point over the runway, there was a weary stoop of defeat to his shoulders.

For a long while Tom stood there shading his eyes, looking westward into the setting sun for Sunny's plane. Finally he saw it winking silver in the light, growing bigger and coming closer, the waiting relatives shouting and pointing, the plane finally circling wide over the Gulf and landing with squeals and thuds and bounces on the concrete. It took an eternity for the Arab workers to roll up the portable stairway, to unlatch the locks and throw open the door. A swarm of excited men surged down the stairway - Saudis in long white robes, Saudis in business suits, other Arabs in cheap cotton shirts and pants. After a pause three disheveled Western men stood poised in the doorway as though unsure whether they wanted to get off here or not. Finally Tom saw a trim, familiar figure in the shadows at the top of the stairway. He caught his breath as he saw Rashid hesitate, reach back, and pull something forward. Tom tore off his sunglasses and squinted until his eyes were slits, but all he could see was a shadowy figure, wearing a long dark skirt that came to the floor, swathed in a shapeless veil and a cloak from her head to below her waist. Rashid helped the veiled woman navigate the steep steps and once, when she stumbled, he caught her in his arms before she could fall. 'Sunny!' Vainly Tom screamed a welcome to his daughter. He waved, he strained to see more of her, he yelled her name again and again until she disappeared inside the terminal.

Tom sank back into his folding chair. He would take his time before joining that unruly mob outside the Customs gate. It would surely take Sunny and Rashid an hour or more to retrieve their luggage and pass through the bureaucratic mazes of Immigration and Customs. He reached inside his pocket and opened his wallet with trembling fingers. He looked at the collection of snapshots his mother had sent him over the years. Sunny in her frilly white First Communion dress. In her Girl Scout uniform. With her horse. In her high school graduation robes. He studied those photographs as if they could tell him how his daughter had gone from here to there to back here again. He had seen her last when she was a baby small enough to hold in a bundle in his arms. Now, bundled in that veil, she was in the arms of a Saudi husband.

Tom wondered where all those squandered years had gone. He dug further into his pocket until he found a creased envelope that held even older, more faded photographs. Tom took a deep breath and looked at all he had left from the happy times. Sally in high school. Sally in her wedding dress. Sally in Saudi. Sally holding Sunny. He forced himself to look at the old photographs, as though they would resolve something unresolved inside him. He shook his head and tucked the past back into the soiled envelope. As if it were yesterday, he remembered why he had sent Sunny away. As if the grief were fresh, he mourned the loss of his Sally. The baby, when she had still been here with him, had only made his loss more bitter. Sunny had been *theirs*, his and Sally's. With Sally gone, the baby had to go as well. With Sally gone, he had devoted the prime years of his life to trying to forget. Still he loved that old Arab story about the doomed lovers Layla and Majnun whose passion survived the grave, who did little with their lives other than love and lose. The long, sad years he had spent since Sally's death, here in his own private Arabian hell, had been parched and shriveled. But in a way these had been perfect years. Perfectly faithful, perfectly mourning, perfectly dedicated to one who was no more.

Tom sat fidgeting on his wooden folding chair, waiting the final moments for the daughter he had sent away as a baby to return to him a married woman. He tried to make himself believe he had been right to devote the prime years of his life to mourning the dead rather than nurturing the living. Tom wiped his eyes. His women had been dead to him for twenty years, but now one of them was being resurrected. He had thought photographs would be the closest he would ever come to Sunny again. So when that telegram had arrived from Boston, he had not known whether the news was punishment or salvation. Sunny coming here as Rashid's wife? His daughter married to Abdullah's son?

Tom was dizzy with drink and heat and excitement. His head ached, and he could hardly bear to think of the bitter ironies of this marriage. In a way, it could be the final manifestation of the ancient life for a life code of Bedouin justice. That day in the Gulf, Abdullah had died because he himself refused to sacrifice the dead body of his own wife. Now, a generation later, his own daughter had been taken by the son of that dead Arab. Was Sunny the final payment for his letting Abdullah die? Was this the ultimate retribution for Abdullah's blood sacrifice?

He had to get hold of himself. He should be glad his daughter had married a young man who was as dear to him as a son.

Tom wiped the sweat off his forehead. All of Rashid's character, integrity, and courage did not alter the fact that he already had an Arab wife. The big block letters of the telegram had not explained away the contradiction of the two wives. He supposed Rashid might already have divorced Nura. It was easy enough for Muslims to divorce unwanted wives. But the Rashid Tom knew and loved could never discard that Arab girl so callously. What kind of man would Rashid be if he snapped his fingers to rid himself of one wife just to make room for another?

As Tom sat on the folding chair and watched the round orange ball of the sun sink toward the horizon, his thoughts strayed to that other major worry. Rashid was an Arab and Sunny an American. It would not be easy for the two of them to be man and wife here, whether they lived in the American compound at Dhahran or among the Arabs in any of the nearby towns. The Americans and the Arabs lived in segregated worlds. Yet Tom had used the weeks since the arrival of the telegram to try to integrate a new world for his daughter and her husband. Rashid's own position in Aramco would be exceptional. There were few Arabs with 'senior staff' status, even though the company was publicly committed to training and hiring a new generation of Arab supervisors. Although Rashid's education had won him a good job, Aramco had still not decided how a rare Arab like Rashid should be treated off the job. Tom had argued that Rashid was entitled to a bungalow inside the 'senior staff' compound. But when the housing supervisor had equivocated that no such housing was available, Tom had lost his Irish temper. Twice in the past few years, Tom had reminded him, rioting Saudi workers had charged that imported American workers were paid more and lived better than native Arab citizens. Even though the Arabs had been assured by King Saud and Aramco that eventually they would earn the same wages and share the same living standards, so far those promises had not been kept.

Tom had insisted that Rashid must have the senior-staff bungalow to which he was entitled, but the housing supervisor reminded him that many American husbands came out here alone at first and had to wait for a year or more before they were assigned houses and could send for their families. But when Tom persisted, the supervisor had finally offered a compromise of sorts. He could still not assign a house to Rashid, but he could assign a very long overdue two-bedroom unit to the family of Tom Shannon. Tom had wanted to hold out, on principle, for Rashid's being assigned a house in his own right. But all these negotiations over where the newlyweds would live had taken time, and Sunny and Rashid had been due in only a few more days. He had finally agreed to have 'his family' stay temporarily in a house whose tenants were away on leave. Tom had tried to take pleasure in at least his partial success at being a good father. He had lined up an Indian cook who could come in five days a week and a gardener. He had checked personally to see that the sheets on the bed were fresh and the kitchen stocked with food. He had bought them what would pass for a wedding cake, and in the refrigerator was an iced bottle of apple juice euphemistically known as 'Saudi champagne.' He had even arranged a small reception for the two of them tomorrow.

Tom lurched to his feet when he heard a howl from the mob outside Customs. He craned his neck to see if the passengers were coming out yet, but then he settled back in his chair when he saw it was simply an argument over who stood where in line. He hoped Sunny wasn't having too bad a time of it inside the terminal. Saudi bureaucrats were notoriously slow and puffed up with their own importance.

Tom stared at the closed door of the terminal. He had heard stories over the years about Aramco workers who arrived at Dhahran airport and were so appalled by the heat and the chaos that they turned right around and left the kingdom on the same plane. He prayed that that would not happen now.

At last Tom heard a sort of moan from the crowd. The passengers were starting to emerge, but still Tom hung back. Saudi men were the first ones out, and joyous knots of kinsmen escorted them off to the parking lot. Bewildered Americans and Europeans were greeted by their Arab guides.

Tom took a deep breath and walked toward the gate. He had known Rashid would keep his wife as far apart from the throng as possible. Tom removed his sunglasses and stood at the head of the crowd of Al-Murrahs. Finally

Rashid emerged from the fastness of the terminal and was immediately swamped by his tribesmen. But then Rashid broke away and waved, calling, 'Mr. Tom!' Rashid took a step toward him, but Tom was looking at the one Rashid was leading by the hand.

Sunny walked slowly behind her husband. She placed one foot gingerly in front of the other and followed blindly wherever Rashid was leading her. Since she had gone into the lavatory and donned this veil just before landing, she had seen nothing but indistinct shapes and high fences and mysterious barriers. She had been utterly dependent on her husband to steer her to safety, and she had felt helpless and fearful alone in her own shadow world.

But now, as Rashid let go of her hand, as she heard her husband call out her father's name, Sunny knew she was alone no longer. She was about to see him. She was about to be with her father.

Sunny seemed to stare at her father through the thickness of the veil. Slowly, then, she threw off her cloak and lifted her hand and pulled back the curtain of the veil. Just in front of her stood a sunburnt, weather-beaten, grizzled old man. His clothes didn't fit him right, he reeked of liquor, but to Sunny all that mattered was the shine of recognition, of gratitude, of deliverance in his eyes.

Tom gasped, and as he stared at this vibrant, rosy, blooming young girl, for him time receded. 'Sally!' He stumbled a step toward the apparition. 'Sweet Jesus, Sally!'

She reached out for the father who, finally, she was sure loved her. She cradled the lost treasure of her father in her arms.

12

Sunny took a deep breath, but the hot, humid, dusty morning air of Dhahran seemed to stick in her craw. She stood on the stoop of the Aramco bungalow, raised her hand to knock on the door, but instead nervously smoothed out her new floor-length black cotton Arab robe where it stuck to the sweaty skin beneath her breasts and armpits. She ran her finger along the pink flowers embroidered on the bodice and smiled, remembering how irresistible she had found this robe when she and her father had spotted it fluttering above their heads like a flag of exotica in a nearby souk. A merchant had climbed to the top of his stall to get it, and she had buried her face in its rough scratchy fabric, fragrant with cinnamon and cloves and musk and mystery. But now, as she hesitated here this morning, reluctant to face a handful of possibly hostile American wives, the robe's black magic did not seem to be working. She wondered if she was dressed right, if they would like her, if they would invite her back and ask her to join their clubs.

Sunny resented having to care so much about what these women might think of her. She did not want to need the women who waited on the other side of this closed door. She had not come halfway around the world to ingratiate herself with a pack of small-town housewives. She had thought she was forever leaving America behind when she had climbed into that pressurized airplane cabin at Idlewild. But three weeks among Dhahran's homesick expatriates had taught her that instead of leaving American conventions behind she had come to their tabernacle. Here in the desert Aramco had constructed a sanitized, air-conditioned, prefabricated make-believe American bubble complete with bridge clubs, softball teams, garden clubs, bowling leagues, and - Sunny suspected - the narrowest of small-town attitudes.

She had thought Saudi would be a sensual assault of palpitating marvels and luscious surprises, but so far the only surprise had been how ordinary and confining life was here in Dhahran. Sunny supposed it had taken longer than it should have for this disappointing reality to sink in, but at first she had been entirely wrapped up in finally being with her father. He had taken two weeks off from his job, and they had spent it talking, laughing, shyly confiding, trying to make up for the lost years. He was different from the way she had imagined he would be - smaller, gentler, less a mountain than a dear worn eroded hill. Yet this father of hers was warm and sweet and good. She loved the way his eyes glowed like the last live embers of a desert campfire when he talked about the Arabs. And she was thrilled at how he would always lean lovingly toward her, as though he yearned to protect her from all that was menacing in life, even when they were doing something as safe as sitting snug on a sofa.

But Sunny could see that her father was a troubled man. He drank too much and was an outcast among the other Americans. Her father had such tragic eyes. Sometimes when he shook his head and teared up and said she was the spitting image of his Sally, Sunny longed to comfort him as if she were his all-forgiving mother instead of only his long-lost daughter. She missed him when he had to go back to his work in the desert, and she began to wilt with boredom in Dhahran. Their houseboy cleaned and shopped and cooked their meals. The books she had sent from America had not yet arrived. When Rashid was with her, he was tender and passionate and more relaxed than he had ever been in America. But he was not with her for too much of the time. Just as he had warned her, Rashid was putting in long hours away from her not only at his Aramco job but with his Arab family and his business and his tribe. So far, except for a few shopping expeditions into Khobar with her father, she had not even been outside the high chain-link fence of the compound. It was the law in Saudi that women, even American wives with valid drivers' licenses from Illinois and Texas and Indiana, were not allowed to drive cars outside the confines of Dhahran. She could not escape what she was beginning to regard as her Aramco kennel unless her father or her husband escorted her as if she were a dog on a very short leash.

Sometimes, in the early evenings, if Rashid was off somewhere, she would wander the perimeter of the fence and stare out at the beckoning wilderness. The desert, lit by the whooshing gas burn-off flares, was so tantalizingly close. She longed so to break out and explore that enticing world. She wanted to lose herself in those high undulating dunes which surely must be just beyond the horizon. She yearned to live in a black tent. She wished she could ride camels and herd goats and sit beside a campfire and belch as Arabs always did in the movies when they wanted to show that yes indeed they had enjoyed that feast of roasted camel or boiled goat. Already she had learned, however, that it was going to be harder than she had thought to go native. Rashid had made one excuse after another to avoid introducing her to his family. First he had said that everyone was far out in the desert, camped by the Al-Murrah wells in the Empty Quarter. Then he had said she must wait because the new house he was building in Khobar wasn't quite ready yet. Then, after he had returned from an entire week alone with his family in the desert, he had said this wasn't the right time to take Sunny out to meet them all because his mother was sick. When Sunny had continued to press him, Rashid had said it would be better to wait until the house in Khobar was finished, and then he had launched into an elaborate explanation of the manifold problems with plumbers and pipes and polluted water and the fixtures for the toilets. When Sunny had finally made him understand that she preferred to meet his family out in the desert - that she itched to get away from this Aramco reservation, that it was ridiculous that she had not yet really met any Arabs in

Saudi Arabia - Rashid had come out with his lamest excuse of all. 'It is too hot,' he had said, masterfully, as if the finality of those words must end all discussion.

But Sunny had refused to take the hint. She had sweetly reminded him it was only July and that therefore it would doubtless be very hot here for many months more. Surely he did not expect her to wait until winter to meet his family? Rashid had laughed and kissed her and stroked the inside of her thighs to distract her. But when she had refused to melt on cue, he had turned away and sat down and opened his favorite copy of the Koran and flatly, before he immersed himself in religious meditation, told her she must work harder to develop the celebrated Arab art of patience. She had stood there helplessly watching him shut her out. He was her husband and she loved him, and she was determined to grit, even grind, her teeth if that would make her a perfect wife to him. And so she had tried not to be jealous and angry and suspicious when Rashid didn't even offer her any explanations about what he had or had not done with his first wife in the desert. Sunny had wanted to believe that when he was away from her overnight he was talking to his mother or meeting late at night with the tribesmen or drilling water wells at dawn. But lying alone in their double bed in Dhahran, Sunny knew precisely why Rashid had not taken her to meet his family. It was that other woman - that Nura. He would not discuss Nura with her. Sunny didn't even know what she looked like, although she fervently hoped Nura was a snaggle-toothed old hag, someone she could pity, someone Rashid could not *possibly* love.

Sunny stood baking under the relentless sun, wishing she were anywhere but here, wishing for any worry but this one. She could not bear to think of Rashid in the arms of that other woman. She could not bear it.

Sunny told herself that this was neither the time nor place to obsess herself about Nura. She had a more immediate problem. She had to do her best to make friends with these Aramco housewives. Sternly Sunny reminded herself not to be supercilious. Like it or not, she needed the friendship of these American women. She had been first introduced to some of them at the reception her father had arranged the day after they arrived. But what Sunny chiefly recalled was the singular triumph of standing there flanked by her husband and her father. Only very dimly, from the radiance of that afternoon, did she remember Mary Lou Simmons, a red-haired, freckled, motherly older woman who had offered to hold a morning 'coffee' to introduce Sunny to the other 'gals.'

At the time, however, Sunny remembered with some trepidation, she had been a little haughty with Mary Lou. She had not thought that Mary Lou, or any of the Americans, especially middle-aged American women who called themselves 'gals,' would be even slightly important to her. She had thought she would make Arab friends in this Arab country. But this past week, standing uncertainly out on the sidewalk after Mass, she had smiled a frozen smile at all the Americans who had coursed past her. She had haunted the supermarket looking vainly for a friendly face. Then finally she had decided her solitary confinement had gone on long enough. With a sense of desperation she had telephoned Mary Lou and gushed that she was ever so eager to meet the other 'gals.'

Sunny knocked hesitantly on the closed door. Finally she heard a slap of sandals, and the door was thrown open by a small, elderly Pakistani houseboy who grinned toothlessly at her as he ushered her into the living room.

Above a babble of voices coming from the far end of the bungalow, Sunny heard a woman's Midwestern twang. 'Who's that, Moe?'

'Missee . . . ?' He cocked his head at Sunny.

'Sunny Shannon. I mean Al-Murrah. Mrs. Al-Murrah.'

'Eh!' The houseboy shouted to the lady of the house. 'The daughter of Majnun!'

Sunny decided the houseboy must not have understood her over the humming of the air conditioner. 'It's Sunny,' she called out. 'Sunny Al-Murrah. Tom Shannon's daughter?'

'Bring her out to the kitchen, Muhammad.'

Sunny followed the houseboy through a living room that, with its Sears-catalogue brown Danish-modern couch and chairs, its brown-toned floral rug, its maple coffee table, its china lamps painted with a design of rosebuds, was first cousin not only to the decor in the bungalow assigned to her and Rashid but to her grand-parents' parlor back in Still River. It depressed her that in this room there was not the slightest clue that they were not in Illinois or Massachusetts but in the Kingdom of Saudi Arabia. There was nothing inherently wrong with Sears or Illinois or Massachusetts. Yet she scorned this living room which could easily have won the Good Housekeeping Seal of Approval. She, a woman of high romance and infinite daring, had not followed the love of her life halfway around the world only to be smothered in the clichés of small-town America. Reminding herself she had to make friends, any friends, Sunny managed to paste a smile on her face.

As the houseboy threw open the kitchen door, she saw a tableful of women drinking coffee and eating cakes. Mary Lou Simmons rose and smiled and took her hand in greeting, but Sunny looked at her with a kind of horror. Mary Lou was wearing a cute pink candy-striped cotton shirtwaist, high heels, and stockings. Sunny glanced at the other women. Every one was dressed in a pastel shirtwaist, a seersucker skirt and blouse, or color-coordinated separates. Too late Sunny remembered that at her wedding reception the Aramco women had been gussied up like farmers' wives at church. On the streets of Dhahran too the women had been dressed demurely, sweetly, girlishly. Sunny wished she could back out of this room and run home and change her clothes; but then she remembered that she had packed more exotic plumage, dramatic long dresses mostly, and sensational red lacy and black satin lingerie. The rebel in her felt proud of her unconventional wardrobe, but the rest of her longed to blend in so she wouldn't be so lonely anymore. She smiled, she hoped disarmingly, and said she guessed she was dressed all wrong.

'Never you mind.' Mary Lou smiled a maternal smile. 'First time out to Khobar, every single one of us wasted good American dollars on one of those cheesy robes.' Mary Lou picked at a loose thread on the sleeve, and Sunny watched as the seam began to unravel. 'See! Didn't I tell you? It'll shrink, too. But don't you worry about looking peculiar, honey. You just sit down here now, and have some coffee, and meet the gals.'

Sunny sat and sipped and smiled fixedly while Mary Lou made the introductions.

'Gert's from Texas, and she has twins. Ellen's from California, and she has two boys and a girl. June's from Oklahoma, and as you can see, she's just about ready to have her baby, her very first. Alma's from Texas, and her kids are all grown up and live back in the States. Peg's from Texas too, and she has three little ones. And Kathy's from . . . I don't remember where Kathy's from.'

'California.' Kathy finished her history. 'And I have six. Four girls. Two boys. And believe me, there are absolutely no more on the way.'

Sunny politely joined in the laughter. 'So.' These ladies seemed as alike as cookies from the same cutter. 'So! Well! I'm from Massachusetts. And I just got married.' She giggled nervously. 'I'm not even pregnant. At least not yet, I don't think! Ha! So! Mary Lou!' Sunny's panicked mind was mostly blank, and so she was as surprised as everyone else at the table to hear what came out of her own mouth. 'So what do you think of Colonel Lawrence?'

'Who?' Mary Lou squinted in confusion at Sunny.

'I think she must mean that guy in Accounting,' Ellen said. 'You know, his wife was playing bridge at Jenny's last week. Her daughter's in my Linda's Girl Scout troop. That the one you mean? Jim Lawrence? Nice guy. How do you know Jim?'

'I don't, exactly.' Sunny was apologetic. 'I meant Colonel T. E. Lawrence. Lawrence of Arabia? The British leader who united the Arabs during World War One? In the Hejaz? He was one of my heroes when I was a kid, but you know there's this big controversy about whether he was really a hero or just an exploiter of the Arab cause. And I've been thinking about him a lot since I arrived here. Or rather, thinking about his book. *Seven Pillars*? Lawrence's book?' Sunny fervently wished she had in fact asked the gals about Jim Lawrence instead of the colonel. 'But enough of that! So! Mary Lou! You've been here in Dhahran how long?'

'Since '48. Almost ten years.'

'That's a really long time.' Sunny sought urgently for common ground. Friends - she had to make friends. 'Of course not as long as my father. He's been here since '34.'

'No one's been here as long as Old Majnun.' Gert laughed. 'No one's wanted to.'

Sunny recognized the word she had first heard from the houseboy. 'What did you call him? Old - what?'

'Majnun.' Mary Lou poured her more coffee.

'You don't know Arabic? Married to a sand nigger, I hear, and you can't even talk like the ragheads?' Gert grinned wolfishly at Sunny. '*Majnun* means "the crazy one." It's your father's nickname. He even calls *himself* that.'

Mary Lou saw the hurt on Sunny's face. 'No one's laughing at your dad, honey. And nobody's saying he's nuts. The name has something to do with an Arab legend. Some sad old love story, as I remember it. Romantic. You'll have to ask your dad all about it.' She squeezed Sunny's hand.

Gratefully Sunny smiled at Mary Lou. Carefully she ignored bitchy Gert. She tried to gather her scattered wits as she sipped her coffee. 'Sand nigger!' 'Raghead!' Was that what they called Arabs here? And they called her father 'the crazy one'? Sunny was not altogether listening when a woman in pearl-toned glasses began telling her all the recreational possibilities of Dhahran - the swimming in the Gulf at Half Moon Bay or in one of the pools, the tennis and the golf and the boating, the classes in crafts and cards and gardening. But she did hear Mary Lou mention something about a riding club.

'Horses?' Sunny's heart leaped. 'You have horses here?'

'The best Arabians in the world.' Mary Lou seemed relieved that finally she had found a niche for Sunny. 'I'll take you over to the stables one day soon.'

Sunny was just about to tell Mary Lou about Princess Camey when Kathy, who could stand to wait no longer, blurted out what was on the tip of all their tongues. 'So you actually *married* an Arab.'

'Tell us about it.' Alma leaned forward in excitement. 'We've all been wondering. What's it like?'

'Does he make you wear a mask at home?'

'And walk twenty paces behind him?'

'Does he beat you? I hear they all beat their women.'

'I suppose it was inevitable this would happen someday.' Gert's eyes were cold. 'First we let them come to America, go to our schools, live in our cities. Then they run after our women. Pretty soon they'll be raping us right here in our own houses.'

'Gert!' Again Mary Lou patted Sunny's hand. 'Now, honey, don't you let Gert here upset you. She's having a hard time of it. Her husband was all set for a big promotion, and they were going to celebrate with a long trip all through Europe, and then a whole lot of new wells came through, and his vacation was cancelled, and they're stuck here for the whole summer.' Mary Lou hesitated. 'And he didn't get that promotion he'd been promised, either.'

'Why don't you tell her the whole truth?' Gert glared at Sunny. 'Billy Joe got cheated out of what was due to him. They gave his job to a sand nigger. A very special and very uppity sand nigger. Someone near and dear to your heart.'

Mary Lou struggled valiantly to keep the peace. 'Gert's

not herself, Sunny. She's homesick, the weather's been bad -'

'I've had it up to here with this place.' Gert made a choppy gesture with her hands at her forehead. 'And I'm not alone. Why pretend we're happy little housewives sitting at a kitchen table back in Kansas? We hate it here, we all hate it. You know what we always say, Sunny? S.A.U.D.I. stands for Savage, Arrogant, Uncouth, Dirty, and Ignorant!'

'That's enough, Gert.' Mary Lou tried to change the subject. 'So what's new back in the States?'

'New?' Sunny frowned as the homesick women chorus-ed questions about the latest fads in clothes and movies and music and slang. She tried to block out Gert and all she had said as she struggled to give them some kind of answers, even though she doubted if her rendition of contemporary American bohemian tastes was what they had in mind. She longed for some pleasant social excuse to get up and say goodbye and never have to endure another morning like this. Yet still it wasn't over. Mary Lou had made another pot of coffee, and Kathy was asking her if she had met her husband's Arab family yet, and Sunny was stiffly answering that she hoped to very soon.

'He'll probably take you to a "goat grab"!' June laughed. 'That's what we call an Arab meal, even though it's usually sheep that they eat. They cook a whole lamb and bring it all out on a big tray on top of a mountain of real greasy rice, and everyone uses his right hand to grab hunks of burnt meat. I went once, and we took a lot of photographs to show everyone back home. But the Lord only *knows* what diseases you could pick up eating like that! I wouldn't touch a bite. I told my George not to eat any either, but he did, said he had to, that it would have been insulting not to. He got so sick he was off work for a week!'

Sunny smiled and nodded and laughed as the others traded similar stories of their brief brushes with Arab life. None of them spoke Arabic or had Arab friends. Mostly they stayed inside the compound pretending they were still back in America. Sunny supposed that most of these women were good wives, good mothers, and good company for one another, but she doubted that any of them ever could be a good friend to her. She felt so different - too different. It hurt that she didn't think they liked her any more than she did them. Back home in Massachusetts, people had always said she was a nice girl, that she had a great sense of humor, that she was sweet and down-to-earth and gutsy and fun to be around. How could it be these women around this table didn't like her?

'See here, Sunny.' Gert cleared her throat. 'I think it's time we got down to brass tacks. I'm a Christian woman, and I think it's time we all did you a Christian service. How much do you actually *know* about this husband of yours?'

Sunny did not look up from her coffee cup. There was a residue of mud in the bottom, and she remembered how Rashid said Al-Murrah women could read the future from the shape of that silt. She didn't have to be able to read the coffee grounds to know she had no future around kitchen tables like this. She was just about to stand up and make her farewells when Gert dropped her bombshell.

'They say he has another wife!'

Sunny was stunned. She raised her eyes slowly and stared back at the waiting women. She could tell they had all known about Nura. Even before she walked into this kitchen, every one of them had known Rashid had another wife. No wonder they didn't like her. Sunny bought some time by pouring herself more coffee, adding some cream, stirring in some sugar. As she blew on the hot brew and took a small careful sip, she reflected that she had probably never had a chance to make friends with these women. They might have forgiven her for marrying an Arab, but she could tell by the scandalized looks on their faces that they would never be able to accept her being the *second* wife of an Arab. Sunny thoughtfully sipped her coffee. Tomorrow she would go out to the stables. Even if the people in the riding club gave her the cold shoulder, at least she could make friends with the horses. She would fill up the empty hours swimming by herself in the Gulf and walking the perimeter of the fence and writing wonderful letters home. She began to wonder about the wonderful letters her own mother had once written home. Had her mother too endured this same loneliness? Sunny wiped her lips with an imported American paper napkin. 'It's getting late.' She stood. 'Thanks for having me over, Mary Lou, but I really have to go.'

'Not so fast.' Gert stood and faced her. 'We want to know if you knew all the time. Did you? Did you know about his other wife?'

Sunny gathered the tattered shreds of her dignity. 'That, I'm afraid, will have to remain one of life's little mysteries.' With great aplomb, she sailed past the Pakistani houseboy and out the front door. It wasn't until she was back inside the security of her own borrowed bungalow that she broke down and began to cry.

Rashid solemnly gave her another chance to back out. 'You are certain you wish to do this?'

Sunny nodded and meekly tied on the first of the mask's three ties. She had vowed she would never tie these hateful ties, but now, after only five weeks in Saudi, she was too worn down and disappointed to fight this particular fight any longer. Finally, after listening to Rashid's repeated evasions, she had realized she would have to wear the mask if she was ever to meet his family.

The third tie pressed it tight against her skin from forehead to chin. The gummy heavy taffeta itched, and Sunny wondered if her skin would erupt in an outraged allergic rash. She would have loved to rip off this mask and shred it to black confetti. But the mask had become her passport. After that abortive debut two weeks ago with the Aramco wives, she had been realist enough to admit she had nowhere else to go but, masked and veiled, to the

Arabs. Rashid, however, had not been so philosophical. Gert's words had reopened his own festering wounds cut years ago by those Texas cowboys. He had fumed and shouted and vowed a blood-price to avenge Sunny's honor. She had barely been able to restrain him from storming up to Gert's husband to demand, at the very least, a public apology. That night Rashid had held her close and buried his head in her soft breasts and admitted he didn't know how long he could endure the strain of living like this, inside the American compound apart from his own people and yet apart, too, from the Americans. He dreaded going to work every morning, for he was a division head, the first token Arab to rise much above the illiterate labor gangs. Americans chafed at taking orders from a 'raghead,' and Arabs resented that one no better than themselves had been elevated above them. As the first of his people to be given rank and command, he must always be better and smarter and more resilient than the Americans who technically were his peers. If he failed, he was betraying not only himself but all Arabs.

Rashid had whispered in anguish to Sunny that he was not born to live like this, that he was born to live free in a tent in the desert. She had held him as if their happiness depended only on how tightly and tenderly she could hold him in her arms. She had tried, then, to make him feel better by minimizing how much the company wives had hurt her. She had declared that she didn't care about those women, that she couldn't change them, that she wasn't sure she even wanted to try. She had allowed herself the release of despairing tears only one more time, when Rashid was at work. But then she had dried her eyes and put the scene in Mary Lou's kitchen behind her. If the Americans wouldn't accept her, she would have to do whatever she had to do to win a kind of acceptance from the Arabs. If that meant wearing a hot and itchy - so ugly! - mask, then so be it.

Sunny walked over to the bedroom mirror, stood inches away from her reflection, and stared through the eye slits at the dark shape that must be herself. She did not look human. Involuntarily she shook her head, and her gold earrings and gold necklaces shimmered. She lifted her hand and touched the gold jewelry her father had sent her on her sixteenth birthday. Rashid had insisted she wear all of it today when she finally met his family. The cold thick jangling gold looked tawdry and somehow pagan framing her masked face. She was glad her father wasn't here to see her now.

Rashid impetuously came up behind her, turned her around, and tenderly took her head between his hands. 'No mask for you, my Sunny.' He reached for the ties. 'You are an American woman. The mask is too hard for you.' He untied the first of the ties. 'You stay here. I will not be gone long. Three days only. A short trip out to the summer wells where my grandfather camps. That is all. I will come back to your bed after only three nights.'

Sunny stiffened and pulled away from his embrace. Three nights with Nura? She would be damned if she willingly sent her husband to her rival's bed for three endless nights. She wasn't going to let the mere wearing of a few black folds of fabric keep her from finally confronting that mysterious other woman. Besides, she knew now that if she was ever to break out of the boundaries of this Aramco reservation, she would have to go masked. Firmly she retied the knot.

Still he tried to talk her out of it. 'It is because of what that horrible Gert said to you, no? I think not all the women are like that. When your father comes back to Dhahran we will talk. Mr. Tom knows many people here. Others will invite you to coffee. Nice women. Friends for you. You can be happy here. It is not necessary to –'

'Do I have to put the veil on today too?'

He sighed in resignation. 'Not this morning. But take it with you. Maybe later, when we arrive, you can wear it too.'

Sunny turned away from him. She slipped her heavy black *abba* robe over her floor-length red dress, the darkness descended, and it was done. Rashid took her in his arms. He muttered endearments she could not quite hear; then he led her out the front door and settled her in the back seat of the car as solicitously as if she were an invalid. Rashid climbed in the front next to his driver. The car sped off in the gray dawn for the short jaunt to the airport where the light plane was waiting to take them off toward the red sands of the Empty Quarter.

Sunny felt the hot morning air streaming in the open windows, and as the car accelerated, a fine rain of sand pelted against her veil. She slumped in her seat to protect herself and tried to imagine how she must look, a bundle of black, prone like a dead body on the back seat. She could hear but could neither see nor understand Rashid and the driver small-talking in Arabic. Rashid had told her he would not speak to her in front of the driver, who was not a relative, merely an employee of his water-well-drilling company. Sunny tried not to think dark thoughts. She had made her choices, and now she would have to make the best of them.

Rashid had sat her down yesterday and once again, at great length, coached her in the customs of his tribe. How to nose-kiss a relative. How to eat with only her right hand, and how to wash herself with only her left. How she must sit on the carpet with her legs tucked under her and never angle the soles of her feet toward another's face. When to sit back and be silent, and when to raise her voice in praise of Allah's mercy. Mostly, however, Rashid strove to make her understand the elaborate rules of etiquette regarding the seclusion of women. Only when she was out in public - on the streets of Khobar, in an automobile or an airplane, or when male strangers came to visit the family tents in the desert - would she have to put on her mask. When she was camping in the desert among the tents of her own family, she could raise her bare face to the sun.

Rashid had told her it was only four miles from Dhahran to the airport, but to Sunny it seemed this journey would never end. She tried to convince herself it wasn't so bad to lie like baggage in this back seat. She would have to put up with this darkness for only a little while, until they landed out in the Al-Murrah encampment. But then the driver took a hairpin turn too recklessly, and Sunny shrieked when she nearly rolled off the seat. She struggled up to a more dignified sitting position. As she endured the stings of the lashing sand, for the first time she let herself doubt not only the wisdom of wearing this infernal mask but of marrying Rashid and coming to this bewildering kingdom. She considered the possibility that Gert and those other Americans knew more than she did about the Arabs. No, she reassured herself hastily - too hastily. She was embarked on a great romantic adventure, and she was going to continue to love it. Under her mask she gritted her teeth.

The car bumped from asphalt to an oil-slick road, then back onto asphalt, and there was a hurried consultation at the airport checkpoint.

Finally the car accelerated with a flourish before it braked one last sudden time. Sunny heard the car doors being opened, and then Rashid was helping her to her feet. She was disoriented and dizzy, but she did not dare to rip off the mask to get her bearings. She let Rashid guide her forward over the tarmac, then up a short metal staircase, and then she heard Americans greeting Rashid and telling him which seats to take in the small aircraft. They would be taking off as soon as everyone was strapped in. She sat where the pressure of Rashid's arm indicated she should. He buckled her belt. She sighed and peered out at the dim shapes in the shadowy cabin. It was odd that she was here and yet not here, that the pilot and the copilot had not said hello to her. She supposed that in time her eyes would adjust to the lack of light, that pretty soon she would be able to see out almost as though there were no barriers between herself and all the world. Silently she prayed for that wondrous moment of revelation to come to her soon, please God, soon. In the meantime she sweltered. She was glad when she felt Rashid take her hand in his. She clung to his hand as the engine started a terrifying bucking vibration, and the plane taxied down the runway perilously fast and finally was up trembling precariously in the air.

Over the scream of the engine, Rashid shouted in the direction of her ear. 'Very exciting, no? More exciting than the big jet from America.'

Was she married to a madman? she wondered. This vulnerable little plane was obviously seconds away from a fiery crash in the desert. She wished she had never agreed to come. Or that she had insisted they travel to his grandfather's camp by truck, even if it did take more than ten hours to get there. 'How long?' she whispered. 'How long till we land?'

'Very quick. Up, down. Less than one hour. We are very lucky Aramco was flying in our direction with supplies for drilling camps. Relax.' He leaned over and slid her cloak down to her shoulders, untied her mask and peeled it off. He smiled at her. 'The pilots are too busy with their work to look at you. So no mask until we land, okay?'

'You bet.' She smiled at him and turned her bare face and dared to look out the window. The earth, dangerously far below them, was a vast sea of uninhabited, chilling, grayish, dirty-looking sand. But as they flew southwest, with the rising sun creeping up behind them, before her eyes the drifting sands seemed to be lighted by purple and pink and mauve fires from one end of the horizon to the other, until they flew over a world stained violent blood red. Ahead she spied the great heaving monster dunes that were hundreds of feet high rippling, it seemed, to beyond the end of the world. 'Rashid! Look! It's beautiful!'

'You like it? You like my people's land?' He laughed and leaned over her to point toward the dunes and the red sands. '*Al-Raml* - "The Sands" - is what we Al-Murrah call them. But the foreigners all call our desert the "Empty Quarter" - *Rub al-Khali*. Is a very big desert, Sunny. Al-Murrah lands are as big as France.'

'I know. I read all the books by the explorers who

crossed them. Bertram Thomas and Philby in the 1930s, Thesinger just a few years ago. It was the last land to be explored in Arabia. The last frontier.'

'You think your Philby and the others *found* these lands here? No! My people were here forever, crossing it north, south, everywhere. We live here. Is our home. Even I, Rashid, know these lands as well as I know your body! Then one foreigner comes, pays bandits much gold to guide him, spends maybe one month in the great sands, and everyone in America and England call him a very big hero. This I do not understand, my Sunny. Tell me why this is so.'

'*Shamsa.*' She looked adoringly at him. 'Call me by my Arabic name now, Rashid. Make me "Sunny" in Arabic, *min fadlak* - "Please."'

'*Shamsa!* Yes! You make me very happy!' His eyes glowed black and his teeth flashed white against his dark skin. 'So, Shamsa, I shall tell you where we go today, yes?' When she nodded, he waved his arms excitedly to take in all the lands below them. 'All this is Al-Murrah country. My tribe has more land than any other in Arabia, but we are one of the small tribes, maybe only fifteen thousand of us for maybe quarter of a million square miles. Much of our land is very dry desert, and so Al-Murrah are called *bedu al-bedu*, "the nomads of the nomads." But in the dry desert we must move our tents to get pastures or water for our camels. We have the best camels in all Arabia. Very famous camels, Al-Murrah. So! In the winter, when the camels need water maybe only every six weeks, we go north, sometimes all the way to Kuwait or southern Iraq, to get the good grazing from the rains. In the spring and in the fall, we move from place to place, hoping for sometimes rain. But in the summer, when it is so very hot and the camels need to have water maybe every four days, we make camp near big well and stay there for long time, maybe from June until September.

'So today is summer and so today we visit my grandfather and the others at the well of Jabrin. He is there with only a few from our clan. He is there because Jabrin is more close to my work at Aramco, so it is possible for me to visit them this summer. The rest of the clan is out at a well in the sands, very far away. In Jabrin now is mostly inferior clan of al-Jaber.' He paused in his torrent of words. 'You understand, Shamsa? You understand! Good! Now listen! In the Al-Murrah we are seven clans, and I am al-Shoraim, which is the best. From my clan come all the chiefs. Shaykh Salim is my great-great grandfather's brother's grandson, you understand? No? Maybe later you understand. Now only know that al-Shoraim is the best clan of the best tribe in Arabia. Long ago, before I was born, when my grandfather was only a boy, Abdul Aziz, who later was the first king of Saudi Arabia, came to live with my clan to learn the ways of the desert. He came to us!' Rashid leaned closer to her. 'Like you, Shamsa. The king was like you.'

Sunny very nearly swooned in her seat. This gorgeous man, sitting beside her in his exotic white robe, with his handsome bearded face framed in the soft white folds of his head scarf, was a dream come true. The mask, the veil, even Gert's abuse - all were worth the glory of this moment. She wished he would kiss her, here and now. She was mad for this man.

The plane dipped its wings and began its descent. Rashid pointed at the tight nest of palm trees. 'Jabrin.' Without being told, Sunny tied her mask on, then threw the veil over her head, and settled the voluminous folds around her face. There was no airstrip, only endless flat sand, and the landing was all bumps and thuds and shakes. Rashid led her to the airplane's door, jumped out, then swung her down beside him. '*Ahlan wa sahlan!* Welcome to Arabia!'

Her head swiveled under blackness, but there was nothing to see but a few dusty brown palm trees, some tumbledown shacks made of bits of cardboard and tin and palm fronds, and, nestled here and there in the sand, spreading black and brown canopied tents. But even as she peered in the direction of these promising tents, she heard a squeal of tires, and a rusty red pickup truck careened toward them in a cloud of sand. Before the truck was at a full stop, a tall gaunt figure leaped from it. 'Rashid! Son of my son! Rashid! *El-hamdulillah* - thank God - Rashid!' With a flap of dusty gray robe, the figure advanced toward them. Sunny caught her breath and stared as centuries receded, the age of airplanes and guided missiles fell away, she traveled back in a time warp to before the Age of Enlightenment, before the Renaissance, before the Dark Ages, before the birth of Christ, to a time when the earth was younger and fresher and there were true faith and miracles and much prophecy. In his robes this barefoot old man with his long white beard and wrinkled raisin face harked back to the Old Testament. This Ibrahim of the Saudi tribe of Al-Murrah looked like a direct descendant of the Prophet Abraham, the ancient holy man who was still called 'father' by all the many tribes of the Arabs. She wouldn't be surprised to see fire sizzle the sand at his step, and then the heavens open and lightning strike and thunder roll and miraculous manna fall from the sky.

Sunny watched Rashid kneel to kiss the hem of his grandfather's robe, but the patriarch instead swept him up in his arms, and the two of them rubbed noses, Rashid kissed Ibrahim's nose, and then they kissed lips and hugged. Finally, arms still intertwined, they turned to face her, and she heard Rashid talking on and on in Arabic and saw him gesturing, and then he motioned for her to approach them. In a quick English aside to her, Rashid told her to kneel and kiss the hem of his grandfather's robe. Sunny did as she was told, and then to her delight the old man was lifting her up and into his strong arms. He was hugging her, squeezing her in a bear hug, welcoming her with his arms into his family and his clan and his tribe. After Rashid was sure the driver wasn't watching, he told her to let Ibrahim see her face. Just for today, Rashid said, because she was really an American woman, not a Saudi woman, and mostly because Ibrahim was consumed with curiosity, they would put aside all the rules and introduce her at once here in public instead of later inside the privacy of their tent.

Sunny cast off cloak and veil, and Ibrahim squinted and reached out and stroked the gold of her hair. 'Now the mask,' Rashid said. She untied the knots and pulled away the mask and smiled a tremulous smile. 'Ah!' Ibrahim caught his breath and pounded Rashid on the back and let loose with a rush of Arabic. 'He says even his weak eyes can see that you are very beautiful,' Rashid translated. 'He says that even though you are a *Nazrani*, an infidel Christian, he would have welcomed you here as his daughter because you are also the daughter of his son Majnun. But he says now that he sees you he means it even more, that it is good not only for me, his grandson Rashid, but also for him that you are one of us now. He says you will light up his tent with your hair like gold and fire. He says now he understands why I had to be crazy and bring home an infidel Christian wife.' Rashid laughed. 'He says maybe next year *he* will go to study in America and bring home beautiful gold girl like you!' Impulsively Sunny threw herself back into Ibrahim's arms and kissed him, as seemed to be tribal fashion, on his great beaked eagle nose.

Sunny smothered herself in mask, veil, and cloak, and they all climbed into the open back of the pickup. She tried to imitate how her husband and Ibrahim sat back on their haunches. But when the truck began ricocheting along the trackless stony desert, she lost her balance and rolled over in a black heap. She joined her men in laughing at her clumsiness, but after that she sat cross-legged and held on to the side of the truck for dear life. Under the hot grilling sun the truck careened over the barren gravel plain. Sunny's skin ran with sweat, and her mask stuck like adhesive. But it dawned on her that out here in the desert her veiling was more protection from the sun than punishment for being born a woman. Rashid and Ibrahim had both wound their head scarves in front of their faces so that they too had only masklike slits for eyes.

Every so often the truck would breast a gentle sway of dune, and nestled below them in a valley between the sandhills would be three or four low dark tents. Sunny would have just enough time to glimpse the small herds of camels and goats and the black-robed figures scurrying away from their prying eyes before they would be over the hump of another dune and the small nomad encampment would vanish like a mirage. For Sunny, all this was *déjà vu*, straight from her childhood fantasies. But this was real, and perfect, and golden.

But finally they crested the right dune, and Ibrahim leaned forward and pointed and began talking in a great rush of words to Rashid. Sunny peered out at three black tents which were exactly like all the others they had passed since Jabrin. The tents were low, long, rectangular sweeping affairs, like festive spreading lawn canopies rented for summer wedding receptions at home. But instead of being striped in mass-produced gold or blue, these dark billowing tents were laboriously hand-woven, Rashid had already told her, by his women from the hair of their own goat herds. The flaps along one whole side were tied invitingly open so she could see how they were divided into shadowy roomlike spaces by rugs and blankets thrown over ropes and poles. Sunny longed to explore the fascinating recesses of these exotic black tents, but already a great crowd of specially assembled relatives were rushing to welcome Rashid and his bride.

'*Ayouououououay!*' From the throats of women shrouded head to toe in black came a blood-curdling, ululating shriek that raised gooseflesh. '*Ayouououououay!*' Sunny tried to cower behind Rashid for protection, but then he laughed and told her that special tongue-flapping trilling was only an Arab woman's joy-cry. Just before the welcoming horde reached them, Rashid had only enough time to tell her she would be going off with his women now, that even though none of them understood English all were eager to welcome her, that she was not only the first foreign Christian they had ever seen but also the first one with wonderful yellow hair like the sun. Before she could beg him not to leave her alone, hands were already lifting them from the truck, men and women were screeching and laughing and pointing and jostling, and Rashid and Ibrahim were being carried off in one direction and Sunny in another. She reached out in bewilderment for her husband. But already Rashid and Ibrahim had disappeared into one tent, and the flaps were being lowered. She was alone among these strangers swaddled like herself from head to toe in dire black. Like it or not, she was borne along toward another tent by these figures screeching torrents of words she could not understand. It was like a nightmare to be in the resolute grip of these faceless strangers. It was so hot and she was so dizzy and disoriented she almost forgot that the women under these shrouds were her new family.

She was inside the shade of a tent, the flaps were lowered, she was drawn forward, fingers plucked off her cloak and veil; through the eye slits of her mask she saw bright lantern lights and many moving shapes coming closer, throwing off their own cloaks and masks and surrounding her, untying and peeling off her mask, laughing and gaping at her. Sunny stared from one face to another, wondering who all these women could be. She smiled uncertainly as the laughing, joking, chattering horde closed in on her. One old woman pawed at her gold jewelry; another pulled at her straight blond hair to see if it was real. Someone pinched the bare white skin of her arm, another possessively stroked her hand, a third came close to poking her in one of her blue eyes. Sunny took a step backward, cringing when the women closed in even more tightly around her. Some reeked of perspiration, others of an excess of cheap perfume. She wanted to beg them not to touch her, to back off, to give her air, but she was more afraid of irrevocably offending them. She wished she could understand what they were saying, but she didn't recognize any of their shouted Arabic. She saw their smiles, and although she assured herself that they must be friendly, that they were surely trying to welcome her in what must be an overwhelming display of Arab hospitality, she felt frightened and assaulted and violated. She wanted to scream for Rashid to come and rescue her, and yet at the same time, she wanted to be able to rise to this occasion and be as warm and boisterous and enthusiastic as all these Arab women.

She wished she could make a perfect first impression on Rashid's mother, whichever one of this yeasty pack she was. She wanted to be especially leery of Rashid's wife, if only she knew which one she was. She looked from face to face, wishing desperately for a flash of recognition, or even one word she could understand. She shut her eyes and held them closed until her panic subsided and she began to breathe normally. When she opened them again, she was finally able to see that most of these women had sallow skin, humpy noses, thick lips, and dumpling bodies. At least by Massachusetts standards, they were not pretty. They looked as plain and honest, as solid and serene as an order of cloistered nuns. Yet some had drawn heavy smudgy lines around their huge fawn eyes, and she liked their soft dark understanding Arab eyes. They wore bright long dresses in electric shades of red and green and orange and purple. They were piled with jewelry, too, chunky silver and thin gold ornaments in their pierced ears and at their necks and on their fingers and circling their pudgy waists. One even had a gold nose-ring. Sunny was glad now that Rashid had made her wear all the gold she owned. When one of the women lifted Sunny's gold necklaces to judge their weight and price, Sunny allowed herself a little flash of pride. She not only had more, and heavier, gold than any other woman in this tent; she was also prettier than any of them. At least, she thought, they're no competition.

But just as Sunny was feeling secure enough to smile back at her new family, she glanced at the far end of the tent where a woman and a small girl stood aloof from the rest. The woman was young and proud and haughty and slender and striking, with black hair that rippled nearly to her waist and black eyes that flashed angrily in Sunny's direction. Oh, no, Sunny thought, please God, no, that can't be *her*. Sunny smiled at the women standing nearest to her, then pointed at the one whose identity she had to know. 'Aisha?' Sunny said, as if she assumed this pretty threat must be Muhammad's wife. A fat homely woman bustled forward, beamed at Sunny, pointed at herself, and said 'Aisha.' Without further ado, Aisha swept Sunny in her arms and smacked her lips to Sunny's. 'Sis-ter!' Aisha proudly screamed the one word of English she had learned for this occasion. 'Sis-ter!' Then a wrinkled older woman - dark like Rashid and Muhammad, with their same high aristocratic nose and intelligent eyes; their mother? - pointed at the sultry Arab beauty and said, 'Nura.'

For a very long charged moment the two wives of Rashid glared at each other. Then Sunny's gaze wavered and fell; tears filled her eyes and to her horror, spilled down her cheeks. Nura's being lovely was too much. Sunny finally gave in to the despair she had been fighting ever since Rashid had first shown her the mask on the airplane. She sank down on the rugs piled on the floor and hid her face in her hands. She cried because she was alone and afraid and confused about everyone and everything in this bizarre country. She cried because she missed her grandparents and New England and her horse. She cried because her father was a broken man, not someone she could lean on, and because he drank too much. She cried because she had lost her self-respect by wearing that horrible mask today and because the Aramco wives had shunned her. She cried because Rashid understood her words but not always what she meant by them. She cried because Saudi was hot and horrible and not wonderful as she had always thought it would be. She cried because she was only twenty years old and she suspected she might already have ruined her life. She cried because Rashid had just abandoned her, because his female relatives were bruising her with their sharp exploratory pinches, and now, worst of all, because the woman she had to share her husband with was a dark and sensual beauty. Sunny felt so utterly defeated she did not care that all of Rashid's relatives were watching her cry and probably despising her for it.

But Sunny reckoned without Rashid's mother, who stepped forward as though about to sweep her daughter-in-law into her arms. Then she seemed to think better of it, and sternly she beckoned to Rashid's other wife. The two stood arguing over Sunny in sibilant Arabic for some moments, the old one adamant and commanding, the young one defiant. But then Nura shrugged, and after another instant of grudging reflection, she sank down on the rugs next to Sunny. Gingerly she touched the American's blond hair, and when Sunny looked up, Nura took her stiffly in the circle of her slim arms. 'Sis-ter,' Nura said. 'Sis-ter.' As one, the watching Arab women broke out in a chorus of joy-cries. '*Ayouououououay!*'

'Sister,' Sunny echoed. She smiled with her lips. But Sunny was not deceived by this charade of sisterhood. One reluctant hug, one carefully parroted word could not erase the fact that they were destined to be rivals. As Rashid's mother barked out another order and Nura obediently hugged her again, Sunny could feel that her enemy's breasts were fuller and softer than her own. What else was better about Nura? With a woman as luscious as this waiting faithfully back in his family's black tent, why had Rashid recited marriage vows to her that day in Vermont?

Rashid's mother plucked Sunny off the floor and into her soft, fat, enveloping arms. 'Shamsa! *Binti!* - My daughter!' Repeatedly the old woman gave her great enthusiastic wet kisses on her nose and her cheeks and her lips. 'Um Muhammad!' Rashid's mother pointed significantly at herself. Sunny nodded. Rashid had already told her that a woman was called by her eldest son's name. *Um* Muhammad was 'the mother of' Muhammad. Sunny laughed into the kind black currant eyes of her mother-in-law and smiled at her sister-in-law. She could not resist the honest nurturing warmth of Um Muhammad and Aisha. She made a resolution to try her best to obliterate all dark thoughts of Nura. A moment later, when the rest closed in again to get a more thorough feel of her hair and her dress and her skin, Sunny did not shrink away. Then they wanted to show her - all of them insistently at once, noisily, merrily - their babies, their dresses, their jewelry, their blankets, their tents, their goats, their camels.

Much later that night, after everyone had feasted on three freshly slaughtered sheep, after the men had sat for hours drinking coffee and swapping stories around their campfire, after the women had cleaned up the tents and tucked the children under their blankets and sat for hours drinking coffee and trading stories around their own other campfire, after almost everyone else was asleep, Rashid led Sunny outside. They stood with their arms intertwined under the inky black velvet Saudi sky, and Sunny remembered her mother's letters about how she had loved the beauty of Arabian nights that must have been just like this one. Sunny reveled in the wonder of feeling close to her mother. The crescent moon and the sharp bright stars washed the brownish desert sand as white as freshly fallen snow. 'A beautiful day,' Rashid whispered to her. 'And maybe now we make a beautiful night?' He took her in his arms and tenderly kissed her on her closed eyes and her open lips. 'I think tonight we make baby, yes?' He guided her inside a tent to where she had spread their blankets, and then he made slow passionate love to her until she fell asleep in his arms.

Only after he was sure she was fast asleep did he ease out of her embrace and creep out into the night to another woman who waited in another tent. For it is written in the Koran that a man may have as many as four wives at once, but only if he treats all of them as perfect equals. With skill, with desire, with affection, Rashid did as it was written in the Koran that he must do. And then he dragged his spent body off to lie alone and snatch an hour or two of dreamless sleep before it was time to rise for the dawn prayers.

Back in their Aramco bungalow at Dhahran one morning two months later, Sunny woke up radiant with the news that she was pregnant. Since the company doctor had confirmed her heart's desire late yesterday afternoon, Sunny had been all smiles and blushes and bliss. She had so wanted to feel Rashid's child moving inside her. She had so wanted to present him with his first son as proof of her love. She had tried to wait up last night for Rashid to return home from visiting his grandfather, but she had fallen asleep in the wee hours.

Sunny resisted her desire to kiss Rashid awake. She wanted to stroke his chest with her fingertips. She loved to touch his body. She longed to coax him into making love to her and then to gasp out her great news when he was bursting inside her. On erotic afternoons and love-struck midnights Rashid was a tiger at sex, but in the mornings he was a bear disturbed from hibernation. He would most definitely not appreciate her throwing herself on him before his eyes even fluttered open. Yet she was aroused by the innocence of her sleeping husband, and she could not resist tenderly stroking the black curls on the crown of his head. She was certain it would be better between them now that she was pregnant. He would spend more time with her, he would love her more, they would truly become everything to each other.

Lately, since Ibrahim and the rest of the family had moved into his new house in Khobar, Rashid had been spending more evenings there with them than with her. He had told Sunny once he couldn't help it, that the on-the-job slights of the Americans and envy of the Arabs was getting to him. At night he wanted the security and comfort of being only with his family. She had retorted that *she* was his family now, that she could be his security, his comfort if only he would give her the chance. Rashid had rumpled her yellow hair and kissed her on the nose, but then he had told her it wasn't enough for him just to sit and talk and make love with her. He missed the masculine camaraderie of his Arab family and friends. He had to visit them in Khobar because it wasn't possible to entertain them in this small Aramco bungalow in front of his unveiled wife. Sunny had leaped at this perfect opportunity to suggest yet again that they both move into the house in Khobar. She had been able to endure her socially isolated life in Dhahran only by viewing it as a short intermission before the real drama of her life began in the bosom of the Arabs.

She had filled her time with intensive daily classes in Arabic and twice-weekly excursions with the riding club, and by firing the Pakistani and doing her own housework. But soon they would have to vacate this bungalow when its permanent renters returned. So far even her father's persistent nagging had not been able to get them the promise of another Aramco cottage. It seemed they would have to move either into the house in Khobar or into a tent. Sunny had ignored Rashid's feeble protests that the plumbing still wasn't connected, that the electricity came and went, that he had bought rugs but no furniture. She had pretended utter deafness when he had finally, with some embarrassment, said that he didn't think she and Nura should live under the same roof.

Sunny banished all acid thoughts of Nura. She would not waste this blessedly beautiful morning of pregnant triumph worrying about her rival. She bounded out of bed, hummed to herself on the way to the bathroom, and was singing out loud fifteen minutes later when she returned from the kitchen carrying Rashid's breakfast tray. She pulled open the draperies, and blinding white light flooded the room. Playfully Sunny hit a brass mortar against a brass pestle, just as the Bedouin do in grinding coffee in the morning. A sound like bells ringing filled the room, and a wild-eyed Rashid sat bolt upright in bed crying out something that sounded like a terrible curse in Arabic.

'Good morning!' Sunny said gaily. Rashid glared at her, lay down again, and moaned. Sunny hastily decided her noisy little wake-up joke had not quite succeeded. She was slightly subdued as she set her husband's tea and pita bread and cheese and boiled egg on the small table beside him. She sat on the edge of the bed watching him sip his black tea in silence. She knew she shouldn't try to talk to him about anything important at breakfast, but she couldn't wait until tonight to tell him about the baby. When half his glass of tea was gone, when the lids of his eyes were finally a little bit raised, she couldn't contain herself any longer.

'I have to tell you something important!'

Stolidly he chewed his bread.

'Today's an important day for us!'

He squinted at her. Vaguely he did know that something important was happening today, but he could not quite remember what it was.

'A baby! I'm going to have a baby!'

His eyes widened.

'Pregnant!' She threw herself into his arms. 'The doctor says I'm pregnant!' He hugged her, patted her back, laughed, kissed her on both cheeks. 'And that's not all,' she exclaimed. 'I want to tell you something else. I want to move to Khobar! With your family! Enough Dhahran!'

He looked quizzically at her face and frowned. 'You want to live with my family?' When she nodded, he shook his head. 'A baby, yes, a thousand times yes. A thousand sons! But live as an Arab wife in an Arab house? I say no. It would be too difficult for you, my Shamsa.'

She disengaged herself from his arms, stood, and glowered down at him. 'You don't give me credit for anything. You're always saying everything will be too difficult for me. Like I'm an imbecile or a child.'

He sighed under his breath and groped for his tea and took a small sip as he restated the obvious. 'You are a woman.'

Sunny chose to let that one pass, for now. She was

learning, by trial and error, about Arab men and Arab ways. She had possibly been too bluntly American when she had demanded they move in with his family. When she forced a confrontation, Rashid always dug in and said slighting things he didn't really mean about women. But it was surprisingly easy to have her way with him if she merely turned kittenish and played coy games with him. She was glad she didn't often have to fall back on such stratagems. As long as she didn't alarm him by being too blatantly bossy, Rashid was tender, considerate, and intensely loving with her. On the deepest of emotional levels, deeper than mere words and gestures, this man understood and needed and cherished her. What mattered this lustrous morning was that they were man and wife, and she was carrying his child. She took his hands in hers and guided them to her belly. 'Feel here! Can you feel him? Your son!'

He smiled as he touched her. He ran his hands over her belly; then he pulled her down on the bed next to him and kissed her lips and her breasts and her belly that soon would swell with the miracle of his son. He loved her especially when she was warm and giving like this, just as he hated it when she acted spoiled and selfish and foreign.

Suddenly, as he remembered what else was special about today, he stopped caressing her. Muhammad was arriving for a short business trip. He was supposed to pick up his brother at the airport, and soon. Rashid gave Sunny a final kiss on the lips, then pulled back the sheet and made for the shower. Soon Sunny was patting his back dry, and he was dressing quickly in his best white robe and head scarf instead of his usual shirt and trousers. As Sunny continued a long happy monologue about the wondrous signs of her pregnancy, he decided he would surprise her by bringing Muhammad home for lunch. The two of them had once been friends in Boston, and Sunny was so lonely here. It would give her such a lift to see her old friend. Rashid kissed her and was almost out of the front door before he remembered to tell her he was bringing home a guest for lunch.

She was in the kitchen trying not to burn the rice when the two brothers came in the front door. Muhammad put his finger to his lips and whispered that he insisted on the pleasure of surprising Sunny. He tiptoed into the kitchen and slapped her soundly on the behind. 'Remember me?'

Sunny whirled and stared at Muhammad's grinning face. 'You!' The last time she had seen him, years ago, had been on the sidewalk outside that sleazy Scollay Square hotel. 'What are *you* doing here?' She flushed at the memory of the most degrading hour of her life. But she was righteously angry, and she stood her ground and hissed at him. 'I never *did* get a chance to tell you what I thought of you, did I? What you did to me that way was degenerate and horrible! And now you come here into my own kitchen and dare to touch me - there! - again?'

'Tch!' Muhammad swiftly pinned back her arms and leaned very close to her. 'Sexy as ever, I daresay. Still doesn't take much to set you off, does it? I wasn't surprised when you settled for second-best. But I wager you still would like more from the old master. Another time, perhaps. But for now don't be cross with me, darling. And let's try a little discretion, unless you want my brother to know all our dirty little secrets.' He released Sunny's hands, and by the time Rashid came into the kitchen with the bouquet of flowers his brother had brought them, Muhammad was chastely kissing her cheek.

Sunny endured the brush of Muhammad's lips only by promising herself she would scrub her skin raw where he had touched it. She smiled, took the flowers, and arranged them. And finally, after these stolen desperate instants of second thoughts, she decided she had no choice but to do as Muhammad said. Rashid did not know - Rashid must *never* know about that one sordid encounter. She prayed that Muhammad was here only for a visit. God only knew what she would do if he moved permanently back to Saudi.

What if, by some cynical twist of fate, she found herself living under the same roof as her tormenter? If he dared to make sexual demands on her, could she possibly dare to resist? Her mind raced ahead to a lurid future of guilty blackmailed sex. No, she decided, before it came to that she would tell Rashid the truth and face the consequences. She turned finally back to the brothers, held out the vase of flowers, and forced up the corners of her mouth as if she were smiling. 'Lovely roses. And such a surprise!' She could feel her cheeks burning. 'If you had told me your brother was coming, I would have fixed something special. It isn't every day we have your brother for lunch. Or is it? Muhammad isn't coming back here to live, is he, Rashid?'

Rashid was looking from his wife to his brother. He had heard that same throb of fear in Sunny's voice once when a snake had slithered just in front of her where they walked in the desert.

'Alas, dear sister, I am only here for a few short hours. Lunch here with you, and dinner in Khobar with the rest of the family. Then I must dash off to Riyadh for some most important business.' Muhammad smiled smugly at Sunny. 'But how charming that you thought I was back to stay. I do so hate to disappoint a lady. I suppose you remembered that. I would imagine you have an excellent memory.'

Sunny's eyes flashed, and Rashid thoughtfully studied the merest suggestion of a leer on Muhammad's face. He tried to recall exactly what he knew about her and him. He distinctly remembered that Sunny had preferred Muhammad the night they had all first met at her grandparents' farm. And then Muhammad had boasted in a letter to him in Texas that he had become close to Mr. Tom's daughter. Yet later, when he and Sunny had fallen in love in Boston, Rashid could not recall her saying a single word - not one word - about his brother. And she had insisted they bypass London, where Muhammad still lived, on their honeymoon. She had been eager to go and see everything in Europe except London and Muhammad.

Rashid's eyes narrowed with contempt as he watched

Muhammad rummaging in their kitchen cupboards for a contraband bottle of gin. Rashid did not doubt his brother was capable of every corrupt act known to man or beast. Had Muhammad once made a pass at Sunny? Rashid's eyes softened as he stared at the wife of his heart. He was ashamed of his own jealous suspicions. He shouldn't implicate Sunny in his own tangled lifelong rivalry with his brother. Muhammad had probably once taken Sunny to a movie or out to dinner and then tried to kiss her, that was all. Rashid tried to control his quick hot flash of jealousy as he considered the possibility that maybe Sunny had even kissed him back. But he assured himself she would never have allowed anything further to happen with Muhammad. She had definitely been a virgin on their wedding night. He himself had secretly examined the small brownish bloodstain on the sheets the next morning when she was in the shower. Surely there were many reasons, having nothing whatsoever to do with sex, that could have caused Sunny and Muhammad to have a falling-out in Boston.

Yet Rashid was glad his brother was here for only a few short hours. Recently he had considered asking Ibrahim to order Muhammad to return home and run the family business, which was growing and diversifying at an almost alarming rate. Rashid had been buying up all the available real estate in Khobar and Jubail and Dammam. He had put scores of the cousins to work on a new contracting wing of the company, and soon he would be ready to negotiate with Aramco to provide the American compound with a cornucopia of supplies. He was even trying to import bulldozers and heavy construction equipment. If only a fraction of his enterprises made good, his family would one day be extremely rich and powerful. But it was too much for Rashid to handle both the family business and his demanding job at Aramco. Muhammad should be at the helm of the company; but Muhammad was still enamoured of the sweet life in London.

Rashid knew it would have been easy to persuade

Ibrahim to recall Muhammad, for the patriarch had never been reconciled to the idea of one of the sons of his sons living among the infidels. Yet with this dangerous current running between Sunny and Muhammad, Rashid decided to postpone any such campaign. He reminded himself that by representing the interests of the Saudi government and the royal family in London, Muhammad was bringing more glory and power to the family and the tribe. Rashid decided he should be pumping Muhammad about the interests of the royals and the political and financial climate of the kingdom instead of stewing about imaginary indiscretions. 'So, brother! I think it is time to talk. About the oil and the king and the rumors that his royal extravagance will soon have us back in the desert herding camels.' He wrapped his arm around Muhammad's shoulder and very nearly dragged him away from Sunny into the living room.

From where she stood brooding over the stove, ruining lunch, Sunny could hear the brothers getting down to the serious business they had in common. Rashid and Muhammad might be opposites in temperament and character, but they were equally ruthless and talented in their pursuit of money and power. Muhammad was admitting that the rumors of a financial crisis in the kingdom had not been exaggerated. Even millions of dollars in increased oil revenues had not been able to keep pace with the profligate spending of King Saud. Since taking power seven years ago, Saud had mortgaged the once bright future of the oil-rich kingdom. His extravagances were a page out of *Tales from the Arabian Nights*. He had taken a dislike to his newly built, eight-million-dollar Nasriyah Palace, ordered bulldozers to level it, and then, on the same site, built another one even more grandiose at a cost of twenty million dollars. He had stocked and restocked his harem with foreign and native ladies, and it was said he had sired a hundred children. He had amused himself on trips to Europe buying up entire inventories of jewelry stores and china patterns and couture designers. He bought airplanes and stereo equipment and enough flashing neon lights to make his palace garden light up the desert like Las Vegas.

Still the king had continued his mad sprees, and a percentage of all that spending had swollen the Swiss bank accounts of advisers and assistants and chamberlains and fawning flunkies from Egypt and Lebanon and Palestine and Britain and Germany, who had all descended on Saudi Arabia like a cloud of flies on a freshly killed carcass. King Saud ignored the advice of his brothers and instead made policy by consulting his former chauffeur, whom he had made the controller of royal budgets. He dabbled disastrously in foreign policy, and the Arab world was scandalized when it was revealed he had offered Syria a four-million-dollar bribe to sabotage its planned union with Egypt and even - some whispered - to assassinate President Nasser. But worst of all, King Saud had brought the kingdom to the brink of bankruptcy. He owed ninety-two million dollars to Chase Manhattan and other New York banks, and the Saudi riyal had fallen sharply against the dollar.

Sunny heard Rashid sighing and mumbling pious sentiments about God and goodness and eventual justice. He told Muhammad then what he knew about the coming shakeup in the royal family. If someone didn't do something about King Saud - and soon - what had happened in Egypt nearly eighty years ago could happen before another season passed in Saudi. When the extravagances of Khedive Ishmael had bankrupted Egypt in the late nineteenth century, Britain had stepped in to safeguard its extensive investments, and Egypt had become a glorified British colony. Rashid fretted that the pretext of a similar Saudi bankruptcy might soon have a caravan of American tanks on the camel tracks outside Riyadh. Make no mistake, Rashid said. The American oil industry would tolerate the Saudi monarchy in power only as long as king and court served American interests. If the Saudis couldn't run their country in a stable manner, then the Americans would take off the velvet gloves and come out in the open to run it for them. To forestall such a catastrophe, the rumor was that an intrapalace coup was being planned in behalf of Crown Prince Faisal. He was Saud's half-brother and already not only the heir apparent and the foreign minister but also most assuredly the sanest head in Riyadh. King Saud would be allowed to continue to rule in name only, but Prince Faisal would be the real power. He would put King Saud on a strict budget, he would stop the mad cycle of extravagance, he would make all the hard choices that must be made to avert American intervention.

As Sunny brought in the charred meat and the sticky rice and the limp salads, the brothers were so engrossed with the business of politics and finance that it seemed they had forgotten her. Sunny for once reveled in the silent role of the demure Arab wife.

She pushed her food around her plate, and when she speared her pieces of overcooked meat, she pretended she was cutting into Muhammad. She hoped Rashid hadn't noticed how his brother's arrival had shaken her. She didn't want to face a battery of jealous questions from him tonight. She had been in Saudi long enough to know that what had happened in the Scollay Square hotel was enough to make Rashid divorce her. It was a deadly offense for a woman to be seduced by a stranger, but it was unspeakable that a woman be sexually intimate with her husband's brother. She had most definitely broken one of the greatest taboos. If a man couldn't trust his wife around his brother, how could he trust her at all?

The Saudis were such fanatics about the virtue and honor of their women that Sunny doubted it would make one whit of difference that she had done what she had done with Muhammad against her will and in innocence long before she had even begun keeping company with Rashid. Maybe her husband would be understanding and forgiving, but Sunny did not think it wise to put him to that excruciating test. Sunny felt nauseated as she patted her lips with her napkin. The juices in her mouth were sour, as if she were about to vomit. Fear, she thought; that's what fear tastes like. For the first time in her life she was experiencing the sour sickening taste of fear. She stared across the table at Rashid and Muhammad and was afraid.

—13—

Inside the dark recesses of the black tent Sunny bent over the letter she was writing to her grandparents. But the intense wet summer heat made the ink of her fountain pen run, and she frowned as it made a mess of her letter. She shook the pen, wiped off its point, and tore a new sheet out of the grade-school composition notebook. She had run out of her stock of airmail stationery, and this cheap childish gray lined paper had been the best she could buy. She began again, and this time the pen skipped and spurted. She sighed and put away pen and paper with quiet resignation. This letter was not to be, at least not today. Maybe tonight or tomorrow or after tomorrow she would write that letter she owed her grandparents. There was no rush. She wouldn't be able to mail it for two or three more weeks, until Ramadan was over and they had celebrated the *Eid el-Fitr* feast and returned from their desert camp back to the family compound in Khobar.

Sunny lay back on the rugs spread upon the sand and listened to the lonesome silence of the desert. She watched the rhythmic rise and fall of the two slight forms of her children near her on the rugs. Four-year-old Khalid and two-year-old Sarah, like everyone else in their encampment, were still fast asleep. She wished the sun would go down so the family would awake and break their fasts and keep her company. She was the only adult in their camp who did not observe the Ramadan fast. Everyone else slept away the hot midday hours until it was lawful to eat and drink once again. Usually Sunny could doze through the scorching afternoons. But Rashid was away in Kuwait at a conference of that new Arab organization that was taking up so much of his time and energy.

After the oil companies had slashed the posted price of oil twice in the late '50s, Rashid and other Western-educated Saudis had been instrumental in forming the Organization of Petroleum Exporting Countries to pressure the companies to restore the price of oil to its former levels. Now Rashid was always dashing off not only for OPEC organizing conferences but to meet with Arabs and Iranians up and down the Gulf. Sunny always felt restless and sundered and vaguely worried when he was apart from her. She wished her father weren't away so much, too. In the past few years he had been working either deep in the Empty Quarter desert or offshore in the Safaniya underwater fields of the Gulf. Sunny worried that her father worked far too hard. She hoped he would do as Rashid repeatedly begged him to do: retire from Aramco, move in with them, and spend his days and nights in the shelter of the Al-Murrah tents.

Longingly Sunny looked at her paper and pen. She had so wanted to write a long letter to her grandparents. Instead she snuggled against the rug, twisting this way and that until she had contoured a shallow well in the sand. She lay back, put her arms behind her head, and looked up at the shards of white light that beat down through the loose threads of the tent cloth. Here in the desert she was moved, as always, by an impulse to solitary reflection. The desert heat seemed to burn away life's trivial surface, and the silence seemed to drown out all voices but the implacable one inside her own head. If she had learned one thing in her five years in Saudi, it was to listen to her own loud clear thoughts and feel her own sharp strong emotions and remember her own deep dense dreams.

The shadowy fears and forebodings she remembered

from Muhammad's visit had been painted over by a wash of brighter, warmer, gentler emotions. For these years had mostly been sunlight seasons of innocence and joy and splendor, not only for her and hers but for the desert kingdom she finally had learned to love - not only mythically from afar, but intimately from inside its pumping heart.

For her, these were the nurturing years of birth and suckling and growing, first of her son, Khalid, and then of her daughter, Sarah, lovely bronze-skinned babies with flashing dark Arabian eyes and rosy placid good natures. These were the quiet years of simplicity and laughter and sharing, in a world that had shrunk back to the snug human dimensions of mothers and fathers and sons and daughters and aunts and uncles and cousins, in a world where masks shut out strangers, in a world where there was only really family. These were the chummy years of chatter and gossip and joking, of finally commanding Arabic well enough for heart-to-heart confidences with her ubiquitous in-laws, thoughtful Um Muhammad and sweet Aisha and wise Ibrahim and a supporting cast of fascinating heroes and fools and saints and villains who were the cousins camping just out of earshot beyond the dunes.

These were the slow hot years of exploring the many faces of married love, the hurt of sharp misunderstandings and the healing of graceful reconciliations, the gradual melding of desire and ecstasy with calmer emotions of affection and compassion, the merging of dazzling hopes for the future with the shining memories of a newly shared past, the blunt longings to be utterly as one and the dawning acceptance that that could never be, that it was their separateness that they had to treasure and respect and forgive. These were the tender years of the quiet discovery of answers to questions she had never thought before to ask about family and freedom and serenity and a peace that began deep inside and spread outward in a radiance that made her eyes glow. These were the years when Sunny had grown to maturity, when her will and her character had been tested and fired in a crucible of scorching Saudi summers and hot Saudi autumns and warm Saudi winters and burning Saudi springs.

For the kingdom, too, these were the glory years of untested promise and eager stretching and fevered expectation of rich destiny. These were the years when dour smart King Faisal eclipsed King Saud, when Saudi Arabia squared off against Egypt in the Yemeni Civil War, when the national budget was balanced by young bureaucrats with fancy college degrees, when the Saudis assumed control of half the assets of Aramco, when opportunities were so very ripe that only later could it be diagnosed that in fact they might all along have been rotten at the core. These were the benign years, the last gasp of certainty, when the Western gods of development and technology and modernization secured long-term Saudi visas, when progress seemed inevitable and without ambiguity, when armies of experts descended on Riyadh and Jeddah and Dhahran with their blueprints and their full-color glossy brochures and their five-year plans that promised prosperity and longer lives and the best of everything. These were the believing years, when for the first time ever in Arabia all seemed possible, when new schools and hospitals opened their doors to the ignorant and the sick, when electricity and telephones and radios and television sets became an everyday matter, when trucks replaced camels, when pilgrims from all over the world flew to Mecca on airplanes in a matter of hours instead of the years it used to take some to arrive by foot and by boat and by slow caravan. These were the naive years before the great arrogance began, before self-interest quickened and honed minds realized just what economic and political power could come with this oil - their oil - not Aramco's oil but Saudi's oil.

These were the boom years, the years before conservation, the wildly productive years of straining growth, when the bargain-basement barrels of black gold pumped from the rich new fields increased from the thousands to the tens of thousands to the hundreds of thousands to the millions of barrels per day. These were the pauper years, when the Western oil companies capriciously slashed, and slashed again, oil's posted price of less than two dollars a barrel, when the kingdom seemed not to carry a grudge for its sharply decreased revenue, when the Saudis were docile, resigned, and inscrutable, when the Arabs merely sighed and made the best of this as their ancestors had sighed and made the best of whatever calamities Allah had sent them.

For Sunny and for Saudi, these were the Eden years before the fall.

Sunny sat up and crossed her legs Buddha-like and let her mind drift to the troubles of this paradise. Even she, with her bright determined enthusiasm for all things Saudi, could not be blind to the daily irritations of life in a culture sometimes still too darkly alien to her.

The damp sultry heat raised boils on her skin, she was always erupting in mysterious rashes, and fleas and flies and mosquitoes continued to find her white foreign flesh irresistible. She had been immobilized one year by a light but lingering case of hepatitis she contracted from contaminated food. After that she was as abstemious as the most pious Muslim in the kingdom, for after that wine and beer and liquor made her very sick. She had taken good health for granted in America, but she had begun to cringe inside every time she saw an outlandish tribal woman kissing one of her children. She worried so about Khalid or Sarah's getting sick and dying of some dread disease here in this land of typhoid and malaria and smallpox and tuberculosis and polio and blinding eye diseases Sunny had never even *heard* of in New England. She hated it when she saw other foreigners shaking their heads in disgust at how unspeakably dirty Saudi was, and she was well aware that nothing outraged the thin-skinned Arabs more than aspersions on their living in filth. Every day she had to weigh her concern about her children's and her own health against her fear of hurting her family's delicate sensibilities, and every day whatever compromises she struck left her uneasy.

Sunny glanced around her beloved black *bait el-shaar*, the 'house of hair' that was her tent of contentment. Against all reason, she loved life in this tent. It was most certainly less medically risky and altogether more convenient to live in one of the family's houses in town. She was not so romantic that she scorned air conditioning and electricity and a refrigerator stocked with ice. But the family compound at Khobar was so jagged with the sounds of drivers honking their horns and peddlers hawking their wares and muezzins calling their faithful to prayer. Khobar reeked, too, of gas and oil and exhaust fumes. There was no silent purity to life in that town.

For Sunny as for all the born Al-Murrah, life was sweeter and truer and brimming with more psychic comfort when they camped deep in the desert. Always they took to the desert to mark the most important passings of the yearly calendar. Toward the end of each long languorous summer they would limp out to this desert to keep midnight vigils atop the dunes for the first glimpse of the bright sinking arc of Canopus, the star that marked the end of the season of killing heat, the star that promised the long-awaited rains in only fifty more days. Always they would celebrate the appearance of Canopus as a promise of resurrection in the desert. Sentimentally, too, every fall they would move out to the desert and wait for the wondrous life-giving release of the rains that would raise a fragrant fuzzy carpet of miniature flowers on the desert floor. Sometimes even in the winter, after a flash thunderstorm, they would impetuously rush out to the desert and splash in the lakes and ponds and rivers that made fertile mud of the dead sands. For a time, too, every summer they would move out to the desert so Ibrahim and Rashid could visit with the *shaykhs* and the graybeards as they rested for the hot months by the big wells. And they would always spend at least the end of each Ramadan, whether it fell in the winter or spring or summer or fall, camping in the desert so they would be where their hearts longed to be for the celebration of the cycle of great feasts that came inevitably after the great fast.

Sunny had grown to love the natural ebb and flow of these seasonal migrations from town to wilderness, and she loved, too, being part of the gregarious team of an Arab household. She liked the spicy smells of Arab life - the garlic, the charcoal, the cardamom, the heavy perfumes that never quite masked the honest human sweat. She liked the ever-present grainy sight and earthy smell and dusty taste of desert in the air. She had even accustomed herself to eat what was put in front of her on those huge tin trays the servants brought out for the group feasts. She liked the yoghurt, she loved the rice, she had learned to crave fistfuls of sweet dates as if they were hand-dipped chocolates.

But despite the hustle and bustle and the happy human warmth of this sprawling Arab family, still, even now, Sunny sometimes longed to be not here but home. Her grandmother's formidably cheerful letters chatted of births and courtships and marriages of people whose strengths and weaknesses Sunny had known all her life. She loved her grandmother's gossip, her tart comments about that lopsided addition Dr. Grady had tacked onto his house, her finely detailed account of the contents of Mrs. Roebuck's estate sold at public auction, her judgments of the conduct of beaux and babies and in-laws who came home to Still River for the holidays. Her grandfather's letters were brisker and more quantitative, but they too multiplied her yearning for New England. Gramps marked the seasons not by migrations under the tropical stars but by fertile planting and growth and harvesting. He described in precise numerical detail every change of season on the farm: the number of bushels of McIntosh from the apple harvest, how many dozen pints and quarts of corn and strawberry jam and pickles Gran had canned, how far up on the side of the house the snow had drifted, the exact dates on which the first fuzzy pussy willows had blossomed by the barn.

Her grandparents' letters affected her so intensely that sometimes they worked their way into her dreams. Sunny had intricate, twisting dreams in Saudi, dreams of standing on her lookout hill in the orchards of home, dreams of green fields and white snow and harvests of wondrous abundance. Often, too, she dreamed of her horse. She had a recurring dream of going to the barn and finding Princess Camey crying great human salty tears. Sunny would sometimes find tears on her own cheeks when she awoke from this sad anxious dream. Time and again she and Rashid had planned a trip back to America, but always some pressing Saudi crisis - a sick child, a new oil field, problems in the tribe - had made them postpone it. In a way Sunny wasn't sorry. In a way it was easier not to be a visitor in that other world she had renounced.

Yet she worried a mother's worries as she snuggled her babies and felt the needy soft perfection of their flesh against hers. She stretched down to kiss the tender spots at their temples where their wispy black hair curled. She was determined that they would grow up with a window onto that other world. She must make them remember that they were not only Arabian but also American. When they were older she would teach her son and daughter about her own American heritage, which was theirs too. Already she was talking some English to Khalid and telling him and his sister stories not only about Sindbad and Aladdin but about Peter Rabbit and Sleeping Beauty and Br'er Fox and Superman and Snow White. She returned from shopping expeditions inside the Aramco compound with picture books and baseball cards and cans of chicken noodle soup and packs of chewing gum and Oreo cookies. She told them about her own childhood in New England, about ice skating on frozen ponds, about dressing up like a fairy princess on Halloween, about dyeing Easter eggs, about wearing her Girl Scout uniform and marching down the center of the town in a parade on the Fourth of July. Khalid's wide eyes would grow even wider and Sarah would clap her pudgy hands when she promised that, yes, she would someday take them back to New England to visit her grandparents and watch the leaves change color from green to red to gold and then months later the snow fall white from the gray sky. Sometimes when she heard herself dwelling with too much longing on all this Americana she would make a supreme effort to live in the present instead. She would throw away her remaining Hershey bars and bring out the even sweeter Arabian *halawah tahini* candy. She did not want to confuse her children, only widen their worlds.

She was confused enough herself.

At first it had been exhilarating to immerse herself in a world so fascinatingly different from home. But after the novelty wore off, she had found it disturbed her on a deep and lasting level to live in a culture whose values were so very different from her own. Here right and wrong, good and bad, grace and sin were not the same as at home. Here values that had seemed fixed and irrevocable and absolute in America were blurred and changed and transformed. Here a good woman was a masked and secluded woman. Here God was a joyous constant presence, prayer was better than sleep, and sure salvation belonged only to the believers. Here the common good of family and clan and tribe superseded individual desire. Here a man worried about the shame of others' passing judgment rather than the guilt of judging himself. Here a father knew best even when a son was sixty. Here no legendary national hero had ever rashly vowed he could not tell a lie. Here generosity ranked above the accumulation of wealth. Here a son was a blessing and a daughter another mouth to feed. Here, in the bright sunlight and dark shadows of Arab culture, Sunny found herself grappling with the soul-wrenching abstractions of the philosopher. In America a good man did one thing, and here a good man did another. If good, then, was relative, if it was no longer possible for one society to tell her with total assurance what was good or bad, by what standards could she judge herself and all that happened around her?

She was neither altogether American nor altogether Arabian, and the life she lived in the margins was one of compromise and uncertainty. Her own impulses carried her in one direction, and Rashid's expectations drove her in another. She was never quite sure exactly how she should be acting in any given situation, and so she muddled along, one day acting one way, the next day the opposite. Often she was bewildered, and sometimes she simply yearned to shed her American past as a snake sheds its skin and become more Arab than the Arabs. But like it or not, she was American more than skin deep. She could not slough off her heart, her mind, her soul.

She could not, would not, to begin with, believe that woman was born man's inferior. She had grown accustomed to the mysterious dark sensual swirls of fabric that were women in the streets. She herself had even sometimes enjoyed slinking through the labyrinthine alleyways swathed in black, flicking her veil this way and that, playing at being a Woman of the East. But for her, masks and veils remained mostly a masquerade, the exotic trappings of an elusive gossamer world. It was possible for her to continue to live in this secluded woman's world only if she persisted in seeing it through eye slits as narrow as those of her mask.

Besides, from the perspective of her new moral limbo, the life she was leading didn't *feel* oppressed and deprived. Life here in the bosom of her Arab family felt secure and rich and snug. She was one of them, one of the primal group, and they accepted and cherished her as if she were not a separate and distinct person but only one of the group's arms or legs or organs. Fleetingly, however, she did wish for privacy and did wonder what had ever happened to her *self*. She had her grandparents send her old psychology books from college, and she pored over Freud and Jung and Adler looking for clues to the mysteries of her own mind and the minds of these Arabs she had learned to love.

She was also deeply touched by the spirituality of her new family and her new country. At home most people with college degrees would be faintly embarrassed if called upon to make a public profession of faith. At home religion was secluded behind closed doors. But here God was on everyone's lips every hour of every day. Men dropped to their knees where they walked on the streets to pray to God. At first all this godliness had made Sunny ill at ease. Cynically she assumed there must be a bitter joke or some nasty twist of hypocrisy at the root of all this excess.

Finally she had accepted the fact that the faith of these people was deep and true. Islam wasn't her faith, but nonetheless she respected, even envied its awesome hold on these people. She had to answer her in-laws' repeated questions about Christianity, about how she kept the rules of her faith, about whether she ever intended to take Muhammad as her Prophet. By some mysterious spiritual transference, then, she found some of their faith seeping into her. She would be camping out in the desert, watching a sun rise or a sun set or a star light up the night, and she would find her heart and her mind turning inevitably to God. Churches were forbidden in the mosque-filled kingdom, but in the Aramco compound, Christian services were clandestinely held in homes and meeting rooms. Sunny attended when she could, and as she knelt, sometimes with her father alongside her, watching the priest consecrate the Host, she felt at peace with herself and this world and the next world, with all worlds.

Yet life outside the security of the immediate family could be harsh and cruel. What passed for justice - the amputations of hands for theft, the beheadings for rape or murder, the floggings for a constellation of lesser offences - was sickeningly brutal. There was, too, a feverish - even fanatic - side to Saudi morality. Sunny detested the swaggering *mutawiyah*, the religious police, who prowled the streets with their long heavy canes, occasionally beating men on the spot for missing a call to prayer or even smoking a cigarette. And Saudis who worked in the swollen government bureaucracy were at best lethargic and at worst criminally arrogant. The simplest transaction often dragged on for weeks until at last all the layers of clerks were properly bribed. In this frustrating medieval kingdom, Sunny sometimes thought it was more a pleasure than a punishment that a woman spent all her life inside the loving protection of her family.

'Ahhhhhhh! . . . '

A weird sound from somewhere outside her tent startled Sunny out of her reverie. She heard the sound again. Neither shriek nor moan nor word, but something – human? animal? – in between. It was a terrible cry of despair and pain. Sunny told herself it must just be the camels carrying on again. No creature on earth had a camel's range of mutters and groans and whines.

'Allaaaah! . . . '

When she heard it again, her hackles rose. That was no camel. That was a human cry of agony. She leaned over to make sure her children were still fast asleep, then went to investigate. Outside the tent, the sun beat down on the five black family tents. Sunny staggered in the heat. It must, she thought, be one hundred twenty or above today. No wonder everyone in the family was in a deep sleep coma.

But not everyone. 'Allaaaah! . . .' Again she heard that cry. It was coming from their own camp, from the far side of their camp, from the tent pitched farthest away. From Nura's tent.

Sunny froze in the heat. Whatever happened in Nura's tent was no business of hers. She and Nura did their best to ignore each other. Back in the family compound, Rashid had built two exactly identical houses for his wives and a far more grandiose one in the middle for his mother. When the family was out camping like this, always Sunny and Nura smoldered at opposite ends of a campfire, always they went off in different directions to search for firewood; always they tried to avoid repetitions of their ugly little spats by keeping a cautious distance. Rashid had made it absolutely clear he would not tolerate his wives' being openly jealous or possessive. Once and only once he had sat them down together in the neutral territory of his mother's house and told them how it was going to be. He would do his best, as the Holy Koran said he must, to treat them both exactly the same, night by night, season by season, year by year. His wives could be friends or foes, 'as you like,' he said, but he would not listen to even a whisper of reproach for the existence of a rival. Either peace would reign in all his houses, or he would divorce the trouble-maker and make do with only one sweet and docile wife.

Sunny did not relish breaking her sullen truce with the unmentionable Nura by pulling open the closed flap of the tent to investigate that terrible sound. She remembered, then, what she mostly succeeded in forgetting. Nura, who was the mother of six little girls, was very pregnant again. Sunny wished she could believe either that Nura's girls had been asexually conceived or that Rashid did what he did with his hot-eyed Arab wife only out of duty. Sunny wondered if this time Nura would be delivered of her heart's desire. An old Arab proverb held that one son was worth seven daughters. Sunny knew Nura burned with jealousy because she had given Rashid his first and only son.

Sunny had already turned her back on Nura's cries when a sharper howl rent the air, and then Nura moaned heartbreakingly. Finally there was an answering chorus of squeaky soprano shrieks: Nura's daughters. Sunny swore furiously under her breath even as she turned around and marched the length of the encampment toward Nura's tent.

She threw back the flap, strode inside, and blinked until she could distinguish the shapes strewn on the floor. 'Um

Khalid!' Small hands clutched in terror at her legs, calling her by the name that she, the mother of Khalid, was known by in the family. 'Um Khalid! *Bismallah*, in the name of Allah, help our mother!'

Sunny muttered soothing words to the frantic girls, she hugged some, she stroked others, but she couldn't understand what the girls were trying to tell her. Usually Sunny could comprehend almost everything said to her in Arabic, but sometimes when she was tired or upset all of it became a grunting mystery. She had taken lessons, practiced diligently, and waited for the happy night when she would even start dreaming in Arabic. But when her dreams finally began to unfold in Arabic, they had turned out to be nightmares, for in her sleep she couldn't understand a single word. Lately Sunny had even begun to have trouble speaking English. She had formed the habit of speaking English like an Arab, constructing her sentences with the adverbs in the wrong place, using only a grade-school vocabulary, fluttering her hands passionately about, saying every word slowly and distinctly, accenting the wrong syllables, stumbling as badly in her native tongue as she did in Arabic.

Cautiously Sunny knelt on the rugs beside Rashid's first wife. Nura's mouth was set in an animal snarl as she stared fiercely back. But then another spasm shook her, and her eyes went vacant with pain. 'Allaaaah! . . .' Again Nura cried out to God to save her from such suffering. Sunny bent and stroked Nura's matted hair and wiped beads of sweat from her forehead. She crooned to her rival. When finally Nura lay quietly panting with her eyes shut, Sunny crept down on the rug and lifted the blanket that covered Nura below the waist. She looked between the shuddering spread thighs and frowned. She was no midwife, but she had often been pressed into service at births. Nura's contractions were only a few minutes apart, and so surely she should be about to have her baby. Yet Nura had not even begun to dilate. This was Nura's seventh child, and always before the births had been swift and easy. Gingerly Sunny reached out a finger and lightly touched Nura's unnaturally narrow birth canal. Sunny quickly withdrew her finger when Nura screamed. But she had felt that Nura's flesh was as hard and dry as stone just where it should have been soft and slippery. In a rush of commanding Arabic, Sunny sent Nura's daughters to wake all the other women.

Um Muhammad was soon kneeling beside them, making sympathetic 'tch-tch' sounds with her tongue, coaxing a smile from Nura, chattering about Ramadan and sunsets and the dream she had just had about her daughter-in-law's giving birth to that long-awaited son. Maybe they would call him Abdullah, after her own dear husband, Allah keep him. All the while that Um Muhammad's gentle, practiced hands were probing Nura, she smiled and joked and assured her daughter-in-law that all was well. It wasn't until she had left Nura in the loving care of Aisha, and she and Sunny were outside the tent, that Um Muhammad told the truth. Nura was too narrow and inelastic. With her own hands Um Muhammad had felt the baby pressing vainly against the ungiving walls of the birth canal. Tears filled Um Muhammad's eyes. She had seen other prolonged, painful labors like this one. She had seen other rocklike vaginas that would not stretch wide enough for the passage of a baby. She had seen other women dead and buried after abortive labors like this. Um Muhammad's tears spilled down her cheeks. Nura would die soon. She looked at the sun dipping toward the western horizon. Nura would die, *inshallah* - if Allah willed it - before the sun set again on the morrow. Um Muhammad wiped her eyes, shrugged in hopeless resignation, and began stacking wood on the fire to brew the tea and the coffee with which the camp would break the Ramadan fast.

Sunny looked from the sun to her mother-in-law to the black tent where the women were beginning to keen over Nura. She heard them screeching their death shrieks, and then she heard Nura's daughters starting to sob and wail and scream that they wanted their mother. So this, Sunny thought, was the dark side of fatalism? A healthy woman in the prime of life has a complicated birth, and everyone shrugs and says *inshallah* and starts digging her grave? Sunny put her hands on her hips and considered. No one would fault her if she merely joined in the general mourning and helped the family bury poor Nura before the sun set tomorrow. When Rashid returned from Kuwait, her rival would be gone. Sunny shook her head. She detested sharing Rashid with another wife, but she did not hate Nura so much she would let her die before her time. If she and Nura were destined to compete for Rashid's affections, then so be it. She would fight for Rashid fair and square, when Nura was well enough to fight. But Sunny would not let the mother of those six little girls die without a struggle.

Sunny shaded her eyes and looked across the desert to the far horizon. They were camping out in God's country, an eight- or ten- or twelve-hour drive across the open desert from the nearest hospital in Dhahran. Rashid had taken the one truck equipped with the ham radio, so there was no way they could call for help. Nura would have to be rushed across the desert to the Aramco hospital. But in Saudi only men were permitted to drive. Rashid was in Kuwait, and a party of nephews and cousins were off representing the family at a tribal wedding at a distant well. Ibrahim was still here, but Ibrahim was almost blind and had never learned to drive. Sunny supposed they could put out a call far and wide that an Al-Murrah woman had to be taken to the American hospital. In time, after search parties found all the neighboring encampments and everyone had awakened and prayed and broken the Ramadan fast and talked this predicament over, some fine young man would perhaps finally step forward long after midnight and volunteer to drive Nura and a bevy of Al-Murrah chaperons across the desert to Dhahran. But what if no one took mercy in his own hands? Um Muhammad, who was not only Nura's mother-in-law but her loving aunt, had just shrugged and sighed and consigned Nura's fate to Allah's will.

'Allaaaah! . . .'

Sunny shook her head. Nura might not live long enough for Arab compassion to run its circuitous course. She would have to take charge herself. She would save Nura.

Sunny rushed back to her own tent and dug in the camel bags until she found Rashid's oldest, dustiest robes. She pinned back her hair, pulled his loose-fitting gray *thobe* over her dress, and wound a red-checkered *ghutra* around her hair. But still she hesitated to sweep Nura into a car and begin the long dash across the desert. It was *haram* – 'forbidden' – for a woman to drive. She was afraid of the consequences if she broke that taboo, and so she resolved to confide her plan to Ibrahim. Maybe, if he would give her his blessing, she could violate the rule. As she ran to Ibrahim's tent, she wondered at the picture she must be making. Always as a child when she had dreamed of Saudi, she had imagined herself dressed in a man's robe and head scarf, dashing over the desert on some derring-do mission that would have amazed even brave Colonel Lawrence. But tonight there was no time to revel in childish fantasy.

Sunny pulled off her head scarf and let her yellow hair stream over her shoulders as she threw herself dramatically down on her knees inside Ibrahim's tent. The old man stroked her hair and listened and shook his head as she told him her plan. Finally he took her soft white face between his brown callused hands and gently told her it was impossible for him to allow her and Nura to drive alone over the desert. It was *haram* for a woman to drive, and it was unsafe for women to travel such a distance without the protection of a man. Yet Ibrahim was smiling as Sunny began passionately protesting that they couldn't give up and let Nura die. 'You beg for her life?' he said. 'Even though you do not love her, you fight for her? You would try to teach the Bedouin a new lesson in generosity?' Ibrahim sighed an exaggerated sigh and grumbled that Sunny acted more like a man than a woman, as he gravely stood and threw on his cloak. Yet Ibrahim's eyes were aglow as he held out his hands to Sunny. 'I will drive,' he said, 'if you, my daughter, will be my eyes.' She hugged him, and she kissed the backs of his hands, and then they ran together to Nura's tent.

Ibrahim barked imperious orders. 'Pack food and water and blankets and masks and veils. Carry Nura to the Mercedes. Um Muhammad, you get in too. That's it, daughter, hold Nura in your arms in the back seat. Faster, daughters - move faster.' As the woman scurried to do his bidding, Sunny tucked her hair back under her head scarf, slid in beside Ibrahim in the driver's seat, and showed him how to turn the key in the ignition. Ibrahim gave an elated war cry as the engine caught. 'Now the gears,' she said. Her hands on top of his guided the car into low, and she directed him to push down on the gas and up on the clutch. '*Yalla!*' Ibrahim shouted - 'Let's go!' Sunny leaned on the horn as a warning for the women to disperse as the car jerked slowly ahead through the crowd. The women screamed, hesitated, then finally broke and scattered. 'Now push down hard,' Sunny said. Ibrahim laughed as they picked up speed until the encampment was lost in a cloud of dust. 'Easy, Grandfather,' Sunny cautioned. But when she let go of the rim of the steering wheel to wipe the sweat off her face, Ibrahim laughed and started turning the wheel in playful twisting circles round and round in the sand. Driving a car, he said, was more fun even than riding a camel.

For a long while, then, as Sunny kept a white-knuckled grip on her side of the wheel, only Ibrahim's merry laughter broke the silence inside the car. In the back seat Um Muhammad's lips moved in prayer for Allah to save them from the sure death of a blind man and a woman driving a car. Even Nura kept her cries to strangled little moans. Sunny concentrated on finding her way through the trackless strip of desert that lay between the family camp and the oasis of Jabrin. As she remembered it, this time they had pitched their tents maybe a half-hour's drive due south of Jabrin. She kept the setting sun to her left and prayed, because if her memory was not on course, they were heading toward the certain death of the Empty Quarter. She breathed a heartfelt sigh of relief when ahead, silhouetted under the fabulous light show of the setting sun, she saw the dear dusty palm groves of Jabrin. Now they must find and follow the primitive path Aramco had laid through the desert, a broad black oil-drenched stripe north from Jabrin to Haradh and Abqaiq and then northeast to Dhahran. With God's blessings, sometime before dawn they might finally pull up before the high chain-link fence of the compound. Sunny prayed Nura would be able to hold out that long.

Sunny and Ibrahim gave the palm groves of Jabrin a wide berth, for they didn't want to take the time to stop and exchange greetings with passing tribesmen. They bumped slowly over the gravel and sand, searching for the track until finally, after they had circled most of the oasis, they found the thin black oil slick snaking north to Haradh.

As she helped Ibrahim swing the Mercedes toward salvation, Sunny exultantly told the old man to step on the gas. In the dark Sunny ripped off her head scarf and let her hair stream behind her in the hot wind. She felt wild and good and very free, driving like this, fast, across the open desert. Radiantly she smiled and snuggled closer to Ibrahim. She wished the car radio could pick up a station playing very loud American rock-and-roll and that she could sing along at the top of her lungs to the Everly Brothers or Elvis Presley.

She showed Ibrahim how to turn on the high beams and took her eyes off the slick black ribbon only when Um Muhammad began pounding on the seat demanding blankets and the water jug and explanations about why she and Nura had been commandeered on this madcap drive. Ibrahim guiltily rolled his eyes at Sunny. The two of them had been so intent on their conspiracy that they had forgotten to share the good news with the terrified women in the back seat. After Ibrahim jolted the car to a stop, Sunny tucked a blanket around Nura and gave Um Muhammad water while Ibrahim explained Sunny's plan to get Nura to the American hospital in Dhahran.

'Ah!' Um Muhammad kissed Ibrahim's hand, then Sunny's, finally Nura's. 'Ah! Allah *karim*!' - 'God is generous!' Ecstatically Um Muhammad began babbling that Nura's baby would be a good child, a fine man, a brave warrior of the Al-Murrah. Shyly and uncertainly Nura looked up at Sunny, and when Sunny let a smile curve her lips, Nura almost smiled back. But then another pain convulsed her, and Nura cried out. Ibrahim stripped the gears, and the Mercedes bucked, then leaped under the silver crescent moon.

Once again they were off across the desert, but this time they were all united by a thrill of purpose and adventure. Nura's cries were softer, less urgent. Um Muhammad mopped her brow and murmured she should lie quiet, she should not push down, she should let the baby rest until dawn came and the doctor was there to help. Um Muhammad sang a lullaby for Nura's baby, and then she sang an ancient love song from the old days before too much religion made everyone believe music was the work of the devil. Then Ibrahim began chanting the old songs the men used to sing on camel raids, and when he finished Um Muhammad sang more songs, the lyrics women once sang as they spun their wool and children once sang as they splashed in wells as big as lakes. Um Muhammad sang until she lulled Nura and Nura's unborn baby into a childlike daze of innocent slumber, and still she hummed her sweet songs as they drove through the night to Dhahran.

Sunny kept her eyes on the black streak ahead and her hands firmly on the steering wheel as Ibrahim rested his foot heavy on the gas. It was easy driving on this hard-packed gravel. When she lost track of the oil slick, she would poke her head out the window and navigate north by the stars blazing in the sky. She was tempted when she saw campfires to beg Ibrahim to stop and ask for help with their grueling marathon. But she resisted that temptation, for tonight she wanted the satisfaction of a family solution to a family crisis. She and Ibrahim and Um Muhammad would rescue Nura all by themselves. Ibrahim kept his foot on the gas even as Sunny refreshed him by splashing water on his face. Twice the car got stuck in soft drifting sand, and Sunny and Um Muhammad had to grunt and groan as they pushed it back on course. When they were hungry, they ate handfuls of dates as they drove. Once, when Sunny found her eyes almost drooping shut, she caught the car just as it began drifting off the path. After that Sunny sat up straight and willed herself to be alert. She kept her mind focused on all those wonderful tales she had read so long ago about how Colonel Lawrence would ride on through the desert on a raid or to capture a fort, how he would be tired and hungry and thirsty, how he would triumph over his weakness, and how he would always win. As they raced on, Sunny told herself she would be a hero like Lawrence.

She wondered if Ibrahim would understand what she meant if she confided her feelings to him. But just then Ibrahim turned his head and looked lovingly at her with his dim dark eyes, and she knew this man she loved like a father understood all that, and more. It occurred to her that perhaps everything in her life had led up to this night of truth and testing. Maybe, she thought, she had been born to live out this bright brave night when she turned rival into sister. Tears stung her eyes, and they were not tears of sorrow. She reveled in the joy of every moment of the long hours of this bright, just ride through the night.

Sunny thought she was seeing a mirage when the first gray slivers of dawn cracked the sky. Surely not dawn already? She let out a cheer when she saw fire at the horizon, for that meant Haradh was just ahead. They raced past the eternal flames of the burn-off flares at the gas-separation points and made for Abqaiq. Dhahran was only a few hours away.

Ibrahim floored the Mercedes, for they were on smooth asphalt highway for this last leg of the journey. Nura was beginning to moan softly again, Um Muhammad was soothing her with caressing words, and Sunny prayed to God that her rival would be able to endure until they roared into Dhahran.

Against the gray sky, the sunrise was a rainbow of all the colors of hope, bright purples and pinks and mauves and scarlet orange at the center, where the new day was beginning. Around them were coils of other highways, shanty Arab villages, the silvery glitter of monstrous storage tanks, and steel catwalks climbing almost all the way to heaven. Sunny thanked God when she heard moaning from the back seat. Nura must be still alive, and they were almost there.

With a flourish they pulled up to the front gate of clean, modern, antiseptic Dhahran. Sunny leaned over Ibrahim and flashed her pass, and then the patriarch hit the gas and headed for the hospital. Ibrahim pulled up to the emergency entrance, and Sunny ran inside and gasped out to a nurse that a woman outside was in labor. She heaved a sigh of relief as efficient orderlies whisked Nura away on a stretcher behind closed doors. Ibrahim and Um Muhammad sank down in chairs in the waiting room, and Sunny burst into tears of exhaustion and triumph.

But it was a long while later, after noon, before the American doctor came out to tell them about Nura. As soon as she saw the frowning doctor heading their way, Um Muhammad broke out in a loud howling wail. It was all Sunny could do to quiet her, as they sat and listened to what the doctor had to say.

'No, no, she's fine; mother and daughter are fine. The baby's seven pounds and healthy.' The doctor waited for Sunny to translate that news to the others. Then he smiled a thin angry smile. 'But we had to do a cesarean, and it was touch and go for a while. . . . Another hour or two and it would have been too late.' Ibrahim put a protective arm around Um Muhammad as the doctor paused and ran his tired fingers through his bristling crew cut. 'Look, ma'am, I don't know how you're mixed up in all this, an American girl like you, but I think you should be told what's going on here.'

'What's wrong?' Sunny was almost in tears. 'Something's wrong with Nura? Or the baby? But I thought you said –'

'What's wrong is what we call "atresia."' The doctor sighed heavily. 'We see a lot of cases like the young woman you brought in. Sometimes we can save them, sometimes not. The only way we'll ever be able to lick this is by education, I suppose. Ignorance!' The doctor's eyes blazed as though ignorance were anathema. 'It's like this,' he began curtly. 'A normal woman's vagina is lined with membranes that can both expand and contract. So it's tight when it needs to be tight for sexual intercourse, then wide when it needs to be wide for a baby's passage at birth. But some of the women in the more primitive tribes around the Gulf – and apparently that includes this woman's tribe – don't want their vaginas to be stretched out after they have had a baby. So just after childbirth a woman packs her birth canal with rock salt.'

'Salt!' Sunny was aghast. 'I've never heard of anything like that. I've been living with the Arabs for five years, and I don't think what you said could be true. Not the Arabs I know. No!'

The doctor held up his hand to silence Sunny. 'The young woman you brought in here this morning almost died because she had packed her vagina with salt after the birth of her last child.' The doctor sighed. 'I suppose it must seem hard for you to believe. I had never heard of anything like this either, before I came here.' He shook his head. 'From what we've been able to figure out, the women do this because they're afraid their husbands won't want them, that they'll be divorced and sent back to their fathers, unless their vaginas are as tight and snug as a virgin's. We're told that usually the women do this when they're having trouble with their marriages, when the husband is either threatening divorce or to take another younger or prettier wife. To hold on to their man, they pack their vaginas with rock salt so their husbands will like them better in bed. It must be agonizing when they put salt on their raw skin like that, but the real trouble doesn't begin until after they get pregnant. Some of them abort their fetuses. Others, like your friend, get along fine until they're in labor. The fetus presses down, but the walls of the vagina are as solid as a rock. Unless we can get to the woman in time, and perform a cesarean, both the mother and the baby die. It's a terrible thing.'

'Terrible.' Sunny held her aching head in her hands. Just when she thought she understood everything about Saudi and its people, she would be appalled by some new evidence of barbaric brutality. What Nura had done to herself was almost as bad as the routine genital mutilation of every little Saudi girl. Last year Sunny had first become aware of these 'circumcisions' when she had witnessed one of Rashid's aunts cutting off the clitoris of Nura's five-year-old daughter with a pair of rusty scissors. The other women of the family had explained to her that it was necessary to do this to a girl before puberty so she would not be wild and act as bad as a prostitute. Even though Sunny had done all she could to persuade them to stop these grotesque mutilations, the most Um Muhammad and the others would concede was that she wouldn't have to circumcise her own Sarah. Try as she might, Sunny could not reconcile the Saudi Arabia which was gentle and slow and serene in its everyday rhythms with these sudden, violent, primitive explosions of physical cruelty. 'Will Nura be all right?'

'As long as she doesn't have any more children, she should be fine.' The doctor hesitated. 'Sometimes they do it again, you know. They're rushed in here, we barely save them, and then they go back to the tents and pack themselves with salt again. I'm hoping that doesn't happen this time. You seem to know these people pretty well. Maybe you can talk some sense to them. What are you, anyway? An anthropologist or a writer or something?'

'Yes, or something,' Sunny said vaguely. She was too embarrassed to tell this doctor she was the other wife. She was too ashamed to tell this young man she was the reason Nura had nearly killed herself. Sunny shook the doctor's hand and thanked him for his care and his advice. Slowly, with a leaden guilty step, she headed down the hallway behind Ibrahim and Um Muhammad to visit Nura. She had never imagined Nura could regard her as such a terrible threat, and now she wondered what she could ever say or do to make life better for this wronged woman. Sunny dragged her feet on the polished plastic tiles of the hospital corridor as, for the first time, she tried to see things from Nura's perspective. Her adored cousin Rashid, promised to her since birth, had left her pregnant and gone off to a foreign country for too many years. And when he finally came home, he had brought another wife, an exotic educated lady with yellow hair and money and a father who was a boss man at Aramco. Finally, the golden wife had added insult to injury by giving Rashid his only son, and poor Nura had been so desperate she had even rubbed salt into her own wounds.

Nura was lying in a white-sheeted bed in a ward with other Arab women. As her newborn daughter fed at her breast, tears streamed down Nura's cheeks. 'A daughter,' she repeated over and over to herself in Arabic, as if she couldn't believe the cruelties of fate. 'Another daughter. Seven daughters. Seven daughters and no sons.'

Sunny leaned over and kissed Nura on the forehead and on the nose and on the lips. She wanted to try to be kind to this woman who had never wronged her. 'Sister,' she said in English and then in Arabic. '*Anti ukhtee* – "You are my sister." My sister today, always, my sister.' Sunny sensed that in the days and months and years ahead, having to share Rashid would surely strain her sorority. Yet here and now, Sunny began to forge a bond that was as true as any she was to have in her life. For as she smiled tremulously down at Nura, she had a sudden unselfish inspiration. She would try to be more than kind to this woman who had been destined to be closer than a sister to her. She groped for the words she wanted in Arabic. 'We share one man, and also now we will share one son, yes? You can also be mother now to my Khalid. One family. All ours. You understand? You know?'

'Sis-ter,' Nura repeated in English. She smiled through her tears. 'My sis-ter! *Ukhtee!*'

Um Muhammad swept her daughters and her newborn granddaughter all up in her wide embracing arms.

—14—

The hot winter sun sizzled down on the glassy sapphire waters of the Gulf as Tom Shannon stood with his daughter and his grandchildren on the deck of the family cabin cruiser about to cast off for a picnic at sea.

'Ready here, sir,' called the Pakistani boatman.

'*Yalla*,' Tom ordered. 'Let's go!'

Khalid and Sarah waved to their seven half-sisters straining at the edge of the dock, and from the throats of the ghostly black-shrouded female relatives standing beside the girls came the trill of *zaghareit* joy-cries: '*Ayououououououay!*'

Tom flinched when Sunny, standing beside him, shrouded like those women on shore in a black mask and cloak, let loose an answering cry, '*Awwwwwouoouk!*' He hated to see his daughter in that getup, screeching that eerie screech. 'Stop that, Sunny. Stop that noise.'

'But it's fun! *Awwwwouoouk!*' Sunny laughed. 'It took me months to learn how to do it, sort of. I'm teaching Sarah now. Honey, show your grandfather how you can do it.'

'*Awwwwwwk!*' Sarah clapped her hands together in glee. 'Did you hear? Did you hear me?'

'*Wallah*' - 'By God' - 'you must practice more.' Khalid withheld his approval, as he thought was his right as Sarah's lord. But then as Sarah's face crumpled, Khalid put his arm around her, as he thought was his responsibility as Sarah's protector. 'You sounded very wonderful, my sister.'

'Truly?' Sarah's black eyes blinked adoringly up at him.

'*Bismallah*' - 'In the name of Allah' - 'you do it as well as our mother!' Khalid nudged his mother to see if she had understood his little joke about how badly both of them had imitated the *zaghareit*.

But Sunny was more intent on waving one final wave of regret to those left behind. 'I wish you had let me bring the rest of the girls, Father. There was room here for the sisters, and Nura, and Um Muhammad, and Aisha and -'

'The aunts and the cousins and the uncles and the half-nephews and the granddaughters and the sisters of the wives once removed!' Tom laughed. 'I hardly ever get the chance to be alone with you, and the kids, like this. Humor me just this once. Another time we'll take the whole tribe. But today it's just you and me and your babies.'

'Babies!' At six years old, Khalid fancied himself very nearly a young man.

'Sorry, sport.' Tom rumpled Khalid's hair. 'Suppose you go and get the rods and the tackle box, and the two of us men will settle down with our favorite little girl here, and show Sarah what serious fishing is all about.' As a delighted Khalid ran off to do his grandfather's bidding, with Sarah a devoted shadow behind him, Tom's eyes clouded. 'So like his grandfather,' he said mostly to himself. 'The same eyes; the same trusting look in those great dark eyes.' He shook his head.

'You have blue eyes,' Sunny said absently as she watched the shore, trying to decide if they were far enough away so she could shed her black cocoon.

'I meant Khalid's other grandfather. Rashid's father.

Abdullah.' Tom's brooding eyes were still locked on his grandson. 'I meant my great friend Abdullah. My great regret Abdullah.'

But Sunny was untying her mask, slipping off her cloak, unzipping her outer robe, and stretching out on the deck in her red one-piece swimsuit as she rubbed suntan lotion on her long pale legs and arms.

'Christ!' In an instant Sunny had been transformed from a shapeless black muddle of cloth to an erotic vision of a mostly naked modern American woman. Tom wondered if one of the reasons the Arabs covered their women up the way they did was for the thrill of moments like this, when, in utter privacy, off came the wraps and even the most modest of matrons looked as if she had been conjured up from a pornographic dream.

'Nice suit, isn't it?' Sunny lowered her straps so she could get an even tan on her shoulders. 'One of Aisha's cousins was in London, and she bought four dozen bathing suits just like this for all the women of the family. All red! Every one exactly alike! Too bad we hardly ever get to wear them.' Sunny frowned as she looked herself over. 'Hope I get a little color today. All this sun all the time, and yet I'm so white!'

Tom looked out to sea, away from the sight of his daughter in that sensationally tight red swimsuit. He had seen one, and only one, like her before. Tom stared at the hot blue sea where that other one had died. He sighed and swallowed hard, but the lump was still in his throat. His eyes were drawn back to Sunny. The daughter was so like the mother. Sometimes it was such a joy, sometimes too much anguish. Today, Tom thought with resignation, was apparently going to be one of his maudlin days. He was glad he had fortified himself with a few quick snorts from his bottle of bootleg vodka just before Sunny and the children had come aboard. Usually he had to drink before he could bear to be with her. Vodka was the best, for vodka didn't leave a telltale smell on his breath. He was so ashamed when he saw her sniffing him for signs of liquor.

Guilt, longing, regret, grief . . . Would it, he wondered, never end? Since Sunny had stepped off that plane, the exact replica of her mother, Tom had been engulfed with thrills and shudders of remembrance watching his daughter be so happy with Rashid. He and Sally had been happy just like that. He shut his eyes. 'No,' he muttered. 'No, not today.' He had been looking forward to this family outing for months.

As he had endured this last lonesome stretch out on that hateful offshore drilling platform in this wretched Gulf, he had planned the food Sunny would pack, where they would cruise, how many fish they would catch, what she would say, what he would answer. Tom hated his assignments on the offshore rigs. He hated to be adrift in the deep dark swirling memories of these killing waters. Every night out on the drilling platform, he had tried, and failed, to drown those unquenchable memories in whiskey. He supposed it was perverse, feeling as he did about the Gulf, to bring his family out here for a recreational cruise. Or had he brought them out here in the hope of finally exorcising those family demons? Tom shook his head. He had most certainly not planned to be haunted today. But he held on to the rail as if again he could feel the engine rumbling, the deck bucking, Sally in his arms, her dying in the Gulf, Abdullah . . .

Tom concentrated, as if his sanity depended on it, on the details of the here and now. Sunny had fried chicken and mixed potato salad and baked a chocolate cake for their picnic today. He had bought Kaki cola and candy bars for the kids. And he had even succeeded in finding two hundred-dollar, contraband six-packs of Budweiser for himself. He thanked God when he felt his mouth go dry at the thought of that beer. He wasn't back on that ship of the death; he was here on the cabin cruiser with his daughter and his grandchildren. He went below decks and swiftly drained two beers.

When he came back, Sunny was shading her eyes as she watched Khalid and Sarah dragging the rods and tackle box to the edge of the deck. 'Watch out! Not too close, now! Remember what I told you about the sharks!'

And the barracuda, Tom thought as he anxiously made for the children. Don't forget the barracuda. He called back to Sunny. 'You lie there and relax, princess. I'll watch them - don't worry.' He told the boatman to kill the engines and drop anchor, and he untangled the rods and hooked the bait and cast the lines. Only then did he dare to look for the sinister sheen of silver fins cutting through the mirror-still water. Nervously he laughed. 'No sharks today, that's for sure. And no barracuda.' He wiped the sweat off his forehead and showed Khalid and Sarah how to hold the rods. For a while he was calm as he sat between his grandchildren, telling them stories of how he used to row out on the wide green ponds of New England very early in the morning when it was foggy and the fish were biting. Khalid caught a foot-long grouper, and Sarah's line broke and had to be restrung. When Tom felt a heavy tug on his line and reeled in a pretty chunk of pink coral, he launched into a credible lecture about how reefs were formed ages ago under the sea. But then he signaled for the boatman to come and fish beside the children until it was time for lunch.

Belowdecks he took another icy beer from the refrigerator chest, poured it into a stoneware mug so the children would think he was drinking coffee, and joined Sunny, who was sprawled out like a lizard on the deck. 'Better watch it. Sun's even stronger out here than in the desert. I remember how burned I got that day . . .' Tom stopped himself before he described the burns he had sustained the day Sally and Abdullah had died. Silently Tom tied the awning in place over the deck. 'That's better.' Awkwardly he settled down next to Sunny. He was still a self-conscious father. Aside from kissing Sunny hello and goodbye and calling her 'princess,' he still didn't know exactly how he was supposed to act when he wanted to be loving with her. He wished the mantle of his paternity had settled more naturally on his shoulders. He could hardly pull this full-grown stranger into his lap and ask her to tell him where life hurt. Gruffly he turned to her. 'So how's my little princess?'

She smelled the beer on his breath and wondered where he had managed to buy it this time. But she decided not to make it an issue today. Beer wasn't as bad as that bathtub vodka he was addicted to, or the rotgut whiskey. Always she worried that someday the Saudis would catch him with forbidden alcohol, then flog him and banish him from Arabia forever. 'I'm fine, Father.' Sunny looked out at the murky coast she could still see faintly outlined like a mirage on the horizon. 'Everything's terrific.' Her voice, however, lacked conviction. Although she and Nura had mostly succeeded in becoming friends, still Sunny endured flashes of jealousy when Rashid slept in that other bed. But that didn't trouble her as much as her increasing worries that Rashid's work was eating him up. Even in bed he brooded about petroleum and the Americans and the extreme conservatism of the Saudi royal family. She repeatedly tried to get him to share his problems with her, but he had become so secretive that sometimes she thought he didn't even trust her. Yet stoutly she insisted to her father that nothing was wrong. 'The kids, you, the family . . . Allah *karim* - God is generous.'

'Allah *karim*? I've been here long enough to worry every time I hear that. The Arabs reserve their "Allah *karims*" for the worst of times, when their tents are collapsing round their heads.' He narrowed his eyes in speculation. 'You didn't count Rashid among your blessings just now. Any reason for that?'

'No! Not at all!' Sunny was too emphatic. 'He . . . no, us . . . we're very happy, happier than I ever thought anyone could be. We are extremely happy!' Unhappily she looked at the coast. What she had said was mostly true, except for all those increasing blocks of time when he was apart from her. She had once thought she would make the point of her life to run to Rashid, but instead she had discovered it was to wait for him. He was always away on oil business or tribal business or family business. Yet she had spent some of the most sensual hours of her life not with him but waiting for him, imagining how he would touch her and where he would touch her. She had talked about this with the other women, and they all said it was the same for them. The men arrived unannounced and left without apologies, and the women spent the hot sultry hours of their loneliness in a daze of erotic longing. Sometimes, as Sunny waited in the ever-present heat for Rashid to sweep back to her tent and make her writhe in his arms, she reveled in every exquisite instant of her own breathlessly mounting desire. She would leisurely bathe her body, and shave off her latest fuzz of pubic hair, and smooth scented lotions on her legs and arms and breasts and belly, and brush her hair with long caressive strokes, and paint her fingernails and toenails a glossy scarlet. Hours later, when she was fresh and oiled and ready for him, she would lie down and smile at the seams of the tent and remember the last time he had come to her, and the time before that, and so the hot carnal days and nights would pass, and she was obsessed with the thrill of never getting enough of him.

Yet of course she could not explain all this to her father. 'Rashid's away a lot. He's still working too hard, what with OPEC, and his job at Aramco, and that family conglomerate of his. You know he's thinking of leaving Aramco, don't you? That Tariki offered him a job in the petroleum ministry?'

'Tariki wants him? That hothead? Rashid's one of Tariki's boys?' Abdullah Tariki was the controversial head of the Saudi Ministry of Petroleum, and the nemesis of Western oil interests in the Middle East. It had been Tariki's idea to bond the Third World oil-producing nations together in OPEC, and he was doing all he could to radicalize the Saudi oil industry. He wanted more Saudis in higher positions, he wanted more Saudi control at all levels of Aramco affairs, he wanted Saudis involved in the transporting, refining, and marketing of oil once it left ıa, and he wanted Saudis to renegotiate Aramco's .cession territory. 'If Rashid's as smart as I think he is, 'll go for it. But I think he should be careful with Tariki. I hear he's on the way out, that King Faisal thinks he's a revolutionary. But so long as Rashid keeps at least a little distance between himself and Tariki, now's a good time to join the government team. That's where the future is. Before long the Saudis will be calling the shots, and all those big cheeses at Aramco will be glorified flunkies.'

'That'll be the day.'

'You'll live to see it, I think.' A note of satisfaction swept into Tom's voice. He had no illusions about Standard Oil and Mobil and the other oil giants who were behind Aramco. 'Mark my words, there will be a day of reckoning. Aramco has made a bloody fortune out of Saudi Arabia. Oh, I know the company's built hospitals and schools here, and jumped when the kings and the princes have said to jump, and filled a lot of numbered royal bank accounts in Switzerland. But all that's been too little, too late. The American oil companies have robbed Saudi blind for nearly thirty years. They've had unlimited amounts of incredibly cheap Saudi Arabian oil at their disposal since the Number Seven well came in on the day you were born, Sunny. But that oil's going to run out some day. By the time your Khalid's an old man, there won't be much left. It's a real shame the Arabs weren't paid a fair price for their oil, and that simple conservation wasn't practiced before it was too late.' Tom sighed. 'There will be hell to pay when the Arabs wise up. Already it's started, with your husband's OPEC.'

'You really think OPEC is going to work? You think the oil companies will ever actually agree to negotiate prices?'

'A better question, princess, is whether the Arabs and the Iranians and all the others will ever be able to make a united front for this or any other reason. *That's* the sticking point.'

'True.' Sunny sighed. 'Between the Iraqis and the Kuwaitis and those awful Iranians, Rashid's almost always in a bad mood these days.' Sunny quickly changed the subject away from Rashid's moods. 'Why don't *you* get out now too? Retire. Come live with us. Everyone wants you. Not just me and Rashid but Ibrahim, the cousins, everyone. I hate your working out on those rigs. I'm always afraid you'll be in one of those fires again out there.' Sunny shuddered. 'God! The fire, the burning oil on the water - sometimes I have bad dreams about that.'

Tom looked at her strangely. He licked his dry lips with his tongue. 'You do?'

'Let's not talk about it. Let's talk about other things.'

'Sometimes I think there *are* no other things.' Tom drained his mug of beer and looked out at the glassy blue surface water. 'That and only that. That day. Only that day.' He studied Sunny. 'You're like her, you know. You look like her, move like her, laugh like her. Like your mother. Like my Sally.'

Sunny felt suddenly chilled. Too much sun, she decided. She laughed off her premonition. 'I wish I really were as pretty as her. When I was a little girl I used to sit there on my favorite lookout hill in the orchards and pore over her pictures and letters. . . . You know, I think that was when I fell in love with Saudi, reading her letters. I used to be able to recite them all by heart. She made it sound so wonderful! No wonder I couldn't wait to come here.'

Morosely he looked out over the waters, remembering when he had sat on a deck like this and Sally had delivered her ultimatum - Saudi or her, she had made him choose - and on the day she had died, he had promised, too late, to take her away from this kingdom she had feared and despised. Tears filled Tom's eyes. An irresistible impulse finally to confess gripped him. Before he changed his mind, he let the past spill out into the present. 'Wonderful? No, no, your mother hated almost every minute she ever spent here. She was afraid here, and she wanted to go back home to New England almost from the first moment she arrived.' Tom swallowed hard but went on. 'The day your mother died, I promised her we'd leave. She was pregnant again, and she didn't want to have the baby here.'

'What?' Sunny wondered if her father was more drunk than she had thought. Often he babbled imagined tales from the past and burst into sentimental tears when he had been drinking too much.

But this time Tom was almost soberly determined to tell all. 'I failed all of them. Sally. Abdullah. You.' He leaned over and gripped Sunny's arm and pulled her closer so she would have to listen. 'There's something I've been meaning to tell you, princess. Something I think you should know. Something I've only told one other person. Only old Ibrahim. I had to tell him, long ago, so he would understand. I told him, and he forgave me, and he said it was Allah's will. "*Inshallah!*" He said, "*Inshallah.*" But now I have to tell you, so you'll understand. So you'll understand everything.' Tom shook his head. 'You know, the Muslims believe that everything is fated, foretold by God, that everything happens for a reason and in its own just time. Sometimes I think they're right. When I got that cable about your marrying Rashid, I thought, "So *this* is how it all ends. So *this* is the final price."'

'What are you talking about?' Sunny was alarmed. She tried not to remember that the Arabs and the Americans all called her father Majnun, 'the crazy one.'

'Killed him. I as good as killed him.'

'Father, maybe we should go below, out of the sun.'

But Tom had waited too many years to make this confession. He would not stop until he had told it all, and he would not gloss over his own guilt for the worst of it. 'The Gulf that day. The day Sally died. Him, too.' For a moment as he stared at his daughter, Tom seemed entirely sober. 'She died first, she must have died as soon as the boat exploded and we hit the water. Fire, there was so much fire.' Tom brushed the tears from his cheeks. 'I couldn't have saved her; God took her right away.' Tom crossed himself.

'Father, that's enough. You're upset. It's time for lunch, and –'

'But him!' Relentlessly Tom brushed aside her protests. 'I *could* have saved Abdullah but I didn't. He had saved my life, he got me out of the water and up on a hatch cover, got Sally's body up there too, Lord knows how he ever had the strength, but he did. I was holding her, I still thought she was alive. I was holding on to my Sally for her dear life. And then the barracuda were coming, and he wanted me to let Sally go into the water so he could take her place and escape the barracuda. But I wouldn't do it.'

'Barracuda?' Sunny stared open-mouthed at her father. She had never heard anything about barracuda the day her mother had died. She looked out to sea and listened with growing horror.

'At first I didn't really understand what was happening. The fire, the smoke, the sun, the cries of the dead and dying. Abdullah was screaming in Arabic. Sally was dead in my arms. And those horrible glittering silver fins were coming closer. But then all of a sudden I knew, I understood everything. And still I wouldn't do it. Still I wouldn't save Abdullah. I let that poor man die. I just couldn't let go of her. Couldn't let the barracuda get her, even though she was dead, even though it meant Abdullah would have to die too. He saved my life, and then I let him die. I thought Sally's dead body mattered more than that man's live one.' Tom was so intent on reliving his past he didn't notice Sunny recoiling in horror. 'Damned. Ever since that day, I've been damned. I tried to atone. I stayed here, with Sally. I sent you back home so I couldn't ruin your life too. I paid for Abdullah's boys to go to school, sent them to Beirut, Cairo, London, Boston, Texas - would have sent them to the moon if they wanted it and it had been in my power. But that wasn't enough, no . . . Rashid took you. When I got that telegram, I thought . . .' Tom's stricken eyes searched his daughter's shocked face. 'I told you already what I thought. Told you too much, probably.'

Sunny could not look at her father. What she had just heard was horrible. How could he have done that? And her mother – had her mother really felt the way her father said – had she hated Saudi? Were those letters she had always treasured all a lie? And Abdullah, Rashid's father, the other grandfather of her son and her daughter – had that poor man really died that grisly death? Sunny could feel her father's needy eyes upon her, but still she could not meet them. She wished he would go away and leave her alone so she could sort all this out. But dully she realized that he wanted something from her here and now. He wanted her to say something soothing, she supposed, or even to take him in her arms and comfort him as she did Khalid or Sarah when they woke from a terrifying nightmare. Instead Sunny hid her face in her hands and began to cry.

'Ummie! Ummie! What's wrong?' Khalid was standing over her, touching her hair. 'Are you crying?' Khalid's eyes, so like his paternal grandfather's, accused Tom Shannon of making his mother cry.

'Lunch!' The boatman was carrying the hampers of food and the chests of drink onto the deck.

'Sunny . . .' Tom tried to put his arm around his daughter. 'Honey, I'm sorry. I'm so sorry. You have to believe me, princess, I'm so sorry.'

'It's okay, Father.' Sunny could manage only a slight, formal smile as she dried her eyes on a towel. But still she couldn't look him in the eye. 'We'll talk about it later, maybe after lunch.'

'Sure, princess. That'll be fine. Later. Yes, later. Maybe we'll talk later, after lunch.'

Tom sat huddled by himself in the cabin cruiser, morosely drinking beer after beer, long after Sunny and the children had gone. After lunch, he and Sunny had never gotten around to talking more about the death of all their illusions.

On his lips, in his mouth, down his throat, the beer had a bitter taste. Tom wished he could call back his confession. He should have known better. Of course the horror of what he had done would make a difference to Sunny - to any decent person. It had certainly made a difference to him. All these long sad years of remorse and atonement . . . Again Tom drained his bottle of beer and opened another. He wondered how long it would take for Sunny to hate him, and what form her hatred would take. She might come right out and accuse him of being a killer and a coward. Or she could start picking at him for lesser sins. Perhaps she would simply freeze him out as if he had ceased to exist. Or maybe she would turn away from him without warning someday - like today - when he needed her most. He finished his beer and reached into the refrigerator for another. But there were no more. Tom counted the twelve empty bottles on the counter and in the garbage. Two hundred dollars' worth of Budweiser in his gut, and he wasn't even drunk or forgetful. He dug in the back of the cupboard until he found the little that was left of his bottle of vodka. He drank it off in one greedy gulp, and yet that wasn't enough either. He had to have more to drink, and soon. He was so terribly thirsty tonight.

Tom cursed as he stumbled from the deck to the pier. His limp from that oil-field fire so long ago was always worse when he was a little drunk. He would feel better when he had anesthetized that pain, and all pain, with some more liquid balm. He lurched inside his car and headed back toward the commercial docks where he could usually buy a bottle of smuggled gin for a hundred dollars or more. But it was the time of the sunset prayers, and the docks were deserted. It could be tomorrow morning before the men he knew down here came back on the job. Tom scowled and headed for Abdul Rahman's camera shop in the center of Khobar. Abdul Rahman always had a bottle of Scotch for sale in his back room, for a price - sometimes twenty-five dollars more here than on the docks. But when Tom shambled into Abdul Rahman's, the Arab shook his head and shrugged and told him he had just sold his last bottle. He would not have a new case until maybe tomorrow or after tomorrow. But Abdul Rahman beckoned for Tom to come closer. Hashish, the Arab whispered in his ear. He had good-quality Lebanese hash, the best hash in the world, cheaper and better than British whiskey. Tom brushed off Abdul Rahman as if he were an insect.

Tom muttered to himself all the way out to Dhahran. So Abdul Rahman was peddling hashish along with his Nikons? He remembered Abdul's father, poor old dour old Hassan, who used to chant the Koran out loud as he stitched leather shoes in his shop off an alley. Tom supposed it was a good thing Hassan hadn't lived to see the day when his eldest son sold hashish and contraband whiskey. Tom whizzed past the grimy walled houses and the litter-strewn streets and the neon-lit stores which specialized in all that once had been forbidden in the Islamic Kingdom of Saudi Arabia. When he had first come here, all this had been desolate salt marsh and desert. Then he and those like him had sunk their wells, and the oil had gushed up, and the great transformation of Arabia had begun. Again, as always, Tom wondered whether the oil was blessing or curse. Was it true that everyone in Arabia was either on the take or on the make?

Tom for once was glad to pull inside the Aramco gate into Little America. Tonight he wanted nothing more than to come home, even if this was not truly home but only a poor and incomplete sham of home. Thirty years ago he had left New England. He shook his head as he cruised the sterile streets of Dhahran. He missed Still River's orchards, the white steeples of the churches on the village greens, the snow on the rolling hills, the greenness and the fertility and the optimism of life back there at home.

If only he could have a drink, he was certain he would feel better. Today he had made a terrible, perhaps an unforgivable, mistake in telling Sunny far too much about his own and her own past history. Tomorrow he would have to try to make it up to her. But first he had to get through this night. Liquor had worked its stupefying wonders for him for years, and he was certain it would work again tonight. Tom and alcohol and Aramco were old comrades. In the good old days before 1952, King Abdul Aziz had allowed foreigners to drink all they wanted so long as they didn't pass on their habits to his Muslim subjects. Looking back on those rowdy pioneer days, Tom sometimes wondered when he and his drinking buddies had ever sobered up long enough to find the greatest oil fields in the world. But then one night in Jeddah a young drunken prince had shot the British consul dead because he wouldn't fork over a bottle of whiskey. The scandalized king had responded by banning liquor even in the foreign enclaves. Aramco had soberly said its workers could drink up whatever alcohol they had on hand, but after that Dhahran would be dry. No one who had lived through those next sodden months on the American reservation would ever forget them. First they had drunk up all the whiskey, next the wine, then the beer. Finally they had brought out from the back of their cupboards the brandies, the cordials, the syrupy fruit cocktails none of them had ever before been thirsty enough to drink to the dregs. Tom remembered how they had drained the very last drop of every one of those sickeningly sweet fruit brandies on their last binge.

Tom cruised uncertainly along the busy streets. He supposed that hidden inside virtually every one of these bungalows was at least one contraband bottle of home-made gin or vodka or whiskey. Prohibition here had worked much as it did at home during the Roaring Twenties. People had learned to drink secretly behind closed doors with trusted friends. A few years back, he would have had his pick of friendly living rooms where he could tip a few with his boon companions. But Tom's old buddies had long ago retired to greener pastures. He still got Christmas cards from the old men who now lived in quiet little cabins on the coast of Oregon and in Maine and down in the Florida Keys. He was the last of the grizzled pioneers who had known Saudi when it was still something, before the decay and the corruption set in, and Arabs and Americans alike went for the easy money. He couldn't very well knock on a closed door and beg an illegal drink from a stranger.

Tom pursed his thirsty lips. Maybe he *could* get away with doing just that. The new people considered him a character. Maybe they would enjoy giving this old wreck of a drunk a drink.

But the sudden recollection of Howard Anderson spared Tom that final humiliation. There were only the two of them left from the old bunch, and Howard was top management now. Mostly he was in The Hague overseeing the European business or back making important decisions in New York or Houston, but Tom thought Howard still kept his bungalow here in Dhahran. Maybe he even still hid his keys under the doormat and his whiskey behind the Bible on his bookshelf. Tom shambled up to Howard's front door and was jubilant when he found the key.

'Hi there!' A pleasantly open-faced young man who was not Howard was sitting on the sofa reading a book. A child's bicycle was in the hallway, and there was a playpen in the living room.

'Guess I got the wrong house. I was looking for Howard's place.'

'Howard Anderson? He doesn't live here anymore. But if you're one of his old friends, sit on down. Any friend of Howard's . . .' The young man smiled. 'Can I get you a drink? What'll it be? Vodka or whiskey? Mary made me a nice big pitcher of orange juice for screwdrivers before she went out with the kids. I'd be with them, but I'm sitting the still tonight.' He held out his hand. 'Peter Mitchell.'

'Tom Shannon.'

'Majnun?' The young man's face lit up. 'Hey, I've heard about you. What're you drinking, Tom?'

'Whiskey.'

'Coming right up.

Tom followed him out to the kitchen and sat at the table and felt like kissing the bootleg still that was busily engaged in its intoxicating alchemy. Peter handed him a tumbler of ice and a mean colorless brew that could pass for whiskey if a thirsty man shut his eyes. Tom downed it in four great fiery gulps and waited for this obliging young man to give him a refill.

'You *sure* can drink.' Peter put the bottle and ice out on the table so Tom could help himself, and then he turned to watch attentively as his liquor coursed through its final run. 'I'm new at this,' he confided. 'We're having a party next week, so I had to buckle down and make a batch all by myself. I started three weeks ago with the sugar and the water and the yeast. Hard to believe that by the time this baby finishes tonight I'll have one-hundred-and-ninety-five-proof ethyl alcohol.'

Tom licked his lips and smiled. It was about time his luck changed. He would be drunk as a skunk by the time he hit the hay tonight. He hoped his new young friend would let him bunk on their living-room sofa.

'I suppose you're an old hand, Tom, at this liquor business.'

'You might say that.' Tom drained another glass.

'It's real nice talking to you, and I'd like to talk some more.' Peter looked at his watch. 'But would you mind if I dashed out just for a little while? There's a science fair at the school, and Pete Junior has this miniature oil well on display, and it would mean the world to the boy if I showed up. If you'll just sit here and watch the still for me, I'll be back in an hour or so with Mary and the kids. They'd love to meet you.'

'Sure.' Tom eyed the bottle, which was three-quarters full. 'Happy to oblige.'

He breathed a sigh of relief when Peter shut the front door and left him alone with his liquor and his regrets. He had thought he might have a chance to atone here in Saudi in an endless vigil by Sally's grave. Once he had romantically even imagined he might have been spared for a reason. He had so wanted to believe there could be salvation waiting here. But now he admitted that all there was in the desert was death and suffering. Redemption and resurrection were a Christian mirage in this Muslim wasteland.

Tom poured himself another whiskey and judged that another sort of salvation was almost at hand. He would pass out soon, and by the time he woke up tomorrow he would have forgotten the exact dimensions of his anguish. He would weather this crisis just as he had so many others. But then, as if it had happened yesterday, he saw again the cold sapphire waters of the Gulf, Sally pleading with him to take her home, then the explosion, Sally's death, Abdullah's cries, his own terrible failure. He admitted now what he supposed he had always known. He would never be free of that failure. Never, no matter how he tried, could he forgive or forget what he had done.

Tom shook his head at himself. He supposed he shouldn't be so despairing. It was only human to fail and then to sin and sin again. But if he was truly contrite and meant to sin no more, there were forgiveness and salvation. Tom examined his conscience and decided no man had ever been sorrier for anything than he was for the deaths of Sally and Abdullah. And no man had ever struggled harder to perform his self-inflicted penance. But Tom supposed that, being human, he was guilty of new sins. He drank too much, despaired too much, believed too much in hell and not enough in heaven. Yet Tom decided that he had, after his own fashion, atoned.

Tom sat up and rubbed his eyes and decided he would start all over again tomorrow. He would talk to Sunny until she understood everything. If she still wanted him then, he would come live with her and the children. Maybe he should have told Sunny long ago. He felt almost like a free man, with all that finally off his chest.

Tom also felt sick at his stomach. The air in the kitchen was nauseating him. He could smell the alcohol fumes all around him. That volatile alcohol could blow up any minute. He jumped up in alarm to see if the pipe to the condenser had sprung a leak, then reached to pull out the plug to the hot plate. But he was too late. There was time only for Tom to cry out the last, and the dearest, word of his life before a flash and a shuddering explosion rocked the kitchen of the Aramco bungalow. 'Sally! . . .'

Weeks later Sunny thrashed in bed next to Rashid as the dream of forgiveness, the nightmare of regret gripped her again.

It was very real, this dream. Sunny and her father were sitting on the deck of the boat, at blissful rest at anchor in the Gulf, and as the hot Saudi sun beat down, Tom was telling Sunny the same terrible story he had told her the afternoon of the day he died. But this time in her dream as Sunny listened to her father, her lips curled into a Madonna smile of understanding and compassion, and Sunny leaned over and enfolded her father in her arms as he cried like a child. In her dream Sunny was wise and loving, for in her dream she knew that what mattered was not her father's one fatal and bitterly regretted mistake thirty years ago but her father's present crying need for simple compassion and peace. In her dream there was only a sweet true rush of gentle selfless forgiveness. In her dream Sunny did not flinch away and judge harshly how her father had betrayed his Arab friend. In her dream she only held this broken man like a sick child in her arms. In her dream she was content tenderly to stroke her father's thinning hair. Generously in her dream she knew that many other men at many other times had done far worse. Wisely in her dream she understood that it was a measure of her father's decency that he had never been able to live with his betrayal.

In her dream Sunny understood that if her father had committed a crime or a sin against Abdullah, he had atoned for it long ago. In the dream when Sunny was the perfect daughter she wished she had been able to be, she looked out at the blue waters and imagined how it must have been for him that day, the boat blowing up, the fire, the panic, the terror, the confusion, his wife dead in his arms, his friend in the water, the sinister slide of the barracuda fins. It did not seem so very terrible that her father had stubbornly held on to what was dearest to him in life. As she held on to her father with a daughter's perfect love and concern, it seemed that what had happened long ago could have happened to anyone, could have happened even to her. Then, suddenly, everything shifted, the world turned, the smoke was choking her, she was in the burning water, she was screaming, and it was not her father who had let the Arab die but herself who had done it - she was the guilty one now in her dream that was suddenly a nightmare, and the fins were coming for her. . . .

She awoke and Rashid's strong virile body was holding hers, Rashid was stroking her hair, Rashid was telling her everything was all right, she was safe, he was here, stop crying now, tell him what was wrong, he would hold her, he was here for her now and always, he was here.

'My fault.' Still Sunny was caught in the guilty terror of the nightmare. Around her even Rashid's arms were a reproach. Her father had let his father die, long ago. 'My fault he died, mine, my fault.'

Rashid stroked her hair, tried to reason with her, did what he could to help his wife stop blaming herself for the accident of her father's death, which was no one's fault, which was only Allah's will.

As the horror of her nightmare finally receded, Sunny was left with a sick sense of failure. She should have loved her father more that day on the Gulf. She should have taken him in her arms, as she now took him in her arms in her dreams. Sick with guilt, she lay depressed in Rashid's embrace.

When, hours later, the muezzin cried his call for the dawn prayers, she was still awake with her regrets.

*

Um Muhammad was in the lead; then came Nura, next Aisha, finally Sunny, all swathed head to toe in black as they ducked out the kitchen door and slinked through the courtyard toward their secret women's rendezvous on the seamy side of the town. Um Muhammad stealthily unlatched the back gate. It had been her own desperate inspiration to try this forbidden ritual today to help her American daughter. Sunny's father had been dead for two months, and still Sunny would not ease her grip on her grief.

Nura and Aisha and Sunny listened to the howl of the cold north wind. It was March, *shemal* weather, the season of the harsh bitter blinding sandstorms that swept the Saudi deserts from the Iraqi border straight through to Yemen. Nervously the women huddled together as the wind made their robes billow out like sheets on a clothesline.

Inside her mask and veil Um Muhammad's wary old woman's eyes flicked from one end of the street to the other, and then she nodded in satisfaction. If anyone was watching, they would be taken for maids or washerwomen going home from work. No one would ever even suspect that under these coarse scratchy cloaks they had borrowed from the servants were the women of one of the richest young men of Khobar. No one would ever dare imagine that Rashid Al-Murrah's women were on their way to a *zar*, the exorcism rite banned by the government.

Silently the four of them moved down the narrow street. They walked single file close to the wall, the hidden slits of their eyes trained on the sandy ground beneath their bare feet. It would never do for a woman to meet the glance of a passing man. It would be even less prudent to walk carelessly through the littered heaps of discarded rubbish and filth, the orange peels and the tin cans, the rusty nails and broken glass, the rock-hard mounds of sheep dung. Um Muhammad's black skirts swirled through the urban debris as she picked her way down the reeking alley with a precisely calibrated pace, purposeful enough so that none of the other servants would expect her to stop and chat but plodding enough so as not to excite suspicion; no Saudi ever rushes anywhere at any time unless absolute disaster or salacious gossip or fantastic profits are at stake. As Sunny shadowed her mother-in-law, inside the black shells of her mask and her veil and her cloak she could smell the rank familiar smell of her own sweat. Around her head swarmed a buzzing black cloud of flies.

Wearily the women walked Khobar's streets, down the entire length of one long alley, across three thin streets, up more narrow alleys, always checking to make sure they weren't being followed. The men in the Saudi royal family and the men in the Saudi religious hierarchy had long ago outlawed the ancient exorcism rites that had given millennia of women such comfort. The *zar* rituals had been branded pagan superstitions that had no place in the Islamic kingdom where the Prophet had lived and preached and died. Yet still the frustrated, unhappy women of Arabia held their secret rites to purge their private devils. Childlessness was one demon, divorce and polygamy two others. It was to exorcise these real-life fears and disasters that women would gather together in hairy black tents and shadowy windowless houses to howl and dance and frighten away the ghosts that haunted them. The desperate women who came in secret to dance at *zars* were no less devout Muslims than their husbands, only more wishful.

The wild wind was a constantly sighing wail. Shuffling along, fighting the wind, they made first for the harbor, then doubled back toward their villa. Sunny supposed the *shemal* was to blame for how dizzy and disoriented she felt. Her father had once told her there was nothing mysterious or magical or mystical about why a *shemal* made everyone edgy, that these mood fluctuations were merely due to a change in the atmospheric pressure.

Sunny felt the tears beginning again at the thought of her father. Her tears were gluing her mask to her skin. She took deep breaths to help her stop crying and at once the street smells assaulted her, the sharp pungent ammonia reek of urine, the odor of human and animal feces, the smoke of burnt meat, the clouds of heavy cooking spices, the whiffs of expensive musky French perfume.

She listened, then, to the sounds of modern urban Saudi, the hooting horns, the screech of brakes applied in panic as heavily veiled women walked blindly into the paths of oncoming cars. She stood still and listened hard for a moment, but she couldn't hear the growing swell of the *shemal*, much less the gentle sound she liked best in Saudi, the tinkle of camel bells. She thought they must surely be near their destination, but then they veered suddenly into the labyrinthine lanes of the souk. They twisted and weaved their way through the vegetable and fruit stalls, past the spice men and the gold merchants, alongside the money changers and the sellers of camel saddles and live sheep and truck replacement parts. Sunny was weary of so much unaccustomed barefoot walking along so many unfamiliar paths, but she knew better than to pluck at her mother-in-law's robe and whine that she wanted to go home. This, all of this, had to be home now. With the death of her father, she had lost her last hold on the West.

Finally Um Muhammad ducked into the alley she had saved for last. She knocked on a closed gate, whispered a rush of words, and gestured for her daughters to follow her inside. Here only one anonymous veiled woman stood guard. But from a small, squat, square concrete house nestled inside the courtyard came the muffled sounds of cymbals and drums and cries. Here, tucked away on this back street, the howling wind drowned the sounds of heavy traffic. Before their eyes the air was turning gold with the sands of Baghdad and Basra and Kuwait, sweeping south and sweeping west, roaring from Asia across Arabia into Africa. Gold sand, gray sand, white sand, red sand, sand everywhere, sand under mask and robe and veil, sand in the eyes, sand in the hair, *shemal* sand in every pore.

But as Um Muhammad opened the door, a rolling wave of sensation crested and swept away even the *shemal*. Sunny stood at the threshold of the drumbeats and the sweat and the incense and the repressed emotion, and then she sighed and crossed over; she joined the women packed inside the small single shadowy room of the house. From under the darkness of mask and veil, Sunny squinted out at the darkness of the black figures squatting on the sandy dirt floor. She went to pull off her veil and untie her mask, but Um Muhammad stayed her hand and shook her head. Sunny peered again at the other black forms. Like herself, every one of these women was shrouded not only in her usual mask but in a thick opaque veil as well. If the religious police ever questioned any of them, none could ever with any certainty betray friends or foes. As her curious eyes grew used to the murky dimness, Sunny saw that twenty or thirty women were kneeling or sitting or swaying in this tiny ten-by-twelve-foot room. Her eyes were drawn then to the spectacle in the far corner, where three swarthy men crouched, groaning and screaming. One beat a donkeyskin drum; another clashed brass cymbals; a third tossed his shoulder-length hair to and fro as he waved a wand of incense and led a hoarse and deep-throated chant, '*Allah!*'

Um Muhammad pointed and whispered that she had heard they had come all the way from Iran with their traveling exorcism rites - that they were famous men, holy men, bound south through all the shaykhdoms of the Gulf, then across the sea to India and Pakistan and then home to Shiraz. Sunny caught her breath and stared in fascination at these refugees from one of the medieval tales of the *Thousand and One Arabian Nights*. Back home in Still River she had imagined Saudi Arabia would be one great pulsating sideshow of exotica. She had assumed that here in Saudi there would be snake charmers and fakirs and peddlers of magic carpets in the souks. But until now she had found no such sorcery in this kingdom by the sea. Until now she had made do instead with the natural wonders of sunsets and sand dunes and skies full of falling stars. Like a delighted child at her first magic show, Sunny stood transfixed before the trio of holy men. Their eyes were black and vile; they were naked to their waists; one wore purple pants and another loose baggy gold trousers and another bell-bottomed dungarees. The leader had camel bells strung around his neck, and so he jangled as he danced.

'*Al-lah!*'

For a long while, Sunny could not take her eyes off that man, and it seemed he felt the intensity of her gaze, for he turned and stared back at her with his burning eyes rimmed with black smudgy kohl. But Sunny was grateful when Um Muhammad broke his spell by putting her arm around her and leading her to the shadows of the very back of the room. She had felt herself almost sinking into a heavy trance. She had been seeing herself on the deck of a boat in the Gulf again, sitting beside her father, or was it beside her mother, or was she alone, sitting at the edge of the deck, brooding over the chain reaction set in motion thirty years ago by her father and her mother and Abdullah? She had been staring at the deadly blue waters of the Gulf and pondering the sins and the failures and the guilts and the atonement of generations, as that bizarre man with the wild glittering black eyes had very nearly hypnotized her inside her veil.

'*Al-lah!*'

Sunny slid down on her haunches, her thighs wedged safe and secure between Aisha and Nura. Sunny was stifling. Inside the sauna of this overcrowded room it was hard to breathe. A woman paced from one corner to another with a lighted brazier in her hands. The incense was making Sunny swoon. She remembered incense from her other life, High Mass back in Still River. Her thoughts turned to the Good Fridays of her childhood, Christ on the cross, all the statues ominously shrouded in draped purple, prayers she didn't understand in Latin. Sunny wiped her eyes with her veil. Her eyes were tearing; it must be the incense making her eyes burn - or was something making her so sad that she was truly crying?

'*Al-lah! Al-lah! Al-lah!*'

The chant sounded primitive, primal, as steady as a pulse. Sunny reminded herself, nervously, that there was nothing strange or savage about it, *Allah* was only the Arabic for 'the God,' she heard the name of Allah invoked every hour of every day, there was nothing scary about Arabs calling out to Allah. But the drumbeat rolled on, swelled, quickened; one woman screamed; another figure in black lurched to her feet and stood at the heart of the circle of squatting women.

'*Al-lah! Al-lah! Al-lah!*'

The cymbals rang faster, the drumbeat thumped deeper, the chanting climbed an octave higher, shriller, louder. Woodenly, like a marionette, the woman began to jerk in time. She spun her arms in the air, she kicked her heels, she threw her veiled head from side to side, and she screamed, '*Al-lah, Al-lah!*'

Matches were struck, coals were lighted, the incense burned brighter, the heavy choking cloud of spiced air seemed to catch in Sunny's mask and Sunny's veil.

'*Al-lah, Al-lah!*'

Sunny's head began to swing from side to side, like a toe irresistibly tapping out a catchy tune, left to right, back and forth, wagging in time to the chant, '*Al-lah, Al-lah!*'

A second woman scrambled to her feet and danced a trancelike solo of her own beside the first: '*Al-lah, Al-lah!*'

From deep in Sunny's throat came an echo of the chant, as regular and essential as breathing: '*Al-lah, Al-lah!*'

A third woman took the floor and twitched and kicked; the first one screamed and crumpled to her knees; Sunny's own body began to squirm; Nura's was moving; so was Aisha's: '*Al-lah, Al-lah!*'

From every corner the chant swelled; the women were

one; Sunny felt swept away; she was floating atop a wonderful cresting chant: '*Al-lah, Al-lah!*'

The drumbeat was a roll, the cymbals were a roar, Sunny was on her feet and dancing beside Nura, next to Aisha, behind Um Muhammad, all one, all together amid the mass of frenzied women: '*Al-lah, Al-lah!*'

Faster came the beat, wilder was the dance; Sunny could feel another swell this time inside her; she could feel the tension building, building higher; then it was letting go, subsiding, then changing, breaking out or breaking up, she did not know or care. '*Al-lah, Al-lah!*'

Women were moaning, women were screaming, and Sunny was moaning and screaming and letting go. As Sunny shrieked, '*Al-lah! Al-lah!*' finally she was made to understand that one of the great skills in life was knowing when to give up and let go and let it all stream out of her.

'*Al-lah! Al-lah!*'

She screamed in rage and in grief and in despair and in guilt. '*Al-lah! Al-lah!*'

She screamed in grief for her lost father and her lost mother and for her lost self and her lost life, and all life's losses: '*Al-lah, Allah!*'

Beside her a woman fainted, behind her a woman collapsed, and Sunny was transported for an instant away from the hot swooning voodoo of this room back to New England; she was sitting on a white wooden lawn chair atop her favorite green hill in Still River, breathing the clear Massachusetts air, watching the green swells of the pasture and the woods and the mountains of home. '*Al-lah, Al-lah!*'

Suddenly the music stopped, the chanting ended, and Sunny sank in a black heap on the floor. In the utter silence, she could hear outside the *shemal* howl, beating its desolate crescendo against the walls. She looked up, and above the prone forms of the panting women she could see gold dust in the air. The *shemal* was pushing the creeping sand through the cracks in the walls; the air was alive with a benediction of dancing golden desert sands. Sunny reached out; she felt the gold on her fingers; she had handfuls of gold, riches beyond measure, in her grasp; she made a fist so she would not drop even one precious gram. But then she looked down at her hands, and the golden moment of magic had passed.

In her tight fists were only worthless golden grains of sand.

—15—

When Muhammad Al-Murrah leaned his head just so, he could see six reflections of himself mirrored on the shimmering facing wall of the Embassy Club on Old Bond Street in London. Mostly he liked what he saw, even six times over. At thirty-five plus, he was still a handsome devil, still had that French-film-star face, still made the ladies crash and burn. In the mirrors his arm was carelessly but possessively around the shoulders of a willowy eighteen-year-old English blonde who aspired to be an international model like Twiggy or the Shrimp. As he watched himself and the girl in the mirrors, he saw younger men, younger *English* men, casting covetous eyes his way. Eat your hearts out, Muhammad wanted to snarl, it's mine - all of it: the girl, the money, the act.

He raised his champagne glass in a silent toast to his own reflections. Tonight he had shed his customary Savile Row tailoring for this 'mod' bottle-green velvet Nehru jacket, which he thought made him look decidedly younger. He was tan from his recent holidays in the South of France and sleek from his frequent massages at his West End club. He wished, however, that he dared to shave off his mustache and goatee. The Saudi royals were always winging into and out of London, and he always had to be on hand to toady up to them. At an instant's notice he could slip off his tweeds and don a white nightshirt and wind a checkered handkerchief around his hair, but the customary Saudi facial hair had to remain permanently on his chin and lip.

Yet he supposed he shouldn't let this hirsute compromise shadow his otherwise flawless cosmopolitan image. By day he juggled millions in the international banking community and on the world's stock markets in the name of the Saudi government and the Saudi royal family. By night he courted, and won, birds with plumage as rare and as fair as that of the one snuggled up next to him now. Not bad, Muhammad thought, for a tribesman born to herd camels and scratch fleabites and pray with sand in his mouth. Never would he quench his thirst because of the burning memory of that endless sand. He leaned over, pulled the magnum of Roederer Crystal from the ice bucket, and toasted himself in the mirror: 'Happy days.'

At his side Sheila obediently clinked glasses, smiled vacantly with her pouty lips, and plucked nervously at her teased hair which, despite her best efforts, was neither as glossy nor as golden as Julie Christie's. 'Happy days,' she echoed.

Muhammad's eyes were hard as he smiled with his lips at the mirror. He tossed down the champagne as if it were brackish water from a silty desert well. Happy days? He wondered exactly when these decadent years in Swinging London had begun to go as flat as this bottle of champagne. He had been here chasing the beautiful people and pursuing the good life ever since he'd left Boston for the land of his dreams eleven years ago. He had been one of the few Saudis in London with any sort of college education, and so he had landed a job at a merchant bank in the City even though his university degrees were in engineering. In Muhammad's first years back here as the bank's Arabic translator and interpreter, it had been sensational simply to be more than a scholarship student at a second-rate school in Manchester. It had given him immense satisfaction just to order from the à la carte menu and send back bottles of wine and snap his fingers at snooty waiters at the Ritz.

But by the time he had been promoted to the bank's liaison with Saudi investors, his ambitions had begun to know no bounds. He had leased a smashing flat in Beaufort Gardens in Knightsbridge, and ordered forty-guinea black and brown and oxblood leather handmade shoes from Lobbs, and bought a spectacular dark-brown Jaguar. Only after he had acquired all the accoutrements money could buy had he begun to get an inkling that merely manipulating other people's money - especially dirty foreign money earned by a dark-skinned Gypsy people - did not make him acceptable to the discriminating few who truly counted. For some years, however, he still had valiantly but vainly continued to try to buy his way into the British upper class. But even all those profits from all those barrels of Gulf light crude could not purchase invitations to the most exclusive houseparties at the best country estates. He couldn't force his way onto the membership lists of the better clubs. The snubs he continued to receive were subtler than but just as final as the ones he had endured in his youth as a North Country student.

Inside, Muhammad seethed with a rage that burnt ulcers into his stomach, yet he could not bring himself to hate the aristocratic infidels who rejected him. He detested rich vulgar Arabs perhaps even more than the British did. But to take the edge off his hurt and anger and pain, he became a legendary high roller among London's smart set where money meant more than class. He had been known to bathe naked South African air hostesses in twenty-guinea bottles of champagne in his black marble bathtub. He put crisp thousand-pound notes on one roll of the dice at the gaming tables. Once he had even chartered a plane to take cronies to Monte Carlo for a lost weekend. Yet even as he had polished and refined his role as jet-set playboy, Muhammad had become inwardly more skittish and troubled and afraid because for a long while he had been living far beyond his means.

Six years ago a seemingly temporary personal cash-flow crisis had led him to dip into the Saudi royal funds. He had intended at first to make a quick, grand killing in the market to pay back that shortfall, but instead he had had to fly a girlfriend to Sweden for an expensive late-term abortion. When months passed without the royal family's discovering his theft, Muhammad had grown a trifle bolder and considerably more contemptuous of his masters. He started giving himself a ten-percent agent's fee on all his transactions. He offered his services, for a price, to those who wanted to do legitimate or shady business in the lucrative markets of the Middle East. He began indulging in what he liked to think of as 'free' translations of Telexes from Riyadh, changing a word here and there if he could glean any personal profit from it.

Muhammad rationalized that the princes of the House of Saud deserved the stewardship he was giving them. The royal family were nothing but a ragtag band of desert marauders, warlords who had won their oil booty by plunder. Arabia's oil came from under ground that had belonged since ancient times not to the tribe of Al-Saud but to Muhammad's own Al-Murrah. An army of Saudi warriors had seized eastern Arabia only fifty years ago, and so it was a miscarriage of justice that the oil wealth had accrued personally to the fortunate parasites of the House of Saud. In righteous and self-serving indignation, then, Muhammad waved his magic pencil over the Saudi accounts and conjured up creative profits and losses that at least for some years worked to his own savvy advantage. He chewed antacid tablets to lull his ulcer, and in time he almost forgot that he would inevitably have to face a day of judgment.

But the signs of approaching Armageddon – those Telexes from the ministries in Riyadh, those visits from the bankers in Jeddah, those queries even from his worried brother in Dhahran – had been building for some months.

Muhammad supposed it was the chilling effect of that increasing pressure that had panicked him into what he hoped was not his fatal round of errors. He had lost big on copper, tin, and cocoa in those cursedly treacherous commodities markets. Yet even then, if he had coolly juggled the books just one more time in one more way, he might have been able to tough out the growing suspicions of the royal family. Instead, he had tried to recoup his losses by gambling desperately for high stakes on the stock market. But his run of bad luck had continued. The market had gone the other way, and he had been obliged to dig deeper into Saudi royal funds for cash to make his margin calls. In a sweat, then, he had desperately continued to throw more good money after bad - locked into a cycle of loss. Cash he had intended to take from the royals for only two days was lost forever, and Muhammad was a grand total of sixty thousand pounds short. But he still believed that if he laid off the booze and sent away the birds, he could buckle down to the white-knuckle art of pulling off a fabulous recovery.

Yet already the bloodhounds were hot on his trail. A team of shrewd auditors hired by King Faisal were due in London next week to go over his books. Muhammad supposed that for perhaps twenty thousand pounds in cash, he could persuade them into keeping silent for a while longer. But he didn't even have enough for that bribe. For the lack of a paltry twenty thousand, everything - London, the girls, the high life, all he was and all he ever could be - was about to slip out of his grasp forever.

Muhammad stared bleakly at the telltale signs of his own corruption in the mirror. The skin around his weary eyes was getting pouchy, his cheeks were beginning to sag into jowls, and that roll of flesh around his waist would soon have to be held in by a corset. Deep inside him he quivered. His mind was subtle enough to grasp not only the precariousness of his predicament but the sad and sorry reasons for it. He had always deluded himself that the West's superiorities, its irresistible women and its easy money and its wonderful decadence, would ease the aches he carried inside. He hadn't wanted to sit passively under a palm tree and sigh away the years waiting for Allah's blessings in this life or the next. By his own wit and reason and grit he had tried, just as the infidels did, to make his own heaven on earth. Muhammad looked away, then quickly back at his reflection. It was too late now to recant and mewl about how he regretted not having chosen that other path to God and virtue. He would have to brazen out this bittersweet chapter in his bittersweet life. He knew exactly how he could raise that twenty thousand by Tuesday.

Muhammad watched his frowning face in the mirror. He had swung plenty of arms deals before this. He had been the middleman who sold tanks to the Egyptians and machine guns to the Syrians and mortars to the Iraqis. He had even basked in the reflected glory of being a pan-Arab patriot arming his brothers for the continuing battle with the Zionist enemy. Yet in this early spring of 1967, the scent of blood hung over the Middle East. Even though everyone who could pull a trigger was hoarding armaments of any make or vintage, there was more danger than ever in getting involved in these deadly war games. Muhammad had heard that hit teams from Israel's Mossad were on the prowl to intercept Arab arms shipments. An attaché at the Egyptian embassy had even warned him personally that the Israelis were hell-bent on making an intimidating example of anyone who dared to try to sell the Arabs so much as a slingshot. Even more ominous, the Egyptians said, were intelligence reports from Moscow which cautioned that the Israelis had full though discreet CIA backing in their campaign to halt the arms flow to the Arabs.

Yet even in this atmosphere of bloodlust and paranoia, Muhammad considered that he might have to run this risk. Already he had been sounded out by a friend of a friend, a Lebanese who wanted a shipment of automatic guns and grenades for his Christian masters. The logistics would be sweet and simple, for Muhammad knew where he could get his hands on an entire warehouse of surplus World War II arms gathering dust on a Marseille wharf. One brief rendezvous on the Riviera, and he would have the twenty thousand pounds necessary to buy him a new lease on life.

'Michael, could we order now? I'm famished.'

Muhammad blinked in bewilderment until he realized that the girl must be talking to him. With a trembling hand he poured her another glass of champagne. His nerves were getting the better of him. He would have to be careful lest he altogether lose touch with reality. He had forgotten that he had played it safe and told this one too that his name was Michael. He no longer liked to answer to 'Muhammad,' the clichéd and despicable name of all 'filthy Arabs.' He had told many of his glittering new friends his name was Michael and that he was from Brazil and his father was 'in coffee and silver and tin.' He might have even legally changed his name if he hadn't feared how pious King Faisal would react to the news that one of his men in London had stopped calling himself after the Prophet. He had compromised, therefore, and was Muhammad by day and Michael by night. Usually he could adroitly juggle the two identities.

He took another sip of the champagne, and as he lit a Benson & Hedges filter cigarette with his gold-plated Cartier lighter, he indulged his hopes rather than his fears. If he only dared to take one more chance with those Lebanese guns, he might finally extricate himself from the tensions of this double life. All he needed was one nice round sum of money to call his own, and he could finally stop pandering to and for the royals. He even pimped for the princes when they came up to London on holiday. He knew which cousin liked Egyptian whores and which one liked Greek boys. If he only could get out from under what he owed, he could be a financial wizard amassing and investing his own funds. He could double his money in six months, marry a trim little peaches-and-cream English girl, and become - at last - a citizen of the United Kingdom. His own blue-black passport with its embossed gold lettering would be made out to Michael Murrah. Briefly, as Muhammad smiled at himself in the mirrors, he considered that perhaps his British passport should name him Michael Murray or even Moran. He flicked the ash of his cigarette into the ashtray and decided Moran sounded too Irish. The British liked the Irish even less than the Arabs. He would be Michael Morrison, Esquire. He would buy horses and have a kennel of hunting dogs and drink sherry in front of sputtering fireplaces.

'Michael?' The blonde shattered his fantasy by pawing insistently at his thigh.

He smiled, for he liked to think he was always eager for an eager woman. His thoughts trailed to another eager blonde on another night. Sunny had married his brother, and it seemed she had made Rashid happy. Once again, even though he had had his way with that delectable girl first, his brother had been the winner. Yet Muhammad's jealousy was eased by the knowledge that his own secret fling with Sunny had finally given him the ammunition to bring his brother down whenever he wanted. Ever since Rashid's marriage to Sunny, Muhammad had kept his ultimate weapon primed to be fired at will. 'Sorry, darling, I was miles away.'

'Could we order now, Michael?'

He clapped imperiously for a waiter, and then he masterfully ordered more expensive food than either he or the dolly could possibly eat. Muhammad was cynically aware that nothing impressed these half-starved young girls like plates piled high at pricey restaurants. More than a decade of being a man about town had left him with few illusions about women, or anything else. These glamour girls who pranced and swished and postured were as fraudulent as he was. Even some of the prettiest flowers of English womanhood, aglow in their short fragrant blooming seasons, gave themselves away when they opened their mouths and spoke with the wrong accents. These daughters of millworkers and shopkeepers and farmers from the drab Midlands and the North worked as air hostesses for foreign airlines or secretaries in advertising agencies or shopgirls in King's Road boutiques. They squandered most of their meager salaries on the latest fads in crushed-velvet miniskirts and white boots and Mary Quant makeup, and they all dreamed the same witless dreams of becoming movie stars or models or marrying royalty. Yet while they were waiting for lightning to strike, many of them were willing to trade a night in a stranger's bed for soup, steak, fried potatoes, and a pudding.

Muhammad hid a yawn. Lately he had begun to tire of the pathetic availability of girls like this. He had picked Sheila up at a Chelsea art gallery a couple of hours ago, and already she bored him. One supple young female body had begun to seem monotonously interchangeable with another. There was no hunt and chase and capture anymore, no real sport. Bringing down these girls was as much of a bore as it used to be to decimate gazelles with a machine gun. Sometimes he waxed nostalgic for a virtuous and innocent young woman who would be a challenge to all his seductive powers. Even a terrified Arab virgin covered head to toe in black would be a welcome diversion.

Yet by habit Muhammad's hand crept across this girl's lap. As he stroked the inside of her bare thigh under her miniskirt, he was startled to feel her spread her legs so his probing fingers could inch higher. His interest quickened. This one might not be along only for the free champagne and the sole and the chocolate gâteaux. This one might truly be in heat. In an instant he forgot all his perverse romantic yearnings for the good old days of girdles and sin and frustration and thanked God for the hot and hungry sure things of swinging London.

'Lovely shrimps, Michael,' she said as the waiter brought her a double portion of the shellfish cocktail. Greedily she speared the biggest with her fork. When she had eaten it, she caught his eye, and wantonly her tongue flicked out and she licked away the traces of cocktail sauce. 'Rio . . . you said something before about taking me home to Rio for Carnival?'

As he let her feed him a shrimp from her fishy little fingers, he made a snap decision. For the opportunity of a constantly replenished supply of women like this, he would paddle into Beirut harbor at noon with a crate of machine guns strapped to his back. He looked at his gold Rolex watch. Tonight, after he made a quick call to his contact in Marseille, he would ring up that Lebanese friend of a friend. He would seal the deal Sunday in his favorite luxury suite at the Hôtel de Paris in Monte Carlo. He would fly down to the Riviera a day early, get some sun and sexual recreation in Cannes, and while away the night at the casino. A few good cards, some fancy rolls of the dice, and he might never have to show up at the Hôtel de Paris. But meanwhile Muhammad decided to put his worries aside and enjoy this girl who had the long wet flickering tongue of a snake. A few turns around the dance floor here at the Embassy Club, a quick ride through the rain in his Jag, a few more glib promises he would never keep about Rio, and he could surely be in heaven on earth.

As Muhammad picked at his food and daydreamed about what he would do with the whore he would inevitably pick up Saturday on the Croisette, he caught his reflection again in the mirrors. Gone was the image of the careworn man on the wrinkled brink of middle age. He was smiling a warm, expectant, young boy's smile. He raised his glass of champagne and toasted himself, and the girl, and the future. 'Happy days.'

Muhammad drowsed in the hot rich Riviera sun, but then he roused himself as the waiter brought him his Coupe Baccarat, an exquisite goblet of vanilla ice cream smothered with fruit and Chantilly and whipped cream. Muhammad wanted to purr like a sated tomcat as he slowly savored every mouthful and every sensation of Monte Carlo, the *crème de la crème* of the Côte d'Azur. He loved the smell of perfume and money and privilege that was Monte. It amused him to sit near these lacquered ladies perspiring in their sables in the sun. It touched him to watch tanned sleek old men with skin like fine Italian leather lean back and shut their droopy eyes as if they believed basking in the sun would make them live forever. It intrigued him to overhear delicious teasing whispers about the scandals of his betters. Muhammad signaled for *café express* and lit a cigarette and smiled benignly at the gorgeous riot of flowery purples and violets and reds in the gardens that lay between where he sat in the Café de Paris and the front entrance to the casino and the Hôtel de Paris. But then he sucked in his breath, jabbed out his cigarette, and squinted through his black-lensed Ray-Bans at the grim dark man leaning languidly against a palm tree in the garden. He told himself it surely was a coincidence that he had seen this same man outside his Knightsbridge flat yesterday morning and again at Heathrow. Nervously he lit another cigarette and worried that this arms deal might not be all it seemed. That 'friend of a friend' had eagerly acceded to all his demands about price and where they would exchange money for instructions on how to get the guns. At the time Muhammad had thanked his lucky stars the Lebanese hadn't bothered to dicker over the price, but later he had remembered that the Lebanese who would pass up a chance to haggle over money had not yet been born.

Muhammad breathed a little easier when he realized that the man by the palm tree was not looking his way. Muhammad's eyes glinted with satisfaction as he watched the other man watching the front door of the hotel. Smugly Muhammad congratulated himself for taking the precautions of coming to the Riviera a day early and staying under an assumed name at the Carlton in Cannes and stealing into Monte Carlo by taxi early this morning. He had reserved a suite in his own name at the Hôtel de

Paris, but he wouldn't go up to room 224 for his seven-o'clock meeting with the Lebanese until he was satisfied he wasn't walking into a trap. He had watched his fill of spy films. He knew enough to keep his own silent watch on the man by the palm tree.

But after a while Muhammad stretched in the sun and decided that the lookout was probably just one of the paranoid Lebanese's security men. Muhammad ordered another *express* and was glad to let his mind wander away from such distressing conjectures. Cannes had been glorious yesterday. He had strutted the length of the Croisette and watched the small white waves crash from the bright blue water onto the palm-brown sand. He had listened to the sensual staccato of high heels on cement, and then he had felt lust course through him as he gazed at slinky women with tousled blond hair and ruby lips and long lithe legs flashing under the flare of miniskirts. He had sipped Campari at a seaside café and watched the continuous parade of chic careless women clinging to the tanned muscled arms of men with slick black hair and white wolfish teeth. He had amused himself wondering how much it would cost to buy this woman or even that man for a savage hour on the sheets, and when he saw a husky dog with glowing blue devil eyes he had supposed that here in decadent Cannes the favors of that dog were for sale as well.

Then later, as he sauntered around the casino savoring the elegant concentrated greed of high-stakes gamblers, Muhammad had winked at a luscious red-haired beauty in a low-cut sequined gown. As she bent over the blackjack table, her melon breasts had been bare almost to the nipple. Muhammad had lit a cigarette and watched those pale white breasts shiver with delight as she pulled in her pile of chips. He had wanted to stroke her palpitating bare breasts for luck, as he had once seen an American oilman rub a rabbit's foot during a poker game in Vegas. He had wanted to waltz this woman whose hair was like fire back to the Carlton and be her wild rampant Arabian stallion.

But then he had seen her kiss the withered parchment cheek of a doddering millionaire, and he had sighed and gone back to the Croisette and bought himself a different class of whore.

Muhammad paid his bill, looked over to make sure the man by the palm tree was not watching him, then strolled into the embracing golden opulence of the Monte Carlo casino. But it was the afternoon, and the only gamblers were fat working-class women in shiny polyester and workmen in overalls on their lunch breaks. Under frescoes of shepherds and fine ladies and bucolic angels, slot machines incongruously rang and groaned and flashed and occasionally tinkled coins.

Hastily Muhammad fled back out the front door. He wanted to set himself up at a comfortable vantage point in the hotel's Bar Américain without giving himself away, and so he slipped inside the side entrance to the bar. He told the waiter to bring him a gin and tonic, and then he sat tucked in a corner table by an open window that looked out on the man glowering by the palm tree. Muhammad could see not only the entrance to the hotel but the center of the lobby, and so he settled down with a sense of growing security for the final liquid hours of his waiting. The bar was snug and elegant and decorated in dark expensive woods. Here the women were older and dowdier and undoubtedly richer than the erotic sexpots of Cannes, and for a moment Muhammad regretted that he had not thought to be a gigolo before he turned thirty-five and his looks began to go.

Muhammad had just ordered a second gin and tonic when he saw the Lebanese alight from a car in the company of three wiry dark men who could be brothers to the watching one. The Lebanese walked over to that tree and clasped the hands of his man, and the five of them stared at the hotel, then began walking toward Muhammad's window. He ducked his head and listened as some of their words and phrases were carried on the wind. At first he thought they were talking in Arabic, but then he went rigid with fear as he realized it must be Hebrew. Muhammad threw thirty francs down on the table, but as he stood to begin making his getaway he couldn't help casting one final terrified glance out the window. Just then the Lebanese looked up, their eyes locked, and then Muhammad raced for the back door as the dark men ran up the front steps and into the lobby. Muhammad thanked God he knew all the ins and outs of this hotel. He slipped through the bar's back door into the lobby, and then through another door into the rear driveway guests used as a discreet entrance. A plump Italian was just paying off his taxi driver, and Muhammad hurled himself into the empty back seat. 'Nice,' he ordered. '*Vite!*'

As the shiny black Mercedes taxi slid through the steep winding sienna streets of Monaco, Muhammad took deep gulps of fresh air to fight his rising panic. He looked anxiously out the back window to see if his enemies were on his trail, and then he leaned back on the leather seat and shut his eyes and tried to think. He might have just barely escaped before the Israelis' trap snapped shut on him, but they knew his haunts in London and could hunt him down and make a bloody example of him at a time and place of their own choosing. He had to find a safe place to hide. His impulse was to flee on the first available flight from Nice airport bound for anywhere. But he didn't know where in the world he would be absolutely safe. He supposed he could always play his trump card and take asylum in the nearest Saudi embassy. Even the Israelis wouldn't be able to touch him back in the police state of Al-Saud. But then Muhammad remembered that the auditors were coming to London next week, where they would surely discover he had embezzled sixty thousand pounds of the royal funds. Would it be worse to face the Israelis or an infuriated King Faisal? Muhammad broke out in a sweat.

The taxi wended through the sleepy burnt-umber hill towns, past groves of olive trees and almond trees and mimosa blooming yellow in green valleys, alongside villas and cottages and a picturesque shack that clung to the edge of a precipice overlooking the phosphorescent sea. Even when they swung down the great curve in the high Corniche road into the shabby yellowing decay of Nice, Muhammad still was undecided. He jumped out of the taxi at the harbor and ran down the docks in the hope he could hire a luxury cruiser to sail him to safety, but the only boats in port reeked of fish and filth. He decided to try his luck in Marseille.

But as Muhammad hailed another taxi and then settled back for the three-hour drive to that other Mediterranean port, he looked out at the lush and verdant subtropical vegetation along the Bay of Angels. Usually he delighted in contrasting the Corniche's pretty and perfect but stately palm trees with the dry and stunted and dusty ones back in Arabia, but he considered now that it could be a very bad omen that his path was a gantlet of palm trees. On the Saudi Arabian flag there was an emblem of palm trees and crossed swords. Muhammad searched his heart. Even if all was lost here, could he bear to go back there? Which was worse, a quick death here or a dismally long life back there? As the taxi purred past the hotel room he dared not revisit in Cannes, Muhammad lit another cigarette and pondered the permutations of death.

Muhammad stifled a yawn as he watched the taxi's windshield wipers hypnotically beat back and forth in the steady drizzle. It was just after dawn, and they were an hour or two away from Paris. It had been raining since long before midnight, when he had given up trying to hire a boat in Marseille and engaged this taxi instead. Since then, as they had plied their way slowly but surely northward on secondary roads, Muhammad had been too nervous even for fitful naps. Not, he fumed to himself, that it would have been possible for any sane man to sleep with the racket inside this taxi. Muhammad's run of bad luck had included even his draw of this taxi. Instead of the usual haughty young French dandy, this driver was a woolly-haired expatriate Arab from Morocco. Instead of the usual static-filled rock music on the radio, this driver played a wailing cassette of whiny Arab love songs.

At the first blast of the Arab music, Muhammad had considered curtly ordering the driver to pull over and let him out at once. But it had not been easy to find a cab to drive him so far all through the night. He had not dared to risk looking for another cab in case the Israelis were hot on his trail. And so reluctantly Muhammad had tried to endure the caterwauling music on the driver's cassette. But over and over the driver had played that same scratchy tape with the volume turned up full. Kilometer after kilometer, hour after hour, the Arab singer Um Kulthum had shrieked and whined and wailed about every bit of pain and loss in her long and miserable life. Muhammad had hoped that she and her music and her message were not another bad omen. Sullenly he had watched the driver's dark mobile face in the mirror. When Um Kulthum sobbed her most melodramatic chorus about perfidious love, the driver would clench the steering wheel and moan and shake his head and all but wipe his eyes. If there was a God, Muhammad thought, Allah most definitely excelled at irony. Tonight, when he needed peace and quiet so he could decide on his next move in Paris, God had instead tucked him inside Arabia on wheels.

Muhammad had not intended to engage his driver in even the vaguest conversation in French, much less Arabic. He had not wanted to face impertinent questions about why he was taking a slow taxi rather than a fast train or plane to Paris. He had most of all not wanted to admit that he had even the slenderest of ties of brotherhood to this crude and ignorant Arab behind the wheel. But the hours of shattering music had grated on Muhammad's already strained nerves. During each of their brief food and rest stops, he had fought off the desire to confide his predicament to someone, anyone, even a waitress at a restaurant or a bartender at a café. On the long black ride through the night, he had conceived and then discarded a series of daring plans. He would telephone everyone he knew, someone would lend him a great sum of money, somehow he would buy a false passport and assume a new identity maybe in America. But when he had placed a series of calls at three o'clock in the morning from Lyon to London, some of the clique he had thought were his friends had laughed at him and others had hung up and no one had volunteered so much as a shoulder to cry on. Muhammad had wondered, as he dully replaced the receiver after his final call of desperation, how he could have ever thought he could trust the infidels.

It was when he climbed back into the taxi then that Muhammad had finally begun chatting with the astonished driver. Yes, he had admitted, he was an Arab. As he listened to the growl of his native tongue on his own lips, Muhammad had pondered his admission. He had not said he was an Arab for a very long while, and so why now? As the taxi swished through the rain, Muhammad had traded histories with the driver. He had wished he were an illiterate but good-hearted Moroccan who had a loving wife and family waiting for him back in Fez. He had wished to God he could go to Morocco and take refuge in the back alleys of a casbah today. Or he had wished he could go to Beirut. If an Arab had to return to that cursed corner of the world, Beirut was unquestionably the best of it. Or Cairo; willingly would he have winged off to the fleshpots of Cairo to spend long nights of bliss in the knowing arms of a plump brown Egyptian belly dancer. He wouldn't have objected to trading threats with those treacherous Iraqis in bloody Baghdad. Or, God help him, today he would even have flown to grim Damascus. Anything, anywhere was better than that other place.

Moodily Muhammad blew smoke rings in the stale blue air and looked out at the bare trees and the crumbling golden farmhouses and the brown fields plowed and ready for spring planting. Frost and fog shrouded the farms in a luminous eerie whiteness, and Muhammad suppressed a shudder at the possibility of another bad omen. With every fiber of his body he despised Saudi Arabia. He hated it for its ugly withered barren desert terrain. And most of all, he hated Saudi Arabia because he was so terribly ashamed he had been born there. Still he couldn't decide whether he was more afraid of the Israelis' killing him or the Saudis' reclaiming him.

At last the driver turned down the volume on his tape. They were almost to Paris. Where did the Saudi Arabian *shaykh* want to go?

Muhammad took a deep breath. Home. He would have to take his chances and go home. Better the devil he knew than the devil he didn't know. The officials at the embassy would welcome him with open arms, they would hear out his story, and probably then they would whisk him off to Riyadh. Once there, he could try to talk his way out of his predicament. He was smarter than any of those filthy nomads. His family was rich, his tribe was important, and he had worked for more than ten years as a representative of the royal family. He was not without resources, and he was not without recourse. He would exaggerate his heroic role arming brother Arabs in the good fight against the Zionists. He supposed he would have to confess to at least some of his financial chicanery, but he would heap most of the blame on the lying, cheating infidels of London and New York and Paris and everywhere else. He would have to kiss the dusty hems of too many stupid old men's dirty robes. He would have to endure long windy pious lectures. He would have to say his prayers very loudly and perfectly and regularly. He might even have to make the gesture of undertaking one of those ghastly superstitious pilgrimages to Mecca. It would all be wickedly boring, but it was better than being gunned down on a London street. In French he gave what he hoped was not his execution order. '*Avenue Hoche. Cinq, avenue Hoche. L'ambassade de l'Arabie Saoudite.*'

Yet as the taxi swung around the Arc de Triomphe and onto Avenue Hoche, Muhammad had second thoughts. Perhaps the Israelis weren't after him anymore. Perhaps the Israelis had *never* been after him. Perhaps he had blown that chase back on the Riviera entirely out of proportion. As the driver pulled up to the elegant three-story chancellery with its fluttering green Saudi flag, Muhammad blanched at the heavy grillwork that barred the windows and the guards who patrolled the sidewalk with machine guns. With a sinking feeling Muhammad realized that once he stepped inside Saudi diplomatic territory, he might never be able to get out again. He looked down the street where boisterous French children shouted behind the ornate gilded gates of the Parc Monceau. He gazed longingly toward the glorious Seine, and he felt like weeping at the thought of never again seeing the loveliest city in the world. But then he collected himself and remembered that he was Muhammad Al-Murrah, a sophisticated, debonair, and devil-may-care man of the world. If this was the end, he would hold his head up high and go out with style. He inclined his head and gave the nightclubs and the boulevards and the shops and the pleasures of beautiful Paris his best and most regretful French-film-star smile. And then he put the tips of his fingers to his lips and blew beautiful Paris a kiss goodbye.

—16—

The *shaykhs* and the scribes and the graybeards of the tribe were all assembled in the marathon Al-Murrah *majlis* deep in the dry barren heart of Arabia. At noon they had come under this billowing black tent in their ancestral grazing lands on the fringe of the Empty Quarter desert, and still at night they sat and sipped coffee and argued and could not altogether agree. Hotly the debate waxed and waned, reached another crescendo, trailed off again into a tense quiet that made the dogs whine and whimper. In the silence a lone wolf would howl. Outside, over withered miles of undulating desert, lit now by the orange oil-field gas flares, the wolf packs still prowled. But the cheetah and the ostrich were all gone from these deserts. The leopard was rare. The gazelle, the antelope, the oryx were endangered species found not in the wilderness but in pens at the Riyadh zoo. The Al-Murrah, whose nomad way of life was as threatened as that of the other desert wildlife, would listen sagely, sympathetically, nostalgically to the howl of the lone wolf. Then one *shaykh* would say the howl of the wolf was a vengeful omen, and another would counter that even Allah's beasts were calling for mercy. Stolid heads would swivel and shake and nod, and again they would continue to try for consensus in the great matter that had brought them together in this rare assembly once again.

These *bedu al-bedu*, these 'nomads of the nomads,' sat as their ancestors had sat, in their houses of hair, holding this dark midnight assembly. Years ago, not so many years ago, in the lifetime even of the middle-aged Al-Murrah, but before the gushing of the oil, the grandfathers and the fathers and the sons had often come together like this on the long hot summer nights as they camped to the south at the wells with the women and the flocks. Before the nomad life became almost extinct, the generations had often gathered like this in thanksgiving as they camped to the north after the winter rains. In those old days, those simple days, a formal *majlis* like tonight's might have been called to plot a raid on the camels of a nearby tribe, to vow revenge for a blood feud, or to join a brother's war against distant foes. In those old days, those innocent days, a formal *majlis* like tonight's might have been called to trade gossip of births and deaths and marriages, to laugh at a full season's jokes and ironies, to listen with rapt attention as a wandering poet recited the old legends that could make a sentimental boy or a graybeard weep.

Sharply Rashid wished that tonight's business were that old business.

He sat cross-legged between his grandfather Ibrahim and old Salim, the *shaykh* of all the Al-Murrah. They had sat so and talked so until day turned into night. They had sipped coffee and drunk tea and refreshed themselves with fresh frothy camel's milk. Yet still they had not been able to reach unanimous agreement on what must be done with the one who had transgressed. Still, even as they had continued to lament the crime, they had remained divided on the punishment. Over and over again they had measured the shame and tried to apportion the blame.

Yet they had come to some tentative conclusions.

But before they pronounced final judgment, they had agreed they must hear the other side of the story. Two young bucks had been sent in a battered pickup truck to fetch the accused, who was being sequestered in a heavily guarded black tent even deeper in the folds of the desert. As the *shaykhs* and the scribes and the graybeards waited for the next act of their tribal drama to begin, they sat patiently listening to the silence of the night.

Rashid tried to read his brother's fate in the stern set of a chin or the fierceness of an elder's gaze. Yet Rashid knew which of these Al-Murrah had called for vengeance and which for compassion, and the words did not match the faces. The most implacable of the grandfathers, he who had called for the sure swift vindictive fall of the executioner's sword, now sat reciting verses from the Koran to himself. Yet the kindest of the scribes, he who had blamed all the world instead of one erring man, now sat with his weathered face glowering. Muhammad would have to have the gift of tongues to move these righteous warriors of Allah.

Rashid wished he could suddenly wake from the bad dream of these last anxious weeks since his brother had been whisked back to the kingdom in a private jet. Muhammad had been home in Saudi Arabia for nearly a week before Rashid had an inkling of what had happened on the Riviera and in Paris and London. A low-ranking prince of one of the most distant branches of the royal family had hinted to him, after a meeting at the Ministry of Petroleum, that the person closest to him by blood other than his mother had been involved in a shocking scandal whose dimensions were only now beginning to be known. But the prince had refused to say more, and it had taken weeks of discreet probing for the outlines of the scandal to emerge. In London auditors had furrowed their brows over contracts and columns of figures and discovered that Muhammad had been stealing from the royals on a grand scale for years. After that, stories of Muhammad's whoring and drinking and gambling had finally been repeated in Riyadh. But what finally caused King Faisal to order Muhammad isolated in a monklike cell in a mud-brick Saudi fortress was the shocking tale of his secret treason with the enemy. The incriminating documents and the letters and the photographs of Muhammad locked in earnest discussions with a known Israeli agent had been thoughtfully supplied to the Saudis by the American CIA.

Gravely Rashid watched Shaykh Salim try to put the other elders of the tribe at ease by chatting about less consequential matters than the fall of one of the brightest stars in the Al-Murrah firmament. While the small talk swelled around him, Rashid could not keep his mind from the incredible fact that in a few moments his brother would be led in as a criminal, and after he was given a final chance to explain himself, the judgment of the elders would be pronounced upon him. For some hours those who counseled mercy and those who advocated retribution had been edging toward the same recommendation.

Rashid caught his grandfather's eye, and for a moment the younger generation pleaded with the older for reassurance. Ibrahim had insisted they must be here tonight to safeguard Muhammad's interests, to intercede for mercy, and to lend him moral support in his hour of need. When Ibrahim reached out and put his hand on Rashid's shoulder, his grandson tried to smile. Yet still Rashid brooded over the cunning of the Saudi royal family. Men could mutter about the wild extravagances and dissolute behavior of some of the younger princes and the arrogance and the pretensions of the senior ones. But even their harshest critics had to admit that the masters of the House of Saud were very clever. Muhammad Al-Murrah had betrayed the letter and the intent of Koranic injunctions to be just and righteous and keep to the straight path. He had violated the trust of the royal family and besmirched the reputation of his tribe. Worse, he had given perfidious aid and comfort to the enemy. Here in the Islamic Kingdom of Saudi Arabia criminal punishments stipulated thirteen centuries ago in the Koran still prevailed as law.

If Muhammad were brought before an Islamic court, he might be sentenced to have his right hand lopped off as a thief or even his head cut off as a traitor. Muhammad would have been neither the first nor the last Saudi subject to be executed quietly in the dark shadows of a prison yard or publicly in the bright sunlight of a city square. But the royal family had not wanted to risk a possible blood feud with the Al-Murrah, who were not only one of the kingdom's noble ancient tribes but stalwarts in the National Guard. Instead, the wily royals had remanded Muhammad to the custody and justice of his own tribe. If the order went out to spill Muhammad's blood, no one could ever trace the blame to the House of Saud. But if the Al-Murrah should decide to spare Muhammad, the tribe would forever be not only responsible for all his future actions but indebted to the tender mercies of the royal family.

Glumly Rashid looked over at the huge black Nubian slave who stood waiting in the shadows of the tent with his beefy arms folded across his chest. Slavery had officially been abolished by royal proclamation four years ago, yet still this one monstrous family of Nubians served as slaves to the cruelest letter of the law. The father and the grandfather and the great-grandfather of this forbidding Nubian had been the royal executioners, famed throughout central Arabia for the neatness of their bloody work. Just in case the tribe decided that vengeance was the way of the Lord, the royal family had sent their own private enforcer to the Al-Murrah.

Rashid listened to the howls of the lone wolf outside in the wilderness. In a way it would have been simpler if the royal family had walled Muhammad away forever in the Black Hole of Hofuf. Anything would have been more merciful than having to help judge his own brother like this. He had sat and listened and tried to be impartial today, yet he had not been able to bear to join in this public condemnation. From time to time Ibrahim had nudged him to speak up, pro or con, yet still Rashid had kept his silence as the elders debated his brother's fate. It had seemed for a while that Muhammad would be quietly beheaded and so spare the tribe future embarrassment. But then Muhammad's costly education had been recalled, the reputation of his brother and his father and his grandfather had been elaborately praised, and finally Ibrahim himself had interceded to sway the elders away from such a drastic solution.

It had seemed the graybeards were inclining, then, toward agreement to cut off Muhammad's right hand in punishment as a thief, when Rashid had finally cleared his throat and spoken his piece. Eloquently he had pleaded that the fault lay not so much with his brother but with the ways of the infidels. Muhammad had been corrupted by too many years in the lands of the unrighteous. Now that his brother was back in the kingdom of the believers, Muhammad in the deepest recesses of his heart and soul would surely remember the lessons he had forgotten. In weeks, months, years here among his brothers, Muhammad would learn to treasure a spartan life of honor and piety and chivalry.

Finally, after Rashid had moved some of the elders to

tears, Shaykh Salim had proposed that they attempt to rehabilitate Muhammad instead of maiming him. For the rest of his life, Muhammad would live inside the kingdom's Islamic boundaries so that he would never again be tempted by the infidels' evil ways. Moreover, for a year or so Muhammad could be made to live as his ancestors had lived, herding camels from a house of hair in the cleansing purity of the desert. The *shaykh*'s plan seemed a model of mercy; yet Rashid wondered if his brother might not prefer beheading. Could his brother endure to fall from Knightsbridge to the Empty Quarter?

Rashid nervously wrung his hands. Whether the tribe finally decided to cut off Muhammad's head or hand or merely break his heart, Rashid was sick at having to witness his brother's humiliation. Rashid remembered another night when Muhammad had been not villain but hero. When the Ain Dar well had exploded into fire, Muhammad had saved his and Tom Shannon's lives. For the nobility and bravery of that night, Rashid was still in his brother's debt.

Rashid fancied that what might be on trial here tonight was not only Muhammad's transgressions in the West but his own lifelong rivalry with his brother. Muhammad would doubtless blame everyone but himself for his disgrace. He would never forgive Rashid for participating in tonight's tribal council. It took all Rashid's discipline to remain cross-legged, waiting here in the shadows while he longed instead to go off in the desert and mourn the brother he had lost so very long ago. He reproached himself for not trying harder with Muhammad, not just this year but in every year of their lives. They had been born brothers and forever they were fated to be brothers. In the beginning, when they were boys together, they had been so very much alike. Perhaps the trouble had begun between them because they *were* so much alike.

Rashid looked around the circle of his tribal brothers. In their gray robes and red kerchiefs, they looked all cut from the same bolt of cloth. Seven, ten, fifteen generations ago, they had all shared the same father, for a tribe was only a few centuries in the life of an extended family. By rights Muhammad should be sitting here among his contemporaries, an honored man from an honored tribe. Rashid wondered how Muhammad had become such a stranger to these ties of blood and honor and tradition. He thought back to the beginning of his own rivalry with Muhammad. He supposed it had always been easier for him to excel in the years of their boyhood in the desert. With every fiber of his being, Rashid had been inclined toward the old ways, the old values, and the family had richly rewarded him with love and approval. Always Rashid had been everyone's favorite. Looking back now, Rashid supposed he had been gifted by Allah with more of everything than his brother. And so, on this night of judgment, Rashid accused himself of never trying hard enough to share those gifts of Allah. He, the blessed one, should have always been more generous with his brother. Instead, Rashid had delighted in every sweet fierce triumph over Muhammad. Always the two had fought, and always Rashid had struggled to be the better.

It wasn't until Muhammad had begun consorting with the infidels that he had discovered another world in which he could outshine his brother. The Westerners had liked Muhammad better; he had been the natural linguist, and he had excelled at tennis and charades and with the blond daughters of the unbelievers. Over the next decade, after Rashid had returned to Saudi and Muhammad had settled in London, the brothers had become increasingly estranged. But Rashid feared that whatever fragile bond of affection still remained between the two of them would snap tonight. What was at the root of their tragic Cain and Abel rivalry? Brother turned against brother, he supposed, not only here in Arabia but everywhere on earth. But an old Arabic proverb was a litany of descending degrees of distrust. 'I and my cousins against the stranger,' it began. Then 'I and my brothers against my cousins.' Finally, 'I against my brother.' It was not just here in this particular family and tribe that it was brother against brother. Perhaps Allah had placed some terrible fratricidal curse on the Arabs.

Rashid sighed and put the blame where it belonged, not on Allah but on himself. Gladly would he have paid any price tonight to take back these long years of rancor. Even now, after the two of them had long gone their separate ways, still they were more alike than they were different. Especially tonight, when Muhammad was in jeopardy, Rashid wanted to rally loyally to his side. 'I and my brother against my cousins.' Blood ties after all mattered most. A brother was even closer to a man's heart than his wife. He and Muhammad shared the same mother, the same father, the same childhood. Together they had even shared the same shock of being plucked from the traditional culture of the desert nomads and set down willy-nilly into the twentieth-century West. They differed only in how they had responded to the trauma of living in those two worlds. Rashid wished he could intercept the truck carrying Muhammad here to this tent and transform this night of recriminations into one of brotherly reconciliation.

A distant roar cut the night, grew louder; headlights bounced closer; the waiting men of the Al-Murrah stopped talking and drinking and composed their faces into expressions of stoic justice.

Two fierce tribesmen, their cartridge belts crisscrossed over their chests and their gray robes and red-checkered head scarves flapping in the night wind, jumped from the rusty red pickup truck. They waved their loaded carbines impatiently, then aimed their muzzles at the heavens and shot a trigger-happy round to urge their prisoner to get moving. At last Muhammad, immaculate in a snowy robe and head scarf, stalked out of the truck. Like a prince slumming among commoners, he deigned to stoop and enter the hairy black tent as if he, not they, were about to pronounce sentence. He graciously inclined his head to one *shaykh*, smiled haughtily at another, royally ignored graybeards whom he had always known as his enemies. Rashid tried to catch his eye, but Muhammad swept past as if his brother did not exist.

A tribesman guided Muhammad to his appointed place on the rug at the center of the circle of Al-Murrah. Muhammad knelt, arranged his robe in graceful folds, and looked around as if he expected coffee and tea and naked dancing slave girls.

But no one was thirsty for anything but justice. Muhammad had erred, and Muhammad was about to be punished.

In rich and beautiful Arabic, Ibrahim began by delivering a long and ornate history of the tribe here in Arabia, the cradle of life. In the beginning of time, when Allah created the heavens and the earth, the Garden of Eden had lain not far away, just twelve miles off the peninsula on the island of Bahrain. There Eve plucked the fruit, and then sin was born. Adam and Eve were expelled from the garden of earthly delights, and they were the first to wander as the Bedouin still wander on the parched earth of Arabia. Eve, who was the mother not only of Cain and Abel but of pain and suffering, finally died when it was written that she must die. She was buried in what is now the Saudi city of Jeddah, where it is still possible to visit her moldering tomb. Ibrahim recited the genealogy, from father to son, through all the centuries, from Adam to the Patriarch Abraham to Yam, the father of all the People of Murrah. For millennia, for as far back as man had memory, the fathers of the Al-Murrah had been lords of the desert. For millennia, for as far back as man had history, their ancestors had ranked high in the hierarchy of the noblest and the freest and the bravest of the Arabian tribes. Ibrahim chronicled Al-Murrah victories in raids and in battles. He recounted the valor of its warriors and the eloquence of its poets and the wisdom of its chiefs. He extolled its piety and its fierce devout defense of Islam.

But finally, Ibrahim said, even the most honorable of tribes could sometimes, if Allah willed it, be besmirched by shame. A tribe must always carefully guard its reputation and punish its transgressors, for the dishonor of one sullies the honor of all. What the Al-Murrah faced tonight, Ibrahim said, was one such isolated case of moral deviation. His grandson Muhammad was accused of breaking his covenant with his people. And so, here and now, the community of his fathers and his brothers and his grandfathers had to see not only that he made restitution for his crimes but also that he would never repeat them. Tonight Muhammad stood accused of stealing the funds of the House of Saud and living a life contrary to the Koran and committing treason with the enemy. All day and night the tribe had sat assembled to ponder Muhammad's fate. But before the noble brother of the accused delivered the tribe's verdict, *bismallah* - in the name of Allah - Muhammad was to be given a final opportunity to plead his case.

All eyes shifted to the sinner.

Muhammad waited for the tension to build even higher. This was his moment, and he would savor it. If these were his last moments on earth, he would make the most of them. They might cut off his head, but as long as it was still on his shoulders he would hold it up proudly. Contemptuously he studied the faces of his accusers. In the sorry weeks since he had so rashly delivered himself into the hands of his tormentors at the embassy in Paris, Muhammad had had more than ample time to regret throwing himself on the nonexistent mercy of his countrymen. When furious packs of swindled princes had descended on his prison cell, he had feared they might beat him on the soles of his feet or even torture him with jolts of electricity. When they had accused him of selling guns to the Israelis, he had laughed and said they must be joking. It was only when they showed him the photographs the CIA had given the Saudis that Muhammad had stopped laughing and begun sweating. He had met with his Lebanese contact in a King's Road pub only once to arrange their assignation on the Riviera. He blinked in disbelief at the grainy black-and-white photographs of the two of them sitting over their pints.

Too late he remembered the warning the Egyptian diplomat in London had given him about the CIA working covertly to nip Arab armaments in the bud. He supposed that by now every two-bit arms dealer in Europe knew the price Muhammad Al-Murrah was paying for trying to sell arms to the 'Lebanese.' After Muhammad had vainly tried to explain away those incriminating photographs, the princes had nearly broken him with taunts that already the Nubian executioner's sword was sharpened and waiting. He had been terrorized for so many days and nights that by now he was nearly beyond fear. Better a quick death, he had decided, than the long slow torture of living in this Saudi hellhole. But just as he had thought he was about to be led into the prison yard and beheaded, that squad of crazy wild-eyed guards had trucked him deep into the desert to camp in a hairy black tent. When they had forced him into their truck tonight, he had thought they meant to murder him in the desert. Never had he dreamed they would be bringing him here to parade him in shame in front of his grandfather and his brother.

When his eyes finally fell on Rashid, for an unguarded instant an expression of loathing contorted Muhammad's face. He had given his brother credit for more mercy and decency than this. He had not thought his brother would sit and gloat at this, the final act in the drama of his life. In Muhammad's mouth his saliva tasted as vile as vomit. For an instant the *shaykhs* and the scribes and the graybeards all receded, and it was only he and Rashid, circling each other for their final round, just as he had once seen cocks fight to the death in a ring in Havana. But then that vision faded, and Muhammad was conscious again of the eyes of all the others locked upon him. If they expected him to grovel, they were about to be disappointed. 'You all presume to judge me?' Defiantly Muhammad spoke in English, though he knew his choice of an alien language would anger the tribesmen. 'Savages like you? Camel herders? Illiterate tribesmen?' Muhammad spat contemptuously on the rug.

Bitterly Muhammad smiled as he watched the dark faces of the tribesmen grow blacker. He listened to Rashid hesitantly translating his jibes into Arabic, and then Muhammad continued. 'Tell them this, too, my brother, O son of my mother.' Muhammad's voice was silky. 'Tell them they have no authority over me. If I am to be judged, it will be before an Islamic court in Riyadh or Jeddah or Hofuf. I insist that I will be judged by my peers, not by those who always were and always will be my inferiors. I will defend myself in a judicial proceeding at ten o'clock in the morning in a government building, not here in the middle of the night in a tent in this godforsaken desert. You tell them that, noble Rashid. And remember that I am listening to what you say. Leave nothing out, my brother.'

'Muhammad, don't do this.' Rashid pleaded with his brother in a rapid English he hoped the other tribesmen would not be able to follow. 'You're not back in London, demanding civil rights in a British court. Don't insult them like this. Please, in the name of Allah -'

'In the name of the devil, do as I say! Pull yourself together, little brother. Don't be afraid to speak up. Pray to Allah that He may finally give you courage and manhood.'

Rashid flushed at the taunt. He looked over at his grandfather for help, but Ibrahim avoided his eyes. As he translated his brother's insults into Arabic, an angry muttering arose from the tribesmen. Ibrahim caught the *shaykh*'s eye and nodded. Then Salim ordered the executioner to step forward, for the rugs to be rolled back, for the oil to be heated. The Nubian lifted his sword from his scabbard and brandished it in the firelight.

As the dense stink of the burning oil wafted inside the tent, Muhammad could no longer control his growing terror. 'What's going on?' Even though he had not seen the tribesmen move a muscle, it seemed to him the circle had suddenly begun to close in tighter around him. 'What's that smell?' Muhammad began to panic. 'Me? You're going to kill me? Oh, God, you're not going to cut off my head?'

Shaykh Salim's eyes flicked contemptuously over to Muhammad. 'Not your head. . . .'

Muhammad paled. Suddenly he knew. He stared down at his right hand. He pulled back the sleeve of his white robe and looked at his five fingers, his palm, the wrist that joined the flesh and bones and muscle of his hand to his arm. 'No,' he whispered.

Muhammad sank to his knees and began to confess and beg for mercy. 'I admit it - yes, I took the money. I didn't mean to, it was only a little at first, then I was unlucky and it was more than a little, but you're rich, you can pay back the Al-Saud. Don't take my hand off, please, not that.' Muhammad wet his dry lips. 'And you can't punish me for carrying on with women and whiskey. I didn't do anything any worse than the precious princes. Are you going to cut off *their* hands?' The executioner strode to the center of the tent with his meaty hands grasping his long, sharp, glittering curved sword of Damascene steel. 'It's that lie the CIA concocted that you're going to maim me for, isn't it? God, oh, God, you must believe me. I never sold anything, ever, to the Jews. It's their fault I'm here. A man who said he was a Lebanese set me up in a trap in Monte Carlo, the Zionists were waiting for me, I barely escaped with my life. The Israelis and their American masters forged that evidence against me.' Muhammad hung his head. 'You don't believe me,' he whispered. But then he was seized with an inspiration. 'Bring me a Koran. Will you believe me if I swear on the Holy Koran?' The tribesmen watched stonily as he repeated his denial with his right hand on the Koran.

Then one Al-Murrah carried in a sizzling pot of oil, another rolled up more of the rugs, a third spread a gray cloth on the bare sand. For a long moment there was silence inside the black tent as all the dark eyes of the tribesmen locked on the still, silent, kneeling figure of Muhammad in his immaculate white robe.

But then Muhammad slowly raised his head and lifted his arm as he pointed his finger straight as a spear at the heart of his brother. 'You! This was *your* idea, wasn't it? Always you hated me, and now you think I am finished, eh?' Muhammad laughed an angry rasping laugh from deep in his throat. 'You, the blameless one, the one who could never, ever, do any wrong, sit in judgment of me.' A look of cunning crossed Muhammad's face. Most of all, he longed for revenge. He wanted to mortally wound this brother who had always been the world's winner. Now, Muhammad urged himself. Do it now. Show him the same mercy he has just shown you. 'Holy, eh? You think you are so good?' Again Muhammad spat on the ground in contempt. And when he opened his mouth again, it was to spit out his venom not in English but in Arabic, so that all the tribesmen would understand his meaning. 'Your wife, your American wife.' Muhammad's voice dropped to a whisper, and the scandalized but spellbound tribesmen had to lean forward to hear his next words. 'I had her first. In Boston. I took her in Boston, in a hotel room in Boston.' Muhammad slapped his buttocks. 'Here! I took her here!' Muhammad snapped his fingers. '*This* for your virtue! Every night you lie with a whore!' Muhammad looked around the tent at the stunned tribesmen. 'And are any of you who presume to judge me any better?'

Ibrahim was the first to break the shocked silence. 'We are all better than you.'

Every tribesman shrank away in horror from Muhammad, for it was unthinkable to break all the seals of family intimacy as he had done. A wife, a daughter, a mother were never discussed in public, much less fouled by talk as evil as what had just spewed from the mouth of Muhammad. Whether his story of what he had once done with Rashid's wife was true or false, whether that woman was wanton or virtuous, was a matter to be decided inside the high walls of Rashid's own house. They were here tonight to judge Muhammad, not Rashid or Rashid's wife. As one, the tribesmen closed their minds and hearts to Muhammad.

Shaykh Salim shook his head. 'What are we to do with this man who admits that he steals and leads a dirty life? Who goes further and defames his brother, a man of honor, in front of all the tribe? I say it is a very bad man who tries to break his brother's heart.' The *shaykh* reluctantly turned his eyes to Muhammad. 'I must ask if you have proof.'

'Proof of what?' Muhammad wet his lips with his tongue. His eyes darted around the tent for a means of escape. But he knew he would never make it to the truck.

'Proof,' the *shaykh* said, 'of your accusation against the woman.'

'You must be joking.' Nervously Muhammad laughed.

'The Koran,' Shaykh Salim explained wearily, as if to an infidel, 'says very clearly that if a man brings an accusation of dishonor against a woman, he must have four witnesses who have seen her doing that shameful thing. You have these four male witnesses?'

'But that's absurd. Of *course* I didn't have four men watching. I'm not in the habit of inviting in a crowd to watch.'

'Then you must be accused of a new crime. If you do not have witnesses, then you have brought a false accusation against the honor of a woman.'

'Listen, Shaykh Salim.' Muhammad was as earnest as he had ever been in his life. 'She did it. I swear she did it. She let me do it in a hotel in Scollay Square in Boston. Go get her. Bring her here and ask *her*. I demand that! She'll tell you!'

'We will not bring the woman here. But even so, it is possible that we will believe you.' Shaykh Salim's eyes watched hope flicker on Muhammad's flushed face. He pointed to the fire which still burned before them. 'If you insist, we will have the test of fire.'

'Fire?' All Muhammad's bravado was gone. He would

have said or done anything at this moment to escape this horrific nightmare.

The *shaykh* sweetly explained. 'We will put this fire in your mouth. Live coals on your tongue. If you are speaking the truth, your tongue will not burn. It is a very old test. We have not had the test of fire for many years in the tents of the Al-Murrah. But we will do it tonight if you like, if you insist.'

'No! No fire!' Muhammad tried to scramble to his feet, but too many arms pinned him down. 'You're lunatics! Every one of you is stark raving mad.' He screamed at Ibrahim. 'Grandfather! Help me! Don't let them do this! Please, Grandfather! Mercy!'

'Son of my son, I sorrow for you.' Tears ran down Ibrahim's cheeks. 'It will not be necessary to test you with fire.' Ibrahim and Salim exchanged meaningful glances; then the *shaykh* told the Nubian executioner to put away his sword.

'I have heard too much that I never wanted to hear tonight in this tent,' Ibrahim said as he looked over and saw that Rashid still was holding his head in his hands. 'Too much.' He wiped away his tears. 'We will not cut off your hand or your head, Muhammad, though Allah knows you have provoked us enough to justify it. You are a son of the Murrah, not a servant from Pakistan or a lorry driver from the Yemen. We will not strike down one of our own. The Nubian was only to frighten you into repenting the evil inside you.' Ibrahim sighed. 'So much for our plan.' His voice broke, and his eyes pleaded with the *shaykh* to say the rest.

Salim called for the muttering tribesmen to be silent. '*Bismallah*,' he began - 'in the name of Allah - my judgment is that Muhammad will spend all his days and all his nights here among his people, forever in the kingdom, until it is Allah's will that he die.' Ibrahim handed over his grandson's passport, and Shaykh Salim fed the document to the flames. He waited as it caught fire, flamed, and burnt to a gray ashy cinder. '*Khelas* - it is finished.

Further, for the first year of his homecoming, he will live the life of the poorest of his Bedouin brothers. He will roam the deserts of the Empty Quarter, tending the camels, moving his camp now north, now south, following the rains and seeking the wells, living the simple life, the good life of the ancestors.' Even the *shaykh* faltered and looked away from Muhammad's burning eyes, but then he continued. 'Muhammad, here you were born and here you will die, in the fullness of Allah's time.'

Ibrahim had regained his voice and his control. 'We had intended to do no worse to you tonight. But it seems that we must, for you have done worse to us. You have shamed all the family and so, as the head of the family, I tell you that you are no longer the son of my son. You are outcast from my family. We will not talk to you, you will not live with us, if you see us on the street we will turn away from you.' Ibrahim's voice quavered. 'It kills me to say this to you, Muhammad, but say it I must.' Yet despite his anger Ibrahim could not keep from offering Muhammad hope. 'If sometime in the future your brother, the one you have hurt the most, decides to forgive you, then and only then can you be reborn in the family.'

'So be it!' Shaykh Salim nodded his agreement.

Muhammad knelt at the center of the grim tribesmen; then he crawled over and fished out the ashes of his passport from the fire. He held those ashes in his hands and then he screamed an animal cry of loss and pain and misery. He buried his face in his hands and howled louder, longer, wilder than the lone wolves in the desert wasteland. Then his hands fell from his face that was smeared with ashes and he sobbed as if his heart were broken.

Shaykh Salim sighed. '*Wallah*, justice is done.'

17

Rashid slammed the door as he stalked into Sunny's bedroom in the predawn dark of the next night. He stood glowering over her side of the bed, but he did not trust himself to look down at her as she slept. Always she looked to him like an angel, and he did not want to be misled by that superficial resemblance this morning. He did not want what might very well be one of his last glimpses of her to be her sleeping in all innocence with her silky gold hair spread over the pillow. He could not stand more doubts and vacillation.

Since the *majlis* last night he had been brooding about what to do about this one he always thought of as the wife of his heart.

On the long drive back from the Empty Quarter, he had staved off sorting out truth and lies, guilts and shames, responsibilities and recriminations. Finally he had headed for the Dahana dunes to be alone and decide how to deal with Muhammad's accusation about Sunny. He had pitched a black tent before dawn in a deep golden valley between the soft shifting sands of two high dunes.

Rashid had devoutly prayed at daybreak facing Mecca, hoping for revelation and peace. Over and over and over again he had pondered the possible truth or falsehood of Muhammad's words. His brother said he had once used Sunny in a perverted way in a hotel in Boston. Very clearly, as clearly and as truly as a camel bell could be heard across a silent desert at dawn, Rashid remembered how Sunny had flirted with Muhammad the first time the three of them met. He could still remember how jealous he had been that night. He had thought her the most enchanting woman in the world, but he remembered, on that first night, that Sunny had had eyes only for his brother.

Rashid had prayed at high noon, sweating in the hot sun in the cleft between the undulating dunes, remembering the boastful letters his brother had written him a few years later in Texas. He recalled how his Arab friends had marveled at Muhammad's astonishing success with the infidel women. The Iraqis and the Kuwaitis and the Saudis had joked that all Boston must be Muhammad Al-Murrah's personal harem. Rashid distinctly remembered Muhammad's writing that he had become good friends with the daughter of Mr. Tom. But try as he might, he could not recall any sexual innuendos about Sunny.

Rashid had sat outside in the dry pure air until the sweltering early-spring sun made the sky turn yellow, and then he had sat brooding inside the shade of the black tent. Later, when Rashid had begun keeping company with Sunny, he could not remember her saying a single word about his brother. Now that he thought about it, it was odd that she had never so much as mentioned Muhammad. On their honeymoon she had refused even to consider visiting him in London. Rashid's eyes narrowed with growing suspicion as he remembered how Sunny had blushed the day Muhammad had surprised her in their Dhahran kitchen. At the time Sunny had acted so guilty that Rashid had wondered if anything untoward had ever happened between his brother and his wife.

Rashid had prayed the sunset prayers. As night fell, then, he had become more and more depressed. He recalled the day he had spotted Sunny in that coffeehouse in Boston. He had been enraptured to see her, but at first she had been aloof, even antagonistic. Yet very quickly she had thawed into breathless eagerness to spend every second in his company. She had thrown herself into his arms that snowy New Year's Day by Boston Common - *she* had been the one to propose marriage; *she* had even been the one to insist she be his second wife. Had Sunny been just as ardent with Muhammad? In the beginning, Rashid knew, Sunny had been almost as much in love with Saudi as with him. Her bewitching enthusiasms for all he held dear had made it easy for him to adore her, especially after all the snubs and slights he had endured in America, especially after his humiliation by that gang of Texas cowboys.

Rashid had wondered, as the moon and the stars faintly lit the dark heart of the Saudi night, if Sunny's fervent adolescent yearnings for Arabia might have once led her astray with his brother. Sunny had always been willful, hell-bent on getting whatever it was she wanted. Long before they were married, she had confided that all her life she had dreamed of coming to live near her father in Saudi. Rashid supposed it was possible Muhammad had exploited Sunny's hopes and dreams. Sunny might once have been so starry-eyed she had been an easy mark for his unscrupulous brother. Rashid very reluctantly had made himself consider the worst possibilities of all. Had Sunny truly loved his brother? Had he himself been merely her second choice? Or was the truth even darker than that? For all he knew, Sunny might have had many men in that shameful way Muhammad described. She was still, now, even after all these years of marriage, a wild woman in his own bed. Rashid's eyes had flashed in fury as he considered that maybe she was wild in the bed of others. Maybe she slept in the black tents of all his cousins. Maybe she was as much a whore as Muhammad had said.

Rashid had wanted to rend his clothes and howl at the moon and mourn for the death of love and trust and honor as he sat lonely and brooding in the desert. But finally he had faced the fact that he would have to confront her. He had supposed she would deny Muhammad's accusations. But he had fancied he would know the truth when he looked into her eyes. Her clear blue trusting child's eyes had never learned to lie. One look at her angel eyes, and he would know.

Rashid had packed up his tent and, scorning the asphalt highway, had driven the longest possible route across the open desert back to Khobar. He had not been in a hurry to find what he feared would be the bad news waiting for him in his wife's eyes. On impulse, when he was almost home, he had stopped at an uncle's house and donned the humble garments of the penitent pilgrim. The month of the *hajj* had already begun. Whatever happened after he confronted Sunny, whether the proof of her eyes left him broken or troubled or even brimming with thanksgiving, he would make the pilgrimage to Mecca for spiritual comfort, guidance and renewal.

'Wife!' Miserably he stood above her bed waiting for her to wake. 'Get up! We must talk!' He still could not bear to look down at her. When she did not answer, he reached to shake her awake. He looked down at the bed in surprise. The sheets were rumpled, but she was gone. For one quick hateful second he assumed he had caught her in adultery. Even as he had been lamenting the death of their love in the desert, she had been playing the whore with one of the cousins.

But then he realized that the air conditioner was turned off. The hot late-March night air streamed through the open windows. The door leading out to the roof over the kitchen was ajar. It was a balmy tropical night. She liked to sleep under the stars on nights like this.

Swiftly he crossed to the roof. By the moonlight he could see her lying on a mat. But his eyes were playing tricks on him. For one ghastly moment the mosquito netting looked like a shroud. For an instant in the eerie light it looked as if she were lying on a bier. Hesitantly he came closer; he bent; he breathed a sigh of relief when he saw the regular rise and fall of her soft full breasts. For one terrified moment he had feared that a wild and wayward cousin had taken it upon himself to avenge the sullied family honor by killing her as she slept.

Rashid watched her sleeping the sleep of the innocent. He shook his head. He had not wanted to see her like this, to watch her as she slept as if he were making his final farewell, as if he were storing up memories of how lovely she was, how she smelled of jasmine perfume she put behind her ears and musk between her legs. Her hair, her lovely long fair silken infidel hair, was the color of the sun. Always he would love her. Always she would be the wife of his heart. He stood above her hungrily. He had loved this woman for more than eleven years, and still he had not lost his hunger for her. He had already given her the gift of his youth, and he had thought he would give her his middle years and his old age, and that in the fullness of Allah's time they would lie together and turn to dust together here in the land they loved.

He stood above her and wished time would stand still and he would never have to wake her to face her fate. He had never loved her more than now, when he feared he was about to lose her. Never had their love seemed to him sweeter and truer than now, just as he suspected he was about to end it.

He tried to be stern as he stood above the sleeping form of the wife he suspected had been untrue. He knew he would have to send her away if she had once played the whore with his brother. All the tribe - all the men who mattered had heard Muhammad's defamation. It was not possible for her to remain his wife if she was a woman of shame. Yet Rashid was sick at heart. Would he have to choose between honor and love? What good was honor if it meant he must renounce her? He wiped away two tears as they rolled like stones down his cheeks. As a man will press against the rail of a ship as it pulls out of his home port, watching every sandspit and palm tree and dune of his beloved shore recede, he concentrated on the exact tint of her hair, the swell of her breasts and her belly, the flutter of her lashes as she began to wake under the intensity of his stare.

'Rashid?' She murmured his name and moved over on the mat to make room for him. But she was still mostly in the spell of her heavy dreamless sleep, for her eyes closed again and her breathing once again became deep and regular.

He smiled fondly down at her, remembering the hours she had slept without stirring in his embrace. She always said that sleeping in Saudi was like blacking out in coma. She blamed it on the heat, on the torpor of the climate, and - mostly - on the hot annihilating fire of his love-making. He longed to throw himself down beside her and make slow tender love to her as she slept. He wanted her feet on his shoulders as he plunged deep inside the hot truth of her. He wished it were possible to touch her everywhere one last time, to sink himself home deep inside her one last time, before they must deal with the matter that now lay between them like a sword. But then against his skin he felt the itch of the rough simple cotton he had wound around his waist and thrown over his shoulder. He had already donned the costume of the consecrated pilgrim bound for Mecca. He could not touch her, or any woman, until after he had completed the pilgrimage.

Sunny turned in her sleep; her eyelids fluttered again; she opened her eyes and let out a frightened cry, shrinking away from the apparition looming above her. But then she rubbed her eyes. 'Rashid? Is that you?'

His ghostlike body was swaddled in two seamless lengths of white cotton, the *ihram*, the simple covering that the Patriarch Abraham had once worn. Rashid stood silent and waiting, bareheaded, in his pilgrim garb that symbolized piety, the righteous search for peace and purity, and the renunciation of all profane worldly pleasures. Bound for Mecca, in a state of grace, detached from the fleshly possibilities of his wife's body, he waited for Sunny to wake and listen. When she was conscious enough to remember his words, he would talk with her. He would talk with her before this dawn of his pilgrimage, and then he would leave her, if Allah willed it, perhaps forever.

'What time is it?' She sat up and stared at her husband. She recognized his austere garb. 'You're making the *hajj*?' She was awake enough to be thrilled at the thought of Mecca. 'I wish I could go. I wish you didn't have to be a Muslim to go. I've always wanted to see it, not just on TV. I wish I could just slip into Mecca and watch. Or go in disguise, like Burton. I don't suppose you'd help me do that? I could dress like a man, cut my hair . . .' She saw the appalled look on his face. 'I guess not.' She yawned. 'You should have given me some warning.' She threw back the mosquito netting so she could rise and help prepare him for his sudden pilgrimage to Mecca.

He stared at the flash of her naked legs but then averted his eyes. 'Stay where you are. Cover yourself.' He lit a kerosene lantern and put it between them. He sank down cross-legged on the cement roof. 'We must talk.'

'All right.' It wasn't until she had settled back on the mat and wrapped a sheet around her nightgown that she remembered what she could hardly believe she had forgotten. Two days ago Rashid had gone off with the rest of the men for a tribal conference about Muhammad. She had expected them back yesterday. She had waited up past midnight for Rashid to return with the news, but she had waited in vain. 'You look awful. Something bad's happened to your brother, hasn't it? Did he admit it all? Did he really steal all that money and try to sell guns to the Israelis?'

Rashid shrugged. 'I suppose so.'

'What happened to him? What did the tribe decide?' She caught her breath. 'They didn't *kill* him, did they?'

Rashid wearily shook his head. 'The family will pay the money back to the royals. And Muhammad will never be allowed to leave the kingdom again.'

'He probably would rather they had cut off his head.'

'You are very concerned for my brother.' There was a new resonance of suspicion in Rashid's voice. 'I think you maybe care very much for my brother.'

'No.' She was sick at the thought of her tormentor permanently back in Arabia. 'It's just that Muhammad's so worldly and sophisticated. Making him stay here is the worst thing you could do to him.'

Sophisticated. She thought Muhammad was sophisticated. Had she been in love with Muhammad all these years? When she lay in his own arms, was it fantasies of sophisticated Muhammad that had made her cry out with animal pleasure? Rashid steeled himself to put aside his jealousy and continue with the unfinished business of this night. 'But I did not come here to talk about the fate of my brother.'

'Then why did you come? Why else would you wake me up in the middle of the night?' Sunny held her sheet more tightly around her. Sex. He wanted her, and so he had awakened her from a sound sleep. But all this talk of Muhammad had chilled her. She wanted to go back to sleep, not make love. She lay back on the mat and turned her face away from him.

Rashid almost forgot that he was consecrated for the pilgrimage and could not engage in angry words even with this wife who had probably betrayed him. His breath was ragged as he struggled to contain his anger at this wife who had just turned from him. When he finally spoke again, his husky voice was almost melodious. 'Is it true? Tell me, woman, is it true? Is what my brother said about you and him true?'

'Muhammad?' Sunny turned over and stared up at him. 'What are you talking about?'

Rashid prayed to Allah for the grace to love this woman well at their end. He had been gentle with her in the beginning, and so he wanted to be gentle with her in what he suspected was the beginning of their end. He prayed for serenity, balance, and compassion. When he spoke again it was deliberately and with a mournful calmness. 'In the tribal council, Muhammad accused me of being as big a sinner as he is. He said that once, before you and I were married, he lay with you. He described what he did with you, before all the elders of the tribe, in front of all the sons and the fathers and the grandfathers. He said that you had deceived me.'

'Goddamn Muhammad,' Sunny whispered.

Rashid waited for her to say more. He waited for her to explain herself. He waited for her to clear herself. He waited in vain for her to deny what Muhammad had said. After a while, then, Rashid asked her what he had to ask her. 'Is it true?'

She looked anxiously at him, she looked fearfully away from him, she smoothed down the hem of the sheet with her nervous empty hands. She wished he had waited until morning to confront her. It was the middle of the night. She wasn't thinking clearly, she wasn't prepared for any of this, she didn't know what to say. She didn't know how much Muhammad had told him. 'Is what true?'

'Muhammad and you? Sex.' Rashid touched his buttocks. 'In Boston. At a hotel in Scollay Square.'

He knew it all. Muhammad had told them everything. Desperately Sunny tried to think whether it was better to tell Rashid the truth or to lie. But she had always been a poor liar. Rashid had always said he could read all her thoughts just by looking in her eyes. He was looking in her eyes right now. She might as well tell the truth and hope he would be understanding. He loved her. She was utterly certain that he loved her. He loved her, and so of course he would understand as soon as she explained the circumstances. 'What does it matter, Rashid? All that was long ago, before we really met. Before we fell in love and got married. We have been together for years and years. Ten years! We have a son, a daughter. A life! That's what matters. Don't you understand that?'

'I understand that my brother says he did dirty things with my wife. I understand that if that is true, what we have is ruined. Dirty. Shameful. *That* is what I would understand if what my brother said is the truth.'

'But you remember our wedding night, in that inn in Vermont! I was a virgin. You saw the blood.' Her eyes darted to their bedroom, where she kept the stain of her virginal blood as a souvenir. The scrap of white cotton sheeting with its small significant brownish spot was in the third drawer from the bottom in her chest of drawers. 'I even cut it out the next morning. I took scissors and cut the bloodstain. I can show it to you, if you don't remember.' She was pleading now. 'You were my first man. The very first!'

'You do not deny what Muhammad said?' Behind his eyes, at his temples, Rashid's skull throbbed with pain. 'Is it true?'

'Oh, God.' She decided she would have to tell him. 'I should have told you before. I wanted to, but . . .' She would not say out loud that she had been afraid he would divorce her if he knew. She would not speak that word. 'I was so innocent, Rashid. I thought Muhammad loved me, that he was going to marry me. I had never been with a man before. I had never done more than kiss a boy on the lips. I swear it! You have to believe me! I didn't know. I didn't know what he was going to do. He forced me. I tried to get away from him, tried to fight him off. . . .'

'So it's true. So all of it's true.' He raised his head and stared at her searchingly, then longingly, finally with utmost concentration, as though he were memorizing the exact curve of her cheek, the set of her lips, the dying light of her eyes, as though he might never again see this face of the woman he had loved for the young and happy years of his life. A little of what was the best of him died then, a little of his inner harmony left him, some of the goodness soured, what had remained of his innocence and his youth went away, and there was a bitterness on the roof of his mouth and on his tongue and in his throat. He shook his head, sighed, and forced himself to stand. He turned away from her. He placed his right foot before his left, and he took the first step away from her. He transferred his weight to his left foot, and he made himself move a few more inches away from her. The third step came easier.

'Rashid? Rashid! Where are you going?'

'Doubly at Thy service, O God,' he said in Arabic, not to her but to the God he was sure was listening. Again he repeated the *Talbiyah*, the prayer of dedication and submission to the will of Allah which is uttered again and again by every pilgrim seeking God's sacred way. 'Doubly at Thy service, O God.'

'What's that, Rashid? What did you say? Rashid!'

He was already in the shadows, almost over the threshold; already gone from her. She couldn't see his face. She could hardly hear his answer. 'First the dawn prayers. And then the journey. I will make the *hajj*, to Mecca. On the pilgrimage maybe Allah will tell me what is to be done. With me. And with you, my infidel woman, the wife of my heart.' He closed the door to their bedroom, the door to their married life, softly behind him.

Rashid stood on the summit of Jebal el-Rahmah, the Mount of Mercy, one questing and troubled and believing man among a sea of more than one million of the faithful who had assembled from Indonesia and Malaysia and India and Iran and China and America and Africa and every Arab nation of the Middle East. They had come in this Islamic year of 1387, on the ninth day of the twelfth month, Dhu el-Hijjah, by foot and by camel and by horse and by donkey, by automobile and by moped and by truck, by boat and airplane and by caravan, to perform one of the most sacred of the pillars of their faith. Every Muslim, woman no less than man, is required at least once before he dies, if he has enough money to afford it and is healthy enough to survive the rigors of the journey, to make this pilgrimage to the west coast of Saudi Arabia, here, to the holiest shrine in Islam. Once in his life, as the highlight of his life, a Muslim must come here to God's country, on the fringe of the Arabian desert. On a day even more joyful than the day of the birth of his firstborn son, a Muslim must make a pilgrimage here to where the Prophet Muhammad lived and was given the Word of God as revealed in the Holy Koran. Here in Mecca all the races - brown men, black men, yellow men, white men - must pray with one trembling, rapturous voice in the eternal brotherhood of the saved on the Plain of Abraham.

Rashid stood for the third time in his life among the believers making the *hajj* to the Mount of Mercy.

He and his brother had come here first as boys, on camelback, for a pilgrimage of grace and dedication. Grandfather Ibrahim had wanted their first glorious glimpse of Mecca to come after weeks of arduous camping in the desert. Before they ventured beyond the borders of the kingdom to secondary school in Beirut, he had wanted to burn the old ways into their memory. He had wanted them to come as their Bedouin ancestors had always come, dusty and parched and thirsty for salvation. Rashid could never forget catching his breath at first sight of the holy city. They had come upon it suddenly by night. At the crest of a perilous ridge of dark desolate mountains, Rashid had stood transfixed by Mecca. Its minarets, domes, and golden gates had been lit by lights of green and blue, and Mecca had seemed a sapphire city, an emerald city, a city of light so precious it could illuminate the darkest recesses of the heart of man. He had been enchanted by the eternal light of Mecca, and had known most certainly that this city was the closest man could come to paradise. Heaven was like Mecca. From that day forward, for Rashid, heaven had seemed real and attainable if he were but righteous enough.

He had come here the second time as a young man, by limousine, for a pilgrimage of thanksgiving. How happy he had been then, a year after he had returned home to the kingdom with Sunny as his bride, the year his first and only son, Khalid, had been born. With a glad heart he had returned to Mecca, the site of the joy of his youth, to give thanks to Allah for all the blessings of the prime of his life - for Khalid, for the happiness of his marriage to the infidel American who was the love of his life.

And now he had come here the third time in his middle years, by jet, for a pilgrimage of sacrifice and sorrow. He had come for strength and solace. He had come not in joy but in grief to pray for guidance to mend his shattered life.

In preparation for his moment on this mountain, Rashid had flown yesterday from Dhahran to Jeddah and then taken the pilgrim bus forty-five miles north. As he had entered Mecca by the serene and heavenly Gate of Peace, he had sighed as he always sighed at his first glimpse of the black cube of the Kaaba majestically towering fifty feet high in the courtyard. He and all the world's eight hundred million Muslims prayed five times each day facing this sacred rock that was the *Beit Allah*, the 'House of God.' For all time, at the very beginning of time, at the Creation, God had placed his Kaaba just here. Even in pagan times, men had worshiped at this shiny meteorite. But then this rock had been consecrated to the One God by the Prophet Abraham. Yet even after that dark shadows had fallen again on this House of God, for after Abraham the idolatrous had set up their graven images again inside the Kaaba's sacred walls. It wasn't until the Prophet Muhammad was born thirteen centuries ago not far from the shade cast by this sacred stone that the Kaaba was once again consecrated purely to Allah.

Rashid had paced alone then through the opening rituals of the *hajj*, for the other pilgrims had begun their prayers here days ago. As he walked counterclockwise round the Kaaba seven times, chanting his prayers, he had hoped for a flood of understanding, acceptance, and peace. But he had remained troubled even as he proceeded to the next rites of the *hajj*. He had drunk thirstily from the rich mineral water of the Sacred Well of Zamzam, symbol of Allah's font of mercy for the believers, and yet his soul had still been parched. He had run the course of the pious, seven times between the hills of Safu and Marwah, and then he had prayed inside the Sacred Mosque. Finally last night in the village of Mina he had camped humbly in the open on the rocky ground beside more than a million of the pious. He lay that night under the diamond stars that lit the sky above the holy city.

And now Rashid stood among the multitudes praying on the crest of Jebal el-Rahmah. It was a small mountain as mountains go, only two hundred feet high, a shortfall of mercy just outside Mecca. Beside Rashid prayed thousands of other Muslims. Spread below them, all around them, on the wide dusty Plain of Abraham, more than one million stood and prayed in the sun, where the Prophet had once stood and prayed in the sun. *Wuquf* - the 'Standing' - is the most sacred rite of the *hajj*, the heart of the ritual. Since noon the weary pilgrims had been standing so and praying so, and it was now just before sunset. Rashid prayed that Allah would give him the grace to know His will and then the strength to submit. He told himself, and Allah, that she had betrayed him. She had given herself to his brother, and so she must be forever stained in the eyes of the righteous. *Inshallah* - if God willed it - he would divorce her. Without her his life would be as barren and joyless as these desolate mountains in which holy Mecca nestled like a precious jewel. He wished he could believe that in the desolation of the life he would face without her his faith would shine inside him like a precious jewel. 'Doubly at Thy service, O God.' On the crest of the Mount of Mercy, Rashid prayed not for mercy but for strength.

In the distance a cannon boomed, and the time for the 'Standing' was over. The pilgrims surged to a rocky place called Muzdalifah. Rashid walked with the others, prayed with the others, and before he lay on the ground to try to sleep through the night, he bent with the others to gather his own forty-nine sharp pebbles to use in the rituals still to come. All that long night he lay sleepless in a fever of prayer for Allah to show him the way. 'Doubly at Thy service, O God.'

Before daybreak another signal cannon boomed, and again the army of the faithful marched on Mina. A great and angry roar came from the throats of the Muslims when finally they could see looming before them three square, whitewashed masonry pillars which symbolized Satan. Once, very long ago, deep in the racial and religious memory, legend had it that on this very site the devil had tempted the Prophet Abraham to disobey God's command to sacrifice his son, whom the Muslims call not Isaac but Ishmael. But here, just here, Abraham had resisted Satan, and good had triumphed over evil. Rashid took one of his pebbles in his hand and threw it straight and true. A rain of pebbles beat against the pillars, as the believers stoned the devil, repudiating all the evils of the world. Rashid took aim and threw another righteous rock. Sunny? Was Sunny evil? Was she Satan? Or was his brother, Muhammad, the devil in his family? Rashid cast again and again, until he had cast seven stones. Yet still he felt the evil with him, inside him, unpurged. 'Doubly at Thy service, O God,' he prayed.

With the other pilgrims Rashid began the *Eid el-Adha*, the Feast of Sacrifice. He bought a live young sheep from the herds brought to this place by the townsmen from neighboring villages and the Bedouin from the neighboring tribes. He murmured a prayer of consecration, and then with a sharp knife he slit the animal's throat. A river of sacrificial blood spurted on the dry Plain of Abraham. Rashid stared down at his slaughtered lamb, then at the blood dripping from his knife. Long ago, here, the Prophet Abraham had been willing to sacrifice to God his Ishmael, his son who was the dearest thing on earth to him. After that testament of faith, long ago, here, God had taken pity on Abraham and accepted instead the sacrifice of a lamb. Today, here, the sacrifice of these animals symbolized the readiness of all Muslims to surrender whatever was dearest to them if that was God's will. Rashid considered the possibility that he too might be called upon to make that supreme sacrifice in the name of his Lord. But if he submitted, if he vowed to God he would renounce his Sunny, would the Lord relent and spare him as he had Abraham?

Rashid stared at the blood on his knife. He raised his eyes to the heavens. Was God commanding him to renounce her? Or did God want even more from him? Was now the time to stand up and be counted against not only her but all the wickedness of the West? He wondered if there was some oblique divine purpose for all that had happened. Would divorcing her be a ritual act of purification? If he purified himself, hardened himself, made himself like a sharp sure blade of Damascene steel, would he someday be able to strike a mortal blow for Allah against the infidels? As the blood dripped from his knife to his hand, still Rashid pondered guilt and retribution.

Rashid gave the carcass of his slaughtered lamb to the religious authorities for distribution to the poor; then he trudged with heavy heart back inside the sacred gates of Mecca. He stood with his brother and sister pilgrims in the teeming main square. He joined the ecstatic throng circling the Kaaba seven times, praying all the while, meditating on the unity of God and man. He kissed the *Hajar el-Aswad*, the 'Black Stone,' embedded in the south-eastern corner of the Kaaba. 'Doubly at Thy service, O God,' Rashid repeated over and over until the prayer seemed to ring inside his head. In a daze of religious fever, then, he joined the masses of the faithful joyously following the paths of Abraham and the steps of Muhammad. He, and they, ran back and forth seven times from one point in the square to another, just as Hagar, the second wife of Abraham and mother of Ishmael, had once run desperately through the desert in search of life-giving water for her son. Here, on the sacred soil of what would become the square of Mecca, the Angel Gabriel had appeared to Hagar, the angel had stamped his foot on the ground, and a well had miraculously spouted from the barren ground. Rashid, and the others, drank from the Well of Zamzam just outside the Sacred Mosque, in the square of the prophets and angels and miraculous revelation.

The *hajj* rites were almost at an end, and Rashid despaired that God was not going to give him a sign. With the dragging step of a vanquished man, he walked back outside the gates of Mecca to another flat holy plain, where he walked devoutly seven times between two more eroded holy hills. For the third and final time Rashid walked back to Mina, where stood the three pillars of the devil. Slowly he took careful aim at the white pillars, and one by one he threw his remaining stones at these representations of evil, seven stones at each pillar, and more, until he stood empty-handed and disarmed. 'Doubly at Thy service, O God,' he prayed again.

He turned his face to Mecca; then he gazed again upon the Mount of Mercy. Yet nowhere could he see the slightest intimation of Allah's revealing His will. He heaved a hopeless sigh and walked slowly back inside the Gate of Peace. He supposed he had been presumptuous to dream of private revelation. He did not need any sign from heaven, any bolt of lightning, any eclipse of the sun, any shooting star falling from the sky to the earth. He knew right from wrong. He knew God's implacable laws. He must give up his Sunny.

Tears filled his eyes. How he loved her! He loved her more at this moment of grief and renunciation than he had ever loved her when he held her in his arms and thought they would live forever together as man and wife. He loved her now with longing and with pain, just as he had loved her before with the fierce hot joy of possession. He loved her, but he would renounce her.

Again Rashid sighed. He had known in his heart of hearts that it must come to this as soon as Muhammad had made that evil denunciation in the black tents. Yet he had struggled against his fate. He had come on pilgrimage to Mecca. He had hoped that if he prayed fervently enough, Allah might take pity on him. He had dreamed that Allah might in His infinite mercy give him a sign that he could forgive Sunny and keep her as his wife. Yet he had not felt even an instant of special grace during this *hajj*. He had tried, and he had failed, to evade his destiny. But here and now, on the sacred soil of Mecca, he would do what he had to do.

He must divorce her or risk losing his soul. He must divorce her, and so he would divorce her.

He would send her back to America. He would always love his Sunny, but he would never see her again. Yet he shrank from telling her his decision. He did not think he could speak those iron words to the wife of his heart. He would tell his mother, and his mother would tell her. He would of course have to keep Khalid by his side here in the kingdom, but he would take pity on Sunny and let her have the comfort of their daughter. She could take Sarah back to live with her in America at least until the girl was old enough to be married.

Rashid stared at the Black Stone embedded in the Kaaba. Later he would register an official record of his decision with a *shaykh* in Hofuf. But here and now on the most sacred ground on earth he would renounce her. He wiped away his tears. 'I, Rashid, divorce my wife Sunny.' He repeated the assertion. 'I divorce her.' His voice quavered, then, as he prepared to make the third, and final, renunciation. 'I, Rashid, divorce my wife Sunny.'

He bowed his head and let the tears fall on his white pilgrim robe. 'Doubly at Thy service, O God,' he prayed.

Finally, wearily, he put himself in the hands of the barbers for the symbolic shearing of a lock of his hair, the outward sign a *hajj* was completed and a Muslim consecrated to Allah. But Rashid thought that the beginning of his bleak years, the years of his lonely crusade in the service of Allah, required a more dramatic gesture.

Rashid told the barbers to shave his head bare to his skull.

—18—

The main *majlis* reception room of the villa in Khobar was strewn with a disarray of suitcases, cardboard boxes, and reed baskets. Copper trays stacked with used coffee cups, dirty tea glasses, and empty soda bottles littered brass tabletops, and great wads of sodden tissues lay in discarded heaps. Um Muhammad ran hither and yon through the clutter, urging the servants to hurry, to take this, not to forget that, pausing only long enough to wipe away her own tears or to comfort a sobbing little girl. All the Al-Murrah women - all of them, not just the immediate family but distant aunts and cousins and in-laws, a throng of more than fifty women - were packed into the *majlis*, and all of them were weeping with the hopeless grief of mourners at a funeral of a loved one struck down in the prime of life. Women swooned on the gilt chairs ringing the perimeter of the reception room. Women were prostrate on the pinkish Persian carpets on the floor. Women wept even as they sat atop suitcases nursing their babies. As Aisha wailed, she clutched the wide long sleeves of her new black silk robe and deliberately ripped rents into that costly fabric. Nura keened with her head tossed back, like a wild animal. Nura's daughters wept in heaps on the floor. Um Muhammad cried even as she continued to rush in a frenzy from the front door to the main reception hall to the women's quarters, supervising the servants packing up the limousine with the suitcases. All the weeping women kept an anxious watch on the stairway where Sunny and Sarah and Khalid must soon emerge. Outside the driver beat a quick warning tattoo on his horn. It was almost time to leave for the airport. Cousin Hussein and Grandfather Ibrahim were already waiting in the car. Hussein was the official family chaperon who would escort Sunny and Sarah on the airplane all the way to London. But Ibrahim at the last minute had decided he too would go to the Dhahran airport to say goodbye to his American daughter. Again the driver sounded the horn.

There were footfalls in the hallway, and the Al-Murrah women caught their breaths as Sunny came down the stairs. Her one arm was around Khalid, her other around Sarah, and it might be that they were carrying her or that she was carrying them, so intrinsic to each other's support did the mother and the children appear.

Sunny stood in the arch of the *majlis* one last time, and

she willed herself to stop crying as she looked from one dear face to another, from Um Muhammad and Nura and Aisha to the little girls and the aunts and the cousins. She wiped away her tears and steeled herself to say goodbye to the only real family, other than her grandparents, that she had ever known.

She had been despairing and impotently furious ever since Um Muhammad had gently broken the very bad news to her. At first she would not believe that Rashid had divorced her, that he was finished with her, that he refused even to say goodbye. He had merely telephoned his mother from Riyadh and given Um Muhammad the lordly order that Sunny must leave the kingdom within one week. He would see to it her residency visa was made to expire in seven days, that her exit visa was signed and sealed, and that her ticket was ready and her passport entirely in order. As a special concession, he would allow her to take Sarah. But she must leave Khalid with him in Arabia. He would send her and his daughter generous quarterly payments to an account he had opened for them at a Boston bank.

Desperately Sunny had tried to reason with Um Muhammad, but there had been no way to reason with Islamic divorce laws. If a husband repeated three times that he was divorcing his wife - for any reason, good or bad, consequential or frivolous - she had to return to her father's family. When it finally began to sink in on Sunny that this nightmare was real, she had thrown herself on Ibrahim's mercy. The old man had held her in his arms and cried along with her; then he had gone off to plead her case with Rashid in Riyadh. An ashen-faced Ibrahim had come back the next day to tell Sunny that Rashid was unshakable. But Sunny had nonetheless marched off to the American consulate in Dhahran to see if there was anything she could do to fight the divorce or to get custody of Khalid. A polite but preoccupied clerk had informed Sunny that the U.S. government never interfered in Saudi family affairs.

She had done as she was told then. She had packed her suitcases and had begun to make her farewells. She had visited each and every one of the women relatives, and every morning and every afternoon and every evening of this entire last week had been one great womanly weeping and gnashing of teeth. Finally, yesterday, Sunny had made one other last visit: to the grave of her mother and father in Dhahran. She had put doomed roses on their graves, and she had watched their blossoms wither in the heat even as she knelt and prayed. As the rose petals fell to the sand, she wondered whether her father would have seen a bitter irony in this final parting of the ways between the Shannons and the Al-Murrahs. Would her father have seen this sundering as the last shabby act in their family saga? Would he have wondered if now, finally, the ghost of Abdullah was appeased and at rest?

As Sunny looked around the *majlis* at her loved ones, her face crumpled, and she started to cry again. She had wanted to say brave sweet words of parting to these women she loved, but all she could do was simply open her arms mutely to all of them and embrace them, one by one, as they came to say goodbye. Um Muhammad held her and rocked her like an infant; Aisha cried in her arms; Nura wept like a true sister in her embrace; and Nura's daughters held on to her as if she were their second mother.

Sunny broke down altogether as she watched Sarah trying to say goodbye to all her half-sisters. The little girls clung to each other, and Sunny faltered in her resolve to take Sarah back to America. Surely, she thought, her daughter would be happier here with the family. But then Sarah looked up at her, and smiled a tremulous child's smile, and buried her head in her mother's long black skirt. 'Oh, Sarah, Sarah . . .' She would thank God she was at least taking her little girl away with her. Um Muhammad had explained that Rashid did not have to let her take Sarah to America. The girl was seven years old, and Saudi law said a mother had to surrender the children to the father at that age. In practice, moreover, a man could and often did take custody of all the children, no matter what their ages, after a divorce.

Again the horn sounded from outside.

What had to come now was the hardest parting of all.

Sunny let go of her daughter and crouched down and swept her nine-year-old son into her arms for the last time. Nura had promised to raise Khalid as her own, and Sunny knew Nura was a good mother and would take loving care of him. But as Sunny looked into her son's needy tear-filled eyes, she was sure Nura could never love him as she did. For a long while Sunny had lavished extra love and care on her firstborn. Khalid was shy and achingly sensitive, and the bond between the two of them cut to their core. She was heartsick at leaving him. This innocent little boy would suffer even more than she would from the divorce. She hoped he was more resilient than she thought. She would never forgive herself, or Rashid, if this child was scarred forever by what was happening today. 'Khalid, Khalid, my son . . .' she murmured as he clung to her. Khalid stroked her yellow hair, and he touched her cheek and manfully tried to be brave and smile for his mother.

The horn blew again outside, and Sunny kissed him again and again and hugged him desperately. Then she stood and tied on her mask and threw on her cloak and turned to go. But Khalid would not let her leave without a fight. He threw himself at his mother. He clung to his mother's skirts. He hurled himself vainly at his mother's masked face for one last kiss. Sunny reached out to him, she held him, and never, as long as she lived, would she forget her son's frantically clawing at her mask, trying to rip it off so he could touch her, could kiss her, could see her one last time. Nura and Um Muhammad, in the end, had to pry him off her, finger by finger.

Sunny and Sarah finally staggered outside in the midday heat. Just before Cousin Hussein and Grandfather Ibrahim ushered them inside the long black Mercedes,

Sunny stopped and turned and looked back at the house of her happiness. It was not a beautiful house. Like too much construction all through the Middle East, it was a squat, dirty-looking reinforced-concrete box of a house with a flat roof, and it looked more like a dreary transient motel than a home. Yet inside these graceless walls she had been loved and cherished and warm and content. She hesitated a moment longer before forever turning her back on this house and this life. If he were going to change his mind and save her by a last-minute reprieve, Rashid would appear just now and take her hand and lead her back inside. But it was Ibrahim who took her arm, Hussein who helped her into the car. The limousine door clicked softly shut.

Even though the other women were supposed to stay inside, they surged out into the driveway. Sunny and Sarah pressed their faces to the window and looked out at the throng of waving, weeping women. Between the mask and the tinted window glass, Sunny could hardly distinguish her mother-in-law from her sister-in-law from her cousins. But as the car began to roll slowly along the driveway toward the gate, she saw the white-robed figure of a small boy break away from the rest, she saw Khalid running after the limousine, she heard him crying out her name. As the car passed through the high-walled gate and picked up speed, the last she saw of her family and her life in Arabia was her son, her Khalid, her little boy kneeling in the dust crying for his mother to please come back.

At the Boston airport two days later, Sunny hurled herself into her grandmother's arms. She was home, she was protected, she was safe, and no one was going to hurt her anymore. Sunny had promised herself, on the long flight across the wide Atlantic after a brief stopover in London, that she would stop her endless crying. But she was weeping as she put her daughter's small soft tan hand into her great-grandmother's big rough red one. 'Sarah, this is her. Gran!'

'Lord, she looks just like her father! Come here, you little heathen!' Bess swept the little girl up in her arms and gave her a lip-smacking kiss. 'You can call me Gran too, now, honey. You speak English?'

'Of *course* I speak English.' Sarah was accustomed to being petted and cosseted by women of all shapes and sizes, so she took this raw-boned, white-haired old woman in her stride. As the one she was supposed to call 'Gran' hugged her tightly again, Sarah stared in solemn fascination over her shoulder at the hordes of rushing, impatient Americans sweeping past her. All these women, her mother included, looked so naked and vulnerable with their faces uncovered. She watched as a pretty young woman threw herself into a man's arms, and he spun her around, and they kissed for a long while boldly on their lips. Sarah's intelligent eyes darted around the terminal. She liked how clean it was here, how shiny it was, how everything - even the floor - was spotless and polished as if for the Great Feast or the visit of an important prince. Sarah wished she could show this sparkling country to Um Muhammad, and Nura, and her half-sisters, and Aunt Aisha, and especially to Khalid. Her mother had said America would be wonderful; she had promised her chocolates here, and pretty dresses with ruffles, and a transistor radio, a television set, a record player, and a telephone all for her very own. But Sarah did not think even all those treats would matter much without her brother to share them. Sarah tried not to think of Khalid, or of her father. She had vowed not to ask her mother about either of them anymore. She didn't want to make her mother cry. More than anything, Sarah wanted to make her mother so happy she would never again cry as she had been crying since their world had crumpled last week and they had been hustled out of Saudi. 'I speak very good English,' Sarah said carefully as her great-grandmother released her. 'Also good Arabic.'

'You sound good to me.' Bess stepped back so she could get a better look at Sunny's daughter. 'Look good, too.

She's a pretty little thing, Sunny. But too skinny. Needs some meat on her bones. But we'll take care of that.' She touched Sarah's glossy raven hair and seemed reassured by her flashing dark eyes. 'And spunky, by the looks of her. She may look like *him*, but thank God she has your spirit.' Gran pronounced a benediction on her two descendants. 'I always did like spunky little girls.'

'Is Gramps waiting in the car?' Sunny looked around for the one who was missing.

'No, he's just feeling poorly. It's hard for him to get around after the stroke. With the chair and all.'

'What stroke? Gramps had a stroke? When?'

'A while ago. After Tom died.' Bess put her arm around Sunny again. 'I didn't want to worry you. I thought you had enough worries out there in *that* place.' Her scowl left no doubt about what she thought of Saudi Arabia. 'But let's get out of here.' She gestured for a porter. 'We'll talk about all that later. God, girl, it's good to have you back.' She ruffled Sarah's hair. 'And to have you here too, sweet pea.'

Soon they were all wedged in the maroon Volkswagen and heading for the tunnel under the harbor to Boston.

'Prettiest city on God's earth,' Gran promised Sarah.

The little girl looked from her mother to her great-grandmother with saucer eyes. 'Prettier than Jeddah?'

The old woman snorted, then launched into a monologue about the superior delights and historical importance of the City of Boston and the Commonwealth of Massachusetts. By the time they were out of the tunnel, Sarah was hanging on Bess's every word, laughing, and pointing out the window and asking excited questions.

Sunny sat quietly with her arm around her daughter, reveling in the sensations of finally seeing Gran again and being home where she hoped she would feel she belonged. She cautioned herself that there must have been many changes in the ten years she had been gone. Gran was driving a Volkswagen now, although she used to swear by Chevrolets. But as Sunny listened to her grandmother regaling Sarah with opinionated pronouncements, about the world and life and everything that flashed past their windows, she thanked God that at least Gran was the same.

'We'll take a little detour,' Bess said as she spun off the highway and toward Beacon Hill. 'Show the child a few of the sights.'

Sunny started to cry when she saw the gaslights and the noble red-brick town houses and the flower boxes and the polished brass knockers on the front doors. She pointed in wonder at the sloping gabled roofs and the chimneys. There were no beautiful black tents on West Cedar Street, and Sunny wept for those Bedouin houses of hair. She tried to stop crying. Yet how could she miss Saudi and hate Saudi and love America and find it lacking - how could she feel all of this at once and not cry?

'Don't cry, Ummie. Don't be sad.'

Sunny blew her nose and assured her daughter that everything was going to be just fine now.

Bess slowed down as they drove through a park. 'That's Boston Common over there to the right, where they used to graze cows in the old days. And that's the Public Gardens to the left. Next time we're in town, sweet pea, we'll come here and go for a ride on the swan boats in the middle of that pond.'

'What's a swan?'

'You don't know what a *swan* is? Sunny, how can this child not know that?'

But Sunny was staring toward the Commonwealth Avenue Mall. 'You are my sunshine,' she had sung to him here. She had sung to him that he was 'her only sunshine,' and then he had kissed her. Her eyes misted over again, and she sobbed into a tissue.

'I just feel so bad, Gran.' Sunny shook her head. 'As if everything's over for me now. You know?'

'I don't know, child, but I expect you'll be telling me all the gruesome details later.' Bess looped past the State House and dipped through the bustling streets of afternoon shoppers. 'First, though, I want to show you what they've done to Scollay Square.'

Sunny braced herself for another round of tears when she came face to face with the sleazy hotel where Muhammad had ruined her life. She waited for Scollay Square's flashing neon and decrepit buildings and the prostitutes and bands of predatory sailors. But as she stared at the formidable new office buildings and the clean sweeping boulevards, she decided they must have made a wrong turn. 'Where are we?'

'Scollay Square.' Bess waved her hand as if she held a magic wand. 'They tore down the old red-light district, and good riddance. It's called Government Center now. That peculiar thing you're looking at is the new city hall. That'll be a federal building there. And a state one on the corner.'

'It's so different!' Sunny was glad they had obliterated Scollay Square, but she was suddenly afraid that perhaps Boston and America and everything outside the sheltered confines of her walled family compound in the Kingdom of Saudi Arabia had changed too much. She had wanted every fiber that was home to remain frozen in place, and instead the wrecking balls and bulldozers had torn down and built up and transformed this whole world in her absence. Sunny sank deeper into desperation as the Volkswagen raced down the Boston side of the Charles. Even venerable Back Bay was dwarfed by the stark new skyscrapers of Prudential Center. Sunny's heart sank as she looked out the window at the altered skyline and sinews of Boston.

'Recognize your alma mater?' Gran waved toward the two graceful Gothic spires of Boston University that were surrounded by grimy buzzing nests of dormitories and classrooms and parking lots. 'I suppose you'll be going back there in the fall. How long do you have to go to get your degree? One year or two?'

'My degree?' Sunny shrugged. 'Two years I suppose.' Until this moment she had not given a thought to reconstructing her life in America. Until now it had been all she could do to make her farewells and hold herself and her daughter together as they journeyed from the old life to the new. She couldn't believe her grandmother was rushing her so much. She had just gotten off the plane, and Gran was zooming her around Boston and all but registering her in a full semester's courses. Sunny wanted to tell her grandmother, and Boston, and all America, to slow down, to be gentler, to give her time. In Saudi . . . Sunny reminded herself again she was no longer in that kingdom. She looked back dubiously over her shoulder at the Gothic spires of Boston University. She could go back and get her psychology degree. But she was almost thirty – surely too old to be a student.

'Next stop Harvard Square.' Bess pointed to the red-brick buildings, white steeples, and shady green trees on the other side of the river. 'That's the most famous university in America, sweet pea. That's where Kennedy went.' She shook her shaggy head. 'I still can't get used to his being gone. Tragic; it was tragic. That riderless black horse at the funeral! And her with those two little ones. I've never seen anything as sad as that in my life. I don't care what the Warren Court said. There was a plot. I think it was either Castro or the Mafia. But *we'll* never know for sure. It's all been hushed up. It was a conspiracy, and it'll be the ruination of this country, you mark my words.' Bess sighed. 'Gramps and I were at the meat counter at Tom's Food World, when all of a sudden one of the stock boys came running out of the back room yelling what he had just heard on the radio.'

'What's that, Gran?' It was just over there, on the far bank of the Charles, that she had once walked with Muhammad. He had kissed her as they stood just there, and then he had rushed her to her doom in Scollay Square.

'Why, the assassination! What I was doing when I first heard they'd shot President Kennedy. What were you doing when you heard?'

Sunny tried to remember. She must have been out

camping with some of the cousins, for Kennedy had been dead and buried before Ibrahim had told her the news. Weeks later she had borrowed an old news-magazine to read about the details of the killing and the funeral and about Oswald and Ruby. But the rise and the fall of John Kennedy had seemed more remote to her than one of the old *Tales from the Arabian Nights*. She had left America in the Eisenhower heyday of the '50s, when Kennedy had been merely a glamorous young senator from her home state. Hearing Gran mourn him now like a beloved son only increased Sunny's growing sense of alienation. But as they drove over the bridge and up Boylston Street toward the center of Harvard Square, she was relieved to spot the homely landmarks, the dear narrow winding streets, the worn red-brick sidewalks, the musty storefront bookshops, the elegant open gates of Harvard College, the crowded kiosk with its newspapers from all around the world and its teletype bulletins rolling electronically along the roof. Harvard Square had not, thank God, been torn down or spruced up or renovated into something slick and modernistic and shoddy. But then Sunny took a closer look. The streets were the same, the buildings were the same, but what sorcery had been worked on this younger generation? Sunny stared in astonishment at the carnival of costumed young people lounging in purple caftans and Indian feathers and combat flak jackets and tie-dyed blue jeans. She fancied she could hear the tinkle of camel bells, and as she looked she saw a bearded youth dancing with a girl on the sidewalk while he jingled a string of camel bells on a red velvet ribbon. Strangely, Sunny thought of that *zar* and the dancing wizard who cast out women's demons. Here in Harvard Square, Sunny watched a breathless young coed skip and prance and dip and laugh, and as she moved her full breasts jiggled as if she was not wearing any underwear.

'Hippies,' Gran snorted. 'Trash, I call them. Drug addicts and trash. Need a good bath and a haircut, if you ask me.' She hit the brakes as her lane of traffic came to an abrupt halt. Ahead in the street in front of the Coop, there was a growing sound of chanting. 'The Commies are at it again! They've got these kids brainwashed with their Red propaganda. Marching here, marching there. The war! That's all you see on the news anymore.'

Sunny craned her neck. Young people in blue jeans were waving signs she was too far away to read. They were shouting something that sounded almost like a high school football cheer. 'What's that they're yelling?'

'Treason,' Bess said.

'Vietnam? They're demonstrating against the Vietnam war, aren't they?' Sunny had to get closer to see more. She could not help opening the car door and getting out and taking Sarah by the hand and walking up by the kiosk so she could read the signs and watch the protesters' faces. Sunny had heard about the antiwar movement. In Saudi she had been isolated from most but not all the currents of home. Sometimes Rashid had brought her a stray copy of *Time* or *Newsweek* or the *International Herald Tribune*, and always the news had been severely scissored by Saudi censors who excised any mention of Israel or Communism or sex or subversion, or progress. Yet even Sunny knew that in this spring of 1967, President Lyndon Johnson was increasingly being blamed, especially here in Boston, for leading the country into an unjust war in Vietnam. Sunny stared at the howling protesters. Another lifetime ago, she had hung out here in the Harvard Square coffeehouses, where beatniks had smoked cigarettes and denounced Jim Crow in the South and talked cynically about the American dream souring into a materialistic nightmare. Sunny studied the faces of the demonstrators, hoping she might see someone she recognized from her own youth. But these protesters were too young to have been a part of her tame Bohemian days in those beatnik cafés. Standing here in Harvard Square, watching a bold new generation parade by, the fantastic dancing hippies with their bells and the fierce chanting militants with their causes, Sunny felt tired and alien and very much past her prime. She hustled Sarah back to the car. 'Can we go home now, Gran?'

On the hour-and-a-half ride out to the farm, Sunny tuned out as her grandmother described the state of the orchards, how hot the spring had been, the health of Sunny's ancient great-aunts, soaring property values in Still River, the new priest who had come to the parish with ecumenical ideas that bordered on the Protestant.

As they sped along the smooth highway, Sunny tried to take in the immensity of her homecoming. She looked up at the trees arching and blooming and swaying in the spring wind. It was so very green here, Sunny thought. So beautifully green. Muslims believed green was the color of paradise, but Muslims were wrong. Green was the color of Massachusetts. Green was the color of hope. Beautiful green. Every tree they passed seemed like an old friend. Wonderful trees, orchards of trees, forests of trees, so much greenness here, so much life. How fruitful this land was, how bountiful, how blessed.

Sunny would have sung 'America the Beautiful' out loud except that she knew it would have made her weep again. She had not known she had it in her to be so sentimental about America. She had not known she had been so very homesick for so very many years. She had never seen anything as beautiful as these elms and these maples and these weeping willows.

When at last they turned into the driveway to the farm, a fresh shower of tears fell from Sunny's eyes. She looked from that dear house to those wonderful rolling hills to that fragrant countryside, and she cried in relief finally to be home. Bess pulled on the hand brake, and Sunny heard another familiar voice from the past. For a moment she forgot all about her marriage and her divorce and her son and her sorrows, and she leaped from the car and raced up to the front porch, where her grandfather sat patiently waiting in his wheelchair. They kissed and hugged, and in a way it wasn't a lie when she told this withered old man who used to be her virile grandfather that he looked wonderful. She presented Sarah, and Gran wheeled Gramps inside, and they drank coffee and devoured an entire apple pie. But then Sunny's attention began to wander. She found her eyes turning outside, as she searched for the last member of the family.

'Go on!' Gran nudged her. 'We'll take care of Sarah. You'll find her in the upper meadow.'

Sunny raced out the back door, up past the garden, out by the orchards, and followed the bridle path around the bend. She was breathless when she spotted her. Princess Camey! The mare - older now, but still the horse of Sunny's youth and dreams - stood grazing in the far end of the meadow. 'Princess Camey!'

The mare's head jerked up, she whinnied, she began galloping toward Sunny. But she stopped twenty feet away, she shyly dropped her head, she looked up at Sunny through her long lashes. You? Is it you? Can it truly be you? After all these years you've come back to me? And then she trembled and waited in an agony of anticipation for her Sunny to touch her once more.

Sunny ran the last steps to her horse. She threw her arms around Princess Camey's neck. She nuzzled the horse and rained tears on the russet hair of her old friend. She kissed Princess Camey again and again, and the wise, gentle, forgiving animal eyes of the mare looked out at her with infinite compassion. 'You know, old girl, don't you?' Sunny whispered. 'It's been tough times for both of us, hasn't it? Lonely years, huh? Wait till I tell you all that's happened. . . .' Sunny could not go on, just now, with the news of her failed life in that other world. 'But I'm back now; everything will be better now! I even have a little girl. I brought my Sarah back! Wait till you see my Sarah, you'll love her, she's like I used to be, like I was the first time we saw each other, on my birthday. . . .' Sunny wept into her mare's thick mane. 'Oh, Princess, how I've missed you!'

At last Sunny wiped away her tears and set about the last loving step of her homecoming. She led Princess

Camey through the meadow gate and down the bridle path and through the orchards, out to the crest of their favorite lookout hill.

Sunny stood and looked out over the green rolling emerald vista of home. Always in Saudi, when she had despaired the most, when she had felt lonely and defeated and forever alien, she had held herself together by imagining herself back here, centered on the crest of this hill. On the darkest days, on the worst days, she had fantasized herself back here. On the worst of all the days, on the day she had broken down at the *zar* and howled like a madwoman, on that day especially, she had feared she was losing her mind. She had imagined herself back here that day, sitting atop this hill on a white wooden lawn chair, drinking in the tranquil undulations of these meadows and these fields.

Sunny began to cry again. She cried in great heaving sobs, and she was not comforted when Princess Camey nuzzled her neck. Sunny wondered if she was having a nervous breakdown. It had been the thought of the view from this hill that had kept her sane. Now that she was truly here, truly back, would the view stop working that same magic for her? Were the peace and the safety of this vista only a mirage? She looked out at the shimmer of the river and the bloom of the orchards and again she tried to assure herself she would be all right. Rashid had sent her into exile, but she would be all right. With an effort she said the words out loud: 'I'll be all right.' But she did not believe it. She did not believe she would ever be all right again, not without him. Sunny was very much afraid.

Sunny dragged her feet down the narrow, tree-lined North Cambridge street, looking for the psychologist's address. But these sprawling old wooden Victorian three-deckers and brick town houses were too quiet, too middle-class and normal for anyone who specialized in neurosis.

She wished she hadn't let her old college adviser talk her into this. When she had gone over to Boston University to meet with Professor Hunter about resuming her studies in September, she had ended up crying again, and pouring out personal details about Saudi and Rashid and Khalid and the divorce and her fears that she had been on the brink of a breakdown since she had come home two months ago. She had been insulted and alarmed and had only cried harder when Professor Hunter suggested that before she came back to school she might 'talk' to a therapist. She wasn't crazy, she told him, she was just sad, she just couldn't stop crying. As she had wiped her eyes, Professor Hunter had gently assured her he hadn't said she was crazy, just troubled. He had leaned back in his chair and confided that he had been in therapy when he was her age, and not only because it was required as part of his training. Therapy, he said with the shining eyes of the true believer, had been the single most rewarding episode in his life. It was wonderful to have someone to talk everything over with, someone who listened and understood and helped you learn to listen and understand. Besides, he had said more briskly, if Sunny was serious about coming back to study psychology, how could it hurt to find out about the discipline firsthand?

The two of them had talked, then, about what sort of therapist she might want to see. Just as the professor had begun to describe the differences between psychiatrists and psychologists and psychiatric social workers, before he had the chance to launch into an impromptu lecture about Freudians and Neo-Freudians and Anti-Freudians, Sunny had blurted out that she wanted to talk to a woman. She had looked away from him, out of his office window at the traffic coursing past on Storrow Drive, and admitted she was too angry at men - at all men - now, that men had always failed her. If she had to go to a therapist, she wanted her to be a woman, someone sympathetic and honest and true. Someone motherly, someone like the mother she had never known. 'I see,' Professor Hunter had said, and he had smiled as he wrote down a name and number. Dr. Rebecca Rosen, he had explained, was a Harvard Ph.D., a psychologist who was in private practice only a few afternoons and evenings a week, and only for a very limited number of women patients, since she spent most of her time as the supervisor of a school for problem children in Newton. Sunny had liked the sound of this Dr. Rosen. If she had to see someone, she wanted to see someone with those priorities.

Sunny reached into her pocket, and the sweaty palms of her hands smeared the ink as she smoothed out the scrap of paper with the address. She looked doubtfully up at the two-story red-brick town house. But a Mercedes was parked in the driveway. Maybe, Sunny decided, a psychologist who charged forty-five dollars for fifty minutes of her time did live here. She followed the instructions Dr. Rosen had given her on the phone and knocked on the ground-floor office door.

A woman stood there, a plump rumpled woman in her mid-forties, wearing baggy beige pants, a wildly patterned African *dashiki*, sandals with socks. The woman had a mass of kinky mouse-colored hair, wonderfully gentle but wounded, wise light eyes, and lips that pursed a lighted filter cigarette. 'I'm Dr. Rosen.'

Sunny smiled and tried to do the right social thing; she shook the doctor's hand, and said what a nice neighborhood the doctor lived in; she volunteered the half-truth that she had had no trouble at all finding the office. But all the time she babbled pleasantries, her eyes were riveted on the doctor's kind, serene, caring face. A lump came into Sunny's throat. This one looked the way a mother should look. As the doctor took her seat in the easy chair facing her, Sunny had an impulse to climb into her well-padded, wrinkled lap. A mother. She had always longed for her mother. She could not fight off a welling emotion of irrational love for this woman. She was embarrassed to love her so at first sight. She must have loved her mother so at first sight, she thought, at birth, and she looked away from the doctor, shaken by a fleeting memory of bliss, of mother love.

Sunny sank down into an orange easy chair facing the doctor. She leaned her head back so tightly against the back of the chair she could almost feel the corduroy ridges pressing into the bones of her skull. There was an ottoman in front of her chair, and the brown towel on top of the ottoman seemed to her an invitation to get comfortable. Sunny slipped off her shoes and put up her feet and sighed and looked around the small, cozy, womblike basement office. To her left was a wall of books, but Sunny looked away when she saw too many titles about madness. There was a sofa to her right, a small table with an open box of tissues next to her chair, and on the wall above Dr. Rosen's head the wallpaper was a *trompe-l'oeil*, a thicket of stark chartreuse trees leading upward toward the summit of a hill. She'll take me there, Sunny thought. Through those woods, she'll show me a path through those dense chartreuse trees to the top of that hill.

Later, in the long years that were to come, in her Mondays and Wednesdays and Fridays here in this womblike basement haven, Sunny would tell Dr. Rosen about that extraordinary wellspring of love she had felt at first sight of this woman who was to be not her mother but her therapist, her mentor, and her friend. She would tell Dr. Rosen about the premonition she had felt when she had looked at the chartreuse wallpaper woods, about what it meant to her to find a path through that forbidding thicket. They would talk endlessly, intimately, painfully, about that, and everything else, in all the long years that were to come.

But on this first visit to Dr. Rosen's lair, when at last Sunny looked back at the doctor, as she watched her lighting another cigarette, inhaling, blowing smoke up into the air so that it curled like mist through the thicket of chartreuse trees, Sunny initially could not speak at all. She opened her mouth to say something bright and pleasant to Dr. Rosen - she wanted to say *the right thing* to this nice motherly woman - but instead, as she looked the doctor in the eye, she shook her head, and the tears began again, and to her shame she sobbed out loud. She cried with her head in her hands as the expensive minutes ticked by, and then she plucked a tissue from the box on the table next to her and she blew her nose. Finally she let herself look back at Dr. Rosen.

'Would you like to tell me about it?'

Sunny heaved a great sigh of relief, she blew her nose again, and she began to do just that.

Sunny sat snugly between her daughter and her grandmother in the balcony of the Cambridge cinema waiting for the projector to roll the first reel of *Lawrence of Arabia*. It was ironic, Sunny thought, that she, with her lifelong obsession with both Lawrence and Arabia, must be one of the last people in America to see this movie. It had been a box-office smash when it opened several years ago, but the movie house was virtually empty for this matinee revival.

Bess passed the popcorn to Sunny and Sarah. The old woman had overridden all Sunny's objections and insisted she had to see this movie. Bess was worried about her granddaughter. She was hoping that *Lawrence of Arabia* might help Sunny sort things out. In the four months since her homecoming, Sunny had turned very bitter about Saudi, about Arabs, about men, about everything connected with the disaster of her marriage.

Sunny had even confided to her grandmother, in the aftermath of this summer's Six Day War in the Middle East, that she had taken personal satisfaction in Saudi Arabia's failed attempt to use its oil as a weapon against the Israelis. During the brief bloody duration of that war, however, Sunny had been terrified that the fighting might spread to Arabia. She had known very well how vulnerable Saudi was and always would be to terrorist attacks or even a full-scale invasion. The Saudi oil installations were a sitting target for radical Arabs who wanted revenge for America's support of Israel. She had worried, too, that the Soviets or even the Iranians might use the war as a pretext to seize the oil fields.

It had taken her nine desperate days to get a telephone call through to Khobar, and to find out that Khalid and everyone else she loved in that world were safe and secure and abuzz with excitement. Ibrahim told her an Arab mob had ripped down the flag at the American consulate, then demolished a canteen at the nearby air base before they marched to Dhahran burning cars and breaking windows. Local police and then the National Guard were called out to quell the riot, and since then Saudi troops had been guarding the pipelines and the oil fields and the American compounds. Sunny had been able to follow the next flurry of news in the papers, for the fighting had no sooner stopped than Saudi Arabia threatened to halt its oil production and all shipments to the West unless Israel withdrew from the occupied Arab territories. Sunny had enjoyed picturing Rashid wringing his hands in his Ministry of Petroleum office when the 'oil weapon' had turned out to be a dud. Greedy Iran had immediately volunteered to step up its oil supplies to America and Europe and Japan, and after a few weeks Saudi Arabia had quietly resumed its exports.

But Sunny had taken care not to poison her daughter with her own bitterness. Sunny would have preferred to feel noble and forgiving about what Rashid had done to her. But she was not a saint. As she told Dr. Rosen, she felt she had been unjustly punished, abused, and scorned. And most of all she felt wildly, deeply, intensely enraged. But at least since she had been pouring out her anger to Dr. Rosen, she hadn't been so weepy. Depression, Dr. Rosen had told her many times, was anger turned inward. Every time Sunny felt like crying, she asked herself if she was angry at someone or something. She had been startled to discover seas of dark, fathomless anger inside herself. She was furious at Rashid, at Muhammad, at her father, at her mother, at Saudi Arabia, at America, at fate, at God, and above all at herself. Sunny had not thought it possible to be so angry. She was furious even at her own dreams. She blamed her silly romantic girlish dreams for deluding her into making a wreck of her life.

Sunny took a handful of popcorn. She did not want to see this movie that doubtless glamorized Saudi and the Arabs and Lawrence, the shining hero of her youth.

Sunny was even angry at T. E. Lawrence, for first leading her down the sandy desert path toward disaster. Lawrence should have written less about the wild freedoms and spiritual solace of the shifting golden Arabian desert sands and more about the slavery of Arab women and the cruelties of Islamic injustice. One night last month when she couldn't sleep, she had opened her dog-eared copy of *Seven Pillars*. She had wept over Lawrence's images of Arabia, but then she had thrown the book across the room and wished she had the guts to feed every deceitful page to the fire. Lawrence was a liar and a fraud - a literary criminal.

Sunny sat tensely in her seat. She decided cynically that she might have been spared great personal anguish if Hollywood had made this movie twenty years ago. She could have experienced the exotic and romantic aspects of Saudi in air-conditioned comfort for the price of a two-dollar movie ticket. She should have been smart and waited for the movie instead of trying to make her arabesque dreams come true. She wouldn't have got prickly heat or boils or hepatitis or a broken heart sitting in Harvard Square watching a celluloid fantasy.

The house lights went down, the curtain rose, and the loudspeakers swelled with a thrilling heartthrob of music. Sarah clapped her hands in delight as a beautiful vista of desert lit the screen, and Sunny put her arm around her, as though she were afraid that even the sight of Arabia would steal her daughter away. Sunny wished she could sit with her ears plugged and her eyes locked shut, deaf and blind to the bewitching spell of this movie. She reminded herself she had already paid too high a price for her Saudi fantasies. She had to put all that behind her now. She must forget the searing Saudi realities of her life.

But of course she watched the movie. Of course she could not resist it. She had no mask to hide behind in this deserted movie house.

Sunny looked up, at first unwillingly, at the flickering images on the screen. She watched Peter O'Toole - pale as Lawrence had been in his white Arabian robes, handsome and dashing as Lawrence had been in his flowing Arabian robes - ride his camels and his horses, raid his Turkish trains, and be noble and brave and mad with his love of Arabia.

Sunny munched on a handful of popcorn and sighed at first sight of a flashy-eyed new actor named Omar Sharif. Yes, she thought, Arabs could be like that, and she remembered her first glimpse of Rashid and Muhammad at the Ayer train station long ago. She was misty-eyed with longing as the cameras panned over the dunes and the mountains and the black tents of Arabia. She longed to get up and climb back inside that well-loved world.

Her face was radiant as she sat in the darkened theater, caught up again in the mystique of a dream world that was more than a dream to her. The sand, the sun, the robes, the tents . . . She did not hate that world; she had *never* hated that world where she had spent the best years of her life. She could not believe, now, suddenly, that in these last months of bitter pain and disillusion she had almost forgotten that the love she had felt for so many years for Rashid and for Saudi Arabia - even for dashing Colonel Lawrence - had been a true love. Later, she knew, she would have to talk to Dr. Rosen about all of this. Dimly, she knew it was going to hurt to admit she still wanted Rashid even if he didn't want her. She was going to have to examine the painful ambiguities of all her feelings - the good and the bad, the sweet and the bitter, the sad and the angry. Somehow she was going to have to try to reconcile the romance and the realities not only of loving Rashid but of loving Arabia. Yet as she watched the Saudi she had loved so unfold again before her eyes, Sunny felt the healing begin.

After the final credit had rolled, after the music had stopped, after the lights had come back up, still some of the magic lingered in her heart and her soul. When Gran went back to Still River to fix supper for Gramps, Sunny and Sarah stayed in Cambridge to watch the second showing.

19

'When can we go home, Ummie?'

Sunny suppressed a shudder of fear, put down her Boston Sunday *Globe*, and smiled nervously at Sarah across the breakfast table. Always before, in their four years of exile, Sunny had shrugged off such painful questions. But Sarah was eleven years old and had to be told the truth someday. Sunny wished she could make the hard truth soft and tender. 'You mean, when can you and I go back to Saudi Arabia?'

'Home! I said home! You understood! I want to go home!'

When Sarah's black eyes flashed in anger like this, Sunny thought she looked just like her father. Sunny stared sadly out the window at the green forests and rolling pastures and neat white frame historic houses of Concord. More than fifteen years ago, when she and Rashid had fallen so impetuously in love, neither of them had considered the consequences a failure of that love could have on their children. Sunny knew now from reading learned articles on sociology and psychology that the odds had been stacked against a modern American woman and a traditional Saudi man's living happily ever after. Yet there was a fresh hot anguish in her when she looked back at Sarah. 'I'm sorry.'

'Is that all you can say - "I'm sorry"?' Always before Sarah had been her mother's fierce partisan, but this time she fought her own battle. 'I guess you'll start to cry now, and make me feel even worse, and so I'll shut up again, and you'll *never* tell me the truth.'

Sunny did not notice the two tears that slid down her cheeks as she shook her head at the daughter who knew too much for her age. 'Talk,' she said dully. 'You want to talk. All right, we'll talk.' But Sunny shut her trembling lips.

Sarah mercilessly continued. 'I want to know when we're going home to my father and brother and Grand-father Ibrahim and everyone else.'

Sunny steeled herself to say it. 'I don't think I'll ever be going back. You know your father divorced me. So I can't go back. But *you* can. You can go back anytime. If you want.' She tried to smile. 'As you like.'

'I can?' Sarah's face was radiant. 'I can see everybody! Khalid - I can see Khalid!' Sarah bounded over and threw herself into her mother's arms. 'Ummie, oh Ummie!' But then she looked up at her mother. 'You can't go home too? I'd have to go without *you*?' When Sunny nodded wordlessly, Sarah reached out and wiped away her mother's tears.

Sunny kissed Sarah on her right cheek, on her left cheek, on her right cheek again, as the Arabs do, and then she settled her daughter in her lap. 'Let me tell you something. I miss it too, Sarah.' Her voice caught. 'I miss him - your father - of course.' She loved Rashid still and she was furious at him still and despite everything she yearned for him still. Except for his very generous quarterly bank drafts, he had cut her cleanly from his life. Yet Sunny wished she didn't find every decent man she met here in America drab once she measured him next to the fireworks of Rashid. Her husband had spoken to her from his heart always. He had been so intensely careful with her hopes and her dreams and herself, at least until the end. She turned aside from the familiar dull ache of missing him. 'And Khalid - oh!' She had never ceased grieving at the separation from her son. 'And all the rest of them - Ibrahim, and Um Muhammad, and Nura, and Aisha, and Nura's girls. And I miss other things, too. The sound of the prayer calls. The hot dusty smell of the desert. The sun - I'm always looking for the sun here; the sun doesn't shine the same way in Massachusetts.' Sunny's voice was a whisper. 'I miss it, all of it, just like you do.'

'Then let's sneak back! We can buy you a forged passport and cross over the border from the mountains and pitch a tent in the desert and be happy again!'

'Where ever do you get such ideas?' Sunny laughed, and remembering her own romantic fantasies, she knew exactly where. She stroked her daughter's raven hair. 'What's really the trouble, Sarah?' Her sudden demand to return home had taken Sunny by surprise, for Sarah had seemed to embrace every facet of American life and reject everything that reminded her of Saudi. She had grumbled every time her mother insisted they speak Arabic together, and she performed the daily Muslim prayers only when her mother was watching. Once she had even poured a bottle of peroxide over her black Arabian hair to bleach it American blond. Sarah tried hard, perhaps too hard, to seem exactly like the other girls who attended day classes at Concord Academy. 'Aren't you even a little bit happy here?'

'I liked it a lot at first, even though I missed Khalid and everybody all the time. It was fun, everything being different, and everybody making a big fuss over me. But it's not so much fun anymore. Sometimes I just feel so confused, and tired of trying so hard, and never really fitting in. At school they say I'm a foreigner. The teachers make me stand up in class and talk about my country, and then the other girls look at me like I'm weird.' Sarah chewed her lip. 'I *am* weird, Ummie. I'm not like the other girls. And I'm tired of that. I want to be back where I'm just like everybody else.' Anxiously Sarah scanned her mother's face. 'You know?'

'I know exactly.' Sunny sighed. She too felt like a foreigner. She had been stunned to discover it was harder for her to adjust to life back in America than it had been to adapt to life in Saudi. Often she talked to Dr. Rosen about how bewildered, how rootless she felt, and it wasn't much comfort to be told that culture shock was often the most severe when an expatriate tried to come home and pick up the threads of a life come unraveled. Somehow, somewhere between Still River and Saudi Arabia, Sunny feared she had lost her soul. She had never suspected that staying in Saudi so long would put her certainty about life and values and herself in such jeopardy. In a way, now, she could understand Muhammad's terrible fall from grace. He too had been dazzled by a beguiling way of life that was enticingly different. He too had truly been unable to go home again. And he too had lost his soul. Yet Sunny hoped that, unlike Muhammad, even living in this limbo somewhere in the emotional middle between America and Arabia, she had succeeded in salvaging a sense of what was important in life.

She had tried not to complain out loud about how lonely she found contemporary America, about its emotional and spiritual sterility, about how cold and calculating and competitive and unloving men and women seemed with one another. She had not wanted to offend her new American friends by implying she had found her life in Saudi Arabia - a country everyone else seemed to think was primitive and uncivilized - to be rich and vivid and brimming with contentment. She had mostly broken herself of her bad habit of starting wistful sentences with, 'In Saudi, we used to . . .'

When the telephone rang, and Sarah leaped to answer it, Sunny poured herself another cup of coffee and wondered if it was ever going to be possible for her to feel at home here in America. She wished not only that she had not changed so much in Saudi but that America had not changed so much. The old values of family and religion and home didn't count for very much anymore, and in their place was a cynicism that made her heart ache for her country. Maybe she didn't want to feel at home in this brittle new America. Yet she had tried to make a life for herself here. At Boston University she had earned her bachelor's and master's degrees and was now working on her doctorate in psychology, so that someday she could be a therapist like Dr. Rosen. Sunny loved the justice of school, where she went to class and studied and earned the grades she deserved. School wasn't like life, where a woman could do everything right and still fail.

Sunny frowned and turned her head as she heard Sarah squeal. And then she was on her feet and running to the telephone in a panic, for Sarah was talking and then Sarah was shrieking not in English but in Arabic. 'Khalid! Sarah! Oh, my God, Sarah, something's wrong with Khalid, isn't it! Khalid!' Sunny snatched the receiver and screamed. 'My son?' She heard a buzz of static and a faint whisper of Arabic, and so hastily she shouted her question about Khalid again in that other language. Sunny shrieked, then, too when she finally understood that Ibrahim and Um Muhammad and Nura were on the line, that they were in Saudi, that Khalid was more than all right, that all of them except Ibrahim were coming to London this very week and that they wanted her to come there too. Ibrahim had taken the responsibility of calling her secretly and against Rashid's wishes because he said it was a crime that Sunny was never allowed to see her son. Rashid was thinking about letting Khalid go to an English boarding school next fall, and so he was taking him to London for interviews. Um Muhammad and Nura had been hounding him to take them and Nura's daughters along, and Rashid had finally given in and said they could come to shop and see the sights. They would be staying at the Dorchester, beginning the day after tomorrow, and just as soon as Rashid went off to some business meeting, they would smuggle

Sunny and Sarah in to see Khalid. Would Shamsa and Sarah come?

'Yes!' Sunny shouted down the telephone. 'Yes!' She and Sarah were jumping up and down for joy before Sunny even hung up the telephone.

Sunny and Sarah slipped down the corridor of the sixth floor of the Dorchester Hotel toward the Al-Murrah suite. Um Muhammad had telephoned them yesterday at the Park Lane before afternoon tea, while the rest of the family were all taking their siestas, to whisper that everything was in readiness. Sunny and Sarah should come to the Dorchester lobby just after eleven, when Rashid had gone off to meet the broker who watched over the family's European investments. Just to be on the safe side, Cousin Hussein would stand guard in the corridor all the time Sunny and Sarah were inside. Rashid was in such a terrible temper these days, Um Muhammad had confided, that Sunny would hardly recognize him. Since the royal family had nipped a military and civilian revolutionary conspiracy in the bud two years ago, the pitch of paranoia in the kingdom had been so sharply elevated that it was no longer safe even to whisper words of complaint against government graft and corruption. To make matters even worse, the kingdom had also been in the grip of an economic slowdown, for oil revenues had not kept pace with massive Saudi payments to prop up the Egyptian and Jordanian regimes after the disastrous 1967 war.

Nothing, Um Muhammad had fretted on the telphone, was the way it had been in the good old days. The old woman had complained to Sunny that London frightened her, that she was bewildered here, that she didn't understand a word anyone said, that she had been terrified on the airplane, that she trembled at the thought of defying her favorite son. Yet bravely Um Muhammad had committed herself. *Inshallah*, the family would be reunited.

Sunny heard a door open around the corner, and she and Sarah froze. But then they heard the birdlike twitter of an Englishwoman's voice, and they both laughed out loud at their fears. Rashid had left only a few moments ago, and Cousin Hussein had assured them on the house telephone that he would be gone all afternoon. Yet still Sunny and Sarah were as nervous as though they were about to steal furs or jewels instead of only an hour with their loved ones.

They tiptoed ahead on the costly blue swirls of the Aubusson rug. They were leery of any lurking shadows that might be Rashid. They had been waiting for six tense days at the Park Lane. Two days ago, when Rashid took Khalid off to Dorset for an interview at Brineston, they had tried to persuade Um Muhammad and Nura and Nura's daughters to meet them by the Serpentine. But Um Muhammad and Nura insisted on wearing their masks and cloaks out on the London streets, and Hussein had been afraid they would attract too much attention. The Arab community in London was small and gossipy. He hadn't wanted a passing Kuwaiti to witness Sunny and the Al-Murrahs and casually pass on that news a few days later to Rashid. And so until now the women had contented themselves with snatches of talk on the telephone. Sarah had whispered confidences to her half-sisters and been enthralled by every delectable detail of Wahda's betrothal to a second cousin.

Sunny and Sarah cringed as they crept around the final corner and saw a man in a ghostly white robe and head scarf staring back at them.

'*Ahlan wa sahlan!*' Cousin Hussein shouted a welcome and raced toward them. He embraced Sunny and hugged Sarah and grinned and winked and escorted them proudly toward the door of the suite. He would stand guard out here, he said, like a eunuch outside the sultan's harem.

The door flew open. 'Shamsa! Sarah! *Habibi!*'

Brown arms in black robes swept Sunny and her daughter into the sitting room of the suite on a tide of rapid happy Arabic. Um Muhammad was wailing and thanking God that they all were reunited, Nura was screaming and thanking God that they had lived to see this great day, Nura's girls were laughing and squealing and thanking God that they all at last were back with their long-lost sister. While the women noisily shrieked and laughed and wiped their eyes and thanked God again and again, Sunny and Khalid merely stood still and silently drank in the sight of each other.

He had grown up, she thought. He had been a little needy-eyed boy when they had pried his hands off her at the house in Khobar; now he was tall and manly in his austere white cotton Saudi robe. But it seemed he had regressed to being as shy as a toddler, for he blushed and his eyes at first would not meet hers. Her mother's heart ached as he finally looked at her. He was thirteen, but still he was needy-eyed. Still he was her boy, her son, her Khalid. The photographs Nura sent her every few months had mercifully not recorded how wounded and questioning his dark eyes had become. Was that how her banishment had affected him? Had he heard gossip about his mother's old disgrace? Was it that family scandal that had made her Khalid so timid and withdrawn? Oh Khalid, she thought in anguish, what has he done to you? What have *we* done to you, my beautiful sad wounded son?

Khalid took a first uncertain step toward this lovely vision of the lady who was his mother. She was even more beautiful than he remembered. Her hair was longer, straighter, more angelic. She was wearing an angel dress, a filmy long white lacy garment with a ruffle around her lovely ivory face. He tried to stop the insistent voice inside his head even as he looked at her. He had heard dirty rumours about his mother. Yet to him she was as beautiful and pure and perfect and unreal as an angel.

The angel swept him into her arms, no spirit but a woman of flesh, his mother come back to him. He brought his hand from behind his back, where he had been hiding the red roses he had bought for her this morning. 'For you,' he whispered in English. His voice cracked. 'For you, my mother.' They clung tightly to each other, they laughed, they kissed each other, they laughed some more. 'Khalid, Khalid, Khalid . . .' She sang with the full range and resonance of a symphony the name of her son. She kissed his hair, his cheeks, his lips, his eyes, she embraced him as though one perfect caress could make up for four years of mother love lost.

Then he turned his starry eyes to his sister, and it was Sarah's turn to kiss him and hug him and love him. He laughed again, this time with pure delight. 'You look very fantastic,' he said to her in English as he looked at her in wonder. As he stroked her long lustrous ebony hair, he told her in Arabic that they had to talk, they had so much to say, she wouldn't believe everything that had happened to them all at home since she'd left, they were even richer now, they were moving again into a new family compound right on the beach, maybe if he did get accepted into one of these fancy English schools she could come over and see him all the time, they could be together again, it would be so wonderful to be together again, he couldn't possibly write her everything in his letters, just as soon as he had talked more with Mother - Khalid's eyes glowed as he looked back at his mother - he would sit down and pour out all that was in his heart to his little sister.

Everyone was kissing and hugging and jabbering to everyone else, Nura's girls were wriggling and giggling, Um Muhammad was weeping, Nura was beaming. In the pandemonium Sunny and Sarah and Khalid sank down finally in an oasis of silent contentment on a green print sofa in the middle of the room. She put an arm around each of her children, and the three of them smiled radiantly as one of Nura's daughters snapped their photograph, with Khalid's roses on Sunny's lap. He was just feeling brave enough to reach out his hand and smooth back a tendril of his mother's silky yellow hair, they were just deciding which important confidences must be shared first, when suddenly there was the sound of running feet out in the corridor.

'Rashid!' Cousin Hussein burst in through the door. 'He comes!'

Khalid and all the women of the family froze.

None of them had moved a second later, when the door opened again.

'I forgot my . . .' Rashid stood transfixed in the doorway.

Sunny's eyes widened at the sight of him. Always she had loved him best in his exotic flowing white robes. But he was wearing a custom-tailored three-piece gray-flannel suit, and his hair and his mustache and his beard were all freshly barbered, and in his hands he carried a slim crocodile-skin briefcase. Looking at him turned out like a Western executive, she could not imagine him ever being handsomer even if he had been sheathed in a robe of solid gold. She had forgotten how even a glimpse of him used to affect her like a jolt of electricity. When she sat in Dr. Rosen's office, dissecting all the many moments of her long years with this man, the electricity of him had eluded her, and she had been at a loss to explain why she had adored him so.

But now it all came back to her in a flush of passion, how he had always moved her, how nothing on earth mattered to her like the love of this man. She had been chaste since he sent her away. She had turned down this man and that man, and as the years of banked desire had gone by she had wondered why everyone else except her seemed to think sex was worth the price of heaven or earth. But now, looking at Rashid, she felt again that old hot burning between her thighs. She cast down her eyes in confusion, and when she looked up, she had her libido more under control. He had lost weight, she noticed. He was all fierce sharp angles now, his cheeks were hollow, there were blue shadows under his burning eyes, his eyes were perhaps too dark now, she could understand why Um Muhammad had sounded not only concerned for Rashid but even a little afraid of him. Cares and troubles had etched new lines on his face. But Sunny fancied she could erase those unhappy lines if she but touched him softly enough with the tips of her fingers and with her lips and with butterfly flutters of her eyelashes. She sighed for their loss.

Rashid stared back at the wife he had divorced and banished, he thought forever, from his sight. He stared at Sunny sitting on the couch with one arm around Khalid and the other around the little girl he had seen for the past four years only in photographs. At night sometimes he had gone through his mother's and Nura's and Khalid's private papers until he found the latest batch of pictures of Sunny and Sarah. The child was even prettier than her photographs. The mother and the daughter, the one so fair, the other so dark, the two of them sitting with their heads so close together, were so very beautiful. For a long moment Rashid did not move as he let his eyes feast hungrily on Sunny and Sarah. A wild, he thought, irresistible impulse to sweep them both into his arms coursed through him. He wanted his daughter back, and he wanted the wife of his heart back. He took one involuntary step; but then he had second thoughts. He remembered she had deceived him. He reminded himself she had betrayed him. Rashid shut his eyes, and the spell was broken. He remembered Muhammad and shame. He told himself a strong man had to do difficult things. It was not necessary that a strong man enjoy doing these difficult things, or that he do them without doubts. It was necessary only that he continue to do them. It was important only that he be strong.

With a supreme effort of will, he stopped himself from taking even one step closer. His face worked for an instant, but then one by one he made its muscles go rigid. He looked at her again. Four years had passed, and yet she looked younger than when he had seen her last. America agreed with her. She had that soft, fresh, dewy, ageless American glow again. Always the Americans looked like that. Even the very old ones looked as untroubled and hopeful as children. Rashid suddenly hated Sunny and all Americans for their eternal, expectant, grasping youth. They all assumed the world, and everything in it, was theirs for the taking. His resolve not to give in to her and all she represented stiffened.

Bitterly his eyes swept the suite. Every person in this room was guilty. Each one of them had gone behind his back. His son, his mother, his wife, his daughters, even his faithful Cousin Hussein had defied him. They all knew he had forbidden any contact with this woman. Yet as soon as he had let them out of Saudi, they had sought her out. Rashid felt fury begin in his stomach and burn up his heart. They were all in league against him.

Rashid glowered at Khalid. He could especially not trust his son. He could not understand what was wrong with Khalid. He was such an unhappy boy, he kept to himself too much, he pined and brooded and persisted in making himself a misfit even in the family. Rashid had been so worried about Khalid that he had been ready even to send him to school in England, if that might make him happy. But if this was how Khalid acted behind his back, how could he trust his son among the infidels? He supposed Nura and Um Muhammad must be coddling him too much. He would have to take Khalid firmly in hand. He would not allow his son to come to school in England after all. Khalid could get a good Islamic education at home, within the boundaries of the kingdom. Grimly, without saying a word, Rashid stepped back out into the corridor and firmly closed the door behind him.

Sunny and the others cowered more closely together as they listened to his footsteps receding down the hallway. Then they heard another nearby door open. They could hear Rashid moving around in the adjoining bedroom.

Finally Rashid opened the door to the sitting room, but only a crack. 'Hussein! Come here, please, Hussein.'

The cousin hung his head and shuffled his feet as he went through the door to the bedroom.

Back in the sitting room the women listened in silence to the muffled sounds of angry Arabic, as Rashid questioned his cousin at length. Ibrahim's name was repeatedly mentioned, and for a while it seemed Rashid's anger at his women had softened. Sunny pulled her children closer to her. She stroked Khalid's hair, and Sarah put her head on her mother's shoulder.

'Mother! I would like to see you please, Mother!'

Um Muhammad gnawed her lip, she crossed the room and embraced Sunny, she kissed Sarah on her cheeks and her eyes and her forehead; she was weeping as she joined Rashid on the far side of the bedroom door.

Again Khalid and the remaining women listened as the old woman explained that all this was Ibrahim's idea. Then they overheard Rashid's deep-pitched murmur that this must never happen again, and finally Um Muhammad started to cry again.

'Nura! In here!'

Nura did not move. Her eyes met Sunny's, and Nura smiled defiantly. She sat back in her easy chair as if it were her throne.

'Nura? Did you hear me?'

Nura's daughters crept closer to her. One took her hand, two more perched on the arms of her chair, the youngest sat on the floor beside her and leaned her head on her mother's knee. The rest stood behind her.

A somber and morose Hussein opened the door, raised his right hand, and crooked his index finger at Nura.

'Shamsa. . . .' Nura held out her arms to Sunny in a kind of plea for understanding.

'Wife!'

Nura's eyes fell, she swallowed hard, she shrugged. She wiped the beads of perspiration off her forehead; then very reluctantly she stood. She smiled sheepishly at Sunny, then turned and went to answer her husband's command.

'Daughters of Nura!'

The seven girls grumbled, but they followed their

mother and their grandmother and their uncle to the far side of the bedroom door.

On the couch Sunny held her son and her daughter very tight. There was an inevitability to what must come next. Rashid was going to punish not only her but Khalid. Rashid was going to make his son walk away from her. Rashid was going to force Khalid to have to live with his own renunciation of his mother. She knew Rashid would call Khalid, and she knew Khalid would have to answer his father's call. She knew too that Rashid would probably not stop at that. Rashid was going to try to punish her even more terribly than he was going to punish Khalid. When Rashid called Sarah to him, would her daughter abandon her as well? When she herself finally had to get up and walk out of this cursed room, would she be alone?

'Khalid!'

Khalid held on to his mother all the more fiercely. His two arms were nearly in a stranglehold around her neck. He pressed his head into her shoulder.

'Son!'

Khalid groaned. Sunny could feel him turning his head from left to right, from right to left, shaking his head, saying no with his head.

'Khalid *ibn* Rashid *ibn* Abdullah *ibn* Ibrahim Al-Murrah!'

Finger by finger Khalid's grip on his mother's neck loosened, until one hand was on her shoulder and the other in her lap. Still Khalid shook his head; but then he sighed, and he pulled away, and he looked his mother full in the face. His eyes filled with tears, and silently he kissed her on her nose, on her lips, on her cheeks, on her eyelids.

'Son!'

He kissed the palms of his mother's hands; he stood up; he swept Sarah into his arms and hugged her; tenderly he tucked Sarah back into his mother's arms. He bent and kissed his mother on the eyelids again, and with his finger he wiped away the tears that were streaming down her cheeks. He smiled tremulously at her, he touched her yellow hair, he wished he were strong enough to defy his father and his tribe and his tradition and stay here forever on this couch with his mother. He hated himself as he turned his back on her. He walked with the stooped defeated shoulders of a very old man across the sitting room and into the bedroom where his father and the rest of the family waited.

For a long while the final summons did not come. For a long while, as Sunny sat on the couch holding her daughter tight in her embrace, it seemed there would *be* no final summons. But then, in the dead silence on the far side of the door, there was a collective family sigh, and the command.

'Daughter!'

Sarah went rigid in her mother's arms. Sarah hardly dared breathe at all as she listened to hear if her father truly wanted her.

'Sarah!'

The little girl listened hard, as though she were memorizing the rare secure beauty of that sound. She concentrated on the unfamiliar timbre and tone of that voice, on how her father seemed to caress her even with the sound of her name on his lips. She frowned. She did not altogether trust what she heard in her father's voice. Did her father really want her, or did he only want to use her to hurt her mother?

'Sarah!'

The little girl shook off her mother's clinging arms, and her own doubts. As though bewitched by a siren's call, she rose from the couch and turned away from her mother and toward where her father and her brother and her grandmother and her half-sisters all waited. She took the first step toward them and away from her mother. But then she looked back at her mother sitting utterly alone in this room that only a few moments ago had been crowded with all the loving, laughing members of her family. As she looked at her mother, the memories flashed by her: Mother laughing as they camped in the black tents when she was only a very little girl, Mother weeping as she packed their suitcases in Saudi, Mother crying in her great-grandmother's arms at the airport, Mother teaching her how to ride that Princess horse, Mother putting Father's photograph by her bedside in Concord, Mother showing her that old pearl-inlaid box with its faded photographs of her parents, Mother standing all alone on the top of that hill back on the farm in Still River. She remembered once watching her mother open an airmail envelope from Saudi and vainly running her finger inside the crinkly envelope for a personal message, and finally crying and kissing the paper of the birthday check Rashid had written Sarah with his own firm hand.

Sarah wished she could forget all those images of her mother crying. She wished she could believe that if she turned and ran from her mother and threw herself back into the soft happy bosom of her Arab family, her mother wouldn't miss her very much. Sarah shook her head, but the image of her mother standing all alone on the crest of that windswept Still River hill, with only that old faithful mare of hers for company, still haunted her.

'Sarah!'

The little girl stood irresolute. She loved her mother, but she had had her mother for all the years of her life. She missed her father. She hardly knew what her father was like. And Khalid - she wanted her brother back. And all her sisters, and her grandmother, and Nura. Sarah yearned for the domestic happiness that lay on the other side of that door. She longed to go home to Saudi, to go back to the desert, to be in a place where she didn't have to carry the constant burden of being alien from everyone else. For a second she considered the possibility of going over to the far side of the bedroom door only long enough to persuade her father to let her mother cross over as well. She knew her mother would run over that threshold if her father so much as whispered her name. Sarah looked back at her mother, all alone and so afraid. Sarah could not bear to see her look like that. A fierce, hot flood of loyalty surged through her. Let them all go away, but *she* would stay. Sarah threw herself back into her mother's arms, and they clung to each other, proudly.

'Daughter!'

Sunny and Sarah huddled on the sofa and listened as Rashid called in vain, and then finally they heard him firmly shut and lock the bedroom door. They sat waiting and listening and holding on to each other for dear life for a long while. It was as though everyone they loved had disappeared in a puff of smoke or in an evil spell cast by a *jinn*. When they could not bear the abandonment of this silence any longer, the mother and the daughter finally stood and collected their coats and their purses and carried Khalid's bouquet of red roses out of the suite.

Sunny telephoned the hotel repeatedly that night, but always a clerk told her very politely that the line was engaged.

When she called again the next morning, the concierge sang a different tune. He had no record of any guests of the name of Al-Murrah. No one by that name had been registered in this hotel. Except for the roses her son had given her, Khalid and all the others had vanished without trace back inside the boundaries of the kingdom.

20

Rashid stood at the bulletproof windows of the penthouse suite of Vienna's Intercontinental Hotel, waiting. He had waited, it seemed, almost all his life. But on this October night in 1973, with his waiting almost at an end, he could hardly bear the tension of these final seconds, minutes, hours.

Thoughtfully he stared at the dimming lights of the infidel city below him. It was late, later than Vienna or any of the West thought. While this sparkling infidel city of waltzes and chocolate and *Gemütlichkeit* slept blissfully below in featherbeds, here in the penthouse of the Intercontinental long-overdue decisions that might soon seem a nightmare to the Viennese burghers were about to be made. Rashid watched more lights wink out, and he imaged all Vienna going dark before his very eyes. He looked out beyond the city where it was already black, beyond the Ringstrasse where the medieval city walls had once stood. Twice in the past five centuries the Turks and their armies of Allah had swept all the way to the city's gates. Just out there, Islam had been turned back. Rashid did not think he and his would be turned back this time. God had put that oil in the ground under Saudi and Kuwait and Iraq and Iran. *Inshallah* - if God willed it - at last the Muslims would use their oil as a weapon for a good cause, for the best cause.

Rashid looked out at the dark Viennese sky, where an Islamic crescent moon lit the night. He studied the lie of the heavens and did not doubt that just as Allah had arranged the cycles of the moon and the constellations of the stars, He had predestined the precise timing of the chain of events that was approaching its inevitable cataclysmic climax. A week ago the armies of the Egyptians and the Syrians had surged across Suez and up the heights of the Golan in a crusade of honor to win back the lost soil of Palestine. It had been a surprise attack on the Jewish religious holiday of Yom Kippur, the Day of Atonement. Rashid and the other Arab oilmen had already been en route to Vienna for price negotiations on Saturday when the bulletins about the war had flashed around the world. Already, even without this new outbreak of hostilities, the stage had been set for a long-overdue confrontation between the oil-producing countries and the oil companies. International market conditions had been pointing not only to a massive increase in the price of oil but to a crucial shift in the structure and the power of the industry itself.

But the euphoria of the stunning early Arab supremacy

in the war had strengthened the resolve of the Arabs in Vienna. On Monday they had told the negotiators they wanted nearly to double the price of oil, from less than three to more than five dollars per barrel. But the oil companies had countered with an offer of a seventy-cent-per-barrel price increase. On Tuesday, when the Arabs had refused to budge, the negotiators had stalled and said they had to wait for instructions. On Wednesday the Arabs had warned the oil companies they had only until Friday midnight to accept their offer. Next week the Gulf oil-producing nations were meeting in Kuwait for a hastily called conference linking oil-production levels to the war. The OPEC negotiators said it was in the best interest of the oil companies to accept this reasonable final offer. *Inshallah*, after Kuwait, OPEC might have a far more radical agenda.

Rashid looked at his watch. The oilmen would be trooping up to the penthouse at any moment. Time was running out for all the West, for the era of cheap and abundant oil was at an end. During the worldwide glut of oil in the 1960s, the price had hovered at less than two dollars per barrel. But in the past few years demand had finally outpaced supply, and in 1971 in Teheran OPEC had succeeded in negotiating its first price increase with the majors. Yet inflation in the West and devaluations of the dollar had chipped away at the producer-country profits. Even before the October war, the stage had been set for an entirely new pricing accord.

Rashid took a deep breath and reassured himself that there was no reason to be nervous. Even if the West refused the price hike, OPEC would unilaterally impose it. Rashid's thoughts wandered from the price wars to the real war. He and the other Arabs here for the OPEC talks had thrilled so to the winning news from the front. After the shameful humiliations of '48 and '56 and '67, the early victories in Sinai and on the Golan had tasted all the sweeter. But Rashid was worried about possible American intervention. What would happen if push came to shove and the Americans had to choose between Israel and a cheap unlimited supply of Saudi oil? In the end would they choose love or money?

Rashid looked down at his watch. He himself knew more about money than he did about love these days. Since Sunny's departure, he had put his passion into his work. He had immersed himself in the restructuring of the Middle East petroleum industry. As he had worked obsessively long hours at the Ministry of Petroleum, Rashid had felt his own bitterness eat at him. On a day of shame long ago, he had vowed vengeance as he knelt in the dust of that Texas college town. He regretted that by marrying an American he had tried with all his heart to live with an incompatible other world. Rashid was not the only Arab to sour on the West, but he was considered a radical in ultraconservative Saudi. All he wanted was a constitution for his country, a curbing of the unlimited feudal power of the royal family, and a more equitable sharing of the oil wealth. Yet Rashid had been intimidated into mostly keeping even his cautious dreams of reform to himself. Abdullah Tariki, the fiery Saudi Arabian oil minister who had been most responsible for the formation of OPEC, had been fired by King Faisal when Tariki spoke up once too often. His replacement, Zaki Yamani, was as gradualist and pro-American as the king he served. Yet even the Saudi princes could work themselves up into righteous anger at the oil companies for their exploitation of Mideastern oil resources and at the Americans for their unyielding support of Israel. In addition, the most reactionary forces within the kingdom were still leery of all Western influences. The old religious leaders liked to say that the malignant infidel growths, from television and radio to airplanes and automobiles, should be cut out like a cancer.

Rashid and his colleagues in the Ministry of Petroleum did what they could to convert these Saudi angers and prejudices into what they considered rational and enlightened policies of economic self-interest. Rashid wanted Saudis to run Aramco, and he wanted Arabs to get a reasonable share of the astronomical profits. He wanted to slow down the rate of production and conserve Saudi's resources for future generations. Rashid's speciality had become Saudi relations with other Arab oil-producing states, and he had spent increasing blocks of time at OPEC meetings and visiting the Mideast oil fields. He was one of the first generation of Western-educated Arabs who were ready, willing, and able to run their own industry. Rashid had long ago understood that Aramco and the 'Seven Sisters' oil giants had never paid the Arab governments more than a slight fraction of the profits from the petroleum industry. But what was different now in 1973 was that finally Rashid and his colleagues had the means to force a change. It had taken decades for the Mideast oil industry to learn the value of joint economic action, but finally OPEC spoke powerfully and persuasively for the oil-producing nations.

Rashid reached into the vest pocket of his dark herringbone jacket and pulled out a packet of cigarettes. His hand was trembling as he lit a Kent filter with his gold Dunhill lighter. He had accepted his first cigarette two years ago in a tense smoke-filled room when he joined the OPEC negotiating team. At first he had felt so sinful he had not inhaled, for at home smoking was still officially frowned upon. But in time his yearning to be in the Arab fraternity had overcome his fundamentalist guilt. The other Arabs chain-smoked as if the slim cylinders of Players and Craven and Marlboro were written in the genetic code of their race. And so Rashid had smoked and watched and waited at conference tables and in luxury hotel suites with his brothers from Kuwait and Iraq and Libya. They had waited for the world's demand for oil to exceed its supply, for the Arab states to be ready to act in concert, for the season to play the bittersweet trump card of Arab vengeance.

Rashid stood on the top floor of the Vienna Intercontinental looking down at the once proud imperial city sleeping below him. His time of waiting was at an end. Finally even cautious Saudi Arabia was about to unsheath the oil weapon and use its economic power to force the West to redress thirty years of wrongs against the Palestinian people.

Rashid and all the other Saudis lounging in this suite eavesdropped as Zaki Yamani bargained on the phone with one of the princes in Riyadh about whether Saudi would cut its production five percent or ten percent or twenty percent per month. To Rashid there was a melodious music to any of these numbers, just so long as Saudi linked the delivery of oil to the West with international politics. For years Rashid had despaired that King Faisal would ever dare to take this step. The king had been specifically threatening for some time that America must moderate its support of Israel if it wanted a continuing supply of oil. Yet the Americans had persisted in believing Faisal was bluffing.

Rashid listened intently to Zaki Yamani. That familiar throb and thrill to the oil minister's voice meant he must be closing a deal. This time Arab unity was going to be more than coffeehouse talk. Next week in Kuwait, Saudi Arabia would vote to cut production back five percent a month until America and the West pressured Israel to withdraw from the Arab territories it had occupied in 1967. Finally Rashid would not be ashamed to call himself a Saudi Arab.

On the telephone Yamani was reassuring a prince that the oil companies had no choice but to accede to the price increase. Yesterday over coffee, Yamani said, one of the negotiators had winked and said they would simply pass on the increase to the consumers. More money for OPEC would also mean more money for the oil companies, which had never once turned down the possibility of an extra penny of profit.

Rashid heard Yamani's voice suddenly change and become velvety and deferential. The king must be on the line. Yamani said he understood that the king did not want to leave Vienna without a pricing accord, that he did not want to throw the loaded issue of oil prices onto the floor of the Kuwait conference, that he wanted not to break but only curb the West.

Yamani bid a hasty farewell to the king as a knock finally sounded on the door. Rashid lit another cigarette, sat beside Yamani, and studied the bland closed faces of the man from Exxon and the man from Shell. For five minutes everyone exchanged the requisite pleasantries. But even before the barman had taken the orders for orange juice or Cokes or coffee, the Exxon representative talked turkey. 'More time,' he said bluntly. 'We're going to have to ask you fellas for two more weeks.'

Rashid blew a smoke ring, and as he watched the blue haze hover between the Arabs and the Westerners, he wondered how these men could be so dense. He studied the confident faces of the oilmen. Could it be that they did not understand that the oil companies were no longer calling the shots?

Zaki Yamani shook his head as the man from Exxon earnestly explained that OPEC's demand to double petroleum prices had caught them unaware. A price increase of that magnitude would have an impact on every fiber of the Western economy, and so the companies must take the time to go to their own governments first for approval.

Yamani was still shaking his head as he politely fulfilled his responsibilities as host. He handed one of the executives a glass of fresh-squeezed orange juice; then he prepared a Coke the way he knew the other one liked it, with ice and a slice of lime. Solicitously, symbolically, mischievously, he squeezed the lime dry. 'Two weeks?' Yamani shrugged. 'I can tell you, OPEC is not going to like this.'

The oil executives continued to try to justify the two-week adjournment. They talked about national pricing boards and the mechanisms of democracy and the past thirty years of mostly smooth company relations with the governments of the Middle East. But the oilmen were talking to themselves. Yamani began consulting the airline timetables to see how quickly he could whisk his delegation home.

The oilmen were not accustomed to being dismissed by Arabs, and so they sat for a very long while waiting for Yamani to haggle back at them. By the time it dawned on them that tonight's negotiations were at an end, the Saudis were already packing. Finally the two bewildered executives got to their feet and walked to the door. But at the threshold the man from Exxon paused until he finally caught Yamani's eyes. 'Zaki, what happens now?' For the very first time, the anxious West was waiting for a cue from the Arabs.

For one long exquisite moment, no one in the penthouse moved, as the Arabs savored the first luscious taste of victory. For one long arrogant moment, Rashid fancied that here on the top floor of Vienna's Intercontinental he was watching power and ascendancy and world domination pass from West to East.

Yamani smiled a very slight dismissive smile and waved his hand airily at the oil executives. 'You'll be hearing it on the radio.'

The oilmen shut the penthouse door softly, even respectfully, behind them.

Rashid was calm and silent and watchful as all around him in the Kuwait Sheraton, Arabs from Iraq and Libya and Egypt and Bahrain and Abu Dhabi and Qatar vowed eternal brotherhood and solidarity with those dying for the cause. In this second week of the October War, the tide had turned against the Arabs. The Israelis had launched a successful counteroffensive across Suez and had rewon the Golan from the Syrians. But here in this air-conditioned hotel auditorium the OPEC delegates still talked like winners. Some wanted dollars; some wanted blood; others wanted power, vengeance, and every last inch of occupied Palestine.

Even before this conference began, Iran and the Arabian Gulf members of OPEC had announced that the posted price of crude oil would be five dollars and twelve cents per barrel.

But then at this meeting, matters had taken murkier political and economic turns. As soon as the radical Arabs insisted oil must be used as a political weapon against Israel and its friends, the Iranian delegation had hurriedly exited for Teheran. Iran would vote to raise oil prices but wanted no part in any economic campaign against Israel. The Shah had been selling oil to Israeli customers for many years.

The Arabs then launched into a daylong debate on how to calibrate their use of the oil weapon. Ever since the founding of Israel, Arabs had dreamed of using the economic clout of Mideastern oil against the Zionist state. In 1948 the world hardly noticed when Iraq stopped its pipeline shipments to Haifa. In 1956 Iraq and other anti-Western states imposed a limited embargo on Britain and France, but the United States filled the gap by sending its own domestic oil to Western Europe. Again in 1967 Arabs tried a short-lived oil boycott of the West, yet they had to abandon it when the oil companies again shipped surplus oil wherever the Arabs were withholding it. Until the October War their strategies had failed both because international market conditions were against them and because the powerful Gulf oil-producing nations were not united. But the Arabs vowed in the Kuwait Sheraton that 1973 was to be the year of the oil weapon.

An Iraqi was maintaining that they could not put a price tag on honor, on blood, on glory. He pleaded for the total nationalization of all American oil interests, the withdrawal of all Arab funds invested in the United States, the sundering of diplomatic relations between the Arabs and the Americans.

The delegates lit cigarettes, motioned to the coffee boys to bring them fresh brew, and looked uneasily down at the figures they had been scrawling on the notepads before them. If they decreased production, would they be cutting oil production or their own throats?

A Libyan was standing on his chair as he shouted for the Arab expropriation of all foreign oil companies. For a moment the delegates were so caught up with his exciting rhetoric that they surged to their feet and cheered.

All the while Rashid and the other Saudis sat in a quiet huddle. King Faisal had made it infinitely clear that today they were to keep a steadfast vigil with the radical Arab states who were fighting the good fight against Israel. But they were not to get carried away and promise the Palestinians the moon and the stars and their homeland. Even before Rashid and the others had met in Vienna, Saudi Arabia had agreed to a joint economic and political strategy with the Egyptians. Cairo wanted to regain its Sinai territory, and Riyadh wanted more money for its oil and more recognition of its role as a world power. If in the course of this struggle Israel were humbled and Jerusalem regained, all Arabs would offer prayers of heartfelt thanksgiving. But here in Kuwait, Saudi would vote cautiously for *modest* monthly cutbacks in oil production and *selected* embargoes against Israel's staunchest supporters. King Faisal still hoped his moderation would keep America from launching a massive arms airlift to Israel.

With hooded eyes and a sense of futility Rashid watched the others parlay the oil weapon. In the end all that would matter was whatever black words were said in the White House in Washington. Even as the Arab oil ministers were meeting in Kuwait, a delegation of Arab foreign ministers were cooling their heels in Washington as they sought a personal meeting with President Nixon.

Rashid hunched miserably inside his ceremonial white silk robes as the whirlpools of Arab rhetoric swirled around him. He hated sitting mute as the chance for his country's greatness slipped away. He wished with all his heart that the Saudi nation dared stand up and be counted among its brothers. He longed to shout that Saudi Arabia would not sell America one drop of oil until Israel was brought to heel. He did not care what President Nixon might say to the Saudi foreign minister. By now, he thought, even King Faisal should have had enough of this gossamer web of American lies.

Yet Rashid kept his thoughts and his fury to himself. He had been sent here by his king to help hold the line against the wild men of the Arab world, and hold the line he would. After the Iraqis and the Libyans were utterly exhausted from pleading their militant message all day long, Rashid and the other Saudis smoothly stepped in and imposed moderation. Oil production was to be cut back ten percent now, and five percent more every month until there was a Middle East settlement agreeable to the Arabs. In the meantime, each Arab oil-producing nation was to be free to stop any and all oil shipments to any countries supporting Israel.

Rashid looked up at the night sky as he stood outside the Kuwait Sheraton waiting for the limousines to take the Saudi delegation to the airport. The bright stars that had seemed to light the Viennese night with the promise of so great a destiny seemed dimmer now. The great adventure begun so auspiciously last week seemed to have ended in anticlimax in Kuwait. Back in the desert the Bedouin said the heavens were dark like this when a storm was brewing. As the limousines pulled up to the curb, Rashid murmured an automatic prayer under his breath for rain. It was October, beginning the season of the life-giving winter thunderstorms.

He could not know that just three nights from now, the biggest storm since the triumph of Muhammad the Prophet was about to break over all Arabia.

Tensely Rashid lit another cigarette; he inhaled three times in quick succession, then stubbed out the tasteless cigarette in an ashtray and lit another. He raised his hand to signal for coffee, and when the boy bustled over with a full brass beaker, he drank two thimble-size cups. He pulled back the long sleeve of his white robe and saw that it was eight minutes to the nine-o'clock television news.

Rashid looked around the Ministry of Petroleum's *majlis* conference room in Dhahran, at the pearly muted tones of the Persian carpet on the floor, at the massive mahogany desk Zaki Yamani used when he was in the Eastern Province, at the ornately framed portraits of King Faisal and his father, King Abdul Aziz, and his brother, Crown Prince Khalid. Perched on each of the spindle-legged gilt French Provincial chairs ranged all around the perimeter of this vast room was a white-robed Saudi bureaucrat. Each of them had rushed here after frantic calls from Riyadh summoned them to stand by for an emergency. The king had been meeting with Yamani and the royal Cabinet all evening at Riyassa Palace. In a few minutes their decision on how Saudi Arabia would respond to the thunderbolt of America's financial intervention in the war in Israel's behalf would be announced to the world.

Two dark dwarflike Yemeni servants carried in a twenty-five-inch Sony color television set and placed it in the empty center of the *majlis* floor. But the cord wouldn't reach to an outlet, and the servants had to scurry off to find an extension in time for the broadcast.

Rashid tried to temper his rising excitement. There probably wasn't going to be any earth-shaking news, just another mildly worded rebuke cautioning the Americans that Saudi might be forced to take drastic measures someday if the United States persisted in its support of Israel. Rashid doubted that even President Nixon's shocking duplicity this week had shaken King Faisal's confidence. Two days ago in a meeting with the foreign ministers of Saudi Arabia and the other Arab states, Nixon had promised a 'peaceful, just, and honorable settlement' in the Middle East. What Nixon had not told the Arab dignitaries was that a massive American airlift of military armaments was already under way to Israel. Nor did he warn the Arabs that the very next day he would ask

Congress for more than two billion dollars in emergency military aid for Israel. King Faisal had taken Nixon's actions as a deep personal insult, and so he had gathered the royal family together to plot revenge.

The servants finally found an extension cord, they switched on the television set, and Rashid and the other Saudi oil officials sat on the edge of their chairs. Rashid cautioned himself that what he was about to hear would be just another serving up of lukewarm threats and ancient resentments.

On the screen the announcer cleared his throat and grimly began to read from a brief prepared statement. The Kingdom of Saudi Arabia was immediately suspending all oil exports to the United States.

Rashid was so stunned he hardly heard the announcer repeating his bulletin. Until now more than six hundred thousand barrels of Saudi oil had been shipped every day to the United States, but now all shipments were to be stopped. The announcer issued a dramatic call to economic war. 'At the instruction of King Faisal,' the announcer read, 'a *jihad*, a holy war, is being called. In this *jihad* it is the duty of all Muslims to back the freedom fight.'

Rashid and hundreds of thousands of Saudis listening to this electrifying news on radio and television were on their feet and cheering in the kingdom's offices and coffeehouses and black tents deep in the desert. '*El-jihad!*' Rashid shouted along with his brothers. '*El-jihad!*'

The Al-Murrah rode slowly in a line, out into the desert.

They rode out into the wilderness not as in the old days, in a caravan of dancing black Arabian stallions and atop fleet white racing camels. This time, in the dawning of this new Islamic era, four generations of Al-Murrah rode out to their ancestral tribal hunting grounds in a cavalcade of cars and trucks powered by the Arab oil that had made them the new righteous kings of Allah's earth.

Rashid rode in solitary splendor in the lead car. He was a *shaykh* now, one of the leaders not only of his tribe but of all the tribes of the Arabs. His white robe was silken, his black cloak was edged with gold, and his face was regal and imperious. He turned and waved like a prince to old Ibrahim, who rode standing in the back of the pickup truck just behind him with his arm around young Khalid. He looked back over his shoulder at the cousins and the uncles and the nephews fanning out like an army on the march. All but one of the men of the family had come together to return to the desert and celebrate the change in their people's fortune. Ibrahim had pleaded with Rashid to let Muhammad join the victory procession, but the one brother had refused to forgive the other even on this day of fraternal Arab triumph.

Yet as he rode into the desert Rashid had a sudden impulse to send for his disgraced brother. Perhaps now, he thought, even that fallen star of all the Al-Murrah could have rightfully held his head high. Rashid was just about to send someone back to Khobar for Muhammad when he remembered what his brother had done to him and his. Rashid decided there were some things a man cannot forgive. Perhaps there were too many things that he himself could not forgive. But he let his hand drop, and he hardened his heart once again against his brother.

Rashid rode standing erect, holding on to the handrails he had had installed in the back seat of his custom-made Mercedes convertible. A cartridge belt crossed his chest, a hawk was on one wrist, a carbine was in his other hand. He rode in valor as his ancestors had long ago coursed over the desert celebrating their victorious battles. Three months ago, when he had felt that first wonderful euphoria as King Faisal proclaimed holy war against the infidels, he had longed to sweep out to the desert. He had yearned to ride fast and high and far atop a camel up and down the dunes, with God's wind and sun and sand on his skin and his hair and his soul. He had wanted to ride out into the desert at the head of his family, just as he was riding now on this dawn of triumph. But in those first wild dizzy weeks of the oil embargo, there had been no time for hawking and hunting and a manly gathering of the tribe. Since October it had been one conference and negotiation and oil auction after another, as Rashid had plied back and forth across the Middle East meeting with the other OPEC oilmen. King Faisal's call to *jihad* had been fervently embraced by the Arab world, so that one month after the embargo was imposed Middle Eastern oil imports were down to two-thirds their normal levels. Western Europe and Japan had been heavily dependent on Arab oil, and so as winter approached brokers had bid in panic for the little petroleum available. An auction of oil in Iran in December had brought offers of twelve to seventeen dollars per barrel, and when OPEC met in Teheran just before the end of the year the oil ministers had boosted the posted price to nearly twelve dollars per barrel. In the ten weeks since OPEC had met with the oil companies in Vienna, petroleum prices had quadrupled.

Rashid savored the sweetness of Saudi's international triumph. He was forty-two years old, and already he had achieved every glorious goal he had ever set for his entire life. The West had most definitely been humbled. At the height of the October War, President Nixon had made a Saudi diplomat wait for days before he deigned to meet with him at the White House. Yet just three weeks after the oil embargo, Secretary of State Henry Kissinger had flown to Riyadh to beg for oil. Two weeks after the embargo was imposed, the European Community had passed a resolution calling on Israel to withdraw to its pre-1967 borders. The Japanese had sent their foreign minister to Riyadh for emergency talks, and the sly French had signed a separate pact with the Arabs. Most of the needy nations of Europe had come crawling to meet King Faisal's terms. With an awesome speed, the West had begun at least to pay lip service to 'the violated human rights' and 'the legitimate territorial claims' of the Palestinian people.

But for Rashid more had been won than money and the promise of belated justice for the Palestinians. For him, the victory in the blood feud with the West was fiercer and more primal. He believed the West deserved every bit of misery the Arabs were meting out to them. He believed that for too many vicious generations the West had humiliated and exploited the Arabs and every other culture in the world that wasn't white or European or American. He remembered that Ramadan fast when the cowboys had made him drink forbidden beer until he vomited. For that act, and for the perpetration of thousands of stupid imperialist acts exactly like it, Rashid savored the retribution of the oil embargo.

He looked out over the harsh, parched desert where his ancestors had lived in poverty and privation since the beginning of time. Let the West suffer.

Rashid felt the hot sun soak into his skin and the hot wind beat against his robes. Let the West shiver.

Rashid felt the powerful throb of the Mercedes engine under his feet. Let the West pay.

Rashid felt the lord not only of all he could see before him in the undulating folds of the desert but of all the world. Finally, he thought, it's *our* turn. After centuries as a stagnant backwater of the world, Arabia had become the center of the earth. Finally, after centuries of ignorance and squalor and humiliation, Arabs were taking their rightful place as *shaykhs* among the nations of the world. Finally Arabs and Arabia had gloriously come of age. Finally they had cast off the role of passive victims to become powerful predators.

Rashid squinted at the sky. He thought he could see something moving up there. He knitted his brows together, he crouched as though he had just spotted his prey from atop a camel, he called out to Ibrahim and Khalid and pointed to the black speck flying almost to the clouds. He shouted to his chauffeur to go faster, onward, out to the desert. As the car lurched ahead, Rashid untied the lashings on his wrist. He plucked the hood off the falcon and raised his hand and let the bird fly. Up it soared, as fast and true as Sufis say their prayers ascend to Allah. Then the falcon veered in pursuit of the black eagle that had flown too near the waiting hunters.

The army of Arabs waved their guns in the air and cried out in delight as the chauffeurs stepped on the gas and raced behind Rashid. The eyes of the Al-Murrah were fixed to the sky where the coming battle would be fought. The fleet falcon was small but fierce and out for blood. Yet the proud eagle wheeled and banked and fluttered its wings under the sun, as though a mere falcon were not worth fight or flight. The falcon came at the eagle like a surface-to-air missile. The eagle turned and screeched and faltered as it tried to make its escape, but it was too late. The smaller bird hit the larger one, bird-screams filled the air, the Arabs fired encouraging rounds of automatic gunfire at the clouds. Finally the mortally wounded eagle lost altitude, screamed one last time, and plummeted to earth.

Rashid's car sped to where the eagle had fallen. He called the hawk back to his wrist, hooded it, tied it down, and stared down at the bloody gore of feathers and skin and muscle that only a moment ago had been a mighty eagle. He remembered then how he had always hated the blood and death and waste of a kill. He looked down at the fallen eagle and tried to rejoice that he had triumphed. The eagle was dead. He had achieved exactly what he had set out to achieve.

'*Bismallah al-rahman al-rahim*,' he prayed, consecrating this sacrifice to Allah 'in the name of God the merciful and the compassionate.'

Yet as Rashid stood over the fallen eagle, it seemed to him that the bitter flavor of revenge was not exactly to his taste today. He had imagined revenge would taste sweeter three months ago, too, when the king had declared *jihad* against the West.

He felt his gorge rise at the sight of the dead eagle. A vague contrite sorrow settled over his spirit. Only a moment ago he had been so certain this just retribution was the will of God. He wondered why, then, he felt so sad. He remembered Ibrahim's saying once when he was a boy that he should be altogether certain what he was asking for when he prayed, or he might end up getting something for which he had not bargained. Was that, Rashid wondered, what had happened not only to him but to all his people? His thoughts narrowed from the world's woes to his own. He had sent his own happiness away when he had sent Sunny packing. Still he missed her. Still sometimes he lay sleepless with the missing of the wife of his heart. But swiftly Rashid banished his doubts and his sorrow. 'Allah's will be done,' he whispered as he looked down at the arrogant imperial eagle dead on the sand.

But then Rashid was engulfed in the triumphant throng of Al-Murrah who had left their cars to gloat over the fallen eagle. Grandfather Ibrahim was all but dancing on the sand. The other men were gathering around to congratulate him on his kill. Then Khalid motioned everyone away, and he cocked his shotgun and released a full magazine on the carcass of the eagle. Rashid was startled as he watched his son's eyes glitter as he blew the remains to kingdom come. His son had always been such a gentle, quiet boy. Rashid wondered exactly when, while he was away on his important business, his son had learned this bloodlust. But Rashid decided this was neither the time nor place to indulge his own growing doubts about the possible price his son and all his people might have to pay for so much heady victory. Here and now he would celebrate this new order in Allah's world. Rashid threw back his head and let out the ancient war cry uttered by his ancestors centuries ago when they stormed out of Arabia to conquer most of the world for Islam. '*Allahu akbar!* God is most great!' He waved his carbine in the air in triumph.

'*Allahu akbar!*' From the throats of the Al-Murrah came a mighty cry, so that it seemed every grain of the desert sands rang with an epiphany that reached all the way to the heavens. '*Allahu akbar!*'

21

A wet, sleety midwinter snow had transformed wedding-cake Vienna into a gray world of arctic slush, and the American and the Arab who was young enough to be her son stood shivering in the cold. Sunny had just let go of Musa Elemy's arm to hail a cab when an arrogant black limousine pulled up with a screech of brakes and sprayed soot-encrusted ice over her legs and coat. She was still glaring when the doors opened and a cluster of haughty Arabs stepped out on the curb.

Sunny caught her breath. She had eyes only for the slender man in the black cashmere overcoat who was already striding up the front steps of the Intercontinental Hotel. 'Musa,' she whispered. 'Oh, my God, that's *him*!'

But the young Egyptian had not understood that she had just seen a ghost. 'Come, Um Khalid, we will walk, it is cold, and that terrible car made you very wet.' Musa was solicitous of the kind lady who had been his mentor, friend, and surrogate mother since they both had arrived in Vienna on very separate missions four months ago. 'You will be more happy after we drink coffee and eat cakes. Come!'

Sunny was about to call out to Rashid when she remembered that he probably would not answer. As he walked away from her into the hotel, she remembered him turning his back and leaving her in Saudi seven years ago and again in London four years later. He had made it painfully plain, in the long years of their separation, that he was finished with her. He was prompt and methodical about sending her the very generous allowance that had enabled her to stay in graduate school for five years and to enroll Sarah in a Swiss boarding school. But he had never acknowledged Sunny's impassioned letters. She still did receive communications of a sort at regular intervals from Ibrahim and Um Muhammad and Nura and Aisha. But since none of them could read or write, their replies were all written in the careful hand of a local *shaykh* who listened to their messages and then composed formal, flowery sentiments in stilted English.

Reading between those enigmatic lines, Sunny had tried to follow the course of her son's life back in Saudi. Khalid himself had abruptly stopped writing to her a year or so after their abortive reunion in London. But still he wrote long anguished letters to his sister, and Sarah had confided that she thought Khalid was becoming, as she put it, a 'religious freak.' He was studying the Koran at the Islamic university in the Prophet's birthplace of Medina, and the letters Sarah shared with Sunny were rife with religious ranting and studded with odd juxtapositions of quotations from the Koran. Yet when Sunny asked in her letters what was wrong with Khalid, all she got was polite evasions in the cursive script of the *shaykh*. As Sunny stood in the snow, she almost threw caution to the winds and raced after Rashid. Surely he would not turn her away without putting her mind at ease about her son.

'Um Khalid!' Musa plucked at her arm. '*Yalla!*'

Even as she watched, another limousine pulled up, and the doorman ushered the last of the Saudi delegation inside the Intercontinental. She had missed her first opportunity to confront him as if by accident on the street. She had telephoned all the luxury hotels after she read in yesterday's newspapers that the OPEC ministers were due to arrive for another round of talks. Most of the other Arabs had reservations at the Intercontinental, but she could discover no trace of Rashid anywhere. Yet she had been haunting the sidewalk of this hotel all afternoon in the hope of catching a glimpse of him, until finally she had given up and called Musa to invite him to tea. She craned her neck, but when it seemed Rashid had disappeared from the lobby she consoled herself that she could come back to stalk him tomorrow. She had been shocked at how thin and gaunt and drained he looked. She had not imagined her Rashid would look so sad.

As Sunny and Musa set off across the cupid's heart of Old Vienna for Demel's pastry shop, she wondered if it would soon be transparent to Rashid and Musa and everyone else in her narrow arabesque world just why she had chosen to come here to Freud's Vienna for the last stage of her doctorate in clinical psychology. She was writing her dissertation on the culture shock of Arab women who had recently moved from a traditional Eastern culture to a modern Western one. But instead of setting her research in the sizable Arab communities of New York or London or Paris, she had constructed an elaborate but flimsy constellation of reasons why the small, clustered, and transient Arab community of Vienna was ideal for her research. Yet she knew very well that she was here because this was the permanent European headquarters of OPEC. Back in Boston she had seen Rashid's grave, harried face on television as he ducked into OPEC meetings in Vienna.

For once, as she paced the narrow curving streets with Musa, she was too preoccupied to notice the stone angels and gold imperial eagles atop the graceful yellowing palaces, the apothecary shops decorated with hundred-year-old mosaic frescoes, the filigree and flowers and priceless antiques lovingly displayed in shop windows. Firmly she told herself it was none of her business how miserable Rashid had looked. It was all over between them. She had to accept that she could not have him and that he did not want her. She had worked so very hard in her psychotherapy three times a week, for seven long years, to get to the point where she could accept the ending of their love.

In a window Sunny caught a glimpse of herself arm in arm with Musa. She was glad to have this young man who reminded her so of her son beside her today, and every day. It had been such a lucky chance that she had met Musa during her first bewildering week in Vienna. She had been wandering through the fruit and vegetable stalls at the open-air Saturday morning *Naschmarkt* when she spotted a crowd of Arabs congregating before bins of spices and Middle Eastern food. When her gaze fell on Musa, his resemblance to Khalid had made her stop and stare at his thick curly hair and limpid brown eyes and wiry compact body. Impulsively she had tapped him on the shoulder and asked him in Arabic if he was from Saudi. His face had lit up so, to hear this pretty foreign lady speak his native language, even though he had to disappoint her with the news he was Egyptian. But they had struck up an animated conversation and strolled the adjoining carnival of the flea market, and arranged to meet the next day for coffee. They had commiserated over the trouble they were both having in their intensive German classes, and they had talked at loving length about those they had left behind in Khobar and Cairo. Before long he knew all about Khalid and Sarah and Rashid, and he was addressing her with respect as Um Khalid, 'the mother of Khalid.' He showed her his treasured photographs of his parents and brothers and sisters back in Egypt and confided how he had come to be in Vienna.

After he graduated from Cairo University with a degree in archeology, Musa had found himself in a dead-end job in a musty back room of the Cairo Museum. Yet he had turned down a dazzlingly high-paid offer to teach in a secondary school in a Gulf emirate, for he told Sunny earnestly that he had not wanted to be a slave in bondage to the petrodollars. He wanted to use all his heart and mind and soul to build up his own country. She had thought Musa meant only Egypt, but instead he instructed her with his eyes aglow that his 'country' was all the Arab world. As an archeologist, he wanted to probe the cultures of his people's past so he could help to make them proud not only of what they once were but what they still were and what they could be if only they stood together as true brothers. He was on a partial scholarship from the

Egyptian government to study for his doctorate at the University of Vienna. Many Third World students flocked to this Austrian capital where visas were easy to come by and they didn't have to pay university tuition. Still, Musa said with a sigh, he didn't like being exiled from his family and the world he loved. His academic courses would all be taught in German, and he had to pass examinations in Latin, Greek, history, and philosophy before he would be allowed to study his beloved archeology. It would be five to ten years before he could go home again.

Sunny and Musa swept into Demel's as though she were the countess of chocolate and he the marquis of all tortes. They sighed rapturous sighs at the sumptuous spread of cakes and strudels and cookies and candies, he settled on Sacher torte and she on *Apfelstrudel*, and then they laughed and greedily decided to split a wedge of that heavenly pastry filled with vanilla and whipped cream and bliss. In the golden smoky haven of the *Rauchsalon*, they were lucky enough to win one of the two choice chintz sofas. Musa ordered coffee and whipped cream for two, and Sunny leaned back and let the coffeehouse's comforting essence of snug caloric conviviality calm her. When she had decided to leave America, she had chosen Vienna because Rashid was here, because Sarah's Swiss school was not far away, and because its Arab community suited her research. But now one of the reasons she rejoiced to be in Vienna was the jolly sugary confection of its coffeehouses. Demel's, with its gilded mirrors and its nostalgic Old World ambience and its elegant icing everywhere but on the tabletops, was her favorite place to snuggle down on cold afternoons for long cozy chats over coffee and cakes.

As the waitress brought them their sweets and coffee, Sunny savored the even sweeter knowledge that Rashid was a ten-minute walk away at the Intercontinental. If she put a few schillings in a public telephone, there would be one of those quaint Viennese buzzings in the circuits, the desk clerk would answer, and one of the Saudi suites would be rung. Her heart leaped at the thought of hearing his voice.

She picked at her strudel and considered not the mechanics of reaching him but the dicier question of whether she should even try. Seven years was a long time to be apart. Rationally she could mostly accept that what they had once had was dead. Yet she had learned in therapy to listen not only to her mind but to her heart. It wasn't over – at least, not for her. Seeing him for that instant on that snowy street had moved her. Even after everything that had happened, still she wanted him. Sunny believed that the woman she had become was of sterner stuff than the wide-eyed girl who had thrown herself at Rashid. Yet still she had the same old passionate impulse to go and get the man she wanted. But time and pain had taught her she should be more cautious in her loving. Rashid had wounded her to the core. It would be wiser to let things be.

Moodily Sunny watched the plump, ruddy, sad-eyed Viennese gossiping away the cold gray afternoon. Vienna, to her, was the world capital of faded romance. More than a hundred years ago this had been the Imperial City of Europe, the glittering center of the Habsburgs, the most splendid and gilded and pampered metropolis west of Constantinople. But now all that remained was hints and whiffs and husks, the echoes of lovely gliding waltzes, the aroma of extravagant tortes, the beautiful baroque buildings that stood like white marble mausoleums along the wide sweeping boulevards. Sunny remembered how happy she and Rashid had once been here in Vienna on their honeymoon. When they and their love had been fresh and blooming, he had bought her nosegays of violets and they had sighed to the strains of Gypsy violins. But it could be that the faded romance of Vienna was the perfect setting for a rendezvous with Rashid. In sad and wistful and courtly Vienna, perhaps they could be nostalgic enough to be at least kind to each other again.

'Um Khalid! I have said something to make you so sad?'

Impetuously Musa took both her hands in his and looked into her eyes. His heart went out to this lovely woman who had the mind and body of an American but the heart of an Arab. Sometimes he wished she were a generation younger so he could make her his own and dedicate his life to chasing away the shadows of tragedy he saw in her eyes. 'I have made you cry? But what did I say? I will take it back, deny it, never say whatever I said again!'

Sunny laughed. 'No, Musa, it was nothing you said.' She decided not to tell him about seeing Rashid on the street. Already Musa had said many times she must forget that Saudi man. If she wanted a new husband and she still fancied Arabs, he said that in Cairo he would introduce her to the sons of pashas and military war heroes and other fine upstanding men, who would treat her like the daughter of a pharaoh. 'I just get sad sometimes,' she said, 'watching you talk, thinking of my Khalid.'

'Ah!' Musa's compassionate eyes clouded with concern. 'It is very wrong, I think, to keep you from your son. Those heartless Saudis! What kind of man would keep a woman from her own son?'

Absently she patted Musa's hands and ordered them more coffee. If she telephoned Rashid, she would probably just get a secretary who would put her off with promises and excuses. But he might not turn her away if she came in person on a family mission of mercy. She had a moral right to see her son, and he had a moral responsibility to see their daughter.

She sipped her *Kaffee mit Schlag* and decided she would make a sentimental journey to Doktor Karl Lueger Ring. She would see him again, talk to him again, and *inshallah* even love him again, as early as tomorrow.

Two months later, she sat numbly waiting in the coffeehouse near Rashid's office on the Ringstrasse. She had lost count of how many hours she had wasted waiting for an audience. She had repeatedly begged his motherly

English secretary that she must talk to her estranged husband about their children, and yet the secretary had put her off with one polite evasion after another. Shaykh Rashid was in conference, he was away in Geneva or Teheran or Caracas on business, he had been summoned back to Riyadh for urgent consultations. The secretary had finally volunteered that her boss had left word that if it was money she wanted, she was to be given however much she asked.

Sunny sat waiting in opulent impatience amid the velvet and damask and cut-crystal splendor of the Café Landtmann. As she sipped her coffee, she kept watch at the window in case Rashid passed by on the Ringstrasse. Her secretary had once again suggested this morning that she should try back later, in an hour or a day or a week. Sunny was tired of this anxious charade of politesse. She wished she knew the address of his Viennese apartment so she could corner him alone. She decided to burst into his office and insist she be allowed to see Khalid and that he visit Sarah.

She marched down the sidewalk and up the stairs and past the receptionist when suddenly Rashid's secretary came rushing out to her with elaborate apologies for so many weeks of delay. Shaykh Rashid had just told her to usher madam in the next time she called. He was winding up a meeting in the conference room, but meanwhile she could wait in his office.

Sunny had expected his office to be as grandiose as Saudi Arabia's new pretensions in the world, yet his was a tiny no-nonsense hole in a corner. As she told the solicitous secretary she wanted her Arabic coffee without sugar, she sat in one of the utilitarian steel chairs facing the wide cluttered desk and started to perspire. It was almost as hot as Arabian summer in this small windowless room. Sunny stared at the six space heaters with their reflectors aimed at Rashid's chair. The secretary explained that her boss had chosen this humblest of offices because he thought it would be easier to warm up such a small space. Yet Vienna's damp chill winter had still left the *shaykh* shivering, and so he had ordered the ring of space heaters.

As the secretary scurried off for her coffee, Sunny looked for personal clues about how Rashid was and what Rashid had become, besides a cold man. There were file folders and cabinets and piles of papers and four telephones atop the desk. But the only sign of the man who worked here was a copper ashtray overflowing with butts. Yet he and all the Al-Murrah had always denounced cigarettes as satanic. Had Rashid truly gone to the devil?

She smelled smoke and felt eyes burning upon her, and she looked up and flushed. His eyes were blazing at her as he stood in the doorway smoking a cigarette. As he exhaled, he seemed like a dragon to her. She wished she had not come. Better she had not learned she was afraid of him now. She was the first to look away from the death of love and the birth of fear.

He took a deep elated breath. She was the same. No, he thought with the mellow magnanimity that had come to him with the new wealth and power, she was even more than he had remembered her to be. She was more confident, lovelier and stronger and graver in her womanhood than she had ever been as a girl. He wished it were possible to take photographs of her, so he could keep her image here with him even after she had gone away. His voice was husky. 'I am so very sorry for keeping you waiting for such a long time.'

When she dared to look at him, his smile dazzled her. She conquered her immediate impulse to forgive him utterly, for keeping her waiting today, and for the past two months, and for the past seven years. She reminded herself she had every right in her world to be angry at this man. 'This is the umpteenth time I've come here to see you. And I've sent notes and telephoned.'

He was taken aback, and he waved his hand dismissively in the air. 'Calls, letters, visits, everyone comes here now, everyone wants to talk.' He shrugged. 'I am a very busy man.'

She held her ground. 'I'm not everyone.'

'No. No, you're not.' He sank down into the warm nest of his chair. He had agonized over whether it was kinder to see her and tell her face to face how it had to continue to be with them, or simply to evade her until she gave up and went away of her own accord. The messages about her calls and visits and letters had brought it all back to him – how she had made him feel when they were young and foolish, how he had loved her, how she might still have the power to make him feel now that he was middle-aged and worn and disillusioned. His thoughts trailed back over the past fifteen months since the October War and the oil embargo. How naive he and some of the others had been at the beginning, when they had all still believed Saudi Arabia was leading a crusade to build a grand new Islamic world that would cleanse mankind of corruption. Rashid had been outraged when, in March of 1974, King Faisal had ended the oil boycott before Israel returned even one inch of lost Palestine. All the embargo had done was enrich the oil companies and the Arab governments who catered to them. Even before the price increase, the Saudi economy had been so underdeveloped it had been unable to spend the nine billion dollars it earned every year in oil revenues. So in 1974, when Saudi found itself with thirty-four billion dollars to spend, hasty and extravagant and ill-considered development had sprouted from the Red Sea to the Gulf.

The princes of the House of Saud grew even fatter and greedier and more impossibly arrogant. Airplanes full of Western carpetbaggers and con men and pimps of all persuasions darkened the skies over Dhahran and Riyadh and Jeddah as they flocked to pander to the baser instincts of the newly rich Arabs. Billions of petrodollars ended up in the banks and on the stock markets of the industrialized Western states, but a complex and severe international depression had been triggered by the embargo. Stock-market prices collapsed, unemployment soared, economic production faltered, and inflation spiraled. The Arabs faced an economic dilemma. The value of the money they invested in the West was eroded by inflation, and so Arab oil was worth more in the ground than after it was pumped out and sold and converted into shaky Western currencies.

Yet the investment of the recycled petrodollars in America and Europe had intrinsically bound the Arabs to the continued health of the Western economies. If they didn't keep pumping oil at maximum production, their Western investments would be at risk. Instead of a glorious victory for Islam, the oil embargo and price increase had merely made the West suffer mildly, pay extravagantly, and learn truly to hate the Arab people. Rashid did not know whether he should be proud or ashamed of that day last spring in Riyadh when he had finally poured out two repressed decades of angry recriminations to the king. Passionately he had said Saudi Arabia should nationalize its oil and enforce a real boycott to bring America and Israel to their knees. The inscrutable king had politely listened to his every word, but the very next day Shaykh Yamani had informed him he was to be banished to Vienna to serve a minimum of six years as a member of the OPEC Secretariat.

Rashid wished he could have confided all these troubles to Sunny tonight and every night after dinner, before they went to bed. He leaned forward in his swivel chair. He must not let himself think of her back in his bed. He did his best to be very businesslike. 'Shall I be frank with you?'

She nodded and narrowed her eyes and did not know what to make of him. She used to know him better than she knew herself, and on some deep abiding level she believed they would always remain utterly intimate. But it was unsettling to feel that she knew him absolutely, yet not at all. He had changed so in their years apart. His English had greatly improved, he was dressed like a Western businessman in a Savile Row suit, and he had learned how to dominate and control a one-to-one meeting. He was treating her like a client at a disadvantage. Again she wished she hadn't come.

'I hesitated to see you today or any other day.' He toyed with a gold-plated pen. 'I did not think it would be good for you or for me.' His burning eyes scorched her. 'I don't think we should open this again, Sunny.' But his imploring eyes were saying something else. . . .

She blushed and looked away in confusion. *He still loves me*, she thought. Radiantly she smiled at him. He was smiling back at her as the secretary came in with two tiny cups and two glasses of water on a brass tray. Behind her padded the coffee boy carrying a steaming beaker. With a flourish the secretary poured the cups.

They sipped in silence until they were alone again. She could not take her eyes from his face. His once bronze and glowing skin was sallow, premature lines of worry were etched in his face, his hair was tinged with silver, and his once beautiful wild-animal eyes were disappointed and wary. As she looked at him, secure now in the knowledge he still loved her, she forgot her own desperation over these long years of separation. He needs me, she thought, even more now than when we were young.

'So!' Anxiously Rashid's eyes raked her. 'So what now?'

She laughed a giddy frightened little laugh. She did not know what now. It was wonderful that he said with his eyes that he still loved her, and she knew in her heart that she still loved him. But so much stood between them. She could not shrug off all the lonely wrongs of the past seven years. He had sent her into exile from the family and the country that were home to her; he had cut her off not only from himself but from her son; he had been cruel to her and Sarah when he had surprised them at the Dorchester. Suddenly she felt so much anger burning in her throat she doubted she could speak even if she knew what to say.

Rashid saw a fire that was not love in her eyes, and so, swiftly, he retreated to neutral ground. 'I think,' he said gently, 'that we should begin by talking about the children. Tell me about Sarah. Where she is, how she is.'

'You know she's at Brilliantmont in Lausanne?' She was surprised when he shook his head. 'But I wrote you about that in my letters.'

'I regret to say that I do not always see all your letters.' He frowned. 'Why isn't she here with you?'

'I wasn't sure if I'd stay that long in Vienna. But next fall, when I have my own flat, I've enrolled her here at the American School.' Sunny's voice was tremulous as she fought tears. He had not even read all her letters. It was too much to feel all this love and fear and hurt and anger in one brief encounter in a small office heated to the temperature of a sauna. She swallowed hard, but still she had a lump in her throat. 'Last spring I decided we should leave America. Sarah was having trouble in school. You know, with the embargo, and the energy crisis, and the gas rationing, some of the children were giving her a hard time.'

'I have heard this.' Rashid sighed and shook his head. He knew very well that 'Arab' had become a dirty word in much of the West. But it pained him that his own daughter had paid a personal price for the oil embargo.

'I was ready to start the research for my dissertation. You know about that? About my work here in Vienna with Arab women who are having trouble adjusting to life in the West?'

He nodded. 'Too bad you missed Nura. You could have asked her all about that.'

'Nura was here?'

'Briefly. Last fall for two months. She's back in Khobar now. Where she insists she will stay.'

'I see.' She could hear no affection in his voice as he talked of her rival. 'I think I have some idea what she must have gone through.' When Rashid looked startled, she elaborated. 'I mean being away from home. It was hard for me back in America. You know, I never felt more American than when I was in Arabia. Or more Arabian than when I was in America. Sometimes I think I don't really belong anywhere. I suppose that's why I decided to come here to live.' She smiled. 'They say Vienna is an international city. But I think of it as neutral ground, somewhere between America and Arabia.'

'I understand,' he said quietly. They smiled at each other and remembered that it had always been like this between them. Despite all their differences, they could achieve a perfect emotional understanding.

'I suppose you know I'll be here at OPEC for at least six years.'

'That long!' She was elated. But when she sipped again at her coffee, instead she took in a bitter grainy mouthful of grounds. She spat them out into a napkin and remembered why she had come to him. 'The children. Sarah and Khalid. I think you should go to Switzerland and visit her. She needs you. I know what she's going through. My father treated me just like you're treating her. I missed him so much, growing up. I needed him, and he wasn't there. She needs you, just as Khalid needs me.'

'Go on.' His eyes were hooded.

'Well, that's it, really.' All her eloquence seemed to have deserted her. She was drained and exhausted and she couldn't bear many more minutes of this unsettling audience. 'I want you to get me a visa so I can go to Saudi to visit Khalid. Sarah thinks there's something wrong with her brother, that he's . . . too religious.'

'Is it possible, I wonder, for a man to be too religious?'

'Get me this visa and let me see Khalid, and then I'll tell you.'

He smiled. 'So!' He stood up, as though their interview were at an end.

She sat rooted to her seat. 'So? So what?'

'Yes on Sarah. No answer yet on Khalid.' He was brisk. He pushed a button on his telephone and picked up the receiver and summoned his secretary.

'What's that supposed to mean?'

'No problem – I will go to Switzerland to visit Sarah. As

for Khalid, I can say only that I will try. Soon I must go back to the kingdom on business, and I will see if what you ask is possible.' Rashid shrugged. 'Maybe he will come here, maybe you can go there, who knows but Allah?' He came from behind his desk and held out his hand to her. 'About Sarah. It may be a little difficult, because I go there, and I go here, and I never can be sure about the changes at the last minute. But my secretary will arrange a time. Perhaps we can visit her together. As you like.'

She was dizzy with emotion as she got to her feet. When she swayed, he caught her at the elbows. They were still looking yearningly into each other's eyes when they heard the door opening. He held her hands in his an instant longer than courtesy demanded; then, as the secretary escorted Sunny back out the door, he sighed and opened the dossiers waiting on his desk. But a moment later he bent and unplugged all the space heaters. Finally, after all these cold months in drafty Vienna, he was warm enough. Being with the wife of his heart had finally warmed him like the sun on an Arabian afternoon.

Ibrahim sat waiting in solitary splendor for Rashid to come and pay his respects at his morning *majlis*. As he sat waiting, Ibrahim's lips moved as he silently recited his favorite passages from the Koran, the wise sweet *surahs* that urged the faithful to compassion and forgiveness. He beseeched every heavenly blessing for the delicate family matters he would lay before Rashid today about his wife and brother and son.

'Grandfather!' Rashid was resplendent in white *thobe* and *ghutra* as he strode into the cavernous reception room with its lines of empty gilt chairs against the four walls. He kissed the hem of his grandfather's robe, and his shoulder and his cheeks, and touched noses, and only after he had intoned the solicitous ritual questions about the health of all those in Ibrahim's loving world did he ask why the rest of the family and tribe were missing.

'Later they will come,' Ibrahim said as the coffee boy brought in the bubbling beakers. 'But first I wanted to see you and talk with you alone. You have been away for so many months. Closer, my son, so I can try to see what living in the land of the infidels has done to you.' Ibrahim squinted, and he reached out his hand and traced the lines of stress on Rashid's face. 'So it is like that,' the old man sighed. He regretted that he was about to increase the troubles of this one whom he loved the most. For a long while he chatted with his grandson about matters great and small, and then he steeled himself to say what had to be said as quickly and mercifully as a knife slashes the throat of a sheep.

'Problems,' he said, mostly to himself. 'Always my family has so many problems.' He sighed. 'I must talk to you about Nura. You are the son of my son, and she is the daughter of my daughter, and always you my children have been dear to me. But you know that, yes?' Ibrahim smiled, and he reached out and stroked Rashid's cheek. 'Yet for too many years I have been silent as I watched that girl suffer - first when you went away to school in the West, and then when you came back with your Sunny whom you know you loved more, and then when you went away again. She even tried and failed to endure that life in Vienna with you, and so once again she is here alone like a widow.' Ibrahim shook his head. 'I am the head of the family. It is my duty to protect all our women. Nura came to me and begged me to speak for her, and so I am bound by honor to say what I say now. Son of my son, you must either treat this woman as your wife or release her so she may have that in another marriage.'

'She loves another?' Rashid flushed with a rush of quick hot jealousy. 'My wife wants a divorce so she can marry another? Who is this man who wants my wife? *Who?*'

'*You* are the problem, not Nura,' Ibrahim said mildly. Tomorrow or after tomorrow, or perhaps later than that, maybe even after Rashid was safely back in Vienna, was soon enough to let him know that Nura and Cousin

Hussein longed to marry. 'Let her go, my son.'

Rashid was silent for long moments until he mastered his jealousy. Everything Ibrahim had said about his long neglect of Nura was true. He searched his heart and admitted he had loved Nura like a wife only in their first rapturous months together. He supposed he should love her or let her go, and yet he had always liked the security of his pliant cousin's waiting in the wings while he played out the real drama of his life with Sunny. He knew he was being selfish, but he was reluctant to give up Nura even now. 'I suppose I could take her back to Vienna with me again.'

'Yes, you could choose to make her unhappy in Vienna again. You are her husband. You can take her back to the West or you can divorce her, or not, as you like.' Ibrahim paused. 'Life is difficult, my son, especially if a man chooses to be brave and fine and generous.'

'You think I should divorce her?'

'I think you should do whatever your conscience and your heart tell you to do. I am not your master, only your old frail grandfather.'

Rashid hid a smile and told himself he could still learn a thing or two about manipulation from his frail old grandfather. He bent and kissed Ibrahim's hand. 'I don't know what I would ever do without you.' He held Ibrahim's hand to his cheek. 'What would we all do without you?'

Wisely Ibrahim said not another word about Nura. In a few minutes or hours or days, he was certain Rashid would announce he was divorcing her. Ibrahim hoped for as great a success in his second, even more delicate diplomatic mission. For a long while he had wished for a reconciliation between his estranged grandsons. Ibrahim had never abandoned all hope for Muhammad's rehabilitation. He had taken it as an excellent sign that Muhammad had spent so much loving time over the years with Khalid, and he liked to think the time was right to welcome the prodigal back. 'I must speak now of another problem.

Your brother lives like a pariah dog, without family and honor and pride and –'

'A dog lives as a dog must live.' Rashid snapped his fingers. 'What do I care about a man who has made himself as low as an animal?'

'He's your brother.'

'I know what he is and who he is, and I remember *all* that he has done.' Rashid's features hardened as an outrageous suspicion occurred to him. 'He's the one who wants to marry Nura, isn't he? Wasn't it enough that he took Sunny?'

'No, no, that's not it.' Soothingly Ibrahim patted Rashid's hand. '*Wallah*, I promise you, that's not it. I just hoped that now, after all this time, you might be ready to forgive –'

'Not now. Not ever.'

'So be it.' Ibrahim let out a long sigh of defeat. 'And there's one more thing.'

'Isn't this enough for one morning, Grandfather? I come home for the first time in nine months, and all I hear about is problems. In Vienna I have still more problems. Where is the peace? Where is there peace for me?'

'Not in this kingdom but the next,' Ibrahim said gently before he went on. 'Khalid worries me. You haven't been here, so you haven't seen the change in him. Ever since what happened in London between Sunny and you, he's been even more shy and withdrawn than he was as a boy. You weren't here. He needed you then, and you weren't here.'

'I was busy.' Rashid's eyes flashed bitterly. 'I had no choice. And you know that now I still have no choice. The royal family sent me into exile.'

Ibrahim lowered his voice to a whisper lest they be overheard by a spying servant in the pay of the Al-Saud. 'I hear rumors that Khalid spends more time in Medina listening to bad men say dangerous words than listening to the holy men reciting the Koran. I ordered him home as soon as you sent word you were coming. Maybe you can talk to the boy, find out what's wrong, make him come back here to the family compound where I can keep my dim eyes on him.'

'My son is here?' Rashid leaped to his feet and shouted. 'Khalid!'

Softly the door opened. Silently Khalid crept into the *majlis*. Humbly the youngest Al-Murrah knelt and kissed the hem of the robes of his elders. But Khalid's eyes, when he finally lifted them to his father and grandfather, burned with resentment even as he mumbled all the proper filial sentiments.

Yet Rashid seemed not to have noticed that something was amiss as he swept his tall straight handsome Khalid into his arms and hugged him. 'My son; my only son.' He shut his eyes and sighed as he held his and Sunny's son.

But Khalid's eyes were wide open as he endured his father's embrace, and he stared without blinking at his grandfather. It had taken Khalid long years of anguish before he finally had been able to see his way out of his confusion and come to a series of conclusions about what was to blame for the ruin of his father and his mother and himself. The foul pollutions of the West had corrupted them all. His mother, who had left him when he was a boy and needed her the most, was evil and immoral. His father, who had turned on him in London and then left him when he was a young man and needed him the most, was venal and compromised and damned. Khalid had struggled to accept the doom of his genes. He had inherited the taint of infidel corruption from his mother's womb, yet he thanked God that, through the intercession of Juhayman *ibn* Muhammad *ibn* Saif Al-Otaybi in Medina, he had finally been struck by the light of personal Islamic revolution and was working to purge himself of his own seeds of corruption.

Ever since the charismatic Juhayman had explained everything to him, Khalid's loneliness and doubts, even his tormenting headaches, had begun to go away. This evil all around and even inside us, Juhayman had whispered, is because of the corruption that grows like a cancer here in the heart of Islam. The evil of the decadent West has infected the House of Saud, and so the royal princes must repent and reform either by choice or force. Khalid had been fascinated by Juhayman's religious sedition. He had been bewitched when Juhayman spoke those dark words of blood and revolution. He had been enthralled when Juhayman said they would be a new *Ikhwan* - a 'Brotherhood' - of religious warriors just like the glorious legendary *Ikhwan* whose legions had forcibly united Arabia under the banners of King Abdul Aziz sixty years ago.

Khalid had first met Juhayman a year ago when they both sat cross-legged at the feet of Abdul Aziz *ibn* Baz, a blind *shaykh* of the Islamic University at Medina who said the world was flat and that all that had happened since the Prophet walked these very streets thirteen centuries ago was wrong and profane. Khalid wished he were still back at Medina hearing Juhayman and the blind old *shaykh* debate Islamic doctrine. Everything seemed so wondrously simple when Juhayman explained it, but here with his father's arms around him the complexities of life and love and sin began to befuddle him again.

The three generations sat and drank coffee, and Rashid beamed at Khalid, and Khalid looked away, and Ibrahim did his best to hide his misgivings. 'I have a surprise for you, my son,' Rashid finally said as he smiled even more broadly. 'In Vienna I have talked with your mother. She thinks, and I think also, that it is time for a coming together. Either she will come here to you, or you can go there to her.'

'Her?' Khalid's mind whirled, and his heart beat faster. He had loved her so, once. Yet when he had confessed the story of his life, Juhayman had said his mother was a blight and a pestilence. He had finally promised Juhayman he would never fall under the influence of such a daughter of darkness again. Unhappily Khalid sighed. 'I will never again visit the lands of the ungodly. Never, Father. And I beg you not to bring her here.' He hesitated. 'At least, not now.' Khalid bit his lower lip to keep it from trembling. 'Please, Father.' His voice rose with passion. 'All day, all night, always now I live only for the Holy Koran. I read it, I say it, I dream it, in Medina, where the Prophet was born. I have no time now for women, only for God.' Khalid's eyes were ashine. 'You must respect that.'

The eyes of Rashid and Ibrahim met over the bowed head of the youngest of the Al-Murrah. And even though Ibrahim slightly but firmly shook his head, Rashid reached out and pulled aside Khalid's head scarf and stroked his son's black curls in an indulgent blessing. Khalid had asked him for so little in his lifetime. The least he could do was humor the boy's request, at least for now. There was no harm in Khalid's being consumed by the marvels of the Koran. Rashid wished he had the luxury of sitting for days talking to Khalid about its wonders. But he had to bring this conversation to a close and catch his plane back to Vienna. 'As you like, son. As you like.'

Sunny and Sarah paced nervously on the promenade in the Jardin Anglais beside luminous, misty Lac Leman. A stiff gusty wind snapped some of the blossoms off the tulips, and birds shivered along the budding branches of the sycamore trees. It was early spring, the beginning of a new season of hope, and the Geneva air was heady with the promise of renewal. Yet there was still a chill of winter in the air.

'He's not coming, Mother. I just know it. We're crazy to wait out here like this for him. We came all the way around the lake from Lausanne, and he's not going to turn up.'

'He's late, that's all. Forty minutes late. He'll be along soon. Saudis are always late.'

'No, he's not coming. I just know he's not. He promised to come before, and he didn't. It will be the same today. He's going to make fools of us today too.'

'No, honey, he'll come.' As Sunny put her arm around her daughter, she tried to sound more confident than she felt. 'He couldn't help it that the king called him back to Saudi last month. He sent flowers, didn't he? He had one of his assistants telephone you, and then he set another day to see you as soon as he could. He's your father. You're going to have to learn to trust him.'

'Trust *him*?' Sarah shook her head with the bitterness of a cynical old woman. 'I could *never* trust him. Not after what he did to you. And to Khalid in London. And I haven't forgotten how he even tried to get me to abandon you.'

'Sarah, Sarah . . .' Sunny sank down on a bench that looked out on the soft curtain of water spouting high in the air from the Jet d'Eau. She patted the seat beside her. 'Sit down, Sarah.' The time was long overdue to teach her daughter some healing lessons about reconciliation. She wanted Sarah to have a chance to be happy someday with a man of her choice, or even alone by her choice, but Sunny was afraid her own broken marriage might have damaged Sarah's capacity for loving. Yet Sunny did not ever want to be a hypocrite with her daughter. She had always tried to be honest with Sarah. She could not counsel forgiveness when she herself could not quite find it in her heart to forgive Rashid for all he had done. The wounds were too deep, in a way still too fresh even after seven years, for her to forgive him after a few words and imploring looks. But she hoped she and Rashid could at least try to begin to be kind to each other again. She was willing at least to risk being kind. If that was the first tentative step toward forgiveness, she was ready to take it here on the promenade by the lake.

'You're not going to try to defend him, are you?' Sarah anxiously studied her mother's face. 'Since when did you start believing all his promises again?'

Sunny looked from the gray lake to the gray sky. It had rained this morning, and she could glimpse the faint pastel colors of a rainbow inside the white water geyser on the *jetée.* A swan flapped its wings and flew low over the whitecaps on the vast lake. She would not utter hypocritical words to persuade her wary daughter to believe. Instead Sunny put her arm around the girl and stroked her hair as Sarah rested her head on her shoulder. They sat hunched together against the cold on the park bench, looking out at the choppy lake, until finally behind them on the road they heard squealing brakes and an imperious horn, then a car door slamming shut.

Sarah leaped to her feet, she turned, she shrieked like a fan at a rock concert. 'He's here! Mother, he came!' Sarah started running down the path toward the one who had finally come back to her.

Sunny smiled and shook her head in wonder as she followed Sarah down the path. She had just been worrying about her daughter's capacity for forgiveness, but now she could see that Sarah was light-years ahead of her. Intentionally Sunny lagged even farther behind. She wanted to be a witness but not a participant in their reunion. Whatever happened between herself and Rashid, she wanted Sarah to have the chance to re-establish a relationship with him. As she watched the distance narrowing between father and daughter, Sunny remembered how she had felt when she had finally been reunited with her own lost father. When they had fallen into each other's arms at the Dhahran airport, she had felt she had found a lost treasure. She would let Sarah savor the wonder of that triumphant discovery all for herself.

Rashid's empty arms ached for his women, for not only his daughter but his wife. 'Sarah!' Her warm body was in his arms, and they hugged, and he kissed her glowing cheeks. '*Habibi*, Sarah!' Finally she pulled away, and she laughed, and he greedily devoured every detail of the face and the figure and the presence of his and Sunny's daughter. She was a glorious girl with a tall slim athletic American figure, slanty almond-shaped dancing dark Arab eyes, and a lustrous mane of black hair. Only a generation ago, Rashid remembered, before the oil changed all Arabia, the tribes used to march into battle behind a barefaced maiden with long flowing black hair like Sarah's. The tribes used to rally behind a beautiful maiden perched on a thronelike canopy high atop a sleek white racing camel. It was said that a tribe could never lose behind the standard of a lovely Arabian desert princess such as Sarah.

He touched her rippling black Arabian hair. And as he wished there were words he could say to make up for all the lost years, some of the joy died in his eyes. He had let her go away from Saudi so that Sunny would still have someone to love. At the time it had seemed right to make that sacrifice so her mother would not be altogether alone. But here and now, looking down into his daughter's eyes, it seemed to Rashid that any feeble reason to send this lovely vulnerable girl away had to have been very wrong.

Sarah reached up and wiped away the two tears that fell down her father's cheeks.

'I am sorry,' he said. 'I want you to know that, to know that I am sorry.'

She buried her head in her father's chest, and he patted her shoulders as she cried her heart out in her father's arms. They were still standing like that, as still as weeping statues, when Sunny finally came up and joined them and the three of them walked hesitantly along the windswept promenade by the stormy lake.

—22—

On this morning of mornings Muhammad lay abed smiling as a loudspeaker outside on the street blared a static-filled call to the dawn prayers. It was his grudging custom to stumble out to the mosque to pray the requisite five times each day, but at last he could dispense with that tiresome charade. No hypocrisy for him today. Let the other poor gullible fools of Arabia bow and scrape to their overbearing God. Today he would lie languorously in bed, defying the cliché that prayer was better than sleep. If any of his sanctimonious cousins who took such self-righteous glee in ignoring him could see him now, Muhammad thought they would probably whisper to one another that the devil must be in him this morning. The superstitious men and women of Khobar had long ago decided he served not God but *Iblis*, 'the devil.' So be it, Muhammad thought. If Iblis be my master today and through all eternity, then so be it. At least the devil hasn't disowned me.

It felt good to lie in bed while others were all groaning and rising and kneeling and making themselves miserable in the name of the Lord. All the men prayed, because all the men had to pray. The *mutawiyah* religious police took careful note of which men missed their daily prayers in the mosques, and they would hunt down and flog the culprits with their heavy canes. Since he had been hauled back to Saudi, Muhammad had thought twice before outwardly rebelling against the kingdom's mandated morality. He had detested all this pious muttering into his beard, but nonetheless he had contemptuously bowed to the inevitable. That one terrifying night in the black tents of the Al-Murrah had been enough for him. He had never wanted to test Saudi retribution again. He had fasted during Ramadan, and he had even made one desultory pilgrimage of fear to Mecca. And day after day he had prayed facing the Mecca he scorned.

All but for today. To hell with all that hideous piety today. He would do what he damn well pleased today.

Muhammad looked around, as though for the last time, at his austere bedroom, grim as a prison cell. For furniture there were a clumsy free-standing wooden wardrobe, a rickety metal table, and a hard single bed that creaked on rusty springs when he turned over in his restless dreams. A plastic chamber pot and a clay pitcher and basin were on the grimy concrete floor by his shoes. A far cry not only from his old flat in London but also from the palatial seaside villas where the rest of his family lived. Yet Muhammad tried to console himself that at least he had a kind of freedom here in his sordid little lair with his carefully concealed bottles of whiskey, his pornography, his cards, his dice, and his memories. If he had still been a member in good standing of the family, he would have had to deal with his mother and his aunts and his cousins bursting into his room at all hours, pleading with him to do this or to do that, judging him always, comparing him constantly with the shining example of his cursed brother, reminding him with their big sorrowful doe eyes that he was the major failure of his generation. Yet sometimes he longed even for their censure. Ever since that night of dread in the tribal tent, he had been as good as dead to all the family except that young one and that old one who had never quite been able to leave him alone.

Muhammad scratched a fleabite. This little room was a lousy place for him to wind up. He, who had slept on silks and satins and the fragrant alabaster skin of beautiful white women, was ending his days in this smelly cement shack in Saudi Arabia. He had come full circle. He had begun even more pathetically than this out in the desert in a hot black tent, and now this hot dark room was where he was waking on the day that he had decided to make his last stand. Muhammad wished there were someone with whom he could share that final rich bitter irony, but there was no one here who could understand that, or anything else.

He could hear a bustle and a clanking and a hissing of water out in the kitchen. That would be Aisha, the wife he had despised when he had first glimpsed her face nearly twenty years ago in their bridal tent. Perhaps it was just as well that Aisha most certainly was not capable of irony. That sly woman who had mocked him for not being man enough on their wedding night still sometimes came to this squalid room and watched him sweat and curse and try to be the Arabian stallion he had once been. But he had lost his virility too, here in this kingdom. His brother and his grandfather and the *shaykhs* and the graybeards had unmanned him that terrible night. Yet Muhammad cherished the belief that he would still have been able to be rampant in the bed of the right woman, a West End whore in red lingerie or a French tart in black boots or any of those naked spread-eagled blondes whose graphic pictures he labored over by lantern light. It was not his fault that he couldn't do it anymore. It was Aisha's fault, and Arabia's fault. That bovine witch who masqueraded as his wife would surely not mourn his passing. Nor would Arabia.

Muhammad noticed that the faint gray pearlish dawn light had brightened into white hot morning, and so he pulled back his sheet and jumped out of bed. He wanted everything to be perfect today. For seven miserable years he had truckled to the primitive folkways of this dusty little backwater. For too long he had lived here with a sort of animal resignation. He had eked out a scavenger living on scraps thrown his way by the foreigners. But he would endure no more sad miserable days. Today - not by God's will but by an act of his own devilish will - he would release himself from this purgatory. He would go out with a final glorious flash of his old inimitable style.

He padded down the hallway to the small humid room that was euphemistically called the bathroom. He curled his lip at the porcelain footprints flanking the hole in the floor that served as a toilet. For *him* to have to live like this! He looked longingly at the shiny black porcelain toilet with its marble pedestal seat, and at the massive ornate pink sunken bathtub, and at the chrome shower stall with its sliding fiberglass mirrored doors. He had pored lovingly over catalogues from Italy and America and Germany before he decided on these beautifully designed bathroom fixtures. He had been rapturous with anticipation when the crates had finally arrived at Dammam, and he had paid the extravagant customs duty and brought home what he had thought would be his own sybaritic spa. But the Arab plumber had cracked the porcelain of the toilet, and said he didn't have the right pipes for the shower stall, and that there was something else awry with the sunken tub. For two long years the servants had dutifully scrubbed and polished these unconnected fixtures that sat in useless reproach in this bathroom, a monument, like so much in Saudi, to what might have been.

Muhammad reached up high on the cement wall and twisted a faucet far to the right, and after a while a trickle of rusty water dripped from a nozzle in the ceiling. There was no hot water today, and not much pressure, either. But Muhammad stood awhile under the dripping nozzle and indulged in a fantasy that he was back at Claridge's, standing under a hot steaming luxurious gush of shower water. He wanted to believe he was starting off this day clean and fresh and invigorated. Muhammad had flown far higher on far more rocket-propelled flights of imagination than this during his monotonous years of exile from the good life. Mostly he pretended that none of this was truly happening. He wasn't living in Saudi in this squalid house with that horrid woman. Soon, please God, very soon, he would wake to the fresh rain of a London springtime morning.

Muhammad stood under the lukewarm trickle of rusty water and let himself ponder yet again the cruelties of fate. Bad enough he was here living this shadow life, but harder to endure even than the reality of Saudi was the knowledge of the life he *could* have been enjoying now in London and Paris and Cannes. He, who had pioneered Arab decadence even before the great explosion of oil wealth, could have been the leader of the pack now that it was fashionable to be an Arab loose in the fleshpots of Europe. Even here in Saudi he had heard fantastic rumors of wild parties and wild women and wild spending. Government censors scissored out any references to this new international phenomenon of Arab playboys in newspapers and magazines, but the government could not stop coffeehouse gossip.

Muhammad would sit, spellbound, as young men just back from London or Paris or Rome boasted that the world now belonged to the Arabs. Arabs owned vast luxury yachts anchored off Antibes. Arabs gambled tens of thousands of dollars on one roll of the dice at Marbella. Arabs danced with movie stars under the electronic throb of discotheque strobe lights in Paris. Arabs owned their own private helicopters and jets and stables of Thoroughbreds and women. Arabs owned manor houses and villages and forests. Muhammad burned to be part of that flamboyant excess. He would have been a king of society if he had been living in Knightsbridge now. It was rotten luck that his timing had been off by a decade. He had been one of the first of his race to bite the apple, and he had been expelled from that luscious paradise for doing what an entire new generation of rich Arabs were now routinely doing without censure. His mistake was simply to have done it all first - and to have been caught at it. Muhammad stood under the rusty trickle of tepid water and seethed at the injustices of life.

Back in his bedroom he opened his wardrobe and took out the poor excuse for a dinner jacket his Indian tailor had just made him. He hung the black formal suit on the front of the closet and brushed off a few stray grains of sand which clung to the lapels. The fabric was coarse and shiny, the cheap plastic buttons were all wrong, the fit was too baggy in the knees and too tight through the shoulders. It would never do if he were going to the Folies Bergère in Paris or the Palladium in London. But the tuxedo was more than elegant enough for its purpose today.

Muhammad cursed when he could scarcely button his trousers. That wog of a tailor had done it again. Muhammad had accused the Indian before of intentionally shaving an inch or two off the waistline of his pants just to torment him into believing he was putting on weight. Muhammad stood sideways, sucked in his gut and gazed at his portly reflection. He could not wish away the fact that he had gained forty-five pounds since his homecoming. He had discovered that sometimes it filled up the empty places inside if he ate and ate until he could stand to eat no more. At least here in the kingdom he could indulge one of his sensual appetites. It had made him sick to his stomach at first, however, to have to eat that stringy charred mutton and that greasy sticky rice served on those foul trays set on the floor as if for animals. But he had learned to make up in quantity what was lacking in quality. He would gorge himself by cramming handfuls of meat and rice into his mouth; then he would belch and lie down and sleep off the food the way he would a hangover. In time, too, he had made the right contacts for contraband drugs and bootleg alcohol. Hashish sold for ninety dollars an ounce, and Johnnie Walker went for upwards of a hundred dollars a bottle. Muhammad supposed some of his excess poundage was the fault of the booze. Since the oil rush had hit the Eastern Province, whiskey was available on Khobar's every back street.

Muhammad smiled at his reflection. He still cut a handsome figure even in this tight shabby dinner jacket. Usually, when he was wearing his shapeless Saudi nightshirt, his protruding stomach was completely camouflaged. He fancied, however, that he could carry these few extra pounds without affecting his French-film-star looks. If he were back in London now, the dollies wouldn't give a damn if he weighed three hundred pounds. And here in Saudi, no one cared what he weighed. Here in Saudi, no one cared anything about him, one way or another. That black night in that black tent he had howled at the moon when they burnt his passport. And since then he had finally understood that the doom Ibrahim had pronounced on him was even more devastating. It was a living death to pass his days and nights here without a family, for there was no life in Saudi except for family life. He was sick to death of being a leper. Sick to death.

He rooted in the bottom of his cupboard until he finally found his opera glasses. He slipped on the patent leather evening pumps he had ordered from a London catalogue. He knotted his tie just right. He looked in the mirror and decided his image was perfection. Today he would write the appropriate denouement to the story of his life. He would go out with style, with élan, with class - and with just a little dash of mystery. At the end he would leave the Bedouin guessing.

The roof of his mouth was dry. Already he was thirsty. He was dying for a jolt of morning coffee. But it would only prolong the end if he slaked his thirst with coffee or water. He calculated it would take him at least three days to die in the desert without food or water.

He strode outside and settled himself in the driver's seat of his battered gray secondhand Toyota. As he switched on the air conditioning, he wished he could have begged or borrowed a better deathmobile. He would have liked to go out in a Rolls-Royce. It would have been a perfect final touch to make his last stand in the lap of British luxury.

A melancholy wisp of an impulse made him drive out to the lavish miniature city his brother had built for the family alongside a muddy stretch of the Gulf beach north of Khobar. He would have loved to peek wistfully over the high white wall at the wonders Aisha had told him were inside. Nine air-conditioned villas were scattered around the landscaped grounds for Ibrahim and Um Muhammad and Nura and her new husband Cousin Hussein, and Nura's married daughters. There were a mosque, a swimming pool, a playground for the children of Nura's daughters, a grove of date palms, separate buildings for the kitchens and the laundry, even a small zoo where Rashid kept camels, horses, falcons, gazelles, goats, and an ostrich.

But Aisha said what was truly unusual about Rashid's minikingdom by the sea was its architecture. Instead of the usual squat flat-roofed Arabian blockhouses, Rashid had ordered his architect to design graceful white modern houses shaped with fanciful peaked roofs like the old black Bedouin houses of hair, so that the family compound resembled not only a Bedouin encampment but some marvelous fantasy in *Tales from the Arabian Nights*. Muhammad wished he could barge inside to say goodbye to his mother and the others he had once loved long ago. But he had been turned back before by the servants stationed at that high black ironwork gate. Muhammad regretted that Rashid was in Vienna. He would have liked his brother to be in the search party that found his body. He would have liked Rashid to stand weeping over his bier. He wanted him to feel remorse for the role he had played in the downfall of his only brother. He wanted Rashid to wonder if his death had been suicide or an ironical accident. Most of all he wanted to haunt Rashid forever.

Muhammad had to pass back through the pulsating bottleneck of Khobar to get to the desert. But some mishap ahead on the main street had created a traffic jam, so he leaned on his horn, turned up the air conditioning, and sat and waited. Since oil revenues had skyrocketed, Khobar and every other hamlet in the Eastern Province had been transformed into a boomtown. The many thousands of Western hucksters who had arrived here had quickly exceeded the limited supply of Saudi hotel rooms. Desperate salesmen from California and London and Hamburg paid one hundred dollars to sleep in the hallways of sleazy hotels and even fifty dollars to rest overnight in the back seat of taxis. The salesmen came and the salesmen stayed because the Saudis were doing their extravagant best to spend the three hundred million dollars their country made every day on its oil. Bureaucrats concocted grandiose five-year plans to transform Saudi into one huge bustling urban garden. Contracts were signed to build factories and refineries and schools and hospitals and housing projects. Ground was broken for two giant urban industrial centers, Yanbu on the Red Sea and Jubail on the Arabian Gulf. So many roads were laid it seemed the planners wanted to cement over all the deserts. To work these wonders, an army of laborers had been imported from the squalid tenements of the Middle

East and from the teeming ghettoes of India and, especially, from the orderly civilian compounds of South Korea. Even after the foreigners outnumbered the natives in the work force, still more labor gangs came and stayed and sweated to build Arabian dreams.

Only a few years after the oil boom had begun, the boulevards of Riyadh were lined with imposing new government ministries. A four-and-a-half-billion-dollar contract was awarded for a national telephone and telecommunications system. Sprawling airports were commissioned for Jeddah and Riyadh and Dhahran. Warplanes, tanks, artillery, and the world's most modern weapons systems were bought from America, France, and Britain. Consumer goods of every description - videotape recorders, designer blue jeans, color television sets, cosmetics, freezers, washing machines, blenders, video games, Paris *haute couture*, prefabricated houses - everything under the sun was being imported to an Arabian population which had begun to wonder how it had ever lived without all this convenience and progress and civilization. The congested docks of Jeddah and Dammam could not handle it all. Some shipments waited outside the harbors for three months. Whole shiploads of perishable goods rotted in the holds. Car imports tripled in one year. Real-estate values increased astronomically, so that land worth ten Saudi riyals in the mid-1960s sold a decade later for twenty thousand. For a while this year the cost of renting a flat in Riyadh had doubled every week. A pleasant four-bedroom villa rented for fifty thousand dollars a year. A luxury villa went for as much as one hundred fifty thousand. The annual rate of inflation fluctuated between thirty and seventy percent. With millions seemingly up for grabs on every street corner, a frenzy of graft and greed and corruption touched every fiber of Saudi society.

Muhammad's knowing eyes darted around him at the bustle of street life. Any other morning he too would have been trying to turn a quick buck from the befuddled foreigners who swarmed these filthy streets trying to get rich quick. His speciality was hanging out in the luxury hotels making extravagant promises that, for a price, he could introduce salesmen to princes and guarantee lucrative contracts that would make them millionaires in a month. He conned the gullible, greedy foreigners until their money and their visas ran out, and then he did it all over again with the next generation who came to town gripped by oil fever.

Yet Muhammad despised himself for being a parasite on the parasites. Once he had been so much more than he was now.

He looked out in disgust at the hucksters plying their shoddy wares, at the mountains of sand piled up in front of the innumerable construction sites, at everything that was crass and slick and overpriced on this Khobar street. Muhammad remembered an old Bedouin proverb. *Jild far ma yistuwi minnuh tabil*: 'A drum can't be made from a rat's skin' - or as they said in the West, You can't make a silk purse from a sow's ear.

He was glad finally when he headed out of town and inland toward the ancestral grazing grounds of the Al-Murrah. All his life he had turned his back on his tribal past, but now at his end he would confront it.

But first he had to endure one more Saudi eyesore. Khobar was tacky and honky-tonk and gaudy. But Aramco's ugly utilitarian sprawl of pipelines and conversion plants and refineries and pumping stations was pollution of a different sort. Muhammad drove past Arab shantytowns and American real-estate developments. He sailed past the rusted-out automobiles left to rot by the roadway, for the reckless carnage on Saudi roads was a national disaster. The government estimated that seventeen thousand Saudis had been killed on the highways last year, and that an astonishing *eighty thousand* wrecked cars were abandoned by the roadside of Jeddah alone.

He drove for a very long while, then finally turned off the highway that fingered into the desert. He made his own tracks into the wasteland. He bumped along until he was certain he was so far from the last outposts of civilization that no one would be able to stop him from doing what he had decided to do.

He parked the car, turned off the engine, opened the windows, and sat listening to the terrible silence of the desert.

What, he wondered, would Khalid think when they found his uncle's body out here?

Muhammad sighed softly to himself. He had managed so far today to keep his thoughts away from Rashid's son. But he knew very well that he probably would not be out here now in this vehicle of death if it weren't for Khalid. He wished that poor troubled boy hadn't come blundering in, uninvited, to his room last week when Muhammad was drunk. He wished Khalid hadn't cornered him with too many pointed questions. He wished he himself had not supplied too many precise answers about what he had done to Sunny so long ago in Boston. That brief, bitter *tête-à-tête* with Khalid had been the final straw.

Muhammad wiped the sweat off his forehead. More than anything in his life, he regretted that one careless confession to that boy in the dead of that night. He was a little surprised he had it in him to care so much about how he had hurt that boy. Although he had sown his seed far and wide for more years than he wanted to remember, Muhammad had no children of his own. But he had always fancied a son. He had always thought it would feel wonderful to have a walking, talking clone of himself at loose in the world. A son would have been a stab at immortality.

It was only after he had been exiled here in the kingdom that Muhammad had discovered there were other deeper, sweeter, and less selfish pleasures in a son, even in his brother's son. Muhammad supposed Ibrahim had looked the other way in those first years when he had begun secretly spending long afternoons with young Khalid. The old man knew everything that happened in his family kingdom, so surely he had been told that Muhammad had taken Khalid out to the desert and taught him to shoot, that they went hunting together, that he regaled the boy with stories of life in the West, that he helped him with his studies. Muhammad was grateful to his grandfather for the gift of those stolen hours with young Khalid.

At times, in those early years, he had sometimes even imagined that this quiet sensitive aching boy who missed his mother so was not Rashid's son but his own and Sunny's. But then Khalid and the others had gone off to London for that ill-fated reunion, and when the boy came back he had sought solace not with his prodigal uncle but in the Glorious Koran. Muhammad had not been able to stomach such an excess of religion, and so the two of them had begun to drift apart. He had rarely even seen Khalid in these last years since he had gone off to Medina.

He had never expected his nephew to show up last week and demand an accounting of what had happened long ago with his mother. Muhammad had been shocked. Khalid was emaciated and grim, and Muhammad had thought the boy must have a fever because his eyes glittered so. Khalid had also learned to speak up and to make demands and to refuse to take 'no' for an answer. Muhammad had been taken by surprise and Muhammad had been drunk, and Muhammad bitterly regretted that he had given his young hypersensitive nephew a very graphic description of *exactly* what had happened in that Scollay Square hotel long ago.

Muhammad reached into the glove compartment and pulled out a notepad and a pen. He could at least leave a final message for young Khalid. As his last will and testament, he could finally tell the whole truth. He could take full responsibility for seducing Sunny. He could admit he had forced her against her will. He could make his last message to the world a stroke of decency and kindness and honor. He would do that for the nephew he loved like a son. Muhammad scribbled on the paper; he squinted at what he had written; he sighed and felt his conscience was finally clear. He put the paper under the windshield wiper, where whoever found him would be sure to see it. He hoped it was Ibrahim who finally found the truth. Muhammad wished he could have seen the old man one last time, too. It had been Ibrahim who had cast him out of the family, and yet it was Ibrahim who refused to utterly abandon him. Every December on Muhammad's birthday, his grandfather met him as if by accident in the mosque. Always Ibrahim would insist they pray together, and then they would sit cross-legged while the old one sagely questioned the young one to see if finally Muhammad had experienced a change of heart. Last winter Ibrahim had raised his hopes when he promised to plead his case to Rashid, but last spring he had dashed them again when he sent word his brother had refused a reprieve.

Muhammad looked around at the sand and scrub and the nothingness of the desert. This was, he thought, a hell of a way he had picked to die. He wondered at what had led him to this particular bleak and lonely end. A good Muslim would never court the instant damnation of suicide, but Muhammad was not a good Muslim. He could have taken an overdose of sleeping pills, or blown his brains out or hanged himself. So why this? Anything would have been easier than this.

But nothing, Muhammad thought, could possibly be more ironic than for Muhammad Al-Murrah to dress in a tuxedo and drive his air-conditioned car out to the desert to die in the end like a true Bedouin. By rights, he thought, all Arabia should self-destruct like this in its infernal deserts. Muhammad supposed that dour old King Faisal would have liked to have a death like this. But less than two years after he declared his *jihad* against the West, Faisal had been shot by a nephew who resented being hauled back to Saudi after disgracing himself with drugs and women in America. Muhammad had been in utter sympathy with the assassin. The day the Saudis cut the nephew's head off in a main square in Riyadh, Muhammad had raised a glass or two in honor of his passing.

Muhammad sat for a long while thinking about the poetic justice of his own end. He had begun here, and here he would end. He let the silence and the stillness of the desert seep inside him. He recalled that arduous year his tribe had forced him to spend in the desert after his disgrace. He had been sick that year, and hungry, and tired, but despite all the hardship he had experienced a rare serenity. As he sat alone in the desert waiting for death, he again felt that contentment begin to creep over him, and he could not help wondering if this desert he had tried so hard to escape was the essence of his life and himself after all. Perhaps this contentment had always been waiting for him in the desert. Maybe it had truly been his destiny to live and die here as his ancestors had.

Muhammad longed to blot out these unbearable thoughts with a long fiery drink of whiskey. It had been hard enough to live an ambiguous life. He could not bear an ambiguous death.

He looked up at the sun and wondered if it would truly take him three days to die. He considered hurrying things along by leaving the shelter of the car and running out bareheaded into the shimmering wasteland. But then he shuddered. He did not want to court such pain at the end. He would wait here in the car for an easier but more protracted death. Finally, here at the end, waiting for death in the desert, he would cultivate the celebrated Bedouin art of patience.

He dozed off and slept through the heat of the day. The shadows of the coming night were making a purple tapestry of the sand, and the night wind was beginning to howl when he finally woke. His first thought was how thirsty he was. His mouth felt cracked and dry. He yearned for a frothing glass of beer that was icy cold the way the Americans drank it. He imagined that beer: how the head would smell, how the glass would sweat in the heat, how the beer would soak into his tongue and slide down his throat. Beer, lovely beer, how he longed for a beer. . . .

'Kaki!'

Muhammad was so certain he had to be alone in this desert wilderness that he ignored the word boomed almost in his ear.

'Kaki!'

A bottle was thrust inside his open window. A cold glass bottle of Kaki cola was thrust before his parched lips. Muhammad decided it must be a mirage. His mind must be playing tricks on him. He had heard that this happened in the desert, before a man went crazy or died of the thirst and heat and dehydration. Yet he could not help reaching out for the mirage.

He blinked in surprise when his hand seized the icy bottle. He raised it to his lips and was about to drink deeply when he remembered that drinking was taboo for him. He had come to the desert to die of thirst, not to drink from a bottle that miraculously appeared from out of nowhere. From nowhere? He turned his head. Just inches away was the grinning face of a Bedouin.

'You want Kaki?' Again the Arab waggled the bottle in front of Muhammad's lips.

Through a daze of thirst Muhammad wondered what this man could be doing here in the middle of nowhere.

Without having to be asked, the Bedouin proceeded to tell him. He had been out riding the desert by himself, in his pickup truck, bringing water to his family camped to the south, when he saw the car and came over to chat. The Bedouin said he was Bandar of the Al-Murrah, and he thought he recognized this brother of the famous Shaykh Rashid. Maybe he would like to share his campfire this evening? He could erect his tent right here. He had meat, dates, tins of soup, and chocolate cookies. Maybe they would even make a party of it, because four Al-Murrah tents were pitched over that big dune on the horizon. And just beyond that, there were more Al-Murrah. Maybe he could tell them stories about his famous brother by the campfire tonight? Bandar broke off his excited monologue and looked at the sky. The sun was setting. It was time, he said, for the sunset prayers. It was always better to pray with others than to pray alone. Would the *shaykh*'s brother join him for the prayers?

Finally Muhammad found his voice. 'No,' he croaked.

Bandar poured water from the tank in the back of his truck and performed the proper ablutions. Then he drew a half-circle in the sand facing northwest toward Mecca and began to pray.

Muhammad stared at the Bedouin. Even here at the end of this earth, that confounded religion hounded him. Even here at the end of this earth, he was besieged by not only religion but the ways of a people he had always despised and tried to forget. He had been a fool to sit in the sun today and waste his sympathy on a people and a way of life that were anathema to him. Even as Muhammad ground his teeth and watched Bandar pray, a gust of wind dislodged the scrap of paper he had tucked under the windshield wiper. Muhammad watched the truth blow away on the wind, up into the air, out of his mind and out of his sight. So be it, he thought.

As Bandar prayed, Muhammad started the engine of his car, put it into reverse, and left the Bedouin behind in a rain of sand. Like a demon, or like a man possessed of demons, Muhammad drove fast and reckless back toward the main highway. He had tried to end it all with an ironic, elegant arabesque of an allegory, yet his lovely plans had come to naught. The cursed Bedouin would not even leave him in peace to die in their cursed desert. But despite the interfering interventions of God and man, he was determined to die today. If the old way was to be denied him, he would go out the new way. He would die in one of those spectacular head-on collisions on one of those smooth and expensive new highways. His end would be quick and bloody and very, very modern. He would make himself one of those abandoned wrecks in the graveyard alongside a Saudi roadway. It was not the witty and dramatic end that he had imagined, but it would be quick and it would be certain.

It was night when he reached the highway, but he turned off his high beams. He sped along for twenty minutes before he saw a pair of bright lights approaching. The lights came nearer; he saw that they were too high above the roadway to be those of an automobile. Good, he thought; a truck. His own end would be even more certain if he slammed into a two-ton semi at high speed. He pressed down on the accelerator, the Toyota surged forward, the lights came brighter and closer, he could hear the throb of the truck's powerful diesel engine. At the last moment Muhammad swerved hard to the left, into the path of the oncoming truck. The other driver vainly hit his brakes, the vehicles hurtled together, and at the last instant before they collided, one final desperate and involuntary scream, a plea for forgiveness and salvation and resurrection, came from Muhammad's heart and Muhammad's soul and Muhammad's lips.

'*Allah!*'

Silence descended like a veil over the desert.

—23—

The welcome rumble of the tea cart coming down the hallway could just be heard over the drone of the Iraqi minister, who was making an interminably elegant point about the price-cutting of certain grades of Gulf light crude. Rashid fidgeted in his seat near the miniature green-and-gold Saudi Arabian flag arrayed with the other national emblems on the green baize-covered conference table. It was nearly noon on this Sunday morning, and the concentration of the seventy OPEC officials and their aides packed into the narrow conference room wavered. They had opened their twice-yearly conference yesterday with an agenda of routine business guaranteed not to make world headlines. Jet-lagged delegates from the far-flung oil-rich countries of the world, from Indonesia and Nigeria and Venezuela as well as the Arab Middle East, diplomatically hid their yawns. Any minute now they would recess, drink tea together for a few social moments, then disperse through the city to rest up for this evening's official reception at the Hilton.

Faintly Rashid could hear church bells ringing from across Vienna's gabled medieval rooftops. He felt a pang of homesickness and wished instead for flat roofs and a deep hoarse masculine voice calling the faithful to prayer. He was weary of his assignment to the OPEC Secretariat and sorry he was still banished to this cold place. Outside, under the slate sky, a soft wet snow fell on this late-December morning. Below on the icy pavements alongside the Ringstrasse, Viennese burghers bustled about preparing for this week's Christmas holiday. Across the street in the *Christkindlmarkt*, loudspeakers blared the gentle lyrics of carols. Sunny had invited him to spend the Christian festival with her and Sarah in Switzerland.

Rashid glanced around the crowded room, alert to any slight modulations of tone among the always touchy delegates. Next to him Saudi's Zaki Yamani fingered a gold Mark Cross pen. Across the table Jamshid Amouzegar, the Iranian representative, stared with hooded cobra eyes at the Iraqi who was still delivering his flowery, predictable speech. Rashid allowed his attention to drift inward, to his own troubled world. With Muhammad dead, with his doomed and broken brother finally in the peace of death, he felt more inclined to spend the coming holiday with Sunny and Sarah. Muhammad's death had almost but not quite laid something ugly to rest between himself and Sunny. Still Rashid could not forgive or forget what she had done long ago with his brother. Yet he wanted to spend the holiday with Sarah. Had it been only she that he was to meet at Gstaad, he would not hesitate to go.

Rashid worried his chapped lower lip with his front teeth. He would have to come to some sort of decision soon about Sunny. He still loved her, yes. That had never changed. Renouncing her in Saudi long ago had been the most wrenching decision of his life. It had hurt so much to break with her that he was still wary of resurrecting so much as their friendship. Rashid stared at the palm tree and crossed swords on the Saudi flag. In his heart he would never finish with her. Always he would reserve the most secret and needy part of himself only for her. Until now he had hurt only himself by continuing to love her in his secret way, but he had seen in her eyes how it still was for her. He was as certain she still loved him as he was of the existence of God. Yet he did not want her to hope for the impossible again. They could never reconcile. Privately he might still yearn for her, but he could never publicly forgive her for shaming him with his brother. He was Saudi, and she was American. If they had failed in their love when they were young and fresh and full of hopes and dreams, how could they possibly succeed now, in their middle age, after all the dashed hopes of these years as gray as the winter skies of Vienna?

Suddenly, from the other side of the closed conference door there were loud staccato noises, a rattle of broken crockery on the tea cart, then shouts and the sound of running feet. A current of fear coursed through the OPEC ministers. Bursts of automatic gunfire came from the corridor, the reception rooms, the library. The distinguished ministers and their secretaries and translators dived for their lives under the cover of the conference table. In the hallway high-pitched screams were drowned out by swells of gunfire. The lights went out in the corridor. From a rasping throat came a savage battle cry. The conference door flew open, and two swarthy men wearing shaggy brown fur hats hurtled inside brandishing submachine guns. As the OPEC ministers flattened themselves under the table, the intruders sprayed random shots at the walls and the ceiling. The women secretaries were shrieking, there was a terrified babble of Spanish and an African dialect and guttural Arabic, the floor was a tangle of arms and legs and papers.

'Yusef! Put the explosives there!' The command came in Arabic. 'Down there!'

Outside in the corridor the battle still raged. A woman gunned down an Austrian policeman who had already surrendered, then killed an Iraqi security guard who tried to wrest her submachine gun away. In a flanking office another armed intruder grappled with a Libyan delegate, then shot the delegate dead, and finally pumped four more shots into the Libyan at close range before leaving his body to slide into a pool of blood.

An Austrian woman screamed and screamed as a man with wild eyes dragged her by the hair through the doorway of the conference room. Another gunman shot a telephone out of the woman's hand, then raked the switchboard with automatic fire. OPEC delegates were herded from the hallways and offices into the conference room. 'Down,' they were ordered: 'get down!' The smell of blood and fear lay as acrid as cordite smoke over the conference room. Four minutes after the attack had begun, three men lay dead and the six gunmen had captured the seventy most important oil princes of the world.

'Yamani! Where's Yamani?' one gunman screamed in English at the others. 'Have you found Yamani?'

'Allah,' groaned Shaykh Yamani. Rashid saw the lips of the Saudi oil minister move in silent prayer.

'No moving!' The gunmen shouted the command in English, German, Spanish and Arabic.

From where he lay under the conference table Rashid heard more shots, running feet, a moaning from not far away. Outside on the street there was a screech of brakes. Gunmen fired out the window, and from the hallway came withering bursts of automatic fire, screams, the terrifying thud of a grenade exploding inside narrow walls. Choking fumes began to waft into the conference room, and clouds of plaster fell from the walls and ceilings. Another gunman staggered through the door, sank into an empty chair, and pulled up his shirt to show his comrades a bullet hole just below his navel. Outside in the corridors there was finally silence.

Rashid lay still while the enormity of what was happening seeped through him. Terrorists were raiding the OPEC foreign ministers' meeting. The cartel of men who had been able to hold the world for ransom were themselves being held at gunpoint. Dully Rashid wondered which righteous cause this particular desperate band espoused. In 1975, this year of international terrorism, every faction in the world was armed and on the march. Were these German or Irish or Armenian or Indonesian or South American? They could be from anywhere or everywhere, for the world hated OPEC for more than quadrupling the price of oil. They could even be solid citizens from America or Britain or France who were sick of being victimized by those they publicly called the thugs of the world. Cautiously Rashid angled his body into a crouch and peered up at two slender dark-haired men wiring sticks of gelignite to the windowsill. As they worked, one gave the other terse commands in the flat accents of Palestinian Arabic. Rashid shut his eyes and shook his head. He had hoped and prayed in these last moments that his captors were anything but fellow Arabs. Back in Saudi, Rashid had argued that the time was overripe for the rich and conservative Arab states to concern themselves with the needs of the poor rather than the whims of the wealthy. But the cynical, cautious royals had instead continued propping up the moderate Arab states and hoping and praying the less-than-moderate ones would self-destruct. Rashid sighed. Even if the Saudis had refused to make policy changes that might have averted this day of reckoning, still they might have thwarted the raid simply by tightening their meager security measures. But the Saudis had joked that OPEC was headquartered in safe, jolly Vienna, not in lunatic Beirut. In whispered asides, the oil ministers had reminded him of the millions they paid the PLO to let them alone. Rashid had been wasting his breath when he warned them that the more radical fringes of the Palestinian resistance could not be bought off so easily.

Rashid's suspicious mind turned to treachery. Could disaffected delegates from Algeria or Libya or Iraq have provided the terrorists with floor plans and meeting times and even a secret way into the meeting room? Rashid lay prone, his face to the nap of the rug, and gloomily remembered that today's bloody work was perhaps not history's first Arab fratricide. He considered the bitter possibility that Arab brotherhood was nothing but a beautiful myth, more fantastical than the most fanciful tale woven by Scheherazade.

There were more hoarsely shouted commands. 'Up, one at a time, up. Stand up!' Slowly Rashid and the others got to their feet, and they held their arms in the air in surrender as the terrorists frisked them. The oil ministers stared from the precisely aimed barrels of the submachine guns to the face of the terrorist who apparently was calling the shots.

The tall, steely chief of the commando squad searched the faces of his captives until he bared his teeth in a wolfish smile at Yamani and then the Iranian Amouzegar. 'You die first,' he promised in heavily accented English. With the butt of his gun he began to separate his hostages into groups of conservative Gulf Arabs, Third World ministers, and representatives of the more radical Mideast states.

As Rashid joined the huddle of frightened Iranians and Gulf Arabs, he feared the terrorists might assassinate them all in the next few instants. Rashid's mind groped toward a comforting verse from the Koran. 'To the righteous soul will be said: O thou soul, in complete rest and satisfaction! Come back to the Lord, well content thyself and well pleasing unto Him! Enter thou, then, among thy devotees! Yea, enter thou my heaven.'

But instead of signaling his comrades to open fire, the leader stood before them like a general about to scold his rawest recruits. 'Reactionaries! You are the prisoners of the Arm of the Arab Revolution!' With his cold dark boastful Spanish eyes, the young chieftan took the measure of his cowering middle-aged captives. 'Some of you will have heard of me already, eh? I am the famous Carlos, the one they call "the jackal"!'

Rashid stared back in horrified fascination at the Venezuelan-born terrorist who styled himself a revolutionary Marxist liberator of the world. Carlos had gunned down a Zionist financier on the streets of London. Carlos had killed two French gendarmes and a Lebanese informer who tried to question him in his Paris hideout. Carlos had organized an attack on the French embassy in The Hague and was suspected of masterminding the Black September massacre of Israeli athletes at the Munich Olympics. Carlos was a seasoned killer, one of the darlings of international terrorism. Rashid's eyes flicked to the other members of the gang. The lone woman stood with her menacing machine gun at the ready; she looked more savage than any of the men. Rashid had already overheard her bragging to her comrades that she was the one who had gunned down the two guards in the initial assault. The wounded terrorist who still sat rubbing his belly was tall, sturdy, fair, and surely German. He and the woman might be from the Baader-Meinhof gang. The three lean, hard-faced Arabs were probably younger than their lined and bitter faces made them appear. With their dark hair, dark mustaches, and dark brooding looks, they resembled his Khalid. But Rashid thanked God his son was not armed and desperate and lost like these three old young men. Rashid bowed his head and silently grieved for the broken lives of a generation of Arabs like this trio before him, young men irreparably scarred by the corroding impact of acid rage. Just a moment ago Rashid had despaired of elusive Arab brotherhood. Yet he cherished at least the idea of that Holy Grail. Still he liked to think that Yamani's, and his own, chances for survival would have been better if one of these Arabs had been the leader of this raid.

Meanwhile the chilling Carlos paced back and forth before his captive audience. 'Criminals! You have so much money, but do you help your *people*? No, you make allies with the *imperialist enemy*, the Americans! You have the power to bring the capitalist world to its knees, and instead you join with them against your own people! The oil belongs to the poor people of the Third World, and to the Arabs, your brothers, the homeless brothers and sisters of the Palestine you have forgotten!' Carlos pulled a typed seven-page manifesto from his pocket and began reading it out loud.

Rashid heard Carlos denounce the Zionists, the Americans, and the Iranians and praise the Syrians and the Iraqis as he waved his machine gun in the air. 'Pay! We will make all of you pay!'

Carlos chose a British woman to carry his political manifesto out to the Austrians. 'Unless they broadcast our demands over the radio by three-thirty this afternoon, I will execute a member of the United Arab Emirates' delegation. An hour later a Saudi will die. Then an Iranian.' Carlos took another page of demands from his pocket. 'By seven tomorrow morning, a bus with curtained windows will take us all to the airport. There we will board a fully tanked DC-9 with a crew of three. But in the meantime they must send an ambulance for our wounded comrade, who will be treated, then taken aboard our plane in the morning. Every delay, every provocation, every attempt to hinder us, under whatever pretext, will only risk the lives of our hostages. Understand?' The English girl nodded timidly as he handed her the manifesto. 'Then go!' Carlos roared.

As the door closed behind the fleeing woman, a tense silence fell. Below them on the wide boulevard of the Ringstrasse there were the sounds of trucks and police wagons surrounding the building. Across the street where Sigmund Freud once had lectured at the University of Vienna, sharpshooters trained their sights on the second floor of the OPEC building. Sirens wailed, ambulance doors opened, bullhorns filled the air with nervous static. At a command from Carlos, the Arabs shot long bursts of warning fire out the windows at the police vans pulled up in the snowbanks. The curtains were drawn then, the lights were turned out, and there was a dark collective sigh from inside the OPEC conference room as the siege began.

Carlos called for a transistor radio and fiddled with the dial until he found a station playing schmaltzy Viennese waltzes. He glided toward the window to inspect the explosives his comrades had already wired from there to the center of the conference table. He turned theatrically to his captives and then struck a match. As he waved it dangerously close to the dynamite, he watched the play of fear on the mesmerized faces. Carlos laughed, pulled a Havana cigar from the pocket of his brown leather jacket, and lit it. He drew on the cigar slowly, meditatively, and with obvious pleasure. 'Now,' Carlos said: 'now we wait.'

Musa waited patiently as the love of his life sat poring over the latest letter from her brother in Saudi. He had loved his Sarah, he thought, ever since that magic morning when Sunny had first brought the two of them together at her villa in Grinzing. It had been spring, and they all had gone walking in the Vienna Woods, and he had picked Sarah wildflowers and lost his heart forever to this girl with the flashing eyes and the fiery spirit and the lissome body he yearned someday to touch and hold and treasure. Musa's eyes misted with emotion as he looked adoringly at the sixteen-year-old Arabian beauty who already had secretly consented to be his bride. As soon as she graduated from the American School next year, they would go hand in hand to ask Sunny's blessing. And perhaps as early as the year after that, when he was finally awarded his doctorate, they would marry and return in triumph to Cairo, where he had been promised the job of his dreams working on the excavations at Sakkara. As Musa let his gaze wander around the seedy bohemian student clutter of the Café Leopold Haweeka, he didn't see the wild-haired Germans in their torn faded blue jeans and the pouty French in their tight faded blue jeans and the sensitive Austrians in their baggy faded blue jeans. He imagined himself instead sitting with his love at a rickety table in a dirty corner of Groppi's in Cairo. Almost he could feel the sultry heat, hear the honking horns, see the laughter and camaraderie and chaos of the city and the country of his heart. He would rent a flat with a garden, and Sarah could study at Cairo University to be a teacher, and together they would work hard and love greatly and do their best to build a great Islamic nation. In time, *inshallah*, their own sons and daughters might be able to live lives free and unbowed and brimming with contentments pleasing to the sight of God and man.

Yet here and now in the Viennese café Sarah was frowning. 'No - oh, no, Khalid, no.'

Musa took her hand in his and longed to kiss the tip of every finger, and her wrist, and more, and protect her from all sadness and pain. 'Is he ranting on about your mother again?'

'That's only the beginning. Now he's saying the same sort of thing about Father, and Ibrahim, and everyone else in the family except me.' Sarah threw down her letter in despair. 'It's hard to tell with just these letters, but sometimes I think he's getting a little crazy. Maybe he needs me. Maybe I should go see him.'

'I'm sure your father would be delighted to get you a visa.'

Sarah shook her head. 'No. I said it before, and I'm sticking to it. I won't go back unless my mother can go too.' Sarah's black eyes were thoughtful. 'It's funny. For a long time I hated Saudi for breaking my mother's heart, and I used to say I would never set foot back there. Then the very next day I'd sneak into my mother's room and get out her old photographs and put on a cassette of the prayer calls and cry because there's nowhere on earth that I belong except right there where I was born.'

Musa was just about to assure her he understood exactly what she meant when he heard the blare of a radio turned up too loud and then chairs being scraped back as students ran closer to hear the bulletin. He caught the words 'Arab' and 'OPEC' and 'Palestinian terrorists,' and then he and Sarah were hunched over the radio listening to the first details of the raid in which Sarah's father was surely a hostage. Musa took her in his arms and murmured that she must trust in Allah and not be afraid: 'Allah *karim* – "God is generous" '; but then Sarah's wild eyes met his. 'Mother. We've got to tell my mother. *Yalla*, I know just where she is.'

Sunny was sitting in a flat near the Prater, talking about marriage and childbirth and despair with two tired, beaten Palestinian women of an uncertain age, when she heard running feet, then an urgent pounding on the door and finally Sarah and Musa's frantic cries for her. Gently they broke the bad news, and Sunny sank down on a wooden chair at the kitchen table and saw the look of fierce joy for a moment light up the bleak faces of the Palestinians. But then the women remembered their manners and their humanity. They made tea and assured Sunny that of course the Palestinian freedom fighters would never hurt her husband. Sunny was too close to hysteria to ponder the bitter ironies of revolution and reaction and the women who suffered on both sides. She hid her face and cried for the estranged husband she had never ceased to love.

But then she insisted she had to see with her own eyes where they were holding him. In the taxi she mumbled Rashid's name as if it were a prayer. Three blocks from the OPEC office a roadblock sealed off the Ringstrasse, and Sunny stared transfixed by horror at the sharpshooters and the bullhorns and the ambulances. For the rest of that long gray afternoon Sunny and Sarah and Musa wandered the old streets and alleys of Vienna in a miserable daze, until Sunny finally gave in to her impulse and stumbled alone inside St. Stephen's Cathedral.

She hesitated before the medieval splendor of the gold

and precious stones and ivory and shimmering purple satin of the high altar. Soon the church would close for the night, and only a few other lost souls in babushkas knelt to offer muffled prayers in the wintry shadows. For many years Sunny had been indifferent to the eternal encircling dimness of religious sanctuaries like this one. At the depth of her depression after Rashid had divorced her, she had stopped crying out to God to have mercy on her. But now instincts she had thought she had long ago outgrown had led her to this place. She bent her right knee in genuflection, and she crossed herself. She had not forgotten how to make those gestures of worship and respect.

Sunny knelt at the marble communion rail; but prayers did not come easily. She had forgotten much of what she had once known by heart and soul. She whispered an 'Our Father,' a 'Hail Mary,' but she could not remember all the faithful assertions of the formulized 'Credo.' She had neither a book to guide her through the old devotions nor a faith to lead her toward the exaltation of personalized petitions to God. She bowed her head and prepared to leave. It had been a mistake to come to a place where she no longer belonged.

Yet as she walked with a leaden step up the nave, she saw a knot of women fervently praying before the small snug shrine to Saint Maria Potsch. She came closer, she crossed herself, she knelt before the miraculous icon that was venerated by the Viennese as a last resort for those in mortal danger. The simple golden painting of the sad-eyed Virgin and child looked Oriental and otherworldly. Legend had it that nearly three hundred years ago in a small monastery in Hungary this wooden icon had cried human tears. Save my Rashid, Sunny prayed. Save him for me. Then, just as the pure true sound of a young boy's unbroken voice can for one perfect instant fill a cathedral with the essence of paradise, Sunny raised her eyes to the icon and was comforted. She slid a hundred-dollar bill into the black wrought-iron offering slot to the left of the shrine, and she lit a great mass of tall white waxy tapers and row after row of small squat candles inside flickering red glass votive lights. She prayed then, woman to woman, for Saint Maria Potsch to intercede for Rashid. She was so afraid he would be killed. All the news reports said the terrorists would surely murder the Saudis and the Iranians. She was terrified she would never see him again. She could not endure the thought that she would never have the opportunity to tell him what he still was to her. She did not want him to die without knowing she loved him. When those candles burned low and finally sputtered out, she lit new ones and prayed for the safety of her husband, for his return to her, and for the grace of their being given a second chance.

The muted pearl of the creeping Viennese dawn faintly stained the heavens. Rashid looked at God's light and remembered that in the desert Bedouin knew it was time for the dawn prayers when there was enough light for them to distinguish a white thread from a black. Surely if he pulled threads from his shirt and jacket, he would be able to distinguish white from black.

It was time to pray, yet neither captors nor captives so much as yawned or stretched. All through this long anxious night, the oil ministers and their aides had sat rigidly awake while the terrorists paced and glowered and showed increasing signs of strain. After the gang all took amphetamines to help them stay alert, the one they called Yusef had spent hours tossing a grenade from his left hand to his right, sometimes even loosening the pin with his teeth, before Carlos sharply ordered him to stop it. The tension was so unbearable the hostages had sometimes even prayed for the quick deliverance of a police counter-attack.

The jittery night had been studded with comings and goings. The Iraqi *chargé d'affaires* had bustled in and out in his role as official mediator. The voluble, impetuous Venezuelan ambassador had arrived to pay a goodwill visit to his friend the oil minister. As the hours dragged, the Algerian oil minister had begun to assume an important role. He was seen talking earnestly with Carlos and the Iraqi mediator, the outside telephone lines rang repeatedly for him, and shortly after midnight he assured everyone there would be no more violence. In the dead of night, the Libyan ambassador had sidled inside for a mysterious private conference with Carlos.

And most of all, that long awful night, Carlos had seemed to revel in every moment of his role at center stage. He tried out his pidgin Arabic on the oil ministers. He screamed on the telephone when the Austrians sent in trays of ham sandwiches, which his Muslim captives could not eat. He stalked the room conferring with his comrades, he engaged in rambling Spanish confidences with the Venezuelan oil minister, he played the solicitous *caballero* with his handful of female hostages.

Carlos took his deepest delight, however, in toying with the strained nerves of the Saudi oil minister. Three times that night he drew Yamani aside and, in between threats to kill him, confided that from Vienna they would all make a madcap odyssey by air from Libya to Baghdad, then perhaps even to Kuwait, before reaching their final destination in revolutionary Aden. There, at the foot of the Arabian Peninsula, after all possibilities for international publicity had been exhausted, the terrorists would finally do what they had meant to do all the time. Carlos waved his automatic pistol. The first round would be for Yamani, the next for Amouzegar.

Before dawn the stale air of the conference room was blue and thick from too much nervous chain-smoking. Ashtrays overflowed, and crumpled cigarette packs littered the floor alongside discarded paper plates and cups. Rashid looked from the garbage-strewn conference room to the paling sky and thought of dying. He sighed and remembered happier sunrises at home in a black tent in the desert. He remembered a lifetime of Saudi's spectacular sunrises of mauve and bronze and gold. He yearned for the peace of the desert, its solitude, its certainties. If this dawn was to be his last, he would have liked a sunrise so glorious it assured him of the inevitable triumph of the forces of light against darkness. But today the world was still draped in shadows. His eyes fell from the effete grayish European dawn.

From outside came the tremble of a heavy tread, the whoosh of air brakes, the crunch of wide tires forcing passage through icy snowbanks. One of the Arabs looked out the window and gave Carlos the high sign. Like a film star Carlos moved through the forty European and clerical hostages he was releasing, signing an autograph for one, giving another a spent ammunition case as a souvenir. The lucky ones were led into the adjoining library, and the door was firmly shut behind them. Carlos clapped his hands and told the forty-two remaining hostages to put on their coats and get ready to go.

Outside it was cold and dark as Rashid and the others stumbled up the steps of the bus. Carlos stood by the door, the webbing strap of his machine gun slung across his chest as he aimed the muzzle at his hostages. Inside, the woman terrorist stalked the aisle, her finger on the firing pin. The Arabs carried an armory of grenades and ammunition and spare pistols and automatic weapons. Carlos was the last to swing aboard.

Gently the bus driver shifted gears and the cavalcade began to wind its way through the deserted streets for the airport. In the lead were two police cars, then an ambulance carrying the wounded German terrorist, next the busload of hostages, finally another bus loaded with steel-helmeted special-duty *Einsatzkommando* police. At the airport the scene was set for more guerrilla theater. Television crews had already aimed their lights, powered by portable generators, at the twin-engine Austrian Airlines DC-9 that was to be the getaway plane. Cameramen, producers, sound men, and reporters crowded the tarmac in readiness for live transmission of whatever happened. Hidden on the observation decks of the airport building, sharpshooters took aim in case all hell broke loose.

Aboard the airplane, Rashid sank into his seat, rubbed his bloodshot eyes, and looked around at his fellow hostages as he carefully buckled his safety belt. After their nineteen hours of sleepless anxiety, they were all exhausted, rumpled, and bleary-eyed. The conservative Gulf Arabs sat in one silent uneasy nest. The more radical oil ministers from Libya and Algeria and Iraq formed another more confident and chattering group. The Third World representatives seemed alternately bewildered and frightened and as detached as if they were watching a television drama. The plane thundered down the runway, lifted, and was airborne heading south for Arab North Africa.

Rashid leaned back and tried to discipline his overtired mind into rational patterns of thought. Now that Europe had been left behind, the hostages were less likely to be killed during a rescue attempt. But from now on they would be more at the mercy of their captors because they would land only in territory the captors considered friendly. Rashid looked out at the pristine sea of clouds and wondered if the terrorists meant in the end to murder them all, or ransom them all, or simply dramatize their political causes. Rashid wanted to believe that even the most radical revolutionaries in the world would not dare to slaughter such important captives. But one terrorist stood in the cockpit with a gun melodramatically held to the pilot's head, and two more armed Arabs prowled the aisle. Even as Carlos strutted through the cabin signing autographs for the Africans and joking with the Venezuelans, there was still menace to his swagger.

Rashid brooded as he slowly lit a cigarette. If he died today, he would leave unfinished business. Outwardly he had renounced Sunny, but inwardly he had never stopped loving her. And then after he had chosen duty over love and sent her away, he had tried and failed to find consolation in his work. He had dedicated his life to using the oil to better the lives of his people, but perversely

Arabia's explosion of wealth had destroyed the very way of life he loved. It grieved him to see so much Saudi graft and corruption and spiritual alienation. Especially he was repelled by the extravagant greed and decadent indulgences of the royal family. The House of Saud had turned Arabia into a police state, with barbed wire and tank patrols and a network of paid informers spying on every level of society. But most of all, Rashid was sick at heart that the royal family had not used its bonanza of oil wealth to make Saudi Arabia an international moral force for peace and prosperity. Despite the magnificent lies and the fanciful wishful thinking of the Saudi national propaganda machine, even in the kingdom itself there were still pockets of grinding poverty and not enough food for some hungry mouths. Rashid believed that the royal family, too, should have done far more to help brother Arab states where the poverty and the deprivations of daily life were an Islamic scandal.

Yet as he sat on his hijacked airliner with his life in jeopardy, Rashid tried and convicted himself of moral crimes not so very different from those of the royal family. He had amassed a private fortune by being in the right place at the right time and making the most of every opportunity that had come his way. He had used his wealth to enrich his family and his tribe, and he had built high walls around his lavish villas and tried to believe the cruelties of the world could never scale them to hurt those he loved. He knew he was not the only well-meaning Saudi of his generation who had made these compromises and who lived these doubts. He had been one of the first Western-educated Saudis to return home and cast his lot with the oil industry and the profits of private business. But he wondered now what role he might have played in the true development of his country if he had chosen a different path.

Once, when he was a young man of fire, he had tacked a photograph of Egypt's Nasser up on the wall of his apartment in Texas. Once he and young men like him could have decided to be like Nasser and change the feudal government of Arabia into something truly progressive. Rashid hoped it might still not be too late, for himself and for his people. It was not enough that once he had spoken his mind to King Faisal. He vowed he would be truer to his beliefs if he survived this siege. Yet he had been silent for so long about so much that counted, he wondered if he would still have the power to speak his own heart and mind. He loved Sunny, yet he had persisted in rejecting her. He detested the royal family, yet he had continued to work in their best interests. How long could a man repress himself before he lost his essence? Rashid wanted to live to find out. Please, God, he prayed, let me live.

As the plane began its descent to Algiers, the hostages hoped Carlos would make good his promise to release some or all of them here. They were reassured when they overheard him asking the Venezuelan oil minister to mail a letter to his mother. But then Carlos contradicted himself and said they would only be making a brief sociable stopover in Algiers before proceeding onward to a more pressing rendezvous in Libya. Yet the terrorists made wary preparations before touchdown. They pulled shut the window shades, checked their ammunition, and held their guns in firing positions. After the plane shuddered to a stop, Carlos stood guard with his machine gun aimed at the rear door. When an Algerian diplomat tried to climb aboard, Carlos howled at him to stay out. For a long while, then, after the wounded German guerrilla was carried off to a hospital, the terrorists played out a period of tense negotiations with their supposed Algerian friends. As the nervous hours ticked by, the Arab ministers sighed and shrugged and prayed, the Asian and African delegates muttered among themselves, and the terrorists toyed with their grenades. Finally Carlos set the Third World oil ministers free but kept fifteen Arabs and Iranians hostage. After five frayed hours on the runway, finally the jet was airborne for Libya.

On this next leg of the journey the snug, smoky, talky

atmosphere of the cabin began to resemble that of an Arab coffeehouse. Carlos settled down beside Yamani, and while the terrorist spun out a long tale of his past loves and adventures and dreams, the Saudi oil minister listened and nodded and offered sage advice. From one end of the cabin to the other the confiding, disputing, bargaining, joking sound of Arabic rose and fell. The Iraqi oil minister began to argue recent politics and ancient territorial boundaries with the Iranian across the aisle. A Kuwaiti pondered future posted prices for light and heavy crude with a Qatari. Coffee was served, and cigarettes were smoked. All that was missing was the click of backgammon tokens and a blind old man reciting the Koran off in a corner.

All the while Rashid covertly continued to study the three Arab terrorists. Kemal, the second in command, called himself a Palestinian but spoke in the rushed blurry accents of a Lebanese. The one called Salim seldom spoke, but by his round cherub face, his squat peasant body, and his bronzed brown skin, Rashid thought he might be from one of the Dhofar guerrilla units fighting their sporadic Omani 'people's war' on the revolutionary southern fringe of the Arabian Peninsula. It was Yusef, however, the youngest, clumsiest, and most vulnerable of all, who intrigued Rashid. He got up and walked over and offered Yusef a cigarette, and for a while they stood together smoking and talking.

Dully Yusef recited the pathetic losses of his dismal life. His family had forever lived and died in Jerusalem, but he himself had been born in *aam el-nakbah* - the 'year of the disaster' - in late '48 in a refugee camp on the east bank of the Jordan. In the camps a sister had died young of tuberculosis, and an older brother had been killed when he strayed too near the Israeli border patrols. His father had died young, Yusef said, 'of a broken heart.' After that, to support his younger brothers and sisters and his mother, Yusef had made his way to Kuwait to work as a laborer in the oil fields. He had lived in a cardboard shack, and more than half his salary had gone for expensive food and water, and he had learned to hate the arrogant dandified Kuwaitis. Later, after one of his younger brothers had died in King Hussein's 1970 Black September campaign against the Palestinians, Yusef had returned to his family's camp in Jordan and joined the Resistance. In the past five years he had wandered from faction to faction before finally committing himself to the Popular Front for the Liberation of Palestine. 'Our number one enemies now,' Yusef told him as he shifted the weight of the machine gun in his hands, 'are the reactionary Arab states who oppress our own people. First we must deal with them, then the Israelis.' He read the sympathy in Rashid's eyes. 'Join us,' he whispered. 'It is not too late for you Saudis. You can help. You are rich, powerful, so rich and so powerful. The Americans would *have* to listen to you. Fight beside us like men!'

Rashid looked away from Yusef's glittering eyes. Instead of shouldering a machine gun himself, he wished he could persuade this bitterly passionate young man to surrender his own. He wanted to offer him a secure, predictable job in the Saudi oil fields and convert him to the serene pleasures of family and tradition and quiet deaths that came to content old men as they slept. Again he grieved that the best and the brightest of this new Arab generation seemed destined only to fight and die young. Rashid simply clasped Yusef's hand, and smiled, and quietly returned to his seat. He had not dared speak provocative words of compromise to this young man with the cocked machine gun. Yusef's dark eyes had been dilated not only by amphetamines but by a rage perhaps too deep to be quenched by anything but death. Rashid stared gloomily out the window, where a nasty storm was breaking. He was sick at heart for the waste of this doomed Yusef and all his tragic nation. As the plane started its descent into Tripoli, the rains began and jagged red-blue bolts of lightning lit the sunset sky.

'Home!' Carlos cried out in relief. 'Finally! I promise

you, here the prime minister himself will welcome us! Libya will hail us as heroes of the revolution!'

But again, something was amiss in this radical Arab haven. The hostages overheard Carlos shouting into the cockpit radio that of course he had permission to land here. But the plane leveled off and began circling the airfield for a half-hour, for forty-five minutes, for an hour until they were running dangerously low on fuel and had to land. Yet the control tower made them park on an isolated runway, remote from the airport buildings. Carlos took Kemal into the cockpit for another long spell of negotiations on the radio. After a jittery hour and a half, finally Kemal went off to the terminal for a round of urgent talks. Carlos told his captives he wanted a plane with a larger fuel tank for the long hop to Baghdad, but the Libyans were hedging with a string of suspicious excuses. The other terrorists seemed more agitated now than in the first murderous moments of the raid. The German woman crept into a corner of the cabin and began to cry. Salim vomited in the lavatory. Yusef once again began caressing a hand grenade. Every half-hour Carlos went to the cockpit to confer tautly over the radio with Kemal. By midnight the cabin was cold and miserable and ashiver with tension. The siege was in its second day, and the terrorists had kept themselves awake with the aid of drugs for thirty-six hours. The German stretched out on a row of seats and covered herself with a thin gray airline blanket. One by one the hostages fell into a fitful sleep.

Rashid woke up shaking with chill at twenty minutes to three. As he padded to the lavatory past the sleeping hostages and terrorists, through the open cabin door he could see a Libyan sentry standing guard on the tarmac with his bayonet fixed. A sullen mist hugged the runway, and the rain still fell in torrents. Rashid was about to settle back in his seat to try to sleep when he heard muffled sounds of elation from the other side of the cockpit curtain. He crept close enough to be able to distinguish words. 'Ransom,' Carlos was saying. And then the familiar voice of the Algerian oil minister was assuring Carlos something about a 'Swiss account' and Saudi's King Khalid and the Shah of Iran. Carlos mumbled a sum, but Rashid couldn't hear whether it was five or fifty million. The voices trailed off into exclamations and congratulations and laughter.

Rashid sank down in the nearest seat and held his head in his hands and thanked God. Surely the terrorists must just have agreed to accept a ransom paid by Saudi Arabia and Iran. He considered waking Yamani to share the good news, but he was afraid to do anything that could jeopardize their still fragile security. He shut his eyes - he thought - for only an instant; but hours later he was awakened by rough hands shaking him. He looked up into Yusef's piercing Palestinian eyes. 'You must go now. Quickly, before we change our minds.' Rashid and four other OPEC aides were being released as a goodwill gesture, but Yamani and the other oil ministers were flying back with the terrorists to Algiers. Carlos poked Yamani in the ribs, and taunted him, and pretended he was going to put a bullet into his brain. Rashid squinted his puffy eyes and wondered why this final melodrama. He had heard Carlos gloating last night about millions in ransom, but here and now he was acting as if he had yet to play out a final bloody scene.

Yusef nudged Rashid with the butt of his gun. 'Go! Now!'

Rashid emerged from the stale blue air of the cabin into the wet predawn darkness of the Libyan airfield. He ran a few steps, he breathed in the pure heady air of freedom, and thanked God he was still alive. He turned and looked back at the red-and-white Austrian Airlines jet sitting motionless in the heavy mist like a ghost ship. He had thought he would die in that airplane, but instead Allah, in His eternal wisdom, had given him a reprieve. Rashid squared his shoulders and walked with the other released Arab hostages back toward the airline terminal, and his destiny.

*

Rashid was so eager that he ran from the driveway through the garden and up the steps to the front door of her villa at Grinzing. But like the middle-aged man he was, he panted as he stood at her doorway. He would catch his breath before he rang her bell.

It was early Thursday morning. He had slept for seventeen hours in the Libyan hotel room before finally waking to the welcome news that Yamani and the other hostages had been released in Algiers. Rashid had eaten, showered, and tried unsuccessfully to get through to her on the telephone. Then he had raced back to the airport to catch the first flight to Europe. He had flown from Tripoli to Rome to Vienna, and he had hoped against all reason she would somehow know he was on that flight and be waiting for him at the airport. He had been the one whose life was in danger during the long anxious hours of the raid, but as soon as he was safe he had feared that somehow she had been struck down and forever taken from him. He had come straight here from the airport. But as he looked down at his rumpled suit, he considered slinking down the steps and back to his flat and telephoning her tonight, as though contact with her were not a life-and-death matter. He took a deep breath and remembered the resolutions he had made to be true to himself when he had trembled in mortal fear on the hijacked airplane.

He pressed his finger to the doorbell. When there was no answer, he rang it again and again. Surely she would be there. He needed her. He pounded on the door until at last he heard footsteps, the chain on the door being lifted, the door opening.

Sunny's face was swollen with the evidence of tears. But at the sight of him, her eyes lit up and the years dropped away and once again the two of them were young together on Commonwealth Avenue, where she had sung to him that he was her sunshine. 'Rashid!' Sunny threw herself into his arms. 'Rashid. Oh, my God, Rashid, you're safe, you're all right, you're here. They said on television that everyone was safe, but I didn't know for sure; no one would tell me at the embassy. Oh, Rashid!'

They held on to each other and rocked together in the doorway of her villa as if on the threshold finally of sanity after years in a madhouse of their own making. Their arms were intertwined as they shut the door behind them and sank down on the Persian rugs and silky cushions in the living room Sunny had furnished as if she were still in Arabia.

'I have so much to tell you, so much to explain,' he began. But she put her finger to his lips. 'Later,' she whispered. 'We'll talk later.' He tried to kiss her, but she shook her head - 'Not yet,' and instead snuggled close to him as though he were a quilt and she were cold and tired and finally snug in her own bed after too long a journey away from the home of his arms. His shoulders encircled her, her hand curled on his cheek, they sighed and were finally warm enough after the long years of chill. When after a while his hand stroked the small of her back, she raised her head and smiled to let him know without words that their time of waiting was over.

Slowly they drew closer together; their lips touched; gently she turned in his arms so that their bodies pressed together on the soft carpet. There was a new element of tenderness to this kiss, a mutual desire not so much for the ecstasy of thrill and touch as for the comfort and reassurance of intimacy made flesh. He loved her with butterfly kisses on her cheeks and her eyes; she loved him with the faint tracery of her finger trailing from his eyes to his lips to his neck to his chest. They kissed with a groping, growing passion until she staggered to her feet and led him to her bed of feathers and they undressed and lay under eiderdown. For a long while they made slow gentle sacramental love with their eyes wide open.

Finally, in the full faint sun of that Viennese afternoon, they fell asleep cradled in each other's arms.

—24—

As the *bateau mouche* glided under the Pont Neuf, Sarah leaned yearningly closer in Musa's arms and their lips touched and dizzily they kissed until the boat emerged back into the sunlight.

'Paris!' Sarah laughed and blew a kiss to *la Rive Gauche* and *la Rive Droite* of this city of romance and light and perfection. 'God, don't you love it!'

'I love you better,' he whispered, and they kissed again, this time in broad daylight.

Sarah sighed when they broke apart. 'I wish we were married. I wish you were my husband and I was your wife and we were in bed back in the Ritz like my mother and father are right now, that's what I wish.'

'*Saabrah*,' Musa said in Arabic: 'patience.' But as he put his finger to Sarah's lips, she bit it with her sharp bright polished American teeth. Musa grinned at her, then pulled away and lit a cigarette. His being in Paris with Sarah and Sunny was the first leg of the longer journey they were all taking tomorrow to Saudi Arabia. He was along for this reunion only because Sarah had insisted. Even though Musa had been flattered to be already considered almost in the family, he had worried that what Sarah had in the back of her mind was talking him into eventually living with her not in Egypt but in Arabia. She had taken great pride and pleasure in pointing out to him that her homeland had launched a massive and very well funded archeological campaign to dig up the deserts for links with the fabled past. Sweetly she had suggested he might make an international reputation for himself by finding the lost queendom of Sheba or King Solomon's mines or even the Garden of Eden under Arabia's vast shifting sands.

Musa had finally given in and corresponded with the

antiquities department for his three-week student visa. He would spend a few days with Sarah's family in the Eastern Province, then set out for the excavations in the desert. He would do this and more willingly for his Sarah, although he was beginning to wonder whether this adorable little lady of his dreams was made of sugar or of steel. Sometimes she was as bossy as the Egyptian girls back home, who were legendary throughout the Arab world for leading their men around on leashes. But Musa was determined to be everything and to go anywhere and to do anything for his Sarah, today and every day of their lives. He gave her a wink. 'You truly think your mother and father are together, you know, *like that* now?'

'You bet I do.' Sarah giggled. 'We were all set to go shopping after lunch. But then she got that call from him at the airport, and she blushed when she told me that just this once you and I could go off together without a chaperon.'

'So maybe she went out shopping with him.' Musa had been astounded at Sunny and Sarah's capacity for shopping. For the past three days in Paris they had haunted boutiques and salons, even sidewalk stalls, searching for presents to take home to their Arabian family. Musa had trudged behind the two of them as they bought silk shirts and gold cuff links for Khalid, sumptuous black silks and satins for Um Muhammad, an inlaid ebony walking stick for Ibrahim, custom-blended perfume for Nura and Aisha, and scarves and stockings and cosmetics for Nura's daughters. Musa had joked as they piled package after package in his arms that they had asked him along only to be their beast of burden. It cheered him to think of haughty Shaykh Rashid carrying Sunny's parcels all over Paris.

'Mother does not go shopping in a slinky white satin negligee.' Sarah smiled at Musa, but then she sighed and stared down at the swirling waters of the Seine. She hoped her mother wasn't getting in over her head with her father back in their suite at the Ritz. Sarah didn't altogether approve of their reconciliation. She didn't trust that man who had wounded her mother and herself so deeply. At times she still found it hard to forgive him for his long neglect. And most of all she was furious that her father was trying to interfere with her romance with Musa. He said he didn't think much of Egyptians and that Musa wasn't good enough for her. He insisted she come home and do as all her half-sisters were doing and marry Saudi cousins or the scions of rich Arabian merchant dynasties. Sarah had even overheard her father vainly trying to pressure her mother to forbid her ever to see Musa again. But Sarah laughed off her forebodings as she pointed at the next bridge which they were fast approaching. She and Musa had solemnly promised each other a kiss every time they passed under every one of the many bridges on the Seine, and they had kept that promise all afternoon as they repeatedly rode and rerode this riverboat. She laced her hands around his neck, he threw his cigarette into the river, and he crushed her to him and kissed not only her lips but her eyes and her cheeks and her hair.

'We could check into a hotel,' Sarah murmured in his ear. 'We could go over by the Boul' Mich' and find a nice little quiet hotel and be alone together. We're in Paris, Musa. We're young and in love and we're in Paris!'

'But we are not animals.' Firmly he disengaged her arms from around him. 'You are a good Muslim woman, and I am a good Muslim man. We will be patient.' She bewildered, yet she fascinated him when she acted like a liberated American girl one moment and a secluded Arab maiden the next. But if God was willing, he would spend all his life trying to understand Sarah's passionate complexities. He smiled at her as he bent his head and kissed her hands. 'Besides, I think maybe your father would kill me if he saw us even kissing like this. Can you *imagine* if we went to a hotel room!'

She hurled herself back into his arms and kissed him full on the lips. 'I can imagine,' she whispered. 'I imagine our being like that all the time.'

They sat with their arms around each other and their heads together, kissing, as the boat drifted drowsily under the sun. And when that boat ride was finished, they bought another pair of tickets and settled back in their seats and kissed their way down the Seine again and again, until the sun finally set.

Sunny and Rashid stood with their arms intertwined at the bedroom windows looking down at the sun setting on the slither of the shining river. 'Remember when we were here on our honeymoon,' she said as she tilted her head up and smiled into his eyes. 'We walked along the river and for once you didn't care if the whole world saw us when you kissed me.'

'I remember. I remember that, and everything.' He turned and bent his head and kissed her with as much tenderness and wonder as if this were their first kiss a generation ago in the winter wonderland of the Commonwealth Avenue Mall. And then he simply held her close to him and rocked with her in the dappled Paris sunlight. He did not dare to speak another word. Today, here, now, he wanted only to touch her and hold her and love her. The two of them had lost their sexual nerve and had not made love for the past eight months since that one sunny afternoon of featherbed reconciliation after the OPEC raid. He, and she, had eventually owned up to fears that the same things which had sundered them once would inevitably divide them again. He had worried not only that the rigidity of Saudi ways would still be too much for her but also that his tribe would remember too many scandalous details about her and Muhammad. She had doubts not only about their cultural differences but about her own inability to trust Rashid or any other man again.

Yet they had not been able to keep away from each other. Usually they had treated each other as brother and sister as they made the diplomatic and cultural circuit from dinner parties to gala premieres. Yet sometimes, when they had touched by accident, his eyes had taken on that wild-animal flash of his youth. She would glance away then, and cross her legs, and he would light a cigarette and chain-smoke until the sexual charge between them dissipated like his blue wreathy clouds.

But this afternoon, when she had greeted him at the door to her suite in this low-cut white satin negligee, when he had glimpsed flashes of bare white thigh through the high-cut slits, he had known that this afternoon they were most certainly not going to sip coffee and talk about the opera. He told himself he should immediately take his hands off her and sit her down on a sofa and tell her what he had come to tell her - that he was not going to return to Saudi Arabia with her after all. He should make his excuses about pressing OPEC business in Caracas, and then he should go one step further and talk to her heart to heart about why she shouldn't go back to Saudi either. Once and for all he should be doing his best to make her understand what the years had done to their son. Yet instead Rashid held her closer and kissed her neck, and slid the lacy straps off her shoulders, and held her naked in his arms, and touched her breasts with his mouth until she moaned.

Sunny felt triumphant when he threw off his clothes and she felt his skin next to hers as they stood kissing in the sunlight. She had always known in these past chaste months that it would be very easy to seduce him back to her bed. A look, a touch, a word - not to mention this sensational negligee - and she had known he would be hers again. She had not forgotten how she had prayed before that sympathetic golden icon at St. Stephen's for a second chance with the only man she had ever loved. Tomorrow he and she and their children would finally all be reunited; but she had decided just this once to throw caution to the winds and indulge in a more carnal reunion.

'Sunny, I don't think -' She cut off whatever he was going to say with a long tantalizing kiss. As they walked arm in arm to the bed, he seemed to have lost not only his voice but also his compunctions about making love to her just before leaving her. She twined her arms around him, and he kissed her lips and her neck and her breasts again until they fell down on the bed. He wanted to be inside her without even one more impatient instant of waiting, but she slithered away from him on the satin coverlet. 'Slowly,' she whispered. They lay apart, unmoving, not touching, staring into each other's eyes, until they were both breathing heavily from the erotic charge building between them. Then she reached out and traced the outline of his lips with her fingertips, and he shuddered when after a long exquisite pause she lightly trailed all five fingers of her hand from his neck to his chest to his belly, and lower. Always she had loved to stroke his body until he quivered, but this time he would not let her coax and tease him into a fevered afternoon of leisurely desire. He leaned over her and brushed her long silky yellow hair back from her face. 'Beautiful,' he crooned; 'always you are so beautiful.' As he kissed her lips, she was parting her legs and then he was inside her. She had been willing to settle for familiar, comfortable sex that was slow and sweet and lingering, but instead he loved her with a young man's fast hot fierce passion. When it was over, they lay silent.

She would have liked for him to hold her then, and tell her again and again that he loved her, and for the two of them to plan every second they were going to spend together in Saudi. But instead he leaped up from the bed and made for the bathroom. She lay staring at the ceiling and wondered how she could have forgotten the Muslim habit of racing straight from sex to shower. Obviously all those people who always said Arabs were filthy had never been in love with one. Wearily she dragged herself out of bed. As soon as he was done in the shower, she stepped under the warm stream of water.

But when she finally came out wrapped in a white terry cloth robe, Rashid was already dressed and engrossed in an intense conversation in Arabic on the telephone. He smiled at her and waved her over to the sofa as for the next ten minutes he continued his discussion of petroleum prices. By the time he finally hung up the phone, she was so annoyed she almost forgot the two of them had just made love.

'Sorry.' Nervously he ran his fingers through his hair. 'That could not wait.' Uncertainly he smiled. 'Well, that was quite a surprise you had waiting for me. That beautiful negligee!'

'I thought we should start off my homecoming, and our family reunion, just right.'

The smile died on his lips. 'I am afraid I have a little bit of bad news.' He cleared his throat. 'You know OPEC! So many problems with the Africans, and the Asians, and the South Americans. Not to mention always the Iranians!'

'Out with it, Rashid. What's the bad news this time?'

'Caracas. I am being sent to Venezuela. Today.' He had dreaded her fury when he told her he wouldn't be going to Saudi with her. But he felt worse when instead she put her face in her hands and started to cry. He sat beside her on the sofa and tried to take her in his arms, but she pushed him away.

She raised her head and looked him straight in the eye. 'How could you do what we just did when you knew?'

'I tried to tell you. . . .'

'Not very hard. . . .' But she wiped away her tears and made an effort, once again in their relationship, to be fair. It was true she had seduced him and he *had* been trying to tell her something when she lured him to bed. It was also true he had spent the past months gently trying to persuade her not to venture back to the kingdom. Rashid was usually so kind with her, but he had become thin-lipped and evasive every time she insisted she had to visit Khalid. Repeatedly he had talked her into postponing this trip, or persuaded her and Sarah to go somewhere else for a holiday, or even announced at the last minute that unexpected problems with Sunny's visa had made the trip impossible. She supposed she had to accept responsibility for disregarding all the clues he had left about his disapproval. 'It's just that I'm so disappointed. I thought we'd all finally be together.' Two more tears rolled down her cheeks. 'Khalid, you, me, Sarah. You know?'

'I know.' His heart ached for her as he held her in his arms. He smoothed back her hair, and he kissed the soft vulnerable skin at her temples. He wondered if he should after all be blunt and share all his misgivings about Khalid. But he hated to see her cry, and he still believed Khalid might after all welcome his mother with open arms at the Dhahran airport. There would be time enough later for tears and guilt and recriminations if their son in the end failed them. But for now he could not bear once again to hurt his Sunny. As he kissed her on the forehead, he looked at his watch. 'I must go.'

'Already? Not already?'

'I am sorry.' He stood and picked up his attaché case. 'I Telexed Cousin Hussein yesterday. He's arriving in Paris tonight and will be your chaperon back to the kingdom.'

'For God's sake, are they *still* doing that?' She had assumed that by now Saudi Arabia would allow women to travel on airplanes without being under the protection of a male member of the family.

'You always liked Hussein.'

'But I never liked being on a leash.'

'Hush, now.' He took her in his arms once again and kissed her chastely, Arab fashion, on her right cheek, left cheek, and right cheek again. He called down all God's blessings upon her and her journey and her reunion, and then once again he turned his back and walked away, leaving her alone.

The mother and daughter, in identical cocoons of black masks and black cloaks, sat very close together on the back seat of the shiny air-conditioned black Mercedes. Beside the driver Musa turned and aimed a dazzling smile at the women he hoped would one day soon be his wife and his mother-in-law. Yet it grieved him to see Sarah and Sunny wearing those outlandish Saudi masks. In Cairo, Western women wore smart Western clothes, and even the poorest and most conservative woman in the slums would never dream of wearing a mask or a veil. No one, Musa thought, would ever have guessed that these two just this week had flitted like gorgeous butterflies through the trendiest Parisian boutiques clad in turtlenecks and designer jeans and high-heeled suede boots.

'Do you really think Khalid will like them?' Sunny anxiously touched the presents, gaily wrapped in embossed gold paper and tied with glittery red ribbons, which lay stacked beside her on the seat.

'Like what?' Buried under mask and cloak for the first time in her life, Sarah couldn't hear her mother. The few muffled words she had tried to exchange had already convinced her she was not only nearly blind but deaf and dumb inside this stifling black shroud. But when Sunny repeated herself in a shout, Sarah reached over and patted her mother's hand. 'He'll love them, don't worry.'

Sunny bit her lip and kept holding tight to her daughter's hand and stared unseeing through the mask and hoped she hadn't made a terrible mistake to come back. On the long flight out, she had repeatedly tried and failed to get Hussein to talk about her son. She had assumed Khalid would be waiting at the airport, but instead there had been only the limousine and the driver and Hussein's lame mumbled excuses that Khalid, like his father, must have been called away at the last minute by pressing business. Sunny sighed and reminded herself she had had to come back sometime if she and Rashid were ever to lay the ghosts of their loving to rest. Her two weeks in the seaside family compound outside Khobar would be both reunion and test. Even though Rashid still had to endure more long years of banishment in Vienna, she would have to return here with him on visits if they remarried. Sunny leaned back in her seat and crossed her fingers. If on this visit she discovered that both she and Saudi had changed enough, she would allow herself to love Rashid all the way.

From behind the barrier of her mask and cloak, Sarah tried to see if her mother looked as apprehensive as she sounded. Sarah put her arm protectively around her, and as their black *abbas* blended together, Sarah's eyes stared out from her mask to meet Musa's. She thanked God he had been able to get his visa and join them on this long journey back in time to the medieval kingdom of her childhood. She was afraid she was going to need Musa's strong shoulder to lean on if and when her mother finally came face to face with what Khalid had become. Her brother's harsh, howling letters had left Sarah with the foreboding that he might try to hurt their mother in some irreparable way. As Sarah sat with her arm around her mother, she wished she could turn back the clock fifty years, to a time when it had taken intrepid travelers long months by boat and by camel to reach these burning Arabian sands. She wished there were something she could do to spare her mother the heartbreak of trying to make these utterly different worlds converge after only a few hours of boredom on a jet.

Sarah looked out at the ocean of beige sand that drifted over onto the narrow asphalt ribbon of the highway. She feared Saudi's ways still remained as distant from the West now as a half-century ago. She had an impulse to tell the driver to turn around and take them back to the airport so they could catch the first plane out. Her memories of her homeland were faint and childish and shadowed by a heartfelt sense of dread. Until her reunion with her father that cold windy day on the bank of the lake in Geneva, she had been ambivalent about her wistful yearnings both for him and for his Arabia.

Wedged in the front seat between fat Hussein and the plump driver, Musa nursed anxieties of his own. Musa considered himself a progressive man, and he thought Saudi Arabia was the most reactionary of all the Arab states, and so he could think of no logical reason to be in this feudal kingdom. But then Musa reminded himself there was nothing logical about love, and he craned his neck around and gave his reason for being in Saudi Arabia a good-humored wink.

Sunny watched the younger generation exchanging loving glances and wished Rashid were here to look at her like that. Fretfully she wished he were with her today. Once again she couldn't understand why he had acted so forbidding every time the subject of her return to Saudi Arabia had come up. It was hot in the limousine even with the air conditioning, and Sunny started to do a slow burn in the back seat. Rashid should have been with her today. For the first time in many years, he and she and the children could have been home together under the same roof. She resented being here without him, and she hated having to wear this horrible mask again. But she finally noticed that the windows were tinted so that no one on the outside could see them. She threw off her cloak and nudged Sarah and pointed at the window, and they both tore off their masks and took deep breaths of freedom.

'Thank God!' Once Sarah had seen a crazy old *clochard* outside St.-Germain-des-Prés in Paris dangling a dead rat from the tips of his fingers. The crazy old man would swing that dead rat back and forth like a pendulum as he ran through the ranks of horrified tourists. Just so, Sarah dangled the mask disdainfully in front of their eyes. 'I can't believe, Mother, that you used to wear these things all the time.'

'Believe it.' Sunny wiped the perspiration off her face with a tissue, then brushed her long yellow hair with hard angry strokes. 'Your grandmother still wears one. And your aunts. And your half-sisters. And I suppose you would have to too, if you were ever rash enough to come back here to live.'

Sarah wondered if her mother was really warning herself. She looked out the window at the monotonous dun-colored sandscape spreading to the gray horizon. 'So this is it,' she said softly. 'Saudi.' Sarah shook her head. 'After all this time I expected something else.' She shrugged. 'Something more.'

'Don't jump to conclusions, Sarah. It gets a lot better away from the oil fields and the highways and the heavy industry. Out in the desert, it's God's country.'

But Sarah was not convinced. 'You're just a sucker for the desert, Mother. I remember how you made me keep going to see *Lawrence of Arabia* with you.' Sarah laughed and patted her mother's hand again to take some of the sting from her words.

Mother and daughter leaned back and fell silent as, for the first time since their plane had banked over the Eastern Province, they had their blinders off and could see what changes had been wrought in the kingdom. On the berm of the road every few miles or so were rusty wrecked Buicks and Datsuns and Land-Rovers left to decay where they had stopped, just as camel carcasses had once been left to rot to white bleached bones beside caravan trails. Muhammad had died not so long ago in a tangle of machinery like this, and Sunny wanted to tell the driver to pull over so she could pay her symbolic respects to one of these wrecks. When her eyes teared, she told herself the glare from the sun must be bothering her.

'I bet you're thinking about Uncle Muhammad.' Sarah handed her a tissue. 'You've never said a word to me about him, but I've seen the old photographs. I think he was handsome enough to be a movie star.'

'He thought so too.' Sunny wiped her eyes and remembered some of Muhammad's deadlier sins. Yet she supposed that in the end Muhammad, just like everyone else, had finally been made to pay for his mistakes. 'But the less you know about your uncle, the better.'

She donned her new pair of sleek Italian designer sunglasses and pointed ahead at the skyline of a city that had been little more than a village when she had seen it last. 'Look at it! Khobar!' From this distance, silhouetted against the sky, the clean modern outlines and the sheer sprawling dimensions of the town were impressive. But as their Mercedes slowed to a crawl on the congested streets, Sunny met Sarah's eyes and they both shook their heads. Khobar was a hive of frantic commerce. Clouds of exhaust enveloped the town in a noxious smog, and the thick air was grainy from the swirls of gritty sand that blew in from the desert. Even with the car windows rolled tight shut, Sunny coughed and held her cloak in front of her mouth for protection. She took off her sunglasses in the hope Khobar would look better and cleaner to the naked eye.

'Mother, why doesn't it look this bad in the photographs? Everything's so *dirty*! You never told me it was so *dirty* here.'

Sunny took a deep breath of the foul air and shrugged. It seemed to her the entire town had become one giant, teeming building site. Cranes swung huge blocks of concrete up in the air, brown men wire-walked on girders high in the sky, traffic was snarled, horns pounded, jackhammers screeched, and curses rose in an angry babble of Arabic and English and tongues Sunny had never even heard before. She watched small yellow men plodding down streets carrying baskets of concrete and sand and gravel on their shoulders with the patient drudgery of human donkeys. She asked Hussein what nationality those hordes of foreign workers were.

'Many Korean,' he said. 'Some from Pakistan and Yemen. Palestinians and Egyptians, of course, have been here too for many years.' Hussein explained that the big bosses imported Koreans by the tens of thousands. They worked in gangs and lived in labor camps and left the country when they had completed their contracts. 'Koreans very good,' he said. 'Work like slaves. Koreans no problem. Not like Palestinians and Egyptians, very bossy.'

Musa turned around and gave Sarah an I-told-you-so look. Even back in Vienna he had denounced this Saudi arrogance which considered all the world a slave market where human beings could be bought and sold for a price.

Sarah didn't like what she was seeing any more than he

did. She nudged her mother. 'Just tell me one thing. We're supposed to be in Saudi, right? So where are the Saudis?'

Again Sunny shrugged. She was too depressed to talk, and so she simply put her finger to her lips and stared at the sights. Towering reinforced-concrete and steel and glass blocks of business and residential buildings were uniformly modern and functional and altogether alike except for gaudy electric neon and garish plastic touches on the doorways and facades. Gleaming luxury cars waited behind plate-glass showroom windows, there were an unusual number of jewelry stores, and shop after shop bristled with displays of cameras and electronics and appliances. High man-made dunes of sand and gravel were piled in the middle of streets and upon sidewalks and in alleyways to mark the spots where construction had once been intended. Billboards on this corner, atop that fence, and on this half-completed high-rise proclaimed that the government or a ministry or a prince was graciously allowing an American or a British or a German contracting firm to erect this particular tower of modern enterprise.

Yet scattered here and there among all the barely dried plaster of this slick newness were reminders of the not very distant ancient past. Goats scavenged on reeking rubbish piles that looked like the same ones Sunny had left behind more than a decade ago. Pariah dogs slinked in dusty shadows. A masked woman scuttled down a side street. Just off a busy traffic circle a pack of small boys in ragged robes tormented a donkey tethered to a stunted palm tree.

'This is Saudi?' Sarah shook her head in disgust. 'This is my country? But I thought Saudi was supposed to be so rich! Why don't they clean it up? Can't they even be bothered to collect the garbage? I don't know, Mother. I don't know why we came back here.'

Sunny did not know either. She looked from the old Khobar to the new and could not decide which was worse. She reminded herself she had never been able to tolerate the seedy squalor of Saudi towns. She remembered that for her, only the desert had ever qualified as one of the wonders of the world. When she had longed to return to this place, she had yearned to dwell in the black tents out in the golden sands of the open desert. She leaned her weary head back on her seat and shut her eyes and recalled that Arabs never did lavish much care on how their homes and their businesses appeared from the streets.

Arabs always did prefer their beauties to be secret and private and possessive. They encased their homes inside high walls and their women inside dark masks. But she thought she should try to reassure Sarah. 'We'll be at your father's house soon. It'll be better there.' She faltered. 'At least, I think so.' Inside the welcoming shade of Rashid's family compound, she would be reunited with Ibrahim, with Um Muhammad – and most of all with Khalid. Sunny reminded herself that if she did remarry Rashid, she would be spending her visits back here not in the premature decay of this young town but with her loved ones inside the sheltering walls of the family compound. Sunny remembered what she had forgotten about life in Saudi. The mask, the veil, the wall could be welcome defense against a hostile world.

The driver sped out of Khobar and along the Gulf coast where the air was salty and the sand was near. At last the car slowed and turned off onto an unpaved track and then after a while pulled up before high whitewashed walls. A servant opened a wrought-iron gate, and as the Mercedes purred inside, Sunny and Sarah gasped in delight at this oasis of the good life. Clusters of sleek, whitewashed tent-shaped villas were scattered around manicured grounds that looked out on the tropical blue Gulf. There were beds of bright red flowers that were as big as beach balls, and groves of palm trees waved in the wind. Outside these walls it might be gritty, seedy Saudi. But inside was a mirage of the mythical glories of Araby the blest.

Sunny and Sarah had time only to squeeze each other's hands in relief before doors slammed and a band of excited women ran out to welcome them home. Sunny threw herself into Um Muhammad's arms and kissed her mother-in-law's kind, dear, wrinkled brown raisin face. Sarah was embraced by her Aunt Aisha and then engulfed in a tide of shrieking half-sisters. Sunny and Nura ran to each other, but a current of shyness flowed between these two who had always been rivals yet somehow loving sisters as well. For a moment the two former wives of Rashid stood hesitantly apart. But then Cousin Hussein came running out of the villa carrying his and Nura's six-month-old baby in his arms. As Sunny watched Nura's face grow radiant at the approach of her husband and her son, the twenty years of jealousy she had felt for this lovely Arabian woman fell back into another life, and so she laid that old competition finally and forever to rest. This time, as Sunny and Nura embraced, there was no real or imagined barrier to their sisterhood. The crowd parted, then, when old Ibrahim hobbled out and kissed Sunny and held Sarah in his withered arms. Every cheek was wet with tears by the time Um Muhammad guided them inside the main house to feast Sunny and Sarah's homecoming with a freshly slaughtered sheep.

It was such a warm welcome, so very nearly perfect in every way, that Sunny couldn't bear to ask the question about the one pair of arms that had not been here to enfold her. Only when they all had opened their presents, only when they all had eaten their meal, only when they all had drunk coffee and tea and been refreshed with braziers of incense and perfume did Sunny finally allow herself to take Nura aside and ask where Khalid was. She evaded Sunny's eyes, she shrugged, she said he was away on important business. He would return, *inshallah* - God willing - maybe tomorrow or after tomorrow or maybe even after that. But then Nura's eyes filled with tears, and silently she led Sunny over to where her own young son slept in a nest of blankets on the floor. Tenderly she picked up the child and held him out to Sunny. 'He will be your son too,' she whispered. 'One son for us both, yes? You remember in the hospital when you said that to me after Ibrahim drove us to Dhahran? Sisters then, sisters now.' Sunny took the baby and rocked him in her arms and thanked Nura for being so generous with her heart's desire. But after Nura laid the baby back in his bed and took Sunny in her arms as though she were comforting her for a grief beyond words, Sunny could not bear to admit to herself what she was trying to tell her with the symbolism of their sons. In Nura's embrace there was a subtle message about the loss of Khalid. But Sunny refused to acknowledge its finality.

Yet that night, when Sunny lay like all the rest of Rashid's family sprawled out on a balcony, she stared up at the brilliant jeweled stars in the black velvet sky and was afraid. Just as she could see the constellations outlined so starkly above her in the heavens, so could she clearly understand the meaning of her son's behavior. A Saudi son was always, above all, adoring and dutiful toward his mother. It was unthinkable that a son would not welcome back his mother. Khalid must no longer love her. Khalid must not want her here. Khalid must blame her for the divorce and for leaving him motherless. Khalid might even have finally heard the old scandal of her and Muhammad. Sunny stared up at the bright winking stars in the indigo Saudi night and wondered if she had done right to return. She lay sleepless and fearful until, near dawn, she faintly heard the calls to prayer drifting on the wind from Khobar. 'Prayer is better than sleep,' the muezzin cried. Always she had loved the sonorous, sensual bleat of those prayer calls. Even before she had understood Arabic, she had loved to listen to their singsong monotone shouted from the rooftops. Finally she drifted off to sleep, lulled as if by a lullaby, while around her on the rooftops men and women and children rubbed their eyes and crawled to their feet and made their ablutions and lined up to perform the dawn prayers.

Several nights later Sarah lay in wait until long after midnight, when she was sure her mother was fast asleep, before she crept in from the rooftops and slipped on a mask and cloak and tiptoed down to where Hussein was waiting for her in the garage.

'Is that my little Sarah?' he whispered.

She grinned behind her mask at the fat jolly man who had, it seemed, finally made Nura happy. '*Aywah!*'

Hussein took her hand lest she stumble as he led her stealthily out the front gate and helped her inside the bright blue pickup truck he had parked outside the wall. Yet he ruined his elaborate precautions to keep his niece's rendezvous secret when he playfully sounded the horn as he ground the truck into gear. '*Yalla!*'

Sarah laughed as she ripped off her mask and let her cloak fall to her shoulders. At moments like this, racing through the midnight desert on a clandestine mission, she felt wilder and freer here at home than she ever had barefaced in Boston or Geneva or Vienna. She had been talking nonstop to her half-sisters ever since she had thrown herself into their arms three days ago. She had sat at her grandmother's feet and confided her hopes and dreams about how wonderful life was going to be once she married Musa. So wrapped up with her family had she been that she had scarcely noticed when Musa went off to visit the Saudi archeological excavations deep in the Empty Quarter. She had forgotten how secure it could feel to be snug in the bosom of her family. But the smile died on her lips as she thought of her coming reunion with the one who had so far done his best to wreck that illusion of family security.

'You've seen him, uncle, talked with him. Maybe you can tell me what to expect when I finally get to see my brother.'

Hussein shrugged. 'Khalid is Khalid.' He reached down and, to forestall a repetition of other questions he couldn't or wouldn't answer, he inserted a tape into the truck's cassette machine.

Sarah waited for the melodramatic whine of an Arab love song to boom out of the speakers, but instead an old man's voice began to drone verses from the Koran. Hussein was subtler than she had thought. Instead of telling Sarah about Khalid, he had vividly painted the limits, the excesses, and the triumphs of his nephew's character by playing an electronic rendition of the Koran.

She had expected this to be a long mad dash across the desert; but Hussein braked and slid off the road onto an oil track when they were less than half an hour away from the compound. Expertly he settled into a nest of limp dunes lying silvery in the moonlight. Then he pointed down in the next valley at a red pickup truck parked beside a lone black tent. 'He waits there.'

Sarah already had the car door open and was running ankle deep in the soft sand. 'Khalid! Brother! It's me!' A slender ghostly figure in white ducked from inside the tent and waved and ran to meet her more than halfway. They laughed as they collided, and he lifted her off the ground and swung her round and round in his arms. She was breathless when he finally put her down, and her eyes danced as she feasted on the brother she had always adored. He was tall now, even taller than their father, and bony thin, and his bristling black beard needed to be trimmed and shaped. Yet she would have known her big brother anywhere. 'You look wonderful.'

He kept his arm protectively around her as he led her inside his tent. 'And you are beautiful. Not at all the funny little duck of a girl I remember.'

'Khalid! You take that back or I'll get right back in the car and go away for another ten years.'

'You were always beautiful, little sister.' He kissed her firmly on her right cheek, on her left cheek, on her right cheek once again. 'Don't go away and leave me all alone again. Please don't, Sarah.'

Her eyes were wet as she followed him inside the tent, and they sat back on their haunches and drank the coffee he brewed, and they began to talk about everything except their mother. She told him all the things she had never quite been able to write him in her letters about what it was like living in exile in America and Europe. And he entertained her with a lively rendition of a decade of family gossip.

She leaned forward confidentially, then, and began to tell him about the man she loved, but she faltered when his face suddenly darkened and he fired a series of questions. Did this Eygptian pray five times a day? Did he keep the Ramadan fast? Could he recite the Koran? Yet even though she assured him that Musa was as pious as a *mullah*, Khalid stalked back and forth in the tent in outrage that his sister wanted to marry a man from Cairo. 'Egyptians!' he muttered. 'They all have spines of rubber; they're not true Arabs; only Allah knows if they are even true Muslims!'

Sarah bowed her head in despair as she listened to the brother she loved raging about the man she was determined to marry. She would take Musa as her husband whether Khalid or even her own father liked it or not, but she was sick at heart to hear her brother rave like this. She could not imagine how the gentle little boy she had shadowed with devotion for the happy first years of her life had turned into this ferocious young bigot.

Khalid suddenly broke off his attack on Musa, smiled radiantly, snapped his fingers, and said he could choose a good pious Muslim husband for his sister from among his comrades who followed the true path of Allah. He sat back down, and for a while as he told her about the greatness of Juhayman and the brotherhood of his followers, Khalid's face glowed with a beatific peace. Khalid told her admiringly that Juhayman was so intense and wild-eyed that he was nicknamed *el-wahash*, 'the one who is like a wild beast.'

But then Khalid's face darkened again, and his voice rose in anguish as he told her how the cowards at the university had wrongfully expelled Juhayman when he spoke out against the corruptions of the royal family. 'The House of Saud!' Khalid's voice was a hiss. 'Juhayman is right that we must rise up and cleanse the kingdom of the

House of Saud! The Holy Koran says it is the duty of all Muslims to depose a ruler who lives not and rules not according to God's laws. We must revolt, as Juhayman says! We must establish a true Islamic republic here in the Muslim heart of Arabia! For too long the House of Saud has been corrupting the kingdom with the foul stench of Western ways! Juhayman says, and Juhayman is right, that the radio, television, video machines, telephones, and telegraphs spread lies from one end of the kingdom to the other. Men miss the calls to prayer and instead assemble in stadiums to watch paid athletes play the devil game of soccer. And the blame for all these horrors can be laid at the perfumed and impure feet of the royal family. Its princes are known throughout the world for their gambling and their whoring and their drunkenness and their drug addiction and their decadence. Juhayman says it is almost time to right these wrongs. First Saudi Arabia, and then all Islam, must be made clean and pure. We are almost ready, little sister! And when we are ready, we will strike and cut off the head of the snake!'

Sarah did not dare to interrupt his tirade even after Khalid's breathing was normal again. Instead she leaned over, took his hands in hers, and kissed them, and then she drew Khalid's head into her lap and stroked his curly hair. She crooned to him as though he were not her brother but her son. 'We should never have left you,' she finally whispered. 'Mother and I never should have left you alone here. My brother, my brother, what have they done to you, my brother?' After a long while, then, she asked him what she had to ask him. 'Will you come to the villa and see her?'

His black eyes stared up into her black eyes, and he shuddered and shook his head. 'I hope not.'

'I think you should, Khalid. It will break her heart if you don't come.'

'Break her heart?' Khalid laughed bitterly. 'What do you, or she, know about a breaking heart?' He stood and pulled back the flap of his tent. 'Pray, little sister, not that

I come to see her but that I do *not* come.' He looked up at the faint gray predawn sky. 'Enough; you must go. We must make another goodbye.'

'Khalid, I think –'

He put his finger to her lips to silence her. Swiftly, then, he embraced her and resolutely led her out of the tent and up the dune to where Hussein was parked. As her uncle started the engine, Sarah watched her brother walk back to his lonely tent pitched under the cold night sky.

A week later Sunny, Um Muhammad, and Nura drowsed in the shade of the family's palm grove. It was deep in the heavy heat of the long hours of late afternoon, and most of the other women in the family were fast asleep in the villas. But Sunny was still bravely fighting off the comatose rhythm of daily siestas. Already half her visit here had slipped away with the speed and nonchalance of a deep breath. She and Sarah had spent happy days striking out into the desert to visit Al-Murrah who still kept to the old ways. They had spent gorgeous afternoons sliding atop the luminous phosphorescent waters of the Gulf in one of Rashid's sailboats. And mostly, every morning, every evening, they had gone visiting all the intricately woven webs of aunts and cousins, of sisters and grandmothers, of in-laws and stepdaughters of aunts and cousins and sisters and grandmothers, so that it seemed they were destined to visit every household that women called home in the kingdom's entire sprawling Eastern Province. But today Sarah had rushed off with two of her half-sisters to shop for bargains in jewelry at the gold souks of Khobar.

Sunny sat content in the sultry palm shadows. After lunch she had said she would sit awhile in the shade and sew bridal clothes for one of Nura's about-to-be-married daughters. She had almost forgotten how serene it could make her feel to be here, how mercifully uneventful and soothing it could be to sit back and smile and let whatever would happen happen. Her gaze fell on Nura, asleep in her chair, and she was glad her old rival had finally found happiness in marriage with her Hussein. Last year, when Nura had defied the doctors and risked another pregnancy, she had checked into a London hospital and had another cesarean. Finally, she had been delivered of the son for whom she had always yearned. Sunny thanked God that at least there had been a happy ending for Nura.

But it was very hot, and Sunny would sew one gold sequin on the orange satin bodice, then she would yawn, and her eyes would flutter shut. She would wake with a start then, and take another stitch, and let herself think and dream. Mostly her thoughts were of the lost years spent away from this slumbering land. It was a relief to be back drifting in these quiet currents, and it was a revelation to be back in this secluded world of women. Sunny loved the daily visits to all the many tiers of Rashid's women. She loved sitting with them sipping tea, hearing confidences about their husbands and their children and their desires and fears. It was to be with and to help and to understand all the many needy varieties of modern Arab women - the quiet desperate barren women, the triumphant glorious twittering women, the troubled seething repressed women - that she had begun her graduate studies years ago. It had been the memory of women like this that had led her to the Arab community of Vienna.

But now, back in Saudi, Sunny finally understood that her real life's work might lie not with the transplanted Arab women who drooped in Europe and America but back here in Saudi among women like her mother-in-law, Um Muhammad, and her sister-in-law, Aisha, and Nura's seven nubile daughters. The women Sunny had known and loved in Saudi were as likely to be powerful and fulfilled as they were to be passive and neurotic. She loved the emotional warmth that can radiate from an earth mother's hearth. To Sunny, as to the women of Saudi, the family was the emotional bread of life. She wished she could sit eternally under this palm tree and try to knit these various threads of insight and thought into a fabric of higher meaning. As a psychologist, she thought she might be able to do exciting work here in Saudi. If she and Rashid were to remarry and eventually return here, perhaps in this segregated women's society she might finally begin the most important work of her life. But these were dense, heavy thoughts for such a hot, humid afternoon. Sunny's eyelids drooped, and the needle fell from her fingers.

Sagely Um Muhammad watched sleep claim the one she still called her American daughter. In a moment she would summon one of the servants to fetch cushions so Sunny could sleep in greater comfort. But just then Um Muhammad heard the swing of the front gate and the crunch of tires on gravel. She shaded her eyes with her hand and watched Khalid's red pickup truck pull into the compound. At once Um Muhammad woke Nura, and both women scrambled to their feet. Khalid had promised them he would try to stay away until his mother had gone. Um Muhammad and Nura rushed over, they embraced Khalid, they talked, they gestured and argued with their hands. Finally Um Muhammad pointed to the palm grove and shook her head, and she and Nura walked with their shoulders stooped in defeat back inside the main villa.

Khalid stood for some moments looking at his mother sleeping under the date palm. He had not seen her since that awful day when he had betrayed her years ago at the Dorchester. And in those years he had forgotten how to love her and learned how to hate her. He had begun to believe what he had heard about her. She was a creature of darkness, and she had tempted both his father and his uncle to impure acts. Yet this pale white woman with her long straight yellow hair spread loose on her shoulders like a virgin did not look like sin made flesh. She looked like the mother he had lost long ago. As she slept so near now, he remembered when he had loved his mother more than anyone else in the world, how he had clung to her, how he had lived for her smiles, how she had once been the embodiment of all that was good and true and tender in his world.

Khalid fought an impulse to tiptoe over to his sleeping mother, to kneel at her feet, and to put his aching head in her lap. It seemed to him, for one weak, wavering instant, that it would be right for him to welcome her - and himself - home. Instead, Khalid climbed back into his truck and almost backed out of the driveway and away from her temptations. It would be easy to stay away for the few more days until she left. He could let her go away without speaking the bitter words that burned like acid in his mouth. He could let his silence and his absence speak an eloquent rebuff. But then Khalid hardened his heart against such girlish sentiment. The righteous path to Allah's grace, he reminded himself, was stony and steep. He climbed back down from his truck, squared his shoulders, and remembered what he had promised Juhayman in Riyadh yesterday. Stone the whore. He had promised he would at least symbolically stone the whore. Khalid slammed the truck door shut so that she would wake up and face his judgment.

Sunny's eyes opened, and she looked around in confusion. 'Um Muhammad?' But her mother-in-law and Nura were gone. She saw a splash of color in the driveway, then an unfamiliar truck, and finally the tall spare youth in an immaculate starched white robe and head scarf. The young man was standing almost hidden in the shadows of a palm tree, and so Sunny couldn't get a look at him. He must be one of the cousins, she decided. Since Rashid had become so rich, it seemed that most of the thousands of Al-Murrah tribesmen claimed to be his cousin. But then she remembered the gatekeeper would admit only very close male relatives inside this compound where Rashid's women walked with their faces bare to the sun. She would welcome the visitor and call for one of the servants to serve him coffee. Sunny groped for her sunglasses and stood up so she could begin to fulfill the demands of hospitality.

'Stay where you are.'

To Sunny, the youth's voice seemed familiar. She tried to remember if she had met this young man this week at one of the family gatherings. She squinted and saw that his skin was nearly as fair as her own, but his features - his aquiline nose, deep-set limpid dark eyes, narrow lips - were purely Arab. She thought she saw a family resemblance not only in his face but in the arrogance of his carriage. She tried to remember which aunt had sons his age. 'Welcome,' she said. 'I welcome you to the house of my husband.' She prepared to begin the long, convoluted courteous ritual of host welcoming guest.

But the youth did not respond as he was supposed to. 'The house of your husband?' His tone was mocking. 'What husband is that?'

'Rashid *ibn* Abdullah *ibn* Ibrahim *ibn* Khalid.'

'I know this man,' the youth said. 'And he *has* no wife now.'

'I am Sunny Shannon.' She continued to stare in confusion at the young man in the shadows who was questioning her so rudely. She had seen him before and heard him before. But his voice and his face came from deeper in her past. 'And you? Who are you?'

'By Allah, you don't know? In the name of Allah, you can't guess?' The youth walked out of the shadows and into the sun.

Sunny stared transfixed for a moment, and then her face lit up. 'Khalid! My son! You came! I knew you would!' She opened her arms, she took several quick running steps toward him, but she stopped when he roared for her to come no closer.

'Stop there, stay there, I tell you to stand where you are, woman. From here I can see all of you I want to see, woman.' Khalid's voice was low and husky with emotion. 'Finally you return. Finally you bring your sickness and your sin back here to pollute us. First my uncle, then my father! But you will not corrupt me! You will not fool me, trick me, ensnare me!'

'What?' Sunny hardly heard his accusations. Instead of trying to translate the sibilant hiss of his Arabic, she had been feasting her eyes on the fine figure of her son. He was tall and slim and handsome. He reminded her so of how Rashid had been when they were married. She wanted to touch the black curls that surely must lie under his white cotton head scarf. She wanted to stroke his hair and his cheek and walk in the shade of this date palm grove with her head resting on one of her son's broad shoulders. She drew a step closer to him.

'Stop! I told you, not one step closer!'

But Sunny still was not listening. She moved closer to her son.

Khalid backed away. He could not bear for her to come any closer. If she were very near, if he were forced to look into her clear trusting blue eyes, his resolve might fail. He remembered what he had come here to do, and he bent and picked up a dusty stone from the driveway. He felt its weight in the palm of his hand. It was not a large stone, but it was big enough for the job it must do. 'Whore! Infidel whore!' He ignored the tears that had formed in his eyes, he drew back his arm, and he threw the stone at his mother.

She felt the thump on the bodice of her dress, near the breasts that once had nursed her son. She looked down at the brown dusty smear. She touched that smear; she looked down at the ground where the stone her son had thrown at her had fallen. She bent and picked up the stone and stared at it as though she had never before seen a rock. She held the stone out to her son in her open palm.

Again he retreated from her. 'Go away. Go away and do not come back to this place. I beg you, go away, please, in the name of Allah.' Khalid's voice was a whisper. 'You are the great shame of my life.' He turned and fled to his truck, he turned the key in the ignition, the red pickup roared to life and careened out the driveway.

Sunny stood in the cloud of dust, the stone in her hand. She was still standing there in a daze a moment later when

Sarah leaped out of another car that pulled inside the driveway.

'Mother! Mother, *look* at me! Look what they *did* to me!' Sarah pointed to her legs. When she had gone off shopping in Khobar this morning, she had decided to abandon her mask and long black cloak, and instead had worn a demure knee-length red cotton dress she had bought in a Paris boutique. Sarah had looked chic and pretty in a modest sort of way, but she looked that way no more. Her bare legs were coated from ankle to knee with shiny black paint. 'They sprayed me with a can of paint! One of the *mutawiyah* religious police cornered me in broad daylight out on the sidewalk in Khobar. He called me a dirty whore and sprayed me!' Sarah burst into tears and threw herself into her mother's arms. 'Why did they do that to me? It was horrible! Little boys were pointing at me and laughing, and grown-up men were rubbing their crotches! I was so embarrassed!' Sarah wept like a child. 'Why, Mummy, why? Why did they do that to me?'

Sunny held her daughter in the sun inside the high walls of her estranged husband's estate. She could not explain to Sarah, or to herself, how something like this could happen. How a son could stone a mother, how police could attack a girl at high noon on a city street, how both she and Sarah had been called 'whore' in the space of one ugly afternoon. She had no explanations, but she did have one precise answer. Tenderly she patted her daughter's head, and then grimly she guided her inside the villa so that they could pack and leave the Kingdom of Saudi Arabia before another setting of the sun.

Sunny fumed as the limousine swished through the streets of Vienna en route to the Opera. 'You were supposed to come at five, Rashid. We were supposed to have dinner and talk, and instead you don't turn up until quarter to seven, and you say we don't have time to talk, that we have to get to the Opera. Well, I don't care about Mozart and

The Marriage of Figaro. I care about the fruits of our own marriage. Khalid. And Sarah. What happened in Saudi was outrageous.'

'As you like.' Rashid shivered inside his raincoat. Outside, a cold drizzle was falling in the early-October night. Even after all these years in Vienna, the climate distressed him. 'We will talk, just as you like. But later. After the Opera. It was not easy to get these tickets.' Sunny had developed a recent fervent but untutored passion for the opera. 'A premiere! I thought this would please you. I bought these tickets for you, my Sunny.'

'Don't try to sweet-talk me. Not this time, not tonight. I don't care about your tickets, or what you did for me buying them. I've been back from Saudi for more than a month, Rashid, and *still* we haven't talked about what happened there.'

'I was away. Venezuela, Indonesia, then Geneva.' He shrugged. 'It is my work.'

'I don't care if you were off in the Land of Oz. You've been back at least a week that I know of - maybe you've been back longer - and so far you haven't been able to find the time to talk about your children.'

'So you want to talk now? Here in this car?'

'I just want to know what's going on. First Khalid tries to stone me, and then some religious maniac attacks Sarah with a can of paint. I tell you, Rashid, never, ever, have I been angrier in my life. What the hell is going on in that country of yours?'

Rashid shrugged as if to displace an unsupportable weight from his shoulders. 'Saudi - you know how it is there.' Again he shrugged. Rashid had been nearly sick with worry over what Khalid might do if and when he ever saw his mother again. In these last unhappy few years, Rashid had begun to despair that he had failed his son. If only the royals hadn't banished him to Vienna, he thought, he might have been able to reach Khalid before it was too late. Rashid was desperately afraid it was now already too late for his son. Ibrahim had telephoned him with the news of what Khalid had done to Sunny, and Rashid had once again begged the princes to transfer him back to the Ministry of Petroleum in Saudi. But the royals had said they were pleased with his work at OPEC. They had reminded him that they let him come home to visit his family as often as he liked. They had said perhaps it was for the best if he cooled his heels in Vienna awhile longer before coming home to his old job in the oil ministry. Rashid had not even been able to reach his son on the telephone to ask for an explanation of what he had done to Sunny. Yet now pride made him try to assure her, and himself, that everything would work out for the best. 'I think my country is changing, getting better, but some of the old ones are not happy with so much change.' He hoped he sounded more convincing than he felt. 'They want to make the clock stop and go back. It takes time, you know, *inshallah*, to change the old attitudes.'

'Old attitudes! Khalid is eighteen years old. He's not old, he's young. And *educated*. He's studying at a Saudi university, and yet the first time he sees me after nine years - nine years! - he picks up a stone and throws it at me!'

'The old Koranic punishment for the adulteress,' Rashid explained as if he were the narrator in a travelogue or an anthropologist giving a university lecture.

'I *know* that,' Sunny snapped. 'I got his message. But how could he dare to do something like that, as though we were living back in the Dark Ages? What kind of boy have you raised? What has our son become?'

Rashid's quick temper flared. 'And our daughter? What of her? In her short skirts and her bare arms? You let her run wild. Here in Vienna you let her do only Allah knows what with that Egyptian peasant. I have seen how that Musa looks at her, how she looks at him. I tell you, I would like to take a knife and cut his throat.'

'Musa is a fine young man. I would be proud to have a young man like Musa for my son. A lot prouder than I am of Khalid.'

'You let her out on the streets like a whore.'

'Oh, so that's what you really think of your daughter? I suppose you approve of those fanatics' spraying paint on Sarah's legs?'

He shook his head. 'They were extreme. That was not necessary.' He lit a cigarette. 'But she had no business going out in public in Saudi with her face and legs bare. You should have known better than to let her.'

'Everyone made such a point of telling me how things had changed. How everything was so modern now, especially in the Eastern Province. Khobar was supposed to be a new model Saudi city. All the American women from Aramco go shopping there every day, and they don't wear masks and long black robes.'

'Sarah is Arab, not American. We expect more of our own women. And I tell you, sometimes the religious police get a little crazy and spray-paint the American women too.'

'Barbarous,' Sunny muttered. 'Saudi has changed, all right. And not for the better. It's even more narrow and fanatic than before. Now you have a little money, you're all arrogant on top of the old ignorance. What a combination! What a place!'

'Arrogant? Ignorant? You accuse me and all my country of this?'

'Damn right.' But Sunny was glad that just at this moment the limousine had pulled up to the front entrance of the Staatsoper. She was afraid she had just gone one step too far with Rashid. 'Later,' she murmured to him as he helped her out of the car. 'We will talk about this later.'

He too seemed as eager as ever to back away from any final confrontation. He smiled down at her as though nothing were amiss between them as they glided into the resplendent crystal and creamy gold and red plush rococo citadel of Western culture. She was like an intense burning flame next to him in her filmy floor-length red chiffon gown, her long golden hair free on her shoulders, her eyes lit with a rage he had not yet appeased. He nodded to acquaintances as from the corner of his eye he watched her burn beside him. This was neither the time nor the place for carnal passion, but he wished he could take her in his arms here and now and kiss away all her troubles, her anger. He wished he could channel that passion she seemed to be radiating against him into its proper place toward him.

If she were a Saudi woman, he would not be having these problems. Sometimes Rashid wished a Saudi woman had been fated to be the wife of his heart. Sunny was so very difficult for him to love. But he tucked her arm tighter to him and enjoyed the possessive satisfaction of watching masculine heads turn to watch his beautiful woman promenade through the opulent foyer. He loved this exciting passionate woman, he loved all the fight that was in her, he loved her pride and her will and her sharp-honed mind. But he fervently hoped she would stop nagging him about what had happened with their children on that doomed return to Saudi. He had done his best to discourage her from going back, but once again she had done as she pleased.

They took their choice parquet seats. They waved to friends in the loggia, they leafed through the libretto, they did not speak a word to each other. They were relieved when the maestro waved his baton, the orchestra struck up, and the heavy sparkling gold curtain was raised.

But Sunny was not in the mood for Mozart on the frailties of love. *The Marriage of Figaro* was being performed in Italian, the notes in the program Rashid had bought her were in German, and so she was not altogether certain of what was happening on the stage. She could pick out gestures and emotions and the general melodramatic drift of events, but she missed the subtle currents of the play.

Her confusion here tonight, she thought, was so like the perplexity she had always felt and feared she always would feel when she immersed herself in all that was alien in Arabia. Sitting here in her seat at the Viennese State

Opera, she was as much the estranged and bewildered observer as when she tried to fathom all the intricacies of life in Saudi. As she stared up at the stage, a wave of futility swept over her. She would never understand Rashid, and he would never understand her. It was not enough to love each other, to show each other a rare sort of beauty, to soar at times together on notes as lovely as those from the throat of the diva on this stage. The weight of too much tradition and history and culture was against them. Their romance had been born under a dark star. It would be cleaner and kinder to admit that sad truth now and to cut their ties before they damaged each other any further. As the curtain descended at the end of the first act, she nudged Rashid. 'Let's go. We must talk. Now. It can't wait.'

But she did wait to say what she had to say until they were back at her villa in Grinzing. She made them tea, she sat down Arab style on the soft Persian carpets of her parlor, she finally simply shook her head. 'It won't work. We have to face the fact that it won't work.'

He had dreaded her saying those words all the way back here from the Opera. He did not want to lose her. There were problems, yes, and difficulties, but he was not ready yet to admit they were insurmountable. And the Arab in him could not quite accept that his woman was rejecting him. He could not bear to understand what she was saying. 'What will not work?'

'Us. We can't be together. We tried once and we failed. We're trying again, and we have to face the fact that we're failing again.'

'I think you are tired tonight. Discouraged. Maybe you had a very bad time in Saudi. Maybe what happened there was not very good. Khalid is a confused boy, he listens to the wrong people, he did maybe a terrible thing to you. I will tell him this when I see him. I will order him to write you a letter. An apology. Or – yes! – I will make him come here to visit you. I will order him to kiss the hem of your dress. He will do this because I am his father and you are his mother, and it is wrong in the eyes of Allah to go against what a father says to do.'

'No, for God's sake, Rashid, I've had enough of this Arabic melodrama. He tries to stone me, and you want him to kiss the hem of my dress! I don't *want* all that. I just want a normal relationship with my son. And with you. But apparently I'm to have neither. It's too late for that. And for us.'

'Sunny, I beg you, in the name of Allah, do not be impulsive. We need time, we need –'

'We need to leave each other alone.' But he looked so miserable she could not bear it. She stood and began pacing. She would have to offend him, or else he would never let her be the one to end it tonight. 'You weren't there that day in Saudi. But I suppose I shouldn't have been surprised at that.' Unfeigned bitterness crept into her voice. 'You're a Saudi man, you go about your business, you were *never* there when I needed you.'

'You have said this to me before. Always you say things like this that I do not understand.'

'That's just it, Rashid. You don't understand. You can't help it, but you don't understand even when we speak the same language. There's not much we can do about that, other than to leave each other alone.'

'You want me no more?'

'No more, Rashid.'

'I did not want it to be like this with you.' He sighed. 'I wanted . . . what I suppose was not possible.'

She looked at him hunched over like a thin-shouldered old man on her floor and wished she could take him in her arms and make the impossible possible by the sheer strength of her will. But she had already tried and failed to do just that, not once but twice. Yet still there were the children of their love, and for the sake of the most troubled of those children, she had one more thing she had to say. 'Rashid, I beg you, please do all you can to help our son.'

'I do not want to talk about him. Khalid will be all right.

He is young, full of fire, but he is a good boy. I want to talk about us.'

'There's nothing more to say. But we have to talk about Khalid. I wish I could be there to help him; I wish he would have let me be there for him. The look on his face when he threw that stone at me!' Her blue eyes shone with tears. 'Rashid, you must listen to me. I'm a trained psychologist. I know what madness looks like. It's my business to be able to see when someone is crying out for help. Khalid needs help. I'm afraid our son will be in very grave danger if you can't help him.'

When Rashid stood up to take his leave of her, he was in a cold rage. This overbearing, meddling American woman fancied she could love him and leave him as she liked? And as her parting shot, she accused his son of lunacy? Rashid stood erect and haughty and distant as he said what he supposed was his final farewell. 'So kind of you to be so concerned about my son.' He nodded to her. 'And I have a warning for you as well. Look to your own house, to your own daughter, so that she too does not become a daughter of shame.' He turned on his heel, and after he strode out the door, he slammed it behind him.

—25—

One picture, one image, one dream unites six hundred million Muslims from Arabia to Africa to Asia to America. It is a picture of one place, a symbolization of one dream that can be found in flimsy grass shacks that bake in the African equatorial sun, in fetid, flyblown slums that wallow in the Indian monsoons, in air-conditioned stucco villas that look out over the blue Mediterranean, in the lavish marble palaces of Asian and African and Arabian millionaires and generals and kings. The poor rip out magazine photographs of this place and tape them to their walls. The prosperous buy gaudy three-dimensional reproductions which can be made to wiggle back and forth in primitive moving pictures and fix them to their walls. The rich buy oil paintings framed in velvets and gilt and even lit by green flashing neon and hang them on their walls. But always, the rich and the poor share the same picture and the same yearning.

Mecca. Come pray in Mecca. Come pray with the faithful in Mecca at least once before you die. See Mecca and die.

It is the salvation of that message that matters, not the quality of the photograph or the skill of the painter or even the physical beauty of the scene itself. The haunting graphic image is always mass on mass shadowed by mass, a big black cube surrounded by teeming antlike forms hemmed in by high mountainlike man-made courtyard walls. In and of itself, this cube and this throng are not an inspiring sight. Yet desperately poor old Egyptian women look up twenty times a day at this representation of Mecca on their mud walls and yearn to go there, to be there, to pray there, to die there. Mecca means sanctity and grace and a gateway to paradise; if they were rich for a day, they would spend that day in Mecca.

In the *hajj* season of 1979, which fell that year in November, a record-breaking two million Muslims had come to Mecca to pray. The hostels and campgrounds and hotels had been crammed with pilgrims from every corner of the world, for this was the fifteenth century of the Muslim calendar, a special anniversary year. But in these troubled times, the peace of Allah clearly had not yet come to the world. In this season Ayatollah Khomeini's Iranian militants had seized American hostages in Iran, and the Muslim world was divided against itself on whether this act of wild defiance was the work of God or of the devil. Muslim public opinion united, however, in grief and anger when the atheist Soviets invaded Afghanistan and began to persecute God-fearing believers. In the long hot Ramadan that had preceded the *hajj*, there had been public signs of religious reaction even in tightly controlled Saudi Arabia. Posters had been tacked up in the souks warning infidel foreigners not to dare to wear gold crosses around their necks or to let their shameless women walk in the streets of the kingdom with naked arms and legs and faces.

Yet still, before dawn on this Tuesday morning on the twentieth of November, a week after the formal *hajj* was over, the devout continued to swarm past the tamarisk trees on the Mecca Road. The lame hobbled on their walking sticks, the sick were being carried on their stretchers, even the dead were carried in their simple wooden caskets to Mecca for a final blessing.

Khalid *ibn* Rashid *ibn* Abdullah *ibh* Ibrahim Al-Murrah carried one such wooden casket draped in white gauzy shrouds.

He and the five other young mourners seemed to stagger under the weight, as if the body in this bier were the remains of a fat Jeddah merchant, or maybe an obese distant cousin of the royal family, or perhaps merely one of the porcine takers of bribes who haunted the cavernous walls of all the government ministries. But occasionally one of the pallbearers would lean slightly while he mopped the sweat off his brow, and inside the casket there would be not the thud of flesh but a rattle of heavy iron and steel. This casket, and fourteen others just like it on this road, carried Russian AK-47 rifles, submachine guns and enough ammunition to stand off the armies of iniquity almost forever.

The heavy casket dug into Khalid's shoulder as he and his comrades marched toward their destiny at the Grand Mosque. Faint stars still shone in the western sky, while to the east the horizon burned with the coming of the sun. It was cold in the predawn darkness, and Khalid and the others were covered only by the thin coarse cotton of their austere shin-length white robes. But Khalid and his bushy-bearded comrades did not complain on their long forced march toward the most sacred shrine on earth.

Theirs was a holy mission, theirs was a march of consecration, they believed a higher morality allowed them to violate the taboos of their faith and carry their forbidden warlike cargo into the sacred peaceful boundaries of Mecca.

As Khalid trudged along with his silent comrades, it seemed to him that every event in the twenty-one years of his life had inevitably led him to the culminating glory of what was to happen in a few revolutionary moments when they passed inside one of the sacred gates into the holy courtyard of the House of God. Here, this morning, just as soon as a *shaykh* intoned the dawn prayers, he and his fellows would strike a righteous blow for the purity of Islam. They would proclaim the coming of the new *Mahdi* who would return the brotherhood of Muslims to their lost graces and holy destiny.

The casket was so heavy it was digging a ridge into the muscle of Khalid's shoulder. He reveled in the pain as personal atonement for the impure inheritance of his very life. Still he longed to exorcise the personal demon who was his mother. He could scarcely believe now that once he had loved that woman so, that her abandonment of him when he was a boy had hurt him so, that she had so poisoned his soul it had taken years and years of fervent prayer finally to come to his righteous rejection of her and all she represented. Juhayman had told him it had not been enough to throw that one dusty stone at his mother three years ago. Juhayman had told him his demon could be purged only by blood and violence. Khalid was certain Juhayman's answers were the right ones. Signs, portents, dreams all reinforced Juhayman's message.

Khalid had already inclined toward becoming a follower of Juhayman the day he had picked up that stone. But he had not formally committed himself to the cause until last summer, after Juhayman and nearly a hundred of his comrades had been jailed by the secret police in Riyadh for six weeks. Khalid had dreamed disquieting dreams and thought disquieting thoughts, and finally Khalid had abandoned his studies and gone to Riyadh and followed wherever Juhayman led. Today in the courtyard of the Grand Mosque at Mecca, Khalid and his three hundred consecrated comrades would fire the first shots to proclaim the beginning of their righteous movement, foretold by the Prophet Muhammad himself long ago, to cleanse all Islam.

Yet the burden of knowledge of what was to come this morning weighed heavier on Khalid than the weapons in the casket. Mecca was sacred ground. No man was allowed into Mecca even carrying a gun, much less intent on shooting to kill with it. What Khalid was going to be a part of today would defile the shrine. If they failed, and the House of Saud brought them to trial, they would face the death penalty for the capital crime of desecrating Mecca. A foreboding passed through Khalid like a shudder, and for a second the bier tilted so sharply on his shoulder that the guns almost clattered out, exposed, to the ground.

Fear of detection and failure made Khalid stand straighter and more resolute. There was no room today, he sternly reminded himself, for doubts about the inevitability of their messianic destiny. Juhayman dreamed strange and terrifying and wonderful dreams about what was to happen today.

The first dream had shown Juhayman that the new *Mahdi*, the 'right-guided one,' foretold centuries ago by the Prophet Muhammad, was already among them. An obscure passage in one of the *Hadiths*, or Traditions of the Prophet, prophesied that in a forthcoming time of tumult a savior would arise to restore God's kingdom on earth. 'The princes will corrupt the earth,' Muhammad was said to have said many long centuries before the Saudi royal family discovered a taste for gambling and women and wine, 'so one of my people will be sent to bring back justice.' The *Hadith* said the *Mahdi* would be called Muhammad, son of Abdullah, and that he would be a blood descendant of the Prophet and would be revealed at the dawn of a new century. Juhayman announced that

Muhammad *ibn* Abdullah Al-Qahtani, whose mother was of the tribe of the Prophet, was Allah's new *Mahdi*.

A second dream had shown Juhayman exactly what to do with the revelation. Just as the *Hadith* predicted, the new *Mahdi* was to be proclaimed to the faithful before the Grand Mosque at Mecca. The people would rally to him, they would make of him a battle cry, and the House of Saud would fall. From the sanctity of the Grand Mosque the *Mahdi* would proclaim a new holy war - *jihad* - and millions of pious Muslims the world over would flock to answer the call to arms.

Juhayman's third dream was apocalyptic. There would be violence and death in Mecca when the *Mahdi* was proclaimed. Where the righteous battle was joined, the white marble would run in thick rivers of red blood. Unholy men would come to battle against them, but Allah would make the earth swallow up the armies of the defilers who dared resist the word and the flesh of the *Mahdi*. Ten years, finally, after the epiphany of the *Mahdi*, the Antichrist would appear to wreak havoc; then finally Jesus Christ would descend again from paradise to destroy the Antichrist and restore the everlasting peace of Muhammad.

Today, here, now, this morning, Khalid and the others were to play their roles in the great drama foretold by the Prophet Muhammad so long ago and by his follower Juhayman only this year. First the shots and the blood, then the holy miracle, finally the great Islamic heavenly peace. As Khalid trudged through the stone gate and into the courtyard of *Beit Allah*, the House of God, he repeated that sequence to himself as if it were an incantation. Shots, blood, miracle, peace. First the darkness, then the light.

Fifty thousand of the faithful were already assembled in the emerald city for the dawn prayers that would usher in a new Islamic century. But this blessed courtyard that could hold a quarter of a million worshipers was so vast it seemed to Khalid at first sight as though there were no men and women here, only he and his comrades and their caskets of arms, and the great fierce black cube. He stared at the meteoritic sheen of the Kaaba that seemed to glow from within even before the rising of the sun. He would have liked to set down his burden of death for a moment and pray privately before this holy citadel. He would have liked to meditate and maybe even think second thoughts before the action irrevocably began.

But it was too late for prayers or doubt. It was past four o'clock in the morning, almost dawn, and Khalid's comrades were weaving their way toward the front of the mosque where a *shaykh* was summoning one and all to prayer. Muslims were washing themselves and lining up and bending and kneeling in homage to God. Khalid and his comrades prayed with the others. But as their lips moved in the familiar words, their eyes were shifting the length and breadth of the courtyard, watching for danger, preparing for the threats that would soon be brought against them.

'*Allahu akbar* - God is most great!'

As the final words echoed on the lips of the faithful, there was a commotion in the center of the crowd, a tussle, the microphone was seized, the *shaykh* was pushed aside, rifles were pulled out from under robes, shots were fired into the air, the public-address system squealed and then Juhayman's hoarse, excited voice screeched loud and clear. 'The *Mahdi*! Behold the right-guided one!' Khalid and his comrades bent over the bier, ripped aside the burial shrouds, tore open the casket, and seized their submachine guns. 'The *Mahdi*! The *Mahdi* will bring justice to the earth! Recognize the *Mahdi* who will cleanse the kingdom of its corruptors!' Juhayman waved Muhammad *ibn* Abdullah's arm to the heavens. 'The *Mahdi*! Behold the right-guided one!' Khalid and his squad ran, as they had been trained to run, to block one of the thirty-nine double gateways to the courtyard. 'The *Mahdi*! The *Mahdi*!'

But pandemonium broke out among the thousands of

terrified worshipers even as Juhayman's proclamation echoed over the courtyard. Men and women screamed and ran for the exits as the clatter of automatic fire came from here, from there, from near the entrance to the Grand Mosque and at the doorway to the Kaaba. Warning shots, Khalid told himself as he stationed himself at his gate with his machine gun at hip level in the firing position before him. Screams rent the air. As the gunfire continued, Khalid wondered why Juhayman was commanding his followers to fire so very many warning shots. He had secured his own gate as ordered, and as he looked to the center of the square it seemed Juhayman and his crack guard were doing all they could to restore order. They fired repeated rounds into the air, but some of the shots ricocheted against walls and hit the old men, young men, middle-aged women. Bloodstained bodies lay before the Grand Mosque. Red blood flowed in thick rivers on white marble. Khalid shuddered as he remembered Juhayman's prophecy.

Then his eyes were caught by a movement that horrified him even more. A panicked stampede of men were running his way to escape the wrath of God. Khalid had hoped and prayed that he could be a silent, passive accomplice in the initial violence that had to come before the *Mahdi* was proclaimed and all the world's Muslims flocked to their standard. But God's infallible will was sending these profane pilgrims his way, and so Khalid bowed to the will of Allah and clicked his firing pin and aimed his gun to the heavens. Yet still he did not fire. Surely, he prayed, this mob would see him here and turn and go back to listen as Juhayman told them of the wondrous new dawning of Islam. But the mob ran closer. In a few moments they would be upon him. 'Stop!' Khalid cried. He could see the enlarged whites of their terrified eyes. 'Go back!' Closer they came. They were running away from the will of God, the word of God, the message of God. They were running away, and it was his destiny to stop them.

'In the name of Allah!' Khalid pulled the firing pin for

his warning shots. But he had aimed low; some of the bullets hit a ledge, bounced back, struck the crowd. Khalid saw the man closest to him stumble, saw his blood spurt like the arc of a fountain, saw him fall, saw others bleed and fall on top of him, saw a heap of writhing bodies before him.

'In the name of Allah!' Khalid's eyes were shut, but his finger still pressed the firing pin as his gun continued to rake the empty air before him where only a moment before the panicked mass of men had made a last desperate run for freedom. When Khalid opened his eyes again, nothing moved before him.

'The *Mahdi*! I proclaim the *Mahdi*!' In the center of the courtyard Juhayman was still waving Muhammad *ibn* Abdullah's arm in triumph. A knot of zealots surrounded the *Mahdi* and raised their carbines to the sky. They shot triumphant round after round into the air. 'The *Mahdi*! The *Mahdi*!'

Khalid waved his machine gun in triumph as well. He did not grieve for the dead as he stepped past the pile of corpses and made his way to join the company of the elect. As he walked, he saw that his sandals smeared a slick trail of blood on the shiny white marble. 'The *Mahdi*!' Khalid shouted. 'The *Mahdi*!' He cheered with his comrades, he fired his machine gun to where Allah surely watched and smiled from the heavens, and then he climbed the winding steps of the tall slender minaret so he would be ready to defend their sacred killing ground when the army of the wicked princes came against them. Thus had it been foretold fifteen Islamic centuries ago by the Prophet Muhammad, and thus, *inshallah* - God willing - it would be.

Six hundred miles east of Mecca, more than one week after the seizure of the Grand Mosque, in the dark of night Rashid approached the military minibus. He and the government officials assembled in this Eastern Province parking lot had been routed out of their beds by youths with machine guns and ordered to inspect the havoc that had been wrought on their usually tightly policed little corner of the Arab world.

The commander of the National Guard division dispatched to quell tonight's bloody rioting welcomed each bureaucrat. 'Everything is under control,' he said once, twice, fifteen times as the officials filed on board. 'No problem. All is under control.'

The problem, Rashid thought dourly as the bus backed out onto the highway and struck out north under the moonlight toward the center of this latest disturbance in Qatif, was that everything was *out* of control. While the madmen who had attacked Mecca still suicidally fought on from the labyrinthine cellars under the vast courtyard, the Saudi royal family was being denounced by Muslims all over the world for allowing such an outrage to occur. The House of Saud had failed in its most sacred duty to keep the holy places undefiled, and there were those even in Arabia who said it must be deposed for that crime. Then yesterday, here in the Eastern Province, the Shia religious minority had rioted in the streets. In such an atmosphere of bloody chaos and wild rumors, not only the security but the continuity of the kingdom was utterly in peril. One false move and the House of Saud might fall.

As Rashid peered through the darkness of this sullen night for the dusty date groves of Qatif, he wished sharply that his son were sitting safely beside him. In a time of such fear and uncertainty, a man fell back even more on the traditional sureties of family and kinship and tribe. Rashid's mind wandered to his private worries about the son he was beginning to realize was a stranger to him.

Rashid had been at a conference in Riyadh when the first electrifying bulletin of the attack on Mecca had been blurted over the radio, and since then he had searched everywhere it was possible to search for Khalid. But he had found not even a whisper of his son in the family compound, in the nearby mosques, in the homes of his childhood friends, in the ancient haunts of the Al-Murrah in the desert. All he had been able to find was a mounting body of disturbing evidence that there was much that was mysterious and even suspicious about Khalid's behavior. Young men who had once been his boon companions told Rashid they had not prayed beside him for years. With a heavy heart Rashid had listened to them saying Khalid had changed, that he had become forbidding and distant, that he criticized them for not being pious enough, that he ranted on and on about bloody dreams and dark prophecies. He wished he had heeded Sunny's warnings about Khalid when he had seen her that last time in Vienna three years ago.

Rashid finally admitted to himself that he had long ago lost touch with his son. Instead of gadding about playing the international oil diplomat, he should have spent these past years teaching his son the ways of God and the world. When he discovered where Khalid had been stranded during this national emergency, he would start off afresh with his son. He regretted he had allowed him to go off to that hotbed of religious reaction at the university of Medina. It was past time Khalid stopped steeping himself in pious frenzies and learned to play his life's predestined role as son and heir to a great business fortune and an even greater tribal heritage.

Rashid came out of his reverie when he saw an American-made tank blocking the road ahead. Saudi National Guardsmen stood shoulder to shoulder with their guns in a firing position aimed at the sparse oncoming traffic.

'Roadblock,' the National Guard commander explained. 'Since yesterday Qatif and other Shia villages have been cut off in all directions. All were trapped inside.' He snapped his fingers. 'Like rats!' He smiled. 'Now all is under control.'

At the approach of the government van, the soldiers saluted, then scattered so the vehicle could skirt the tank through the packed sand beside the highway. Rashid looked at the familiar grim silhouette of the tank. As soon as the news had been flashed of the attack on Mecca, the National Guardsmen had sealed off all the oil fields, the refinery, the docks, the transportation centers, the Aramco compound at Dhahran itself. No one had known in those first hysterical hours if the Mecca siege had been the beginning of a coordinated rebellion. The royal family, assuming the worst, had prepared for a coup. Someone, anyone - the Soviets, the Israelis, the Iranians, even the American Central Intelligence Agency - could be trying to seize the oil fields. The skies had buzzed with helicopters and fighter-bombers in formation and reconnaissance planes photographing everything that moved. A curfew had been slapped on the Eastern Province, suspected dissidents had been rounded up and thrown into the Black Hole of Hofuf, all communications with the outside world had been severed. From the roof of one of Rashid's villas, he had been able to look out on a roadblock much like this one on the main road to Qatif.

'All is under control,' the commander repeated. 'I am authorized to tell you that all is under control here in the Eastern Province. And that soon, we think very soon, all will be under control in Mecca.'

'*El-hamdulillah!*' Rashid and the others chorused their thanks to God and waited for the commander to give them the latest news. But he merely lit a cigarette and smoked vigorously and blew perfectly formed smoke rings.

The fierce fighting at Mecca had already been the scandal of the Muslim world for eight days of carnage. Sacrilege mounted upon sacrilege. Gun battles between the followers of Juhayman and Saudi National Guardsmen had left hundreds dead in the courtyard before the Grand Mosque, and for the first few days of the siege the terrorist sniper fire from the minarets had been so heavy it was not possible even to remove the corpses. The stench of rotting flesh, grilling in the intense midday sun, had profaned the House of Allah. In the first frantic hours after the siege had begun, Saudi officials were perplexed about whether they even dared to fire against the rebels, for it was forbidden to bear arms in Mecca's holy environs. But the learned Muslim *ulema* had given the Saudi army dispensation to shoot to kill. Saudi soldiers were told that if they died in this holy fight, their souls would instantly gain entrance to paradise. Intoxicated by that heady promise, soldiers loyal to the royal family walked unshielded into rains of zealot fire.

But the followers of Juhayman also believed their cause so righteous that to die in its defense would win them heaven. The rebels fought like cornered animals. When one died, his comrades shot his face off where he fell so the secret police would not later be able to identify his body and take vengeance on his family. The gamy stench of the dead and the acrid fumes of cordite lay like a pestilence over the slaughterhouse Mecca had become. Yet still, despite the best efforts of the elite of the Saudi army, despite the best advice of seasoned American and French advisers, the followers of the *Mahdi* had continued to hold the most sacred ground on earth. If the rebels had made their stand anywhere else, the firepower of the Saudi army would by now have crushed them to the size of grains of sand.

But the Saudis could not level the holy citadel of Mecca. They had to fight the zealots inch by bloody inch with light-arms fire. The Saudis first assaulted three of the main courtyard gates, but Juhayman's men easily picked them off from their vantage points atop the minarets. Then the Saudis tried a daylight commando assault by helicopter to the center of the courtyard, but again the zealots cut them down to a man. The slaughter had continued for one day, two days, three days and still the Saudis had failed to win a foothold inside the courtyard. Finally on Friday, the fourth day of siege, the government forces won the high ground of the minarets and the upper stories of the surrounding buildings. American-made tear-gas canisters were thrown to cover the advance of Saudi forces, column by column, around the courtyard.

Then it was the government's turn to rake the exposed flanks of the zealots from the minarets.

Juhayman and his men erected barricades of mattresses and prayer mats; but slowly, inexorably, they were beaten back by the superior force of the government troops. By the sixth day of siege, Juhayman had retreated underground with his surviving rebels. They barricaded themselves in the warren of cellar supply rooms and prayer alcoves that honeycombed under the courtyard. Saudi officials told the world media they would simply starve the terrorists to death.

But the world, especially the devout Muslim world, was not satisfied by that answer.

The first sketchy news of the attack had enraged the Muslim world. But their fury had to be based in a certain ignorance, for the Saudi royal family had immediately sealed off the kingdom from the rest of the world as soon as the attack occurred. Telephone lines were cut, and the government hunkered down for what its officials feared was a coup to overthrow the House of Saud. Yet garbled accounts of the assault inevitably leaked out, and the first hysterical assumption made in Muslim capitals was that the Americans and the Israelis had seized the heart of Islam. In Iran, the Ayatollah denounced the West and called on all Muslims to unite and triumph over the hated infidels. Furious mobs laid siege to American consulates in Pakistan, where two Marines were killed when the embassy in the capital city of Islamabad was overrun and burned to the ground.

But then more details filtered out of Saudi. Russian AK-47 rifles had been found beside dead terrorist bodies, and the rumor had spread through the bazaars of the Middle East that it was the Soviets who had attacked Mecca, that this was an attempt at a leftist coup by the South Yemenis or one of the Palestinian fringe groups or maybe even some fanatic cells of Maoists who had been training in remote desert camps. But gradually saner heads arrived at the truth. Russian rifles that had been used in the recent civil war in Yemen still glutted desert arms bazaars just across the southern Saudi border. It would have been easy for the zealots to buy as many AK-47s as they needed. Saudi leaders thanked God their own Red scare had been so short-lived.

'We were ready for them here last night,' the National Guard commander was saying. 'We had taken certain precautions. But we did not want anyone to die here. We told them to stay inside. Off the streets.' He shook his head. 'We tried to keep the peace. We tried!' Rashid and the others clucked their tongues in sympathy. 'Khomeini! It was his fault what happened here! We would have had no trouble but for Khomeini! He whipped them up to a frenzy, and they believed that madman's lies! May Allàh curse Iran!'

Rashid sighed under his breath. In the twenty years he had been sitting in the councils of the kingdom, he had heard no one and nothing denounced with so much fear and fervor as Iran. The Saudi royal family despised the godless Soviets, were embarrassed by the insult of Israel's existence, and had nasty but short-lived family spats with the Americans. But it was only and always bad neighbor Iran who terrified the power brokers of Arabia. Rich, militant, grasping Iran at some time or other had laid claim to virtually all the oil-rich lands lapped by the Persian Gulf, and the Saudi-Iranian power rivalry was complicated by passionate religious loathing.

The ancient bitter schism between the Shias of Iran and the Sunnis of Saudi Arabia and most of the rest of the Muslim world festered as though blood that had been spilled twelve centuries ago were still wet and unavenged. Not long after the death of Muhammad, Islam had split into two antagonistic sects over the issue of whether Muslim leadership should be inherited or elected. Wars were fought between rival caliphs, and in the end the most prominent blood descendants of the Prophet were murdered. But the blood feud did not stop with those first martyrs. Those who had fought the losing battle to keep the Prophet's relatives in power became known as the Shias, and in Saudi Arabia two hundred thousand of these Shias were clustered in segregated communities in the oil-rich Eastern Province. Always the insular Saudi Bedouin had treated this despised minority as second-class citizens.

In Aramco's first years in the kingdom, it was mostly the poor and unemployed Shias who had dirtied their hands working as day laborers on the rigs. Even now, forty percent of Aramco's Arab workers were Shias. The most vital economic center of Saudi Arabia was manned by a dissident minority work force. It had been a recurring Saudi nightmare that someday the Iranians would exploit their fellow Shias who worked in the oil fields to foment a revolution in the kingdom. The Saudis had feared that Iran posed a threat to their sovereignty even before the American-backed Shah fell. But after the Ayatollah Khomeini publicly threatened to 'export' his militant Islamic revolution, there was a new dimension of religious hysteria to Saudi paranoia about the designs of Iran.

'They are Shias! All crazy! Fanatics! We always knew they would fight us here, there, everywhere! What else could happen with us and the Shias?' The military chief spat in contempt on the floor of the van. 'But we tried not to kill them. We warned them. We rode through the villages with sound trucks and broadcast over the loudspeakers that it was forbidden for them this year - as it has been forbidden every year - to hold their unholy parades. We warned them, but they did not listen. Fanatics! Madmen! Always the Shias are the same!'

Rashid sighed very softly and sadly under his breath again. He had no quarrel with the Shias, who were, after all, his brothers in the fraternity of Islam. He was even tolerant of their rituals during Muharram when young men in a swoon of religious ecstasy would whip themselves to bloody pulps with heavy chains as a reminder of how the Prophet's grandsons had been martyred long ago. But what was an annual religious festival in Iran had always been absolutely forbidden within the boundaries of Saudi Arabia. Yet for months this year it had been rumored the Shias in the Eastern Province were going to stage public parades of flagellation to demonstrate their solidarity with the militants of Iran. Even before the attack on Mecca, the royal family had feared the emotional frenzy of Muharram parades might excite the volatile Shias into suicidal attacks on the oil fields. Now with terrorists in control of Mecca, the Saudis were in no mood to tolerate even the slightest act of Shia rebellion. It had even been feared that Shia fanatics might be in conspiracy with the Mecca outlaws to topple the House of Saud.

'We had to do what we did,' the commander said. 'We had no choice. It was the will of Allah.'

Rashid gazed apprehensively at the man in uniform. If the rumors he had heard about what happened last night in the Shia villages were accurate, then he was apologizing too profusely. Rashid had heard that there had been rioting in the streets, that buses and cars had been burnt, that shops and a bank had been looted, that warning shots had been fired, that a few of the criminal demonstrators had been shot and wounded and hospitalized, and that hundreds or even thousands had been arrested. Rashid asked the question that had to be asked. 'Tell us, exactly what happened yesterday?'

The commander lit a new cigarette, dragged deeply, and sighed out the smoke. 'It started at sundown. In Safwa, a small Shia village not far from Qatif, a place of no consequence - who would have thought it would happen in Safwa? No matter. I will tell you what happened. I was there, I gave the orders, it was I. . . .' He ground out his half-smoked cigarette and lit another. 'We knew they were going to march in Safwa. I had the crack units of my best men there. We had sealed off the village, blocked every street with tanks, had troops on the roofs of the houses overlooking the square and the mosque. The Shias had been inside the mosque for many hours. We had listened to them screaming and chanting as Shias will. Fanatics! What else could we do with such fanatics? I ask you, what else? The sun was going down when we heard them coming out to the square, singing, chanting. The first one out was their cursed *mullah*, an old man in a black robe like a crow, with a wild white beard and eyes that burnt like those of Khomeini himself. I screamed to him to halt, but he kept coming ahead right at me, right at my guns.'

The commander shook his head, as though he still could not believe what he had seen and done. The hand that held his lighted cigarette trembled. 'You have to understand how it was. The old *mullah* was crazy. He kept marching toward the barrels of our guns, and behind him was a parade of men. Six, eight, ten, I didn't count how many behind him weaving like snakes, naked to the waist, with heavy black chains in their hands. They would scream, all together, and then they would beat their skin with those chains. Terrible! The blood! I think they must have started beating themselves in the mosque, for already their skin was torn and bleeding. I tell you, they were like a vision of devils in hell. Bloody, sweaty, terrible! Hundreds of Shias were behind the devils with the chains, all of them screaming, chanting about God and blood and martyrs! My men were nervous, angered, maybe a little bit scared. I had to do something. If I had not done something, very soon my men would have run away. I screamed again and again for the Shias to stop, to go home, to obey the curfew.' His voice was a whisper. 'Finally they were very close to us - ten, twenty, thirty feet away. I gave the order, and they came no closer.'

In utter silence Rashid and the government officials waited for the commander to finish his story.

'That is all,' he finally said. 'That is what happened in Safwa.' He swallowed hard. 'Later in the night, in Qatif, some of the Shias ran through the streets and set cars on fire and broke shop windows. We stopped them, too. A short while after I gave my men the order to stop the rioting, the town was quiet. It is still quiet. Safwa, Qatif, all are under curfew. Tonight no one has dared to leave the houses. Not even to take away the bodies.' Grimly he smiled.

'I wish to see the situation in Safwa,' Rashid said. There was an assenting murmur from all the seats in the van.

'I will take you to Qatif to see the cars and the buses and the broken windows. There is much to see in Qatif.' The commander could not meet the stares of the others. 'Not much to see in Safwa. It is a very small village. Not important like Qatif.'

'We would like to see Safwa,' Rashid repeated.

The commander shrugged and sighed. 'As you like.' He gave new orders to the driver. They rode in silence until just ahead they could see the lonely meager date grove that was Safwa and smell the rotting stench that was Safwa. 'Only a few hundred people live here,' he explained. 'We think maybe they came here last night from Qatif, from all the other Shia villages, to have their one big march together from the Safwa mosque.'

Under the predawn silvery sky, ghostly Safwa was silent and deserted. The van drove past concrete houses, date-palm huts, ramshackle shelters of cardboard and tin and discarded wood. The driver parked facing the mosque. The government oil officials and representatives of the education and interior and social-welfare ministries gasped and stared. From one end of the square to the other, men and women lay unmoving on the ground. Rashid desperately wanted to believe they must be asleep. Once he had seen a photograph taken in Calcutta of thousands of poor, homeless people sleeping in the open streets. But even in the uncertain light of this false dawn, Rashid could nurse his delusion for only a few seconds. There were bloody corpses lying in the square. The dead lay where they had fallen outside the mosque the night before. Already clouds of flies were buzzing in swarms, and vultures and pariah dogs had very obviously eaten their fill under the cover of night.

'Seventeen Shias were killed yesterday by our security forces,' the commander said.

Rashid's head whipped around from the carnage in the square to the inscrutable face of the general. Far more than seventeen bodies lay rotting before them. He swallowed hard as his gorge rose. 'Seventeen?'

'Eleven here in Safwa, six more in Qatif,' the commander said blandly.

Rashid concentrated on fighting his desire to vomit. He shut his eyes, he rocked for an instant, his fingers dug into his scalp. He seemed to shrink inside himself, and he pulled his red-checkered cotton head scarf closer around his face. He hid his face in his scarf for the shame of this atrocity. But when he finally opened his eyes again, he had regained control of himself. He was angry now. 'The government will say that seventeen Shias died last night?'

'That information is for you only,' the commander replied. 'We tell only you the whole truth. For your eyes – no, your ears – only. The others – the foreign press, the embassies, all those whose business this is not – we tell them nothing. Nothing! Nothing happened here last night in Safwa. A few demonstrators had to be shot when they defied the National Guard. But that was all. Safwa is only a tiny village. Not important. But it is important you understand that. And that you agree.'

Rashid's face was a mask. An animal sense of self-preservation made him avoid the eyes of the other officials. He had most certainly understood the implied threat. The House of Saud would brook no opposition. The princes had wanted their ministers to see the carnage in Safwa. The commander was not only warning them. He was also trying to force their complicity in both the atrocity and the cover-up. Rashid supposed the commander had all along intended to drive them not to Qatif but here to Safwa, even though he had pretended to be reluctant to show them the bloody consequences of going against the might of the royal family. Madness, Rashid now knew, was abroad in the kingdom.

He and the other numbed government ministers were utterly silent as they rode back to National Guard headquarters in Hofuf.

Khalid groaned behind the mattress he was using as a barricade in the storage alcove deep in the cellars beneath Mecca's Grand Mosque. His left shoulder ached from the festering bullet wound he had taken five days ago, and he had no feeling at all in his right thigh. He had been immobilized since he had been hit in that last government attack. He lay in the darkness in a pool of his own blood and urine. He knew he would die soon, here, buried under Mecca, unless Juhayman let them surrender and a doctor could look at his wounds. Khalid longed for the release of quick merciful death. He envied those of his comrades who had already fallen for Allah. Already they were in paradise, lolling on silken divans, being caressed by *houris* whose kisses were as sweet as mango nectar.

Grimly Khalid lay with his rifle propped in a firing position. If the mercenaries of the royal family summoned their meager courage and came at them again, he was ready. He wished they would empty a whole magazine of iron and steel into his wasted body. There was eternal glory for those who died defending the righteousness of Allah. He shut his eyes and let his cramped fingers fall from the trigger. He would die soon either here, fighting in this last stronghold, or up there under interrogation in a torture chamber or by the executioner's sword in a public square at dawn.

Juhayman had searched out every one of his men a few hours ago and told them, one by one, that they could not hold out much longer. The day before they had unveiled the *Mahdi* here in Mecca, Juhayman had prudently secreted a pickup truck full of dates, water, and ammunition down in these unguarded cellars. But their stockpile was running low. For the past four days Juhayman had been rationing dates and water so strictly his comrades were faint. Worse, there was scarcely enough ammunition to repel even one more assault. Tonight or tomorrow they would either have to fight to the death in hand-to-hand combat or surrender to sure slow death at the hands of the Saudis. When Juhayman had asked Khalid how he voted, Khalid had echoed the battle cry he had heard time and again from the throats of his dying comrades: '*Amr Allah* - at the command of God!' Allah would decide how and where and when his slave Khalid died in his service. He voted with his heart and mind and soul to fulfill Allah's will.

Khalid lay waiting for death, yet even though all was mostly lost, he was still a proud, unvanquished warrior of Allah. He and his comrades had proved to themselves and the world that they were God's true soldiers. For two long bloody weeks they had defied the might of the entire kingdom. They had fought bravely, wildly, savagely: '*Amr Allah* - at the command of God!' Yet that defiant scream had rung out too many times. More than one hundred of their comrades had fallen. Now maybe two hundred were left, counting the women and children who had chosen to make this last stand with Juhayman. Together all of them had endured great suffering. They had withstood every attempt by the House of Saud to expel them from their sacred subterranean nests. When they had first taken to the cellars, Juhayman had ordered them to black their faces, to hide behind makeshift mattress barricades, and to wait like carnivorous animals in their lairs for the sinful armies of the Saud. Again and again, day after day, they had repelled the Saudi attacks. Then they had had to endure less soldierly efforts to dislodge them by fire and smoke and electricity and water. The Saudis had thrown tear-gas bombs down the shafts of the tunnels. They had hurled down burning tires. They had flooded the tunnels with water, and then they had tried to electrocute the survivors by tossing down live main cables. They had done everything except unleash sacks of cobras or resort to the medieval tactic of throwing down vats of burning pitch.

Khalid could scarcely breathe. He wondered if he would die from inhaling the poisons hurled at them by the House of Saud. But then he remembered the scores of hostages Juhayman still held at his command post. He doubted the Saudis would risk killing the hostages by pumping lethal poison down the tunnels. The gases were meant to make them abandon their underground fortress and surrender into the clean, fresh, deadly air of the corrupt kingdom.

Khalid could not understand why it all appeared to be ending sadly, wrongly, like this. Juhayman had promised them a better fate than the fetid air of this tomblike tunnel. As soon as they had unveiled the *Mahdi* on the dawn of the new year before the Grand Mosque in Mecca, the entire kingdom had been supposed to rise in their support. In Jeddah, in Riyadh, in Hofuf, in every desert encampment of the Peninsula from the Persian Gulf to the Red Sea, all the God-fearing Muslims were supposed to flock to the *Mahdi*'s banner. Juhayman had assured them that what had happened in Iran would happen in Arabia. Just as the Ayatollah had brought down the discredited House of Pahlavi, so the *Mahdi* would bring down the House of Saud. And the work of Allah would not have ended there. The international brotherhood of Muslims, six hundred million strong, would have united in triumph, and God's kingdom would have been made manifest in this sorry world. The peace of Muhammad would finally have dawned.The forces of light would forever have vanquished darkness. Thus had Juhayman dreamt, and thus had all his comrades believed.

How could it be, then, that the *Mahdi* himself had fallen on the fourth morning of the battle? Half the face of the 'right-guided one' had been blown off by Saudi fire, and the *Mahdi* had bled and died every bit as quickly as the others. Juhayman had never dreamt a prophecy that the *Mahdi* would die like that. Khalid puzzled over the unforeseen death of the *Mahdi*.

He could hear footfalls along the tunnel floor behind him where his comrades were. Khalid heard them coming closer; he heard men crawling and stumbling along the tunnel.

'Khalid, son of Rashid!' Juhayman himself put his hand on Khalid's shoulder. 'It is time, Khalid. Time for this.' Juhayman handed him a length of cloth, and Khalid felt the thin handwoven cotton of the shroud. Juhayman had told them that if he decided they would all surrender together, first they would all wrap themselves in winding sheets. When they gave themselves up to the Saudis, they would already be clothed for the tomb. Silently Khalid wrapped himself in the shroud. One of his comrades helped him to his feet, and Khalid had to lean on his arm as they inched through the tunnel behind Juhayman.

At last they were at the stairs leading to the courtyard. Juhayman turned to face his bedraggled band. 'The fight is not over! We will give them our bodies, but our minds and souls are Allah's alone! Up there, in the sacred courtyard, make them fight to the end to take us! To our dying breaths, we will resist! Cameras! They will have the television cameras there! All over the kingdom, maybe all over the world, people will see us fighting, they will see our faces, and no matter what the House of Saud says, they will understand our cause is the cause of the righteous!' Juhayman raised his arm in the air in triumph.

'*Amr Allah* - at the command of Allah!' The cry was taken up by the zealots. Their battle cries echoed one final time along the tunnels. '*Amr Allah! Amr Allah!*'

Juhayman disappeared up the stairway, and then one by one his lieutenants followed. Khalid leaned heavily on another warrior who helped him climb up to where their enemies waited.

Khalid had thought it would be daylight outside, but as he climbed higher and the air grew fresher, he could see that it was night. He looked up at the sky; the stars were bright and beautiful - so many stars in Allah's heaven.

He reeled when he emerged into the starlight. Then he saw the soldiers wearing gas masks and bulletproof vests, television producers with clipboards and lights and cameras, Juhayman and the others kicking and screaming. Resist, Khalid repeated to himself. Resist to the end; never surrender. Tears of rage stained his cheeks, and he wished it were in his power to kill them all. But already someone had grabbed his gun. And when he tried to stand he tottered and would have fallen but for a Saudi soldier who grasped him by the shoulder. Khalid summoned strength from only Allah knew where and threw off the soldier. He stood with his weight full on both his legs, he crouched like a wrestler, he screamed a dare for them to try to take him.

To a man the Saudi soldiers shrank from him, for Khalid looked like an apparition from hell. His bushy beard was matted with sweat and blood, his white burial shroud hung ghostly on his thin shanks, and he stank like one who had maggots already eating his flesh. 'Take me – I dare you to take me!' he screamed. '*Amr Allah!*' Khalid beat his chest with his fists for the cameras, but at last the Saudis closed in a tight ring around him. He struggled and he kicked and he bit until the soldiers had to manacle his wrists behind him and put irons on his ankles. The Saudi soldiers spat on him, they punched him, they called him a blasphemer and a defiler of the House of God. But still, shackled, Khalid fought them with his voice: '*Amr Allah!*' They gagged him before they led him away to prison.

Rashid paced nervously in the waiting room of the Riyadh jail. Six anxious weeks ago he had sat riveted before his television set in Khobar watching the Mecca terrorists emerge from their underground hell. He had held his breath every time one of the filthy, tattered, savage young fanatics faced the camera and hissed and spat. By then Khalid had been missing for more than two weeks, yet never once as the Mecca siege unfolded had Rashid allowed himself to admit his growing fears that his son was one of the terrorists. But finally, before Rashid's horrified eyes, a wraithlike Khalid had arisen from the depths under Mecca. Ibrahim, sitting next to Rashid on the rugs and the cushions of the *majlis* floor, had sucked in his breath and pointed an accusing finger at the television screen. Rashid had put his arm around the old man, had patted his shoulders, and had held on to his grandfather with all the love and concern he wished he had lavished on his lost son five years, ten years, fifteen years ago, when there still might have been time to save him from such a sorry destiny. Rashid shook his head when he saw Khalid - Sunny's boy, his son, their boy! - kicking and thrashing with the soldiers, being handcuffed, spitting at the camera, screeching and muttering and raving like a lunatic about Allah.

Rashid and Ibrahim had cried that night not only for the shame of it but for the pity and the waste of it. Rashid had been able to do nothing but cry for his son on that first terrible night.

But then he had wiped away his tears. He had resigned his OPEC post, retired from public life, and done what he could do to help his son. He had been deathly afraid Saudi justice would be as swift as it was vengeful, and that Khalid was already being tortured and would soon be beheaded. Feverishly Rashid had redeemed a lifetime of favors performed for court secretaries and assistant government ministers and National Guard officers and distant cousins of the royal family. He had purchased information and attention, and he had tried to buy time for Khalid. He had sent petitions and paid bribes and all but licked royal boots.

Yet still, in those first sullen weeks after Mecca was recovered, it had seemed nothing Rashid could say or do would make any difference. Again and again everyone had made the same implacable gesture when Rashid pleaded for mercy for his son. The courtier or the prince or the minister would hold a finger to his neck, that finger would flick from ear to ear, and the courtier or the prince or the minister would shrug. Juhayman and his followers would have to die because the House of Saud had been publicly humiliated throughout the Muslim world by the blasphemous sacrilege of that assault on the holy of holies.

But first the terrorists were being interrogated by the ministry of interior. It was not only the royal family who suspected that a wider conspiracy must have led to the violence in Mecca. All Arabia still wondered if the Iranians or the Soviets or the Americans or even the Israelis had paid or duped or drugged Juhayman and the others to do what they had done. But electrodes placed strategically on terrorist genitals had uncovered no wider plot. Saudi intelligence officers had learned more than they ever wanted to learn about Juhayman's dreams, about the imagined corruptions of the royal family, about religious prophecies and obscure Koranic interpretations and the approaching raptures of paradise. But finally the intelligence officers had pronounced themselves satisfied the conspiracy went no higher, no deeper, and no wider than Juhayman and his wild young men.

It was then, about a month after Mecca was rewon, that Rashid had noticed subtle differences in the attitudes of the important men he was besieging. They still made that ghastly cutting motion when he asked them about Khalid's fate, but sometimes now they laughed as they did it. They had begun to inquire solicitously, too, about the health of Rashid's grandfather. And one prince from a minor branch of the family had even offered him marriage with his cousin's young daughter so that, he guaranteed, in 'one year only,' Rashid would have a new son to replace the one he was about to lose so tragically.

Rashid had interpreted these new signals as permission to begin hard and earnest bargaining for his son's life. He greased more than one palm with thousands of riyals. He gave others deeds to valuable plots of land. He drew up contracts promising to construct new high-rises in Riyadh at a loss, and he authorized funds to be switched from one Swiss bank account to another. He even delivered a gleaming white motorboat to a royal marina. And finally he cut his secret deal. Khalid could keep his head. The others would die, but Khalid could live. Enough of a public example would be made with the other executions. All Khalid would have to do to save himself was publicly denounce Juhayman for leading him astray with false prophecies. Khalid would have to sign a document accusing Juhayman of homosexuality, drug addiction, and other degeneracies. And then Khalid would be banished forever from the kingdom he had betrayed.

Rashid paced the prison waiting room. In his briefcase he carried the document Khalid must sign. As soon as he was released, Rashid would whisk him to the airport before anyone in authority had an opportunity to remand the stay of execution. He had a chartered jet waiting, and *inshallah*, he and Khalid would be in Vienna before another dawn broke. He had talked to Sunny and Sarah before he left for the prison. Sunny had broken down and wept when he gave her his message of hope.

A steel door opened, and four burly black-skinned guards gestured with their machine guns that Rashid should follow them. The guards carried kerosene lanterns as they marched single file down the winding dark, dank corridor, down, down, deep underground, on stones worn smooth by the bare feet of generations of the condemned, down to the ancient dungeons. The hallway reeked with the sharp ammonia odor of urine and the flat gagging smell of fresh feces. Not once as they walked past padlocked metal doors did the guards pause to look or listen to the wrenching cries for Allah's justice, Allah's compassion. Rashid fought an onrush of panic as they marched deeper into the dungeon. His son, his only son, his beloved son, had lain in this foul place for more than a month. He had hardly recognized Khalid's distorted face on the television screen when he had arisen from the depths under Mecca. What sort of animal would he have become after a month in this hellhole?

At last they stopped before a padlocked iron door. One guard handed him a lantern, another fitted a key into the lock, a third aimed his gun at the darkness within. 'Ten minutes,' one of the guards said. 'Ten minutes only.'

Rashid held the lantern before him. 'Khalid?' In the darkness at first it seemed the guards had made a mistake, that they had opened the wrong door, that no one was inside. 'Son? It's me! Are you there, Khalid?' But then Rashid shined his light into the farthest reach of the narrow dark reeking cell, and he saw a huddled form and heard a muffled growl. 'Khalid? Son? Is that you?'

Khalid rubbed his eyes against the shock of the lantern light. He cringed against the wall away from the threat of the light. He looked as if he were trying to disappear like a cockroach into a crack. 'No, please,' he muttered. 'Mercy, the mercy of Allah, please, mercy, no more, not again, please.'

Rashid wheeled and hissed at the guards. 'You *tortured* him! They told me you hadn't touched him, but you tortured him! Out! All of you out! Shut the door! Leave me alone with my son!' When he heard the door slam behind him, Rashid tried to keep his voice steady as he slowly advanced toward Khalid cowering in the corner. 'It's me, son. Your father. Don't be afraid, Khalid. I've come to take you away from this place. It's all over, son. I promise you, they won't hurt you anymore.'

'Father?' Still the form in the corner hid its face. The cracked voice was less wheedling but still suspicious. 'My father?' The voice suddenly screamed the primal scream of an animal caught in a steel trap. 'A trick! A new torture! You lie! Go! Let me be! Leave me alone!'

Rashid knelt down beside him. He put down the lantern and reached out and tenderly took Khalid's hand in his. 'No trick. I'm here, son. I've come for you. It's going to be all right, son. I'm taking you out of here today.'

'Truly?' Khalid still thrust the weight of his body against the wall, but slowly he let his hands drop away from his face. 'Father? You! You came here for me. Oh, truly Allah is good, Allah is wondrous, Allah is merciful, Allah, Allah, Allah . . . Allah so compassionate, so understanding, Allah, Allah, Allah . . . Allah *karim*.'

As Rashid took his son in his arms, Khalid continued his incoherent muttering. Rashid stroked his son's matted hair, he wiped the tears off his son's gaunt cheeks, he felt for the first time how frail his once strong son had become. Khalid frantically clung to him as though only his father's arms were keeping him from plunging into the abyss. All the while, however, Khalid did not cease his muttering about God.

Rashid's flesh was beginning to crawl not only with lice and with fleas but with an awful new suspicion. He possessively, protectively stroked the wasted body of his son and wondered if Khalid was mad. Had he cracked under torture? Was his mind forever gone? Had it been that fanatic Juhayman or the House of Saud who had made his son crazy?

'Khalid, my son, we have to talk. Then you have to sign a paper. And then we can leave together. This morning.' Gently Rashid disengaged his son's arms from around him. He opened his briefcase. 'I brought a paper, son, that you must sign. I will call the guards to witness your signing, and then we can go.'

Khalid frowned, shook his head, and continued to mouth the name of Allah.

Rashid pulled out the document and waved it at his son. 'Just sign this, and we can get you out of here. I'm taking you to Vienna. Your sister's waiting for you there. And your mother. We'll be together, Khalid. It will be just as it was when you were a little boy. All you have to do is sign.'

'Mother? My mother?' For an instant the madness receded and Khalid's eyes seemed to focus. 'My mother waits for me?'

Rashid spoke quickly now, lest that spark of sanity be extinguished before he could get Khalid to do what had to be done. 'You and I will go see your mother and your sister Sarah in Vienna as soon as you sign this document. All you have to do is sign this paper about Juhayman and all the others, and you can go free. We'll go right to the airport, get on a plane, and you'll be with your mother and Sarah today. Today, son! It will all be over today!'

But from that rush of words, Khalid extracted only one. 'Juhayman?' Khalid looked puzzled, then dreamy, and then a small secretive smile twisted on the corners of his mouth. 'Juhayman! The *Mahdi*! Now I remember! All! I remember all! Mecca! The *Mahdi*! Allah be praised!'

Rashid lunged at his son and clapped his hand over Khalid's mouth before he could utter subversion that the guards outside might overhear.

'Listen to me, Khalid,' he whispered. Rashid stared deep into his son's eyes. 'You can understand me now, can't you?' Khalid nodded his head slightly. 'We don't have much time left, son. I was given only ten minutes with you here, and most of that is gone. Now you listen to me. This paper here is about Juhayman and the others in the Mecca attack. It says certain things that the royal family wants known about Juhayman and the others.' Rashid could feel Khalid's body stiffen as if a jolt of electricity had just coursed through him. 'You maybe will not like what this paper says about the men you thought were your friends. But I tell you, son, you must sign it. If you do not sign, then I can do nothing more to help you. They will cut off your head, just as they will cut off the heads of Juhayman and the others. You will die, Khalid, if you do not sign this paper.' Rashid stared at his son with all the intensity there was inside him, as if the concentrated power of all that he was could keep his son sane and reasonable long enough for him to scrawl his name. 'You understand?' When his son nodded, Rashid released him.

Khalid sank back against the wall, shut his eyes, furrowed his brow and seemed to be trying to reason out something complex and elusive. He shook his head, he shuddered, he turned terrified eyes to his father. 'I think it would be terrible to die like that,' he whispered. He touched his neck. 'A terrible death.'

'An avoidable one,' Rashid said firmly, as though he were about to close an important deal. He pulled a gold pen from his pocket. 'Just sign here, son.'

But finally Khalid seemed to understand the implications of what was required. 'Lie? Betray my comrades?' Khalid shook his head with finality. 'It will be a great shame for you, when I die like that?' Khalid sighed. 'In the family, in the tribe, it will be a great shame?' Tears welled in Khalid's eyes. 'I never wanted to make you ashamed. Always I wanted to honor you, my father.' The tears overflowed and ran down Khalid's cheeks. 'I hope you will not be shamed too much. That maybe you will understand even a little bit why this had to be.' Khalid reached out and touched his father's face. With the soft caressive touch of a lover he traced his father's lips, his father's nose, his father's wet eyelashes. When Rashid opened his mouth to protest, to begin to try again to talk sense to his son, Khalid put his finger to his father's lips. 'Shhh,' Khalid crooned. 'Everyone must die. Everyone must die at the time and place that Allah wills. All must be as Allah wills. Yes, as Allah wills. Allah! Allah, Allah, Allah . . . Allah . . .'

'No!' As Rashid watched the madness once again cloud his son's eyes, he was frantic to save him. Desperately he struck him with the flat of his palm in a last frantic effort to bring him back to his senses.

Khalid cowered away from him. 'Please, no more, in the name of Allah, Allah, Allah . . . please don't hit me again, I've told you all I know, truly, in the name of Allah, mercy, please. . . .'

Rashid was sobbing as he reached over and smoothed back Khalid's hair from his face. But Khalid flinched from his touch and screamed for Allah's mercy. Rashid stumbled to his feet, he gathered his useless document and his briefcase, and he staggered out into the corridor where the guards waited. For a long time as they climbed up from the depths of the dungeon Rashid could hear his son screaming to Allah for mercy and compassion and forgiveness and justice and redemption.

*

Rashid and Ibrahim stood in the front ranks of the crowd in the public square outside the mosque in Dammam. They stood with their heads held high and their faces set in grim masks. It was Friday, the ninth of January, just after the dawn prayers, and Rashid and Ibrahim stood waiting in the throng for the executions to begin. Today in eight towns spread throughout the kingdom, the sixty-three condemned Mecca zealots would be beheaded. In Riyadh, in Medina, in Buraydah, in Hail, in Abha, in Tabuk, in Mecca itself and here, in the heart of the Eastern Province, the zealots would lose their heads. They had been accused and convicted of defiling the most sacred shrine in Islam with murder. In a few moments they would pay for their crime.

Rashid prayed silently for Allah to aid him in the coming moments. He had to stand here in the cold Saudi dawn and watch his only son cruelly put to death before his eyes. Honor required that he stand here. To do less, to cower at home and bemoan fate while his son's blood was being spilled, would bring a deeper veil of shame upon his family and his tribe. Rashid could not afford to court any more disgrace, even though he had already divested himself of the last remnants of his former status in the government. He was glad to be out of public life. He had lost his taste for ambition and power and soldiering for the Saudi state on the bitter morning when he had visited the mad cringing remnant of his son in his cell.

Rashid stared straight ahead. Around him stood many hundreds of men who had assembled from far and wide for the spectacle of Allah's just and sure retribution. Six men would die soon here in this square. Rashid bit his lips before they could tremble. He had done the little he could to help his son through this final passage. Khalid had looked so frightened at the thought of the sword on his neck. Rashid hoped the painkilling drugs he had smuggled into the prison would help his son endure the ride in the police car to this dusty public square, the walk to where the executioner waited, the kneeling and the waiting that final agonizing moment for the stroke of the sword that would end his life. Rashid had also seen to it that his son would be the first to die. When Khalid was led to his death, the square would not yet stink with the scent of human blood, and the flies would not yet be abuzz. Rashid had been able to do only that and nothing more for his son.

Ibrahim leaned on Rashid's arm, pointed, and Rashid watched the two police cars inch through the press of the crowd toward the center of the square. He met his grandfather's eyes. The old man mouthed one word: 'Courage.' Rashid nodded slightly. Ibrahim kept his bony hand on Rashid's arm, as if the old patriarch of the Al-Murrah needed to lean on his grandson for support. But of the two of them it was Ibrahim who was the stronger. Ibrahim all but pumped bravery and fortitude from his own veins into Rashid.

The crowd pressed forward eagerly as the doors of the police car opened, then recoiled in horror as the executioner emerged - the dire personification of death.

Rashid moistened his dry lips with the tip of his tongue. He stared at the man who was to kill his son. This Nubian executioner was kin to that other enforcer the Saudis had sent long ago to the black tents of the Al-Murrah on the night of Muhammad's judgment. He was more than six and a half feet tall, and beefy, with skin as black and gleaming as the night sky when there is no moon. He was wearing a fresh, starched, spotless white robe, a ceremonial bandolier crossing his broad chest and a broad black sash at his waist. Atop that sash was the scabbard of his sword. Rashid quickly looked away from the instrument of his only son's death.

The rear door of the second police car opened, and two guards helped out the first of the condemned prisoners. Rashid's eyes bored into the tall form of the victim in his austere white robe. A broad black blindfold was wound around the prisoner's eyes, and his hands were tied behind his back. At first Rashid could not be sure this was his son. But he watched how the victim walked, how he held his shoulders back, how he held his head high. Surely this was Khalid. When the victim stumbled and almost fell, Rashid took that as a sign his son had been given the drugs that would dull the pain of his ordeal. Khalid was led to the center of the crowd, where a large square of cardboard had been laid out in the dust. The guards made Khalid kneel.

A loudspeaker crackled with static; then a hoarse dire avenging voice sounded the length of the square. 'There is no God but God, and Muhammad is the Messenger of God!'

Rashid stared grimly ahead as the deep voice told of the freely confessed crimes of Khalid *ibn* Rashid *ibn* Abdullah *ibn* Ibrahim Al-Murrah. Rashid recoiled inside when he heard his son's name, but the carefully controlled muscles of his face did not betray him. Rashid's thoughts were elsewhere as the singsong monotone over the loudspeaker reprised the well-known facts: how Khalid and his comrades had seized the Grand Mosque, killed twenty-five hostages, killed one hundred and seventy-six government soldiers, and caused the deaths of at least seventy-five of the zealot criminals themselves. All the while the accusing voice droned on, Rashid dwelt on happier days. He was on the train pulling into Ayer station, and he was seeing for the first time the one who was to be the wife of his heart. He and Sunny were walking toward Boston Common, and she was telling him he was her sunshine, and he was kissing her. She was lying in the hospital bed in Dhahran, smiling up at him, as their son fed at her breast. What had begun long ago in New England with such hope and splendor was about to end here in the hot dry Saudi sun.

Rashid swayed dizzily, but Ibrahim held tight to him with a talon grip. Rashid took a deep breath. He willed himself not to think of anything at all. He must stand here erect and unwavering and endure the horror of these next few minutes. Others would be watching him, judging him, suspecting him, in these next moments. He swallowed hard. He would pretend this was only a television drama being made by the Egyptians or the British or the Americans. He would delude himself that the evidence of his eyes was a lie. He would watch what must happen, but he would not really see it or feel it or comprehend it. His eyes would seem to watch the executioner, but he would focus to the right of where Khalid knelt and waited. Rashid stared as if his life depended on it, as if his son's life depended on it, at a guard who fidgeted in the sun. The guard was tall, young, grim of face, but not so disciplined he could manage to stand properly at attention. The guard looked out at the crowd, he waved, he motioned some message to his friends. Rashid concentrated on that guard. He tried to create an entire history for him. He decided he might be a Shammar tribesman whose ancestral grazing lands were the other side of Riyadh, a Shammar whose grandfathers had raised camels and prayed for good grazing land and lived simple free uncomplicated lives by the grace of Allah.

Rashid stood unmoving, watching that guard, as the voice of doom inexorably continued over the loudspeaker. An Islamic court had met privately to try the criminals for their crimes. They had been found guilty of murder and of desecrating Mecca. King Khalid himself had determined these men must die for their crimes. In the name of Allah, this prisoner must die.

The crowd sighed as the voice stopped. The crowd craned their necks as the executioner neatly rolled up the right sleeve of his robe. The crowd surged forward as the executioner drew his sword from his scabbard in one long clean graceful sweeping movement. He brandished the sword above his head, pointing toward heaven. The sunlight caught the gleam of the shining double-edged Arabian blade. It was an old sword, a relic of past Bedouin campaigns in the desert. It was a long sword, three feet long and curving. It was a newly sharpened sword. The crowd caught its breath as the executioner nodded, as a guard deftly pricked Khalid's skin with a sharp stick, as Khalid's neck stiffened in a quick automatic reflex. The executioner whirled the sword above his head as he took four quick prancing warm-up steps; and then he swung that sword as high as he could. With one great mighty merciful whoosh he brought the blade down hard, fast, for one swift bloody instant of butchery. A fountain of scarlet blood spurted five feet into the air. Khalid's head bounced into the front ranks of the crowd. Khalid's trunk quivered, convulsed, twitched, then fell forward onto the sodden cardboard.

The crowd gasped, then roared its approval that the Mecca murderer had been punished. One guard picked up Khalid's severed head and put it on a waiting stretcher. Two other guards lifted up Khalid's body and placed it with the head on the stretcher. They loaded Khalid's body into an ambulance. The executioner cleaned the blood off his sword. A squad of Yemeni workmen removed the cardboard, wet and sticky with Khalid's blood, then placed a fresh piece down in the dust of the square. As the ambulance carrying Khalid's body inched away through the crowd, another police car carrying the second condemned Mecca zealot moved slowly toward the center of the square.

Ibrahim dug his fingers into Rashid's arm. 'We can go now. Come, Rashid, we can go.'

'*Khelas?* It is over?' Rashid blinked and turned his anguished eyes to Ibrahim. 'Finished?'

Ibrahim nodded very slightly. The two of them turned, and as they began to make their way through the tightly packed press of onlookers, the crowd parted before them. Silently they walked through the crowd to where their car was parked. They would have to go home and wash Khalid's body and bury the boy before sundown, with his severed head turned to face Mecca even in his grave.

26

Outside the black tent in the desert the winter wind howled so wildly that Rashid woke. He heard the rasping cough then, the gasping for air, the muttered verses from the Koran, and he was alert to any changes for the worse in Ibrahim's condition. As soon as they had buried Khalid, the two of them had turned their backs on progress and convenience and all their dangerous corruptions and packed up the camels from their pens in the family compound and struck out home to the purifying desert. They had made their camps away from the ribbons of asphalt. They had zigzagged to avoid railroad tracks and pipelines and gas flares. They had skirted the prefabricated oil-exploration camps that dotted the desert. Already they had been traveling without map or plan or worldly ambition for the waxing and waning of two moons. But in the cold and frosty winter heart of the desert, the biting winds had cut them to their marrow, and Ibrahim had developed a lingering cough. The patriarch had continued to weaken in the rains and the thunderstorms of the past weeks as they had camped on the old tribal grazing grounds on the northern fringe of the Empty Quarter. Each day, as they had struck deeper into the red sands, Ibrahim's physical strength had ebbed, but his spirit had seemed to gather strength and the expectant joy of a young virile man about to know his first woman. Ibrahim was not only returning home to the great sands of his youth but also taking the first steps on a longer, lonelier journey to the eternal home. His and Rashid's odyssey back into the desert had found a purpose. Ibrahim was coming home to the desert to die, and Rashid was with him to witness that death and to wash the old man's body and bless and bury it so that Ibrahim's flesh would not become carrion for the vultures and the jackals and the wolves.

But not yet.

Rashid crawled from under his blanket, added some twigs to the coals of the fire in the corner, and poured water into a cup to take to his grandfather. He would sit and talk with him and comfort and be comforted by him.

The old man lay in a warm nest of wool blankets and animal skins on the cold sandy ground. He tried to sit up to greet Rashid and take his proffered cup, but he could not do it. 'Weak, Rashid. I am so weak. Every hour Allah makes me more weak.'

'You are more strong than any other I have ever known. Even when you are weak you are strong.' Rashid knelt beside his grandfather. Tenderly he circled the old man's neck with his hand and raised him so that he could drink. He held the cup to his lips, tipped it, and watched Ibrahim swallow.

'I woke you. I am sorry a sick old man's sleepless noises keep a young man from his sweet dreams.'

'No dreams tonight. No sweet dreams any night. Nightmares sometimes. But no sweet dreams.' Rashid settled down on his haunches at the feet of his grandfather. 'And I am not such a young man. Not young at all.'

'To me you are.' Ibrahim squinted at Rashid in the firelight. 'I must have been more than forty years old before you were born out here in a tent like this one in the great sands. And you are how old now?'

'Forty-eight.'

'Allah! I am more than eighty-eight years on this earth? Has the Lord forgotten me? Allah! I am here; your Ibrahim is here, in the desert! Come and get him!' Ibrahim laughed when there was a rumble of distant thunder. But then a coughing spell seized him, and gratefully he drank again from Rashid's cup. 'Camel's milk,' he mumbled. 'Tonight I should drink the milk of a camel.'

Rashid shivered. It was an old Bedouin custom always

to drink one last time of the frothy milk of a camel just before death. 'I will milk her in the morning. Not now.' He listened to the thunder coming nearer. 'It will rain soon. Then after the rain, and the dawn prayers, I will milk the camel.' He was greedy for the company and solace of his grandfather. He could not bear to let him go now, in the dead of this cold storming night.

Ibrahim sighed softly. 'Everyone dies, my son. And it is written that when it is a man's time, nothing on earth can change that by so much as a second.'

'In the morning, after dawn, I will milk the camel.' Rashid rooted in one of the saddlebags until he triumphantly waved a bottle of cough medicine. 'This will help.' He held the syrup to Ibrahim's lips.

'You think to cheat Allah's clock with this sticky foul Western stuff?' But Ibrahim drank, and it seemed to ease the pain. Thoughtfully he smiled at his grandson and considered that perhaps it was not yet quite time to die after all. Maybe it was Allah's will that important words be said first to this son of his son. He reached out a hand and stroked Rashid's hair. In the shadows of the tent his failing eyes could not see the silver streaks in the black curls. 'A good boy. Always you were a good boy. I am not sorry to leave this life, but I grieve to leave you now, with your great sorrow. Such a hard life you have had, son of my son! So much trouble in your life! I think life has always been more difficult for you, and for those others who were very young when you were young, than it ever was for me. When I was young - oh, Rashid! - life then was rich and full of freedom and triumph and joy!'

'Yes?' Rashid smiled radiantly at his grandfather. 'We will talk of the old times in the desert? Of the raids against the Rashidi and the Saar and the Beni Khalid? Of when Abdul Aziz, the son of Saud, came here as a boy to learn the ways of the desert with our Al-Murrah? Of when you and your father rode out under the banners of Abdul Aziz to fight for Allah in the camps of the Wahhabi?'

'I think already you have heard all my stories of the old

days. I think maybe I have already told you these stories too many times.'

'Never! I can never hear them enough.'

'No?' Ibrahim shook his head. 'I wonder.' He gestured for more water, moistened his lips, sighed. 'Did I tell you rightly, my son? Did I ever make you understand all there was to understand about the old days? About the generations of children who died because they were too weak for the harshness of that life? About the swollen hungry bellies of the women and the children and the men? Of the famines? Of the shallow graves of the Al-Murrah that lie from one end of the great sands to the other? Of the sun that killed with its fierceness? Of the locusts that ate all the grass? Of the camels that sickened and died? Of the poisoned well water? Of how a man's tongue swells when he dies of thirst?'

Rashid held his hands up to his ears. 'Enough, Grandfather. I know what I must know of those days of glory.'

'Glory, is it? Glory! They were days of ignorance and suffering!'

'Then why did your eyes shine so just a moment ago when you told me what a joy it was to be young in this desert?'

'An old man always remembers the joy of being young. Even if it was not so joyful, an old man remembers that it was.'

'I don't believe you. The old days were the best days. We were a strong people. A good people. A pious people. Before the infidels came, and they found the oil, all Arabia was like a paradise.'

Ibrahim snorted in derision. 'You joke with me? Arabia was never paradise. At least, I hope not. As a man about to die and, I pray, enter the heavenly gates of Allah's kingdom, I tell you most truly I hope that His land here, in my youth, was not paradise on earth. Hunger! Pestilence! Poverty! War! Does that sound to you like paradise?'

'You are in a strange mood tonight, Grandfather. Never have I heard you talk like this. So many times I have heard you say that you wish the infidels had never come here with their gold and their oil and their temptations.'

'That is true. I have said that many times, as you say. So much I worried. With reason. With very good reason. None of us wanted them here. Many times we thought it was a mistake to let them come.'

'So you do regret the coming of the oil and the Americans?'

'Sometimes yes, sometimes not. Does it matter what I do and do not regret? It was inevitable that they come. It was Allah's will the oil be here and that the infidels come and find it. Can I make a fight with Allah's will?'

'No, no, that's not what I'm asking you. I just wanted to make sure . . . Grandfather, if you had it all to do over again, would you do the same?'

'You play devil games with me? You want me to say here, as I lie dying, that Allah in His infinite wisdom and compassion and mercy did wrong?'

'I suppose I only want to hear from your lips again, here, now, that it was better before they all came. That it is the fault of the Americans and the other infidels that things are as they are now.'

'And how are they?'

'Bad, very bad.' Rashid stared into the fire. 'Too much has happened too fast. Too many bad ways to spend money. Liquor. Gambling. Women. It is not only the royal family, although Allah knows they are bad enough. It is everywhere bad here now. Children do not obey their parents. Men do not pray. Men and women do not work. They sit at home and watch American television on their video machines and hire men from Pakistan and Korea and Palestine to do their work. They have forgotten too much that was good of the old ways. God, family, courage, loyalty, generosity. They don't live by the old rules of the East. Or even by the new rules of the West. They live and die by *no* rules. My head hurts sometimes when I think of how it is here now with my people.'

'So what do you want? You want everyone to give up air

conditioning and pickup trucks and automatic washing machines and turn back time and go back to the desert and live as you and I are living now? I think most of them would not like that bargain. Maybe sometimes they miss the desert, when the winter rains come and the desert is green, and there are cool winds and soft nights, yes, then they all yearn to go back to their desert. Like all men, they like to remember the good and forget the bad. They remember the beauty and forget the poverty and pain and fear. But I do not think most of them would choose the old ways. Most of them like the comfort that has come to them with the finding of the oil. It is an easier life for them now. And who is to say that is bad? I think, Rashid, you must admit that the oil has brought us both good and bad.'

'No, no. I think our people were more happy out here in the desert. Here at least there is peace. Freedom. It is very quiet and beautiful here. I feel always that God is near, here in the desert. Here, as nowhere else I have ever been, I am content.'

'You speak, Rashid, like a romantic boy, not like a man in his prime who all his life has been prepared to be a leader of his people. But do not delude yourself. You are not like me, a simple man of the desert, with no education, no life outside the sands. You have higher degrees from universities in America! Your life is more than mine!'

'I am less than you.' Rashid's voice was a whisper. 'Much less a man in every way.'

Ibrahim sighed. 'When I see you so sad, almost I do regret the decisions I made for you long ago. But not quite. It was Allah's will it happened - that all of it happened - exactly as it did. I remember the night that Majnun, the father of your Sunny, came here to us. We were camped maybe two days' march by camel to the east, beside the well that stands near the grove of date palms by the high red dunes. I remember that night as if it were yesterday. It was not the first time Majnun sat beside our campfires. Abdullah had brought him here before. Your father loved

Majnun. He said he was like a brother to him. Majnun was an infidel, but he was a good man. He had eyes that did not lie. His daughter has the same eyes. A child's eyes.'

Rashid quickly steered the conversation away from the tender subject of that one woman he still wished he could forget. 'I always wondered if you regretted your decision. It all started then, you know, when you agreed to send Muhammad and me to school to learn the ways of the infidel.'

Ibrahim looked appraisingly at Rashid; he hesitated; then he finally decided to share the secret he had thought he would carry to the grave. 'It all started before that. In the waters of the Gulf the day your father died.'

Rashid shrugged. 'When does a story begin or end? You could as easily say this all started with Adam and Eve and a snake.'

'Listen to me, Rashid, and listen well. Majnun never told you about the day your father died? No? I can see he did not. Then I will tell you. As a lesson to you I will tell you. But first I wish to eat dates and drink water and be strong again for a little while.' Silently he ate and drank. Then he told Rashid all that Tom Shannon had confessed to him long ago. How Sunny's mother had died. How Abdullah had carried her body through the burning water. How Abdullah had lifted Tom up to safety. Ibrahim's voice dropped to a whisper as he told Rashid the end of his story which was also the beginning of his story, about how Tom had let Abdullah die that terrible death, about Tom's despair at his own failure, about how Tom had devoted the rest of his life to penance for that day of death and courage and cowardice in the Gulf. When Ibrahim had finished, he was silent as he waited for Rashid's reaction. 'Well?' he finally prompted him. 'So what do you think?'

'So that was the secret; so that is what truly happened. Always I thought there was a secret, but I never imagined . . .' Tears were coursing down Rashid's cheeks. 'He let my father die like that? My Mr. Tom? He let the barracuda eat my father! Terrible! And he could have saved him! Easily! It would have been so easy to save my father! The woman was dead, but still he thought she mattered more - dead! - than my father alive! Allah! I never knew until now that Mr. Tom was such a terrible man! And I loved Mr. Tom! I loved him like a father!'

'As well you should have, for he loved you like a son.' Ibrahim sighed. 'You don't understand yet, do you, Rashid? You still do not understand, even a little, Allah's wonderful ways. Do not grieve for Abdullah. Your father had a good death, an honorable end to an honorable life. It is your Mr. Tom you should grieve for. He suffered more than your father. Always, for twenty, thirty years after that day in the Gulf, he suffered. But I like to think that in the end, in the fullness of Allah's time, mercy and forgiveness were granted him. For Allah is all-merciful, all-compassionate.' Intently Ibrahim looked into Rashid's eyes. 'Do you understand this lesson? Do you understand why I tell it to you on this night of nights?'

'I loved Mr. Tom.' Rashid was clenching and unclenching his fists as if he longed to wreak vengeance on the ghost and memory of Tom Shannon. 'All those years I loved him and honored him. All those years I did not know how he had murdered my own father.'

'What am I to do with you, Rashid? How am I to make you understand?' Ibrahim sighed. 'I am old, too old. These dim eyes have maybe seen too much. So much in the lifetime of one man. When I was born we were just poor men living with our camels in our rags in the desert. Now I am told we are such a rich nation but I wonder, I wonder!' Ibrahim's attention wandered. 'I saw my son Abdullah die. I saw Muhammad, the son of my son, die. And most terrible of all, I saw Khalid, the son of the son of my son, die. What justice is there in this world, that a man must watch his great-grandson die? Willingly I would have died in his place! But now at last it is my own time. And I say, *el-hamdulillah* - thank God! Old, so old. My Abdullah died serving the infidels too well. Muhammad died because of the infidels too, but also because he was so weak that their temptations made him bad like a devil. And Khalid - poor Khalid - why did he die? Did he die because of the infidels too? Would he have died as he did if they had never come here for the oil? In his way, he was a good boy. A boy like the boys of my youth. Tall, strong, full of fight. How he loved the old ways and how he hated all the new! Rashid, Rashid! How did we all fail that boy? To die so young, so lost, so bitter!'

'It was terrible what he and that Juhayman and the others did in Mecca. If only they had stormed the palaces of the royal family instead! The whole kingdom might have risen with them if they had attacked anywhere but Mecca. Khalid was my son, and I loved him, but I know that what he did was very wrong.'

'I am older than you, Rashid. And I say to you that it is more terrible what we do every day to one another than what Khalid and his foolish friends did in Mecca.'

'You defend Khalid?'

'I was thinking of the mother more than of the son. *Her*. We must talk of *her*. Sunny - your Shamsa! - now, there was a woman!' Ibrahim seemed to rally at her memory. 'Are they all like that in America? I wonder.' Ibrahim shook his head admiringly. 'She was a woman of fire! You know how we used to say of a warrior that he was *ainah hamrah* - red of eye? I think your Shamsa was a woman with red in her eyes! I miss her.' Ibrahim grasped Rashid's hand. 'You do too. I think always you miss her. Now, Nura, she was a good girl too. But your Sunny was always more. Always I liked to talk with her so much.' Fretfully Ibrahim looked around the tent. 'Why isn't she here now, out with us? Always she loved the desert as much as we do. She was not an Arab. Yet how she loved our desert! And loved us, loved us Arabs; not just you, Rashid, she loved all of us - loved our way of life, what we were, what we could have been - your Sunny was always in love with the *idea* of us! Yes, that's it! That is why we loved her too! She was like us! She too loved us for what we could have been, for what we once were, not for what we are. She was in love with the dream of us, and in that she was exactly like us, for we Arabs too are in love with what we dream we are. Shamsa! A wonderful woman!' Ibrahim narrowed his eyes. 'You think someday she will become a Muslim? Maybe you have not asked her enough? Sweet words! Use sweet words and help her accept Allah and Muhammad His Prophet! You must make a greater effort to teach her the true religion! I think I want to see that wonderful woman Sunny in paradise with us! How could it be paradise without her?' Ibrahim chuckled. 'Maybe I will steal her away from you in paradise. . . .' Ibrahim looked around the tent, as though he were again searching for Sunny. 'Where is she?' he muttered.

With a gigantic effort of will, then, he seemed to remember why Sunny had long ago left Saudi. 'Muhammad!' Ibrahim shook his head. 'He was a bad one, that boy. A lost soul. I failed with him. I am afraid he roasts in *Gehenna* - in hell.' Ibrahim sank back exhausted on his animal-skin pillows. 'You made a mistake, you know, Rashid. When your brother accused your wife, you made a very bad mistake.'

Rashid stiffened. He still could hardly bear to think of that terrible night. 'It's late,' he said. 'You must sleep now. I think we have talked enough for this night.'

But Ibrahim would not be silenced. 'You will listen to me, son of my son. Because you must. You know, and I know, that I will not live to see the sun rise again. I should have said what I am about to say to you long ago, but I knew you would not listen. You are stubborn like a camel, Rashid. You are a good man, but you have the stubborn and contrary heart of a very mean camel.'

Rashid smiled and gave in. 'Speak, then.'

'You never should have sent her away. Never. So she did shameful things with your brother when she was a young innocent girl? So?' Ibrahim weakly snapped his fingers. 'So you should have fought with your brother. But not her. She confessed to you, she told you how it happened, and yet you could never find it in your heart to forgive her.' Ibrahim shook his head. 'Rashid, *ya* Rashid, so learned are you, so smart, so much school, and yet you did not learn that lesson from the Koran? Over and over, Muhammad said that Allah was all-forgiving, all-compassionate. How does every *surah* of the Koran begin? "*Bismallah, al-rahman al-rahim*" - "in the name of God the merciful, the compassionate"! Always mercy and compassion is said to be the first and most important Face of Allah. Have you forgotten that always the Koran says that a man or a woman should be forgiven if he sins in ignorance and then repents? How then could you send that woman away? How? I think that for a smart man you are very stupid.'

'It is not so simple as all that.' Rashid's lips were set in a thin line.

'No? I think you are wrong. I think it *is* that simple. I think you have forgotten that the most important lessons of life are very simple. Love, laughter, mercy, faith, forgiveness. Reconciliation, Rashid. Making peace takes more strength and more courage than making war. The peace is worth more, too, I think. And in the end it is not so difficult. Long ago I forgave Majnun for letting my son die to the barracuda. And not once after that did I regret the great gift of compassion Allah gave to me. It can be yours too, Rashid. Easily, it can be yours! Even for you, my stubborn camel, it does not have to be so difficult as you make it.'

'Some things are too bad to be forgiven.' Rashid clenched his teeth. 'Honor too is important. And vengeance. And justice.'

'I think Allah will give you a very long life, for I think that you have many lessons still to learn before you die.' Ibrahim stared off into the distance. 'But for me, I think it is time. . . .'

'Grandfather! Not yet! We must talk! There is much yet that we still must say!'

'I am tired, son of my son. So tired. But we will talk more if you like. If you like. . . .'

Desperately Rashid searched his heart and mind for the questions that mattered most. Now, at the end, he should be asking Ibrahim for the accumulated wisdom of his long, eventful life. He thought of what they had already talked about - about love, and compassion, and forgiveness, and vengeance - but instead he blurted out something else. 'Palestine? What of Palestine?'

Ibrahim blinked uncomprehendingly at him. 'Palestine?'

'What is to be done about Palestine?'

'You call me back from the gates of paradise to ask me about Palestine?' Ibrahim shrugged. 'What do I know of Palestine? So much talk always about Palestine. I have heard some men say that they would like to pray there in the holy mosque where the Prophet Muhammad once went in the night. But for me it was enough to pray in Mecca. Palestine - yes, it is true, honor requires us to win it back. But that is a problem for young men like you to fix. I care only about my own land, about the grazing lands of the Al-Murrah.'

'But what can we do now, today, to help the Palestinians?'

'They are Arabs, they are Muslims, they are our brothers. Yes, we must help them. Maybe we should buy them land. Homes somewhere.'

'But they want only their own homes, back in Palestine.'

'Many souls in *Gehenna* want paradise. But they do not get paradise unless it is Allah's will. Life is difficult, no? The Palestinians lost their country and we here in the desert lost our way of life. Which of us lost more?'

'Yes, yes, we lost our way. I think so, Grandfather. But what should we do about it? What of our own country? What of the kingdom, and the princes of the House of Saud?'

'I have told you, many times, that I am not a man of politics!' Ibrahim sighed. 'Again it seems I must tell you. So listen to me, Rashid; for the last time, listen. The government? The kingdom? Saudi Arabia? What are they? What do I care about them? *I think they really do not matter*. For me, there are only the family and the tribe. Only us, the Al-Murrah, our sons and daughters and wives and fathers and grandfathers. There are the Al-Murrah, and then there is everyone else. Do I care about everyone else? Do you? I tell you, Rashid, here, now, at the end, there are only the family and the tribe and the camels and the sand and the sky. And Allah. Allah above all. Nothing else matters. Nothing!'

Ibrahim was seized by a coughing fit; he bent over. Rashid put his arm around him and he could feel the body of the old man grow weaker in his arms. 'Lie back now, Grandfather. Lie back and rest.'

But Ibrahim was not quite ready to begin his long rest. He shook his head as if perplexed. 'Was the oil a test? I wonder. Was Allah testing us, giving us riches beyond the wildest imagining of the most greedy man on earth? Was he teasing us, giving us such exceeding wealth, to see if we really were a pious people, a God-fearing people, *His* people? Is our time of testing already over? Has our time run out? Is it too late for us? In the end what have we made of His bounty with the oil? Are we a force for darkness or light in this world? Did we pass or fail His test? I wonder, Rashid.' Ibrahim shut his eyes and lay back and sighed.

Rashid held his grandfather in his arms and waited for the end in the black tent in the desert. Long ago, he thought, it must have been like this when his grandfather's namesake Abraham the patriarch, the father of the Arabs, died in his tent in the desert.

'I am so happy, son of my son, that you are here with me. A good boy. Always, Rashid, you were a good boy.' Ibrahim's eyes were half-closed. And the others, he thought, are they here in this black tent of death? Abdullah? Muhammad? Khalid? My boys, do my boys wait to take me up to Allah in heaven? He heard a gentle rain falling outside on the red sands, and he smiled. Finally, then, Ibrahim opened his eyes wide with an effort. 'The women, my women: you will always care for my women? For the wife of Abdullah, your mother? For my daughters? My granddaughters? All the wives and the daughters? Protect them, Rashid. Promise me that you will always be a father to all of them.'

'I promise, Grandfather.'

'Good boy. Always a good boy. Such a good boy, Rashid.' Ibrahim smiled. 'Allah's blessings upon you, my son. His mercy, His blessing, His compassion, His peace upon you, always, the best of my boys, Rashid. . . .' Ibrahim breathed one last gentle whisper of a breath and then was still.

Rashid sat holding his grandfather in his arms until he felt the body growing cold and stiff. He laid his grandfather's body out on the animal skins then, he washed the body, he wrapped it in a clean white length of cotton so that Ibrahim would be clean and pure and ready for the grave. Later he would bury his grandfather in the desert that was his home.

But first he would pray the dawn prayers. Rashid went outside the tent and caught his breath. In the golden dawn light, the desert was a garden of miniature flowers that had sprung to life in this night of rain. As far as his eyes could see, the desert was a sea of blooming fragrant flowers. So the desert had burst into life as if for the joy of welcoming home its son Ibrahim.

Silently Rashid watched the play of light in the sky, and he looked out at the blooming desert and thanked God for this scented sign of flowery grace. Then he took a stick and marked the direction of Mecca. He bent and washed himself in preparation for the dawn prayers. But a terrible loneliness overtook him as he stood facing Mecca. He was the last of his line, standing utterly alone to pray to his God from the heart of his desert.

But not entirely alone. He went back into the tent, found his transistor radio, and clicked it on. At once he heard the call to the dawn prayers. It was a call riddled with static, coming from hundreds of miles away, where a blind muezzin stood not atop a minaret but in front of a microphone in a radio studio. But nonetheless the fraternity of the call to prayer warmed Rashid. He was not alone. He was one of six hundred million who would bow and kneel and pray to Allah. He propped the radio up in the sand among the flowers.

'*Allahu akbar* - God is most great!'

Rashid bowed and knelt in the flowers and prayed.

—27—

Rashid's expectant smile died as it was neither Sunny nor Sarah but Musa who opened the front door to the Grinzing villa. 'What are you doing here?'

Musa bit off the quick retort that he could ask the same question. The two Arabs eyed each other warily until Musa's eyes fell. He meant no disrespect to the father of the woman he was going to marry at the end of the summer. But he was loyal to Sunny, and he didn't want to help Shaykh Rashid hurt her again. Musa nodded uncertainly and smiled with his lips yet did not invite Rashid to cross the threshold.

'Who's that, Musa?' Sarah was peering over her fiancé's shoulder at her father standing there solemn-faced and unsure of himself. Sarah's eyes lit up for an instant, and she began to reach out to embrace him. But then as she remembered how her brother had died, the light in her dimmed, and she took Musa's hands in hers and stared irresolutely at her father.

'I know you children mean well . . .' They could all hear Sunny's voice coming closer. '. . . but I wish you'd go without me. I'm just not in the mood -' When Sunny saw Rashid standing in her doorway, she faltered, the color draining from her face. She was dressed in a tailored black sheath, and her hair was pulled severely back from her face. Even the subdued way she walked across the room suggested mourning.

'I am welcome?' Rashid looked past the Egyptian to his daughter and the wife of his heart. Now that he had swallowed his pride and come for them, he wondered if all he was to get here today was a lesson in humility. If they were this doubtful even about inviting him inside their house, how was he ever to persuade them to return with him to Arabia? Ibrahim's deathbed advice to reconcile with Sunny had been only an old man's senile wishfulness. 'Very sorry,' he said as he began to back away from the doorway. 'It was a mistake to come here.'

But Sarah was taking matters firmly into her own capable hands. She pulled Rashid inside and closed the door behind him. 'Not welcome? Of course you're welcome. You're my father, aren't you?' But even as she was kissing the back of his hand, his shoulder, his nose, and his forehead, she seemed more conscious of her mother than of her father. It was only after she had seen her mother's telltale blush and her mother's involuntary quick little steps toward her father that Sarah had let him in. If despite all that had happened her mother still wanted something from this man she had once loved so very much, Sarah was going to do all in her power to help her get it. She hoped it would at least comfort her to talk to him about Khalid. It was four months since the execution, and still her mother dressed only in black. Sometimes at night Sarah still overheard her mother crying herself to sleep. But worst of all was when her mother would break into a conversation about the weather or music or politics and shake her head and insist it was her fault and Rashid's fault that their son had become such a tragedy.

'Such a late spring,' Sarah said brightly as she helped her father out of his coat and took his hat, gloves, and scarf. 'But then, it's always cold in Vienna. But *el-hamdulillah*, it's almost May. The flowers will be out anytime now.' Sarah took Musa by the arm and all but dragged him with her toward the kitchen. 'Coffee? Yes, we'll make the coffee. You two must have a lot to talk about.'

Sunny and Rashid stood staring in silence from the opposite sides of the room.

She had never thought she would see him again. She was certain he must blame her for the tragedy of their son. She wondered if he had been there in Dammam the day Khalid died. Had he watched? She felt unsteady on her feet, thinking of that. She warned herself not to think of that again. She studied Rashid's face. They had parted three years ago in this very room, after she had decided to wash her hands of all that was the once and future kingdom. Was Rashid really here? Perhaps this was just another nightmare from which she would wake in a sweat, alone in that same Viennese featherbed where they had once made such exquisite love.

She was bewildered by a fireworks of emotions - love, hate, longing, disillusion, fury, tenderness, guilt, all of them at once - for this man who stood glowering at her. She wished a blink of her eyes could make this disturbing man go away at least until she had time and space to sort out this welter of emotions. But when she blinked, he did not go away. He still stood there concentrating all his intensity on her, only on her, as if they were the only two people left in the world. As if all that were left in the world were he and she and the featherbed in the other room. A slow rosy flush burned Sunny's cheeks. She was very much embarrassed not only at her thoughts but at the knowledge that he would surely understand why she was blushing.

'So beautiful, my Sunny. Still so beautiful when you look at me like that.' A small sensual smile played on his lips. How was it he had forgotten what hot magic there had always been between them? He was relieved to see she still burned for him. He had been afraid she would turn him down flat or that she would at the very least need weeks and months of persuasion before she agreed to give him another chance. He would say whatever had to be said with his lips and his arms and his naked flesh against hers. She would understand that better than the sweetest of honey words. In the end he was man and she was woman, and instinct and impulse and desire and emotion were all that mattered. He would sweep her into his arms and carry her into the bedroom.

'Back off, buster!' Sunny held a hand up before him like a traffic cop.

Rashid frowned in bewilderment. What was this? One second she had been all cream and surrender, the next she was ice and war. His eyes narrowed as he tried to understand this unpredictable American woman.

She pursed her lips and clamped a tight rein on her weaker self. She would not succumb to ecstatic remembrance again. She remembered how very angry she was at this man. 'Let's start this all over, shall we? You, Rashid, out in the hallway. You knock on the door, I answer it, I slam the door in your face. Got that? Ready?' Briskly she shooed him toward the door. '*Yalla!*'

He did not budge. 'You mock me? You make a joke of me? If you wish to fight with me, Shamsa, then we will fight. But you will not mock me, understand? There has been too much between us for that.'

'Damn right there's been too much between us.' Sunny glared at him; but then her anger too seemed to fade as quickly as her desire. Just now she had very nearly surrendered to this man who had abandoned her in every important way. But he and she had shared more than sex and anger in all the long troubled years of their loving. Her eyes softened as she remembered Rashid's essential decency and the resilience of their friendship and that she had always liked him and respected him and treasured the essence of him. She should at least be able to treat him with the warmth of an old friend. She sighed and led him into the living room she still maintained as a shrine to her Arabia. She gestured toward a pile of cushions on the carpet beside a huge gleaming round engraved brass tray slightly elevated off the floor. 'Please sit down so we can talk like civilized people.' But her smile was wintry.

He sat where he had been told and unhappily studied her closed face. He had badly miscalculated how easy it would be to win her back. He would need all his tact and diplomacy to persuade this woman even to consider loving him again. He wondered, with odds like this, if it was worth humbling himself. But then he remembered the hot magic of that instant when she had flushed at the sight of him. She was worth it. Worth everything. He let his eyes tell her that for a long silent moment, and he was pleased when he saw her have to cross her legs as a shield against what he was telling her with that look in his eyes.

'I want you back.' He blurted out his intention as baldly as if he were an American man. 'Marry me. I want you to marry me again and come back with me to Saudi.'

She sat silent and still, listening to her heart beat faster inside her breast for one long, breathless moment. But then she regained control, and she snapped her fingers. 'Like that? Just like that? You want me back? Marry me, come back to Saudi, just like that?' She shook her head. 'No. Just like that you ask me, and just like that I tell you my answer. No, absolutely not.'

'You must not be so quick to answer such an important question.'

'I'll never go back there again. Not after Khalid. I hate everything about Saudi. After all that's happened, you're crazy even to come here and ask me.'

'You hate only Saudi or you hate me *and* Saudi?'

She shrugged. 'Does it matter?'

'So I think we begin with your turning down my country but maybe accepting me, eh?'

'No, Rashid. My answer is no. Period. For you, your country, for any combination thereof.'

But the vehemence of her refusal did not faze him. He began bargaining with her as though they were sitting at a stall in the souk. 'Not so fast! Listen to me! Sit, look, listen to me before you say no.' His voice took on the singsong pleading of an Arab peddler's pidgin English. 'One moment, please, lady!'

Despite herself, Sunny was smiling as Sarah sailed in with a brass tray and small cups and Musa trailed behind with a beaker of Arab coffee.

'We will drink coffee, yes?' Rashid gestured imperiously for the younger generation to serve the older.

'Thanks, Sarah.' But it was Rashid at whom Sunny was smiling as she sipped from her tiny cup. 'So you think you're going to make me a bargain, Rashid? Well, I warn you, I've bought your whole line before, and all of it was very shoddy. Loose threads, seams that came open, fabric that came unraveled. I was fooled once, but it won't be so easy to fool me again.'

'No?' He smiled wickedly at her.

'No.' She laughed.

Sarah and Musa's eyes met, and discreetly they retired to the kitchen.

'So, Shamsa! I think finally I say something right to you today. At least I make you laugh. It is very good to be here and to hear you laugh. I have not heard you laugh for a very long time.'

The smile died on her lips, and she smoothed non-existent wrinkles from the skirt of the black dress she wore in mourning for her son. 'There hasn't been much to laugh about.'

'I am sorry that I have more bad news.' He sighed. 'Ibrahim is dead.'

'Oh, no! Not Ibrahim too.' Her blue eyes glittered with sudden tears. 'He was my favorite, you know. He was so good to me. Good to everyone. You know, Um Muhammad wrote to me that when he heard the religious police had painted Sarah's legs, he drove into Khobar and went after them with his cane. I can just see it. The avenging patriarch. God, I wish I had been there to see that.' She wiped her eyes. 'You were with him when he died?'

'Of course. In January . . . after what happened in January, in Dammam, we went out into the desert together with the camels. Just the two of us, camping by the old wells in the red sands. He died out there, in the night, in his black tent. It rained the night he died. The desert was a carpet of flowers the day I buried him.'

'Rain and flowers? Ah, that's good. . . . Good for Ibrahim. The last of the Arabs. And the best of them.'

Rashid cleared his throat. 'He talked to me about you the night he died. I think he was a little bit in love with you, you know. By God, if it were not forbidden by Islam, I think he would have married you himself after our divorce.'

But this time she did not smile. 'It's not Ibrahim's death that we should be talking about, is it?' She tipped the cup to moisten her lips, but instead she took in the dregs. 'You saw - you know - Khalid - that day?'

'I stood in the square beside Ibrahim. But did I *see*? Rashid shook his head. 'Even now, even with you, his mother, I don't think I can talk about that.' His voice broke. 'You know?'

She nodded. 'Go on.'

'I want you to know I did all I could to save him.'

'You couldn't just *buy* his way out? I thought everything was for sale in the kingdom.' Her eyes were bitter.

'Not this time. I tried everything, paid everyone, but the royals wouldn't pardon him unless he signed a paper betraying his comrades. I went to his cell. I pleaded and begged -'

'But of course he turned you down. You asked the impossible. You must have a very inflated idea, Rashid, of what the world will do even if you ask the impossible.'

'Not all the world. Just those I love.'

'Ah, so now you tell me that you love me?'

'Always. That has never changed. Like the sun. To me you are the sun.'

'Rashid, Rashid, don't you understand it's too late for all that? I'm not a girl of sixteen you can dazzle with pretty words. I'm forty-two years old, and I don't believe in knights in shining armor anymore. Or in an Arab Prince

Charming riding up on a white horse to sweep me off to a mythical kingdom by the sea.' Sunny's voice was rising with emotion. 'For God's sake - all of you are always talking about God so much, so I will too - for God's sake, go away and leave me alone. Haven't you already brought me enough grief?' Tears were running down her cheeks, and her shoulders were shaking, and she was almost incoherent. 'Bad enough that I once went to live with you in that godforsaken - Yes, godforsaken! Saudi is absolutely godforsaken! - that godforsaken country! Now, after those savages killed my son - my only son, my poor, lost only son!' A great desolate sob wrenched out of her. '*They cut off his head!* Oh, my God, my God, they cut off his head!' She covered her face with her hands and she wept.

Swiftly Rashid reached over and took her in his arms. He stroked her hair, he crooned to her, he listened as she sobbed out her grief. He held her close and tight and safe in his arms. 'I know,' he murmured. 'I know, I know.'

She cried for a long while; then her sobs turned into one long mournful sigh. 'I will never get over this,' she whispered. 'Never, as long as I live, will I ever get over how and why my boy died. It was *our* fault. *We* did that to our son.'

'Let me be with you.' He did not heed the tears that rolled down his own cheeks. 'Maybe it won't be so bad if we're together.'

She pulled slightly away from and dabbed at her eyes with the sleeve of her dress. 'I don't know how you stood it. To see him in that prison, and then to have to watch them . . .' She looked up into Rashid's eyes and shook her head. 'I am so very sorry for you. I know how I feel. But you . . .' She touched his cheek and wiped away his tears with the tip of her finger. 'How much more terrible it must have been for you.'

He held her close in his arms. But this time he was the one who cried and she was the one who crooned. 'There, there. . . .' She patted his black curls streaked with silver.

They clung to each other and rocked on the carpet.

Finally he stirred, pulling just far enough away from her so that he could see her face. 'This feels right,' he said. 'To be finally here with you like this. I think this is right. Do you feel it too?'

She was so tired of trying to be resilient and strong. Her arms were still warm from the touch of him. She nodded. 'But -'

He put his finger to her lips to stop her from saying whatever she had been about to say. ' Listen - please, just listen to me. I have been so wrong for so many years about so many things that I can understand that maybe you still doubt me. You are a very strong girl - American woman, sorry! - and so maybe you think I come to you with bad tricks. That maybe I want to hurt you again. I am right? Yes!' He picked up her hand and kissed every finger, then the palm, then the inside of the wrist. 'Please marry me. I need you, Sunny. I loved you when I was a very young man, I love you now that I am a man in the middle, and I swear to Allah I will love you when I am very old and maybe finally wise like Ibrahim!'

'I believe that you . . . love . . . me. But that's not enough. You loved me before, and it wasn't enough then. Why would it be any different this time?'

'Can you believe I am less stupid this time?' When she smiled, he was encouraged enough to continue. 'I will change. No, already I have changed. I talked with Ibrahim, he told me I was stubborn like a camel, that I made bad mistakes with you and with everything else. He gave me a lecture about mercy and forgiveness and compassion and told me to go back and read my Koran again. He made me very angry, but then he died and I could not fight him anymore. So I read the Koran once again. I was alone in the desert. I had much time to think. And I came to important decisions. About you and me and Sarah.' He took a deep breath. 'Both back! I want you both back! I want you both to come back with me.'

'Sarah and Musa are getting married in August.'

'Is that so?' He scowled. 'I haven't heard anyone asking my permission for my daughter to marry this - person.'

'Why should she ask you, Rashid? What sort of father have you ever been to her?' But for Sarah's sake, Sunny tried to mollify Rashid. She still remembered how much her own father's approval had meant to her, despite or maybe because of his long neglect. 'She loves him. And with good reason. He's a good man. He's a *Doktor* of archeology now, and he's up for a prestigious position back in Cairo. I'll miss him, and her, when they get married. Musa's been more like a son to me than . . .'

Rashid took her hand and squeezed it sympathetically at that veiled reference to Khalid. But he was thoughtful as he mused out loud. 'For my child to marry an Egyptian? I had Hussein's nephew Fahd in mind for her. She should have a Saudi husband. All men from Egypt are too much different from us. Always they are not satisfied. Change this, change that, change everything their way. Egyptians are very arrogant. They think they are so superior.'

'The pot calls the kettle black.' Sunny threw her hands up in the air.

Rashid ignored her accusation. 'This Musa, he is not a troublemaker, is he? A professor of revolution?'

'Aren't you the one the royals banished for speaking out of turn?'

'I don't think they ever really trusted me.' Rashid shook his head. 'I had such great dreams, once. I was going to do so much for my people. But I failed. I failed with everything. My work. My marriage. My children.'

'Maybe not with everything.' Her smile was tender.

'So finally you decide to give me hope?' Gratefully he kissed her hand again. 'So now I must persuade you to trust me all the way.' He thought for a moment. 'This Egyptian teacher, you are sure he is a good man?'

'He has my total trust.'

'Maybe, then, I should have gone to Musa before I came to you. Maybe this very trustworthy Musa could have given me lessons before I came to see you?'

'Maybe.' A smile twitched at the corners of her mouth.

'And our daughter loves him? Truly? She says that she must have him? She says that she will kill herself for love of him if she is not allowed to marry him?'

'Sarah's an intelligent young woman and a sensible one. She loves Musa, but she doesn't show her heart all over Vienna as if she were acting out some melodramatic Arab opera of love.'

'Then how can you be sure she loves him?' Rashid gave Sunny a shrewd look of calculation. 'Listen to me. Suppose I give Sarah my permission to marry this Egyptian you say you trust so much. But say I make them promise they will come back to live in the kingdom. Say I promise to get him a good job in Saudi. He's an archeologist. I will build him a museum. Two museums. Whatever he wants. If I do that, will you promise to consider what else I have asked you?'

'You think you can negotiate my affection like you did the price of oil with the Iranians and the Venezuelans and the Libyans?'

But he could scent the closing of the deal, and he would not be sidetracked. He sweetened the pot. 'A big wedding for her wherever she wants. Here, in Switzerland, in Massachusetts, or back in Saudi. A job for her, too. She can go to study at a university at home. And then they both can teach subversion in the kingdom. Yes! I will get jobs for both of them.'

Sunny was tempted. Rashid's blessing would mean a great deal to Sarah. At heart neither she nor Musa had cast off all the old ways. Sarah would marry Musa with or without Rashid's permission, but she would be happier if her father approved. Yet would they like the idea of going to live in Saudi? And did she herself want them back there? Sarah was all she had left of the old days. If Sarah went back to the kingdom, she herself might find its pull irresistible. As Sunny looked at Rashid with newly dawning respect, she wondered if he had concocted this scheme on the spot. 'Suppose you ask them yourself.

Sarah! Musa! Come here for a moment, please.'

Sarah's eyes were asparkle as she came bounding ahead of Musa into the living room. 'I shall die - *die!* - I shall throw myself from the highest minaret in the kingdom, if I do not get my man!' Sarah giggled.

'Sarah! You've been eavesdropping.' But Sunny laughed, too.

Rashid looked from the daughter to the mother. 'Both of you are having a good laugh mocking me?' He stood. 'I see you did not teach her respect.' He turned to go.

Musa frowned at Sarah. 'Is that any way to treat your father?'

'Wait!' Sarah impulsively threw herself into Rashid's arms. 'It was a joke, just a joke! I wasn't making fun of you, truly!'

'I did not think your joke funny,' Rashid said quietly. 'I was very serious, and you laughed. I do not think the question of whether you marry this Musa a joke.'

'Neither do I.' Sarah was suddenly solemn. 'I would like to marry Musa, yes, Father. I would be very happy if I can marry him with your permission and your blessing.'

'Truly, daughter?'

'Truly, Father!'

Musa stepped forward. 'I beg you please to give us your blessing.' His warm brown eyes were earnest. 'I will love her and honor her and protect her forever, as Allah be my witness.'

Rashid gave Sarah a kiss on the forehead before releasing her and turning his full attention to the young man who was evidently so beloved by both his women. 'You are a good Muslim man?'

'As Allah be my judge.'

'He is, Father. He does everything right. Prays, fasts, gives alms, everything.'

'Quiet while we men are talking.' Rashid studied Musa's honest broad strong Egyptian face and decided his daughter could do worse. 'You are a man of politics?'

'I like to think I am more a man of religion.' There was a

ghost of a smile on Musa's lips. 'Of course there is politics in the religion. I believe, as the Holy Koran tells us, that it is the community of the believers who decide who our rulers should be. And that if the rulers do not follow God's laws, they should be replaced by others who are more worthy.'

'Is that so?' Rashid too was almost smiling. 'I take it you mean that the Saudi royal family must fall.'

'I did not say that.' But Musa was encouraged enough to elaborate. 'Always I have dreamed of one great Arab state that puts no boundaries between the brotherhood of the believers. Our problems are not just with the House of Saud. Since Nasser died, nowhere in all the Arab world has there been a leader worthy of his people. But someday there will be. I hope in my lifetime.' He smiled at Sarah. 'Or in my son's.'

'Ah!' For a second Rashid's eyes flashed with that wild-animal spark of his youth. He looked from Musa to Sarah, and he allowed himself the hope that this younger generation would do better than his own. His daughter, he decided, had chosen a man after his own heart. Yet he couldn't resist making his approval for their match conditional on their returning to Saudi. 'Will you promise to live in the kingdom?'

'I'll have to talk that over with Sarah.'

'Don't rush us, Father. And tell us this. What if we decide *not* to live there? And I heard you trying to talk Mother into coming back, too. What if none of us will go back there with you? Will you still give me your blessing to marry Musa?'

'You act more like an American woman than an Arabian girl. Demands, so many demands!' He narrowed his eyes at her. 'You are your mother's daughter.'

'And yours.'

'American women! One Saudi man against two American women! Okay! I give up!' Rashid hugged Sarah. 'You win! You both win. Or maybe even we all win! Yes, you may marry him. God help us all, you may marry your

Egyptian!' As he hugged her again, he smiled at Sunny. 'So what do you say? You maybe believe me now? You promise you will marry me now?'

As Sunny smiled at Rashid, finally in her clear blue eyes there was a glimmer of the old trust and affection. 'I'll think about it. I'm going back to New England for a visit next week, and I will promise you only that I will think about it tomorrow or after tomorrow.'

—28—

Still Sunny stared - wondering, remembering, imagining - at the faded sepia photograph of her mother, her father, and Abdullah. She stared so long and hard she lost track of time, and when a shadow fell across the photograph she assumed it must be almost night.

'I came for you.'

Startled, she looked up at Rashid standing silhouetted between her and the sun. He was dressed like a *shaykh* in an immaculate snowy white robe, a white head scarf, and a black *igal* band holding his *ghutra* headdress in place like a crown. She had not seen Rashid in Arab robes for years, and she was flustered because her heart raced at the sight of him dressed for the desert. She had known this man for nearly thirty years. She knew his weaknesses almost better than she knew his strengths. She was a modern woman, liberated, psychoanalyzed, proud of her hard-won independence, a woman not only of the world but of herself, and yet her hand still trembled at the sight of him. She didn't know whether she was glad or angry that she could still feel like this.

Princess Camey whinnied, and another horse whinnied back.

Sunny scrambled to her feet and looked over in the meadow where she had left her mare grazing, and she saw the white Arabian stallion prancing up to Princess Camey. 'A white horse! Oh, no! Rashid!'

'I told you that I came for you. I was tired of waiting, and so I came for you. Even on a white horse. *How* can you say no to me?' He laughed. 'I am ruthless, no? I will stop at nothing to get you back.'

'You think it's that easy? You rent a horse and dress up in costume and sweep me off my feet like I'm still some deluded, romantic girl?' But she grinned at him.

'I think now I am supposed to take you up on my horse and ride away? Is that the way it is supposed to be?'

'You bet. We're supposed to ride away into the sunset and live happily ever after.'

Solemnly he offered her his arm. 'Shall we?'

'Not so fast.' She studied him speculatively. 'Was that what you thought I would do? Hop up behind you on the horse, and off we'd go, and that would be that?'

'I hoped so.' He shrugged. 'Maybe yes or maybe no. But at least I thought you would laugh. Then a little later we would get on the horse and go away together.'

'I see. You're very sure of yourself.'

'Not sure at all. If I were sure, I would not have thought I had to rent the horse. Twenty-five dollars an hour.'

She laughed, then shook her head. 'It's going to take more than charm for you to get me back. Sorry, but I'm not that easy. Not anymore. You wasted your money on the horse. I don't want fantasy from you.'

'You are so old and gray, my Sunny, that you no longer want your dreams to come true?'

Part of her did want to get up on that white horse with the man of her dreams and ride away, and the hell with life's being difficult and real and gritty. But Sunny sighed and answered him the way she knew she should answer him. 'If I do decide that I want you - if! - it won't be because of costumes and fantasy and delusions and our own private tales of Arabian nights.'

'You did not like our Arabian nights?' He reached out and brushed the blond hair away from her forehead. 'They were nights that I liked very much.' His voice was caressive. 'I promise you more nights that do not end until the call for dawn prayers! All night I will keep you awake, we will burn, I will give you a thousand kisses, all night, every night.'

She drew away from him before he could sweep her into his arms and show her how he meant to keep her awake all night long in Saudi. She did her best not to let him see she was smiling. How, she wondered, could he still be so impetuous with her? He had first kissed her - at her own instigation on Commonwealth Avenue - twenty-three years ago. Surely after all these years he could not still be so boyish and passionate and so full of yearning to touch her? From under lowered lashes she looked up and saw his eyes burning with that old wild-animal fire, and she was not a little alarmed to feel an answering heat start to simmer between her thighs.

She walked a few frightened paces away from him, where it might be safer. She wasn't going to make a shambles of the rest of her life just for the sake of a little - or even a lot of - hot sex in the desert. She had built a decent, reasonable, productive life for herself without this man who had brought her such extremes of grief and ecstasy. She was comfortable with the compromises she had made with herself and with life. She liked the woman she had become. At least with Sarah, she had been a good mother. She was very proud that Sarah had not only an enduring character but an unblemished capacity to love. Sunny had an enormous sense of accomplishment, too, that she finally had finished her dissertation and was a psychologist with a clinical practice among the Arab émigrée women of Vienna. Her work was fascinating and challenging, and she dreamt that someday she might write a book that would break new ground about the psychology of Third World Women.

In Vienna, Sunny had wonderful friends, urbane men who took her to the Opera, witty women she ate chocolate cake with in the coffeehouses, a sophisticated and cultivated circle who came to her elegant parties. She tried to convince herself all this was more than enough for one woman's life - even for the life of one woman who had always been hungry for the most and the best that life could offer. She dared to shoot a quick nervous glance in Rashid's direction. Was he - still! - the most and the best that life could offer? She would not let herself look at him again until her breathing slowed. She hoped he had not noticed how he was affecting her. She hoped he was deaf and dumb and blind and that he had forgotten how he had always moved her. She wished her pulse would slow down and he would stop looking at her like that. But at the same time she also wished he would just take her in his arms and sweep her away in an excess of passion that would obliterate all her scruples, doubts, and fears.

More than anything else, however, she was deeply afraid of Rashid's fatal power over her. She stood very still, she searched her heart and her mind, and she faced her fear. If she let herself love him again, she might willingly and eagerly annihilate herself in an excess of love so powerful it would destroy her. It had almost destroyed her once, and it could again. She considered that perhaps she was better off alone than risking everything she was for this man. Sunny smiled faintly to herself. She had taken such pride in being in touch with her feelings, yet she had not realized until now that she harbored this deep and abiding fear of the power of love.

'I think at this moment you are very far away from me, my Sunny. I will go now, then?'

'No, don't go.' She ran her hand through her hair. 'Sorry.' She supposed it might take more strength and courage to love this man than to resist loving him. She remembered she had always prided herself on her courage. She took a deep breath. 'I'm sorry about a lot of things.'

'So!' His face was wreathed in smiles, and he took a step closer to her. 'So you give me hope? So! So there are the horses! *Yalla*, let's go! So after all we get on and ride off into the sun!'

'Not so fast, Rashid.' She laughed. 'This is important. We have to talk about all of this. It's a lot more complicated than that.'

'Always, American woman, you *make* everything so complicated. I think you like things very complicated.' Glumly he sat down on her blanket. 'Sometimes I do not understand why always I want you. You are, I think, very much trouble.'

'You're not so easy yourself.' Gingerly she sat just out of reach on the edge of the blanket. 'If we are even going to consider a reconciliation, we're going to have to be honest with each other. We have to talk about all the things that have gone wrong in the past, about our cultural differences, about how we might avoid them the next time around.'

'You make us sound like a difficult and maybe very boring course in the university.' He grinned wickedly at her. 'Why not just reconcile and later on talk about it? Why not reconcile here and now on this blanket?'

'Not a chance.' She would not smile back at him.

'Very well, then.' His demeanor changed. 'Words, you want words from me? You want to bargain, you and me, like we are at a table in Geneva? You trust words more than how you feel and how I feel? The love? Such love! It is not enough for you?' He shook his head, and his eyes were disappointed. 'If words are what you want, that is what you will get. So? We begin now?'

'All right.' Nervously she smoothed down the edge of the blanket. 'Let's start with what you want, what you're offering me. Exactly what do you want?'

'To marry you again. I will marry you here, or in Europe, or in Saudi. As you like.'

'And then what? You don't work for OPEC or the oil ministry anymore. So where will you - where would we - live?'

'In Saudi. In the compound at Khobar. I'll go back to running the family interests from there. Or if you like I will build you a new villa. Or we can get very romantic and live in a black tent in the desert. Up to you. I want you anywhere, as you like.'

'I don't think I could stand to go back to Saudi.'

'You loved it once.'

'I loved you once, too. But I don't know if I'll choose to act on that love again.'

'I think you still love me, yes?'

'Maybe.' She avoided his eyes. 'Let's talk about how Saudi twisted our son into such a creature of hate. I will never forget his face when he threw that stone at me. Our son was dead in the most important human way long before a single shot was fired in Mecca.'

'Ah, so it is our son who stands between us now. I had hoped that maybe our grief would bring us together rather than apart. I had thought we would need each other more now.'

'I'm sure we do.' She hung her head. 'Rashid, *we* did that to our son, didn't we? It was *our* fault, wasn't it?'

'I wish you were a Muslim, for then you would not torment yourself with guilt like this. Khalid's life and Khalid's death were Allah's will.'

'You really believe that, don't you?' She shook her head. 'I envy you that. I wish I could take that same comfort. But I think it was you and me, and Saudi, that made Khalid a tragedy. How could I ever go back to that barbarous place where they cut off our son's head? Where women have to wear masks or veils? Where women still can't work in offices with men or drive cars or live with any sort of freedom or independence or dignity? Where you have a feudal king and thousands of rich and decadent princes who waste billions of dollars while some of your poor nomads all but starve out in the desert just like their ancestors did thousands of years ago? Once I thought Saudi was the most romantic place on earth. Now I know better. I can't go back there, Rashid.' Her voice broke. 'Even if means I'll never see you again.'

'Yes? You tell me with your eyes that I am still so important to you? You give me hope, my Sunny?'

'Honest to God, Rashid, haven't you listened to a word I've said? I just told you all the reasons why I can't go back to Saudi with you. And all you heard was my saying I couldn't stand the thought of never seeing you again.'

'All else is negotiable. All but that most important thing. If you want me, you shall have me. Here, there, wherever you want.'

'You'll give up Saudi for me?'

He looked at the wooded Massachusetts horizon. 'Not exactly,' he finally said. 'I am an Arab. Not American or European. An Arab. I am proud that I am an Arab. I wish to live nowhere in the world except Arabia. Nowhere but at home can I be happy. I love my desert and my people and my God. But my life is complicated because of you. I think I have loved you since I was just a boy and your father showed me your photograph.' Rashid laughed. 'Never did I see a girl so beautiful!' His voice was soft and low. 'I think it is very wonderful for me that I am a favorite of Allah, to be given this love for you all my life long. I have lived with you, and I have lived without you, but always – with you, without you – still the feeling I have inside me for you is the same. I am a most lucky man. But so! Such a lover I am! Rashid, he loves so much! His country, his woman! Too much love! What can he do? His country does not love his woman and his woman does not love his country!'

'So tell me: what does this lover do?'

'Whatever he can to make his country love his woman and his woman love his country. The great lover makes great compromises, eh?'

'Compromises? Yours or mine? I suppose your idea of a great compromise is that I give in and go back to Saudi with you.'

'Slowly, slowly. . . . Always you Americans want to jump to your answers. Such a fast people!' He shook his head. 'I think we should trackback.'

She smiled. 'You mean backtrack?'

'As you like. I love so to see you smile again at me. I will talk more very bad English if that makes you smile so!' He reached over and took her hand. 'I warned you, I am a ruthless man and will stop at nothing to get you back! So! So I think we will stop smiling and be serious now. You say you hate Saudi. I do not believe this. I was with you in Saudi, you remember. Before Ibrahim died, he said to me that you loved the desert like an Arab.'

'Ibrahim always understood everything there was to understand.' She smiled. 'But the Saudi you're offering me isn't the Arabia I loved. The simplicity and harmony of the old life is gone now. What Saudi is now is ugly and crass and arrogant.'

'There is some truth to what you say. I would not say it so bluntly –'

'I wish for once you would, Rashid. I wish for once you would just say what you mean. Right now are you being sincere, or are you just mouthing pretty Arab sentimental words so you can humor me into coming back to Saudi with you?'

'So many suspicions. Still I think you do not trust me.' Shrewdly he assessed her. 'Is it me only you do not trust, or all men, any men?'

She looked away from him in confusion. Always he startled her when he exactly read her mind and heart like that. He misunderstood so much of the little things about her, but then he took her breath away when he saw into her soul.

'Bull's-eye, eh? So how will I convince you then to trust me? You ask me to be blunt like you, so I will try. I would not be here now if it was not for Ibrahim. He made me listen to him talk about you before he died. At first I did not want to hear him. He gave me a lecture about love and compassion and forgiveness and mercy. And then he told me how your father let my father die by the barracuda. He told me that, Sunny.' Rashid shook his head and his eyes shone with tears.

'So you finally know.' Sunny picked up the photograph taken of the Shannons and Abdullah on the pier the day that her mother and his father died. 'My father told me he owed you and Muhammad more than he would ever be able to repay. I suppose I thought that I owed you too. Maybe I still feel it.'

'I do not want your guilt. I do not want you to come back to me because more than forty years ago your father once was not brave when it was necessary for him to be brave. Your father was a good man. Like a father to me. Maybe he was more like a father to me than to you. If you are angry at your father, it should be for failing you, not for failing my father.'

'No.' She shook her head. 'I can't hold anything against my father. What he did to me and your father was so very long ago. My father paid for everything he ever did that was wrong. The problem with my father was that he could never forgive *himself*.'

'And you, his daughter - is it the same with you?'

At that instant she felt like throwing herself into his arms and putting her head on his chest and letting him be so wise and strong that nothing could ever hurt her again in life. She wanted to crawl inside his arms and let him protect her forever, not only as a lover might but as a father - as her father - never had. She was shocked at her ferocious sudden need to hide inside the supposed safety of his arms. She was relieved when that impulse to surrender faded.

'I think, Sunny, it is very hard for me to forgive, too. Maybe it is hard for everyone. But Ibrahim told me about my father and Mr. Tom and the barracuda as a lesson in how to forgive. Before Ibrahim died, I think he wanted everyone, everywhere, to forgive. He told me to beg you to come back to me. But I tell you, Shamsa, that this was very hard for me. Maybe I had even more doubts than you. You hurt me very much before. I thought I would die for shame the night Muhammad told all the tribe what he did to you. In your world maybe what you did was not so bad. But in my world, maybe there is nothing worse that a wife could do to her husband. I spent many days after Ibrahim died alone in the desert thinking about you and about me. At last I decide. At last I forgive. At last I choose. You! I want you!'

'And what about shame? That hasn't changed. Aren't you worried what the tribe will say about Muhammad and me?'

'After Khalid and Mecca, you and Muhammad do not matter. Forever, now, our family is disgraced.' Rashid shrugged. 'Besides, so much is different now in Saudi, there are so many shames in so many families now, that no one will care about one hour in a Boston hotel a lifetime ago.'

She studied him for a long moment, but then she shook her head. 'No. My final answer is still no. You threw me out, Rashid, as if I were dirty. You took my son away from me and wouldn't let him see me again. Now years later, Ibrahim says a few sweet words to you on his deathbed, and suddenly you see the light, and you come back to me dressed in your white robes riding a white horse you rented by the hour, and I'm supposed to melt in your arms and tell you I forgive everything and that I'm yours? Life doesn't work that way!'

'No? Why not?'

'Why not?' She was exasperated. 'Because it just doesn't, that's why not!'

'Yes, yes, that's good. Get very angry. Yell at me, scream at me, spit it all out, Sunny. Good. I am here. I will listen. I will sit and listen and understand all the bad things you want to say to me. I am not going away this time. Shoot!'

She was bewildered. She fought her rising desire to burst into tears. He had never been like this before with her. She had thought that by now he would have stalked off and ridden that damn white stallion back to wherever he had rented it. 'Go away!' She shook her head, and she could no longer keep the tears from welling in her eyes. 'I don't want to love you, Rashid. I don't want to love any man. Too much trouble. You're all too much trouble. Too much heartache. Enough, too much, go away. . . .'

He let her cry. He wished, as he watched her shoulders shake, that it would have been right to take her in his arms and kiss her into agreeing to be his woman again. Instead, while she was so vulnerable, he kept his distance. If she chose to love him, it would be of her own free will. He did not ever want to break the brave spirit of the wife of his heart. Sitting here on this blanket in Still River, listening as Sunny cried out her confusion, Rashid felt very sorry for this woman he loved. When she had been younger and unmarked by life's defeats, she had been the easiest, the freshest, the most entrancing woman in the world to love. Now she was so wary, so mistrustful of her own best impulses. Rashid sighed and blamed himself for her disillusionment. If he had loved her better the first time around, she would still be soft and giving and loving with him now. But in their years apart, she had grown so accustomed to being strong and lonely that he wondered if she wanted or needed him. If she took him back again, it would be because she was strong enough to love him as he never had been loved before.

'I just hate it when I cry like that.' She blew her nose on the black Saudi veil that was still lying on the blanket. 'I just hope you don't take that for a sign of weakness.' She sniffled.

'Never that.' He chose his next words with care. 'You and I have been through many good and bad things together. With us now I think it is not possible simply to smile and laugh and kiss and marry like happy children. What sort of man would I be if that were so? And what sort of woman would you be? I think it is a good sign - good, yes! - that your tears come and at first you say no and that you are still full of doubt.'

'You do? You think that's all right?'

'Remember that it took me many days in the desert before I decided to come to you and - how do you say it? - forget and forgive?'

'Forgive and forget.' She yearned to take him in her

arms and forgive him everything. She wondered whether that yearning was good or bad, strong or weak. Would she be the bigger fool to take him back or to refuse him?

'I think, Sunny, it is time to move on, yes? Or move back, as you wish. To my offer. I said we would go back to Saudi to live, and you said no. So I make a new offer. We live part of the year in Saudi, part in the West.'

Her eyes widened. 'How and where? Doing what?'

'Maybe I could move from oil into finance. Investments. In Saudi, and out of Saudi. I don't know, we must talk more about this. We could live in London, in New York, maybe even Vienna, if you insist, but London or New York is better. I think London, really. Many Arabs there - almost like Saudi, I hear.'

'You'd be a broker? Like your brother used to be in London?'

'I would invest my money and money of families like mine. But I think not for the government or the royals. I think I have had more than enough already of the royals. Enough of the oil, and enough of the royal family. I do not think the future of my country is with either of them. I think, too, that OPEC's time in the sun is almost over. We were too greedy last year when the revolution in Iran made the world fear a new oil shortage. We went too far when we doubled oil prices again. But soon the world will have a glut of oil. Britain, Norway, and Mexico are new major producers who are not in OPEC, and I think they will do all they can to undercut our prices. Another thing to worry about is what will happen if and when war breaks out between Iran and Iraq. If either of them closes shipping in the Gulf, only Allah knows what will happen to my country.' His voice took on a tinge of bitterness. 'I like to think the days of the House of Saud are numbered as well.' He shrugged. 'I hope that God in His infinite mercy and compassion will have pity on His people the Arabs. Maybe there is still time for me to make a difference to my country. I hear that men meet in small groups everywhere to talk, to plan, to prepare for the day when they can strike and win. I do not give up hope. Already there is much change in Saudi. As you say, much of the change is for the bad. But it can be different. I – Rashid! – could help to make it different!'

'How would you like to see Saudi change?'

He threw his hands up in the air. 'Some other time, I think many other times, we talk about this. But now I think we must talk about you and about me, yes? You see, Sunny, I think it is possible not only for Saudi to change but for you and me to change. Already I try with myself. But is it your wish to change? Will you love me again?'

He fascinated her, intrigued her, moved her, more now than when they had been young and foolish together. She liked not only what they had been talking about today but the way they had been talking. He had never been quite so honest with her about how he felt about his country and the oil and the royal family. He had always charmed her, seduced her, but he had never before taken her quite so seriously. She watched the play of light from the setting sun on his face. His were the most expressive eyes she had ever seen. His eyes could flash amber fire, his eyes could be as cold as ice, his eyes could speak more eloquently than any mere words. Just now, however, his soulful Arab eyes were utterly watchful. This is it, his eyes told her. Now you must decide. Now.

Miserably her uncertain eyes met his certain ones. 'How can you be so sure, Rashid? How can you be sure that what happened before won't happen again?'

'I am not sure. You want insurance of our love? Or contract? You would trust a paper more than how I feel and how you feel?'

'Trust. That's the whole thing. Trust. The one essential. And the one thing I don't seem to have anymore.'

'You used to. Your eyes used to be so clear, like a baby's.'

'And now?'

'Now they have much doubt in them.' He leaned over

and earnestly took her hands in his. 'Listen to me, Sunny. It's my fault. I put that doubt there. My mistakes. I hurt you before, but I won't again. Believe me, Shamsa! Trust me!'

His hands were warm and reassuring and strong intertwined in hers. His eyes were hot and loving and insistent locked upon hers. There were so many intelligent reasons to refuse him. But what, she wondered, about the joy that could be hers if she let herself love him again? She had almost forgotten the possibility that he might make her happy this time. Her heart leaped with hope she thought she had lost forever. It could be such a joy to love this man again.

'I will love you right this time, my Sunny.'

Her whole body was beginning to lean toward his. He drew her hands toward him, and her arms came closer, he was kissing her hands, she could not help arching her neck closer to watch his lips touch the tips of all ten of her fingers, his arm was around her shoulder, his lips touched hers, for a very long while they lay on the blanket kissing. She was dizzy with his kisses. She had forgotten how his kisses made her tremble. She wanted only for him to keep kissing her. She could suddenly not understand why it was she had ever doubted him, why she had sat on this blanket hesitating all day long, why she had wasted all that time when they could have been kissing and touching and making up for all those cold lonely years.

'You will marry me, my Sunny, yes?'

Whether this turned out in the end to be surrender or victory, whether when she was very old and altogether gray she would look back on this as her finest moment or her weakest one, Sunny made her commitment. 'Yes, I will marry you, Rashid, yes!'

They sat hand in hand in the leather-upholstered seats of the chartered jet. Each of them stared into space, lost in the separate worlds of their private thoughts, but every so often he would squeeze her hand or she would turn and smile tremulously at him.

Sunny looked out the window at the wild baking wasteland of Saudi Arabia thousands of feet below. Except for the silver ribbons of oil pipelines slicing through the desert, there were no signs of life, just raw umber mountains and gray barren steppes and glittering snowlike salt flats. Saudi was a world alien from the fruitful American and European earth of green pastures, winding rivers, and wooded hills. The jet streaked over the wilderness, hurtling them into the unknown. It was too late now to turn back, for soon the airplane would be banking and circling, descending to Dhahran. Sunny twisted the gold wedding band on her finger. She was glad she had chosen to win at life by loving and forgiving and risking a reconciliation. And yet sometimes she still endured twinges of doubt and wondered if, after all, she had not won but lost.

She was doing her best to live with this ambiguity. She reminded herself every day that she couldn't expect paradise on earth with Rashid. Even after the emotional high point of her reconciliation on that blanket of bliss atop the highest hill in Still River, she and Rashid had continued to walk through a mine field of problems. They had finally agreed they would look for a second home outside London, that they would encourage Sarah and Musa to live in the family compound in Saudi, that Sunny would wear the mask when she went out in public in the kingdom, and that she would set up a private therapeutic practice among the women of Khobar. Once the initial great leaping joy of having Rashid as her man again had faded, Sunny had faced the fact that with the loving of Rashid - and maybe with the loving of any man - always there would have to be this ambiguity, these compromises, these wishful instants of longing for an impossible perfection.

But finally they had exchanged their marriage vows in a Catholic service in Massachusetts. Sarah and Musa had flown over for the ceremony, and Gran had wheeled in Gramps in his wheelchair. The altar of the small chapel near Still River had been banked with budding white roses, pale lilac orchids, and jasmine in full heavy-scented bloom as the priest pronounced them man and wife.

Sentimentally, then, they had returned to Vermont for their second honeymoon. They had detoured off the interstate on the way up and searched Bellows Falls in vain for the shingle of the justice of the peace who had married them a lifetime ago. But the town's fast-food restaurants and shopping centers and drive-in banks were not as they had remembered the sleepy little hamlet. Finally, however, their pilgrimage wound up in that same picturesque old inn. But this time they had a prepaid computerized reservation, and there was no skeptical Yankee innkeeper to scrutinize their marriage certificate and wonder what kind of 'furriner' Rashid was. Desk clerks no longer cared if couples were married or not, and when Rashid wrote *Saudi Arabia* as his home address, the clerk began respectfully calling him 'sir.' Upstairs, under the snug cover of a patchwork quilt, they had finally been able to laugh at some of the changes time had dealt them. And then they had made a love that was sanctified and approved and legalized by both their worlds.

In the airplane Rashid leaned over and pointed. The lunar landscape was now cluttered by clusters of steel and iron and stone and fiberglass buildings and storage tanks and factories and houses and shops that were the Eastern Province of the oil-rich Kingdom of Saudi Arabia. Even now, in the afternoon, from high up in the cloudless sky, they could see pinpricks of fire from the gas-burn-off flares. They were too far away to smell the inevitable sulfurous stink of the Gulf light crude that hung over Saudi. From here they could see only its gleam and the fire of it, flaring below at their destination.

'Almost there.' Rashid was holding Sunny's hands in his as the jet began its descent to Dhahran. 'Almost home.'

Sunny turned her head and looked at her husband's handsome swarthy face framed in the folds of his white cotton head scarf and at his comforting strong body clothed in the plumage of his long spotless white robe. She had chosen freely to love this exotic man not once but twice. The first time she had loved him out of ignorance, from a romantic girlish longing for adventure and passion and a life that was different and therefore intrinsically better than the lives of other girls of her day and her age. This second and final time she loved him out of knowledge, from the pain of tragedies shared, in the hope of companionship and comfort and compassion and a trust that would only deepen in the coming years. She wondered now if those first hot passionate years when she had loved him without reservation had been their best years, or if the best were yet to come. It was possible she could learn to treasure the new ambiguities of their loving as proof of their own new maturity and mutuality and interdependency. But she hoped she never would give up all her hopes and her dreams. She was not so old and so gray that she would abandon all hope in happy endings and beginnings. In these brittle, angry, often loveless times, still Sunny optimistically hoped that love in the end could just possibly be true. She smiled radiantly at Rashid.

Then she sighed and did what had to be done. She quietly bent and opened her carry-on bag and lifted out the things she had packed there. She shook out the black folds of the inevitable cloak and smoothed out the black ties of the inevitable mask. Rashid lifted her hands to his lips and kissed them.

The jet descended; the desert seemed to rush up to engulf them in its heat; the wheels touched down; the jet bounced on the concrete runway and taxied toward the terminal.

Slowly Sunny lifted the stiff black mask up to her face. She shut her eyes and tied the three ties across the back of her head. She opened her eyes and looked through the narrow slits at the cloak in her lap. She smoothed down its olds again, and then she threw the heavy enveloping hroud over her head. Rashid took her hand and guided er to the rear of the cabin. When at last the steward pened the door, Sunny faltered and might have stumbled f Rashid had not caught her at the head of the portable taircase. The two of them looked out at the hot barren esolation of Saudi Arabia. Behind her mask, Sunny's eyes wam with tears. She didn't know whether the tears were or joy or anger or fear. But when she looked up at Rashid, he could see the glitter of tears in his eyes as well. She was eassured by the loving proof of his tears. He took her arm o that they would not stumble a second time as they escended the stairs home to Saudi.

On the following pages are details of Arrow books that will be of interest.

MONTE CARLO

Stephen Sheppard

It is May 1940 when Harry Pilikian, a young American, drives his Rolls Royce through the French night. By the time he reaches the principality of Monaco, the Germans have invaded France – and the war begins in earnest.

In neutral Monte Carlo, for the next two years, an uncertain peace prevails. The Italian army pays a token visit, Gestapo men move about in plain clothes, and refugees from all parts of the world – the rich, beautiful and bizarre – gather to sit out the war in safety and comfort.

But amidst the glitter and elegance of this famous resort, the menace of engulfing war is never far away. And those who fled to Monte Carlo for sanctuary are inescapably drawn into the anguish and horror of the conflict . . .

BASIKASINGO

John Matthews

It was a name of mystery, of secrecy and of vengeance – the one clue linking a circle of death and duplicity that stretched across the globe . . . terror in London, a diamond heist in Africa, a kidnapping in Bangkok . . . All that connected them were whispers, rumours and chance remarks – but they were part of a gory trail with no beginning and the very deadliest of ends . . .

Caught in its spell, the innocent and the diabolical, the hunted and the hunters act out their desperate dance of death . . . Not since *The Bourne Identity* has there been a thriller so intricate, so vivid and so terrifyingly real.

NILE

Laurie Devine

Egypt . . . and a small Muslim village where life has remained almost unchanged since the time of the Pharaohs. It is a world of fear, danger, and magic. But most fearful and dangerous of all is a woman who violates the ancient taboos. A woman such as Mona . . .

Meanwhile, in the sleek westernized world of Alexandria, Youssef al-Masri is growing up in a rich, powerful Arab-Jewish family. He seems destined for a life of wealth – or dissipation.

Until he and Mona meet and fall in love . . . and until history tears their world apart.

And for two generations their children and their children's children will try to repair that fatal rift.

Nile is a superb epic of high romance set against a background of seductive richness.

1985

Anthony Burgess

Ingenious, chilling and darkly comic, *1985* combines a devastating critique of Orwell's *1984* with a terrifying vision of the future. As memorable as *A Clockwork Orange*, it is as powerful and unsettling as anything Burgess has written.

'Fully demonstrates Burgess's brilliance' *Francis King, Spectator*

'A book as important as it is frightening' *Daily Telegraph*

'There is too much which is truly excellent for anyone to ignore it' *Auberon Waugh, Evening Standard*

PROMISES

Charlotte Vale Allen

Just a girl – too young to know the world, too innocent to know the human heart – Jess made one last promise to her dying father: to look after her eleven-year-old sister Tillie. *Promises* is an unforgettable novel which tells the story of how Jess is forced to take to the streets to fulfil this promise and how Tillie, beautiful but selfish and spoilt, almost turns the promise into a curse.

Set in the Great Depression, *Promises* is that rare combination, a powerful saga of human drama and emotional conflict, and an absorbing story of discovery and suspense.